STRANGE COMPANY

HEARTS OF DARKNESS

NICK COLE

Strange Company: Hearts of Darkness

Copyright © 2025 by Nick Cole

All rights reserved.

This is a work of fiction. Any similarity to real persons, living or dead, is coincidental and not intended by the author.

ISBN: 979-8-88922-108-1

No part of this publication may be reproduced, stored in a retrieval system, or transmitted in any form or by any means electronic, mechanical, photocopying, recording, or otherwise without the prior written permission of the publisher and copyright owner.

Edited by David Gatewood
Cover Art: Marc Lee
Cover Design: Mike Corley
Formatting: Greg Franz

Website: NickColeBooks.com

DREAMS OF DEATH. DREAMS OF DESTRUCTION.

The Black Ship fled across the stars… and the Strange Company pursued.

Eventually…

We ran her down. The Black Ship of our mortal enemies. The last… Monarch starship full of our past evils, and the last of our devils. Or so we told ourselves…

The Dark Star.

The boarding op was a hot mess from the get-go. And I knew that going in. Like it was all… a bad dream I'd had a thousand times before, again and again. A real, real bad dream. But isn't it always that way with the thing you've been dreading finally arriving at your doorstep? Finally. Bright, shiny, smiling evil and ready to ruin your day.

It's always the hot mess you knew it would be.

Trust me. We have to be honest about these things.

The whole lead-up to our coming annihilation felt like nothing but pure dread in the pit of my scarred stomach. Scarred by fear, worry, injury, rations… and bad street tacos for which I have no regret. Acid and grease that don't mix and the fire sauce didn't help matters. Meat on the street you never should've eaten, but did anyway because you were alive, had survived the last bad contract's attempts to kill you, and the company had paid out what little it managed to steal.

It's a glamorous life being a PMC. Don't believe the lies, kids. First Sergeant's signing up and you can get in on all this.

No. Street tacos and all the bad coming at you on a hot insert like the one the company has found themselves in this time is like that hot-crazy starport bar beauty you should have said no to… and didn't even though every buddy you had stood in the way and tried to warn ya off. Food poisoning, bad rations, and a hangover with no place or time to catch your breath. She had curves that wouldn't quit and this time things were gonna be different despite that mean little mouth and the bitter eyes she paints up. This time… things are gonna be different. This time the contract's gonna be gold, and the formations parades, and the chow a feast…

We have to…

Be honest about these things.

And sometimes you just can't stand to hear it even though you know it's true and you're the one saying it like it's a chant, a prayer, a warning.

It's just another hot mess, ruck hobo. Different day, same series of disasters to avoid and fires to put out, Sar'nt.

This time things are gonna be different you hear you laughing at you as the first rounds start zipping in, little snaps past your bucket, rips of paper in the audio detectors.

All the bad coming true just like you knew it would. Have dreamed it would. A game you don't want to play but are forced to anyway.

LOL, ruck hobo.

Suck deck and return fire if you wanna find another starport honey and hold on to her tight as your cash disappears and you... try to remember, or try to forget, who you once were... and what it means to be alive on the other side of the X.

Then it was all hot incoming, heavy and relentless, fast moving at twenty hundred feet per second. All of it everywhere at once as I tried to maneuver Reaper into her breaching position on the landing bay of the massive enemy ship we'd been charged to board and destroy.

Thus sayeth the monkey Kong.

Dis one on you, hoomans.

Or die trying. If we wanted a place back among the worlds we once said were ours even though they were really the Monarchs'.

But it was us who did the colonizing and the building, and the dying, in a horrible vacuum or hostile environment. Wasn't it?

The Dark Star.

The company and a small task force has come to get its kill on out here beyond the limit of known human expansion.

The *Spider*, our NewMax destroyer that was five hundred years old, at least, and held together with baling wire and bubble gum on a good day, was holed in a dozen places even as her main gun whined and fired, the entire superstructure shuddering with each powerful shot. Reactors were offline already. Critical damage and hull breach indicators bleating to that effect and screaming for attention like wounded I'd known when they were hit bad.

Known all too well.

That starport honey... never mind she hates your guts... she'll pretend otherwise and there's something about her in your arms that makes the dying wounded... quiet for a little while.

Dying wounded like...

Like Crusher and Honcho and Firsty at the starport assault on Astralon, or Crash, call it whatever you want it doesn't exist on the stellar charts anymore.

Remember that?

But not like Boom Boom who died of his wounds in the night after we escaped the gunfight at the fuel point, and who we later blew up to cross a checkpoint controlled by Ultra special operators with a bonus-round field interrogation team. Choker stapled a smile on Boom Boom's face. Boom had faded in his sleep, bleeding out as we crossed the wastes.

He would have liked that we stapled the smile on his face after we turned him into a bomb to play our trick.

Then later...

Choker slashed his own throat so we could get off the X. On the sands of Mars. But that was later. Stacking Ultras on LZ Heartbreak and then hitting the factory to rescue the kids, the psy-cans. The Bishops.

Monsters made in the Dark Labs like our Voodoo warrants.

So... it was not like some of the wounded I had known. Screaming. And hurt like hell as death rubbed its cold claws while the medics worked and gave the inevitable— the middle finger. Telling time and death they weren't done just yet and to shove off and let them have this one. Telling the inevitable waiting for all of us what it could do with itself.

Medics. They are too good for us.

Medics like Choker... Blender... and Klutz who was still alive despite my firm conviction I'd get him killed soon enough.

XO put our ancient NewMax pocket destroyer into approach-to-assault boarding position as we entered the wide hangar bay of the *Dark Star*. The main aft cargo doors were already open. The panorama of the Battle at Typhon was incredible and all around us as we made ready to board, kill, and die.

Starships burning, C-beams searing across deepest space itself, auto-turrets and defensive cannons off the *Dark Star* doing everything they could to keep the swarming locusts who'd come for her, back. Blurring and blaring deadly light shows.

We'd run the last Monarch ship down at the very edge of named space. Some kind of edge. Some kind of... jumping-off point.

Distant Typhon.

A lonely system long past the edge of all things known, devoid of anything but a cold super gas giant. Purple and angry swirling like a necrotic leviathan in the vast depths of edge-space. An uncaring giant, uninterested in our petty death struggle against our former overlords who'd made themselves our gods.

Punch was the onboard pathfinder for Reaper as the lights on the assault deck went from red to off. He was calling out the assault-boarding commands and readiness checks to hit the cargo ramps once they were down.

To get us onto the enemy deck.

For the killing, and the dying.

Don't think about that part before it happens as much as you can because it's all you're gonna think about when the incoming starts... well, *incoming*.

Belt-fed, emplaced fire starts rattling across the hull as the enemy gunners open fire on the ship itself.

Hey... I've said it before. We have to be honest about these things. And here we were... at the end of this tragedy we'd become... *involved* in.

Check the logs... as far back as the ones I sliced out of the bad contract on Astralon. Someone told me once... *Never get involved, Orion.*

Never.

And as the first sergeant likes to say, "Yeah... and here you are, young Sar'nt."

Involved.

So there's that.

Honest about these things... we must be.

Fifteen seconds out to get-it-on-thirty when Wolfy gets smoked hard right in the noggin by a micro-railgun round from one of the defenders guarding the LZ we've been tasked with hitting aboard the *Dark Star*. Punched right through his EVC bucket, right then and there, and even as Klutz went to do... something...

EVC.

Extra Vacuum Combat armor.

A hardened space suit for combat in exotic environments, and space.

... there was nothing that could be done. For Wolfy.

He was gone and I knew it right there even as it happened.

Sometimes... you just know.

See... *we have to be honest about these things.*

We swore as Wolfy slumped into the assault rack as the *Spider* rattled, braking hard, retro-mains firing in full, hull screaming to hold together. We raged silent for a hot moment and promised payback on installment while someone threw up and others looked away from our first-of-dead, finding a prayer they hadn't thought to make in recent bad years of the wandering and wanton recklessness that is the life of a private military contractor.

PMC.

Or mercenary... if you prefer.

Then we were yelling, getting ourselves ready as the enemy deck got closer and closer and Punch's voice-of-authority commands were shouted to unclip from the airframe of the starship. To put your body into the man in front of you.

Countdown to assault boarding had begun.

Now... it was all inevitable. The hot mess I'd seen coming like some distant storm on the horizon.

The *Dark Star*'s hangar, one of hundreds across the surface of the vast and fantastic ship, this was where command had selected for us to board. The hangar was immense. Polished. A perfect killbox already lit up by intersecting fields of enemy fire from the defending gun teams, punching into our ship and deflecting off the ground shields as the PDCs engaged what they could.

PDCs.

Point Defense Cannons.

Chain guns go *BRRRRRRRRRRRRRT*.

Engines howl.

Massive landing gears whine and extend.

"Ten seconds!" screams Punch as Klutz and I lower Wolfy to the deck. Dead. I quickly grab a strap and clip his body into the starship. He'll wait here for us now.

The engines howl and the ship takes an actual cannon round off some gun the defenders set up on the deck to repel our innocent attempt to murder them all.

Jingo, the ASL for First, assistant squad leader, gets sick and hurls all over the inside of his EVC bucket. The vomit's hot and yellow, reminding me of the protein enrichment broth M.O.M. served three hours ago as we prepped for insert onto the *Dark Star*.

"We're gonna get killed down there!" mumbles Goods, First's M67 Pig gunner.

"Screw it!" screams the enraged Jingo, heaving again, after sucking water off the mouth straw inside his EVC bucket and then spitting all over the inside of the helmet to wash away the filth away he made there.

"Gain fire superiority! Move toward the guns! Kill everything in the way, Strange!" he bellows above all the approach-to-boarding chaos.

Time irises in and we are in it now.

I am in it and it's as real as it gets and it's no dream.

Someone else got hit bad. I couldn't see who it was, but I heard it.

Ballistic hypercloth folding on impact, a loud *THUMP* and then a small wet *slop* which is the sound of the round smashing through flesh, bone, and sometimes brain.

It's almost an afterthought. The *slop*.

I know it's going to be a hot mess. I know it like I'm in a dream. And, knowing it... I'm still going to do it.

"Five seconds, Reaper!" bellows Punch.

I want to hurl too. And I'm in charge of this hot mess.

See this mess? It's mine, sir. All mine.

The Monarch gun teams find their range and hose the cargo deck like ammo is on sale bulk discount and they went with the company card to buy the store out. Rounds tear through open space like small fast-moving rockets. If they were close enough to external EVC audio to detect… they'd sound like small quick rips of paper.

Sudden, unexpected, lethal, deadly rips.

Boarding ops are very—emphasize *very*—unforgiving.

I turn to check my squad and Klutz is hit and choking on his own blood.

See… I knew I'd get him killed. I don't have faith in much. But I do have faith in me to get mine killed.

Ave, Klutz. You made it longer than I thought you would.

"Down and clear!" thunders Punch like some law of the universe that cannot ever be denied. "Go go go!"

There's no time to help Klutz.

He's gonna die.

We're all gonna die on this one.

This… hot mess I saw coming and could do nothing to stop.

Klutz, who wanted only to be a hero, rages at himself, willing his body to move despite the fatal wound as all the life runs out of him. All he ever wanted was to be a hero.

Like any man.

"No…" I whimpered at the universe. *No…* I whimpered in my nightmare coming suddenly awake. Covered in thick viscous sweat and staring around suddenly at the darkness in the weapons cage deep down in the belly of our ship. Our home.

The *Spider*.

We weren't there yet.

En route. We are still… en route to cruel and uncaring Typhon.

And yet… it was real. It *is* real. That hot mess.

Like… PTSD.

But in advance of what would be.

It will be a hot mess, and we will all die.

And yet… we will go.

Strangers to the universe. Brothers to the…

End.

We have to be honest about these things.

EN ROUTE TO TYPHON...

"Captain's thinking about doing a company bonus in Soup's honor, Sar'nt Orion. Wanted to run that by you. Men seemed to really have been inspired by his actions on the LZ at Saffron City."

This might as well happen, I thought.

"What, Sar'nt?" he snaps as though he can read minds. Probably something first sergeants can do.

"Nothing, First Sergeant."

"And also, going forward," he says, "no one better say he was the best of us, Sar'nt Orion. Old Man wants that stuff shut down. It's weird, like some kinda cult."

Then why are you doing a bonus in his honor? I don't ask.

Silence.

"But he was... First Sergeant," I say. "He was the best of us."

He looks up from his paperwork and there's pure cold murder in those eyes. Lately... he's lost that sense of humor he never had. He feels it too.

The hot mess soon coming our way.

You didn't even know him, my soul screams at me the thousand screams of the tired and foot-sore NCO that is me. He was not the best of us and you didn't even like him and you got him killed.

I have... issues.

The first sergeant gives me a look that tells me he knows I'm a damn liar and that Hotsoup was not the best of us.

COMPANY LOG

The Black Ship fled across the galaxy… and the Strange Company pursued.

In those postapocalyptic days after the fall of the Monarch Empire at Marsantyium, and after the Old Man of the company, the captain, had been charged by the monkey Kong with the final hunting down, and destruction, of the last known Monarch ship, *Dark Star*, the Black Ship, a ragtag fleet of humanity's last surviving warships gathered in orbit above Marsantyium, assembling to hunt down and destroy the last of the fleeing Monarchs. The former rulers of human-controlled space who'd fled off toward the most distant frontiers in their strange ship…

Six months we lingered on the red sands of dying-once-again Mars, shaded in the fading green jungles of the last habitable world of the home system.

Humanity's birthplace.

We refitted the *Spider* on the sand dunes of a world that had once been called Mars. The ancient terraforming of that lost world, begun as humanity had once optimistically leapt outward into the darkness of space, was now failing again as the red sands of that world broke up and reclaimed the lush tropical jungles and ancient red marble cities the Monarchs had constructed to reflect their now-lost glory. Towers, temples, sunken cities, and crumbling palaces were mere looted pantheons the fleeing Monarchs had left behind when it had all gone pear-shaped for them.

In the late red afternoons we wandered among these lost and lonely ruins, wondering at what had been.

Dead Ultra Marines rotted in their pillboxes, littered with spent brass being swallowed by the spreading red sands that had always been there beneath all that hard-fought terraforming. Along the crumbling streets we walked in quiet silence, and beneath the skeletal shadow of the last of the great Battle Spires… the remains of the *Red Dragon*. Crashed there for the Ultras to make their final stand against the aggrieved they'd enslaved there for the Monarchs.

We were… the aggrieved. The company and a dozen other alien races. And the Simia… whatever they were.

The slain Ultra Marines rotted where they had died at their guns, and the chimps came and stripped off them what they found useful and left the rest for the hot winds and the scouring, swallowing red sands of fading Mars.

Such is the way of warriors. Always has been. Always ever will be.

I ruminated on these things working a smoke and a cup of coffee as the work continued, and the readiness to finish the job we'd been tasked with… approached.

I had a bad feeling about this one.

Watching all that death, destruction, and ruin felt as old as time itself. Dead warriors stripped of everything they'd collected on the way to their deaths. None of it mattering anymore as the camp followers came and took what they wanted, leaving nothing but rotting flesh and bleaching bones to give some clue as to what exactly had happened here. And no clue as to who the fallen warrior had been who died at his gun, with murder in his heart, and eternity calling, promising him some note among the logs.

Old as time itself. Like I said.

We have to be honest about these things.

The Ultras' final battle had been not so much a defense as a spit in the galactic eye of everyone else. Their death cult had finally achieved its "Dark Salvation in Combat and War," their words not mine, and then they'd slaughtered their own tyrannical rulers when they could get their hands on them, and anyone else who dared come at them.

We dared. And they died.

It is as simple as that and don't let anyone ever tell you anything other than that about war and combat.

To the last bullet, they'd died. Knives out and teeth bared. Eternity calling.

Then, there were no more Ultra Marines and there was only the company and the Simia.

And the ragtag fleet that had begun to assemble for the pursuit. And the revenge.

And… the looting.

For the company, damage repair and damage control was underway aboard the war-battered *Spider*. She was our warship and now that she could spin up and jump, we could transport to contracts on distant worlds where we would kill aliens and sometimes ourselves, for pay.

The winds of autumn on that dying red-sand world grew cruel, and cold, like they'd been in the thousands of years before the Monarchs had made some heaven among the stars just for themselves, and their debaucheries.

Now it was just ruins and red sand spreading and growing like some end-of-days plague.

They'd lost their humanity. The Monarchs. Become aliens, really. But that's another story soon buried among the sinking sands. No longer important to the galactic sprawl as humans, and aliens, spread, slowly, outward and away from where we'd come from. Where we started at the first of it all.

I was there at the end. I recorded the last of them.

For whatever that's worth.

"Who knows dem things like time and da counts o' such, Little King," muttered Stinkeye, the company wizard and chief warrant officer of Voodoo Platoon doing his drunken shaman act that afternoon. "Dey Monarchs made time dey plaything with dere lies dey told jes' to stand on top us all and run da table for dem damned cursed selfs. They know now, Little King. They know now. They know the Heart o' Darkness. But hey…"

The old soldier wizard hit his dented canteen, his sacred totem, and exhaled gustily a hot breath of his special gutter liquor.

It reeked of vinegar and vengeance.

"Da past don't matter no more, Little King. An' maybe… it never did. Da future… dat's been important da whole time, an' you shoulda know'd dat better den anyone. Little King. Know why?"

I don't, you ol' drunk, I don't say and just try to ignore him.

It only encourages him. When you play. Like throwing coins at some bad hissing tragedian on the worst of streets just because you feel sorry for them and instead they only go in harder on their ancient meaningless words and ham-fisted acting.

Reading your impatience and pity wrong. Taking it for enthusiasm and encouragement. Somehow justifying their sad purpose.

"Because, boy, it's been entangled wit' ya for a long, long time though ya never knowed it all 'long. Soldier. Mercenary. But now ya will know, Little King. Now, you will know when we comes to Typhon out dere spinnin' in da big deep dark all by itself. Now we all will know… 'cause we got a date out there in dem Faraways ahead… and I doubts da company come back from dis one. A whole lotta us gonna die out dere. Maybe alls, Little King. Maybe alls dis time."

Then the drunken old soldier looked out toward the stars glistening in the Martian night sky just beginning to appear over the distant dark ruins along the horizon. The chimp hulks were gathering up there, orbiting overhead in great disastrous and ramshackle clusters because they had a galaxy to rule over now. And do so by fang and claw, and the decree of their mighty Kong.

The Simia.

But their silent message was clear to our forming little ragtag-last-of-humanity fleet that would soon hunt the last Monarch ship down. The Black Ship. Then fight them to the death, theirs or ours. The message of the Simia was very clear. Now.

We in charge now, hoomans. All yer base belong to us, as the old chimp proverb goes.

Whatever that means.

"Maybe dat's for da best, Little King…" said the drunk Voodoo chief as he sighed and seemed to know what I was thinking. "Stinkeye gots hisself a feeling dere ain't gonna be much ta come back to dis way. An' anyway once dis all done up and seen ta proper… I been alive a long time, Little King. Maybe too long… dis time."

Then Stinkeye wandered off, grumbling and making threats to the universe, pulling at the old and dented totem flask the company calculated its fortunes by. And he was just like the rest of us, each in our own way. Whether we realized it or not yet.

Hoping things would be different and not the hot mess they must inevitably become.

Things will be different this time, right, Stink?

That was the last night in the home system, the birthplace of all humanity that had flung itself out to the stars. Not that it mattered anymore. Not that it had mattered in a thousand years. Fabled Earth had been blown to bits long ago by the Monarchs for reasons we'd never know. A dying nearby world that had once been dead was all that was left of everything we once were, when at first… we began our long slow crawl out into the stars.

Now, it was dying again.

But that did not matter to the company. Few of us had ever been to Earth.

Instead… we had other things on our collective minds as a company of private military contractors started long ago by a man named John Strange.

We had a settling of accounts on our hearts and minds though it was not openly spoken of. And it was as though the assassination of the Monarch known as the

Seeker had given the company a taste for revenge now. And we were looking for more along the trail of the Black Ship and where that led to.

Wherever that would be.

Not just war for pay. But revenge now.

A note here...

To the next Keeper of the Log, however long I have left... that felt not just a little dangerous. Wild and dangerous in fact. Like somehow... someway, we'd lost, or were losing, our way.

Not just war for pay. But revenge now.

As a mercenary company...

We fought for pay. Not revenge. Generally. Unless we'd been wronged. And... we had, indeed, been wronged. So the company had iced her.

The Seeker.

Chief Cook, the Psyops warrant for the company, on any given day might hiss at me, "There is no *way* for the company, Sergeant Orion. Never had one. We're just making it up now. It's all chaos and death after this. Nothing but. And we..." emphasis on the *we*... "get paid to make it happen. On demand. Now there's talk of revenge, and where's the profit in that, I'm asking? *Ain't* no profit in revenge. Never was. This plan I'm hearing about ain't the company. Ain't us, Orion. We're losing our way."

Then on the next day he'd crow about, "Trusting the plan, Orion. Trust the plan. It's all swinging our way, Orion. Trust the plan."

Then he'd wink, giggle, or snicker, and slink off to cause more of his particular brand of mayhem and mischief.

There were others who'd argued we weren't in the business of revenge. That we had no business going after the Monarchs on that Black Ship like some ghost ship that was an ill omen of bad luck and blight so one never says its name.

The *Dark Star*.

We were mercenaries. Private military contractors. We had a ship. A ton of new weapons. Tech and hoard we'd managed to steal from the chimp sack of the Monarch capital as it burned.

We were, as some say, in tall cotton. Charlie potatoes. Bucks up now.

Revenge was personal and had nothing to do with killing for pay. So what business was it of ours to chase the Monarchs round and round Perdition's Flame in order to pay off some debt the Simia Kong had assessed us? There were other micro-empires out on the edges of the slowly expanding galactic frontier. Rumors and legends.

Surely they needed someone dead. We could go there and provide that service.

Enter the company, stage left. This is a service we provide. On demand. Who do you want murked?

Point and destroy. That is what we do.

But the Old Man, the captain of the company, was our leader, and his case for dusting the Monarch *Dark Star* was that we could never operate in human space, or what had once been human space, ever again, if we did not satisfy the chimp Kong and make sure the last of the Monarchs were good and smoked out there wherever we managed to run them to ground.

Then we could do business. War business. As proper mercenaries.

And that was our business.

He was our leader. The Old Man determined the direction of the company until there was a new Old Man. So say the rules of our founder John Strange.

So, we heaved into orbit up from the winds and sands of Mars, attended the council of the Star Khans of the Technate as they called themselves, and threw in our hat to the pursuit, capture, and slaughter of our once-gods.

The Star Khans, or the Technate, call it what you want like Crash or Astralon, had been a thorn in the Monarchs' side for much of the Insurrection War. It was they who'd brought their old and battered ships to the fleet and allied with the Simia. It was they who took charge of the planning, the tracking, and the traps they intended to waylay the massive Monarch starship with so we could engage her in battle at broadsides. Then units like the company could board her and kill the last of the Monarchs on their own bloody decks.

And, though the Keeper of the Log is a lowly ruck hobo, he is yet the keeper of this account of the days of the company in the aftermath of the Fall of the Monarchs, and so I must tell you my take on the matter of the hunting fleet of the Star Khans. Or the Technate… call it whatever you will. Not everyone, and in fact, again this is just my opinion, but not everyone was as of a single mind as the company was to find and destroy the *Dark Star*.

Find… yes.

Destroy… eh, not so fast there, space marine.

In the "Great Council of the Star Khans"… and if that sounds a little *dramatic*, let me, Sergeant Orion, explain the galacto-politics of how all this came to be… without being too boring.

So just two lines about all this pompous war LARPing on the matter of the Star Khans.

They were little more than "bigwigs" on backwater worlds who'd survived the war with the Monarchs. Insiders who'd fallen out of Bright World favor, corporate raiders who wanted to survive the fall. All of them having in common that the Monarchs had betrayed them in some deal along the way. They had formed a loose yet powerful alliance in the vacuum of the former tyrants, and called themselves Khans to represent their power blocs.

They seemed to think the chimps, who were really in charge, were just a passing fancy. Like a helpful invasion of locusts who'd wiped out your enemies' farms and weakened them for destruction. *Surely*, they almost seemed to think, *the chimps will just move on now and we can be the chief Humans.*

And… humble ruck hobo opinion here…

Trust us, we won't become the Monarchs. We're the good guys. We're the new boss.

Was what they seemed to be saying without saying it.

Trust us, this time. We got this.

Things'll be different.

What's that old saying…?

Same as the old boss.

So this ol' ruck hobo some call Sar'nt Orion, could practically smell it and I think the Old Man could too.

But…

Our position was fragile. So we joined their alliance, their fleet, if only so we could stand in front of the chimp Kong one day and state that we had, *indeed, fulfilled our orders Your Grand Monkey Highness, and smote the Monarchs unto death.*

Or whatever they refer to him as inside the great and dirty monkey tent cities they like to set up on whatever world they've pillaged lately.

Deed done as requested, and we would be allowed transit and opportunity within their area of control. Our old… empire.

Human space. As it was once known.

"Life comes at ya fast and all," says Punch.

Even now there was infighting, treachery, and intrigues among the scumbag Star Khans. And it was into this mix that the company had thrown their lot, because, as the first sergeant related it to me later, "Sar'nt Orion, I very highly doubt I, or any one of us, will be coming back from this voyage out to the Faraways. Them worlds are hell and gone beyond the limits of human exploration, and if half of what I've heard about that area on the star charts is true… Hells of Suth, we'll be lucky to survive orbital insertion much less storm one of the most secure, and advanced, vessels ever known to man. The *Dark Star*. The very name gives me the chills, young Sar'nt. Who in the Hells of Suth names a ship something awful like that? *Penelope's Dream, Calliope of Novas, Nostalgia for Infinity*… those are ship's names. But, it is the opinion of the captain, and myself too, Sar'nt Orion, that it's gonna be one *helluva* a fight out there for sure. And we wouldn't want to miss that, now would we, Sar'nt Orion?"

The senior-most NCO of the company sat down and sighed, looking off into the darkness where he'd managed to track me down in stores deep within the belly of the *Spider* while she was under refit and rearm. The old warrior found me smoking in the darkness, drinking black coffee. Brooding on all these things and the stories told me.

And also the ones I have marked down…

Like I do.

Listening to some old music I liked, once, long ago, when I was someone else I've been missing more and more lately. Missing those days and wondering how things might have been… *different*. Remembering loading ammo with a company brother long dead now.

I think of the company dead often lately. There're a lot of them.

Player, who led Dog after Hannibal.

The Kid, who got killed at the landing gear holding the dustoff after the bank heist.

Junkboy, who got clean and sober and got his head blown off at the bank on Astralon just as the Kid came in for the indoc brief.

And others…

Crisp.

Twopeat.

Two Fingers and…

Sergeant Stix, KIA on Mira.

And the other guy we called Klutz, who got it at Tebibi Field in the early days of Astralon. Crash. Whatever.

They come and stand around me in the darkness of my cage.

"Listen, Orion…" continued the first sergeant after a galaxy-weary sigh as he sat down on one of my weapons crates. "Out of a hundred swinging boots, nine are real killers. Ten ain't fit to be there at all. And the rest o' them eighty are just targets for the enemy to shoot at while you're getting ready to kill 'em dead, Sar'nt Orion. That's my application on why we're throwin' in with this Grand Fleet of these Khans. They got pretty dreams... we just need to get close to get it done so we can get back to official company business. My guess... gonna lose a lotta ships on final approach to target-boarding. Op like that is gonna be hell to pay to get a foothold on the enemy ship, and there ain't no pretty lie I can tell about that. No two ways. It's gonna be downright gruesome. Ask me how I know sometime. Anyway... them Khans, their fleets, their PMCs, that's gonna be our eighty we gonna meatshield behind to get in close for the killin' work. We get a breach solution, crack that hull, then the company can do its thing and *get it on* right and proper with whatever the Monarchs got stashed in there to save themselves from us. It'll be real-deal, close-quarters battle in them compartments and passages, Sar'nt. Dangerous like you ain't never seen before, I suspect. Maybe we split the spine, destroy the engines if we can even identify them, set demo, but I suspect we are just gonna murder our way deck-to-deck through that cursed ship in order to get it done one by one on them cussed bastards."

He was silent for a long moment, seeing it all play out in his mind.

Then he looked at me with a flat stare.

"There ain't gonna be a lot left of us the other side of this one, Sar'nt. But that's the company. *Get it on* never mind the odds. We ain't ever shirked a fight. We ain't never asked for no quarter in one, and we ain't given none either."

I was pretty sure we had. Me mainly.

But the first sergeant was waxing melancholy and recruiting a lot on the sands so his view of the company and its history was... how shall I put it... a little more pristine than mine.

Than reality, in fact. But I say that for the purpose and authenticity of the logs.

People don't become mercenaries because they know the reality.

That's later.

Then they know.

But they're addicted to the juice of combat, life and death, by then, so they're stuck.

Ask me how I know.

But the first sergeant is the first sergeant and I don't feel like getting busted down to New Guy right now going in on this one.

I wanna be in charge of the hot mess, right?

The first sergeant reached over and took a drink of my coffee. In the one overhanging light I keep on down here, he looked tired, and lost. And old.

He was getting old. We all were.

And that made me wonder how I looked.

I don't spend too much time in front of mirrors these days. I don't like the answers.

"That's all we can do, Sar'nt Orion," he grunted as he finished my cup. "Get in there and mix it up and maybe a few of us come out the other side of this and the company of John Strange goes on, deeper and deeper and farther and farther out there into the unknown of the galaxy. One world at a time. One fight after the next. Them players calling themselves the Khans, they're just goin' to see if they can recover all that fabled Monarch tech, or whatever, out there. That's why they want the Black

Ship. Use it to get ahead. Us? We're goin' because that's what we do. Kill. That's what the Strange does, Sar'nt. Kill. Our honor is on the line. We'll go, break their stuff, and then… kill. That's what we do. Then we get paid. Hopefully. Official company business and anything else is just dressin' it up."

He stared at something on the floor, but I could tell he was somewhere else, some-when else, for a long moment.

"We got to kill them bastards, Orion. Got to kill that damned ship too. If we… if humanity's gonna have a chance, we gotta end the Monarch tyrant-thing out there. Otherwise… they'll do it again. Someone will."

Silence.

I felt like I needed to say something. That he needed… an ally. Someone who understood the mission like he did without all the… rest of it. Whatever that is.

Tell me if you know.

"I'm with you, First Sergeant. I believe…" I mumbled to him in the quiet between us.

But I didn't know what I believed.

He looked at me as though only now realizing I was there in my weapons cage with him, listening to his thoughts, his spiel, his vision of the myth of us, the Strange. Drinking coffee and smoking in the dark. Trying to be left alone.

Just like me.

He looked around, as though seeing where he was for the first time.

"Y'know, Sar'nt… it's real nice what you got down here in the dark and the quiet," he whispered softly. "Real nice."

I nodded and refilled his cup.

He sighed as he got up to leave, swallowing the whole hot brew in one go. "You're a good NCO, Orion. Just makin' sure I believe me too, Sar'nt. That's all. Sometimes ya gotta say it just to hear it. You'll know, Sar'nt, someday. You'll know. One day you'll be First Sergeant and it'll be your job to make sure everyone's a real lifetaker and a heartbreaker, that the grass gets cut and every one of us knows what it's all about every day. The fun part is you get to ruin their day. But that's a secret and don't tell no one I told ya that."

They know already, First Sergeant.

"Now… I gotta go tune up that ol' flamethrower 'cause I ain't takin' no chances on that Monarch ship no way, Sar'nt. Combustible oxygen my butt. Only way to be sure they're dead is to burn 'em bulkhead to bulkhead. Know what I mean, Sar'nt Orion? Flame on. Just like back in the Batts."

He got ready to leave.

"They still doing that Hotsoup thing aren't they, Sar'nt?" he muttered.

I rubbed my forehead tiredly. They were.

"It's like a cult now, First Sergeant."

He shrugged and adjusted his pistol belt. He was always strapped. Even during transit. But he was ex-Saturnian Ranger Batts. And they saw some hairy stuff out there in the deep dark during the Frontier Wars long ago.

So… best to be ready. Never could tell when some slavering xeno was gonna come crawling out of the lower decks at ya all fangs and acid saliva.

"Everything's a cult, Orion. Always was," he grumbled. "But… that's how warriors… *men*… are. They get some wacky thing in their hard drives and it becomes a thing to them to remind themselves they're still alive. Like a totem. A… war cry, if you will, something to scream at death when it's coming for ya, knives out and smoking barrel. Like screaming into the void just to let it know you were there, and you didn't blink when it came for ya in the end. Sorta like that, I guess. Don't know, young Sergeant. More and more every day… I just don't know anymore. I just… *don't know*. Anymore."

Then he was gone, off into the darkness to spread his message of the company's lore and honor to the new recruits and us veterans of all the bad contracts past that ever were. Just to make sure we knew *why* we were doing it when we set those hull entry charges on some airlock aboard the *Dark Star*. That everyone was on the same sheet of music about getting it done when it came time.

Get it on time.

We were going to find the last of the Monarchs. And then kill them. All.

Then we would be free.

Or at least, whoever survived would be free. And then the company could go on. Somehow.

In those days humanity watched from her shattered worlds and war-torn decaying orbital cities as the "Last Great Fleet" formed itself up in order to hunt down the monsters who'd once ruled us all.

Some for profit.

Some for revenge.

The company for honor. The irony that we were mercenaries was lost on everyone. Everyone but me.

For the record.

The Black Ship fled across the galaxy… and the Strange Company… pursued.

CHAPTER ONE

A ragtag fleet of all combat types of warships assembled across the remains of the system of humanity's birthplace, orbiting the decaying and shot-to-hell world of Marsantyium. Day by day, the fleet grew. When the *Spider* finally limped up into orbit on three good mains, the few remaining interstellar tracking stations that had survived the conflict were nailing down the flight of the *Dark Star* as she egressed through the known worlds of humanity, racing for the deep dark beyond the official frontier of their fallen empire in order to escape the wrath of her former subjects.

And the Simia.

The Technate fleet intel unit now calling itself "Group Zero Tracking and Termination of Target" had developed what they called "solid intel" that the Monarchs were going after an Andromeda-class super-freighter headed out toward the Faraways for some reason no one was sharing with the general public.

Rumor, however, was the freighter had been collecting deep-jump navigation probes that used a combo fold/jump to skip far out into the galaxy. Unmanned, these experimental probes returned, and autographical and navigation data from unreachable points across the stars was collected in a scanning node aboard the super-freighter.

If the Monarchs could reach that freighter and plunder her collected navigational data, then they could, in theory, use their fold technology to reach those previously unnavigated points in deep space and well beyond our vengeful reach.

The freighter had gone radio-dark. No data could be plundered unless there was a hard connect.

Beyond the Faraways lay another system. The last system officially claimed by the Monarchs. Typhon. The Faraways were the halfway point to Typhon.

In about eighteen months the Andromeda-class super-freighter was scheduled for an extended orbit of Typhon. Onboard refineries and processing facilities could convert the gas giant's raw resources into usable fuel for the long haul back to human-controlled space after draining the tanks on a navigational route that took her through unexplored space well beyond the current frontier.

There were rumors of illegal colonies and outposts out that way. But under the Monarchs all those rumors had been discouraged as… *conspiracy theories*.

The Faraways were a very distant group of paradise worlds in one system. Stellar cartographers called it a *utopian super-cluster*. They had been found at the very edge of human outward expansion some thirty years ago and allowed to develop with private commercial interest.

A pretty decent-sized civilization had formed out there in the Faraways, but they had little contact with the rest of what was once human space, and Monarch civilization. So of course they'd flourished without the heavy hand on the scales of benefit and the jackboot of the Ultras on their throats.

But...

The Faraways were hell-and-gone from known space. Navigational data was sketchy at times and the distances were simply immense. Some ships didn't have the energy reserves, supplies, or jump engines to make the voyage and would need a ship tender and resupply vessels just to execute a series of micro-jumps to get out that far.

Day by day in orbit over Marsantyium, during the company briefs as we recruited new platoons and replacements for Ghost and Reaper, it was becoming increasingly clear the last Monarch ship was aiming for the most distant colony at the farthest limits of human expansion for reasons beyond just getting lost.

"The poop," muttered Chief Cook, "is she's gonna pull a fade like nothing ever seen. The Monarchs aboard *Dark Star*'ll grab that freighter, murder the crew toot-sweet, unlock the data vaults on that node and then possess stellar cartography light years ahead of any of our current maps. Maps we will need to develop for upwards of two to five hundred years never mind how long it takes to fly out there and kill them. Think, Orion... just think what they could get up to out there with all that free time and no trail of killers breathing down their necks constantly. They could make super weapons. Theoretical star cannons and space stations the size of small moons that could vape a planet just like that..."

He snapped his fingers, and it was like the crack of brittle tree limbs in the dead of winter.

"A Death Station! Man... what I could do with one of those. Things would be different then, I'll tell you, Orion. I could jump around and settle some very petty little scores I've been keeping for a very long time in my little write-in-the-rain notebook. Ah yes... there's a certain betting track in the Bright Worlds that would rue the day they ever cut me off from the Jockey Club bar during the Stellar Crown indicating my credit was 'no longer good' and that I was, quote, 'dangerous and unhinged.' Unquote. Rue the day, I tell you, Orion. Oh, they would indeed rue that day."

Then he walked off muttering to himself and swiping at the air around him as he envisioned a revenge that would never take place.

But things were gonna be different.

Everyone in the fleet seemed to say some variation of that same sentiment. Things were gonna be different. Call me an optimist... I had my doubts.

The Faraways, on a digital sand table inside CC of the Technate flagship, looked like a massive resupply point to me, for the last of the Monarchs if they could reach and hit it in time.

If they were going to go dark and build a whole new civ where we could never reach them, they'd need stuff, and my guess was they'd allowed the Faraways to prosper without their "guidance" in order to rip them off when it was time to *di di mao* from Dodgeistan.

Like I said... I'm an optimist. That way.

Then, the Faraways plundered, the Monarchs could pretty much go dark and dumb-thrust their way off into the rest of the galaxy, never to be found again.

And if they supposedly had a space-fold drive on that ship… then they were gonna get away.

We have to be honest about these things.

Some people escape official justice in this life. I have my suspicions about the next though.

Plus, who wants to be the bad guy? Too much work and always looking over your shoulder.

But, and this is another thing we have to be honest about… they'd be back. At least for the payback. Or to just take back what they thought was theirs, by divine right, they being the divine who gave themselves that right.

So, we would need to kill them. Even if we did have to fly five hundred years out into a trap to get it done.

And that made the meeting at Typhon way more attractive.

"Get it done in one, son," said the first sergeant when we discussed the importance of that coming battle I secretly already knew, thanks to my PTSD on installment, was gonna be a real hot mess.

Maybe the last hot mess the company ever got itself in. The tragedy this slice of the logs since Astralon has felt like it was shaping up to be.

Or Crash, if that works for you.

And then after that… the company had made its deal with the Kong.

We'd see the Monarchs buried. Then our credit was good. Right? That was the deal.

LOL.

Mercenaries always get crossed on the contract, silly ruck hobo.

Still… you gotta have faith, even if it's faith in a hot mess coming at you twenty-four hundred feet per second.

Optimist.

Me.

The Faraways were hell and gone. Have I said that yet…? If I have, it can't be overstated. It's really far… away. Hence the name. The distance is mind-numbingly incomprehensible even with space-magic jump engines. In reality, the Faraways are to most just a rumor of a system, or systems, few in the human expansion had ever been out to, much less really heard about. It's literally that place on a map where things get sketchy and the known information matches exactly the amount of rumor, question, ghost stories, and unanswered questions that abound in the areas not marked.

Long-ago mapmakers inked such places with cute little notes like…

Here be dragons.

So we had that going for us.

Already fast messenger ships were hitting the local communications network, broadcasting that the *Dark Star* was hitting small colony worlds near the edge, places already rocked by twenty years of war, overrun by revolts or the chimp raids. Now the Monarchs were looting them for any resources the massive ship could carry off into its deep space salvation run.

We had no idea why they were doing this, but we had our guesses.

Some said it was just for supplies to start their new stellar tyranny wherever they were going off to. Me. I said that. Said it to the captain during a brief.

"Nonsense. Sir. It's all about the caches," muttered Chief Cook during one late afternoon brief before we'd joined the growing battle fleet in orbit around Marsantyium. The wan red light of that world filtered through the windows on the ops deck along the upper hull of the *Spider*. "That would be my guess. Sir!" announced the Voodoo intel and psyops warrant with a little too much gusto. Too much certainty. Like he was selling us something that was the opposite of what was good for us. But that was his standard operating procedure when he was about to lay something really crazy on the company that would involve a dangerously suicidal attack against overwhelming odds, black-market grade pharmaceuticals, or some sort of subterfuge only rubes at local planetary backwater Pleasure Raves would fall for.

And sometimes… in particularly tragic operations he'd planned and executed in the past on behalf of the company… all three at the same time.

"It's the *last heist* mentality, sir," said the chief behind his mirrored aviator sunglasses, smoothing the slicked-back sides of his hair where it was dark as opposed to the balding top he kept neat and shining. "Classic third-worlds Banana Republic dictator thinking. Sir. Colonel Fuller did a huge study on this back in Psyops Command, and it was completely eyes-only black-list classified for the real spooks and deviants that ran that particular circus. But it laid it all out pretty clear as day. It was definitely our jam and the sickos liked it. I should know. I thought it was solid and would've done it myself had I been presented the opportunity to dev such a doomsday plan for high-priority off-books assets that needed to be scooped up if the villagers suddenly came to the castle with pitchforks and torches."

He muttered some angry curse at someone named "Hannerty," waved his hand as if driving someone away, then fixed us with a mirrored stare as though none of that had just happened.

Also no one knew who "Hannerty" was.

Chief Cook lowered both hands to his battle belt, checking that his pistol was there for some reason. Actually that wasn't a bad idea on his part. Why? Company mood was basically, regarding Chief Cook… we were gonna shoot him if his plan, or assessment, was something we immediately recognized as possibly getting half of us killed outright in the first five minutes of contact.

I mean honestly, that was pretty smart of him. To go around armed all the time in those days as we got ready to head out into the deep dark to hunt down our sworn foes.

I knew of at least five company members who'd sworn some kind of dark pact to see the chief dead. Seriously. Cut their fingers and signed their names in blood and all. They'd sworn to shoot him the next time he came up with one of his dangerous half-baked plans.

And…

Full disclosure… I was an honorary member of this *Get Chief Cook* cabal who met on Tuesdays down in the back of Secondary Engineering where no one ever went because that area had been blasted to pieces in a running gunfight with Alpha Prime Six World interdiction cruisers whose government hadn't wanted to pay up on our contract to eliminate their rebels and tried to have us murdered in space instead. It was stupid really, the Tuesday meetups. We drank what found-hooch we'd been able to find in the ruins of Marsantyium, plotted murder, and discussed and assessed whatever the crazed Voodoo warrant psyops chief had been skulking about on that week around the *Spider* and general planetside operations.

I thought it was good for them. The cabal. The conspirators. To get it out of their systems. *Aaaaand...* even an ace hole card I might need to play sometime, if just to save everyone's life. Seriously he wasn't going to drug me, or paralyze me, *again*. Not if I had anything to say about it this time. If it even vaguely went that way, then hell... I was going to kill the Voodoo warrant officer myself.

Trust me... I'm aware of the contradiction that I was keeping an eye on the cult, as any good NCO would, and at the same time pretty much a card-carrying true-believer member willing to fulfill the tenets of our faith with a double tap from behind or just one in the psyop chief's skull.

And...

Everything is a cult.

Soldiers love to start little cults within a unit. The Hotsoup cult was really starting to irritate command. The guys on the line... wouldn't have it any other way.

And then there was Catboi.

Boi with an i. Not a y.

But I'll talk about him later. Not now. I have a headache. And he's a very huge part of it.

Lately the *Get Chief Cook* cult had gotten pretty clever. They were attempting to think up some insult Cook had supposedly directed at Stinkeye, so our drunken space war wizard would make good and show Chief Cook "Da Heart o' Darkness o' the Universe" because of the fallacious slight.

Then... our *Chief Cook problem* was solved.

Yeah, it's wrong. But it's better than dying raving like a lunatic about giant mushroom men in the middle of a gunfight with bad guys, surrounded by drug-fueled visions of bats and melting faces as Chief Cook sucked on some "magic cigar" or slammed handfuls of pills yelling for you to hang on and "*enjoy the ride. It's all part of the battle plan, Orion. So hang on and don't look the bats in the eye because they might actually be entities from the other side... demons, officially. We're dealing with the vagaries of the dark side of the quantum. So, ya never really know, Sergeant. You never really know.*"

Him howling and hooting like the dangerous psychotic I knew he truly was.

Meanwhile you're filling your fatigues with feces and drool and firing full auto, getting hit a dozen times and feeling nothing because you've "bought the ticket" and are taking the ride.

Even though you don't count being drugged against your will in combat as "buying the ticket."

Yeah, not how I wanna go.

So... I joined a cult. Don't @ me.

And...

We have to be honest about these things...

It's something to do.

But also because I felt it was good for the conspirators who wanted to kill Chief Cook. They needed to get it out and it was basically harmless as I believe Chief Cook is unkillable. The drugs and gunshot wounds haven't got him. He wasn't just forward back on LZ Heartbreak calling in fire... turns out he was literally running around the advancing Ultra troops masquerading as one of them and calling in fire on his position.

"Found some gear that identified me as a forward combat air controller. They thought I was one of them. Thought I was saving their wired-tight-shut butts and in reality I was lasing them for effect."

"How'd you find the gear?"

"Shot a guy and took it. It was a little bloody, but the deception worked and that's all that matters, Orion. The deception. Keep moving… the cheese is in at the shop. See the baker on Rigel."

Then he winked and walked off acting like we'd said nothing to each other as though we were being watched by someone who wanted him dead.

We were.

Me. *I* wanted him dead. And by that time the cult was up to fifteen guys.

In truth, putting on my NCO hat, it was good for the cult to just blow off some steam and pretend they were actually going to kill him.

They'd even set up a holo-range down there with sim-targets of the chief running around with needles and pills trying to come at them in a threatening manner. They'd clipped recorded sound bites from his various intel lectures. Sometimes he'd shoot back at you.

Much of what was recorded was incoherent nonsense, even later.

So, I could keep an eye on things down there. In the cult. Monitor *their plan*. Make sure things stayed within *managing*. Then one day Stinkeye showed up, sober, at a cult meeting and just sat there and listened to their reports and terrible plans and schemes about how to do the chief in at a moment's notice should he plan to either drug, paralyze, or commit us to a forward assault against overwhelming odds while wildly claiming some kind of "element of chemical surprise" he'd had arranged that was all but undetectable amid the overwhelming gunfire we'd found ourselves currently in. Or some small moral victory he always claimed might be achieved in "our glorious deaths" made possible by pharmaceutical superiority.

Stinkeye listened to all the reports and grand planning…

Stone. Cold. Sober.

That. Scared the hell outta me.

Then he got up, muttered, "Gud." And left.

I felt the cult had gotten a little more serious than it needed to that day. Still… I let it ride. Let's just say I was keen to see how far it would go…

I know… I have issues and am currently not in therapy even though I should be. But…

That was when I thought I needed to either go to the first sergeant, or at least let him know what was up, *or*, warn the chief about forces and assets lining up against him even now as we spoke.

Give him at least a fighting chance, was how I saw it through a distant haze of nicotine, coffee, some alcohol, and PTSD installments of the coming Hot Mess that was really messing with my sleep schedule.

Maybe, I thought…

Maybe Chief Cook could even be cool about it and do some PR. Deviate from coming up with some plan to use gas, pills, or psychotropics to give us the "high ground in the battle against the Monarchs, Sergeant Orion! I'm working on something I call Thunderballs, and believe me you… this stuff really *kicks*."

He yowled like an alley cat.

"It'll make killing machines of your boys worse than that tin-can-for-a-best-friend you got and have you spitting death like an IG-M89 medium man-portable rapid defense gun made by Colt-Horakawa. *Five hundred rounds* a minute, Orion, nano-cooled barrel, cybernetic assist system, firing seven-six-two going forbidden popsicle in the face of those damned Monarch tyrants. Viva the company, Orion! Sic semper tyrannis! I'm on it right now, codename Thunderballs, and it do… *kick*. Few refinements and it'll sing… you'll see. Now move—we're being watched. Say nothing and don't make eye contact with the bats. They're everywhere today…"

That was the afternoon Chief Cook cornered me in the sprawling market tents beyond the dunes where the local traders processed the looting of all the Monarch treasures taken out of fallen Marsantyium.

"Oh… and I know all about the Tuesday group, Orion," he said smugly, conspiratorially. Smiling soullessly behind his mirrored aviator shades. His wide-spaced teeth broad and gleaming in the late afternoon red heat of that dying world.

The winds had started to blow harder and harder lately, as though sweeping off this world forever. The winds sent ancient red sand everywhere as the terraformed jungle failed and returned to what it had been for thousands of years.

"I'm all over that group, Orion. I've even got an *inside man*. So don't worry, Sergeant. This is all part of the plan. And… you've gotta trust the plan, Orion. It's the only way we're going to see the other side of this. Defeat is victory. We'll burn the starship to save it. Eggs for ten cents, sell 'em for six apiece. Trust the plan, Orion. No matter what, trust… the… plan."

I had no idea what he was talking about regarding *the plan*. But I did know about the plot to kill him and I wasn't totally opposed to it.

In my defense, I thought it would never actually happen. Like I said, I just knew sometimes soldiers needed to do this stuff to deal with what they'd been through, and what was coming next.

So… it was just fun.

I told me.

The fact that the chief had infiltrated it on some level made it even more of… *a game*. Instead of an assassination plot.

Right?

As I write these things now, I realize they were just hopes. I am terrible at *people*. Hence why I sit in the loneliest part of the ship, in my weapons cage, drinking black coffee and smoking in the dark.

As someone once said to me, there's a fine line between fishing and standing on a dock looking like an idiot.

So there the chief was, in ops aboard the *Spider* that afternoon brief, later after the market meeting in Marsantyium, explaining with an almost fervent certainty to the Old Man, a certainty reserved for government types when they tell you how taxing you more and giving you less is going to improve your life, that what the Monarchs were doing, as they fled human space, was looting various tech, or even… I don't know what to call it… *treasure hoards* they'd hidden during their long and tyrannical reign, in secure vaults all across human space. And probably some worlds we didn't even know about.

"Nonsense. Sir. It's all about the caches," muttered the chief.

Which is basically what I had already said it was before he blurted out "Nonsense" and launched into his spiel. Practically foaming at the mouth as spittle flew from between his wide-spaced teeth.

Then he added this little gem…

"Probably slaves too. Sir. That's their thing… usually is. With those selfish bastards. And I've worked with them, close, real close in fact, closer than even I liked, sir, and slaves, someone lesser… that's real big-time for them. That's their thing, those Monarchs. Part of their identity. Having the lesser around to *lick their boots*… even if they are on their way out to the edge of human space and off the history books forever… is like coffee and smoking in the dark for Sergeant Orion down there in his pathetic little lonely-cage he thinks none of us knows about. Someone lesser is the only reason to live for monsters like the Monarchs. The uber drugs and weirdo sex gets played out in time. Trust me… I know. They need someone to kick around just to get out of bed in the morning. Like I said, it's different, but just as morally bankrupt and pathetic as Orion and his lonely-cage."

Lonely-cage.

Everyone was looking at me.

I said nothing. I do have other reasons to live. I just can't name any of them right now.

No one said anything for a long moment. This final hit mission was looking grimmer and grimmer with each briefing. Seriously. Chasing the Monarchs out to the farthest limits of human space where it got real dark and murky, just to finish someone off who was already ancient history as far as the galactic civilization at large was concerned… was a lot to ask.

A lotta guys in the company were thinking about calling it quits for this one. Even with all the new recruits joining up. It felt like a one-way mission.

But there were other factors to consider too.

The chimps were taking control of everything now. And their attitude toward humanity was they wanted nothing to do with the human civilizations still thriving on all the ruined worlds.

Ever again.

Unless they needed trade, repairs, or some kind of expertise, the chimps were too busy with their own strangely enigmatic plans for their new civilization.

And the glimpses I'd gotten of it were… dark. Sometimes, later at night on Marsantyium, you smelled burning flesh. Soldier long enough and you know the smell.

Command's official policy was that was none of our business.

Still, the implications of it… *bothered me.*

And it bothered everyone because many doubted chimp civ was gonna be about bongo drums and bananas.

It was becoming clear that human space, or former human space, was in for some trouble in the near future, and humanity being the apex predator wasn't as assured as it had been up until now.

The chimps were about to assert dominance, and you could feel that. Everyone knew it. These worlds weren't gonna be fun, to put it mildly, for a while. Hard times lay ahead.

So there would be trouble. Eventually. And that meant war. And war meant mercenaries.

Private military contractors.

PMCs.

So that was big for us because there would be work for us to do if we were allowed to do it on the other side of this.

But first…

At the limits of human space, out there in the misty Faraways… who knew what we would find? But we'd go out there and hunt the last of the Monarchs.

The *Dark Star*, at that time in the planning of Group Zero Tracking and Termination of Target's best hopes and dreams… *Dark Star* was headed for one last raid in the Faraways. Much of the fleet could jump out there and hopefully force a conflict before the subsequent hop out to Typhon to intercept the Andromeda-class super-freighter coming in from deep haul out there in the big lonely where it had been collecting skip-probes coming in from distant unreached worlds far beyond our reach.

There were rumors of human micro-civilizations way beyond out there that had gone off the Monarch grid. And explored, and expanded, well beyond the Faraways themselves, even beyond distant Typhon… but who knew?

Myths, lies, legends.

There were a lot of rumors, and not all of them involved undiscovered worlds paved with gold and lost civs with fantastic tech and riches beyond imagining.

Some things heard, occasionally, sounded downright scary to this old ruck hobo.

And for all his faults, our war wizard stayed out of all this because he seemed bothered by something else and kept making irregular treks down to my cage to bother me…? I guess. Sober. Watching me like I was some problem he needed to figure out.

"Dat ain't da Monarch way," hissed Stinkeye from the back of the ops center where the briefing was wrapping up after Chief Cook's lecture about secret tech-caches being the real reason the Monarchs were heading the way they were heading. "Not dem to jes run away and all dat. Turn tail and hide. Nah. Dat ain't dem. Chief Cook is a liar and he don't know what da hell he talkin' 'bout and alls."

The Old Man turned and cleared his throat at the end of Stinkeye's ragged small menacing rant.

"What do *you* think they'll do once they're out there, Chief?" asked the company commander. That clear look of the indigestion of command on his face.

As usual.

Also the captain was the only one who used Stinkeye's actual rank of Chief Warrant Officer, Voodoo Platoon.

No one else ever did or would. He'd been too many times blind drunk and lying in his own filth, or in serious debt through Cheks losses to other company members, to be given the slightest bit of even honorary respect.

Even among mercenaries.

And that's saying something.

On payday Stinkeye's creditors lined up right next to the old drunk. Sometimes they even carried his practically lifeless body, stinking of his foul vinegary drink and personal filth, to prevent him from "playing dead" and missing the company payout. Company rules indicated Cheks debts got paid before the contractor did.

Less company homicides that way. Never none. But… less.

"Goals," First Sergeant would bark at me and the other NCOs. "Not always achievable, but always pursuable."

All Stink's Cheks cards were terrible, loser cards. And yet he remained an unrepentant gambler between payouts. Convinced the next hand was the one that would see him straight out of his numerous unresolved debts.

Fun fact. I don't play Cheks. But I like to watch the cards animate and do their thing against the other cards.

"Don't know," Stinkeye muttered at the Old Man with his one good eye. "Only more a dere mischief I 'spect. But dey ain't headed where you tink dey a-goin'."

Everyone was quiet like we were in church, or something similar. Stinkeye, drunk that he was, bad gambler he ever would be, had that trick of capturing your attention and making you listen, even if it was nonsense. Sometimes.

Heart o' darkness.
Dark places of the universe.
Here be dragons.
We have to be honest about these things.

"Might look that way to ya's all. But dey always go someplace secret ya don't want ta know 'bouts. Yet. Some place real dark. Some place folks dey never come back from at all. Never and no never. And dey a-goin' dere for true dis time, brothers. Dey goin' 'cause dey got some final mischief ta deal out on da big Cheks game for all dem marble-worlds everyone tink is dey's now. And ain't none of you ain't no gonna like it when da dealin's done dis time. Nah… dis a bad draw and dey got cheat cards, says Ol' Stinkeye ya war wizard."

He got real quiet, then looked around like he was seeing ghosts we couldn't see. And yeah, only the recently dead Choker wouldn't have gotten a chill up his spine when Stinkeye did his war-wizard act this way, this deep.

"We headin' into da heart, brothers. Dis time we headin' right into the Heart of Darkness itself. If ya was smart…"

He looked around at all of us. Even the Old Man.

"You'd call dis contract done and final on dis one. Find sumtin' else ta do besides soldier now," he barked suddenly, then dropped back into a hoarse and ragged drunk's whisper. "Ain't no one comin' back from dis one, Strange Company. Dis one is tangled with da Heart o' Darkness itself. Trust me."

He looked around slowly.

Then…

"Mark my words."

He took a hot swig from his totem flask and glared at all of us.

Chief Cook clapped his manicured hands slowly and then did an imitation of someone laughing heartily. Once.

Like a sociopath trying to pretend it was human and just like you.

"And what about you, Stink, ya old fraud… You *goin' on dis one?*" hectored Chief Cook from his spot near the captain. Imitating his archenemy for a moment in his own, bitter way. Chief Cook was standing like a specter in the dark behind the holographic map of known space and the various red glowing reported positions of the last Monarch ship.

Dark Star.

Stinkeye nodded slowly to himself, looking down at the deck of our starship.

"Oh yas," he said softly like he was just some child now. "I'm a-goin', ya sorry excuse for a lyin' spook. If just to see you get killed on dis one, and I hopes dere's suffering like you ain't never seen dis time, ya dark sorcerer from da nether regions of Suth. Plus..."

He smiled and it was... not good. Almost... sly.

"Ah got to see that Heart o' Darkness once more dat dey headed to... one last time. Yeah, one last time for—let's just say how we used ta before any and all of ya's were ever—*for da lulz*. For sure tha's where dey's headed, brothers. So dat's where I'm goin' now. And all of us too no matter what salvation ah tries ta offer, even if some of ya's run, and never no looks none back. Forget who ya were even. No... Stinkeye goes. And the company goes, and ta its death dis time."

He looked at me for a quick second and then turned to scan the rest.

"Even as one see it ta be true dis time. We all die out dere. Brothers and all ta the end."

DEATH AND DESTRUCTION

The entire company, or what's left of it, makes the deck of the vast and immense hangar inside the *Dark Star*.

I don't know the casualties, didn't know them yet. But I knew we were taking them, and it was heavy already. Monarch gunners had us dialed with fire from the gun emplacements and they didn't spare the belt. They threw everything they had at us in the first ten seconds on the deck.

This Hot Mess… it's all mine.

And… I saw it coming even as everyone gets shredded in seconds all around me.

Punch was hit bad but he kept pushing forward to cover… a small trench used for shuttle prep fifty meters into the enemy hangar that's become our last *X*.

I hear Stinkeye laughing raggedly like a rusty screen door banging open and closed in a strong wind even as we die.

I hear it above the calls for aid and the incoming and outgoing blare of automatic gunfire.

"Told ya…" he cackled. "We all's gonna die today on dis one, Strange! All gonna die… let's go crazy…" he croons, summoning his berserking magic for us one last time. Rage and fear building inside dudes being ventilated by staccato bursts of lethal and harsh, and undeniable… gunfire.

"If da elevator try to break down… go crazy!" he's howling over the platoon comm and pushing forward over our mangled dead as I see the wounded Punch dragging Suck, as in Suck It Up, the AG for the First's Pig. Suck was hit in the gut, and the trail of his bowels and blood follow Punch as I watch him haul the mortally wounded assistant gunner out from under fire and down into the trench just to get him out from under the heaviest incoming I've ever taken in all my years of… this… is… the end of the company.

I've already burned two mags and there are dead and not moving all over the LOD, the line of departure, behind us.

We catch a break… kinda. The enemy gunners don't relent and continue to hose us, but the *Spider*'s sandcasters give us fifteen seconds of cover as sand and micro-chaff fill the ship's internal hangar.

The electromagnetic dust won't last long as we are in that halfway zone where most starship hangars are able to maintain atmo between deep space and breathable oxygen.

In seconds the *Dark Star*'s atmo systems will blow our ship-provided concealment and not cover off into space and so… we have to reach the areas we've identified as cover before…

In the first moments of combat, I identified the shuttle maintenance trench as our next objective and ordered the push that has at least half my guys dead.

The *Spider*'s PDCs engage.

Huge *brrrrraAAAappping* burps of chain gun fire erupt as the point defense cannons target the enemy gun positions and hit them with forty-millimeter dumb rounds in extremely high dosage.

About six thousand rounds a minute.

I reached the trench just as the sandcasters' dust storm swirls off past the hulking *Spider* who is deploying her docking hooks to maintain a hold on the enemy ship before XO commits to "gears down" on the deck.

One of the enemy cannons fires and smashes an artillery round right into the flight deck, and I have a hard time telling myself that anyone still there—and most assuredly it would be XO—is anything other than dead.

M.O.M. could still run operations even though she's losing her mind after having her memory banks shotgunned back on LZ Heartbreak at Marsantyium.

Her memory blocks are badly compromised.

But I have no time for even that thinnest of comfort that there's actually going to be an exfil off this last of all *X*'s.

"Told ya not to get involved," whispers the ghost of John Strange at the Bar at the End of the Universe where the waiter wears a small red jacket, there is acid jazz, and the ice burns like the stars of Orion.

Now, in the dark of the shuttle maintenance trench, I ask for a count to see who's made it this far.

I got...

Scooth and Duffy who came over after Dog was no more. Goods the gunner is dead out there on the deck and I can see that his ammo bearer won't make it out of the trench where even now he's dying despite Punch's efforts even as he bleeds all over himself.

Yeah... Hot Mess makes it sound fun.

And it's anything but.

Jingo the ASL, assistant squad leader and SDM, hasn't made it into the trench either and I can't chance a look up because the gunners saw where we went down and now they're laying the hate on thick as Komaloup syrup.

Yeah... we're not *gonna* die.

We're dead already.

There are other shuttle maintenance trenches and some docking cranes the rest of the company made for. Comm is sporadic, broken and distorted when it manages to come through.

The enemy is running jammers.

I huddle in the trench knowing things are already going horribly wrong from the start. I have what remains of Fourth with me which somehow ended up as my New Guy squad. I'd stacked them behind First like that was somehow gonna keep them safe.

Now... I knew they, and we... we are all gonna die on this *X*.

In just the next few seconds.

It's a strange thing to measure your lifespan in seconds. There's a cold clarity you never expected that comes with it.

And then I'm awake in the cage and the dark. Lying with my head on the table where I'd been doing some primary maintenance on the Bastard. Getting her ready for the Hot Mess I should not go to. No one should.

The cage smells like old equipment, issue canvas, gun oil, my smokes, and the coffee I keep in the Perk-O-Max.

It may not smell pretty. But it's life and it's comforting and it's the opposite of all this dreaming PTSD in advance I keep having about what we're heading into and what will surely become of us.

It's as real as real gets, and I swear as I look about at the gun parts and all my little totems of this life I keep here in the dark with me.

I reach for the half pack of smokes, make flame, and tell myself it was just a nightmare as I inhale the dart in the darkness, watching the ember at its length glow to life and thinking how that's a metaphor for something important.

I blow smoke and watch it curl and twist.

"It's just a nightmare…" I hiss.

I'm a liar that way.

But here's the truth.

Sometimes in the business of leading men into combat and managing that unmanageable chaos… you gotta lie to yourself about the odds, their odds, your odds… if only just to go into what no sane or rational man would dare ever do.

Ever.

It's just a nightmare, Orion. That's all.

We have to be honest about these things.

I watch the smoke and think about the eel girl's long arms as she curled about me and made me feel… alive.

What did she say?

CHAPTER TWO

The Star Khans of the Technate decided to call the strange collection of old warships the *Spider* had fallen into… *Rogue Fleet*.

Yeeehawww, boys!!!

After that, everyone got real excited 'cause that name was seven shades of pure D-beam strike and the first shirt was recruiting hard because everyone wanted to march, or rather fly, off to what was being built up as the greatest battle of all time.

For Freedom. And all that. Again, my doubts have been officially registered and the call and pull for me to find a scout vessel and teach myself how to execute a seven-parsec jump without hitting a star or stellar body was as strong a pull as the tides of any given sea.

I could feel the waves crashing against the sand that was my broken soul.

Yes… that's me being literary. That's all you get. Don't ask for more. I'm sure we'll have casualty reports and actions on the objective soon enough and even I can muster the purple for that horror.

So…

Yeah, lotsa young starry-eyed recruits were getting pushed gear by Chungo, evaluated by Cutter, when he was sober, and scared to death by the boys on the line as Top found a place for them to die alongside the rest of us.

Me?

I drank coffee in the cage down there in the dark past aft stores, tried to read some ol' dog-eared paperbacks about cowboys from long times ago I never knew, and waited for first jump to get ready to execute.

I'd been here before, I told myself. I knew how this was gonna go.

Nothing to worry about, right? And those dreams… they were just dreams and certainly not… prophecies.

I'm not a prophet.

Just a merc ruck hobo who's been there, done that, and got the gunshot wound.

But things felt uneasy anyway. Sometimes down there in the dark, alone, listening to all the strange and small, and suddenly great noises, abrupt bangs, unexplained crashes, massive gears or cylinders locking into place… all the terrifying noises a starship makes, reminds you a ship like the *Spider* is half haunted house.

That was when I heard the sound of dry crunching leaves sometimes in the silences in between.

I began, unconsciously, to look around for drifting autumn leaves on a fall day. It had been a long time since we'd seen her friend. Now she was back as a medic, the Little Girl.

And the big question, unspoken mostly, was where was her friend?

The Wild Thing.

The sounds of the starship, barely audible most of the time, made me uneasy.

But I thought it was just the night terrors about our extermination that had me jumpy. I told myself I was drinking too much coffee, smoking too many darts. Told myself as I was pouring another cup and sticking a smoke in the side of my mouth. Told myself that as I sat in the cage on my old chair and watched the shadows, certain there was someone, or something, there in the darkness watching back.

Finally, Rogue Fleet, *yeeehawww, boys!!!*, orbiting around Marsantyium went to jump… and you've never seen a bigger, hotter mess of disorganized stupid. Of the twenty-nine capital ships comprising Rogue Fleet destroyer-class and above… thirteen managed to arrive inside the designated jump window exit around the Faraways' navigational beacon.

Now, if we had been immediately involved in full-bore ship-to-ship combat with the *Dark Star* at max missile engagement range, movement to contact but capital-ship style—C-beams and scatter packs, PDCs and the occasional phason gun battery, and eventually arriving at close-quarters broadsides, then finally boarding, which we'd expected it to be once we ran this bastard down—we would have been annihilated within moments at those projected odds.

Thirteen to one. Disorganized and all over the sky.

Dark Star was what the Monarchs were cooking up to replace the aging Battle Spires was the rumor I heard one day when I accompanied the command team for fleet brief aboard *Thunderer*. But apparently, continued this official rumor from the chief petty officer I shared a smoke with, they only made one and *Dark Star* was what was known, officially, as an X-ship.

An X-ship.

Experimental, multi-generational, advanced tech on board. Dark Labs stuff not available to the rest of us star crawlers and jump-space junkers.

Man, that scout ship I was lusting after and the escape I had planned was strong when I began to consider how advanced a Monarch starship might actually be.

Thirteen capitals to one might not even be "bettable" odds on what used to be Vega.

Nether hipped me to what might have happened.

"There was a weapons system being worked on in the labs I escaped from, Orion…" he rasped as he burned one of my darts in a single go. Which is how he does it. "They managed to use certain Bishops that had an affinity for gravitational control, strangely common in the third-generation colonists who settled out along the edge worlds, a trend we could never tie down the specifics on, to… well… from what I saw of the project, anyway—I was brought in to consult on Bishop candidacy—they, these Bishops, were used as batteries to power what was being called a 'wave-matter' gun."

Batteries.

I shook out another smoke for him. Lit. Watched it disappear. Watched the curling smoke, blue, fade into nonexistence.

It's creepy.

He's my friend.

"Yes… batteries. And just like batteries, one firing burnt them and turned them into little more than… vegetables."

And I don't ask *You were brought in to help work on this weapons system, Nether?*

He's my friend. I know his story. It's here in the logs if you've taken the time to read them all. I don't blame you if you skip that part. It's hard. One of the hardest things I've ever had to listen to.

But that's why they don't pay me the big bucks.

"Yes, Orion. I was a monster too. If Stinkeye ever finds out…"

"He won't, Nether."

Because you are my friend. And I too have played the monster. I'm pretty sure we all have, to greater or lesser degrees, at some point in our lives.

All of us… are someone's monster. Whether you like that or not. It's a fact.

But that doesn't mean you can't change. Or make it right.

And Nether did.

All it cost was everything.

For the record, the moons of Vega are all broken up and that world is now an ecological disaster, never mind the multiple D-beam strikes and the chimps who have taken over the casinos and clubs and made them into the palaces of their local warlords. Heart of Darkness stuff never mind what Stinkeye says we don't know about "da Heart" as he puts it.

Now, Rogue Fleet Tac Plan was guessing we needed at least twenty warships to get our hooks into the beast.

Thirteen weren't gonna do it, fam.

Rogue Fleet, *yeeehawww, boys!!!*

We were gonna win, everyone could just feel it.

Me… I was worried about what else besides a wave-motion gun got cooked up in the Dark Labs and bolted onto the *Dark Star*.

Horrors abounded. No wonder I was having nightmares…

I smoked and drank coffee and was glad I was just an infantryman. A grunt, if you prefer. And I have no heartburn about that. I love that job description even if those who don't know use it to justify mass casualties taken and prices needing to be paid.

Yeeehawww, boys, we gonna win this time!

I could look around on any given training day aboard the *Spider*'s shoot houses and hull crawls and see the *prices to be paid* as they trained to be heroes and knew they'd beat the odds.

Just like the fractured moons of nightmare Vega.

Grunts.

Yes. And if they could get me and mine on board the *Dark Star*, then… I knew how to do that part. Breach and clear. Compartment-to-compartment fighting. Trench guns in effect. Firefights in main passages. Yeah, that was our jam. But up until hard contact… not my circus, not my monkeys.

We just gonna ride the assault racks to LOD.

LOD. Line of Departure. Down and clear. Move toward the gunfire and kill everyone.

That... I could deal with. Even if my PTSD on installment was indicating "no chance of survival on the objective."

So that first jump, thirteen capital ships and various escorts, tenders, and support freighters, made the insertion window within the first hour of jump-window insert. The rest of Rogue Fleet, *yeeehawww, boys!!!*, official trademark, pick up your t-shirts in the onboard commissary, would trickle in for days to come.

Not. Optimal.

In theory, we'd be getting shot to pieces one by one by the powerful X-ship *Dark Star*. With whatever strange weapons the Monarch Dark Science Labs had cooked up to arm her with.

And as Stinkeye would say later, "Thirteen's a bad number for someone anyways... question be, Little King... who number is it gonna be dis time?"

By the time we reached the Faraways, the *Dark Star* was long gone. We arrived around what were known by the official colony logs as the Dandelion Worlds, finding only ruin, madness, and planetary-scale slaughter.

The *Dark Star* in her stellar wake like some raging-deep-sea-of-tempests leviathan swimming off into the outer dark of deeper, darker seas beyond the ports of men.

Purple. In my defense I'm fighting the impending dread and melancholy by trying to be a real writer as it feels like this is the last of the company record and I'd like whoever uncovers it to think well of us.

Yeah, that's what I tell myself. But it doesn't help that Stinkeye's become some kind of spiritual melancholic brother, or believer, with me as we both seem to be locking in on the same wavelength of doom, destruction, and the end of all good things.

Fun, huh?

Even though misery loves company, I do not. Hence the weapons cage in the deep dark parts of our little destroyer where no one goes. Much.

"*Call me Ishmael*, Little King..." Stinkeye muttered drunkenly to himself as he staggered into the shadows near my cage. Then the drunken old space wizard swilled a hot gulp from his totem flask and moved off to torment someone else with his babbling witcheries and promises of debts unpaid and never remembered.

We'd arrived in the Faraways, officially known as "the Dandelion Worlds" in the cartography logs, and also to the inhabitants thereof.

The locals didn't call their home "the Faraways." Self-explanatory.

Now they didn't call them anything at all.

The Dandelions had gone dark on comms two months ago, during flight time out. Now we knew why...

Comm traffic had been, up to then, standard, and they were preparing for our arrival and coordinating rendezvous from local supply freighters.

Six months' jump travel to the truly last civilized worlds at the edge of human existence, chasing *Dark Star*, and we found a dead world, or worlds, instead of a frontier boom-world. If the Monarchs had been here, then we, and the rest of Rogue Fleet, would have been shot to pieces as we trickled into the jump exit window and then got wrecked by the largest warship ever built.

The *Dark Star*.

But they were long gone, leaving only epic-scale death and destruction in their absence.

Everyone had been adding *The* to the ship we were pursuing now. The last Monarch vessel. Side note: that *The* made it more ominous to me.

Calling it *The Dark Star*.

That made it more... *ominous*. Iconic. Not to be messed with. Man... I had the creeps. And I was committed now once we'd jumped for the Faraways. I was going all the way because the chance of finding a junk scout ship to get all together and take myself off somewhere safe and unexplored and probably less dangerous but still dangerous... had passed.

We were hunting now. Badly. But we were hunting.

Rogue Fleet. *Yeeehawww, boys.* Sad trombone sound.

I got a thing for words and their passage, their evolving. So there's that. *The Dark Star*. Perhaps you've guessed that about me by now, having read my time in the logs.

We have to be honest about these things...

In reality, you probably think less of me and have come to the conclusion that I have a tendency to nitpick details. Okay. At least I don't go on and on about coffee.

Man, that'd be annoying. And I love the stuff. So indulge my purple and my small observations. I'm sure the gunfights and boarding that are about to end the company will more than make up for my shortcomings.

Hey, I might even get killed on the first insert and maybe someone like Punch will pick up the logs and you can hear about how much and how often he wants to beat everyone in the company senseless for general stupidity.

The funny thing is, most guys think Punch is really nice and friendly. Very likable. But it's only an act because after the first twenty fights, even though he's a solid soldier, we told him we'd have to let him go if he didn't stop talking with his hands and breaking people's faces. And putting them in the hospital. And killing one guy.

Cuts down on company numbers and the first sergeant likes to keep those up.

So, Punch started smiling more, totally fake but pretty good, letting things go, and learning how to use corrective punishment and a few other leadership and non-violent communication skills to get things done.

Once a month he comes into my cage and I shut the doors and we listen to the silence for fifteen minutes to make sure no one's come down that way. Then I light a smoke, pour another black coffee, lean back in my squeaky chair and listen to his list of people who, and I quote, "absolutely need a beatin' right now, Sarge."

He has even alphabetically organized it, and has a priority rating for each victim, unofficially officially.

Absolutely needs a beating is above *seriously needs a beating* and right between the two is *I will wipe the teeth from their face with* (insert nearest handy object on my card table which I call my desk). But the highest rank definitely is... *I will take them down to aft engineering and all I need you to do, Big Sarge, is show up with two sacks of lime and a coffee to make this happen, right now!*

Once our session is done, usually takes about an hour, Punch takes a deep breath, and I add all the names on his list of perceived wrongs to the training schedule in the form of a combatives session Punch will teach later that week.

The fact that it's a training environment reels Punch's aggression down to an acceptable level of violence but still allows him to strike, beat, kick, chop, choke, and occasionally electrocute them.

I love seeing their faces when they find out they're on the schedule. They know what's coming and they are not happy about it.

This usually rectifies irritating Punch in the future. Guys get better at their soldier skills much faster, which is usually what irritated Punch. That, and trying to do something they saw in a video game, or a spectacuthriller. Once.

This has not worked on Catboi, who has gone on Punch's list a number of times and I feel will soon arrive at the *All I need from you, Big Sarge, is to show up with two sacks of lime and a coffee to make this happen, right now!* level of importance on his list.

But I will get to that. I will get to Catboi.

Unfortunately.

So…

There may have been a lot of tough talk along the passages and on the cargo decks where we were running our shoot houses about the impending boarding action we were expecting, guys going full ghetto war ogre and thundering, "Caps to pop and bodies to drop, *baby!*" when they weren't invoking *Saint Hotsoup*, or just ululating his tag like it was a bodily function for no reason anyone in charge could find a rational explanation for.

It was annoying. All team-level leadership positions and even the new guys, except for Catboi, were taking to it if just to fit in.

So life's real fun for me right now.

Truth was it was the sudden appearance of the article *The* before *Dark Star* that told me guys were fighting hard not to let all the scary stories get to them. Dark rumors of an actual X-ship in play, and the weird mind-bending tech we were possibly going to face inside that hull when it was knives-out-time… there to put paid on the Monarchs once and for all time. If you didn't get cool with the fatally unexpected pretty quickly, then that was a lot to hump in your ruck for the coming boarding action.

Tough-guy talk and general bravado in the face of certain death was how the infantry in all the armies that ever made it… faced such situations.

But that *The* had found a way in. Messed with us. The Cult of Hotsoup comforted themselves with their unjustified saint as some kind of emotional twilight seemed to settle on the stellar horizon for all, despite all efforts to think happy thoughts and run shoot houses and hull-breaching exercises at close-quarters murder.

They needed to process their impending doom. Our… impending doom. My PTSD on layaway seemed to second these notions but I kept all that to myself.

We have to be honest about these things. I am. Even when I don't want to be anymore.

Dark Star was a ship we knew very little about. But, when matched in size and scope, easily measuring larger than one of the fabled ruined Battle Spires the dead Ultra Marines had once flown into combat, it was formidable in the imagining.

Dark Star was a giant disc. A saucer really. A disc-ship as it was known in starship hull identification types. A completely revolutionary concept and design in stellar hull-building according to starship dorks and "experts" all across the company.

Everyone seemed to be one now to some greater or lesser extent. So it has always been with humanity in lieu of hard data or what some call facts. She was rumored to be loaded to the gills with state-of-the-art Dark Tech weapons straight from the Monarch insidious monster-making labs. Add in all the Bishops they'd managed to loot from their various black sites along their way straight outta human-controlled space…

… and it was gonna be a real knife-and-gun show like nothing the company had ever seen before, was the general consensus. So, we ran our war games of fire and movement and fell back on what we knew, intent on honing that to a razor's edge.

Infantry tactics. Door kicking at the pro level for all the marbles.

Bishops, though…

Basically versions of our Voodoo Platoon weirdos. They'd be in the mix in there. Wizards, superheroes, call them whatever you want. We'd be facing monsters of a kind. We had three, and four if you count the Little Girl's Wild Thing. Some of the other mercenary companies on other ships might have one or two, at best.

The company was considered singular for having so many of them, much less just having them. I have no idea how they became a part of the company; they weren't there in the beginning with John Strange.

But the *Dark Star*, she had a lot of them, supposedly. Each and every one of them would be a wildcard of strange powers ranging from the telekinetic to the mind-bending, in there in the dark… of the *Dark Star*.

What they could do was… completely unknown.

So go ahead and train your guys for that one, Sergeant Ruck Hobo.

Okay…

Guys… I'm gonna want you to shoot real fast as soon as anything… weird happens. And a lot, too. Shoot a lot. Hell, mag dump in effect, boys. Only way to be sure.

Again, when using battle rifles as primaries I was not an enthusiastic encourager of automatic fire. You just burnt badly aimed rounds you might need when you found yourself closer to the enemy and swapping a mag.

But with Bishops on the horizon, I began to schedule a lot of sim range time for the squads in which we trained to use automatic fire effectively, and in high dosage. I had squad leaders humping all the extra mags and ammo they could carry on the hull crawls.

In the face of the unknown… the company had decided to deal with its weirdness through full-auto gunfire in adult-sized doses.

If you fail to plan, then you plan to fail. Amirite, fam?

LOL.

We were probably going to get turned into jabbering baboons or roasted alive by some firestarter.

And what the hell was Nether's power, exactly? I had no idea, and Nether didn't really either. Hope they didn't have one of those.

Oh, and then the Monarchs were sure to be sporting any of the old Model 501 combat cyborg teams they'd managed to raid from their supply caches. Hunter-killers, Eight Series combat models. C9-85 infiltration cyborgs optimized for terror and urban combat protocols with a heavy warfare chassis. There were other models specializing in other types of warfare. That was just Hauser's specs.

Terminators, some called them in reference to some ancient spectacuthriller or comic book… I had no idea.

And along with the unknown mag-dump Bishops and the combat cyborg teams like Hauser that the Monarchs no doubt had aboard, they had their personal security teams, probably the best of the best operators who'd been handpicked straight out of the Ultra Marines before they'd made their last stand on Marsantyium, "The Guardians" they were supposedly called, but that was unconfirmed and had long been the subject of boogeyman talk among the PMCs.

In other words, the Monarchs were loaded for bear and expecting trouble when we came knocking.

We arrived in the Faraways, the Dandelion Worlds, and found nothing but silence and planetary levels of death.

The whole system had been turned into a slaughterhouse that no one had bothered to clean up.

Of the battle we expected to fight here and would have lost at the place the maps had once marked the Faraways because of our awful insertion jump window, from the flight deck of the *Spider*, the company's ancient destroyer, all we saw was a dead system where once there had been something else.

Dead wasn't even... the right word.

This system had been murdered like none I'd ever seen.

And I have been to systems the Monarchs erased. This was... somehow worse.

Lights out.

No radio or electronic traffic of any kind.

Just some disturbing emergency broadcasts on repeat warning stellar traffic not to approach as the main worlds had suffered a catastrophic-level bioweapon attack.

A civ ender.

Just two months ago. When we'd been in jump transit.

These messages were badly corrupted and... not pretty to watch. The people making them had died badly, and were dying badly as they made them. We watched these barely living corpses as they tried to get the warning out to anyone hapless enough to wander into the system that interstellar traffic was to avoid these ports of call at all costs.

They'd been attacked by the *Dark Star*.

On the *Spider*'s bridge, strapped into our flight stations after initial jump entry, we waited in the ticking silence of the instruments and readouts for the fleet sensor vessel, the *Raven of Winter*, a Rogue Fleet scout corvette with a heavy scout-ECM platform, to develop a tactical picture of the system that seemed pretty much dead to our eyes, and definitely to our sensors. *Raven* was one of the few ships to survive the Ultra Marine massacre at Hulacco. Their entire navy had gone down in flames before the first pass and the *Raven* had jumped out at the last second to save the crew as the Ultras put that world to the torch for siding with the chimps and supplying them with munitions and operators to train the monkeys in some of the more advanced anti-armor systems that that world was once known for producing.

The Ultras spared no one on Hulacco.

Rumors I'd heard of the massacre defied sanity. The Ultras had gone full death cult, torturing and executing entire local populations even when there was nothing to be gained.

If I were to write a history of that time, I'd definitely list the era of the war between the Monarchs and the chimp/insurrection forces as *The Dark Ages*.

I'd heard some horrorshow stories. For sure.

Apparently, the Ultras just wanted it marked down in the permanent record that they'd been those types of stone-cold killers. I guess. They iced the population just to make a point. *Don't mess with us. Even the memory of us. We really were that hard.*

Like they were writing their own epitaph. Which… they basically had. They saw the end coming and they wanted history to remember them as real live boogeymen. Monsters. They knew the Monarch fall was at hand, the jig was up. So they wanted their place in the history books marked down with the words they'd lived their lives by.

Actions.

Penned in blood.

Ulysses Two Alpha Six, one of us now who'd once been one of them, said nothing and continued his relentless training, and the hardening of the men we'd placed him in charge of. I'd promoted him to assistant squad leader in Jax's squad.

He drove them relentlessly and it was considered a tough draw to end up in his squad.

He was hard.

And they got hard. Or they weren't there anymore.

And I had to admire that. The Old Man did without saying a word. You could tell. Ulysses was just the new him. They were cut from the same cloth.

In a way… in some ways and not all ways… he reminded me of Sergeant Hannibal. And sometimes that gave me a cold shiver because I knew he'd be better at what he did than Hannibal had been.

And Sergeant Amarcus Hannibal would have ended up a warlord if he'd gotten command of the company.

Or maybe that's just what I tell myself to justify murdering him in a burning supply crawler.

But those are my secrets and for now these lines are redacted in the log. You can read them upon my death. Once M.O.M. has me officially listed KIA, they will be unredacted and most of all my secrets will be spilled.

Some, I'll keep. They're harmless now, and mostly… just personal.

Ulysses Two Alpha Six was a killer… but so was my karambit when I put a keen edge on it. Not an easy thing to do and a hassle because of the curved talon blade. But a reminder to do so because the karambit kills, and Hannibal was dead.

Back to the Ultra Marine slaughter at Hulacco…

Joke's on them. I doubt there are going to be any histories left or written down in the real dark ages to come. The chimps seem to be doing their best to erase humanity. One world at a time. They're starting with architecture and statues. Burning books and anything they can find that seems to be human art. And of course there are rumors of vast slave populations on distant colony worlds, and…

… *farms.*

Vast preserves where humans are *free range… cattle…* and sometimes sport… hunted…

… and then harvested.

You do the rest of the math. I'm full up on darkness and we're not even there yet.

But those are just rumors. I cannot confirm them. I cannot deny them. Information isn't a reliable thing these days. It's very hard to find the truth.

We have to be honest… about these things.

So *Raven of Winter* completed her deep scans and downloaded an encrypted survey report and comprehensive sensor scan to all the ships of Rogue Fleet that had managed to thread the jump-insert window.

And oh yeah, hey... what was this ol' ruck-hobo you say... what's he doing on the bridge deck of the *Spider*, inside a flight helmet and running a flight crew station, gazing out through the thin slit of the forward ob, *forward observation*, and trying to figure out where the *Dark Star* was in all this hot mess of stupid jump insert... what's Sergeant Orion doing now, you ask?

Well, I'm officially flight crew now. On the *Spider*.

Got a pay bump too.

I'm legit now, kids.

Here's how...

CHAPTER THREE

Usually six months' jump time would have meant M.O.M., the onboard ship's AI, would stack and rack us in coffin-sleep down beneath the *Spider*'s main general quarters. Deep down inside extended Medical and Biological Transport. But because we knew we were going to be performing light infantry boarding operations against *Dark Star*, at some point when we caught up with her, to put it mildly, we trained our butts off in the meantime. And then some.

We trained... *hard*. Not an understatement.

Zero-g combat.

On-board systems capture.

Shoot-house runs every day on the cargo decks with mocked-up ship's corridors, berthing bays, bulkhead defensive positions, and every possible ship diagram we could come up with.

Marksmanship inside tight quarters on board a ship in the middle of a firefight meant every shot had to count quick.

So we drilled that as much as possible getting our new recruits up to speed. And being ready to mag-dump effectively on any Bishops that got inserted into the combat mix against us. Never mind the cult out to get Chief Cook.

It was here, shoot-house runs, that Catboi excelled. But I'll get into him later. I wished he'd been bad... but he wasn't and so I couldn't wash him off to someone else no matter how badly I really wanted to.

We practiced controlled breaching demos without hull rupture, too.

All that Marine stuff we hadn't needed as ground-pounders in any of the planetary operations we'd been pulling for the highest bidder in recent years.

Two guys came in handy in getting this done for the company. Of course Ulysses Two Alpha Six. The ex-Ultra was a master of everything war. And Ultra Marines were extensively trained in ship-boarding operations.

We had yet to find any soldier skill he did not possess in spades.

And Gunny. Gunny was new to the Strange.

The story of how he came to roll with the company on the galactic mat of PMC warfare goes that the first sergeant was in the weapons bazaar back on Marsantyium one hot fading afternoon shilling for recruits, crawling the pop bars and shady alleys turned gambling establishments, when Gunny appeared like some ramrod colossus of lethality and razor-sharp crisp precision death.

Clearly, he was an NCO.

Of some sort.

Clearly he'd been a Marine. Gunny was black. Cigar clenched between his startling white teeth. Marine fatigues pressed and starched. Black boots highly polished. Which was saying something given all that red dust of Marsantyium being swallowed by its past.

"You private contractors?" growled Gunny crisply and business-like at Top. He was carrying a green duffel in one massive paw. The issue duffel matched his fatigues.

The first sergeant sized up his sudden questioner, knew the deal immediately and dispensed with the usual pitch of combat, pay, and exotic tentacle chicks in every starport the company went and killed people for credits in. Punch was with the first sergeant. So I got the play-by-play later.

"We are in fact the universe's *best* private military contractors, Gunnery Sergeant," replied the first sergeant grandly as he eyed the tall, dark, powerfully built man's rank still affixed to his perfect yet faded fatigues. "What unit were you with in the Marines?"

Gunny's head swiveled, scanning the shaded alley filled with exotic caged birds and easy-comfort girls promising drugs and oblivion for a few hours in exchange for pretties looted from the corpse of Marsantyium's red marble palaces. Then Gunny landed his stone-like gaze back front and center and took them both in. Punch and the first sergeant.

"Three-Nine. Game's over and no one wants to Marine anymore. Lookin' for work," he practically barked.

"Well then, Gunnery Sergeant... we got work," answered the first shirt, dispensing with the pleasantries.

"Good. I'll take it."

Then Gunny was one of us. Just like that.

For better, or worse.

The first sergeant explained the details to the former gunnery sergeant. New Guy status, the platoons, earning a tag. *Brothers to the end*. All that jazz.

Gunny listened, never removing his unlit cigar from his mouth.

Then he just growled at the conclusion of the first sergeant's spiel.

"Ain't no New Guy," rumbled Gunny as Punch would report back to me. "Stacked 'em deep on Call's World and the Mohika. Name's not important, but you will call me Gunny for your... unit *tag* protocols. Gimme a platoon of... whaddya call 'em... new guys," he said this with barely concealed contempt, "and I'll turn 'em into lifetakers and heartbreakers each and every one. That or I'll space 'em out the airlock myself. Deal?"

Deal.

Which wasn't even a question the way Punch tells it.

That wasn't the way it was done in the company, but...

"Deal," said the first sergeant heartily and stuck his scarred old hand out to shake on the terms of the agreement.

Now Gunny was one of our new contracts. The first sergeant seduced him on Marsantyium without lies of glory and pay. He just wanted to... soldier. The rest of the company wondered why he'd even joined up. He was old enough to have received a pension, or... something. I don't know about those things. But I also knew something else because I'd been around the men some called professional killers and some called soldiers, long enough. I knew Gunny couldn't do anything else but

Marine at the lifer-level. Even if there weren't any Monarch Marines anymore. Gunny had served with a Marine unit out along the Lumina Reach. Lots of piracy out there near one of the Bright Worlds' main shipping ports. Massive haulers had to thread a system-wide asteroid belt and navigate a series of brutal gas giants to reach the main port. So the Marines out there patrolled the routes and stormed pirate vessels with extreme violence of action. Gunny knew what he was doing when it came to CQB inside starships. That became apparent immediately, startlingly so… when we introduced him to what we thought a "shoot house run-through" was.

And then there was the Mohika. Gunny had been there.

Straight-up savage tribal jungle warfare on one of the worlds out there. Dark nightmare stuff. So, he probably knew what he was doing…

Gunny's voice was a monotone low growl that sounded like he drank industrial-grade cleaning chemicals for hydration, and fun. The half-cigar chomped between pearl-white teeth, made more bright by chocolate skin, probably didn't help matters when it was lit.

He was scary, instantly.

He drew everyone's attention, and within hours it was clear he straight-up legit knew how to clear tight quarters and maintain security in passages aboard a ship. He made us painfully and publicly aware of our weaknesses and the lack of game we possessed when it came to training boarding ops.

He considered it his "life's calling" to ensure we met Corps standards for this type of warfare or he would "relieve the universe of the drain we provided on its existence."

His standard threat of punishment was to "space you myself."

And, for the record… I do not think that was an idle threat. When Gunny began to run things you were either gonna meet standards… or disappear.

I envied his commitment and knew I would never be him.

Command instantly recognized him as the ace up our sleeves that he was. And that we needed.

Gunny got us squared away in the shoot houses on the main cargo decks pretty darn quickly. Whether we liked it or not.

Spoiler… many did not like it.

The platoon he forged, in the aftermath of Dog's disintegration and the company's official retirement of that named element, was given to Gunny as one of the newly created platoons the company had suddenly grown into. We had lots of recruits now as we headed out to put paid to the Monarchs and their Dark Science ship. That was good—no one doubted there wasn't going to be a lot of death when we stormed *Dark Star* eventually. Best to spread that around.

So Gunny got a platoon and tagged the platoon *Red Devils*.

Devils for short.

He didn't ask permission from anyone to do that. He just did it and the captain let it happen.

The captain was smart enough to know that the kind of warfare we were about to engage in was something we hadn't been doing too much of on all the recent bad contracts we'd been getting dealt a bad hand on. Most of those had been planetside. Having a real live Marine NCO was gonna go a long way to a large percentage of us seeing the other side of this.

Some call it surviving. But... I was pretty sure we weren't gonna, and if so... well, you were gonna live with some stuff after this one.

But surviving...

That made me melancholy happy. Which is something I can do that apparently no one else can.

I'd added too many names to the logs, ending their entries with *Strangers to the Universe. Brothers to the End.*

I was beginning to hate that phrase. The creed. That epitaph.

Hearing the rustle of dry leaves on a fall day each time I thought about someone who hadn't made it... messes with you.

Having Gunny... it felt like punching whatever that feeling was... in the face.

A win, an unattainable win for me... was no more log entries ending with *Strangers to the Universe, Brothers to the End.*

I'm an optimist that way.

But the horror of hull combat inside an enemy starship hung heavy on us all despite Gunny's commitment to make us "lifetakers and heartbreakers" or he'd space us himself.

Then there was Hauser.

His hunter-killer cyborg programming was made for this kind of combat. And as he told me in his typically precise yet understated fashion, "I have detailed files, Sergeant Orion, on these types of operations."

It's just Orion, Hause, I don't say to him for the *many-eth* time.

"I have been developing as much information and intelligence as can be verified regarding the target ship *Dark Star*, Sergeant Orion. Currently I am estimating a seventy-six-point-seven-percent chance the company will perish in active combat within six hours of initial breach. The addition of Gunny has increased our chances of survival by zero-point-two-eight percentage points. He seems very competent. For a human, Sergeant Orion. I consider this an optimization of our survival chances and look forward to updating my calculations given further training. I would very much like to see your and the rest of the men's continued runtime."

Continued runtime.

Life.

That's how Hauser sees it with his fifty-eight seconds and change of runtime left.

"They are my friends, Sergeant Orion."

So...

For six months we got jacked in the onboard gym, ran the ship twice a day, cross-trained in a variety of specialties, medicine, commo, demo, recon, heavy weapons and for fun, got into our EVC armor, enhanced vacuum combat, and crawled the *Spider*'s hull when we weren't under jump. On a good day we went the long way across the *Spider*'s hull. On a bad day we went down one side and up the other.

That's harder. Way harder. And weirder along the bottom. Trust me.

We have to be honest about these things. Some things freak me out.

After that, everyone got released to go die in their racks, or crawl into the showers and fall asleep after gorging themselves on hot chow from the mess. That is, everyone except the seven of us who'd been selected for flight crew duty.

They complained.

I was excited.

My scout plans were coming together. I was getting free training in the operation of an actual starship. I was only rated to fly atmo craft.

After a hard day's training we got the rest of the night inside M.O.M.'s coffins, sleeping and going through flight-school sims regarding our assigned stations on the *Spider*'s bridge. Every three weeks or so we downloaded new sims and cross-trained at another bridge station for a week, then back to our primary stations for the next three weeks.

Here's some inside ultraball… you don't get as well rested inside coffin-sim training as you do with actual real sleep. But the XO had let the captain know that if we were possibly going into real live ship-to-ship contact, then he needed a full bridge crew to run flight control, nav, energy weapons, missiles, defensive systems, engineering, and comm-sensors.

M.O.M. and Hauser could handle the rest.

So, no kidding, there I was… riding nav three rows back on the flight systems side of the bridge, strapped in deep down tight in the g-throne at each station, watching plots and making sure we were clear of all traffic, friendly and foe.

XO was on left seat, which is shorthand for the captain of the destroyer-class warship, far forward near the main ob, and no one in the right seat, which in a fully crewed destroyer like the *Spider* had once been, a long time ago, would have been occupied by a slot. Since I had limited flight ops training… remember that dream of me running off and becoming a scout and earning my Class Two rating? Well then, in the event XO was killed in the battle, then I got to unstrap from navigation, in zero-g, pull myself forward, and take command of the ship.

"Then what?" I asked.

Well, as the severely aging XO put it, "Company's on board, Orion… you fight us out of whatever we're in deep of and get clear of it. Use the main guns. They don't make 'em like Beast One and Two anymore. Release M.O.M., or Hauser if she's gone offline, which is more than likely if we've taken enough damage that I'm dead by that time. They'll plot fire for emergency escape vectors from the conflict window. That's probably the best solution you're gonna get to not die."

"What if the company isn't on board?" I asked.

XO sighed and wiped some grease from his wrinkled forehead. We were working on repairs at the missile targeting and solution engagement station, which had been acting up in the training sims lately.

"That means, Orion, the company is most likely on the hull of the ship, or the target ship, and you've got to keep the *Spider* close till they breach hull and start clearing. You should be with them by that point so it won't matter in any event. But that's all you gotta do. The main rule of flying starships is *always fly the ship*. No matter what. Most ships crash because they aren't being flown and the flight crew is distracted by a non-flight problem they're trying to solve instead of flying the starship which is what they're supposed to be doing. Or they hit a star or some other terrible stellar anomaly that wasn't where the flight computer thought it was supposed to be. Anyway, if I'm dead, Orion, it ain't my problem anymore. I've put in my time with the company, Orion, look at me…"

I did.

He was an old man now. Older than any of us physically, though not technically. Spaceflight had stolen his best years on behalf of the company.

Do you have time for a story? Let me tell you XO's story now because for some reason...

When I look at him... I feel like his time is coming... entered into the logs for the last time with *Strangers to the Universe, Brothers to the End.*

And...

I don't want that to happen, even though... why wouldn't it? Especially given what seems to be a series of all-too-real nightmares that won't stop cycling every time I get some real sleep.

So, that's the upside of coffin-sleep and sim training.

No nightmares.

But... they're there... waiting. I can feel them.

CHAPTER FOUR

A long time ago XO, the executive officer of Strange Company or technically... the second in command, had been a dashing young army officer who graduated from one of the premier Bright World military academies, all fancy and posh-like. I've seen pictures in the logs and one he keeps in his quarters.

He was very handsome in that way some people just are.

Rumors around the company indicated he came from a powerful family back in the worlds. I knew the real story though. They were rich, but not players. They worked for the players though and that made them prosperous. His dad was a local freighter magnate and he'd bought his gifted, handsome son, someday to be our XO, a commission in one of the premier fighting units serving the then-masters of human space, the Monarchs. XO entered the Saturnian Batts as an assault squadron air cav officer flying dropships in support at Escalon. That was a real slog of a conflict from what I've read. Later, when he was who he is now, he told me he saw things he wasn't supposed to see during that war. Things he was supposed to shut up about. Problem was... he didn't shut up about war crimes and outright greed. Profiteering and not just war plunder. The friendly KIAs pushed him over the edge, and he started saying things to people he shouldn't have been talking to. He believed all the lies about a free press and fairness.

Suddenly the commission went bye-bye and his father died, also *suddenly* if you believe in things like accidents and coincidence. Things took a real turn for the worse for his family's fortunes. The family held on to some of their holdings, somehow, deals were made, betrayals completed, knives in backs inserted... and in the end a deal was brokered by XO's eldest brother... the scion of the family who ran the shipping biz. Now. The deal was that whoever XO had been, was no more any longer, as far as the Monarchs were concerned. Commission gone, social connections unpersoned, banks de-banked, opportunities lost like drifting smoke of the dart I worked while I listened to his tale of... not woe. Really... sanctioned betrayal to save what could be saved. Once these things were done and XO was effectively cast out of that tier of society... then the family could retain their position though most of their wealth was gone now.

But they could hold on to the ghost of what they once were. For now.

And XO was nobody. And never would be. Ever again.

Deal's a deal.

XO told me he told his brother to take the deal and that his brother... hadn't really wanted to. I don't know if I believed that so much as XO wanted to believe it.

But a deal's a deal and it was the only one on the table.

"I'd been ready to sacrifice over the rice paddies at Escalon to get the grunts some air support… so why not buy something for my family…"

He paused, held out his fingers for my dart. I handed it over. He held it, studied it, watched the smoke curl. Then handed it back.

"And buy what I could, Orion."

The Monarchs hadn't liked XO *not shutting up* about the war crimes on Escalon. So they'd ruined his entire family and left them with some scraps to pretend they were still better than everyone else back on their home world.

And that XO didn't exist anymore.

They stole his name. That was their price.

After the fall, XO wandered out to the starports near the edge. He found the company when I was just a New Guy. He came in and quickly got placed in the executive officer slot because he had the skills and experience to lead and fly a ship.

And he was an officer. So he knew the business of that side of the house.

In pretty short order everyone knew he'd take the company one day and no one was butt-hurt at all about that because XO was an actual good combat leader. A real killer who kept his head in the middle of a firefight, and… those of us who knew… *knew*… he'd done the right thing when it counted and burned it all down for a good reason. We could follow a guy like that. A man.

He was fair, too.

We were cool with his rise to company leadership when and if someday the Old Man got it or faded away too old to soldier anymore. Highly doubtful. The Old Man liked the action and forward was always where you'd find him if he could justify it.

About twenty-five percent of the company has a similar story to XO's. Though not usually writ so large and grand like some story made into romantic spectacuthrillers, or an old book the kind you never forget and think about through all the years to come. Something with beautiful characters eventually played by classy smoke-show actresses crying that *they can no longer marry him because he is no one*, and of course cruel brothers betraying him in the name of family. A lot of guys did it for their hard-luck families on some colony world or stuck in corporate servitude. XO's was just more… strange word here… *glamorous*. And sad. I'd actually heard guys who had similar tales, smaller, more desperate, hear XO's and then rage-punch something inanimate shouting, "That sucks!"

Maybe it's worse his fall was from so much higher. Marble mansions, country houses, sports cars… classy chicks who never knew a starport bar or a brothel.

The rest of everyone not in that twenty-five percent of family heartbreak are generally evading crimes of all kinds. The company is a great place to get lost in.

But XO's story explains me ending up flying comm/nav on the flight deck of the *Spider*.

So, in the company, doing the right thing… that counts for something among us. Seriously. Even though no one said it out loud, it… *resonated*.

XO was a solid stand-up dude who lived his life in the company in the same way we did, it was just that circumstances, betrayal, and fate had landed him among us instead of robbery, murder, and burning down a series of corporate fried chicken franchises like one of us who shall remain nameless as far as this account is concerned as we suspect the corporation actually put out a bounty on that guy.

Doing the right thing counts for guys in the company, guys who've often done the wrong thing, epically so in some cases, burning chicken franchises across a string of worlds being just one example of the "wrong things" that led many of those who ended up here, to end up here. And there's worse sometimes and we have to be honest about that, don't we? That, too, counts for something. We've all… strayed. Not all of us are fallen heroes. Lemme tell you about the time Punch tried to fight an entire planet sometime.

We had an unspoken code by which we measured ourselves and each other. It wasn't much, but it was ours. Doing the right thing counted. Yeah, maybe not like out there in the galaxy where everyone knifed each other in the back for a bigger slice of the action, where *doing the right thing* didn't count for anything because the money was thin on that side of the equation, but in the company… yeah, that kinda thing counted big for something with us.

And in the end, over time, you knew XO's story was absolutely true by the way he treated and took care of us.

And yeah, he was a stone-cold killer when he got into a fight alongside us on the ground. And one day, when the Old Man went too far forward like he always did, hardballers out and blazing hard-caliber thunder on an *X* he couldn't get us off of, then the day after that, XO would become the Old Man. After that particular bad day.

The captain of Strange Company.

So it has been… so it will be.

And we, the Strange, were good with that when the time came. XO was legit.

Now here's the irony, and ain't the universe a very strange place like that, just like Stinkeye always says it is. But the old destroyer we called home, the *Spider*, it kept breaking down along the way from this bad contract to that bad contract. Mid-jump oftentimes, we'd be forced into sublight haul, which had been standard for most of my contracts. And sublight haul meant anywhere between five and forty years' flight time as we crawled across the stars to our next exotic destination to kill for pay.

Which didn't bother most of the company as we were in the coffins. Living dreams and sometimes nightmares depending on what M.O.M.'s PsychAn thought we needed to improve our ratios in the company.

PsychAn.

Psychological Analysis.

So we slept. But for the guy flying the ship… different story. And XO was that guy.

While we slept, there were many years XO was out of the coffins, crawling the old maintenance tubes and dark greasy passages deep into the arcane wiring and ancient systems, to chase down some critical system failure that would have killed us all during the flight outbound… and we never would've known it deep in coffin-sleep.

Sometimes I think longingly about the great vast silences in deep space, alone on a ship full of sleepers he must've experienced.

We have to be honest about these things.

In the end XO never got command of the company because… *he just got old*. Long gone was the dashing air-cav officer who'd joined the company in disgrace. Here, as we crawled weak as lambs from coffin-sleep, was one of us gone old saving our lives instead. Again as we slept and XO didn't.

Those silences though...

The *Spider*, like one vast sleeping tomb, gently hurtling through the big deep dark.

Man... I got probs. But ask anyone who's ever been in charge of infantry... there's an attractiveness in the grave and the gulag and finally being left alone with no fires to put out.

That was XO's life, silence and saving our lives and keeping the ship running to get to the next gig. The next contract. Eventually, because the *Spider* is actually a giant piece of junk—*but hey, it's our junk* as we say—XO got older than the Old Man by living our years in real time, instead of transit time.

Instead of sleeping dreams and nightmares in M.O.M.'s life-like sims.

He's old now.

He's still handsome, though, in that iron-gray fox sort of way. Handsome where he hasn't been burnt by a cooling leak down near the heat sinks on the lower mains that one time when the ship almost melted and went supernova halfway between contracts, or marred by injury and accident and even a knife fight with a whore one time who swore he'd proposed marriage and rescue from her circumstances instead of just the momentary oblivion she'd offered.

He's old, rugged, lined, but he has good bone structure and seems better cut than the rest of us.

Again... honest... we... have to be about some things. Some people just get dealt better cards.

Being good-looking, even when you're old... is a pretty good card.

He's missing a finger. Some gear suddenly came to life he was repairing during flight, when it shouldn't have, as he tried to keep life support pumping for us while we were sleeping.

So he lost that and healed, suffering and popping in pills alone as we made another dark crossing.

I always told him if he got too lonely he could wake me up and we could talk for a while.

But he never did.

"I like to read, Orion. I have friends in those books and I enjoy listening to them. Hell... sometimes I even talk back."

Then he shrugged, smiled, and continued on with his shipboard chores. He was... always... busy with some task to keep the old destroyer running.

We all have scars, burns, wounds, and missing parts. Some you can see, some you can't quite, even though they're there. Trust me... they are there.

We all have those. Never ever think you're alone in that no matter how horrible your marring, burning, or unseen hurt is.

We all have them.

Or eventually... given enough time... we all will.

I think about that when I look at the New Guys heading out with us this time. And the new platoons forming and acquiring their tags as we get ready to go out there and die breaching the last ship of the humanity that once was.

The *Dark Star*.

The man in black haunting my all-too-real dreams of imminent death and eternal dissolution.

Eventually… we all will be missing something along the way. Eventually, even these new guys will have their scars if they make it past the first firefight, which I highly doubt they will this time.

But that's not why XO will never become the Strange Company's Old Man though. Never take command of the company. Scars, burns, and missing parts. No, it's the years when the company was asleep, and he was awake, begging, borrowing, and praying to get us to the next show. The Big Show. The War Show.

He's paid all our fares with his youth.

He's an old man now whose hands slightly tremble and if he sees you notice, he sticks them where you can't see them in his pockets and carries on with the business at hand.

He keeps more and more to himself lately, though it was only a few years ago he hung with the line guys during training, mastering right alongside us some new weapon system in case he was called to deploy forward and take command of the company in the middle of the next hot mess.

He was always easy to get along with even though he was an officer.

I remember him when he was younger though. Not that long ago in my memory. Now. A shavetail LT with a bad conflict under his belt. Then. Still some kinda true believer in war and the honor that supposedly comes with it. But dashing in a way none of us was. A leader. And strong. The kind of *leader of men in battle* you wish you were, wish your platoon had, instead of the dried-out, skinny ruck hobo they got. A wreck of an NCO with bad tattoos and a penchant for a dark weapons cage and old coffee… on a good day, only desiring to be left alone now, and just waiting for the other shoe to drop. Because it always does. The next bad thing to happen. The next fire to put out, or the next hot mess to buy it in…

You know… me.

"Ain't my problem anymore after that, Orion. Put in my time with the company… *and look at me!*" he said to me as we discussed combat flight tactics after a sim in which I'd managed to kill the whole ship and everyone on board. I'd asked him what would happen if he was dead and I needed to make decisions regarding the ship and the company.

"*And look at me!*" he practically yelled, but still keeping his voice low, a sudden wild look in his eyes.

I do. I did.

I wish I had words, when they do this to me, tell me their story and ask me to judge their lives now that they've spilled it all out after keeping it inside for so long. Too long. I wish I had words that were the right words. Somehow. Words that made them… *whole again*. Somehow.

I wish I had those. If I did, I'd just go around from world to world giving them away. Healing and speaking life. But I don't, and that's not what I do.

I lead killers, and kill, for pay.

Ironic, isn't it?

I wish, though… I had those words of life. Of *right-making*.

But I don't. I'm just the Log Keeper. I'm not Preacher and they don't go to him until they're dead and need to be seen to in the grave.

"I'm too old to fight anymore, Orion," XO whispered quietly that afternoon. "You guys are gonna come out of the coffins one day and find me long dead by a few years at least."

He studied me.

"Then you know what to do, right, Orion?"

I nodded. I did know what to do. It was in his contract, and in the log. Official. He was very specific about what he… *wanted done* in the event of his death.

But that wasn't enough for XO right at that moment. He looked at me hard, old eyes watery, burns and scars livid where he wasn't handsome still in that old successful-guy way he coulda been, if things had gone different for him. If he'd stayed shut and taken a cut of the family biz instead of mouthing off about war crimes that never should've happened… which somehow made it all the worse.

More horrorshow. The scars. The age.

Getting old while we barely aged.

It's hard to watch someone you knew young get old. I hate that part of life right up there with all the other awful parts I hate.

It feels… wrong. Even though they tell me it's natural.

I knew what to do. But right then he wanted to know that I knew. What's *to be done*. It's real important to him. This last… act… he has planned so well. Thought of in all those long crossings, alone in the dark, plotting his last message, or final revenge.

"You… know what to do, Orion."

But it means you'll be dead, I thought to myself. *And I don't want that, XO. I…*

"I'll get it done, sir," I said finally when I could no longer bear his questioning glare. Just a hoarse whisper in the subdued ship lighting and the last watch of the ship's night.

My words.

"I'll get it done, sir."

He sat back into the darkness of the flight deck where he'd been briefing me on the main power plant cutoff in event of direct hit to the reactor. SOP for rerouting power to the defensive systems from the lower batteries in case of damage to the ship's main grid.

You could still keep firing Beast One and Two off the forward battery stacks. Crucial in the event of a running gun battle under fire.

XO smiled darkly there in the shadows, savoring what would happen once he was dead. Seeing it all and… *relishing* it.

What I would… *get done*.

It gave him a great dark pleasure, and it was the only time I can recall seeing such a look on his face. Getting some kind of… final revenge, or satisfaction against those who'd done him wrong long ago in another life, not this one anymore.

In that moment he was not the executive officer of some broke-down hard-luck mercenary company barely gettin' it together enough to get to the next gig, stack bodies, get back to the ship and get paid.

In that moment he was the man of wealth and power and cruel cunning he could have become had he not been a real leader of fighting men, and honest.

I think that... *dark dream of revenge*... is a very common thing among soldiers. Among the company especially. The dream of "settling up" with the ones you've left well behind, or whatever. How things will be after you're dead.

Normal people don't get it. Don't fantasize about spending their life insurance policies after they're dead. We do. As though us dead star grunts will be around, somehow having survived the X we were supposed to have bought it on, but technically dead for tax and law enforcement purposes. Y'know. And as far as a few ex-wives are concerned.

This is the fantasy of the soldier. Maybe not the pro. There's a grim reality those seem to inhabit that's like some armor that can never be penetrated. But the rest of us... we like to dream about the lottery. We're normal like that.

I wish I could tell you every brother in the Strange has this noble thing they want done after their death. Some task we must perform after death. Some final honor, some tribute. Like we go ice some guy who was owed the icing in goblin spades on the Cheks deck. Or we give our dead brother's pay, and usually some extra, to some whore who said she loved him once when he binged out for three days and she fed him soup, made him live, and didn't sell off his gear while he raved and fever-dreamed about a bad ambush or operation gone horrible and six shades of wrong, and then somehow got him back to formation so we could mount up and hurtle off toward the next nasty little war to get paid at. Or maybe... maybe there's even a kid on some world he knew about, and we make sure they know who our brother was, to the kid... and of course there's a fund to see the kid to a better life where he doesn't end up like... *us*. The right thing. It gets done and all that.

I wish I could say that. I wish I could tell you we have those fantasies, and as keeper of the company logs, I know all the rights we will wrong when the Reaper has come to collect on our brother...

I wish I could tell you that and those noble things.

But not all tales are so... I don't know the word. But not all tales are those tales.

Some are just... again, I don't know the word. I just know what the man we call XO wants... *done*.

And so we will do it. When the time comes.

In the event of his death, XO wants us to hit the next world we land on after he dies, hire all the dancers and whores and every fallen woman we can get our hands on... and have them all come, and they have to be dressed in their... well... let's just say... *nightclub clothes*... come to his funeral, and they gotta wail. They gotta sob. Mourn. Scream at death. For him. It's gotta be real. And he's insistent on this point...

"It's got to be exceptionally crass and glitzy and frankly something I would've expected from Punch, Orion."

It's in his contract, with lawyers' signatures and all the money set aside to make it happen.

Seriously.

They, the whores we have to find and pay, then have to follow the open-air vehicle we're supposed to prop him up in, like's he's alive... even though he's dead now, like it's a parade and a wake at the same time. And they gotta wail like it's the end of the world and...

Pause.

They gotta call him *El Gigante*.

But that's not all, kids.

He wants his teeth gold-capped like he's some starport hood rat who just bought his first gat. After he's dead. He wants the dental work. And yes… he's already set aside the gold and pay for the dentist and any local laws that are being violated.

He is absolutely specific and detailed on how he wants this done.

He wants tattoos. The worst. He's already had them drawn up. He wants his handsome features… marred by these, frankly, awful tattoos.

And trust me, I have some.

Even I wouldn't get these. They are… bad in ways that bad has yet to achieve.

XO has beautiful teeth except the one that fell out from radiation poisoning during a leak on the number four reactor. The number four reactor always leaks. He wants them all gold-capped after death, and like I said he's made sure all the funds are available and that yes, the dentist will be well compensated for doing work on a clearly dead guy.

"I hope there's something left to work with, Orion," the XO has told me when we go over his death plans in the late hours of the last watch.

Me too, I guess.

So then the XO wants us to dress him in a legit-gangster track suit, gold-plate some company weapons, put a pile of chopped white lotus in front of his face and push his head down in it while he's toured through the space port we've found ourselves in, everyone crying and screaming and wailing about the death of whoever this *El Gigante* is.

I'm supposed to lift his head up out of the white lotus so the crowd can see the tattoos and the gold-plated teeth. Every one hundred meters.

It's in the contract.

"You'll do it, Orion?" he's asked me with a feverish gleam in his normally cool, placid eyes.

I will, I have told him. Sometimes knowing I'm lying when really I'm not and of course I will. Because that's what I do.

It's just that I want to lie.

I told Punch about the plan.

Punch said, "I know whores—they ain't gonna mean it. It's gonna look fake, Sarge."

"He knows," I answered. "The XO told me it will be even better if they fake it. He likes that better."

I asked why.

XO didn't explain. He just laughed to himself.

He also wants a donkey to sit beside him in the vehicle and bray at everyone, and also the fattest whore we can find to push his lotus-dusted face into her huge boobs and sob with abandon when I'm not doing my contractually obligated business of lifting and pushing his head into the lotus.

"'E is gone! El Gigante is gone! Noooooooooo!'" I imitate.

Punch remains quiet when I tell him this.

Punch, I have found, doesn't judge, and I wonder what he's gonna want when he doesn't make it off the *X* someday. Because I've seen his death now a dozen times in my waking PTSD in advance of the boarding of the *Dark Star*.

So I got that goin' for me.

The XO says that, after paying for everything, he wants us to give her, the fat whore, all his leftover pay and savings. He wants us to put his dead arm around the donkey and for the whore to make the donkey drink tequila shots to *El Gigante*.

"While this whole... parade... cruises around?" asked Punch finally in disbelief. Even this is too much for the very logical Punch. Punch who does not judge.

Yes. Yeah he does.

I have no idea what any of this means. I only know XO wants me to record it all, edit it into a file that can be viewed with a final message at the end. Then the screen goes black.

Then I'm to send it to a dead drop link he's made me put in the logs. I tell Punch this last bit.

"What's the message say, Sar'nt?" Punch asked astutely.

I shrugged.

"It just says... *Happy now?*" I answered. "Then nothing. That's the end. That's... what he wants."

"What does it mean?" asks Punch.

"I have no idea, Punch. But I know he wants to make sure whoever views the whole... parade... sees that message."

Happy now?

Punch says nothing. Only stares at me with his mouth open. Then he goes away scratching his head, leaving me to my darkness and promises made.

We will make it happen.

Those silences though...

I think I know... the story of the message. Without having to know the whole story... at all.

It's easy to decipher if you think about it for a few minutes. In the dark. Alone. Drinking coffee in your weapons cage.

He, XO, destroyed himself for them. Whoever they were. Those he once loved. Or thought he did. The receivers of the message. He destroyed himself so they would live the dream of their fine well-to-do family and "high" station. Even though it was an illusion. He'd taken the fall for them to go on climbing.

And all he was asking...

... from beyond the grave now that he was dead... someday when it happened...

Was...

Were they *happy now?*

And unspoken... if the loss of him, who he was and had once been, had been worth it.

Everything.

***

Orion's note to this slice of the log.

There's a part of me, a stupid dreamer part, that knows when the message transmits, the receiver will view it. And, perhaps, forget it. Never speak of it. XO, who he was, he's been dead to them for a long time.

But I hope...

I hope there's one.

A girl once, now an older woman. Maybe. Someone who would have been his wife, his lady someday, his lover, in their perfect life of wealth and prosperity. And now she's old, older, and she will say nothing to the others when the message is received. And maybe... in the days that follow the delivery of the message, she will go to the place they knew. XO and who he was, she and who she has become. Some small café, some quiet park, the rainy streets below the hotel that had once been a promise of a future together, tasted in stolen advance... and think of him, XO, and who he was, one last time.

With fondness. Perhaps.

Can this old ruck hobo of defeated hopes and dreams and nightmares of promised destruction... have one... dream? Hope? Romantic notion?

For his dead comrade.

I wish that for all of my brothers.

That we are not... completely... forgotten by the universe when the *X* has had its way with us for the last time.

I'm adding a picture of a fall leaf I found in the cage. I have no idea how it got here. But, I think it goes here. In the log. With XO's story.

DESTRUCTION

The PTSD-on-a-payment-plan my mind has apparently booked, like it's some vacation I'm not looking forward to at all but must go on anyway, dreams of nightmares really, keeps happening. Sometimes there are variations, but the major details, bit by bit, stay the same.

So I got that goin' for me as I try to sleep when not sim-learning how to fly a starship and hiding from everyone in my weapons cage between shoot houses where we get to learn how we're gonna die ten to thirty new ways each session.

Gunny is… unforgiving.

"You gonna git gud wit' me," he'll mutter around his chomped cigar. "Or you gonna get dead."

But that's where he's wrong. See, my dreams of PTSD whisper we are all gonna get murdered within seconds of boarding the Monarch ship we must pursue.

We won't make it to passage firefights and compartment clearing.

Sometimes, in my waking terrors, Punch makes it to the shuttle maintenance trench. Most of the time he doesn't. One time he throws himself on a live grenade one of the New Guys manages to fumble because we're gonna toss them into the next defense and go out on three and try to move and cover our way up to the first set of defenses the *Spider*'s PDCs have ruined.

In those horrors I'm shouting orders I can't believe I'm giving. I know… even as I give them… we aren't gonna make it. But I'm the first one out and into fire… surging hard and waking up heaving and breathless to the long-dead smoke that's burnt itself out.

Like we will.

I'm thinking, in that nightmare, that if we can get to the first line of defenses, then maybe we can turn this battle, this nightmare, around.

I think I shout something stupid like that over the comm even though it's clearly apparent we are… going to die… here.

"On three, Reaper! We're gonna turn this around *right now*!"

Usually someone takes a fast-moving round and I hear it move from faraway to close in an instant as it tears straight through the ballistic cloth armor of the EVC and the hit guy grunts as the wind gets knocked out of him and the terror floods in as he goes hot, sweaty, and cold as hell in an instant.

In the PTSD dreams… I feel all of this.

Fun, huh?

The flight deck of the *Spider* always gets hit by a one-oh-five artillery shell the PDCs don't intercept. Deck defense guns. As we hurl ourselves away from cover, the flight deck is always burning, roiling black smoke pumping out through the gaping hole one of the Monarch weapons has just put into our ship's command and control systems.

Where XO is running operations for the battle as best he can.

He's probably dead.

Now M.O.M. has got to get it together and run the defenses and get the ship actually hard-docked with the target vessel because if she doesn't… then we have no way off this *X* if we're even ever going to get that chance.

Not that we're going to make it another minute exposed and under fire and pushing into a wall of intersecting hot lead and tracer fire.

Not to mention the deck defense guns which in some particularly horrid PTSD dreams and nightmares the defenders, the Guardians, load with shot and anti-personnel flechette canisters.

Yikes.

"*We ain't gonna last thirty seconds out there!*" squeals the Third Squad AG, Runs, as I'm rattling off orders to rack a new mag, grab a frag, and get ready to go out there and do our thang.

"Time to get it on one last time, Strange," I mutter as I rock a mag in and tap it to make sure it's secure and I'm not gonna get any misfires, jams, or failures to feed.

"Don't matter, Runs," growls Punch.

"Gonna get it done in one, son!" roars Hoser from nearby as his AG, Hustle, nods and says, "Yeah, yeah… gonna get it done, son!"

They high-five each other and Hoser shrugs the belt he carries draped across his shoulders higher so it won't tangle or fall off as we start our push.

Incoming is chewing up the cover as it explodes all around us and ricochets streak off and slam into our ship, or the high ceiling of the hangar deck.

In one particular waking nightmare, a New Guy, New Guy One I think, fumbles his grenade and drops it, and Punch just swears and throws himself on it, saving all of us even though we are seconds from being cut to shreds by those Monarch heavy gunners defending the far end of the landing bay with everyone, and everything, they've got.

More auto-fired railgun rounds firing one-oh-five from the deck defense guns are punching holes in the *Spider* as I look up from Punch's inert corpse. The frag det was underwhelming, his EVC armored body doing a small jump as the fumbled grenade went off, killing him instantly. Saving us temporarily.

I look up, back out of the trench as I slump into the far wall of the narrow industrial maintenance slit in the decking of the strange and bizarre X-ship we have chosen to storm in order to restore our honor. It's clear to me, once again, from those streaking railgun rounds the defenders are throwing into our ship, our home, there's no chance the *Spider* will ever fly again.

No chance we'll ever make it off this *X*.

Another deck defense gun round tears straight through the top three decks of the ship, filleting hull plating and the decks underneath. Another round of flechettes a few decks below probably smashing into the ship's maneuver and fire control computers.

Ancient and reliable things.

Ruined and unreplaceable in the want of current times and situations.

Oh yeah… then in one dream they manage to strike one of the main gun magazines for Beast One and Beast Two and the whole ship explodes six ways to the Arcturus Maelstrom.

And we all die.

Including a lot of the Monarch defenders. I remember waking up with a smile during that one, my face numb from where I'd been sleeping on the table head down still sitting in my chair.

In the dark of my weapons cage.

It was a dry croak of a laugh I heard in that dream as the ship exploded killing us all. It sounded sinister and ancient. Cruel in a dream like death itself was murmuring, and the universe laughing, at what had been done to us. What had happened.

What had become of the Strange Company when they dared too much, went too far… got involved.

Never get involved, Sergeant Orion, murmured the ghost of John Strange over ice and acid jazz in a bar I didn't and never would have the money for.

Then I woke up smiling, laughing morbidly as I realized the croak of death's laugh I'd heard in the dream… was my own.

A PVC patch of the company's insignia, the laughing ancient Grim Reaper Astronaut… lay on the table next to my drool. I'd been meaning to get it onto my EVC rig. Now it stared up at me. Frozen in laughter as it always was.

Mostly Punch dies on the initial rush to the first maintenance trench, the PTSD on layaway, and so do a lot of other people and I'm left with what remains of First and Fourth with the incoming passing over head like lasers, the tracer in effect is so heavy.

So yeah, when Runs yells *"We won't last thirty seconds out there!"* it's not an understatement, or hyperbole.

It's a fact.

And we all know it.

And yet we go anyway, despite the fact that two of the new platoons have perished already. They tried to defend from the docking anchors at the end of the main runway into the *Dark Star*'s docking bay and got shot to shreds by the deck defense guns.

Bright blue pylons of laser light and chromatic steel are the pylons blinking their docking lights, casting shadows of the shot-to-hell and shredded bodies of our own.

The Monarchs destroy these positions. The volume of fire is so heavy that several of Strange Company are blown off the dock and back out into space off the edge of the hangar deck. They begin to drift away with the wreckage of the battle, blown past the force fields that hold on to the atmo in this docking bay.

Incredible technology I've never seen.

Heard of… yes.

Most dockings were hard-connect through a passage, or with the ship itself. Or, if granted the luxury of space station or ship large enough, an outer hull blast door which opened and closed and then atmo was restored once the ship was hard-docked.

This was, despite all the death and carnage… fantastic. And there was this part of me that had to stop… and grimly admire the spectacle I'd been forced to participate in.

This is real. It will happen. And I know it in the dream, and when I awake sweating and breathing heavily.

I watch as the dead of those two new platoons we'd added to our number in hopes of getting the company back up to what it had once been in its glory days, drift away in slow motion against the backdrop of our fleet, Rogue Fleet—*yeeehawww, boys!!!*—getting devastated out there as they tried to take the prize of the Monarch vessel.

And failed.

I had no idea what was going on with any of my other squads, other than that First was ineffective because Punch was no more. I checked the mini-map on the battle board that's sleeved on the left arm of the EVC.

The *Spider*'s thrusters howled as whatever was left of M.O.M. tried to hold attitude and maintain some kind of support position for all elements on the deck of the docking bay.

We could push forward now to the nearest gun position. But we could not fall back. The *Spider* was still trying to hard-dock and get gears down on the deck. Scans still coming from the *Spider*'s combat information processors indicated those defender positions forward were ruined by PDC fire and that we could take them. Now.

That's when I give the order to move forward.

That's when Runs screams... "*We're not gonna last thirty seconds out there!*"

Coulda gone sideways right there for me. The fear was in us bad and I was surprised the New Guys One Two and Three had made it this far.

Sometimes they don't.

We could bolt to nowhere I figure, but that wouldn't stop someone from taking to their boots, and there was a good chance everyone would follow instead of going forward and doing what we were here to do.

Fear is contagious like that. I'd seen it before, and we have to be honest about these things... done it a time or two.

You tell yourself when the fire is heavy and the situation is hopeless that... you're *just repositioning.*

Not running away.

And sometimes you have to. Don't buy anything from anyone who tells you differently. Sometimes you gotta fade.

So right when Runs stated the obvious and my gunner told him what was what and that we were gonna die, but that didn't matter because he was absolutely the hardest guy in the company, no doubts there...

A moment passed in which it seemed the incoming flying over our heads only got heavier... and then someone shouted, "Let's do it for Soup!"

And then "*Hotsoup!*" went up from everyone and we tossed frags and pushed right into the face of the enemy guns even as we hauled ourselves out of the trench.

In the PTSD I've paid for.

New Guy Two didn't move though.

Just stayed there staring at us in horror as we went. That's the last I ever see of him in these waking promises of future deaths I keep having.

In my dreams... I smell burning fall leaves.

Sometimes I hear those searing guitar licks that come at me like hot acid, and screaming, scouring winds that sound more like trumpets.

Sometimes.

We go up and over the maintenance trench lip. A few slip. Most push forward on legs that don't seem to want to move as fast as they should be if we are going to get to the next cover.

We do catch a break. For a second the enemy gunners and troops are too busy pouring fire into other sectors, other platoons being murdered so we might live, to bother with what looks like an overstrength squad trying to take a forward gun position ruined by PDC fire.

Our grenades have detonated.

Dead corpses of enemy defenders are ruined. The Guardians. A few wounded are reduced to KIAs as we overtake their former positions.

I almost forget to fire as we advance and only do so because I note a supreme lack of outgoing fire from my own beleaguered element.

They are just running forward, lumbering in the EVC armor as best they can.

Halfway to the first gun positions ruined by the *Spider*'s now-silent PDCs that were, last time I checked, fully loaded and good for at least hours of near-continuous fire, I begin to unload. Full auto because I'm just trying to suppress our way into a position we can cover behind.

I've set up the Bastard for CQB and replaced the bolt with one set up for rapid fire and willing to take the heat, damage, and action.

I feel good getting on the gun.

The action… it's the juice, as some say. I've wrapped the barrel in hypothermic grip tape to cut down on the barrel's heat, and the EVC's exoskeleton reinforces my grip and hold on the barking thunder of the gun. So it's just grip and rip and I dump on two Monarch defenders pushing in to take the position we're running… far too slowly, far too sluggishly… to reach in time.

The Bastard tears them to shreds in staccato thunder.

Me. I do. Guns don't kill people. People kill people. We have to be honest about these things.

Good. Kill 'em and let the universe sort, as Chief Cook mutters when advocating some new war crime he calls a plan.

Also… they ain't people. They're targets now. Tangos. Enemy. Bad guys. And it's me or them. I dust two with automatic bursts of steady fire that punch whatever they're wearing for rigs and armor.

They're weird.

Sometimes I can't remember what they look like. In the aftermath of my dreaming horrors all I can remember is the words… Dog Soldiers.

But I don't think that's accurate. It's just the words I use to recall the vague imagery that's all too real in that nightmare moment.

Anyway, ain't got time to do much more than pull on dark silhouettes as Monarch gun teams stationed on the second level of the back of the hangar open fire on us with frenetic abandon.

Like they're really trying to murder us.

That's because they are.

We have ten meters to go when Runs, Fartsack, and the other two New Guys are killed by plunging, and very accurate, high-dosage gun team fire.

Gotta respect the pro-level murder.

Most likely armor-piercing rounds too, as the belt-fed baddies we face do their best to lay the hate and patiently murder us into little pieces.

Hot streaking fire tears armor to shreds, smashing plates, ruining helmets, ripping through gear, and ricocheting off weapons.

It's such a sudden horror show of savage gunfire that as all four die I can hardly believe it.

In the PTSD dream.

Some are probably wounded and go down but the gunner who hit them is pro and he halts his traverse seeing downed enemy and then unloads a long dosage of fire on the area they are spread and bleeding across on the deck of the docking bay.

This gives us time to reach the forward enemy gun position ruined by the *Spider*'s PDC fire. Their deaths do.

In the dream.

Maybe forty-five seconds have passed since the assault started.

Wolfy is dead.

So is Klutz. Punch. All the New Guys. Runs and Fartsack. All of First is KIA.

Hustle and Hoser make it with me as far forward as we'll ever make it.

Hoser is wounded, badly, and I see blood streaming out of his EVC near the upper right thoracic. But he seems unconcerned as he crawls and rolls away from where he went down to cover behind the barricade the enemy gun team had set up to repel us.

Blood pools and smears on the gleaming and polished hangar deck of the *Dark Star* where he rolls and crawls for any cover he can suck onto. It's pretty dark red to the old NCO here.

So… he ain't got long. Arterial wound.

Hoser swears. "Gotta get the gun up!" he grunts.

Hustle pops his head over cover fast to check for targets he can start calling out as soon as the gun is emplaced.

That's their standard MO. Hustle and Hoser. My best gunners. Their MO.

Method of Operation, and they are pros at it, like some sort of sports team that's the best in the league. Hands down.

They were with the company before this tragedy began in full. And they've been there since Astralon, Crash, call it what you will.

But in this moment you can tell they are doing their best because they're both wounded and still going after it at the pro level.

Timing's off. Bad game today, boys. Sorry, we won't get 'em next time.

Hustle's head explodes. He pops over the barrier for a quick check to identify targets as soon as Hoser can engage. Then he would have returned to his ammo management role. Straightening belts. Organizing spent brass to keep the Pig free of interference and malfunction. To keep the light machine gun in operation doing its death machine work.

But he's dead and his body just drapes along the cover as though he is suddenly tired. Even though his head is missing.

Hoser swears and lifts the gun up, already firing.

The Pig blares and the hulking gunner continues to fire even though he's already hit badly and gets hit again. Savagely.

Two squads ruined.

I'm alone and forward. In the nightmare.

And I know, once again… we are all going to die badly if we board that ship.

The *Dark Star*.

I want to wake up. Badly. But I don't. Even though I tell myself to shout, "Wake up, wake up, wake up… this is not happening!"

But it is. It does. And it will.

And other things, things I tell myself when it's time… to wake up.

Turn back.

Escape.

Don't go there.

It will be the end of the company and you're being shown all this, Sar'nt Orion… for a reason.

But in the nightmare, and in the cage dark… smoking and drinking coffee so I never sleep again after waking up and smelling my skin thick with sweat and fear… it all seems *soooo… inevitable.*

I hate my life.

Said every NCO ever.

And…

Never get involved, whispered the ghost of John Strange, *Sergeant Orion.*

CHAPTER FIVE

Thankfully all that EVC time in sim and the extra-hard environment training we put in paid off when we arrived over the Dandelion Worlds, ready to insert and secure the elevator. Because of course as soon as we were out of jump and the *Spider*'s engines were cooling after orbital stabilization, the first sergeant and Gunny had us out on the hull and working hull movement-to-contact and sim-breach operations in real time. Even with all the extra gym time I'd been putting in I was straight smoked, and so was Reaper.

My platoon.

Within hours as the fleet assembled over the main world, we got the first WARNO for a possible op developing planetside.

We needed to secure a critical location so the intel specialists could come in and do their thang.

Like I was saying, thankfully our first combat operation in the Rogue Fleet, *yeeehawww, boys!!!*, as it was being called, wasn't wasted on EVC training. Even though we were getting drop-shipped planetside. And it was, technically, a "ground-based" mission, but there were already problems.

Grim problems. War crimes. Weapons of mass, mass destruction had been used before our arrival.

The Monarchs, on their way through the system, had *chemmed* the entire world. Bio-strike, to be specific.

Everyone down there, on the surface, was just dead.

So we had to go in full EVC combat suits, posture four, in order to protect ourselves from the deadly nerve gas agents still present on the prevailing winds and clustered around the mass grave sites.

Full Protective Posture.

And if that's not fun enough already, kids, I have to listen to everyone now gripe and complain about getting into EVC posture four and staying in it for extended operations planetside.

It's really fun being a platoon sergeant. One star, would not recommend. Ever. Go into the circus or work in a mental health facility if you want something easier.

As the ragtag "fleet" tried to organize itself, Strange was ordered to the surface to investigate what exactly had happened around the central space elevator, and like I said, secure the site for SSI development. The Star Khans were going on and on about collecting documentation on everything for future "war crimes" tribunals the Monarchs were gonna stand for.

LOL.

We were gonna kill 'em. There wouldn't be any trials. But that was maybe the Strange Company's mission and I'd noticed the command team kept that on the DL.

But the Star Khans were trying to get all "official" about everything like they were some kind of legitimate government now. My guess was, it wasn't so much that they wanted evidence, but to give the appearance they had that authority to be one, a legit government, going forward and that they were actually better tyrants than the last batch.

Not my circus, not my monkeys. I was here to collect a debt.

So we got sent planetside along with another element from off one of the other ships in the fleet. Meanwhile warships were still dropping in from jump, more and more every day as the fleet grew, as though everyone with a warship and a fighting force could smell big prizes and loot to be gained from the eventual boarding and sack of the Monarch *Dark Star*. Like it was some fabled treasure hauler of legendary olden days to be taken by pirates and divvied up like a Sunday hog.

You could smell and taste the greed and avarice in the climate-controlled air when we had to go over to the *Thunderer*'s CIC to discuss ops.

Also they didn't let me smoke over there, so maybe it was that.

So we were ordered to the surface, and everyone agreed it seemed like nothing more than make-work as the fleet tried to get its jump formations organized at Gateway Station, the halfway point between the edge of the frontier and the system the Monarchs seemed headed to.

Dark and distant Typhon.

Uninhabited. Just there. The furthest extent of their power, and… what felt like some jumping-off point they might disappear from.

Nightmare of my Dreams.

At Gateway the fleet would link up with a jump-envelope carrier and we would, in theory, beat the Monarchs to where they were going through time dilation. Theoretically.

We'd then reach the limit of known space. And this next jump was gonna be a doozy.

An eighteen-month haul even at max jump speed, but in the jump-*envelope* carrier, a concept beyond the ken of this old ruck hobo, and apparently of most everyone else, to include the scientists and engineers who built the thing, theoretical time dilation would kick in and pull some non-linear quantum tricks and very little time would pass.

Or we would be dead or lost in the void forever.

One of those two things.

So we had that going for us.

The rumors and sudden experts that appeared throughout the company about the jump-envelope carrier ran wild and bizarre, and some of these bizarre theories even scared the hell outta me.

First Sergeant told us it was nothing to be concerned about and that "if you're killed in a time-space dilation accident you probably won't know it until you meet your maker for the first time. So… might wanna get some past crimes straightened out, boys, for that meeting. Just in case, is all I'm sayin'."

These were big, mind- and number-crushing, distances out beyond human-controlled space we were dealing with now. Vast gulfs of interstellar unexplored night, even at max jump speed.

The distances were purely… *incomprehensible*.

So as the fleet tried to get its act together, we dropped on Gateway Station to see if there were any survivors down there, and generally pull a recon and document search for any war crimes we found.

Standard secure site op.

We could handle this, I thought. Also thinking we might be walking into something much more than expected… Hauser had briefed us on the possibilities of combat cyborgs or even HK teams… but in my defense… I was tired. I had all that future PTSD on my mind every time I closed my eyes. Flight-sim.

But also… there are no defenses for platoon sergeants. So there's that.

The elevator was officially called Gateway Station.

The space elevator orbital docking facility needed to be secured above the actual main wheel of the upper station so some of the larger ships could sub-orbitally dock and take on supplies. Or offload and transfer.

Intel and Threat Assessment sections with fleet had suggested that if HK teams were operational in the area that they would most likely attempt to stage an attack at the docks especially if one of the larger ships was attempting to make hard contact. So our mission after securing the station was to go up and trip any traps and hopefully disarm any ship-killer IEDs left behind.

Thus we'd insert midway down the station at Gateway.

Rumor also was the Star Khans wanted to loot the local central banks that had set up trade there and pry open the cyber boxes.

Reasons given for this action…

'Cause they're the government now and it's not stealing when they do it.

Or so I suspect. These things are above my pay grade. Ammo, casualties, equipment, the implementation of the commander's will, and foot care. These are my concerns.

I like to keep it simple even when quantum time dilation and global bank robbery are on the menu. Front sight forward. It's best that way most of the time.

So we were sent down to the station in order to document war crimes. LOL.

Hell, the company had committed more than their unfair share of *war crimes* along the way to the lofty estate we now found ourselves in. Again, LOL. We'd been fined when we'd been caught. And hadn't been, when we hadn't been caught.

War crimes under the Monarchs had been a game of catch me if you can. Nothing more.

But that was all over now. Regardless of what the Star Khans said or thought.

War crimes were everyday business as a new super-real reality settled across all the war-ravaged worlds of the former Monarch empire and the illusion of polite galactic civilization got simply wrecked by chimps with AKs loaded to the gills in a space hulk pulling into low orbit and doing whatever they wanted now that the monkeys and their Kong were in charge.

Reality was super weird now. And super real.

The Monarchs no longer existed and there was no intergalactic body to... *deliberate*... on who exactly had broken which of the various rules of warfare someone had once claimed existed.

Truth...

There are no rules in war. War is just survival until the other side is dead. You use whatever you got to kill the other guy using all he's got so one of you gets another slice of birthday cake.

Only people who've never fought to the death make rules about how fighting to the death should go.

War is, in fact, the opposite of something with rules. It's total chaos even with plans and training.

Like every fight to the death, it's a no-holds-barred brawl for survival for you and no more birthdays for the other guy. You will, when you find yourself in a war or a fight to the death, but I repeat myself, you will do whatever it takes to walk away the winner that day, which just means the guy who lived when the other guy didn't today. And yeah, *If you ain't cheatin', you ain't tryin'*.

Trying real hard to survive in that kind of situation is usually called "a war crime" in someone's book. But they weren't there usually. The real trick is just not to get caught trying to do whatever it takes to save your life so you can... I know I overstate this point... get another slice of birthday cake.

Cake is a big thing for me. I always had great birthdays, and when I feel hopeless or overwhelmed, or unable to cope with Catboi... I remind myself that frosting and cake are the prize if I can just get through what I'm doing.

I like birthdays. I like cake. I show up to everyone's in the company. But mainly just for the cake. It's a guilty pleasure that extends to actually living longer. And birthday cake, and all it means and implies... is worth killing the other guy over.

See... we have to be honest about these things as an explanation for my monstrous truths.

Rules of war was *then* and this was... *now*. And *now* is this: civilization's over for a while... so game on and play to win some cake.

Make it to the other side and then you can stand trial or make up silly rules that get people killed. But if you're dead... you don't.

It's that simple.

Rules. Those are polite illusions. If you think they are anything other than that, I own a fast starship I'd like to sell you right now, no questions asked. Just don't start the main drive.

Hell, the chimps had dispelled the *illusion of rules* when they basically ravaged the entire human expansion over the course of twenty years of war with the Monarchs and just about anyone who stood in their howling mad way.

The Ultras... funny they never got accused of any war crimes, and they always won. Until they didn't.

But maybe that had to do with which team they were playing for.

Still, they knew what it took.

War crimes are one of the few things I get excited about. I mean, the fact that they'd finally been held up for the actual joke they were, made me happy. But I am dark and anti-social that way. I had assumed, as we began what was a new phase to the company's post-Monarch existence, that this manipulation tool would be done away with. And that we could just fight to the death and see who won by getting to eat substandard rations in the mud with his buddies.

And then later that same year... cake.

But then the Star Khans ruined it all and announced the op to go planetside to look for... war crimes. Sigh.

So here they were, sending me and my platoon down into a hazardous environment so someone could play games with reality, truth, repeat the same mistakes, and think they were gonna win this time.

Spoiler... reality always wins with a punch in the face.

War crimes are the ultimate reality and if this makes me a bad person to you... I don't care. You're probably gonna be the most surprised person in the slit trench below the guys with the guns shooting you and your family and shoving their bodies into it.

Bold prediction. If it comes true, I want it to be called Orion's Law. Mark it down. It's in the company logs now. Here it is...

More war crimes, less wars.

There, I have spoken it. So it is, so let the galaxy be measured by suchly. The ruck hobo sayeth.

I'm cool with that. Cool with less wars. Even if that means the company gets a lot less work. And even though I get paid for that kinda work, it would not be a bad thing if there were less wars. I could dig more cake for all involved.

Ask any soldier. Ask the dead if they could tell you... they would.

Let me support my hypothesis, instead of actually continuing with this log and the account of the company's catastrophic insert onto Gateway Station. If war is allowed to be as horrible as it possibly can be, total annihilation of the enemy by any means and by every dirty trick possible, and by "enemy" I mean everyone on that other side, leaders, warfighters, people, then my guess has always been people would be a lot less enthusiastic about going to war when they got a real good up-close-and-personal look at its naked howling madness. If they were made startlingly clear regarding the realities and personal stakes, they'd be a lot less enthusiastic about marching someone else off to get it done. When it costs them personally, they get less enthusiastic about all the rah-rah march-off-to-war stuff. When the cost is borne directly... when war goes totally nuts and not only wipes out your military, but then it goes after the population that allowed stupid greedy leaders to get up to such shenanigans... enthusiasm has a tendency to wane. That's probably a law too. Or at least it should be one. When whole population groups begin to disappear, people think twice about getting all excited about war because someone wanted to make some money and then gave them a "real purty flag" to fly and get all real-emotional about. Told them they were a real good person because they were on the "good side" and the other guys were on the "bad side" and all.

The only thing that would make war happen a lot less often would be if the people who demand wars be fought, political types and generals in the rear with the gear, actually had to get up front and shoot people in the face... then, I'm pretty sure there would be a lot less of this war-silliness by which I make my living.

Silliness.

Yeah, I said it. Don't @ me. I'm probably dead already anyway.

We have to be honest about these things, sayeth the broke ruck hobo once too many times.

So the sub-orbital dropships docked with the *Spider* and we loaded up for the hop and made the drop on Dandelion B once we'd loaded up, onboard the drops, in our bulky combat EVC suits.

Fun times.

I looked at Wolfy who was racked next me as we held on, strapped in and unable to sit because the suits are so bulky.

He had his mirrored visor opaqued. I could see his unshaven rangy wolf's face inside the EVC bucket.

He smiled wanly.

I was tired. But I saw the vampire fangs he was sporting.

So of course I had to look twice. I think that's in my job description. I was tired and the op started early. I'd been up since oh-three-hundred shipboard time, and truth was I hadn't slept well. Which I never do on days that have *incoming* in them.

He had vampire fangs in his mouth and a ceremonial dagger on his chest rig. Old, ornate, and shiny. Like some starship kiosk trinket next to the three-moon wolf t-shirts.

Vampire fangs.

Some kid's toy.

I was too tired to ask, but I did anyway as we stood there racked in the red-lit darkness of the dropship underway to the target.

"What's this?"

Wolfy looked at me and without missing a beat...

"I'm just here for the violence, Sar'nt."

I nodded.

Fine. Whatever.

Then Wolfy added, "Hotsoup!" and a few others nearby finished with what has become annoyingly regular and oft-repeated...

He was the best of us.

Forever in our hearts.

For the Soup!

I am their leader. And I hate all of them.

Hate.

CHAPTER SIX

The drops skimmed atmo and we were eight minutes out from insertion onto the platforms outside the main terminal substation of the elevator at Gateway Station.

A pristine M-class world lay below us, totally devoid of life now. You could still see... if you scanned the atmo ahead of the ships outside the small port windows along the drop's fuselage... you could still see the sickly yellow miasma of the poison the fleeing Monarchs had used to eliminate this world for no reason anyone could fathom.

Causing death on an unimaginable scale.

But they were Monarchs, and they'd shed their humanity, considering it weak, long ago, in order to do the great things that were beyond human capabilities.

Their words. Not mine.

These had been beautiful worlds. *The Dandelions* as they were known among the star routes and ports and charts that marked them so. Three Class M's in one massive system full of habitable satellites and rich mining belts. Three almost perpetually summer-like worlds in one system. An incredible roll of the stellar dice for some scout who dared the impossible well beyond official human expansion. An impossible find, really. The Dandelion Worlds had been the rarest of scout exploration finds. A real gem. And they'd been so far out from the reach of Monarch power that the Ultras had never made it out here to ruin these worlds and go *total Ultra* on it.

As they once said.

A small, mostly peaceful civ had built up around all three worlds comprising continually arriving colony ships willing to make the long trek out to avoid the tyranny of the Monarchs.

So maybe that's why they'd poisoned the system. The Monarchs. They hadn't liked the display of outright disrespect to their persons inherent in this stellar civ far beyond the bounds of their control that was doing quite well without their influence.

Control wasn't enough. For them. There had to be respect, and fear too.

Or as some might put it... *It's not enough that we succeed, but that all others fail.*

The capital world we inserted above, along the length of shining gossamer space elevator broken by intermittent massive bubbled discs of substations at various levels, had turned into a local system trading world running goods back out to the frontier. This world had become a local trading powerhouse with links to a dozen unofficially discovered worlds lying further out in the stellar dark. This was Dandelion B, the main planet, now turned into a bountiful ag world. Dandelion C was a tropical paradise largely undeveloped and very much appreciated by the locals as a getaway and large estate world.

Dandelion A was a rich, very habitable, desert exotic mineral world, and most likely the most valuable of the three.

It too, was dead, hit by a crustbuster that had fractured it along geotechnic faults. The Monarchs didn't want it used as a starship construction base anywhere near where they were going. Or they were just petty and raging. C was now burning and breaking up for the next twenty years, having also been hit by a crustbuster munition. Approach and landings weren't even possible, the surface was so unstable now.

There was a local sentient species that wasn't very intelligent and roamed in packs like dogs because they were, in fact, small intelligent canids that walked on upright legs.

Pacifists, the library files called them. They had dedicated their entire existence to protecting and managing most of the other species on the main world. B. Their whole, practically Bronze Age civilization was based on caring for other local animals and culling predators that preyed too savagely on the various flocks and herds of Dandelion B.

The first explorers had simply called them *the Shepherds*. They looked like medium- height gray-and-white shaggy dogs that walked upright and carried little more than spears and slings. Their jaw strength was so powerful they could snap a basso rhino's neck, a large yet agile local herd predator, right in half.

But the Shepherds were as gentle as anything in their dealings with the first explorers and colonists who'd arrived here.

Things had gone incredibly smoothly for this world after that. That is, until the Monarchs showed up just months ago as they fled their former empire.

Now everyone was all dead. Mostly.

The Technate had thought, maybe, that perhaps there were doomsday bunkers buried deep that had once been old colony hab ships capable of a single outbound flight. Maybe there were survivors there.

And the central bank vaults the corporations that had come out this far to construct their trading empire had started.

The drops we were riding in from fleet brought Reaper and a group of First Team expeditionary forces off the heavy utility carrier *Thunderer*. We came down through clear skies then into yellow drifts of stinking clouds and finally down through the choking green miasma of the chem strike the Monarchs had laid down all across this world in order to kill everyone, and everything, dead.

The drop flight crew were already seeing death fields and mass graves out there across the horizon in every direction.

One of the pilots got sick. None of them said anything. Nothing felt… funny.

On approach to final insertion, we banked high over a dead city, power-climbed to high altitude, about twenty thousand feet, and headed straight in for the main bubble disc of the space elevator at Gateway Station.

We set down on one of the circular landing platforms high up along the central spine of the massive space elevator. The landing lights were still blinking though they seemed to be operating on emergency backup power, as everything else was dark.

The shining metal disc-bubble was shaped and molded in what some called *Retro Futura* stellar architecture. Huge massive viewing windows were emplaced all across it, and through these we could see where the locals had died trying to board any ship that would dock and get them off-world as the bio-strike came for them. Filtration and vent systems had been compromised and the gas had flooded even these hardened locations as the chemical agent swept over the planet, breeding and replicating with nano-mRNA-plague weapon systems.

It was both biological and chemical. A real Dark Labs home run.

The question Fleet Tac Plan wanted answered was… were there any legitimate survivors that could make claim to ownership and grievance rights over the world. The Tech Khans were already scheming as to who owned what. So we were sent in to see who lived.

Not because they needed rescue. Because of *ownership disputes*.

Also it was necessary we do the whole document-war-crimes thing. And the bank-robbing on behalf of the new we're-nothing-like-the-last-government government.

It's fair to say our objective here was… hazy. At best.

Just get down there and see if there's anything in it for us, the Technate seemed to say.

Same as it ever was. Been there, done that, bought the t-shirt.

According to emergency broadcasts, the Monarch ship had departed after demanding, and then being, resupplied. Three days later, the gas started killing cities from the north to the south.

The crustbuster strike on the other two worlds had come as the *Dark Star* accelerated to fantastic speeds and just at the edge of the system launched her planet-killers.

Kind of a going-away present.

As the drops approached the landing platforms, above and within the fleet, local satellites were being hacked by *Raven of Winter*, the ECM scout ship for Rogue Fleet, *yeeehawww, boys!!!*, and intelligence-gathering collection was going on aboard the *Thunderer*, which had become the flagship for Rogue Fleet.

The combat information center aboard *Thunderer* was monitoring all traffic from our insert as well as the feeds off our helmets.

The EVC system made this possible.

Supposedly the deadly bioweapon was still present in lethal doses.

So we had that goin' for us.

All of that, the Monarchs' deadly tantrum, the games of the Khans calling the shots now and saying things would be different this time like some alcoholic two hours outta rehab… made me feel… old and tired.

What was I even doing on this one…

I looked over at Catboi. This would be his first real live combat action. He was where all my doubts lay.

The crew chief on the drop was calling out the exit commands, readying us as the engines howled and braked, and the pilots eased the drops onto the high platforms of the dead station.

I turned to Wolfy.

He smiled once again, his fake vampire fangs dripping saliva.

Yeah, I thought, pushing away the greed of the new masters, the games of the power brokers, the war crimes we'd come to put paid on… and all the dead rotting across an entire world… and muttered to myself…

"Yeah… I'm here for the violence."

That's all.

All that other stuff was someone else's problem. Their games.

Wolfy must've heard me, with our buckets being so close. He reached out an EVC assault glove and fist-bumped me.

"Me too, Sar'nt. Me too."

CHAPTER SEVEN

Before we go any further... *Catboi*.

He must be discussed... or explained now. Though it makes no sense and this won't be much of an explanation. I guess I better insert him into the account before I discuss the mess on Gateway Station and the situation we got into there.

One of our new guys we picked up from the days just after Marsantyium, the first sergeant found him Hells-of-Suth-knew-where and dropped him off in front of me.

This was my first introduction to Catboi.

He was small for a man. Slight with almost no fat, and muscles that would never advance beyond what little mass he could barely get on. Weightlifters like Gains would have called him a *hard gainer*. Slight, scrawny, almost impossible to put muscle on.

Gains would have considered it a mission to do so, and... he would have done it.

So, if you're looking for some kind of defense I'm going to provide on why I let this kid into Reaper when I was perfectly within my rights to say no... blame it on Gains.

Gains wouldn't have given up. He didn't give up on people just because they were *hard gainers*, or *weird*. I was missing Gains a lot lately and maybe that had something to do with why I let what happened... happen.

Catboi joining the Strange. Reaper specifically.

It was... an unusual drop-off. And that *should* have been my first clue. But I ignored it. It was out of the ordinary and my Plat Daddy senses were already tingling that I was being screwed when the first sergeant dragged the kid into the dark passage near my weapons cage and whispered for him to wait while he "sorted this out."

Screwed royally. Me. I was getting.

There were clues. Warnings. I ignored them all.

In the dark passage I saw a small young man. Goofy gear with stickers and painted cat girls. Some kinda carbine that looked fairly slick and high-speed. State-of-the-art hype fatigues that was more like a skin suit. The kind you could dial in different camo patterns with the built-in sleeve device that also worked as a computer with a fair amount of power.

Pretty sure those came with IR and thermal defeating features. They weren't cheap. I wouldn't have minded a pair except they looked like yoga pants that uber-stars wore when they were doing workout videos to pop their latest movie, or thing.

Everyone in Strange would have called someone "ghey" for wearing them. Still... they were... slick.

"Now, Sar'nt Orion..." began the first shirt low and confidential as I studied the kid he'd just brought aboard the grounded *Spider*. "I got a special project for you because I don't know another NCO solid enough, and might I add professional enough, in all my experience that can handle this one… Sergeant Orion. You know you're gonna be company first sergeant soon and this is gonna go a long way to makin' that recommendation to the Old Man."

He smiled broadly. But it was fake, like he knew I knew he was screwing me.

I had no desire to be the first sergeant. I was doing fine ruining Reaper's lives. I didn't need to spread like a virus.

Also…

Solid and *professional* are words no one has ever, ever used about me. See the number of times I've fallen for one of Chief Cook's "schemes." Or what he calls *force multipliers*. Sometimes, *operations*.

Professional… okay I'm passionate about foot care. But I have to state that Amarcus Hannibal was disgusted by the way I ran a platoon and described my movement to contact and patrol techniques and squad management game as something conducted by a mentally handicapped chimpanzee trying to teach ultraball to other mentally handicapped chimpanzees.

Punch thought that was funny and then said chimps were generally very smart.

Again, I'll have to be honest here… Hannibal had valid points regarding my lack of skill. No one was more surprised than me when some operation went off without anyone getting seriously maimed or killed that I was in charge of.

Still, for the sake of Reaper I couldn't allow him to voice those truths without pointing out his various war crimes and other offenses against humanity.

But he's dead now. So I win.

And as to being accused of being *solid*… ha.

Every day when I woke up I whispered the same thing to myself in the darkness as I thought about the litany of problems I'd face in running a light infantry platoon full of killers and amateurs, and various other grease fires I knew in fact were headed right toward me within a few hours that I doubted I could put out in time before they engulfed all of us… and destroyed the company. I always lay in my rack, in the quiet dark, and asked myself, "Hey, why not just run away today? Hell… things might be better without you doing your best. Or what most call sub-max performance."

Solid I was not.

We have to be honest about these things. I was a hair's-breadth away from going AWOL at any given moment. Half the time I didn't blame guys when they just faded and were never seen again.

I suspected they knew I was gonna get them killed somehow.

So I got that goin' for me.

After asking myself that question in the morning dark that was more than just darkness, I spent ten minutes plotting how I'd execute my final fade from the company. Then some out-of-control fire or platoon problem would get messaged to me and since no one else was in charge… I'd find myself sucked in, once more, to the wonderful maelstrom of flying feces that is small unit leadership.

Solid and *professional*.

LOL.

I literally laughed when Top said those words regarding me, and I'll have to be honest… I thought less of him for falling so low as to try and con me with that sell.

C'mon, Top... it's me, Orion. Junkboy who stole Ghost's rifle and went on a shooting spree from an overwatch position into a prisoner-of-war camp was one of my guys.

This is my résumé.

And there are other crimes we don't need to list here that are all my fault.

All he needed to say was, "Hey, Sergeant Orion... got a new guy. Make him a killer. And before you protest... no, I didn't ask you if you wanted a new guy. I in fact order you to take a new guy. Which you will do. Hell, you want me to give you a foot rub next, young sar'nt? See ya. Gotta go ruin some other NCO's life."

Which is what first sergeants live to do. Anything else they tell you is a lie straight from the Hells of Suth.

Fact.

And then disappear like the phantom the first sergeant truly was.

Solid and *professional*, my bad tats.

I was insulted by these lies about me.

Still, he was Top, so I had to listen. I had to listen and pretend that the first sergeant, who I admired and greatly respected and secretly craved the slight approval of, had not just whored himself out to get me to think better of myself because he was clearly trying to give me this year's company problem child.

"Got a kid I just picked up in the bazaars. Good kid. An unusual case. But you are just the NCO for this one. He's a problem though and I won't lie to you," he lied.

Then he burped and said, "But ain't they all, amirite, Sar'nt Orion?"

Then he laughed and slapped his knee like he'd just told the funniest joke ever, and we were long-time buddies so this was totally how it was.

Never was it like this. In fact.

Which told me already this kid was gonna be a nightmare.

I'd already started shaking my head, barely, like I was trying to get ready to have a spine. I just wasn't sure I had one.

It was the first sergeant and all. He was a living legend.

But in my mind I was running off the boarding ramp of the *Spider*, jacking a cargo freighter headed for the outer worlds and getting clear of this whole thing once and for all.

In my mind.

"Define... unusual, First Sar'nt," I asked like I still had some say in the unfolding disaster heading my way.

The first sergeant stopped laughing abruptly, realizing I was not laughing along with him.

Note... in hindsight I am proud of myself for not fake laughing with the first sergeant, fake laughing at his own joke. It would've demeaned us both and I felt like I'd saved some shred of dignity whereas the first sergeant had blown all his like a common low-grade whore.

The first sergeant side-eyed me, and the look was pure coldest murder. I was reminded at that stunning crystal-clear moment of the number of confirmed knife kills in the Saturnian Batts he had accumulated in his time there.

Nine.

He'd been a recon man. Supposedly a legendary point man too. Which was saying something if the tales of the Batts I'd heard were even half-true.

His voice was stone-cold sober next. Low and murder-cold.

"Kid came with his own weapons, Sergeant... and uh... gear. He has no formal training. Formally, Sar'nt. Like some military or other. Nothing like that. But apparently he's paid vets who run these high-speed fancy survival schools for civvies to train him up... for... as he's gonna put it to you, Sar'nt Orion... *total ninja war*. Hell, all war's total to me, but that's how we roll, ain't it. And I don't even know what a ninja is."

Again I said nothing.

But I smelled a *larper*.

Someone who'd never been in but wanted to pretend they had by getting as close to the action as they could take. Either by being a fanboy, a game simmer like a gamer or live-action kind of thing, or... some sort of a badge hound but collecting civilian shooting schooling and vet-taught survival training.

But he'd never served.

"First Sar'nt... is he... a *war boy?*"

The company used the term to refer to these types.

The first sergeant opened his eyes wide and his big white handlebar mustache danced a little. "*Hooo boy*, is he, Orion," he hissed. "But he does know a lot about the company, and he's traveled to Mars just to get a chance to sign up with us."

Silence.

"So... you want me to take an untrained *war boy*, First Sergeant, little more than a fan who's probably got kit that's straight out of the *Danger Dan Survival and Special Operations* gear catalog, which may or may not include a samurai sword, and bet the lives of my guys when we're deep in it on that enemy hull? Is that what you're..."

The first sergeant puffed up and turned florid in that way old men do when they've had enough of your sauce.

Dangerous ground... I was on it.

"Sar'nt Orion, listen here. It's called a *wakizashi*, and it's a legit clay-tempered fighting weapon with a keen edge like you ain't never seen. I knew a guy back in the Batts who carried one and straight-up stacked at the Siege of Jostus in the darkest days of the Sindo. Swear on my scroll and everything, Sar'nt. It's goofy. He's goofy. But... he's done the work and his gear is legit."

Man...

"Mostly," added the first sergeant. "I already got rid of some of the more... egregious items. And you're just gonna have to live with the cat girl stencils on his weapons and pack... part o' the deal. But..."

He trailed off and said nothing and I had a feeling he too was having that *Why not just fade* conversation I had every morning with myself.

Then he was back.

"It's not a samurai sword. It's shorter. He uses it just like I use my Bowie knife, and some of the training he's attended ain't no joke, Sar'nt. He's had commo courses, advanced carbine and CQB carbine, and some survival courses that one of the instructors I knew from back in the Batts founded. He's got his fire and movement down. So... compared to the average local militia guy we turn over to you sometimes, I wanna say he's probably above average, Sar'nt Orion."

"You wanna say, Top?"

Again, that nine-confirmed- knife-kills side-eye.

"Orion... we need every swingin' boot on this one. Kid's got some good kit and I went over it, and it's mostly not ghey as you guys say. He's got a legit carbine even I'd envy. His gear has got some... let's call 'em decorations... but that ain't no never mind in the company. Remember Choker and his teeth necklaces?"

I could see the *decorations*.

My soul was dying inside me. Hyper-manga cats and doe-eyed anime girls. They were even on his weapons.

He was standing at parade rest. About twenty meters away in the dark as our low talk at times got loud and the first sergeant had to remind me who exactly had more stripes than the other guy.

And knife kills.

I couldn't tell him about Hannibal. That would've made my number competitive.

"So... I'm stuck with him, First Sergeant."

The old man turned and studied the kid. Then he nodded. "Yup. Gunny would just space him, Sar'nt Orion. You and me both know it. And listen, don't tell nobody, but remember that obscure rule we don't ever enforce, the one from back in the John Strange days how ya needed to pay your company fee on first contract but we've always been so damn broke we don't make no one pay up ever..."

Yeah.

I'd skipped out on mine, and I didn't even know anyone who'd been asked to pay it in years.

"Well, there's a clause in there that half the fee goes to the recruit's NCO for training purposes. Payment in advance."

The first sergeant was whispering now.

He reached into a bag he'd brought with him and pulled out a gold brick.

"Here's your cut. He paid in advance."

He held it out.

I didn't move to take it. My arms were folded. It was surrender if I did, even though I already knew I'd lost and all the bad things would come and destroy me.

And it would all be my fault.

Even Catboi.

The first sergeant stared at me, trying out first his narrowed nine-confirmed-knife-kills look and seeing that fail, then switching to a look of desperation that passed across his face like some sudden storm, and I realized he was little more than an old man getting... older, frailer, and weaker every day. Just desperately trying to... make it to wherever we were headed.

I didn't want the man I'd known as the rock of the company, and a mentor, and someone I'd always wanted to be proud of me as an NCO... to be that guy I was seeing now.

Desperate and kinda... pathetic.

Less than the legend he was.

So I reached out and took the gold brick and shoved it in my tattered and torn cargo pocket where all the other problems go that I can't face yet.

There. We were both dirty whores now.

CHAPTER EIGHT

Catboi's intake interview into Reaper happened five minutes later as I swallowed what dignity I had left, burned a dart to get myself together for what I could only guess was gonna be… weird, studied the kid, and figured how I was gonna proceed.

Goals. Don't let him get anyone killed.

Solid, if possible.

Secondary goals. Don't let him get himself killed.

Doubtful. But I might live with myself better if I could help out there. I'm an optimist that way.

I walked over and told him to cut that out.

"Cut what out, Sergeant Orion?" His face was emotionless as he stared forward in parade rest. Someone had taught him this is what army men do.

I could only imagine how, when… and where. Some old vet he'd conned into teaching him warboy stuff. Some ol' guy who'd been in made-up ops called *The Storm* and *Urgent Fury*. Two-week recondo school out of his hover van, broke down near the municipal starport park.

Please… I prayed, and realized I don't believe in anything to pray to. So… I was getting what I deserve. And I knew it. Somehow.

We never did parade rest in the company even when the Old Man was sentencing some miscreant to extra duty for the rest of their natural lives for some infraction they'd just committed that involved the local constabulary and perhaps a war crime or two.

"The…"

I mimed what he was doing and immediately went right to my next dart. Any patience or preparation for this seemed to evaporate like the cheap cloying misty pheromone spray of some dancer after she's taken your last mem and moved on to someone… richer.

"Parade rest," I said. "We don't do that. Here. Cut it out."

My foot-care and eat-your-protein-bar speeches escaped my mind like the cheap tricks they were.

Cowards, I hissed at them as I blew smoke out and tried to gather my thoughts.

And then, right there, I point at this memory in my mind from the chair inside my cage like I'm watching some movie of me and the clown I am, I knew I was in big trouble.

"Catboi falling out of parade rest."

That's how he talks. Everything is Catboi doing this. Catboi doing that. A monotone narration of his whole life and every detail.

We… were gonna have to do something about that.

My mouth was hanging open and the lit dart literally fell out and hit the floor of my cage.

Later, when I talked to Hauser about the kid, things got a little clearer. But that's because Hauser has "detailed files" on humanity.

Given to him for the sole intent and purpose of killing us better.

He has repurposed them now so he can be our friend.

Murky, but clearer. If that's a thing.

"Catboi is a high-functioning Asperger's adult with some borderline autistic tendencies. There are a myriad of factors that contribute to this condition, but it is harmless and in some cases can be used to optimize for efficiency in certain professions."

"What does that mean, Hause?"

"He has trouble dealing with reality and enjoys his fantasy cartoons and idol worship as a form of emotional expression he is incapable of in real life. What is interesting about him, Sergeant Orion… is that he is aware of this condition, and has taken steps to *weaponize* it."

Okay… that's a new one. Weaponized autism.

Also…

One… Hauser saying Catboi. Hauser had immediately taken to the insisted-upon tag. Surreal and hilarious. I wanted to laugh abruptly and wildly like someone not dealing with reality on all six thrusters… but that seemed… inappropriate.

Two… and then Hauser went on to conduct an interrogation-level conversation allowing him to use his *human termination* and *biologic target predictive behavior analysis* algorithms to diagnose Catboi for the company.

"How, Hauser, has he… *weaponized*… his condition, as you call it?"

That wild insane laughter burbled up inside me and I clamped down on my dart and inhaled it like a maniac.

Shades of Chief Cook crossed my mind.

Hauser didn't miss a beat because nothing makes him uncomfortable, including uncomfortable conditions about medical stuff, because he is a machine, and only the exchange of data matters to him. Not the delicacies or nuances of difficult issues.

"Humans diagnosed with his condition, Sergeant Orion, are much like my kind. Combat cyborgs. They lack emotion and have a high level of focus. Biologically they are different, of course, but from a programming standpoint… they are almost identical to us and our rational and thinking programs and decision-algorithm matrices. His, and our, processes are optimized for maximum efficiency and survival. Mission is everything to a cyborg, as it is to one with his condition. This is accepted in a cyborg, generally, Sergeant Orion, but in human culture, I have observed… this can cause difficulties for them and make them seem… the term your kind uses is *socially awkward*. They are often intensely aware of this but unable to override their programming to alter their behavior because their code is them."

I agreed with this as I thought about it and recalled examples I'd encountered.

"So… what did he do? How did he *weaponize* it, Hause?"

Hauser smiled. Yes, he does that sometimes. His human learning interface has told him to do this during certain parts of the conversation, and as he puts it, "I have learned so much more from serving alongside humans than I did from killing them. I find this very rewarding, Sergeant Orion."

It doesn't help that he's a six-foot-four murder machine that looks like a perfect human specimen of our kind. He radiates cold killing efficiency and there is nothing he can do about that, even when he speaks softly and calmly... which is pretty much always. You are aware of his ability to kill in large doses under overwhelming odds.

Of course you do, Hause. Of course you find working with humans instead of killing them rewarding. I think that's why you're my friend and I've set myself this mission to make you human.

Or at least an example to the rest of us. On how to be human despite the horror show that is us.

"Rather than be ostracized," continued Hauser, "or marginalized by human society at large, Catboi has adopted a mythic pattern-archetype to emulate that suits his gifts. He has pursued a course of training and study, including physical self-improvement and body modification, to become like that archetype in order to survive in a galaxy and a culture that are very alien to him, even though he is biologically human."

Okay...

"And what... *mythic type*... did he develop himself after, Hause?"

"He is what you call a fan of the human fiction character known as *Super Awesome Amazing Cat Girl Spy*. She is his fixation. But that is not who he has based his emotional defensive armor on. His target-identification emulation, something combat cyborgs do in certain specific operations, has led to self-optimization subroutines and protocols that have made him into what he is, Sergeant Orion."

I have no idea what a *Super Something Cat Girl* is, and I haven't seen a comic book in years. Though when I did, it was a real one. Saw it in one of the smashed and ruined museums and treasury hoards of Marsantyium. Some relic a Monarch had held on to from their long-ago past.

Batman Number One. I snapped a pic.

LOL.

Who'd wanna be a bat...

The molding old yellowed thing had been shot through the cover by a round during the Ultras' defense of that portion of the city against the chimps. It was mostly destroyed within the viewing case. The red-marble pedestal shattered. The art looked lame. But apparently, I'd thought to myself as I snapped the pic... this was something important in our human past.

Honestly, I thought less of my ancestors. Seriously. I thought they were all about great books and epic stories of literature and the climb to the stars.

This ruined thing made them more like us. And that made me think... less of them. Which says a lot about a certain ruck hobo snapping pics of the ruined past after some gunfight.

But hey... you do you. Me... I like me. Which is a lie I tell myself when my thoughts get too uncomfortably close to the heart of the matter.

Now I had a nutcase the first sergeant had forced on me who was into these ridiculous things.

So... gotta deal with that.

Also, this is not covered in the NCO manual for any military I have encountered thus far.

"Super Awesome Amazing Cat Girl Spy..." continued Hauser, "is a half cat, half girl. She is a pop singer and some kind of vampire. And of course, an intelligence operative for an agency known as B.I.T.E., Sergeant Orion."

I can't believe I'm having this conversation.

"Catboi allowed me to scroll his device and take in the images of this character and his collection of materials that catalog her misadventures. They seem very silly and have little to do with the real world, Sergeant Orion. Your kind would think she is very beautiful, though. Her proportions are... unrealistic."

"Okay, Hause. So who does *he*—"

"*Stone*, Sergeant Orion. Stone is a secondary character who appears to rescue Cat Girl from the various troubles she finds herself in. Usually kidnapped by wealthy tech-tyrants and surrounded by assassins, or occasionally, by gangs of other rival cat girls who are jealous of her fame... and proportions. Stone is a soldier of fortune who has fallen in love with her but refuses to reveal his true feelings for Cat Girl. This is optimal for Catboi's architecture. It allows him to have a social interaction that is all but impossible to realize. Catboi, that is. Stone is a warrior without peer, and this is the important part, Sergeant Orion... he cannot be impaired or hurt by any known attack which he perceives. He has trained in every deadly fighting art in order to save and defend Cat Girl. Though the two rarely interact, Stone is always nearby, ensuring her safety despite her at-times-reckless behavior and wild misadventures."

"Stone, huh?"

"Yes, Sergeant Orion. For a high-functioning Asperger's with slight autistic tendencies, this is the perfect patterning. It provides an emotional armor that allows him to justify his sense of purpose in order to survive within human society. One more thing, Sergeant Orion... Stone is a combat cyborg who has released himself from service to the Monarchs. I find this interesting and want to know more about this Stone, but he is featured in only sixty-seven issues for a total of two hundred and fifty-eight panels. They should make one of these entertainment media packages focusing on Stone. But that is just... I am not sure, Sergeant Orion... but... I would like to know more. Is that... wrong, Sergeant Orion?"

No, Hause. It's not wrong. And it's just Orion. Okay? We're friends."

So Catboi is basically, emotionally, a human combat cyborg... hence why you two immediately bonded.

I don't say both of these things because...

We have to be honest about these things, I tell myself and then tell myself to shut up.

But... if I am honest... then...

I was a little hurt, jealous even, that my best friend robot had a new best friend who was basically someone who had difficulty living in reality and making real friends.

This says a lot more about me than the two of them.

I know... I am super bad at being human.

I get that.

Hence the weapons cage and the darkness and smokes and coffee.

Hey, I like me, I lie.

Who cares if no one else does.

So, with all... that... I was able to understand the indoc interview and get Catboi into a squad in Reaper. Then everyone got mad. But that's later.

Punch was gonna of course...

Well, we'll get to that.

"So, First Sergeant says I gotta call you... Catboi..." I began. "Instead of how everyone does it in the unit. Which is wait for us to figure out their tag."

He was making eye contact with me. Technically, looking straight at me. But I could feel that his eyes were off to the left and down, though I could not credibly accuse him of this.

This was after I told him to quit doing the parade-rest thing and he said "Catboi falling out of parade rest" and my smoke fell out of my mouth and rolled across the floor of the weapons cage.

But to my next question he responded in standard monotone.

"Yes, Sergeant Orion."

Just like Hauser except his voice is... immature. Like he's still going through puberty, and he has no modulation or inflection. Again, pretty much like Hause, but even the combat cyborg killing machine is learning and throwing in expected inflections every so often. So... we're all learning here.

This will be important when we all get murdered on the Monarch ghost ship later, thirty seconds after boarding.

"Yes, Sergeant Orion," said Catboi. "Part fourteen, subsection six, paragraph G of the company rules and regulations states that if a potential recruit for Strange Company wishes to choose their own *nom de plume*, or alias, or *tag* as it is currently known in company lingo, then if the recruit pays his membership fees in advance he is allowed the right of choosing. I have paid in advance, Sergeant, so I can be known in the Strange Company as *Catboi*. With an *i*. Not a *y*."

With an *i*. So there's that.

He smiled, but it was not genuine. Guilty almost. It was like a practiced quick move and that's when I saw them for the first time.

Vampire fangs. Small, subtle. But he'd had his canines altered to be shaped to a point.

Unlike Wolfy's cheap starport souvenir shop plastic fangs... these were implants. And they were in no way shape or form meant to be "ironic."

They were, I'm assuming, to be taken quiet literally as his actual fangs.

I almost kicked him out of the company right there on the spot regardless of what shenanigans the first sergeant had gotten up to, to ruin my life this way.

Then I remembered that gold bar, though it wasn't so much that as the first sergeant telling me we needed dudes for the boarding action.

And the first sergeant getting older when I did not want him to.

So this is weird, I sighed to myself. But was it any weirder than Wolfy's three-wolf moon t-shirts or half a dozen other weird dudes just in Reaper alone that had... let's call 'em *quirks*.

No, I told myself. It wasn't. Not at all.

"Soooo... what is a... catboi?"

Without pause. "Me, Sergeant. Half cat, half boi."

Again... I sighed. Loudly. For some reason I'd started circling him and I actually now really wanted to lock his heels and put him into *parade rest*.

I was angry.

It felt that way.

"Okay..."

I reminded myself he was just a kid and that we'd all been... *weird*. Back then. Though I couldn't remember being so. I'm sure I was, somehow, and probably am even still now.

"Don't do that around the other guys," I told him.

I could already feel the trouble coming from this. Punch was gonna lose it.

I was already outta any kind of patience.

"That... half cat, half boi..."

And why the *i*? Why not just *boy*? With a *y*.

None of this made sense.

But the first sergeant had wanted it so, even being diabolical enough to end his desperate pitch with, "I have faith in you, Sar'nt Orion. Don't tell anyone... but you're my best NCO in this here company."

I knew that was a lie.

But it was a lie I desperately wanted to believe. Sometimes. I am weak that way. Look away from me in horror. And so here I was now... living the consequences of my ego with a kid who'd paid his way into the unit and now wanted to merc for reasons I could not fathom, seriously, and which the interview failed to reveal... and he was weird, and no good would come from this.

I knew it.

I sighed. What else could I do.

I gave him the protein-bar speech but it felt off. He nodded as though I'd just given him holy writ, produced a protein bar which he ate very peculiarly and seemed to neither enjoy nor hate as he chewed it precisely.

Then the foot-care speech.

Then I made him dump out his gear and I threw away half of it until I had him... optimized down to a battle belt with a tourniquet, two sidearm mag pouches, one knife, note he had several, a dump pouch, and a holster. Then I went through his assault pack and straightened that mess down to bare essentials. His plate carrier was legit and he wore it action-guy-style, putting the mag pouches across the front instead of my preferred chest rig mission adaptability setup, but I get that's not popular with the kids.

I have to admit, cleansing him of his ridiculous gear was... *fun*. For me. But I am small and petty that way and delight in destroying the false hopes and dreams of young soldiers.

It is the perk of being an NCO and this is the hill I will die on. Don't @ me.

Seriously. He had a blowgun. Flash cubes and other absolutely ridiculous stuff from *Danger Dan's* ridiculous catalog. But I let him keep the tiny "samurai sword." It was just as long as a Bowie, and it was as good as a machete. But he had to keep it strapped to his assault ruck and if I saw it coming out in a firefight before "black on mags" had been declared, I was gonna use my last three rounds to Mozambique him.

"Yes, Sergeant, understood. Catboi will wait for the order to fix bayonets to deploy the sacred blade because Catboi does not wish to be... Mozambiqued."

"Stop that."

"Stop what, Sergeant?"

"The Catboi doing this, doing that."

"Catboi stopping, Sergeant."

I sighed.

And knew I'd be doing a lot of that in the future.

But I was tired from my nightmares, or dreams, I wasn't sure… of the coming destruction of the company. They'd already started then.

I just hadn't realized it.

CHAPTER NINE

Double Tap, the security element off the *Thunderer*, went in at the base of the space elevator that was Gateway Station to secure entry to the complex from that level. Once the area was deemed "secure" they'd use an engineering team that had been attached to their element to go in and restart the facility reactors to get power to the rest of the station. Also, they were effectively conducting a "blocking action" to deny entry into the facility above. That way we didn't get any surprises when we were hitting the main terminal of the elevator station.

They were on other dropships off other vessels in Rogue Fleet, *yeeehawww, boys!!!* They'd be dead in twenty minutes, but we didn't know that yet.

We had no clue what we were walking into. It was about to get real rough.

For them… it was a lot rougher.

Both flights of dropships off the *Thunderer* broke up, and they went to their imminent deaths as we went into the trap a stay-behind hunter-killer team had implemented and about which we had no clue we were walking into.

Fun, huh?

The drops carrying Reaper set down on the high-altitude landing platforms at the main terminal for the heavy cargo lifts that once operated upstream along the elevator to the sub-orbital-relay docks higher up.

Fleet Intel had developed information that the sub-orbital relay station had been hit by indeterminate weapons fire and was considered too unstable for boarding until we secured Gateway and sent repair teams and engineers in to restore and secure the docking facilities above atmo.

So we had to take Gateway Station's main terminal substation. A high-altitude bubble-disc constructed within atmo.

Last-known emergency broadcast transmissions Rogue Fleet had received during inbound jump to the Dandelions had come from Main Departure at Gateway Station. That was where we were going in.

If we were going to find any survivors, we figured we'd find them here.

All four squads got off the drops and the transports howled away, churning up the last wisps of a poisonous yellow gas front that had come in over the station just as we'd made final.

The bioweapon the Monarchs had used drifted in large, deadly storm fronts across the world. There was nothing left to kill—it had wiped out everything. Now it was just churning up into dissipating fronts that refused to completely go away.

We were expected to be within this front for four hours. We would have no external support due to the hurricane-level winds in the storm.

Which made this a particularly idiotic time to start our insertion, if you asked me. Guess who nobody asked.

All four squads in EVC posture were "down and clear" and formed into combat wedges in the short-halt position while we waited to make entry to the station.

The winds were tearing in, and external audio in our enhanced vacuum combat armor picked up the eerie howls as they raced across and through some of the ruined parts of the station, creating uneasy screeching sounds that had some of the new guys jumping and hissing, "What was that?"

"Easy," said Jax, who was running Second, officially on the company books, but with Ulysses Two Alpha Six in the ASL position, and getting ready to take over. "Ain't nothin' to get saucy about right off the bat."

Jax was carrying a liberal amount of high-ex even though the commanders of the Technate had told us not to bring any demo. That was stupid, so we did it anyway.

They weren't the boss of us. Yeah!

"We got no juice, Sar'nt," Punch confirmed from First Squad as he jacked into a local power pylon just off the landing platform. He was confirming what we already knew.

There was no power to the complex. Our secondary mission was to get in there and make sure that the engineering team sent in with Double Tap had the ability to restore power all the way up-elevator via accessing the station batteries at this level, which should have been fully charged…

We'd see.

As I've said, Double Tap was already taking in engineers to get a main-start sequence initiated on the ground-level reactors that powered the complex below and could then reroute to power our batteries high above, if they were depleted. They would also power up the lifts to the sub-orbital docking stations so a repair team inserting here at the midway point could hitch a ride upward to where they could effect repairs so fleet docking ops could begin. The reactors were buried somewhere in the twenty-level-high massive base tower that anchored the fantastic elevator to the crust of the planet.

Departing passengers and cargo stopped here in Main Departure before making the trip up to the orbital docks or transferring to the local platforms. Back when everyone was alive. Now they were dead and I doubted anyone would use this thing ever again once we left.

By the time anyone back from where we came from made it out here, this whole facility would be falling apart from lack of maintenance.

And then there was that whole genocide thing to deal with.

That felt like bad luck to anyone wanting to make the investment on getting this ruined system back online again. But what do I know, I'm just a simple ruck hobo leading his guys into a trap on a poisoned world.

They don't pick the brightest and the best for these kinds o' jobs, now do they?

Mission parameters indicated it would take at least eighteen hours to spin up cold reactors to full working and docking capacity. Apparently, they had been shut down without the permission of the "survivors" who'd held the station until the filtration and venting security systems had either collapsed or been compromised. Somehow they'd gone offline. We did not know how or by what means.

Maybe… someone was still alive here.

Doubtful.

But… someone in mission planning was an optimist.

We'd hold Gateway for those eighteen hours. Once it was considered "clear," the additional engineering teams would be flown in to enable orbital docking by the larger ships in the fleet.

In reality… we'd be lucky to survive six hours.

But of course we didn't find that out until the drops were *down and clear* off the landing platforms at the main terminal substation bubble disc, pushing back into the green-and-pink miasma of the sickly dawn that had become a poisoned world, headed back to *Thunderer* for the second round of teams to be brought in after the eighteen-hour mark once we gave the "all clear and secure."

And once the storm had passed.

I had Reaper. It was just us on this one. Ghost and the other new platoons weren't needed for this kind of work. And other than our snipers and recon, they weren't ready.

The captain could not send in Ghost as our QRF if we got in trouble. They would be unable to conduct external breaching and sniper operations where any potential threat might appear to hinder our mission.

No loss for Ghost there.

That kind of op was pure no-handholds terror.

And it sounded easier than it was. Landing on a hull ten thousand feet in the air on a poisoned world in EVC armor and high winds to put the smack on someone sounded like a great way to fall to your death or get blown to bits by mines someone had left for such an eventuality.

Rogue Fleet Tac weather reports coming off the scout ship *Raven* now breaching atmo in low orbit to support the op, had a major storm front pushing in by late afternoon and according to the operations teams off the *Thunderer* that was a good thing.

"Expect dissipation of the chemical agents once the front passes through, Stormbringer…"

This had the potential to shorten the four hour-window and that, if we got contact we couldn't handle, was a good thing. Ride out the storm, flush the agent, QRFs and air support suddenly became available.

Also… *Stormbringer.*

That's us.

Finally. We got a cool call sign.

I rejoiced.

It's the little things that keep a ruck hobo goin' sometimes. And this was one.

We have to be honest about these things. I am a simple soldier and I will do some dangerous stuff all in the name of "That's cool."

Judge not lest ye be judged, or something…

That was our call sign for the op, and the Old Man was tagged as Stormbringer Actual because he was with us on this one.

I was running comm as platoon leader while the captain was moving in with Second Squad which had now become my recon element, under its soon-to-be new squad leader, Ulysses Two Alpha Six.

Current golden boy of the company. Jax was still banged up badly from being wounded and evac'd at Marsantyium. It took us two weeks to find him on one of the hospital freighters and his medical care hadn't been state-of-the-art.

The current talk was he just needed some time and physical therapy. But the reality was Jax was dinged hard no matter how he tried to hide it. So we were gonna make him our Master Breacher and Training NCO to get him outta having to deal with his knuckleheads on a daily basis.

It was Ulysses's time, though. That was obvious to everyone and it was pretty clear that by the time we caught up with *Dark Star* he'd be Second Squad leader and running things there.

I had no heartburn with this. Jax wasn't up to it anymore and I had yet to deal with that.

"Be advised..."

Static and chop saturated the incoming transmission. The winds were rising across the upper stratosphere of the poisoned world, spreading deadly smart dust into huge twirling maelstroms that made the approaching storm look like some bellowing, heaving, angry demon.

"Intruder... secure... the... subbasement reactor complex. Engineers... starting... Mark as now..."

"That's traffic from Double Tap," noted Punch, whose passion besides shooting, martial arts, archery, and generally punching people, was commo.

Punch had a lot of interests and we were all glad for that because those generally kept him from punching people.

We got bits and pieces of the traffic as the broken-up transmission continued despite the swelling storm pushing at us in our heavy EVC suits.

Bad comm was the surest sign everything was going to be all ate up pretty shortly. Ask me how I know this sometime. But I could deal with this as we broke the doors on the station and went in, Second Squad entering first like predators to thread the boarding lounge and move deeper into the shadows, the other three squads coming in and securing all avenues of attack.

"Catboi moving to secure forward passage," I heard as I listened to all my guys working. I could feel First's leader, Punch, gritting his teeth. I was keeping Punch on my squad's traffic just in case I had to jump on something and needed him to run both. I had Catboi in Fourth where I felt I could protect him from the rest of the platoon.

"Catboi on your six, Squad Leader. Right room clear."

Externally it was quiet except for the wind howling outside the silent station. But I was still uneasy and snapped at the platoon to cut the chatter and watch their corners as they began to invariably talk about how creepy the place was.

And all the bodies.

There were dead everywhere, and after several weeks they looked... not good.

Understatement. They were gaunt and leathery to the point of emaciated as though they'd starved trying to hold out for a rescue that was literally light years away.

I've seen the recent, and not-so-recent dead before.

Something was bothering me...

Why did they looked starved instead of gassed? Had the filtration units here worked where across the entire world they had not?

Unlikely...

File that under more information needed.

"Catboi covering left. Secure. Catboi on the move."

But I was running four squads and I had Catboi. So I didn't give the dead as much time as I should have. In hindsight... I can make that statement.

Add to all this slaughter the creeping feeling of shockingly cold ice water running up and down my spine, and I coulda bet heavy on Cheks we were about to be in it pretty shortly.

So my mind was on impending contact and which of several directions inside the station it was gonna come from at any given moment. I had four squads and the Old Man who was forward with Second on recon. We were securing everything in their wake as they now pushed on the station batteries and generators in order to support the work of the engineers at the bottom doing their thing remotely to get the station batteries charged.

Everyone, even in bulky EVC posture four, was gingerly stepping around the dead as best they could. In some places they'd almost died in every space available. In others they'd died in clusters as though they were fighting for a last breath of air coming from some unseen duct or vent beneath their hideous pile.

Blank dead eyes stared up at us as the EVC buckets' lights caressed their ruined forms.

This, I thought to myself... was gonna leave a mark.

"Catboi reporting, Stormbringer Alpha Four." My callsign for the op. "More dead in this hall. At least twenty. Catboi securing the door."

Hustle, who was my acting ASL in Fourth: "Sarge... he gonna keep that up? That's gonna bother the Hose, and you know how he hits first and thinks later and all."

"Shut up," I grunted at my ASL over the private channel. "I'll deal with it after we get out of this creep show."

"Catboi scanning side passage Six Red. Negative contact. Catboi moving forward."

There were just the dead here. Dead there. Dead everywhere. And they were horrible to look at. But infantry at the first-time-caller long-time-listener level long enough, and you've seen enough dead people get up and kill your men. So I could not help watching them all, scanning and following my primary's red dot, waiting for some dead guy to just spring upright, jaw hanging open, eyes glazed, and start popping caps on one of mine.

Which is stupid. They were dead.

But why was I having that feeling...

"Sometimes bad guys just pretend to be dead, Orion."

And why is Chief Cook's voice in my head now? I tried to remember if he'd given me, or been close to, anything I'd had to drink or eat before the op. I checked my heart rate in the bio-feedback menu of the EVC bucket. I was breathing heavy and right at what most cardiologists would admit you for a heart attack heart-rate level.

But that was pretty standard for me. I'm pretty high-strung on the inside, which I why I try to act so... me. So... nothing to be gained there.

I was probably fine, I told myself, trying to calm down. There was no way Chief Cook had dosed me. I hadn't even seen him prior to the op.

But... gotta be honest about these things... that didn't comfort me. He could have aerosolized us somehow.

"Be cool," I grunted at me, and my whole platoon heard it over open comm. I was trying to calm myself down and not freak out that the warrant had poisoned us all for another "combat multiplier."

Two clicks from the pros.

"Roger, Sar'nt," from the new guys.

"We the ice cream man, Sar'nt," from Punch. "We keepin' it cool when it gets real *hawt*, Sar'nt."

Like I said... I seen "dead guys" kill before.

Saw a general get iced like that on a contract back a ways. Blue I think it was. He'd come in to survey the battle after the battle which is a very *General* thing to do and justify some combat action ribbon they haven't gotten yet.

One o' the dead enemy officers just sits bolt upright with a sidearm he'd kept under his body and dials the general near point blank in the skull.

Then we killed that guy but the general was dead and we had some 'splainin' to do about perimeter security and pulse checks.

Pulse check. We shoot you again after we already dropped you just to make sure you're dead as we pass by your corpse. If you got a bayonet which rarely anyone runs on the end of their primary you can do the double-tap-stab.

Hey... war ain't pretty. Only prizes for the winners.

But here, on Gateway Station... they were just dead. They'd been poisoned. They'd strangled, vomiting and defecating all over themselves as they got choked out by a chemical agent. So...

Pulse checks didn't get done.

"How's it look, Punch?" I asked my First Squad leader, ahead along the main concourse inside the station and watching the captain and Second do their work creeping and clearing ahead to the batteries and generators.

"Livin' the dream, Sar'nt." Static wash. We were getting deeper into the station. It was darker. Shadowy. Fewer open portals on the sickly storm-tossed sky. And frankly, that wasn't a bad thing.

That storm was weird. And deadly.

It was doing my nerves good not to see it.

I took Punch's traffic as *nothin' shakin' but I'm creeped out by all this too, Sar'nt* in standard Punch-ese.

"You know, nightmare's also a dream," rumbled the hulking Hoser over the comm who'd heard the traffic. He passed by me and shifted the Pig to cover a dark hall we were passing, ready to lay copious hate in a blur of frenetic outgoing lead at whatever came out of the dark at us. The Pig's light washed over piles of dead down there.

"True dat, big man," seconded his assistant gunner, Hustle, as he followed behind, draped in belts and humping a huge assault pack loaded with as much ammo as the two of them could do.

Even though life-scan sensors indicated everyone and everything was dead here… it felt like there was *something*… something here. So we were loaded for bear with high-ex and high dose… just in case.

Yeah. Something smelled… wrong.

I got a gift, as Punch likes to say.

"You got a gift, Sar'nt. Sucks it involves usually getting shot at. But hey… you got a gift and that's somethin'."

But it was weirder, deeper… darker than that.

So… lemme explain, if I can…

CHAPTER TEN

One time the company pulled a security-intel and documentation gig on a civil-war-torn world called Bernica. It was bad. Real bad. Genocide stuff. The very definition of a nasty little war with war crimes in abundance and all the horrors that go with that. We found and documented more than a dozen mass graves the "winners" made. Once, we found a particularly large one on a long patrol out into war-ravaged farmlands near what had been the main fighting. A mass grave. Haunted survivors still trying to get the farms up and running eventually pointed us to where it had all happened. So we pulled initial security for the site and waited for the Adjudicators and Ultra Marine detachments to show up in force.

We were on the "right side" that time.

But it was a creepy place in those waiting days, and nights. Stuff started to… *happen*… as we set up near what turned out to be several mass graves. We maintained a watch, keeping away the ghouls and jackals looking to loot and disturb what had happened there once news began to spread we'd found them.

And…

Sometimes, late at night, guys in the company began to… *see things*. Things out there in the fog and dark as the mist hung close and thick.

And yeah. I saw some *things* too. Heard *things* also, and somehow… that was worse than seeing what I can only classify as… *supernatural events*.

Which I don't believe in.

Late at night, when it was quiet, and it was always after oh-two-hundred local, we'd see "fog of war" type events, or so we started calling them. We'd hear whispers, pleas. Bargaining. Threats. Those were the worst because they didn't sound just angry… they sounded… *demonic*.

And hey, I don't believe in that stuff.

But there I was… hearin' it.

It was as creepy as it gets. Electronics and comm got all *canked*. It was… real. And it wasn't funny.

We had a guy, he got killed later, on another contract. He straight-up pissed himself and would never stand LP/OP out near this one mass grave ever again. His hair went gray and he was never the same again until he got it from a very real sniper's bullet during a patrol on another world.

His tag had been Upchuck because he always threw up after company runs. Once he went gray after Bernica, some started calling him Silver Fox because he wasn't that handsome. Fairly ugly. But he'd gone gray from whatever he'd seen, or heard, out there one night and would never talk about.

So… he saw, or heard, the *things* too. The things that don't exist because we don't believe in those things here in the far space frontier future.

But Punch had this to say… "We took our war crimes with us, Sar'nt. So why not our ghosts?"

And I didn't like that because it made sense. And nothing about Bernica made sense.

Some contracts are like that.

Upchuck's tag didn't stick and it wasn't even funny for us. That whole gig on Bernica bothered everyone and we were glad to be free of it. We'd lost our sense of humor there and if I look at the history of the company, even though things weren't going great by then, they got much worse after that. Astralon, Crash, call it what you will. The Seeker. The bad LZ at Marsantyium.

The chase of the *Dark Star* which felt like a curse more than an op.

But maybe that was just me…

So we continued calling him Upchuck even though he didn't throw up anymore because mostly he didn't eat much after that night and he sat in his hooch and smoked a lot, always watching the shadows, like he was listening for something.

Waiting for something to… *speak*.

I never got his story. He timed out before he came to see me, even though now when I look back on it… he was due. Overdue in fact.

Even then I could see it. I just didn't want to admit it.

I was wrong. I should've gotten it out of him.

Maybe… maybe nothing would have changed. Or at least that's what I have to tell myself whenever I think back on Bernica and Upchuck who didn't want to LP/OP near the mass graves of the genocidal slaughter one side had done to the other because they'd had their final disagreement over who buttered their toast which way.

Humans. Absolutely willing to straight-up ice each other over bad ideas.

I try never to argue with someone, philosophically speaking, that I can't go out for a taco with afterward.

Bad ideas.

Which, in this lowly ruck hobo's experience, is what most civil wars, which are the nastiest of conflicts, are about.

Bad ideas.

Who butters their toast this way, as opposed to that way. It's all just some variation on that theme. I hate to be simple about this… but I've exchanged enough gunfire on behalf of others that it has distilled down to this bitterest of liquors. For me.

Your mileage may vary.

That wasn't the only mass grave. Or death field. We found more and more. Others here and there. And we left the farmlands and went up into the drizzly highlands of that world. Like I said, I ain't… religious. But near every "new" one we found it got more and more intense, the voices, the more we found. The happenings. The apparitions begging for their lives, being shot, and worse. Much, much… worse. The weeping. I don't believe in "the supernatural" *per se* because of my lack of faith and exposure to the aftereffects of gunfire, but I'd be lying if I told you I didn't struggle to explain away some of those… *feelings*. Some of those *experiences*.

So, for once, and I've never done this or talked about Bernica in the logs after that world. But because what I was experiencing on this station was something… other…

something non-human… was here and watching, and I was picking up on it and not… acknowledging it in the moments before things went absolutely kinetic…

I put it all down here. What I was feeling back near those mass graves on that cursed world where its own people had decided to just annihilate themselves and it had nothing to do with the Monarchs.

Toast and bad ideas.

I guess they just thought they hated each other enough and that the end of the other side was the answer to all their problems for a better tomorrow.

It wasn't.

The tomorrow I saw on that world absolutely sucked.

But here's what it was like in the misty dark, there, late at night without a sound. That whole world, when there weren't IEDs or sniper fire… it was silent.

Like it knew what had been done on some rainy afternoon before we showed up to find the crimes.

Like the whole place knew what it had done to itself.

Here's what it was like in the night-quiet…

The feeling of dread was like *swimming in mud*. It was surreal. It was like swimming in dark waters that weren't… *waters*. And that wasn't the worst part. The worst part is that in that dark… that mud-water… you knew there were monsters. Not… *were* monsters. But *are* monsters.

They're in there with you. In the mud-water.

Unseen and huge, dark and inhuman.

And here's where it gets worse. Some nights you were convinced they were just apparitions. And then some nights…

You were working with local units. Guys who seemed just like you, some soldier, who'd been part of that whole… *genocide-thing*, the winners, later, when you figured it all out. And those nights, some nights, you knew. It's not just… fiction.

Monsters are real. Not just whispers, cries not to be shot, or raped, or weeping endlessly weeping grief. Sometimes the monsters are standing there at dawn on a cold morning, harder to distinguish from your neighbor than anyone knows. Right there in the chow line with you. Rifles on your back. Scrambled eggs and hot coffee.

Locals who'd been part of it.

The winners.

And these monsters… they looked just like you.

What I learned in those paper-plate scrambled-egg breakfasts with the local militia who'd fought there, was right or wrong, sometimes it just takes the right guy talking to someone at the right time about the right idea to turn a basically normal dude… into a stone-cold… *monster*. Something… *other*.

I walked the Bernican countryside with a couple of them that were by all rights normal family men. But they'd killed dozens of women and kids without question. And never thought twice about it.

They just did it.

And then… they went on. In plain sight. Right there in line for chow with you.

Every fictional monster written about throughout the histories are just men doing… *something other*. From the firewyrm to the Devil Dogs of Belleau Wood. An old Earth battle I'd found some links to once. Or at least that's what I used to tell myself.

Monsters are real. They're just us.

But then those slit trenches and mass graves and the voices, sobs, ghostly images that might have been... but probably... weren't...

I just think those victims had left a "stain" on the living, before finally going.

As a reminder. That they were there. What had been done.

That there are monsters. And each one of us... could be one.

Bernica was at the back of my mind as we threaded those corpse-overrun halls on Gateway Station where they'd made their last stand and tried to avoid the death gas the Monarchs had dusted the world with.

Monsters.

And now, here, stepping over the rotting corpses on the floor of what had once been a bright and shining optimistic vision of stellar travel and hope... I was getting that feeling of *stains* and *other* again.

There was something "other" than human here and I could feel it watching us.

The medic who'd once been the Little Girl passed by me and we worked our way up a huge body-littered corridor that ran the circumference of the station.

She gave me that look she always gives me.

Now that she is a woman, and not the Little Girl anymore.

You've always taken care of me, Sergeant Orion.

And inside my EVC helmet I smelled burning smoke, as I tried to ignore the dead and scan the dark where this other thing might be waiting to consume my platoon.

Monsters.

I am haunted by the death fields of Bernica, and what was done there.

CHAPTER ELEVEN

Reaper was inside an outer donut-shaped terminal that bulged out and away from the massive diamond-fiber cable that was the space elevator. Following the cable upwell led into near-space around the world. Just beyond atmo. The entire terminal was like a graveyard now. There were corpses. Everywhere. But interestingly, not a lot here as Jax breached the doors and we made entry.

My guess was there were more bodies in the central hub surrounding the elevators and the inner secure areas where they'd run to get away from the choking gas as it finally disintegrated the filters and made its way into the station.

Punch had First Squad.

Hauser Third.

Like I said, Ulysses had Second with Jax keeping a close hand and doing demo as we hacked and blasted our way deeper and deeper into the core of Gateway Station.

I was running Fourth and keeping them close, as that squad had Catboi and the New Guys and I was busy just getting them to move and to cover according to Strange SOP, or as we liked to say, "Doing it the Strange Way."

A lot of them were in fact veterans of other stellar conflicts or had some time in service with someone or some-other, so they weren't... *awful*.

Filtering Catboi's constant narration of his actions to make that last statement.

"Catboi in the halt, Sergeant. Scanning sector for contact."

One or two had PMC time. But they still needed to learn to Strange *the Strange Way*. There are nuances to every unit, and it takes a little time to integrate and work cohesively. And until they did, I kept them close, moving around me, setting up short-halt security as I moved through all three elements and ran the securing of the main terminal facility while we waited for the engineers down-cable to power up the station and get things moving in the right direction.

Then we could get off this charnel house of a station.

Like I said, the captain was with us. With Second going into the power generation facilities of Gateway to facilitate remote assistance with the engineers at the base. As was Chief Cook who'd suddenly folded in with us long after entering the station. I hadn't seen him on the drops. Stinkeye, on the other hand, had gone deep into the *Spider*'s weapon stores a few days before the op on a binge and could not be found come departure time.

So we counted him out.

That was probably for the best.

The dead bodies. The green mist. The ice water dripping on the spine feeling. This whole thing gave me the willies.

I didn't need that old drunk doing his *Heart o' Darkness* act to add to the dread and tension already causing my heart to jackhammer.

This type of situation was pure theater for him. He would've sensed that and gone full war wizard going on about "da terrors o' da universe."

Theater. A chance for him to perform.

Or...

Maybe it would have practically turned Stinkeye inside out and right into a truly spooked babbling mess. I could see it going that way. Another thing I didn't need right now.

Honestly, yeah, that was for the best. He would have made things worse right about now even though it was about to get worse by orders of magnitude. Or at least, that's what I was thinking at the time just before it did.

Right... before it got worse.

I took a moment as the engineers down with Double Tap on the ground said they were getting some batteries online and juice should be coming up and Gateway Station would be on grid shortly. A few systems came online around us, startling some, with facility battery reserves powering up on a low, almost ominous hum. It was supposed to take hours to get full power for fleet docking operations up, but the engineers must have done something brilliant to get us a working baseline that fast. Now we could check the external feeds on the ground thousands of feet below at the base of the space elevator.

Instantly, we regretted that.

It was a field of death down there, spreading away from the small city at the base of the space elevator. It made the level of death here seem... paltry.

Literally.

An. Understatement.

Seriously.

The dead spread away from the base in tens of thousands in every direction like some endless corporate industrial farm that grew gassed, choked-out, dead bodies.

I was reminded at that moment the population count for the system was just under forty-five million before the *Dark Star* hauled into orbit and gassed them all as she plundered whatever she'd come for.

That's... a lot of death. Even to look at.

For a moment that thought choked me inside the EVC bucket and I wanted fresh air, desperately. But to take off the EVC helmet at that moment was to invite instant death until the station air could be fixed and secured once again.

Hauser was tapping at cyborg speed through a terminal and the holographic keypad he'd deployed to access it. He was in EVC to protect his "skin" against some of the more caustic elements. The death-dust could also ruin his internal machinery.

But then again... if it was that caustic... why did Gateway Station's corpses look so... intact? Like starvation camp victims.

This was... a warning alarm that kept going off in the back of my mind... but I was running a squad, checking corners, getting guys focused on sectors and dangers we couldn't see...

So I let it go when really... I shouldn't have.

His face was a statue within the EVC bucket as blue data scrawled at near light speed across his features from the terminal display.

"Sergeant Orion... the filtration systems were hacked. Internally. They were opened from within to expose the victims here to the bioweapon. But... it is my assessment... a different gas was used here and not the one the scout vessel *Raven* was detecting large concentrations of across the planet."

He was on a private comms channel with me.

"How is this gas different?"

Pause. Unusual for Hauser.

"I am not equipped for chemical analysis at that level, Sergeant Orion. Only that that the gas used here was different, and that it is no longer in effect. It has long since dissipated. Furthermore, there are only trace elements, unlikely to be lethal... of the original neurotoxin responsible for the planetary-wide casualties in the local atmosphere currently."

We had no idea what had happened here. But now... it was getting weirder.

But how could you have any clue what had happened when everywhere you looked there were dead? The only thing I could've guessed before it all became clear in the next few seconds was that the Monarchs must have come in and docked up-station with their massive, and mysterious ship...

And somehow, a vast chunk of the planet's population had gathered at the base to... I had no clue.

Did the people of Dandelion B release the gas within Gateway Station? A desperate defense of some kind?

These were theories my mind scrambled to come up with.

But it was clear the local population had tried to get off-world here on freighters departing by the hour stuffed to the gills with anyone they could get on board.

Those ships were now in jump or long haul, pulling for formerly human-controlled space.

Good luck.

It must've been chaos in those days just months ago.

Worlds like this one, far out beyond the reach of a lot of major repair facilities, maintained a space elevator just like Gateway to handle incoming cargo and passenger traffic without the hassles of landing and re-entry. Atmo landings were rough on ships, in general, that weren't built for it. And most weren't. Especially the big freighters. Having an elevator facility like this that reached upper atmo and beyond made it a lot easier to keep those ships operating to the outer systems, and the barely discovered systems that were little more than the howling dark wilds of some jungle with no such starports or elevator facilities.

The elevator cut down on wear-and-tear for the incoming and outgoing starships.

So the Monarchs had docked up-station, perhaps, was my guess. And then, I was sure once we could get into the systems and look at some of the logs we'd find out what exactly had happened, but then crazy madness of some sort... must have occurred.

A second gas, or probably first, was released internally to the station and its immediate vicinity, was what Hauser was hacking his way through as the terminals came online.

Even as I thought that, looking at all the dead down there, I knew that line, in the company log, which I would eventually write, wasn't enough to describe what had happened. Here.

It was all… *beyond comprehension*.

I need you, whoever you are that's reading this, to understand the moment we found ourselves in. Six months' training in the EVCs can make you feel fairly invincible. It's space armor, after all. Designed to keep you alive in extremely hostile environments. In the most hostile environment man has ever been to.

Space.

And then fight like the third guy in line for a two-person escape pod, to the death with whoever opposes your will to go on living one minute longer.

We don't wear the EVCs on normal planetside contracts. Sure, they stand up to a lot of incoming and the comm and HUD displays are worth their weight in gold for shooting, moving, and communicating, the fundamentals of small unit combat… but it's hard to move fast and keep a low profile in EVC.

Also, fundamentals for small unit combat, and general survival, tend toward being agile, mobile, and more hostile than the other chump.

The EVC cuts down on two of these fundamentals.

But when you do get to operate in an EVC, you feel like some kind of armored knight of old Earth. Add to that you and your closest friends, sometimes known as your squad, are carrying enough weapons and explosives to devastate a small city and there's a certain feeling of invincibility you start to feel that comes with that kind of firepower.

I was strapping the Bastard and a new sight I'd picked up in one of the bazaars back on Marsantyium. It must have come off an Ultra Marine. It married nicely on the Bastard's pic rail. Night, thermal, and calculated zero at any range with just a dial on the side. It also synced with the EVC and I could see in my HUD exactly where the point of impact was going to be even if I wasn't down on the sight.

Which is great for working in the EVCs. A lot of weapons don't marry with them. And that's a whole other thing. Again, *mucho* squad and platoon complaining and me wishing I was someone else other than the platoon sergeant responsible for all these wayward killer children when they complained about EVC posture four. It's amazing how much hardened killers can bleat like stuck pigs when some little detail doesn't go exactly their way. Especially when weapons are involved as they all have strong opinions—this cannot be emphasized enough—which they are absolutely willing to defend with sharp knives.

But, as protected and heavily armed as we were, the level of death we were witnessing stopped you cold and put everything in perspective.

What we were seeing and hearing on Gateway put us in our places regarding a giant universe that didn't much care one lick for our continued existence.

And again, we have seen, and created, a lot of death. But like weapons, everyone has strong opinions on death and what it's gonna be like after we find out for sure.

Most people think they're gonna get some time to sort things out when it happens.

I have seen more than my fair share of guys' skulls suddenly turned to red mist, especially when the incoming is heavy, unexpected, and all of a sudden.

Junkboy, the Reaper SDM back on Astralon, Crash, call it what you will, leaps to mind at this moment.

And it would be great if I could get that image out of my head someday.

Seriously, galaxy. Throw me a bone.

But the feeds down-station on the ground were…

There were mass graves and death camps down there. There had been death work going on *before* they chemmed the whole planet.

They. The Monarchs, that is.

And now someone… gassed them internally while they were trying to hang on.

Nothing… made sense.

Now, Tac Feed was noting mass graves being detected by the *Raven* running her advanced thermal imaging, and I was monitoring the horror of that particular comm exchange as we probed farther and deeper into the terminal of Gateway Station. Weapon lights covered the green poison darkness ahead, sometimes catching the rictus grin of some corpse leaning against a wall, black tongue hanging out, smiling or screaming at the terrible death they'd been dealt there. Here.

"Look at this guy," someone said, and for half a hot second, it sounded to me like Choker who'd bought it at the last of Marsantyium. But it wasn't. He was dead.

But it sounded like him.

"Guess he didn't like the chow at the gut hut." Classic Choker. He was like that. Pure sociopath. That's why we made him the medic. You gotta be emotionless to deal with light infantry medical problems. Especially after leave on a world with party girls who won't overlook the lack of money a merc might have left to provide some oblivion.

To make you forget places like Bernica.

"Stow that," I hissed, and felt like throwing up afresh which is an ironic thing to write. But I said it so low no one heard me because my voice was that dry and my skin was crawling.

And this time I made sure I wasn't transmitting to the whole platoon which I was the leader of. Apparently.

I was reminded how much I'd hated Bernica. And the nightmares for long years after that place.

Meanwhile the comm operator on the *Raven*, some chick, she was crying in the traffic as she tried to transmit the data collection of the death fields being detected. The drones and scans were picking up a lot of death. In high definition.

So, she had that going for her.

They swapped her out after a dull *hummm* lull in the comm transmission and another operator came on. This one was all business and I silently thanked someone for this.

I felt bad for the comm girl on the *Raven of Winter* who couldn't take it anymore. I understood.

We all have our stories. It's been a rough go for everyone since the end of everything ever known.

We all… have our… *stories*.

I'm sure she had hers.

The death camps could be seen by the drones flying overhead down there. There were stacks of corpses and then just entire fields and roadways where, as far as anyone could tell from high orbit and recon bird passes, large segments of the dead must've just been butchered wholesale.

Like it was a ceremony got out of hand and turned into a fever.

Even for mercenaries, this was… *pretty grim.*

It defied comprehension.

I would have killed for a bad firefight with terrible odds, instead of this rotting dumpster fire of a gig.

And at that point, it all went seriously sideways.

We'd only scouted and secured the middle level of the main terminal substation at that point. There were more levels to the substation below and one above. And of course the central hub. But as we got deeper in, it was remarkably free of corpses.

None in fact.

And that felt… *ominous.*

Things got real wild at that point as the leading edge of the storm lashed out at the pressure windows of the high space elevator terminal we were tasked with securing. The rainy poison winds shifted and some corpse that must've somehow been outside the station's bubble disc slid off and fell past the observation windows. Jingo, one of the survivors from Dog, a former Ghost scout who'd been shifted over to my platoon and was acting as assistant squad leader for First, opened fire. Full auto and putting AP rounds into the safety glass, not punching through and instead making a huge collage of heavy impact rounds spider-webbing the powerfully reinforced windows.

Reminding me he could have made things instantly worse for us all.

But the high-impact safety glass held.

"Sorry," he muttered in the aftermath. "That thing freaked me out."

The wind outside keened now. Like… someone crying in the night near the mass grave they'd been hidden in.

That's when the sitreps of contact started coming in from below.

Ground level.

Double Tap's AO.

Area of Operation.

In seconds, as Punch put it, Double Tap was getting "chewed to pieces" downshaft by a combat cyborg hunter-killer team that suddenly came out of the corpse pile near the station entrance at ground level and began dusting perimeter security.

The firefight got wild and we heard everything as it went down inside mere seconds. It sounded like chaos on cocaine as the killer combat cyborgs sprang their trap.

"Contact right!"

"One comin' outta that pile of bodies! Suth! All elements put fire on that guy!"

"Ain't goin' down!"

"Frag out!"

"Gunner's down. Someone get the gun up, dammit get the bloody damn gun up right now or we are gonna—"

"Where's Sarge?"

"Firing AT! Backblast area clear!"

"Sarge is hit! Head's blown off, man! We gotta evac now! This is bad. All bad…"

"Overlord, requesting evac… grid loc… arrrgghghh!"

Overlord was the operation's shot caller from Fleet Command. Currently he was on board *Raven of Winter*.

"LT's hit! Call for fire and dust the site! Overlord, we need you to drop on our loc. Say again, drop all you got, this loc. We're pulling back..." Static washed the channel for a hot second. "... into bunker beneath tower... Say again, drop everything now. Requesting orbital strike. This loc!"

We didn't know there were Hausers.

Now, we did.

CHAPTER TWELVE

"Combat cyborg team, Sergeant Orion," said Hauser as we listened to the chaos at ground level unfold and the utter elimination of Double Tap, our only friendly unit in the area of operation. "Standard graveyard ambush operation for the CCT elements. Probability indicates there is most likely another HK team on station with us now, Sergeant, and that a similar trap will be executed within one minute and thirty seconds of the initial execution."

Damn.

"This might as well happen," I was saying in the shadowy dark as Fourth had just linked up with First. Red emergency lighting had come on and everything looked hellish. Punch had just turned away from me, ejecting the mag on his battle rifle, tapping down the rounds to the rear to make sure they were seated and wouldn't fail to feed. Then he slammed the mag home.

Punch's way of getting ready for whatever came next was to make sure his ammo feed didn't get in the way of his getting his kill on. He flicked the selector switch to full auto. "Time to cleanse some negative energy, like Wolfy says."

That was when Hauser approached me, walking fast now as he laid out options for taking out the HK team that was about to hit us. He was a giant death machine carrying the Pig.

"The combat cyborg will attempt to ambush and eliminate the threat we pose in order to conduct a security analysis of forces pursuing their masters," he continued, "and then download an algorithmic hack-worm to conduct asymmetrical and infiltration attacks against the fleet in order to waylay the pursuit while they transmit a sitrep of pursuit forces status. This will be a specialized unit optimized for this kind of warfare, Sergeant Orion. My software indicates a ninety-eight-point-nine percent possibility that this is happening now. If they make it into the fleet, there is a good chance they will be able to allow the Monarchs enough time to escape capture."

Punch smiled at me.

Then...

"Terminators, Sarge. Pretty sure we're gonna die on this one. But hey... whaddya want, to live forever?"

CHAPTER THIRTEEN

The first combat cyborg from the enemy HK team came at us just as the "dead" began to rise all across this level of the main terminal bubble disc of Gateway Station.

Yup. Dead people started rattling around… and then getting up.

"Uh… Sarge, we got new probs. Beaucoup probs," said Punch as I tried to follow the comm chaos with all involved across the chain of command for this insert.

Double Tap was already under fire on the ground, and getting chewed to pieces by the sounds of it.

"We got a major situation, Stormbringer. All channels dead with Retaliator…"

That was the new comm operator off the *Raven*.

"We're getting jamming interference local and planetwide. Someone's running heavy gear. Be advised… possible trap getting sprung, Stormbringer."

"No duh," I muttered as I watched the weeks-old "dead" begin to shiver and shake as they pulled themselves off the floor all around us.

Retaliator was the command-and-control team running things from *Thunderer*'s ops center. As soon as I got that message I signaled Hauser and tried to get him through to Retaliator.

No dice.

The storm was beginning to hit hard now and perhaps that had something to do with the interference.

But… nah. It was a trap.

It was midday, but the sky was now a roiling black-as-night howl beyond the giant windows in the ob deck. Trash, debris, and strange flocks of dark birds were being carried and hurled into the skies even at this altitude.

The birds were dead. Corpses now by the poison gas and dust they'd been sucked into.

You ever seen a dead black bird fly…? It's weird.

The scene was apocalyptic. Like some last judgment out of some holy book I'd never read.

And perhaps at that moment, as things began to go pear-shaped, I was glad I'd never read such a book. If at least because I didn't want to know things could get worse than they already were.

Spoiler… they were about to.

Hauser shook his bucket at me, his strong-jawed and scarred face clear behind the glass of the EVC helmet.

Negative contact with Retaliator.

"Storm Actual…" I said desperately, hoping I was gonna get the Old Man who was further into the facility on this level as Second Squad had now moved in to scout the tubes and cables to ensure we could get active transport between this level and the orbital docks higher up along the elevator.

I got through, but there was definitely jamming interference going on, and I'd been around long enough to know this wasn't just interference from the storm.

You could practically feel the scream of the signal scramblers dialing through every channel encryption couldn't cover.

Someone was getting it on, and we were on their X.

"Reaper… get ready!" I shouted.

That was when Hauser made his assessment that we were facing the combat cyborg HK team.

An advanced one, apparently.

And Punch posited, statistics on his side… that we would soon be dead.

If you know, you know, and just so I can get it all down I'm going to continue with what happened next instead of giving you a whole deep dive on combat cyborg teams. Advanced ones.

The company had faced three combat cyborg teams in its entire existence.

One prior to my time with the company that ended up in almost a total kill of the entire company, reducing the company down to one squad that managed to make it off a derelict star freighter the combat cyborg team had been trying to infiltrate into a war zone on.

The first sergeant was the platoon leader that managed to get that squad off that ship and the old company commander died of his wounds later and that was when the Old Man came to us and took over as commander.

The second time was on a world just two weeks from the Ultras showing up to turn the tide of events to the winning side… the Monarchs. Of course. That CCT team had been sent in to destabilize the defenses around the main city, which the forces paying us had just taken.

That was on Marceaux.

It felt like we were being hunted.

Three days and long nights of terror and the company decided to pull out without making direct contact with the cyborg team that was busy picking off other companies with sniper fire, explosives, and a terror campaign Chief Cook found, his words here, "Inspiring, Orion."

The company was six months overdue on pay for that contract anyway and things were starting to get sketchy. So we looted the local armory and munitions yards, stole a drop-hauler, and made it back up to the *Spider*. A few contracts later I did some digging and found out no one made it out of the Green Zone we'd been tasked with holding against the near-unstoppable killer HK cyborgs.

The third time was just back on Marsantyium.

We were on-mission after events at the LZ. We had a cyborg HK team out there around our objective and Hauser went after them on his own so we could extract some hostages.

"That unit was an SAT squad. Strategic Area Termination. I had a better chance against them, Sergeant Orion," Hauser told me after the fact. "Knowing their defended position defeated seventy percent of their combat advantage. They would have killed you, but in a fight against another Eight Series combat model cyborg with front-line combat capabilities… they were no match."

Then Hauser looked at me in that machine-like way he has that sometimes reminds me he's not human even though he's my best friend, the micro-circuitry in his eyes catching the light just right enough to reveal the machine within, and said, simply, flatly, "They were terminated so the mission could continue."

So here we were with comm troubles developing as the storm came in hard and howling with Hauser alerting me that we had a cyborg HK team in the wind somewhere inside our area of operations now.

This was just before the dead began to rattle and shake.

With power coming from the base, Second Squad was probing the central lift core of the elevator at that very moment and out of comm reach and link-up with established lines inside the station. Third and Fourth, me and Hauser, had a small patrol base set up deeper into the main floor, just inside some admin offices that looked out on a glassed lounge filled with dead bodies.

The "dead" began to move.

First was on rear security holding the route back to the external doors that led to the landing platforms on this level in case we needed to get out of the facility and ready for a dust-off at the landing platforms even though I highly doubted they'd get through this storm to make the extraction.

I didn't know a pilot alive that would make that approach.

But hey, I'm an optimist that way.

And you always need a route off the *X* even at ten thousand feet, on a lift station along a space elevator line, in a howling poison storm with dead birds whipping about this way and that.

So… there weren't a lot of routes out of this mess until we secured the inner lift tubes and got them operational.

"Uh… Sarge?" It was Hustle now. He was overloaded with belts for the Pig Hoser was carrying. "The dead guys… they're… shaking."

I'd heard Punch's traffic that the dead were moving and I'd seen it with my own eyes. But I was busy trying to get either Stormbringer Actual, or Retaliator. I already knew we had to *di di mao*. I felt it was best to get drops pointed our way.

Call me a wily ol' ruck hobo that way.

But I hadn't processed the "dead" starting to move.

"What do you mean *shaking*, Hustle?"

At that moment I thought the storm was probably doing it. That's what I think some part of my mind that wanted to remain… sane and rational… was thinking. Bernica had messed with me. I shouldn't have been thinking about the *things* we'd seen and heard there in the misty dark. The high winds were hitting the station's thick diamond-fiber cables and the platforms all along the elevator pretty hard. Most elevators were rated for much more. But… there was a gentle sway that was unsettling more than a little bit.

So, I thought that's probably making the corpses shift around. That's all, right, Sar'nt Orion?

Then Hauser was on the comm destroying all my naive hopes and dreams that this was not a hot mess getting worse by the second.

"This is a standard graveyard protocols attack, Sergeant Orion. The cyborg team, most likely a heavy infiltration unit, gassed most of the survivors on the station with some kind of neurotoxin, effectively sedating them into inactivity. Weeks ago. They are among them now and will make their attack at any moment."

Alarm bells were ringing like damage control sirens in my head now.

That's why they didn't look gassed. They'd been starved to death waiting to attack whoever boarded the station. They weren't dead at all…

Someone swore on the comm and said the "dead" were starting to get up.

"Get to cover," said Hauser in that machine-like monotone he cannot help but effect. It's his programming. But I think, or have falsely deceived myself to believe, because I have known him so long and consider him more human than other humans including my failed self, that I can detect differences, call them nuances, in his sanitized speech patterns.

I knew when he was serious. Urgent even.

And right now, he was deadly serious.

I cannot overstate how much trouble we were in at that moment. How exponentially serious things had just gotten. A combat cyborg team was no joke.

And Hauser didn't have a sense of humor.

Hauser turned, swung the Pig he carried one-handed because he is that strong, other arm draped with a belt of seven-six-two armor-piercing, and opened fire on the dead in the boarding lounge as they began to get to their feet.

"They will use them as cover for their attack. Neutralize all clusters of the 'dead' humans."

Some of the New Guys swore and one even said he didn't "sign up for this."

"Yeah, well you're in it now, bub," was Punch's response as he cut loose and ruined a cluster of the recently dead near the boarding scan station.

"Catboi going hot."

Hauser dumped the whole belt on prone, twitching corpses, some of them shakily getting to their rotting feet and dried bloody knees even as fast-moving AP tore straight through them. Men, women, children.

The continuous blur of light machine gun fire punching through the thin partition glass that separated the admin area we were holding, some kinda transit control documentation facility, then hot streaking rounds impacting the prone and barely standing "dead" in the boarding lounge beyond was… surreal.

Except that it was reality. On crack.

Most of us at that point watched in stunned disbelief. Even horror. There was a lot to process going on.

But the cyborg and the autist who was cyborg-like went right into action and got their smoke on.

Punch doesn't need to be told twice to react to contact. He's always ready.

"That's a war crime!" screamed one of the New Guys.

I turned to him and gave him a look, but then for reasons I couldn't figure out, I felt giddy and wild like Chief Cook had just drugged us for combat operations again, and I wondered about that sandwich we'd all been handed out prior to boarding the drops for the op…

Had Chief Cook…

I didn't have time for that. Drugs or no drugs… it was about to get weird and the only way out was through mass gunfire applied quicker than the killing machines.

So I just turned to the war crimes weenie and said, "First time, huh?"

I thought that was the funniest, and truest thing, I'd ever said. He'd understand someday. If he lived through this.

Hauser was almost through most of the belt, ripping the recently dead to shreds, when his gamble paid off and the first combat cyborg rose up with two sub guns on slings and started firing back in spraying bursts.

Several of us were hit. The HKs have very accurate targeting systems. They can fire and move seamlessly, and their hit factor is very high.

Hence… why they're dangerous.

The EVC armor held for most of us. Sub guns fire nine and the EVC is rated against that. And now we knew the gas that had killed most of the planet wasn't in abundance here. Suit penetrations shouldn't set off any chemical alarms and we wouldn't have to run atropine injections.

And that zombifying neurotoxin the HK team had used to set the ambush… it was gone too. Weeks old. Lying dormant inside the "sleeping dead."

So we caught a break. For once. I didn't expect that to be a pattern though, and it wasn't.

New Guy Three took one through the glass of his combat EVC bucket and his brains went all over the back of his helmet.

But I didn't know that until later.

So, he wouldn't live through this to find out it's all war crimes.

It was on now.

Reaper went at it hard even though those of us who knew… knew we were already on the losing side of this battle.

Which is a hell of a way to start a fight to the death.

CHAPTER FOURTEEN

The first combat cyborg to pull the sudden gunfire surprise on the *X* we found ourselves on looked ragged and bloody.

The asymmetrical perfect killing machine's version of camouflage. Clothes from a dead survivor. Gunshot wounds preferable. Blood and gore applied with the use of detailed files on killing wounds humans receive at the wrong side of the starport-trauma-doctor-level emergency surgery centers.

Like Hauser, like all combat cyborgs, they seemed a genetically pure ideal version of Humanity 1.0.

Jacked, not as tall as Hauser, drawn features that almost looked distinguished in an everyman sort of way. A perfect version of a normal human man.

Maybe that's where their designers had sought to make some statement… or warning.

The blur of sub-gun fire wasn't spray-and-pray. It was suppression. Keep us down and get those "dead" up and surging straight at Third and Fourth Squads right there inside the admin area we'd set up as a patrol base to take Gateway Station before the engineers came in to get the orbital docks back online.

This was the initial contact and it was clear they were causing a distraction, as suddenly we had tangos everywhere. We sent lead in every direction.

It was chaos and nightmare.

Like I said, New Guy Number Three got zapped right in the face by a nine-millimeter round being spat out in high dosage from the two blazing sub guns the cyborg was rocking. The fast-moving round punched the face plate on the EVC helmet and blew the back of the kid's skull all over the rear of his bucket. He stood for a second, primary hanging limply as his body switched off forever, then fell over.

No more birthday cake for you.

Now there were rounds everywhere and Third and Fourth reacted to contact faster than I'd given them credit for given the weirdness of the situation.

We had the odds.

It was only one combat cyborg so far. But generally, they operated in teams of three.

Gunfire cackled, glass shattered, bodies got rag-dolled, and we formed a rough perimeter that cleansed our inner circle of imminent threats while more bad guys, unwilling stick-figure-like bundles of human skin and horrorstruck dark eyes, pushed in at us raving like lunatics being forced against their will to attack us.

They screamed for mercy as they raced in, hands turned to black claws, and we shot them down.

This was rough. I won't lie to you. And it was about to get a lot rougher.

More bad news was coming like some storm racing across the horizon over distant fields and headed straight at you whether you liked it or not.

Several rounds connected with my squad but the armor of the EVC suits handled the kinetic blows, and those that didn't suck deck for cover returned fire on the Monarch-made killing machine that was the combat cyborg as it bobbed and weaved through the wall of "dead" it was pushing at us via some unseen method.

Signal control.

Neurotoxin that simulated death and allowed control or pre-planned actions suddenly stamped into the brain structure.

Defend. Target. Swarm.

Who knew… it was madness made real. And the killing machine used them like the human shields they'd become in an attempt to get close enough to turn us into corpses.

In seconds the cyborg had mag-dumped and began to cross to its right as it let both sub guns dangle on slings and shucked two powerful forty-fives from underneath a filthy long coat, whipping out the old-school hand cannons just like the Old Man carried and began to blaze away near simultaneously at us.

Hauser, who had taken one knee and was swapping in a belt, thundered at me…

"Get down, Sergeant Orion!" just as the enemy killing machine drew down on me and began to dump hot fat stubby rounds of burning death.

I was attempting to get my squad into the fight and was just on the verge of reminding everyone to target for headshots.

The cranial mainframe on any cyborg is the best way to bring it down quickly.

That was when Hauser hit me with one of his open fists and sent me into a desk and straight over it.

Then he stood, turned his back, and took several rounds from the cyborg that was just some shady and pale image of his own self, defending me from incoming and very accurate fire. He was hit multiple times, and as I lay on the floor I watched in amazement as the forty-five rounds hitting his back tore out of his chest, the exit wounds exposed shining bloody metal underneath, and all the while Hauser continued reloading the Pig even as still more rounds slammed into his back.

Then he turned like some pneumatic piston-driven machine in a state-of-the-art factory and unloaded on the enemy cyborg as it faded for cover.

It was a mechanical and near text-perfect exchange of heavy gunfire from two perfect killing machines executed almost perfectly.

It was more like watching a game of chess than a gunfight.

No doubt the killing machine was assessing Hauser as a critical threat to the mission and raising its targeting index numbers on him as it continued to run its game.

The thing ran back to its left, swapping mags in the hand cannons and weaving through the rising dead that had lain there for weeks in a neurotoxin death-like state induced by the HK team to seduce and entrap us.

The "dead" rag-dolled as Hauser's Pig tore them to shreds at close range while chasing the other cyborg shifting for cover.

Power, so recently if only partially restored to this section of the station hub, suddenly went down again and the battlefield inside the admin offices and body-littered boarding processing lounge went shadowy between bursts of staccato gunfire.

Targeting lasers from our weapons sliced through drifting smoke while outside the storm cracked lightning across the poisoned sky.

I spotted the HK cyborg amid another press of rising zombies, its inhuman machine's eyes glowing red like some demon's in the shadowy blue as Reaper engaged more targets and hot brass flew frenetically in every direction. I shouted, "He's there! By the departure boards!" as I began to fire on his next position with the Bastard.

The S-16 in my hands had been configured as a battle rifle instead of squad automatic suppression weapon for this mission. I'd figured targeted fire in tight quarters was gonna be my jam. But right now… suppression would have been gold.

Wishes were fishes, beggars would ride and all. I engaged and tried to hammer the killing machine with explosions from the battle rifle I was working.

The rounds thundered out, echoing across the station above the rest of the gunfire, and my first hits tore into the standing dead shifting around the killing machine I was trying to engage.

One round connected with the cyborg who was just getting his reloaded sub guns up and back into action, each arm tracking independent targets as the weapons began to blare and bleed spent brass like chorus line dancers in some glitzy over-produced show.

I caught him in the upper torso, solidly, and the hit in the machinery there must have taken one trigger finger out of action for a few seconds. The round hammered the cyborg and it spun to the left, fighting the kinetic momentum as it fought to stay on its guns. The left sub gun stuttered and went silent while the right continued to engage.

Later I'd find out Fartsack and Rockstar got hit as they popped from cover and unloaded full auto on the beast of a killing machine that was the cyborg.

Fartsack got drilled in the leg and was down.

Rockstar took one right in the ribs. It skipped through the armor, punched flesh, took out a huge section of his rib cage, and went out the back.

A nasty-looking wound. Bad to be sure. But amazingly it missed everything vital.

"Hurt like hell," he told someone.

At the time Rockstar didn't even know he was hit and instead just kept getting his kill on the cyborg who was now fading back out of admin into the cave-like tunnel of another hallway that led deeper into the boarding facilities on this deck.

Fartsack was bleating over the comm that he was hit bad and needed a medic.

"Medic! *I'm hit!* I'm hit *bad!*"

He wasn't. But his leg was shattered. And it probably hurt like hell.

The New Guys, the two that were left, were returning fire like their lives depended on it.

Which they did.

I saw the killing machine illuminated like some specter from one final blare of its sub guns, then there was a pause, and someone yelled, "Grenade!"

Fast as lightning it had deployed a frag from within its shot-to-hell trench coat and thrown the fragmentary device into the boarding lounge as it faded.

By that time it had been hit no less than a dozen times by our fire, but it was still engaged and on the verge of killing us.

And…

I had no idea where the live grenade I'd seen it throw was.

Hauser did.

He sees everything with his targeting sensors. Scanning on multiple spectra, graphing and calculating incoming hits, always optimizing for performance, he'd tracked the arc and roll of the frag that was about to det all over us.

He grabbed it fast and hurled it into the dark tunnel of the hallway after the fading cyborg.

Like it was a rocket.

A second later a thundering explosion ripped through the hall and some of Third Squad closest to the blast were hit by flying frag.

Then the "dead" came through the shattered glass from the main areas of the substation we'd yet to engage, surging toward us, screaming for mercy and wild-eyed with terror as they sought to get ahold of us and tear us to shreds, their eyes rolling and wild with terror, helpless to stop themselves.

CHAPTER FIFTEEN

Post gunfight... we swore, spitting what we could if we could make saliva, while Bender and Klutz were doing medic stuff on Fartsack and Rockstar who were both down and out for the moment.

Thoughts of death and how close it had suddenly been... we did not have time, nor did we want to dwell on that. It had been a while since we'd been shot at by pros.

Like most NCOs and people who've been shot at, there's a worry between instances of kinetic hole-punching in which you fear you and your guys might have forgotten everything you knew.

We didn't.

Win. Sorta.

"Bro... looks real bad," was Bender's standard opening line as he assessed Fartsack. "Probably never have kids, man."

Fartsack swore and cursed, tears already streaming down his red face inside his bucket.

Medic comedy... it's hilarious. Not. Never. Ever.

And yet they are never dissuaded from their comedy stylings.

"I knew this one was gonna go bad on us!" Sack wailed like some prophet mad at his god, telling his deity he knew he'd get it despite his faith.

"Just kiddin', man. You'll probably never have kids 'cause you so ugly, boss. Leg's shattered though. Bad, too. No joke. Get my vibro-saw, Klutz. We'll take it off here."

Bender. He is stone cold.

Klutz on the other hand is all biz and is working so intently and furiously to get some vitals and stabilize Rockstar that I'm sure he's on the verge of screaming, "Stay away from the light, Rocky!"

Klutz... he wants to be a hero. And he wants to be one for all the right reasons. For others.

Comm was still canked. Bad. Broken. Worthless. We were standing in the middle of a slaughterhouse and we needed to chase that thing off into the dark.

I was ready to push forward now, taking whoever I could, threading the dark hallways, finding more and more bodies as we went. I knew it was gonna get worse, but that killing machine needed to be rolled up before it and its cohorts, because of course it had cohorts, teams of three and all, made more trouble. Other gunfights I was already worried about now that this one was over.

When the dead here began to get up and came at us, we had to murder them for good.

"Catboi activated. Catboi engaging…"

Which is what he said when he went hot on weapons. Again, I tried to counsel him, as had others. He could not be dissuaded.

Still… he's a killer. His shooting is next level like it's some test he's taking every time.

It's just… that self-narration. It's like… *Chillax, bro. We read you.*

Funny note… Punch isn't that bothered by it as I thought he would be. Some things Catboi does get under his skin of course, and more than Catboi's fair share of combatives counseling sessions have appeared on the training schedule. But the narration thing…

"Catboi activated."

"Catboi engaging."

"Catboi moving to support."

That doesn't bother Punch. So… of course that bothered me and I had to ask after one of the shoot-deck runs.

"Aw, that, Sarge? Negative. He's back-briefing, that's all. You always try to get us to do that and no one does. He's doing it. That's all. And frankly… it's nice to know what someone's doing when you're trying to run an element and get your shoot on."

Not good enough. Questions occurred.

"Yeah, but…" I paused, trying to process all this. Felt like another Hotsoup to me. "But what if everyone did it?"

Punch. Not even a slight hesitation.

"Yeah but they don't, Sarge. And… why are you always trying to get us to do it, then?"

My mouth opened and closed.

I turned away.

Then back at Punch.

"How'd you like to be AG for a while and run Hoser's belts?" I hissed petulantly.

Punch: "Fine by me, Sarge. Hustle gets it, I'm on the gun and I do like me some lightning."

Needless to say, I stalked away and hid in my cage for the rest of the week.

We pushed in after the cyborg. The dead all around us now were torn to pieces, shot to shreds, gaping and ruined, bloody and a mess of once-human… but we'd stopped them and the combat cyborg had made its fade even though Hauser was tracking the hydraulic and cooling fluids it was bleeding as it went deeper into the station.

"He went this way, Sergeant Orion," noted Hauser. "He will attempt to lead us to ambush site number two as per HK team protocols. We should proceed with caution. Contact will come violently and fast from at least three quarters."

Transmission interference cleared momentarily and I finally got through to Second and was on the horn with the Old Man, telling him we had HK cyborgs and that one was headed his way now.

A minute later I heard cacophonic gunfire ahead and suddenly more casualty reports in my ear inside the EVC bucket. Oh yeah… and I was hit too. A hot caress of lead across one arm that I didn't notice until I raised my gloved hand to slap the side of the EVC bucket because my comm was getting rough and saw some blood coming through my EVC cloth.

I swore.

"Sar'nt... you're hit!" said Klutz. I waved him away as he tried to assess the wound and ended up doing a quick dose of anti-agent to handle the poison dust still tracing around, and med-sealer sprayed all across the crease in the EVC cloth.

The round and torn suit had left a burnt black scar along the exposed flesh of my arm, ruining one of my better tattoos.

In the end I will be nothing but scars and ruined tattoos.

If I'm lucky and good at this war thing longer than I deserve to be.

So far, so good, said the guy who jumped off the building without a parachute. So far, so good. But it's that end at the bottom that separates the living from the dead, don't it?

Speaking of the dead...

Just before the pursuit deeper into the station I'd encountered Chief Cook, who'd come out of the dark like some unwanted specter. We had the ACE reports up and things were good from an ammo standpoint despite the wild and abundant gunfire we'd expended killing the "dead" and going after the cyborg trying to lay the hit on us. A lot of people were hit, in fact, and our medics were busy trying to do what they could while we tried to establish some kind of perimeter in the shadowy boarding lounge right before we pushed down the dark hall the killing machine had gone down.

The storm hammered the windows. It was... unsettling. But at least the dead birds had stopped streaking by and hitting the windows with harsh slaps.

Klutz had been moved to the medic slot for my squad, Fourth, and was doing his usually over-serious best while fumbling through patches and bandages and talking about pasting an IV drip on Rockstar who'd been hit hard and was looking a little pale now. The round had deflected off the hip and got through two ribs. Hauser's squad's medic, Bender, had already nailed Rockstar with a shot of fetamine to kill the pain without making him go all drooly.

"He's good... look at him," laughed Bender. "He's smiling. See. Fetamine works great, contrary to what Cutter says about it killin' ya easy and all."

Chief Cook came through the darkness like some unholy specter suddenly summoned to make things worse.

"Great," I sighed.

"Fetamine. Child's play, kids. Use it in my coffee every morning to kill the back pain. He'll be great. Get him on his feet, Orion. We got cyborgs to kill. Kill or be killed as I always say. And you know, Orion, which side of the equation the company wants to be on... on this one."

So now I had Chief Cook to deal with. He had insisted on interfacing with me even as we moved with supposed stealth through the darkened corridors in pursuit of a deadly HK cyborg that we'd rather didn't hear us coming.

The warrant had gone missing just before contact. He'd inserted with us and hung back, then faded seconds before contact once we were clearing the outer corridors of the station.

"Where'd you go?" I asked. Not without some irritation. Mostly suspicion.

Don't eat, drink, or breathe anything around him, I reminded myself.

I tried to find an air vent nearby, see some crazy purple or orange chemical agent flooding out without being too obvious about it. If Chief Cook had found the station environmental control and added some fun gas to the equation… well, that probably wouldn't be good for us.

"Hauser's right, Orion. These damned cyborgs ran a graveyard on us. Should have smelled it. Good news is I ran down the signal generator that kept the zekes in a near-dead state until the 'borgs could activate them with their signal gear. I hacked in with the help of your new guy who I just requisitioned on the spot, and lo and behold, he knows his way around a pair of bomb snips. We diffused the IEDs the HK team had surrounded the REM signal generator with, and then… I did a little bit of trickery, Orion, and reconfigured the signal bandwidth to disrupt the zekes…"

"Zekes?"

"Zombies. The cyborgs tranqed them with Zynthol Nine, deadly stuff when mixed improperly, ask me how I know sometime—completely banned chemical weapon but then what isn't that's worth deploying—and put the local survivors here on the station in a near-death state for what looks to be like several weeks prior to our arrival. Brilliant tactical thinking and something I wish I'd thought of myself. Then they just lay there waiting for the order to attack and a signal target identifier to key in on. That's how they triggered the *X*, Orion. The cyborgs."

I turned. I suddenly had momentary comm and chatter from all units everywhere including a starship above.

The jamming was suddenly gone.

"They've turned it off to get us to coordinate," said Hauser. "They're probably monitoring our communications."

The Old Man and Second were now involved in a running gunfight with the cyborg who seemed to be fading around the station along the main circular walk we'd ignored in favor of penetration deeper into the station to take our objectives, exchanging fire and grabbing stashed weapons while unloading at his pursuers.

Its pursuers. It's an it. Not a him.

"So you turned it off?" I said to Cook. "The attack signal?"

Chief Cook looked sheepish.

"Yeah, coulda done that, Orion. Amateur move though. Then I had an idea… not to turn it off… but to turn it on. For us!" He snapped his long fingers theatrically. It was the sound of bones breaking. "And… well… let's just say things haven't gone according to… *plan*."

He was smiling for no reason I could figure. And that worried me. I knew I wasn't gonna like the answer. Platoon sergeants will understand this. But… gotta ask anyway.

"What does that mean, Chief?"

"Well, Sergeant Orion… it means the zekes aren't under the cyborgs' control. Meaning they can't use them for a standard commie human wave attack like they did to us on Bak Lo. Sons of bitches! Shoulda been there, Orion. We had the Pigs running so hard they melted the barrels all kinds of forbidden popsicle and still the little fanged bastards kept coming through the wire. In the end we had to fire final protective fires, all the demo, and get a C-beam strike from orbit real danger-close just to shut down their staging areas. But trust me… it won't be like Bak Lo here. Not this time, not this one. It'll be weird. But… it won't be that weird, Orion."

It'll be weird.

Ummmm, yeah. I wasn't gonna like this one at all. I can tell you that right now.

"So what happened... instead of what you planned to do? Chief."

Again he grinned sheepishly. Like some schoolboy caught cheating. "Interrupted the carrier wave the 'borgs were using to control them, Orion. The wave that kept them in a sedated and highly aware neuro-paralysis state as their minds became hellish prisons and their starving bodies fell apart as they fed on their own calories. If we'd managed to be a few days later they'd probably all be dead, starved to death, and that would have been a real lucky thing for us!"

Yeah, I thought. Lucky. Mass genocide through starvation. I see your point you utter sociopath.

"Only thing I could do after shorting the carrier wave, because I couldn't jack 'em and bend them to my... er, I mean *our* will, wouldn't that have been great though..." he said wistfully and trailed off as though whatever dangerous narcotic he'd just taken had just kicked in big time and he was seeing all the colors of the universe or whatever.

Then he was back.

"But that's neither here nor there!" he snapped angrily. "Only thing I could do was to go ahead and reset the base trance signal and shut down their frontal cortex inhibitors with an Alpha Nine REM wave signal I remembered from a mass mind control program we ran in the Ramataans back in '79 to overthrow the Alazar junta. If you know, you know. And officially that never happened. So, I programmed that in, no small feat as it was from memory, and just dialed up the low signal gain to max interference on the brain carrier wave. Voilà, Orion! Mind control... kinda."

I sighed. Did I even want to know? Answer: no. But also yes because it was my job.

"What will that do, Chief?"

"Everything... and maybe nothing... It's not all easy answers, Sergeant Orion. It's not all one-shot torpedoes against exhaust ports *yay you're the hero* and all... there are no heroes anymore... never were... Anyways, tell the boys they might want to shoot extra. You gotta make sure they're good and dead now."

The Psyops warrant looked away. Made some weird face like he was having a tremor or arguing with something, or someone, unseen.

Then he turned back to me, his face snarling rage within the EVC bucket he wore.

"Aw hell, Orion... what are you always saying? *We have to be honest about these things* and all. We... we don't exactly do honesty where I come from. We, in fact, Sergeant Orion, do the opposite of that."

I breathed in through my nose.

Out through my mouth.

I was dead inside. The needle of *me* was way past *empty* on the fuel gauge of *me caring*. I was pure half-past-this-might-as-well-happen-midnight-thirty.

Then, calmly...

"What are we facing, Chief? Need to know now. Clock's burnin'. Chances they've rigged the entire platform to blow as a denial-of-service attack... high inside my thinking right now."

The chief muttered. A whispering hiss and even the EVC-enhanced comm system didn't catch it.

Something about, "You don't have to tell me about IED-based denial-of-service attacks. I'm the king of that noise, Platoon Sergeant."

I asked him to repeat. I was dead inside.

Embrace the suck, whatever it is this time, I was telling myself when Chief Cook told me he'd turned off the pain centers in the zombies and upped their untapped human potential in strength and ferocity.

"How's that supposed to benefit us against the HK team?" I practically shouted.

Dead inside didn't make this conversation any less irritating.

"That was the deal I had to make with the signal devil, Orion. Not that there's a devil. And not that I ever admit to having tricked him *once*... that's classified. Need-to-know stuff, Orion. But that was the only way to break the signal strength between the zekes and the HK team. Those damn 'borgs are good at that kinda stuff. Straight outta the Monarch Psyops playbook, courtesy of the Dark Labs of Mordun's third moon. Which is where all that type of R&D, the really weird stuff, used to happen. Sergeant."

Silence.

Then...

"Not that I knew that either. Orion. Sergeant. Top secret. OPSEC."

I waited, sensing the punch line was coming.

"The Monarchs don't control the zekes no more, Orion, and neither do we. And... they're more aggressive now. Yeah. A lot more. But at least the 'borgs don't control 'em. Take the win, Orion, even if it isn't one. Anyways... tell the boys they might want to shoot *extra*. You gotta make sure they're good and dead now."

Extra?

Second was under attack again. The Old Man was telling me they were getting it from all sides. The two other members of the cyborg HK team had made their play.

I brought up the station map in my HUD as it glowed blue across my faceplate.

Yeah... we were walking into a major ambush.

When I flicked it off Chief Cook was gone.

Like he'd never even been there.

CHAPTER SIXTEEN

I had Third and Fourth on the hustle down the main concourse to reach the reactor and lifts at the center of the station.

Wounded and one medic were left behind with a two-man security element as First came up to take over.

The rest of us were clearing corners quicker than I would have liked and pushing into the shadowy reaches of the station to relieve Second under fire.

Every passage was an ambush waiting to happen.

"Check those corners… pie those rooms!" I was shouting, practically breathless as we hustled through the dark, the storm erupting in full fury now as weird, wild lightning surged horizontally across the dark storm clouds and ran like sheets of ocean water slamming into the bulb that was the main terminal hub of Gateway Station.

"This facility is becoming increasingly unstable, Sergeant Orion," noted Hauser over comm as Third brought up the rear and I had my guys moving forward trying to link up with the surrounded Second Squad. "With the hunter-killer combat team's loss of control of the chaff…"

Chaff meant the walking dead the cyborgs had pointed at us so they could get close with their weapons and cause as much trouble as they could in this ambush.

"… they will be calculating a loss of mission attainability success within acceptable parameters. My neural processes calculate they will attempt to deny the station as an asset to any ships attempting to dock. Their original mission may have been to attempt to infiltrate one of the docking ships as either refugees or casualties, then attempt to disable several ships in the fleet while en route to the next rendezvous."

That was a lot to take in.

We could hear the wild and frenetic gunfight coming from deeper within the station ahead of us. Second was in it now.

"Hauser, take your squad in to support the captain and Ulysses. We'll move up through this side conduit and try to establish a base of fire on the central shaft. Copy?"

Hauser studied the projective holographic map I was sharing with him in our virtual sand table and the routes I'd sketched with EVC glove we'd take into the fight.

"Affirmative, Sergeant. See you on the *X*."

I rounded up my squad and we pried the sealed security door to the conduit open with some jaws we had New Guy One carrying.

We were thinking about tagging him Bull because he looked stupid and big, a real chunk of meat who barely fit in his EVC and kit. One time, while practicing breaching, the Halligan tool didn't do the trick on a simulated blast door Gunny had us practicing on even after we used a breaching slug on the locking mechanism. So he just threw the tool down and ripped the door off like a bull that didn't care.

He stood there heaving with rage... he even roared as he did and everyone thought that was pretty cool.

But then he'd been silhouetted in the doorframe and the holo-tangos lit him up and "killed him a lot" as Gunny put it later when we AAR'd the whole mess that day's shoot-deck had been.

It was one of our better ones.

After that we all got jammed up in the breach and had three "KIA" before we had to pull back and the tangos owned the room.

Not a good day for Reaper.

Gunny made us crawl the hull twice as punishment for being the worst of all the squads to run the haunted house he called a shoot deck.

Today, inside this weird storm... I was hoping for different, and even better, results.

Note... for no reason I can figure out, even though Gunny is the new platoon sergeant, short of the first sergeant, he has taken senior NCO status, unofficially, and I who have labored in vain to run an effective combat platoon with as few casualties as possible, somehow feel like I'm the new kid on the block. So there I was... crawling the hull, twice, because Gunny, same rank in the command structure of the company as me, said my guys had to.

And... he was right.

So we crawled the hull that day. Twice.

Think of the worst punitive punishment you've ever heard of in any military, and then you're at about halfway to a hull crawl's level of suck.

But we did it anyway.

So... big moment in the company as we pushed into the conduit... I tried out New Guy Number One's tag for the first time right there on the movement to contact inside Gateway Station with a firefight going to full cackle deeper inside, near the internals, near the space elevator at the core of the whole main departure transit substation.

"Bull!" I shouted over the comm as I rallied my squad and got them pointed toward the route we'd take deeper into the station, and the order I wanted it to run in. "Breach that conduit panel and get us in. Hoser, I want you in second on the stack. I'm going in first."

I pushed through my guys to get in place as I barked orders and warnings.

NCO stuff.

And of course...

"Catboi stacked and waiting to go in after Hustle..."

If Hoser with the Pig was second on the stack, his AG, Hustle, would immediately be third.

"Next, Wolfy and New Guy Two," I said. "Then Klutz. That's how we roll on this one, Fourth."

Bull just stood there like I hadn't said anything to him. Everyone else moved into position.

Hoser slapped Bull's helmet.

"Hey, idiot… that's you. You're Bull now. Bust that tin can and get us in, bro."

I wanted the squad automatic gunner close at hand because I had a feeling when we got forward and into contact, I'd want to put as much hate as we could do on those cyborgs as fast as we could.

"Yeah," grunted Bull as though accepting the new reality with little fanfare or ceremony. The last surviving new guy with no tag swore bitterly. He'd been trying to advocate for all of us to call him something cool like *Punisher* or *Death Machine* or whatever he thought was a legit lifetaker tag.

Campaigning, really.

No dice, New Guy. You're gonna learn the hard way with something like Noodle or Warts.

Still, I was enjoying letting him dangle and I knew he'd hate the tag he was gonna get eventually.

I'm a small and petty man.

But hey… ruck hobo gotta have fun where he can.

It's the little things that keep ya goin'.

Bull slammed the pry-jaws into the seam in the conduit panel, brutally, then forced them open, the hydraulics needing to do very little work as the leviathan of a man just pried the door apart and forced our breach.

Then for half a second, I saw him debate whether he should just stand there looking into the darkness like a big ol' target. Just like in the shoot deck.

Or… would training kick in, optimistically hoped the broken NCO?

I experienced a brief mental image of him getting ventilated by a combat cyborg, some version of our own Hauser, just waiting there in the dark with a chopped LMG. Then a blur of hyperkinetic railgun fire and the guy I've just awarded a tag to without making a big deal of it…

… rag-dolls unto death and we push in over his corpse and get our kill on for whatever that's worth.

Hannibal used to have this weird dark ceremony when he handed out tags where they covered one hand and half their face in whatever small animal blood they could find and drew "ancient symbols" on the newly tagged guy's chest.

One time I ran those symbols through a computer, and they matched nothing the computer could come up with. But the weird thing was… they were the same every time.

Man, Hannibal was a weird guy.

He was one of the few people I've killed that I was glad he was dead. And yeah… after I'm gone this part will go unredacted, and whoever the next company Log Keeper is… that's right, I iced one of the platoon sergeants back on a bad contract.

And it's one of the few things… I don't regret.

Log: Redact until KIA.

Redacted.

So in that half second I watched Bull after the breach, he seemed to be mentally running the steps he needed to do his job…

… as I waited for him to get blasted from the darkness beyond by some killing machine the Monarchs had left behind to kill us all, or as many of us as they could.

Then he stepped to the side, stowed the jaws, and got his too-tiny-in-his-paws S16 up and ready to fall into the rear behind our medic Klutz.

I checked the dark, following the Bastard's thermal sight picture, saw nothing and remembered that sometimes cyborgs can run cold when sitting on an ambush… then I pushed in.

Second had casualties already.

The Old Man was hit. Ulysses was covering the medic.

The comm was wild.

CHAPTER SEVENTEEN

They were coming out of the walls.

The "dead" the HK combat cyborgs had turned into unwilling killing machines to throw at us like a massive human wave attack while they sprang their next trap.

Hit us from another direction.

Canalize us into an ambush.

A massive IED to det the station.

Anything terrible was possible.

The "dead" were now untethered from control, while amped for maximum violence thanks to Chief Cook. Screaming in horror, raving mad, uttering nonsense gibberish, their minds broken, their spirits shattered by what had been done to them by the cyborg kill team, they raced at us in a fever-frenzy.

I'll be honest, and this isn't to reflect goodness and hero vibes on yours truly…

Now that I knew they were alive, and not dead… I did give the order to try and not engage them in order to save them. If we could. Stupidly, I gave that order. But also, I was trying to save my guys.

So we engaged. Because we had to if we were going to go on getting continued slices of birthday cake.

We have to be honest about these things too.

We needed to pick up those killing machines quick and do them fast and dirty. They were the priority.

The combat cyborgs were killing machines designed to think about nothing but killing, and killing as much as they possibly could, and then killing.

Killing.

They'd laid their trap for us, and as much of the fleet as they could catch in it. Their algorithms and plans and tactics told them they could pull it off.

So here we were, closing for contact as clusters of our kind came at us, helplessly, preventing us from killing the machines that had killed them, but now… just rage-filled killing machines themselves.

We closed for contact and I could hear the wild shooting in every direction in the central core of the station, Second's rounds punching into the conduit we were flanking along to enter the battle from a hopefully unconsidered direction. I knew we were walking into a trap and we had no choice but to, if, and big if here… we were gonna get Second out of it even with Kid Ulysses running the gunfight.

Kid Ulysses was the slang tag no one used around him. It just indicated that for one of the newer contracts to sign on with Strange Company he sure had risen to the top like some kind of ground-to-air missile that could not be denied by chaff, flares, PDCs, or formal protocols.

Some people are, occasionally, just like that. And you only hate them because you are not them.

Do I need to say it?

Yes.

We have to be honest about these things, also.

There was already talk of making him the new XO and just marking the XO down with his role back on the ship now as the company pilot. It was clear the former Ultra Marine would be company commander.

Someday.

And perhaps today was that day as I had reports that the Old Man was hit and down and the cyborgs had sprung their trap.

It looked bad. Second was fighting for all they were worth.

We threaded the blue dark and glowing red-and-yellow-paneled conduit, meant only for service and maintenance access, displays showing all kinds of warnings of catastrophic damage to Gateway Station and repairs that needed to be conducted or sections that needed to be evacuated.

Alarms urgently indicating atmo-breach…

Yellow flashing hazards warning of unsafe passages and to wait for security or maintenance personnel that would never arrive, to arrive.

Gas and steam vents releasing their stuff to prevent pressure cascades and overheating.

One panel showed some stats and data concerning the reactors in the station's basement far below, and though I was no ship's engineer… what I was seeing didn't look good.

Even with the jamming turned off we'd had no contact with the mercenary company that had gone in down there. Double Tap was probably no more. Perhaps comm was down anyway because of the storm, I tried to tell myself as we problem-solved the route in, but more than likely they were all dead because if the cyborgs had run graveyard protocols down there too, to lay their trap, then Double Tap didn't have enough ammo and high-ex to get it done given the fields of "dead" we'd seen down there.

By orders of magnitude they didn't have it.

My guess… the HKs hadn't gassed the area around the facility… the refugee camps and collection centers… with the gas they'd hit the rest of the planet with. My guess was they'd used the zombifying neurotoxin down there too.

This was bad and getting worse…

Some part of my mind, some hopeful let's-all-gather-around-and-build-a-campfire-to-wait-out-the-storm-everything's-going-to-be-all-right… was wishing that maybe they'd found a survival bunker near the reactors and were fighting and holding there.

Wishing.

A regular little Jennie Sunshine I am.

Like I was saying… I gave the order to do whatever it takes to save my guys.

I in no way regret this course of action. But for some reason that makes no sense, I am ashamed.

Punch often reminds me I'm weak that way and that's why he always pulls off the submission holds when I get combatives times.

We popped the panel that accessed the area Second had fallen back to, and I pushed through, ready to zap whoever got in our way even as I was making the call to Ulysses to know we were coming into position and ready to put rounds on target from his left flank.

"Pushing in now, Bravo Six..."

"Bravo" was Reaper for "Second." Six was the squad leader.

I was Delta Six.

Hauser Charlie Six.

Punch... Alpha Six.

The panel popped, I pushed through following the thermal scope dialed for close-quarters battle mounted atop the Bastard which I'd configured for hot and hasty action in tight quarters... and had tangos immediately even as I scanned the battle space.

Hustle and Hoser were right behind me as we pushed into the fight and the first thing I had to do was see what was really going on at the central lift, where the battle was happening, and identify where the enemy was...

Short story short as possible...

They were everywhere.

My next job was to get my gun team emplaced and ready to deliver maximum hate on the cyborgs, hopefully getting them married to other gun teams and taking up sectors and talking.

Talking.

The gun teams alternate fire in order to keep up continuous fire and cover the inevitable barrel change or prevent forbidden popsicle.

This part, on my part, was... optimistic given the chaos and lead flying in every direction.

But hey... NCO gonna NCO, amirite?

What I pushed into was a torrent of half-mad humans that had been frozen in place by a neurotoxin-based bioweapon for weeks as their bodies fed off their own calories in a kind of stasis in order to keep them alive while the cyborgs laid their trap for a pursuit force they had a pretty good idea would be along shortly.

Fortunately, or unfortunately... the jury was still out... Chief Cook had "unlocked" them by hacking the bio-REM signal the HK team was using to control their human wave attack.

And that... was actually a good thing.

The central hub, the center of the main terminal substation, was the size of an ultraball stadium, and it looked like one too.

Circular, tall, cathedral-like. Glowing lights and search beams.

The far side, opposite the warren of landing pads, terminals, and administrative offices we'd just threaded, extended all the way to the outer hull of the massive disc-bubble halfway up Gateway Station, where massive viewing windows looked out on the maelstrom of the deadly storm front that currently was sweeping through this section of the dead planet.

The space elevator's lines ran from the ground to the low-orbit docking station high above just caressing the planet's touch on space itself. This, the central hub, served as the checkpoint where civilians going up paused for bureaucratic processing and delay before transferring to the big disc-lifters that went up-station to the freighters or starliners berthed there. It was also where the bulk cargo lifters, unenclosed and nothing but flat industrial mega-discs, loaded with cargo and exports, or imports if coming down, passed through and ran the planetary customs gauntlet.

So, imagine a massive pro sports field in some stadium and that was the size of the central hub. Except instead of a thunderball field or an ultraball arena, it was a massive industrial dock in which huge diamond-fiber cables rose through the bottom aperture, currently closed, surrounded by portals that irised open to receive disc lifts both passenger and industrial, and then high above matching portals for the lifts to continue skyward to the low-orbit docks higher above.

It was a big transfer station and nothing more. Wide fields of fire. Emplaced bunkers in the form of admin offices and cargo containers left all these weeks.

There were also mobile crawler mag-lev cranes and other types of loading and utility equipment.

Tracking lights, scanning lasers, and working floods were also on, but instead of being operated in any kind of normal operation, they were set to insane flicker and random activation.

Probably part of the combat cyborg plan.

And surrounding the central lift was a massive flattened bulb of a stadium sculpted in angular towers and massive cargo storage bays and cyclopean blast doors where cargo could be offloaded, if customs or payment was a problem, and stored. There were also hotels for passengers laying over, and cafes and restaurants facing a "Grand Catwalk" as it was called. Shops with duty-free imports and rarities.

All of that was dark now.

Many of the "dead" in their weeks of living survival as the planet below was gassed had holed up here. Then the combat cyborgs had released their neurotoxin.

The central hub was a small city inside the massive structure of Gateway Station, and the killer cyborgs had gassed as many of the workers and passengers as they could in order to lay their final fallback position here if they lost on the ground below…

… or had to hold off breaching teams coming down-station from the low-orbit docks.

This was their command post and they were going to fight to the death… end of runtime is more correct… to hold and deny here.

Hauser had briefed us on possibilities such as this and other scenarios, because we'd expected the Monarchs to leave some kind of surprise. And as our killing machine had briefed us—and he'd actually participated, with his team, in such operations before going rogue and "freeing" himself—but as he'd briefed us, their "mission objective" would be, after achieving optimal kills, to fade and insert somehow into the fleet as it continued its pursuit.

Now, as Hauser assessed the situation and deployed his gun team next to mine, he sent me an update.

"Sergeant Orion… they will have to eliminate our unit and all surviving data in order to effect their escape into the fleet undetected. They will make their last stand here, otherwise further operations and completion of task will be compromised as the fleet will be aware of their presence."

Infiltration of the fleet.

That was another intel-driven reason we'd divided into two elements with Double Tap going in below and Stormbringer above. If there was a surprise, we had a better chance of splitting the damage and making sure the fleet was aware of the threat before we perished. Rogue Fleet, *yeeehawww, boys!!!*, was too far downrange in galactic space to chance an infiltration and loss of assets. There was no resupply for years to come.

So Double Tap went to their deaths below and Reaper—Stormbringer—got to secure Gateway Station above.

Hey, kids, fun fact that will haunt you till your death… we flipped a coin with the Double Tap commander when planning the op to see who went where.

So… I got that goin' for me if I survive this one.

That is *if* we… survive this one. Big if.

Fun, huh?

So instead of facing tens of thousands in the open graves and mass killing fields spreading away in every direction that the Monarchs had left far below, we were facing about two thousand half-mad targets and trying to find the cyborg kill team we knew was in the area and causing trouble. I pushed my squads out into the central hub cargo transfer and portal deck where the main fight was in full fury.

We'd had schematics for the station and in the run-up to the op we studied them extensively. So… it's not like we were totally blind.

Just… mostly.

Like we would be when we boarded the *Dark Star* at the end of this… whatever this was. There were no available plans for the universe's most top-secret X-ship.

Two thousand raving-mad near-skeletal humans that were little more than killer drones for all intents and purposes, and one three-cyborg state-of-the-art killing team armed to the teeth lying in wait for us.

But we'd screwed them a little and we were gonna have to use that to get through this however we could.

Apparently, the HK team was anticipating a docking at Gateway Station, but they'd crunched the numbers and expected us to either enter from the base, as Double Tap did, or come down-station on the lifters from the orbital docks.

But we'd come at them from a different angle and we'd engaged and probably damaged one of them in first contact by starting the insert well below which may have split their element as they sought to deal with any forces coming up-station once the lift reactors were operational. And… we'd made our second insert right in their main command post. The landing pads at the main terminal substation just within atmo along the space elevator rising above the ruined gem that was once Dandelion B.

So back to the contact… I gave the order…

"Try not to kill the zekes. They're just interference and cover for the 'borgs. But… don't hang yourself out too far, Reaper."

Meaning… *kill them all*. In essence. *And let the universe sort.*

That's what I was saying when I pushed out into the battle, scanned the whole hot mess and got body-slammed by a half-mad woman who immediately got tangled up in my rifle sling and chest rig strapped across my EVC.

She was wild-eyed and insane and trying to bite the glass on my bucket.

Her hands were bloody claws. Crusted and black.

There was blood and bits of flesh in her mouth.

In that half second before I blew her brains out, I thought... "Oh... they're attacking each other because Chief Cook screwed the signal... and that's somehow... worse... for them. Everyone's a target to them now."

Then she started slamming her head, bloody matted dirty hair and all, into my EVC bucket. She looked like she could have once been a married thirty-something mom.

Atmo wasn't great here. And despite what Hauser had said, I wasn't about to assume there weren't meaningful traces of that biotox agent the Monarchs had killed much of the planet with still in the air. Taking a major suit breach for an extended period of time without sealing spray-plas was not... optimal for survival.

I should have thought about this when my tat got ruined... but hey... a lot going on. Don't @ me.

She got ahold of the Bastard with both bleeding claws, screaming like a witch unhinged, and then she slammed her head into the viewing glass of the EVC as she tried to jerk the battle rifle off me.

Her first crack at smashing my EVC glass went wide as I jerked my head to the right and tried to get my rifle back.

She broke one of the lights on the helmet though, throwing her nightmare witch's face into half shadow and making it somehow *full* nightmare.

Like some... unholy curse... coming at you out of the dark all around and all of a sudden. Catching you... unready.

Firefights were already going off near and close and as an NCO I felt it was my duty to manage those.

LOL! This half-mad witch was beating the crap out of me.

And as I've noted, EVC armor, though protective, is bulky and not conducive to the agile movement usually preferred by infantry who are little more than predatory hunters looking to get their kill on.

Darker shadows of once-humans streaked by our wrestling match, screaming like tormented ghosts. Some of them bouncing off my troopers as they went after each other or just sought to run away from all the madness everywhere and all at once.

Seriously... weirdest fight I've ever been in.

Hoser straight-up butt-stroked one with the Pig and that guy went down like a scarecrow fallen from its perch in some winter's field late in the night.

The darkness was blue as I backpedaled on my extended forearms. Blue and illuminated by staccato spurts of weapons fire barking at the streaking shadows of once-humans. I shucked my sidearm as she cackled and tried to smother me. I pushed it into her face and pulled the trigger.

There was no thinking now. Just survival.

But I'd been here before.

The look in her wild eyes in that last second was gone and some sudden horrific clarity came into them as she fell backward and away from me in the darkness all around us.

She'd been dealt with.

Not my problem.

Not my circus.

I had things to do now.

Fight. Manage. Survive.

Count the ammo and the dead.

NCO stuff.

A leaf, red like blood, fell across the view of her falling away from me in the blue gunfire-lit darkness, and I turned away from it not even thinking about the oddness of that.

I knew it wasn't real. But that's another story…

I saw where my smoking gun needed to be next. Another fast mover coming for the downed enemy I was. I fired three times and the hoary thing went down.

Maybe four times.

You can never remember when you're in it, contrary to the thoughts that people who call themselves pros have about counting your rounds.

I'd shoot someone else, I was telling myself as I got to my knees, no easy feat in EVC, and then perform a tactical reload.

Swap in another mag. Stow the used one and gas it up later.

That was my plan and I had a small unit to run badly. Again, I'm an optimist that way. But hey… I'm all they've got.

Thoughts every NCO has. If they're honest about these things.

I had an idea where the cyborgs were when I heard the thunder of an anti-materiel rifle straight-up destroy someone in Second Squad.

Later I'd find out it was Jax.

"Hoser… put fire on that customs ob."

Seconds later the gun team was dosing the low tower with heavy outgoing seven-six-two of the armor-piercing variety.

Customs towers are rated as cover.

We were in it now.

CHAPTER EIGHTEEN

I watched as Hoser and Hustle began to wreck the HK cyborg shooting from the customs observation tower they were putting all the hate they could on. The tower was three stories tall and sat between two cables that passed through the floor and the ceiling of the central hub.

Zekes streaked and streamed in every direction all around us. Sometimes attacking one another, sometimes just running awkwardly and screaming as though they were on fire from within, tormented and totally horrified as they lost their minds.

My ruck-hobo mind, along with Hauser's monotone sitreps as he spread his team out into a combat wedge and moved in to try and get Second off the X they were on, put the picture together.

It was like this…

Second had entered the central hub, come down a boarding and entry ramp to the main floor of the primary cargo area, threading their way through all the "dead bodies" we'd been finding all across the station, when…

… the cyborgs activated the signal and they were suddenly not just surrounded, but actually overrun.

The bio-hacked "dead" went berserk and probably started attacking Second who established a perimeter and tried to fight their way off the X.

Problem was it wasn't just a mindless human wave attack, or at least it mostly wasn't. The cyborgs had pre-programmed and stationed "elements" in carefully arranged body fields in order to cut off all avenues of access and canalize Second into the real threat: a cyborg-run ambush.

Second had the Old Man and Kid Ulysses. Both of whom are Ultra Marines. We know Ulysses Two Alpha Six is. And we've always suspected the captain was… so Second had it going for them because both men know how to run small units in hot situations.

The zekes activated and swarmed the patrol. Everyone picked up their sectors and put up a wall of lead to establish a secure perimeter despite circumstances. The bio-hacked ruined "dead" came at them from every direction. Clusters and bunches of them staged and staggered to keep up the pressure and push Second to crime scene number two where the *real* bad guys were waiting with high-powered automatic weapons.

Pro tip. Never go to crime scene number two.

Ulysses and the captain caught wind of that when Ulysses got tasked by the Old Man with probing the canalization they were being offered, and suspected was too good to be true.

Of course the captain volunteered himself to clear the route and… that's when the cyborgs sprang their attack.

The shooter in the tower started firing and the captain was hit by a cyborg anti-materiel rifle firing .338…

Believe me when I tell you that is bad even in EVC.

That was when the calls got urgent and it was clear Second had wounded and was in a bad spot getting worse. We pushed in through the conduit and came out into the central hub while I sent Hauser and Third straight in to establish a base of fire and a friendly line of fire to get Second behind.

Immediately Hoser began to hose the cyborg firing the anti-materiel from the admin tower. He was working it like a machine, because it was, and the sonic booms were steady as the HK worked to destroy what little cover Second had to protect their wounded and return fire.

Now part of the fight, I scanned Second's position on the main floor and saw how deep they were in it.

Neck-deep was the answer I didn't like.

Hauser and Third were dealing with most of the awakened "dead" colonists who were trying to just go through them to escape. Claws, eyes, blood. Whatever it took. They'd lost their minds after what they'd been through. A living paralysis in which their minds were rewired while they were conscious and their bodies fed off themselves to keep them alive.

You can't hate the Monarchs, and "scientists" who work for monsters like that, enough.

Seriously.

The awakened "dead" colonists were getting shot to pieces as they pushed on Third stark raving mad and utterly out of their minds. Gun teams were talking and the fact that the squad leader was an HK combat cyborg who carried a chopped Pig helped matters.

Still… Two Times was flipping and flopping on the ground and even from here… I knew he was dead.

Two Times…

He said everything twice. Innately lively guy who always repeated the lowdown on some new thing twice. He was a likeable guy who wanted to be liked and I can say this now… he was always excited about whatever was next.

So, even as he died, his body danced around in autonomic response to what is commonly referred to as a "switch kill."

"Commonly referred to." I hate that. There's nothing common about it.

Second's medic, the Little Girl, we still call her Little Girl even though she is a young woman now, was trying to hold him down and calling out over the comm for help to get him off the *X*.

But it was a switch kill, I wanted to shout over the comm as she shouted, "Gotta move him now!"

He was dead.

The cyborg running the sniper slot had shot Two Times with what was most likely a .338 round, or something equally just as huge and vicious, and hit Two Times right in the central nervous system somewhere. Probably the spinal column, blowing it out all over the deck along with the EVC armor and synthetic ballistic cloth torn to shreds by high-velocity gunfire that just don't care about such things.

He was gone and some dark shadow flitted across my soul and whispered... *How much can you lose, Orion?*

But I had a gun team to run and a QRF to manage.

His body was just flopping around. I'd seen it before, and it was always... *always...* disturbing to me.

Let me tell you something about Two Times now...

One time, after Blue... I went planetside and got lit pretty hard. Just... dealing with stuff. Let's just put it that way. So, I went after it pretty hard. Harder than I should've but I bet you know where I was. We all get there sometimes. Don't be hard on yourself. It's human. And that ain't bad. Sometimes. I think that was when I blew all my mem on the eel courtesan...

I remember you, estrangier.

I was headed back to the shuttle station and hoping I'd run into somebody who could pay my fare back up to our warship, our home, remember she couldn't make planetary landing then, the *Spider*, and I was shaking and hung over and her words...

Those...

They were fading and I wanted to *remember her, them, forever.*

That was the deal I was making with myself to re-up my contract and keep going. Even though I'd been thinking about... another way of life a lot during those days.

But her pheromones and that electric touch of her kind were... I was coming down off that too, and all the expensive liquor I'd been high-rolling with, in the clubs where I'd met her.

As I walked through the warm rain I felt... hollow. Empty. Spread too thin over too much.

I ran into Two Times. I told him I was broke and asked if he could perhaps cover his platoon sergeant for the fare because that's the kind of responsible leadership I like to display.

"Got ya covered, Sar'nt. I got ya covered on this one."

Two times. Life saver. Twice, saying it that way, made it seem... more true. To me. In that moment. More genuine.

The shuttle was two hours off.

He took me and sprang for some local pho. There was a street bar that served it near the shuttle station.

We ate. He paid. I said nothing because... I was out of excuses and the truth was too damn apparent for me to do anything but apologize. I can't do that as a platoon sergeant even though I pretty much want to every day, and especially on the ones they get killed on.

Two Times said nothing.

He just fed me when I was... down.

That was Two Times.

Now I was watching him, his body, flop around after being hit by the fast-moving round of finality.

He was gone. And there was nothing we could do.

And still the Little Girl was working on him, but he was gone.

I swore and told Hoser to keep shooting at the cyborg.

"Use the whole belt on that damn thing!" I screamed and knife-handed exactly where I wanted to un-runtime that walking mechanical horror.

Look at me… knife-handing.

I was pissed.

The ob windows in the stubby tower were shattering and exploding as hot smoking AP tore them apart. I could see the hulking thing in there, on the top control floor, rag-dolling from Hoser's on-target fire. Its malevolent optical sensors glowing red as its synthetic doppelganger's skin tore away from impacts, revealing the gleaming and remorseless death machine underneath.

I caught sight of Ulysses dragging the Old Man out from under fire where he'd been hit on initial contact with the HKs. Ulysses dragged the captain past the Little Girl who was now a woman. A combat medic in an EVC suit realizing Two Times was dead as his body wound down. Just like the rest of us.

A member of the Strange.

To the end. This end. Here.

She'd once been in her little potato-sack black dress and over-large combat boots. Dark-haired, dark-eyed, always watching us.

I could smell fall and burning leaves as I glanced at her and tried to run the battle as the person who was apparently in charge of this mess now.

"Lost him!" shouted Hoser as the blare of the Pig faded and Hustle attached a new belt. "Faded into the tower!"

I didn't have time for that. But I needed to.

"Shift fire. Put some on that cluster pushing on Second! We'll go in after him."

More zekes were swarming into the hub at us, as though they were being corralled and bubbled up, not under direct Monarch control but probably being herded forward by them all the same, then surging toward where Ulysses was dragging the captain back to cover like some spring torrent of death after the winter icing up.

Ulysses shouted at the Little Girl.

I couldn't hear what was said over the comm. It was too far away due to the distance. And the gunfire. And the nightmare screaming coming from the dead.

Screaming like some sudden terrible catastrophe at some big event that had promised to be a good day, instead of the one it had actually turned into.

A memory day. But another kind you want to forget, and can't. Ever.

Yeah, that other part of my mind thought. We'd remember this day. For sure.

Maybe it was the day we lost our commander, whispered the dark shadow and I told it to shut its whore mouth.

"Not today," I grunted at no one in particular.

But…

The captain wasn't struggling as he was dragged behind Third's blaring gun team by Ulysses. Who suddenly turned to fire one-handed with his primary at the horror show of screaming death coming straight at him.

A cluster of dead, already riddled with gunfire, went screaming in right at the gun team and the thin line there.

He sent a burst into the first one, dropped the captain, engaged two more... went dry and butt-stroked a third, beating it to death with the rifle in the end. The rest of the squad that remained put rounds on the others and then Hauser came in, sweeping the rest with the death ray that is his Pig blaring on full auto and accurate like no human being can do.

It was a legit savage display of gunfire in high dosage.

The Little Girl dashed to the captain's EVC boots, grabbed them, picking up his dead weight, then heaving him to cover just as Hauser pushed through, firing the Pig he carried straight into the mass of zekes being pushed right into what remained of Second's line there at the edge of the hub floor, cutting bodies to shreds thirty meters back.

Hustle and Hoser had now established an intersecting field of fire, and in seconds the horrified "dead" colonist survivors were cut to shreds from two different directions out there on the floor.

We still had one wounded cyborg in the tower.

My guess was the other one was pushing the zekes into Second from the hidden service passages that exited out onto the floor, hanging back, ready to make its attack at a completely inopportune moment. For us.

Number three, most likely the first one we'd encountered with the sub guns, acting as a body, was a mystery for the moment.

"Wolfy..." I said over the squad comm. "You're in charge of the gun team. You two—Bull and Catboi—you're with me. We push on that tower now and ice that HK that just did Two Times. Copy?"

"Hotsoup!" roared Bull, who was apparently in the cult.

"Catboi activated, Sergeant, on your six."

"Forever in our hearts!" shouted Wolfy, who gave the thumbs-up to Bull. Wolfy was the high priest of the cult. *Forever in our hearts!* had become some kind of informal reply in the Hotsoup cult. But I didn't have enough time to get annoyed by it as I usually did.

And Catboi... too. There was that.

But... it was time to get our kill on.

We moved down the nearest ramp, crossed down onto the killing floor, engaged a few more of the tangos...

"Catboi engaging one."

Bull on full auto shredding another and missing more than he hit. But the "dead" colonist was down and not in our way.

We made the wall of the tower and stacked.

Klutz came running in with his aid bag because this was where the hero action was, apparently.

"Don't get everyone killed, Sar'nt," I hissed at me hearing my own voice dry, ragged, and heaving inside my bucket.

But I was seeing red and I knew where this was going and I didn't need Stinkeye to berserk me to get there.

I was already here and panting for blood...

This metal thing was gonna die and I didn't care how it got done right now.

Two Times was dead and the captain was hit bad.

Not today.

"On three we go in. Pick up your sectors fast once we're inside," I thundered at my guys. "We won't get another chance to run this again!"

I began to shout the count.

CHAPTER NINETEEN

Stacked and ready at the entrance to the small ob tower I shouted, "*Two!*" as suddenly music thundered through the PA system that had once announced incoming cargo and passenger discs at the central hub. It was a weird techno bass and drum beat that was instantly hypnotic. At the same time the comm inside our buckets fritzed.

I signaled we had dead comm, meaning we'd have to move to hand and voice to communicate in the shoot, move, and communicate portions of the combat dance.

The cyborgs had turned on the thundering hypno trance music to cause signal confusion while every hazard light, directional laser, display terminal, and everything electronic in the central hub ran through its programming startup sequence with a frenetic intensity generally reserved for starport junkies looking to cage some cainedust for a hit, laying a story on you about bad idents or lost luggage and sleeping in the rain.

I was holding the stack to make sure everyone was understanding we'd need to communicate the old-fashioned way now.

The 'borgs had pulled a fast one on us at just the wrong moment.

I got nods and thumbs-ups and that was all I was gonna get shy of calling "*One!*" and sending us in there guns blazing.

We needed to go now and kill that cyborg before it either pulled a fade and became a "later problem" or detonated some IED it had to deny our attack and ended all our problems, right now and forever.

Four of us.

Me. Catboi. Bull. Klutz the medic who'd somehow appeared and I didn't know if I was... heartened by that. Or keenly aware that I'd get him killed.

I popped the spoon on a frag and checked the action at Second's position. Hauser was advancing, hosing the dead with the Pig as the assault continued there. He'd set up Mad Max, the actual gunner for Third, to suppress a new group pushing from the blue-shadowy reaches of the central hub floor that had suddenly switched over to a bloody wash of red decontamination lasers knifing through the heavy gun smoke and shadowing darkness.

Comm was dead, but I knew that Hause, even as he did the killing work his kind was so good at, was analyzing the situation and calc-ing solutions that would resolve it. I could tell that from where I stood as I tried to assess everything, ready for breach, and holding a live grenade while making sure my primary was easy to get up into action before going in against the best killing machine humanity had ever produced.

Hauser outsmarted the cyborgs and sent a text message that appeared in ghostly holo script across my EVC faceplate.

Smart.

Delta Six… There is a 57.8% chance the other cyborg in this team is running the pushes from the darkness in sector six below the main floor. Switching Max to engage… suggest we use the recoilless rifle there with area denial munitions in effect.

Me, holding a live grenade I'm only keeping from detonating by maintaining a firm hold on the spoon even though I've already pulled the pin and that's not even dangling on my finger like I've trained myself to do because EVC gloves are thicker to protect against vacuum and other hostile environments…

So… there's no going back, as they say. We are committed.

Normally I just cut the index finger of my assault gloves and when I do happen to need to contribute fragmentary high-ex to a difficult problem, I keep the pin dangling just in case cooler heads prevail.

No such case here.

I key text-speech and transmit my reply.

Using the one-twenty in here even with ADM in effect is gonna ruin those viewing windows on the exterior hull of the substation.

Catboi is focused on the entrance to the tower we are about to go into like some kind of patient fiend. Like…

Sigh…

… a cat.

Bull wipes sweat from his head, but it's only a gesture because his head is bucketed by the EVC helmet. Still… I've done that too. Everyone has.

This is not a problem for the operation and mission success parameters, Delta Six, texts Hauser. He can reply fast. *We are protected by the EVC armor. Maiming or terminating the cyborg organizing the distraction and resistance will increase our odds to at least mission-possible.*

There was a sudden massive detonation nearby.

Then someone from Third called, "Sorry!" and quickly, "Frag out!"

Comms were back. Like power to the station, they were on and off and unpredictable.

Spall and frag caressed our position.

Me… holding that frag thinking things couldn't get worse as they got worse.

We needed to go *now*…

This was all interspersed with extreme and horrific levels of violence as everyone continued getting their kill on and shooting the survivors who'd been turned into weapons against us as fast and as desperately as they could.

The line was about to collapse around Third again.

And yeah… I was still holding that live grenade, stacked against the matte-gray wall of the ob tower with three of my not so finest, and especially Klutz who's all enthusiasm and little skill.

He was nodding at me seriously and I could see the sweat on his face and the fear in his eyes as he determined to make a hero out of himself today.

I thought making him a medic would keep him, and everyone else, safer.

I had a feeling I'd been wrong about that one.

Now our clumsy medic was stacked with his slung sub gun out and ready to roll on the breach and smash inside the tower. Or die gloriously trying.

My whole role as an NCO is for no one to die. Even gloriously.

Against a new model hunter-killer combat cyborg, I might add.

He had his finger on the trigger of the sub gun.

It's the little things an NCO notices. The things that make you feel uncomfortable and about which at certain intense moments you can do nothing about. In my defense… I had a lot going on.

I swore.

Sometimes…

You gotta just let go in life and cleanse the negativity… as Wolfy would say.

"Fire the Megoosa, Hauser," I said. Then grunted, "Send now."

I tossed the frag, counted and waited for the det. Then, like every stupid small unit infantry leader ever…

I shouted, "Follow me!"

I was probably gonna get shot in the back, I was thinking.

CHAPTER TWENTY

The detonation practically blew the synthetic flesh off the killing machine thing in there when we went in, each of us taking up our positions and sliced portions of the room beyond the portal that led into the ob tower in the central hub.

What happened next took forty-five seconds.

It was straight-up the most brutal gunfight I'd ever been in. And if it wasn't for EVC armor and suits all of us would be dead.

The Monarch hunter-killer combat cyborg is a state-of-the-art murder machine. It can move faster than a human, shoot even faster than you think possible using an onboard targeting mainframe linked to neural-twitch network that tells the machine, gleaming pistons, precision pneumatic hydraulics, core-reinforced armor as bones and cage, all within a six-foot-four picture of the perfect human warrior, who exactly to engage and at what level as a priority target.

It makes these decisions in an instant.

Data collected is near-instantly assessed and organized for the killing math.

Like Hauser, they all look like Germanic savages of the long ago, but cool and military. Unlike Hauser, who's had to be badly repaired more times than we can count, they look perfect. Flawless skin. Rippling muscles. Perfect hair. White straight teeth. Clear piercing "eyes" with one defect… they glow red in the darkest-dark revealing the thermal and IR scanning optical processors within.

They have files, detailed files of course, on every weapons system ever created, and most machines from ground vehicles to Class Three starships—for hijacking operations—and they can create bioweapons and toxins on the fly from almost any easily found cleaning products.

Here's a fact. At a full run, carrying two weapons, they can engage multiple targets with automatic gunfire over unstable and uneven terrain.

Like some state-of-the-art battle tank.

That was what we were going in against as the overpressure from the frag crushed our minds and ears despite the EVC protection.

I had Klutz with me who can barely group with S16 on a good day at the ship's virtual range. Klutz was holding a Stussy M11 sub gun that spat nine-millimeter rounds like Stinkeye vomiting and cursing at the same time with no break between one or the other. The Stussy had only one firing mode.

Full burp.

We let the medics run them because they were light. Carried a lot of ammo. And you could spray one-handed with them while you dragged guys out from under fire if you needed to.

When we trained up Klutz he'd beamed with pride after absolutely ripping a target to shreds at two meters. He'd held the smoking Stussy up and shouted, "Sub guns out for Hotsoup!"

Everyone cheered.

Yeah. I was annoyed. But my strategy in those days was to pretend I wasn't. 'Cause I'm crafty like that and I was sure my annoyance only encouraged them.

Also... none of the thirty rounds Klutz had just dumped had managed to actually "kill" the holo-tango by any stretch of the imagination. If the target was a real bad guy, after Klutz's entire mag... holo-bad-guy would've had a bad scar on one arm.

At two meters.

In Klutz's defense, the sub guns do tend to drift.

So... that's what I had at my back and that's what I was facing.

Klutz vs. state-of-the-art killing machine some affectionately call terminators in some ancient reference, and also because they... terminate. Humans.

Bull wasn't much better.

Catboi as has been stated is a legit shooter and... aggressive. Which are things that have been pointed out to me by others.

I cannot hear these things as all I hear is...

"Catboi engaging..."

Which annoys the small, very small in fact, NCO that I am. And a very poor human apparently when I conduct my own personal melancholic AAR of my days in my weapons cage, alone in the dark with my memories.

We fragged and went in.

The perfect killing machine shot to shreds already by Hoser putting so much hate on the ob tower windows was there. Its torn flesh and the shredded business suit it had donned in order to fit in with the "dead" survivors who'd been turned against us didn't match the vision of perfect infiltrator. Perfect killer.

The ruined synthetic flesh hung away in ragged strips.

"Bloody" synthetic bio-lube ran down the gleaming core-steel skeleton underneath. Half its face was peeled away revealing that killing machine underneath, turning the mouth into a half-rictus death grin like it was glad we'd finally come to settle things up.

Like it was expecting us.

Spreadsheets on human predictive behavior updated and satisfied as the killing math continued to scroll through its relentless number-crunching processors.

It was holding two combat pistols.

My guess is they were forty-fives of some sort because it sure did hurt to get drilled in the plate by one as I entered the room and took up my position, pointing my primary at it in the dark.

The first round from one barrel knocked me down and knocked the wind out of me all of a sudden. Cracked EVC dura-plates rated to deflect at least seven-six-two fire made me feel like I was gonna black out. Still, I raised the Bastard and shot the thing three times... the last one hitting it right in the gleaming steel and "bloody" synthetic flesh-covered "skull," making its steel head whiplash back and to the right.

No skill. My rifle had gone up as I fired from the ground, knocked down and back by the forty-five round that had just caved in my chest cavity.

I would never breathe another breath again. But I didn't care. I just wanted that thing dead for killing Two Times and the captain who was probably gonna die.

Both forty-fives were hammering away even as the evil thing swung its head back at me after I'd shot it.

It shot both Catboi and Bull.

Catboi took a round in the leg and another one in the chest armor but the duraplate held and didn't penetrate either…

Which is hugely lucky but so go the vagaries of combat.

The one in the leg deflected off the armored shin guard.

Later he told me as I was stretchered off to the dropship, he was real excited about the fact that the armor had held.

"Deflection off the left shin guard, Sergeant. These are rated at the highest level. Catboi survived. Half cat, half boi, Sergeant."

"Well good for you," I croaked through the oxygen being administered to me as the painkillers began to kick in and the dead of the company seemed to be standing around the medics working on me.

About six seconds after initially being hit I was gonna take another round right in the plate as the thing lowered one of the smoking blazing forty-fives in the red laser-show-lit darkness and drilled me again.

Even though the round deflected off the mangled plate, it tore straight across my chest and carved a hot gash in one rib.

My EVC integrity was also violated… again… but that, as they say, at that moment of the killing machine trying its best to kill us… was a "tomorrow problem."

Klutz mag-dumped, closing and screaming at the terminator, "Eat it, you cheap toaster!"

"Hotsoup" was flashing across Klutz's HUD faceplate. Yes… they do that now that they've figured out how to hack the external message settings in the EVC armor. It's supposed to be used for non-verbal distress.

And yes… he was screaming the name as he burned nine-millimeter frenetically and closed on the thing.

"This is for Hotsoup!"

He straight-up wrecked it as he rage-dumped and held the sub fairly, surprisingly, steady.

The HK cyborg fell back, smashed one gleaming fist into the wall, and hole-punched an exit into the next room on the first level of the ob tower.

The room we had our first fight in had been some kind of customs office full of giant displays and glowing holographic local-system regulations that were glitching due to the power irregularities, the ongoing firefight going wild in every direction all around us.

I got to my boots, gasping for air that would not enter my lungs ever again.

Or so I felt at that moment.

Klutz surged after the thing as he ejected a mag from the Stussy, letting it slide to the floor like some action hero who possessed endless "action-guy" mags.

I stopped him and gasped something unintelligible. Pointing to the fact he was inserting the next mag the wrong way.

The skeletal gleaming blood-colored bio-lubed ragged flesh-torn killing thing came right back out of the darkness of the room with a shotgun filled with slugs.

He shot me again in the leg and broke it, but hey, the armor held.

It's rated against penetration. Not physics.

Hit badly and sure my leg was gone, I leaned against the wall, switched the Bastard to full auto, my eyes watering and unable to scream because I couldn't get any air in my lungs ever again, and let go with all I had left in the Bastard on full auto at very close range.

I hit the cyborg. A lot.

Someone else shot it too.

A bunch.

Then Klutz dumped on it again and my EVC boot deflected a stray round from the Stussy and awarded me three broken toes for my efforts not to get my squad killed.

And still... the thing wasn't dead.

It's a combat cyborg after all. No switch kills here. You've just got to hammer it to death with lead.

Its targeting computers must have been damaged though because none of the other five slugs it pumped and fired at us did any good.

But the room and all its crazed displays exploded in every direction. Flying sparks and strange artistic images I remember... vaguely.

That's when someone in Third fired the recoilless rifle and hit the other cyborg, cyborg number two, in its position pushing more "dead" at the line. This action blew a giant series of fragmentary holes in the massive decks-high viewing windows surrounding one side of the main terminal's blister at ten thousand feet during an apocalyptic storm and suddenly new alarms and the storm surge were everywhere, swirling crossfire hurricane chaos as I felt my legs go out from under me and I slid down the wall into darkness for a second.

So, this is death... this time, I was thinking.

Then I was awake, or back from my momentary blackout, and the combat cyborg, bloody and shredded, was kneeling down next to me behind a ruined desk for cover, expertly thumbing more shells into the combat shotty it was carrying like it was on autopilot and this was just another day that ended in 'y'.

This was freaky and surreal. Trust me.

Klutz thought he was covering a short distance off, but he didn't even have concealment. He was down on one knee ejecting the mag in the sub gun, then he dropped the one he'd just pulled off his carrier and was readying to insert.

The terminator thumbed in the last shell looking ghoulishly and intently at Klutz who he was gonna blast in the next second or two.

I swore. Again. My eyes blinked closed, then open again. Barely audible inside my own EVC bucket, I rasped for breath like some ruined bellows. Blood was on my faceplate. Pretty sure it was mine.

One arm didn't want to work. I was outta the fight.

My foot hurt for some reason... but I didn't know about the deflection off my boot from Klutz's wild sub-gun dump. I weakly pulled my sidearm with my good arm, my primary arm, thankfully.

I was surprised the HK let me get away with this. It must have assessed I was dead.

I'm sure its processors were heavily damaged.

Point blank I put my sidearm to the cyborg's gleaming scalp, pushing it in, squeezed my eyes shut, and pulled the trigger... blowing what remained of its mainframe all over the wall and into the next room and the dark beyond.

It fell over and clattered to the ground like the tool, the mere machine that it was. No monster's roar. No demon's scream. No villain's final regret. Just... offline. End of Runtime. Reminding me it was just a machine and not some evil nightmare of man's worst imagining.

Just a machine and nothing more.

I was not comforted.

But they have a dead man's switch too.

Just like Hauser.

Just under the right occipital. Just in case they go rogue. Lucky that was the side of its gleaming "bloody" skull facing me.

Hauser, with fifty-eight point three to live, or the micro-nuke detonates and kills any of the company around him, told me about this one time. Just in case he gets hacked on the battlefield.

"You can switch me off by penetrating the sub-neural engagement processors located there, Sergeant Orion. Just in case I become a danger to the company."

It's just Orion, Hause. We're friends. And I don't think I can do that.

These have that too. The disarm feature. And the micro-nukes.

But there's a chance we can disarm.

Hauser... we can't. Part of his freeing himself was to override the disengagement safety system and wipe the core memory containing those codes.

But Ultra Marines serving with the hunter-killer teams had demanded a way to shut down the doomsday nuke each cyborg carried in what the Monarchs called the *No Joy* protocol.

A cyborg gets taken out by bad guys.

It blows up and kills everyone.

It's a small nuke. It uses the micro fusion reactor each cyborg carries on board.

No Joy.

Imagine the power of a sun the size of a thimble and you'll get the picture.

This was a right now problem. Or there would be no tomorrow in about three minutes.

No continued slices of birthday cake.

"It's down!" shrieked Klutz jubilantly and I'm sure was just about to say "Sub guns out for Hotsoup!" when I stopped him with a pained look and gasped, "Ain't over. Get your scalpel. Shoot me up with the fetamine, Klutz. Double... dose. We... gotta... do... some surger... y. Quick..."

We had two minutes until the thing detonated and I was passing in and out of consciousness.

Puncher was calling Fleet for multiple medevacs. The storm had cleared enough by now for help to attempt a rescue.

"Overlord... Stormbringer Actual is hit bad. Need dustoff ASAP, my location. I repeat. Warlord is hit bad."

The body of the killing machine was right next to me, my hands were trembling, and I had pain centers everywhere.

I pulled off my gloves.

I was already exposed.

Then over the comm… it was back again…

Klutz hit me with two micro hypos through exposed skin in the ragged wounds in my armor.

"Hauser… talk to me. *No Joy* in effect. Need to… disarm… cyborg."

My hands were bloody and shaking.

CHAPTER TWENTY-ONE

"Remove the synthetic flesh by making an incision between where the human fourth and fifth rib are located," began Hauser in his deep but calming voice. His tone resonant and his diction precise and crisp.

I did as he instructed with Klutz's scalpel. My hands were shaking. I was working on the "body" of the combat cyborg I'd just terminated.

"Klutz... gimme some Demurax..."

"Sar'nt, that's a painkiller for burn injuries. That's gonna dumb you out hard..."

I swore.

I was doing a lot of that lately.

"Do it. Pain's killing me."

Klutz bent down to where I was operating on the mess of a cyborg.

Bull, who'd been hit, crawled across the shattered glass from the customs screens and the general ruin and was marking time for us.

"Minute twenty, Sar'nt... unless his clock's different than Hauser's."

Yeah. So we had that going for us.

"What if we just carry him to the breach and throw him out, Sar'nt?"

Oh, I don't know, Bull. You've been shot. I've been shot. That breach is at least an ultraball deep left fence away, and between us are a few hundred living dead who will tear our throats out and at least two unconfirmed HK variant cyborgs looking to optimize mission success parameters by killing the rest of us with high-powered rifles, LMGs, high-ex IEDs, and/or whatever else the kill team has in the weapons package they were left behind with. Seems like a lot to deal with, buddy. I'll just stick with trying to disarm the nuclear weapon lying on the floor beneath my trembling hands and blurred vision.

But I didn't say that. I concentrated on Hauser's voice and what I was doing like my life depended on it. Because it did.

The Demurax kicked in, and I took a deep full breath as my muscles turned to butter and the pain went somewhere else. Klutz had knelt down, popped his med bag, and gotten a needle into my EVC pic line.

I had pressure bandages on my savage wounds... but that was a tomorrow problem as far as the Demurax was concerned.

The pain had gone mostly bye-bye. Mostly. Like it was still there, but at the end of the block, promising me a severe beatdown when it made it back this way.

Comms was hot. Hauser's voice cut through.

Ulysses was going forward to finish the cyborg that had been hit by the recoilless Megoosa.

Thunderer had medical drops inbound to take out wounded.

Thunderer CIC, combat information center, was doing a drone flyover and confirming all Double Tap teams on the ground at the base station were KIA.

I shut down all comm links ... except Hauser.

Just me and him now.

My hands were covered in the cyborg's synthetic blood after making the cut with Klutz's scalpel.

"Nice work, Sar'nt. That's a good cut," said Klutz, hovering too close to me.

The Demurax said... *Chill out 'bout that, my man. It's all good.*

So I did.

"Sar'nt, your blood pressure is dropping."

That's cool, I thought as I waved him away from my work area with his dangerously sharp scalpel.

I tried not to pay any attention to the blackness forming at the edges of my vision. I lowered my head and all that darkness went away for a second. Then I realized Hauser was telling me what to do next and that I shouldn't go into the dark like I was thinking it might be nice to do.

I could smell fall. Burning smoke. Leaves.

"Expose the main micro-reactor plate, Sergeant Orion... where your human lungs would be. You should see the release screws and a click-pull."

I did and told him I did.

I may have been mumbling though.

Someone came into the room where we'd had our brutal gunfight, but I was concentrating on the combat cyborg that was about to blow us all to kingdom come in...

"How much time, Foxy..." I mumbled.

Bull answered. Foxy had died at the LZ back on Mars.

Not much time left. The numbers were meaningless so I kept working. What was I gonna do... bargain? Cut a deal? They were gonna run out... and then... booom. Dark.

I fumbled for my Leatherman on my chest rig as soon as I spotted the titanium screws on the gleaming internal armor of the killing machine. I brushed away the gooey synthetic "blood."

"Klutz... pop the screwdriver. Gonna... need..."

I was drooling on the glass of my blood-smeared EVC faceplate. That pain-drug was hitting me hard.

Real hard.

I wondered if Klutz had used... *the whole vial...* 'cause even I knew... there were five doses in a bottle...

"That's... a lot," I mumbled for no reason anyone around me could figure out.

I continued to work as a stranger in the dark came close, stepping across the debris of the shattered screens. He had nice shoes. Dress shoes. Pleated dress pants. I heard the swirl of rocks in a glass. Like a drink. A cool drink in a bar.

"Keep workin', mate. Company needs you right now, Orion," said the stranger in the dark watching us.

No one else saw him.

"Remove the screws now, Sergeant Orion," instructed Hauser.

It's just Orion. Hauser. Just Orion. "You're my best friend."

I don't know if I said that part. I was pretty stoned and getting... *stonier*... is that the right word... by the second. Drugs were never my thing.

Yup.

Klutz used all five doses of the Demu-whatever.

Well... that's cool and all.

I laughed a little.

The stranger swirled the ice in his cool drink and I had a pretty good idea who'd come to watch us all go boom.

"Time, Fox?"

There wasn't much, answered Bull.

That was bad.

Yeah... my mind sang. *That's... real bad.*

"Forty-five seconds, Sar'nt," said Bull.

"Concentrate, Sergeant Orion. My company needs you," said the stranger in the dark with us.

I came back for a second. Got... a little clear.

Screws out, they fell away across the "dead" cyborg's bullet-riddled and shredded body.

I probably didn't need them.

Did I? Right?

It's all good.

I popped the click plate and removed it, revealing an input panel with a glowing keypad and nothing else. Not even a timer.

"Now... remove the keypad. Carefully, Sergeant Orion," said Hauser.

I already had.

"Okay, Hause... just Orion... we're friends. You're my best friend... buddy." But I'm not sure if I said that part.

"Now... listen clearly..."

Okay, that was gonna be a problem, Hauser. I was hearing... cocktails and jazz. Oh... no.

John Strange, that wolf's grin, knelt down next to me and smiled. He was well dressed. Well groomed. The long-dead founder of the Strange Company.

"Need to tell you what's gonna happen next, mate. Company's in real danger on this one."

"Okay..." I said to Hauser.

Or was it to John Strange?

The black began to form at the soft cottony edges of my vision.

"*Dark Star* is going to be the death of my company. You can't go on this one. Do not board that ship, Sergeant," said John Strange, deadly serious.

I pushed that away. Hauser was telling me how to disarm the cyborg's onboard nuclear weapon.

"You have only one chance to get this correct, Sergeant Orion."

I was stoned to the gills and hallucinating, or... something.

"You have to enter the number eighty-eight… eighty-eight times on the keyboard. Exactly."

"Wait… what?" I drooled.

"Type eight and then eight and repeat this eight-eighty times. If you miss a number, the bomb will immediately detonate and terminate. The company in the central hub of this facility will be killed in the blast, Sergeant Orion."

"The company has to survive, Sergeant Orion," said John Strange as he stood up, swirled ice cubes that weren't there in his drink, and began to walk toward the blown-off entrance to the ob tower we'd just fought for our lives in.

"Remember that, Orion. No matter what choice… company has to survive. There's a lot more going on here… than just us. Always was, Sergeant. Always was. Focus now, Sergeant Orion."

He began to walk away and I could hear his perfectly polished dress shoes crunching across the broken and destroyed glass of the displays in the room.

Eighty-eight.

Eighty-eight times.

There was no way I was going to… get this… right.

The black was taking me now… and I was going… otherwise. Into it.

A red autumn leaf fell down across the glass of the EVC… and landed on my bloody hand as I began to type in the eights and count… cursing, high on all five doses of the drug Klutz had most likely OD'd me with.

I sang a song, focusing on the numbers.

The eel girl slithered around me. Making me feel warm and alive as I slithered down into blue dark waters with her. This is where I'd go, maybe. If I got it all wrong…

Forever.

Come, she whispered, *play with us in forests of azure,* estrangier. *Forever…*

I had thirty-seven eighty-eights inputted.

And then the Little Girl's voice whispered from long ago.

Here he comes, Sergeant…

I was gone from there even as my fingers continued to tap the eight key in the killer cyborg's doomsday bomb.

I am waiting for you, estrangier, she said in her buzzing ancient French accent. *And then you will come with us. Down deep. Down where no man has seen.*

Forty-two so far.

"Here he comes, Sergeant."

I remember you, estrangier. *I… remember you.*

"I'll meet you in the bar, Sergeant. Then we can discuss what's about to happen next. And how to get my company off the *X*. Cheers, mate. Nineteen more inputs to go now."

CHAPTER TWENTY-TWO

Tap, tap, tap...
   88. 88. 88...
   Was I in Hell?
   All I saw was red. Smeared red blood.
   Tap, tap, tap...
   Tap, tap, tap...
   88...
   I heard the thump of boots... or titanic feet? And I felt like I was floating.
   Was some leering demon going to wipe away the blood from my vision, my blood and someone else's probably, that was smeared across the faceplate of the EVC bucket.
   Yeah... I was down and that was all I could see. My bloody bucket.
   I'm probably dying... or dead.
   Now that demon from the other side, the dark side, would be leering and leaning into the camera of eternity that will be my permanent POV, and probably very just reward...
   Though, hey... I'm hoping for a little credit on a few *X*'s and bad LZ's I've had the misfortune to be a part of. Is that a thing?
   Remember that time... because right now I'm not uncertain that this is my last moment... moments... so you gotta remember that time I was a standup guy in heavy incoming...
   Does that count for anything regarding what comes next?
   Fear came and went and I started to get very warm... and chill about... whatever was happening.
   88.
   No... 19.
   No.
   88. 88. 88...
   I was on a collapsible stretcher being hustled out into the rain.
   It was the rain that was tap-tap-tapping on my EVC faceplate.
   All I saw was the blood that lay all across it and now the rain was starting to streak and not really wash it all away.
   I knew I'd been hit. A lot. Going in against the HK cyborg. I knew that.
   I was forgetting where I'd just been, with John Strange.

"Need to get that down… later…" I heard myself mumble. My mouth felt sweet and cottony. I felt like I was still in one of the warm volcano pools with the eel girls back…

Estrangier…

There.

Something landed on the field of blood that was my vision. And I waited…

Demon?

Klutz wiped it away with his EVC glove then took a bottle and sprayed water all across the face shield.

I was being carried out onto the landing platforms.

Klutz leaned down, bucket off… and looked in real close to my face.

"His eyes are open!"

I smiled.

Then remembered I'd been hit and I wasn't feeling much.

"Got you tranqed up, Sar'nt. You have four gunshot wounds, though that fourth is really just a graze. Sorry about that tat you had there, Sar'nt."

I fumbled for my crotch.

But my hands were filled with wet cement and they'd never move again.

Being paralyzed wasn't my first concern. Like every soldier, I had more important things to worry about than never being able to walk or feel again.

"Still…" I mumbled, "… got my junk?"

Klutz leaned in and shook his head, seriously.

I swore.

"Blown clean off, Sar'nt. You'll never be a whole man ever again."

Then I felt another glove grab my stuff. One of the flight medics on the drop who was helping load me in swore at Klutz.

She leaned in. Pretty. Brunette. All business.

She winked at me and gave it a hard squeeze.

"You got nothing to worry about, killer."

I called Klutz a very bad word and swore to myself I'd PT him to death to the end of the universe…

I was drooling.

Time jumped and the drop's engines were spooling up for dustoff.

I saw Ulysses running the casevac on the ground. Saw some of the other wounded being loaded.

Then…

"Stand by!" shouted Ulysses Two Alpha Six who had his hand up to his earpiece. Everyone's EVC bucket was off, so the area must have been declared free of biotoxin.

"Tha's… gud," I mumbled.

Probably due to the effects of the storm passing through. Now, it was merely gray skies, late-afternoon rain, and shafts of sunlight like silver swords shooting down through the skies of a poisoned, ruined world.

My comm was still good.

I could hear chatter.

"Hauser's dumping the cyborg! Det in thirty seconds!" roared Ulysses so everyone could hear. Flight crew started flipping switches to Faraday the bird against the effects of EMP and it was fairly easy for me, even in my drug-addled state, to realize what was happening now.

Chief Cook had just climbed into the bird and sat down on one of the flight seats near me. He was still holding his forty-five and he had a wild yet tired look on his face like he hadn't seen me and was mumbling to himself about something.

Then he turned to me and said, "Only way to deal with those 'borgs if they go, is let them det somewhere safe. If that's an option, Orion."

Then he seemed to see his dangling sidearm in his bloody hand. He heaved himself up and holstered it.

"Hauser and Ulysses got the second cyborg. They tried to disarm but that subroutine kicked in and rebooted halfway through the numerical code input. That reset the nuke and locked them out of the system. Thing had a secondary mainframe running even though they'd shot it to pieces. They're dumping it over the side of the station. The elevator's cables are rated to withstand a direct hit from thermonuclear weapons so... we're gonna see, huh?"

He looked at his watch. Then... "Hang on."

There was a pulse. A flash of light out there in the silver-gray skies now that the storm was gone.

Then nothing at all.

Then a massive explosion. Or at least the sound of one.

The medics were checking me as the bird heaved off the landing platforms at Gateway, and the last thing I saw of that world as the ship turned and banked around the station, climbing for upper-orbit burn... was the edge of a small rising mushroom cloud, far below.

Other dropships were departing.

No one was taking a chance that the station and the space elevator cables would hold.

Did it matter?

The Dandelion Worlds were finished. Forever.

I doubted even the chimps would come this far out for a series of worlds the Monarchs had ruined in their attempt to destroy us and deny us the chase.

After...

I spent a month on a cruise starship that had once specialized in medical rejuvenation for the rich and ultra-famous when there were such luminaries before the galaxy descended into the dark and violence that had always been there, waiting at the edges.

Before the wars of twenty years while we were in hypersleep crossing the great black gulfs to Marsantyium.

Mars.

Call it what you will.

The *Nova* was a beautiful ship, but she was old and she was little more than a hospital ship now. But the medics and docs were good, and my injuries were repaired and I was returned to the company on light duty after a month.

By that time the wave-motion-warp-enabled starship, the theoretical jump-envelope carrier that had never yet done what we were about to attempt to use it to do, had arrived for the rendezvous and the fleet was gathering for the theoretical time-dilation leap to arrive at Typhon before the Monarchs did in the *Dark Star*.

Or die and be lost in the void forever.

One of those two things.

During that time I read some books. Smoked. And tried to organize and remember what John Strange had told me on the other side.

In the Bar at the End of the Universe.

During all those 88's.

And… 19.

So… I probably need to encrypt this part because… it's got knowledge and maybe stuff the company shouldn't know. Yet. If I get killed, it will un-redact when the next Log Keeper can enter his credentials, and he can decide what to do with it. Given whatever current situation the company finds itself in.

And there is the chance… things can be different.

But this is what John Strange told me in the Bar at the End of the Universe.

The last time, according to him, we would ever talk.

CHAPTER TWENTY-THREE

"You're getting too close to the Oblivion Gate, mate," said John Strange as he leaned against the bar. Then he rapped on it twice with his long bony knuckles.

"It's time to let go, Sergeant."

We were in the bar where I'd first *gone*... I don't know how to term it any other way than... *gone*. Now I was back after being hit multiple times in a gunfight against terminators and the Klutz loading me up on the Demurax as I tried to disarm the combat cyborg before it blew everyone inside Gateway Station to hell.

This is me writing it down later aboard the hospital ship.

I think I blacked out. As I was trying to disarm the combat cyborg. I had no idea if I'd gotten that done. At the time I felt like I hadn't. And... at first I guess I thought maybe I was dead as I found myself in that strange bar... listening to John Strange. All I knew was that I was hit, was hopped up on tranqs, and barely able to concentrate on the repeated digits I was inputting into the keypad to avoid total thermonuclear annihilation.

Y'know... Tuesday.

Apparently, according to Klutz and Bull, I did get the digits entered the right amount of times, and just in time with about a few seconds to go.

Klutz told me he had his eyes closed at the last second because he was sure I'd gotten at least one, if not many, of the inputs wrong and that without ceremony we were all gonna get instantly flash-fried.

Klutz eventually opened his eyes and watched as I entered the last string of numbers and the killing machine simply went dark, the barely visible countdown within its cold machine eyes suddenly going dark.

The word DISARMED appeared in red ancient Numerica letters, and then the machine just lay there... offline.

I passed out.

Apparently.

The rest of Reaper came in and carried me out to the casualty collection point inside the main terminal substation as we waited for the drops to come in on casevac runs and get us off-station.

The battle with the last remaining cyborg we could identify on station went down and Hauser and Ulysses dumped it down ten thousand feet.

Of course.

No further attempts were made to dock at the elevator's docking systems. The station was deemed too dangerous to attempt hard-connect.

I write all this down as we get ready to enter the jump envelope the experimental carrier *Winds of Change* will create for us to get ahead of the *Dark Star,* somewhere so far out no one in the fleet has ever been there.

A world called Typhon in a mostly unmapped binary star system identified as Wanderer 189.

The whole thing feels ominous to me.

That's not the very edge of human expansion… it is officially *beyond* the edge of human expansion, by some orders of magnitude, and some primal part of me fears we are heading into a very dark unknown that was meant to be unknown… *for reasons.*

This is where desperate scouts, bounty-laden pirates, unlucky gunfighters, and poor explorers with nothing to lose go. Beyond the limits of the known.

There are rumors of other vast colony ships, never heard from again… that went that way. Where we are headed when the jump-envelope ship *Winds of Change* spools up her barely tested magic drive and attempts to get us there faster than anything thought possible.

Or… lost forever in the void.

But those are just rumors.

So, I'm writing all this down, what comes next in the log, because this is what happened to me after I blacked out and went to the *Bar at the End of the Universe…* and found the founder of the company.

John Strange. Actual legend.

Again, lemme hip you to his CV.

Curriculum vitae.

Ancient logs indicate he was a drinker. Several mention reckless and daring attacks against fortified habs during the pre-colonial Saturnian Conflict. Under the influence, of course. That was the first armed conflict in space of any scale larger than a gunfight inside some rando station.

That's where John Strange entered the histories. Supposedly a sergeant in the Colonial Marines. Promo'd to captain six months in and leading guerilla raids across the frozen tundras of Titan back before it became the economic powerhouse of early expansion. John Strange's rise to power is the stuff of spectacuthrillers.

Sources basically say about him…

Founder of the Strange Company. British. Wolf's grin. Drinker. Adventurer. Slender. Big teeth. Well-cut gray suit. "Intergalactic rogue, wanted criminal, reckless adventurer, and mercenary captain." Hard-bitten and wily.

Died on Caspo after the company boarded a long-overdue ghost ship, the *Lorelei,* found sixty-seven years late and derelict. Then… *something* happened… and all logs curiously say nothing about the *something.*

Only that one platoon—Reaper—and John Strange survived.

There is a mystery here, but I've never been able to get to the bottom of it.

But John Strange is a legend, after all. And he's been long dead. So here he is… drinking a gin and tonic while I bleed all over the floor of the bar and soft jazz plays. Hurricane lamps adorn the tiny tables where glamorous young couples should be sitting.

The bartender smiles at me and asks me what I prefer.

Yeah, it's that kind of bar.

I ask for beer.

As Chief Cook likes to say, "Sometimes, Sergeant Orion... you just buy the ticket and take the ride."

EVC armor is hot as hell, and the first thing you think when you get into mission-protective posture level four in an EVC is how great an ice-cold beer would taste.

Because you can't have one.

You'll be drinking through a rubber life tube for the next thirty-six hours max, according to specs for extended EVC operation. Mission posture four.

Spoiler. I did fifty-six hours once and lost ten pounds. One star. Would not recommend. Ever.

The bartender pulled a cold beer from a classy woodgrain tap handle into a tall frosty glass, then set it down on a thick red cocktail napkin he'd placed on the curving, red-leather padded bar we were standing against.

I unslung my rifle...

I know... surreal, huh?

I leaned it against the bar.

I picked up the beer and I drank it all down.

It was the coldest beer I've ever had. And yeah... I knew this was some kind of hallucination... but it was real. As real as...

It was real.

And it tasted great.

And I was gonna enjoy it even if I had my suspicions the cyborg's micro-nuke had gone boom and this was Hell's waiting room.

Hey, there were salty peanuts in a little bowl.

My hands were bloody.

John Strange clinked my glass.

"You live through this one, mate. Don't worry. It's what's coming next I'm worried about, and why I need to have a little talk with you one last time, Sergeant Orion."

The beer hit me that way the first one does. I felt... good.

"One last time?" I said, digging around in the salty peanuts to get a handful. Fighting makes me hungry. Later. After I didn't get killed.

"Yeah. I'm moving on, Sergeant. The company has gone farther than I ever... let's just say... thought it would. I've done everything I can... made my appearance... but... you're approaching Oblivion Gate, and that will... disentangle me... permanently. I can't help you anymore."

I made a face and set down my half-full tall glass. The silent bartender had refilled it already. Without a word. What a place.

"So, mate... this is goodbye. It's... freedom. For me. You'll understand one day. But the company..."

He stopped.

Set down his drink and looked at it.

"I know I'm the founder. A myth to most all of you, Sergeant. But we are... mate, we are brothers..."

"Strangers to the universe..." I murmured as I studied his angular face and long features.

He smiled that wolf's grin for a moment, then it became a sad and winsome smile. Like a hero at the end of the movie when everyone lives happily ever after except him.

He picked up his drink and drank, smiling a little and looking far away as he held the cut crystal bucket glass beneath his lips.

"Brothers to the end, Sergeant."

Then he looked at me.

"This is the end... Orion."

I was stunned. As I heard those words I knew... right at that moment, I knew exactly what they meant.

The end of the company.

The end of...

"... of everything, Sergeant Orion."

Like he knew what I was thinking. Or was most afraid of.

"Two things can happen from where I'm glassing events, Sergeant. One... the company perishes. Ends. *The End*. Two... humanity... we go bye-bye. Forever. Also... *The End*."

CHAPTER TWENTY-FOUR

"I have to be careful here, Sergeant Orion… what I tell you here now because you are, and have been for a long time, the pivotal force in events for the company at this current moment. If you know too much, then you could, even if you're trying to make happen what I want to happen, mess things up. So, as delicately as I can do it… here it is and it's vague, mate. I get that. But this is… as much as I can give you."

I nodded.

I drank my beer. All options were on the table.

And yeah… I was thinking about packing up and running once I got back to reality. I have to be honest about that.

And then I remembered we were brothers. To the end. Even John Strange.

How… strange… to find yourself here. All I did was… flee something bad that happened… and try to hide in the company years ago.

Like it was just a job. For a while. And now… it's destiny.

That's what marriage must be like. You meet some cute girl one day, thinking nothing, and time happens, marriage, kids, triumphs and defeats, and one of you passes when you're old and you find you can't go on because that person was such a part of your life.

But it all started with… hey… cute chick. Unexpected.

What was that old poem. Something about a path diverging in the forest and that making all the difference since.

That's how I felt as John Strange laid it out and I thought for half a second… not my circus, not my monkeys.

But then I thought of the company. And I knew… knew what I'd do. Right then. Right there. It was just a moment of weakness, selfish weakness, when I thought I could just walk away.

"Okay… when you run this Monarch ship, down two things are gonna happen, Sergeant," began John Strange. "And they're not good."

He was sober and very serious as he stared at me, even though there was a drink in his hand.

He drained that drink in one go and the bartender was busy about the next. John Strange closed his eyes and listened to the jazz, waiting for the drink in order to continue.

Company logs indicate he was a notorious drinker.

The drink was back, delivered silently. And the WARNO I was getting from the ghost, or whatever the legendary founder of our company had become, continued.

"That ship... the *Dark Star*... it's pure entanglement. Quantum entanglement, Sergeant. It's the darkest, deepest... 'science' mankind has ever possessed. Those Monarchs... they've had that kind of science for a long time, longer than anyone's ever known or suspected. And here's the killer secret..."

He leaned in. Whispered. "They didn't invent it. It was given to them."

There must've been some look on my face. Some... apprehension or lack of understanding.

He drank, still leaning in, and landed one long finger on my chest... where I'd been shot. Landing it right on the cracked plates of the EVC.

His finger came away bloody.

He straightened. "I'd suspected, Sergeant... back in my time... what was real, and what was purest *hokum*. Made-up. Propaganda. *Disinformation* they would've called it back then. Even the fact-checkers, and especially those, were nothing but lies... but long story short... most of history was, is, just one big lie. And one of the biggest lies is that the *Dark Star* is an X-ship fresh out of the Monarch yards."

He laughed bitterly and shook his head.

He upended his drink and polished that off, then rapped the bar twice, clean and quick, signaling he was ready for another.

"That *Dark Star* has been around for a long, long time. Longer than anyone suspects. And a big piece of the story about how the Monarchs, in their early hidden form, ancient royalty, the power elite, technocrats at the end... took control of human civilization, and then exported their tyranny to the rest of the local stellar neighborhood, galactically speaking that is, lies within that ship you are going to board. So here's the big spoiler, and then I'll tell you the two things that're gonna happen, Sergeant Orion, when you and the rest of the company board the ship and go at it knives out and all. The *Dark Star* isn't a starship so much as an interdimensional ship."

I truly had no idea what that meant.

"Doesn't matter what that is, Sergeant," said John Strange, reading the look on my face. "Point is... it's a ship and you can board it and you need to do that and you need to kill it, and kill all of them while you're doing it. If you don't..."

He paused.

The jazz played.

My ice-cold beer sat on the bar.

I was pretty sure my mouth was hanging open like some local slack-jawed idiot.

"They, the Monarchs, will come back from the outer dark. And when they do, they'll finish off what's left of humanity good and clean ... and become something new. And... honestly... really awful, Sergeant."

He laughed as he drank down the next gin and tonic, rattling the ice cubes and signaling he was ready for another.

Then he looked away and seemed to perform his next line as though he were some stage actor. He was quite good actually.

"*From Hell's heart I stab at thee...* and they will, Sergeant. They will indeed if there's a next time. Bit of left-over British humor and ancient theater. No, Sergeant Orion..." he continued, growing suddenly serious. "They'll end humanity the next time, if they escape, which is what they've been trying to do. For a really long time, in fact. That's why I've interacted with the company from time to time... trying to save the company for reasons I wasn't made totally aware of at the time. But I trust the source. Trust me, you wouldn't understand that part. But… I was… sent… to save my company because the company plays a part in saving… us. Humans. Humanity, Sergeant. One last time. And this is it. Apparently my little ragtag mercenary company of lost toys and misbegotten children plays a bigger part than any of us ever thought."

"All right…" I said slowly, processing all this.

Then…

"So… what happens when we run into this ship? The two things?" I asked.

Strange sighed and squared his shoulders, looking off toward all the bottles at the back of the bar standing tall and arrayed like the soldiers we'd never be, but were, fancy and dress-right-dress pretty.

"On that ship is pure Monarch Dark Science. It's the very heart of it because it comes from somewhere else. Somewhere… *other*. Somewhere very dark and dangerous in ways that no X you or I have ever been on is dangerous. And deadly. And you know my history, Sergeant. You know I was in some pretty bad scrapes."

I knew.

Also me too.

"So one, that ship is entangled with the Oblivion Gate. Two…"

He looked me in the eye.

"The Little Girl…"

He waited for me to acknowledge I understood where he was going. That I was following.

"She is… one of… the most powerful… Bishops. Ever. Sergeant Orion."

The Little Girl who could summon the Wild Thing. That figures. Some time-stranded soldier we had no idea where… the future, perhaps… it was from, had always been our guess about what the Wild Thing really was.

Stinkeye had always remained quiet on the subject and a few of us suspected he knew more about her than he let on.

"Stinkeye knows her story, Orion. Always has. It's how she protects herself."

I knew it!

Now John Strange looked at me like…

… like he was about to give me some very bad news. News I wasn't gonna like. At all.

"So… sorry… it goes like this, mate. She needed help. Real bad. A long time ago. When she was being raised in their labs. The Monarchs. The Dark Science Labs. The real secret ones no one ever, ever found out about. Also… they're still out there. Probably shouldn't have told you that but gin makes me chatty which was always a weakness of mine. These are the worst… the ones Stinkeye escaped from. Just like she did. I… don't know how she did it, does it… but it's more than just Bishop powers. Post-human augmentation… really. She… she sent some *prayer* up… Orion…"

John Strange laughed like even he couldn't believe it. Believe what he was gonna say next.

"She sent that prayer up and the universe drew out the Wild Thing to protect her from all the bad her life really was in ways few will ever know. That thing she can summon… always reminded me of some game I played when I was a kid. Back in

Old Earth days, as you might call them. The Doom Marine. That's what he seemed like to me, kinda. You wouldn't know it, Sergeant."

John Strange laughed again.

"Here's the part that concerns... *you*, Sergeant. And the company too. She uses the grief and suffering of others, their memories, to summon that Doom Warrior from... I don't even know where he comes from, not cleared that high apparently... to give her justice. To *protect* her. So, there were others along the way before you, and because her power was... wild, and new... they got burned up getting her out of the labs. She never told you guys about... you specifically, Sergeant... about the legion of Ultra Marines sent after her that she burned up with the Wild Thing on Sigma Six. Nah, of course not, mate. She'd... *attach* to someone she thought she could anchor to... then... turn the Wild Thing loose when she got in real big trouble. See, she's gotta have an anchor to make it work. Nine times outta ten the dude got... used up... and that's a part I need to clarify... but... nine times outta ten she got out of whatever sticky wicket she'd been gotten into, escaped. And... then the host for the Wild Thing... well... that's another story I'll tell you soon. Before we finish and you get back to the stretcher you're on so they can get off the *X* before one of the cyborgs detonates.

"Also, inside baseball. You guys only killed two. There's a third one and it made it into the fleet undetected. Good luck with all that. It was an infiltration unit. That's... gonna be a problem. But not your biggest one.

"Anyhow... so when she made it to the company, back on which world I forget, she needed a new... Wild Thing, Sergeant Orion. Someone to look out for her, care for her, protect her when they came looking for her. All that jazz. And trust me... they've been looking for her. That's why the Seeker took her and hid her. If she had been with you on that flight out of Astralon they would have used a UMARSOC unit and boarded the ship during long-flight and slit your sleeping throats. They'd dispatched a special destroyer with a Bishop that could track her. So the Seeker hid her. That was what she was doing. Anyway... that's all background for the logs, Sergeant. But when she came to the company, mate, she needed a new Wild Thing to entangle with the Oblivion Gate, which is where she draws her powers, just like your boy Nether, in order to survive. The company, and its Log Keeper, were a natural fit for her to protect herself. Grief and tragedy are the... touchstones she needs to activate the power. And you, Sergeant Orion, you and all the company's stores... you were perfect. So... she picked you."

John Strange smiled.

It wasn't a warm smile.

It was the smile you use as a sergeant when you gotta tell one of yours to go to hell and be happy to be on their way about it.

Like taking point on a rough patrol full of murderous indigs. And booby traps. And IEDs and whatever else some hellscape of a jungle on a foreign world can throw at you.

"What do you mean, she picked me?"

"You know what I mean... mate. You are the Wild Thing's anchor, and the closer you get to the Oblivion Gate that's at the black swirling heart of the *Dark Star*, the stronger the attachment gets."

CHAPTER TWENTY-FIVE

"When that Monarch ship full of all that Dark Super Science they've been using to run a con on all of us about *who*, and *what*, they really are… entangles with her… all hell's gonna break loose. Her powers… they're really gonna come online then, Sergeant. And you… you'll be him."

Silence.

But I had my *wut?* face on.

"You know who. You will swap places with her… victim."

Hmmm… that sounds bad for me.

"So why don't we avoid it?"

"Can't, mate. If the Monarchs make escape, if the company doesn't kill them… then they come back and…"

He drew an imaginary knife across his throat.

"No more humanity. *The End*. Like I was saying at the beginning of our… little talk."

"And if we board, then she goes superpower and…"

"I don't know. But… the closer any Bishop gets to the Oblivion Gate at the heart of the ship… weirdness happens, locally speaking. But yeah… right. You… will be him any time she wants to protect herself, any time she's in danger… even if she doesn't want it… you… will… transform… into… Doom Guy whatever he is. So, here's what I… not John Strange mercenary legend, but just another squaddie in the Strange, brother… owe you. Stinkeye can help you understand what's really going on with this 'Wild Thing' and how it's you and not you… quantum weirdness and all… but… there's a very high likelihood that if you go with the company, you will be sucked into the Oblivion Gate forever due to the proximity of the Little Girl and the quantum entanglement of the interdimensional ship that is the *Dark Star*. Specifically the localized neutron star at the heart of the ship. It's a small one. But… that's the Oblivion Gate to… Oblivion, which is where Bishops like her and Nether anchor their powers. As I understand it. Again, Sergeant, legendary status aside… I am just a soldier being sent with a message."

He put his hand on my shoulder.

"But if you get close enough to that gate, as an anchor… you will be sucked in. You will be gone forever."

I processed this. It was… a lot.

"Can they do it without me?"

John Strange stepped back, looked at me with… I don't know.

But it was a look.

"That is *so* you, Sergeant Orion. So... *you*. You'll go if the company needs you. I knew that. Came here thinking I'd try to... *change things*. Control events. Give a brother a heads-up to a patrol he ain't comin' back from on this one. But no, mate. Orion. Always Orion. Nah, mate. Chances decrease significantly, for the company, if you don't go. And if the company doesn't lay the smackdown and end the Monarchs, then they come back someday and that's real bad for everyone. Don't ask me how. Don't ask me why. Universe is a very... strange place, Orion."

Then he straightened up, sniffled a little, and saluted me.

I just stood there.

He reached out and touched me one last time as the bar began to fade and I could hear everyone trying to save my life on the *X* I was headed back to.

I was bleeding out.

Klutz was running a drip on me while Bull and Punch were leaning on one of my wounds that wouldn't stop leaking.

"Gotta get him to the casevac fast!" shouted Klutz. Full hero mode engaged.

It's what he'd always, in his own humble way, wanted to be.

He was trying to save my life. To Klutz, that's what a hero does.

A life that, according to John Strange... was already doomed.

Just like every soldier.

Sign the unsigned bill to pay with your life on demand.

Nothing new.

Time... immemorial. Same as it ever was.

I was glad I chose to become one. A soldier. It wasn't even in the cards. Even if it meant... Oblivion.

I wouldn't tell them.

I didn't tell John Strange, legend, that my dreams were telling me the company would die on boarding. Those nightmares, that waking PTSD in advance, seemed to confirm everything he was saying.

John Strange embraced me as we faded.

"Brothers to the end, mate. Brothers."

Then he was gone.

And all I could hear was gunfire and chaos and Klutz trying to save my life as I struggled to open my eyes, and live.

Just a little bit longer.

I had... an idea.

I could see blood on the faceplate of the EVC bucket and I was being carried through the dark body-littered slaughterhouse of Gateway Station.

Heading for the inbound casevac.

"Hang on, Sar'nt," shouted Klutz. Holding my drip and organizing the litter. "You're gonna make it."

But I wasn't.

John Strange had told me so.

CHAPTER TWENTY-SIX

Before the fleet action at Typhon, during the dangerous warp-envelope jump to beat the Monarchs there, after getting transferred back aboard the *Spider*, Stinkeye found me.

He wasn't drunk.

And that scared me.

"Ya's know now, Little King."

He stood there in the dark.

And then said, "And ah'm sorry 'bout dat."

We were in a dark passage deep belowdecks in the *Spider*. I was on my way to my weapons cage after being released from the hospital ship *Nova*. Hoping not to be found. Needing a few days to just drink coffee and process what John Stange had told me. Everything.

Think.

"You know now, do you, Little King?" Stinkeye asked me like some familiar and forgotten ghost down there in the dark when I wouldn't admit he was there or acknowledge what he'd said. Like that would make it real… now.

"I do," I mumbled finally.

"Ya's afraid?"

I didn't say anything. Then…

"Yeah."

Stinkeye said nothing.

"Should be. Dat's part o' bein' a soldier, part o' bein'…"

His voice cracked. Choked. The next word didn't seem to come out and I could hear him, because most of the lighting down there was offline and had been for some time… just rando, ghostly lights in the distance of the long dark passages down there where ancient war machines and weapons waited in the dark for the company to need them next.

The old war wizard warrant muttered curses at himself in the dark.

Then…

"… brave, boy. Part o' it, and den goin' anyways. Always was, Little King, always was."

And then he was gone. Like some old ghost of our haunted ship, wandering the dark passages down there. Forever.

DEATH

The night before the battle at Typhon I dreamed again, one last time. I dreamed of the death of the company in battle around a faraway cold and hellish gas giant if there ever was one.

There was nothing I could do about it.

There was no way we could win.

The words of John Strange echoed like a judge's sentence in my head.

I'd even taken some Narcadol which specifically said "no dreams" on the booster. Cutter told me he used it religiously. Cutter doesn't want to dream either. He's cut on a lot of wounded in some desperate attempt to save the dying even though everyone who carried them to him knew they were dead already.

Cutter has never given up.

And he's lost a lot of dudes in the Strange. But I told you his story and why he drinks, and why he bottoms out and gets sober and promises it's "forever this time, Sar'nt Orion," even though we both know that's another kind of lie too.

He has never given up. On others.

He has given up on himself repeatedly.

True story and I don't know how many more of these I have left with the time left… me. And it's not so much a true story as a true confession.

We have to be honest about these things.

There are times when I've taken a very badly wounded brother to the casevac, maimed, torn, missing body parts and horrifically wounded and in pain regardless of shock and trauma… and I've thought… about just shucking my sidearm and… *making it all better* for the guy.

We have to be honest… *about these things.*

I have had that thought.

See… I'm not the hero of this tragedy. I'm just another monster. A different kind of one. But… just another monster.

We are all monsters.

But the night before the Battle at Typhon, despite the drugs that lied… I dreamt of the death of the company in the battle we'd fight around that lonely loveless giant and it scared the living hell out of me, and left me empty, at the same time.

It wasn't just PTSD.

It was as real as real gets. Real in ways even the M.O.M. sims for coffin-sleep can't quite nail yet. So it wasn't a dream. I am more and more convinced of them as I have them. They ain't dreams.

They're sneak peeks at what's coming.

I can't say… FACT. But it sure feels like one. And it ain't just the usual bad vibes a soldier gets before get-it-on-thirty goes down whether you like it or not.

This is how it ends, I kept thinking. *This is how it ends.*

So… less than a minute into the battle and two of my squads are gone. Dead. I can't tell you it happens any other way than that. It just does.

Starting with Wolfy getting his brains blown out all over the inside of his EVC helmet about fifty-five seconds after rushing for a shuttle maintenance slit. Then getting everyone cut to shreds in that maneuver. Hunker for five to maybe ten seconds and then push for the next cover despite no contact or coordination with friendly elements and incoming like I've rarely seen in my all-too-short life.

Or at least that's the way it feels lately as the timer seems to have been set by the universe regarding me.

Hoser is bleeding out and I know he's gone when his head just slumps forward onto the feed chamber of the Pig even as his grip continues to hold the trigger full back.

He rides the lightning into eternity.

What a way to go, I think as the barrier we were covering behind explodes from incoming fire. It's coming apart around me, flying off in bits and shards.

Hustle's headless body lies prone next to his best friend, the gunner. They went down together.

We are all...

So here's a funny thing that happens in all these... not *flashbacks*... but *flash-forwards*.

Catboi is never in any of them. Never dies. Never goes down doing his... Catboi thing. Whatever you want to call it. It's like he isn't with the company. But in the morning, I know exactly where he'll be when we drop into Typhon and start prepping to greet the arriving *Dark Star* within days, weeks, or months. Her extra-luminal propulsion system is unknown to us, and we can only *best-guess* given her last jumps, or rather appearances, on the arrival time and start of the battle.

We think we'll be first.

But who knows...

Anyway... Catboi is in Fourth. Where I can keep an eye on him. He'll get out of the racks in about five hours and go to the prep rooms and gear lockers to get ready because we're dropping into Typhon expecting contact.

Because why wouldn't you?

So... he's in the company. Fact.

And yet... he ain't in the... *flash-forwards* doing his Catboi thing.

"Catboi activated."

"Catboi going forward."

"Catboi picking up targets."

"Catboi engaging."

His flat, emotionless post-pubescent voice narrating his every action.

And if anyone asks him what the hell he's doing, he just says, "Catboi. Half cat. Half boi." Like it's a totally normal thing to say. And then goes on doing his thing.

I will tell you more about him, if there's time. But I don't think there will be and he's not that important.

It's just... *odd*... that he's not in the flash-forward.

Space and time are weird things. I've seen a lot of weird things out here. So... this is just another... *weird thing*.

Let's just chalk it up that way. Okay?

So there I am, under fire, heavy fire, and there's still two squads operating in Reaper and I have no clue on the status of the other platoons.

Ship's done for. For sure.

I can see that because I've got my back to the barrier the defenders erected, the outward side, placed against one of the reinforcing supports that seemed thicker than the rest and I'm hoping that'll deflect any incoming which might shatter my spine or dome my noggin once and finally for all.

M.O.M. has managed to deploy the main landing gears fully and our behemoth of an ancient destroyer, smoking from a dozen holings, has set down at the far end of the cyclopean internal shuttle bay.

Because there's oxygen here, she's got fires on board and black, violent, ugly smoke is pouring from gaping wounds in several decks along her battered hull. And then Monarch defenders are still putting more of their railgun rounds into her.

She will never fly again. I know this.

We will never get off this hell-ship. I know that too.

We are... going to die here. All of us. The company. Strangers to the universe. Brothers to the end.

This is... *The End*.

Just like John Strange told me in the Bar at the End of the Universe.

It's just gonna take a few more seconds. Probably less than a minute. So... I don't really have time to get all that upset about the end of us.

I'm facing the short distance we've crossed in just under a minute of boarding action... under fire.

Have I mentioned this is the worst type of operation in soldiering? I hate boarding actions. High casualty counts, tight quarters, nasty and instantaneous death if you count getting vented into open space as *instantaneous*.

Spoiler...

It's not.

I've seen the look on guys getting vented in both EVC suits and basic gear. Both have that horrific look on their face knowing they're lost.

I've recovered them too.

Ain't pretty. Trust me.

So... I hate boarding actions.

And as I sit there hoping my cover holds, surrounded by my dead squad, with no hope of movement to get off this *X*... I am reminded of how much I hate this type of fighting and that my death... is imminent.

And I'm scared as hell contrary to various fictions I've read about clarity in the last moments, or a determination to live.

If I could surrender... I would've.

Then I see Ulysses leading a wedge of what remains of his squad across the deck, under fire.

Like the actual hero of some story you might read about of space marines fighting many-tentacled alien beings on strange and bizarre worlds.

He's a perfect soldier.

My EVC helmet tags on the surviving squad members following in combat wedge.

Even as one of the New Guys takes a round in the gut, goes down on one knee, and Little Girl comes in behind blaring away at some target with the sub gun she uses. She grabs Solo who hangs on to his weapon and begins to help him to the cover

Ulysses has them moving toward—a massive shuttle bay cargo vehicle the defenders had canted sideways along with another lesser maintenance vehicle to improv as a sort of fire support base for that section of the giant hangar along this side of the Monarch starship.

PDC fire off the *Spider* cuts the enemy gunners down there, and it appears Ulysses ordered his indirect gunner, a Dog company survivor everyone calls Hobo Mike, to drop some H-E on them. We call Hobo Mike "Hobo Mike" because we picked him up when we were working as boarders for a Monarch-supported pirate operation trying to economically reduce a world on the wrong side of the equation, via interdiction boarding raids.

The work wasn't hard, until it was and that was usually actually having to board a ship and fight it out. Nine times out of ten they usually surrendered and the Monarch re-education transports showed up in the dead of night after we'd placed them in the security hauler that ran with the fleet. Then they were never seen again and the company had a pretty good idea what that was about.

Not good. But that was their problem. We were free. For now.

So Hobo Mike was on a spice runner coming out of Tortuga Station, and we boarded after a running gun battle. The pirate we were supporting captained a six-Alpha-beam-gun corvette which didn't seem like much, but the captain, she was as slick as she was pretty, and she'd chained her low-powered, less-than-one-gigawatt Alpha beams to fire Gatling-style off her ship during the running fight. So she could increase a high rate of ship-to-ship fire slaved to her engines and cut shields to pieces faster than they could re-energize.

Then she'd knock out a few critical nav and maneuver systems with targeted railgun fire and we'd board. Worked for about three weeks until things went south with a Q-freighter loaded with two mercenary companies looking to scrap.

G.H.O.U.L. Security Solutions and Noble Honor.

G.H.O.U.L. stood for Guerilla and Hostile Operations Unlimited Lethality.

Let's just say it was a good thing we didn't meet them on the ground in their natural environment. They were high mountain killers who came from a world colonized a long time ago by what were once called Gurkas. Those guys were stone-cold fighters, and we had to use the flamethrowers to kill them in the lower decks of the Centauri mega-freight hauler they'd decided to fight for when we boarded her.

They had these crazy curved knives and they fought like demons.

So… First Sergeant did his *thang* and we just burned 'em out, deck by deck.

Noble Honor was just a bunch of gear hounds who thought they followed some ancient code of bushido and were trying to form some kind of intergalactic feudal cult based on thick biceps and tats. Apparently.

The Old Man taught them what real compartment-to-compartment fighting was all about. We came at them like mad dogs, pushing behind ballistic shields just to absorb fire. That was the feint. And of course Reaper drew that lot.

Noble Honor was in the high bridge stack above the vast cargo deck, like a small city rising over a plain full of cargo containers in deep space. So as Reaper got sent in to draw fire, Dog with Sergeant Hannibal and the Old Man did a hull crawl and came at them from behind with Ghost.

Ghost made shots from space with railgun sniper systems and punched right through the hull for their kills. Reaper inserted into the rear after a hull breach and ate up Noble House slick as all can get within hours.

Voodoo was in the bowels of the ship, messing with the Gurkas.

Then we went down there and joined them once things were cleaned up on the upper decks.

Side note. We could have detted the ship and just killed G.H.O.U.L. But the Monarch intelligence officer running the operation… and get this, an old friend of Chief Cook even though it seemed like they hated each other's guts… he wanted the ship taken and the corpses disappeared into the local star. Then he wanted the autopilot set for destination arrival with the cargo and all.

The Monarchs wanted a ghost ship, and we provided. They wanted to send a message and strike fear at the same time. But later, after that op… I wondered more and more about all the ghost starship stories I'd ever heard.

And I wondered if it had been… something like we'd participated in instead of aliens and xenos.

So… all that to tell you about Hobo Mike who we picked up on a spice runner boarding about four days before we hit the Centauri mega-freighter.

He surrendered to us.

He was a little older than the rest of the crew, and once we got them processed and headed for the security barge that was coming in for pickup, we fed them in the *Spider*'s mess hall.

Myself and Punch got to talking to Hobo Mike, who was really just Mike, and it turned out he wasn't official crew on the spice runner. He was just some guy who liked to hop starships between worlds like some old transient riding monorails and maglev systems on some of the more developed worlds.

Never in one place for too long.

Out to see the galaxy. That was all.

We knew where he was going. But… not really. Much is not known about the re-education rings people the Monarchs didn't like got sent to.

And that was information in and of itself.

Not good. Definitely.

But we got to like Mike and his hobo stories and he indicated he could be convinced to sign a contract with the company. So we edited the logs, made our pitch to the commander and the first sergeant. We got him listed as killed in the boarding action and we took him on over at Dog. Eventually.

He was in Reaper for a while first and he was good at almost everything. He was super friendly and always had time to tell one of his stories about some world where he'd tramped on, or some local gal, usually an older lady, that he'd enjoyed the company of because she was lonely…

I guess starship hoboing is a real thing, and he told us all about the codes and conduct of this little secret society of men and women, and sometimes children, who lived this way.

Most of them were orphans. Or had started out that way. Facing little opportunity, they'd either joined the military, indentured themselves to some megacorp shipping line, or "gone tramping" as they called it.

Hopping starships to various colonies looking for work, and always, the next ride to the next world.

No responsibilities.

No debts.

Freedom, of a kind.

Time and circumstance and really Hannibal's secret war against me got him moved to Dog where Hannibal tried to ruin his life, except, as usual, Hobo Mike in his friendly way, patient, always a joke or a story, good-natured, endless stories… and understanding like none of us had what it meant to be really down on your luck… Hobo Mike won over everyone in Dog and stayed there.

I was butt-hurt about that.

Why?

Because he was good, and I really liked him.

But then I realized he was a force for good inside Hannibal's death cult. And that might… do something for me.

Many was the time Hobo Mike sidled up and warned me Hannibal was working some angle on me.

So…

"Watch out, Orion. He's got a mean look in his eye and he's been watching you like a rat-raptor lately."

So that was Hobo Mike, and he made a pretty good indirect gunner with the S16 and the underbarrel attachment he had on it. In the waking PTSD he blooped in three rounds at the makeshift fort, and Ulysses's squad who'd been getting shot up coming out of the forward cargo deck on the *Spider* had a window to push on the objective and make it to cover.

The guns targeting me lessened and I could tell that more by feel and actual sensory data than observation. They were lifting and shifting to target Second.

I scrambled up, stabilized the Bastard which I had wisely set up for short-range close-quarters battle, and just dumped on targets at one to two hundred meters on full auto.

I was suppressing and I heard Ulysses call out over the comm that they were down behind cover. Then… "Orion, get ready to move… covering fire on three!"

They were getting me off my own personal *X*, and for a brief moment I felt like we were gonna catch a break and maybe get through at least the first fifty meters of contact and maybe even… dare to dream… make it two full minutes.

Hey… remember how we held that *X* on Marsantyium?

We were really something then.

I pushed up and got hit and kept moving anyway because what else was I gonna do. I slid down behind the maintenance truck Ulysses had his team firing from, already bleeding to death.

The Little Girl, now the Second Squad medic, was on me. I could see she'd drag-handled Solo behind cover, and it was clear from the gray look behind his faceplate that he was dead.

The eyes rolled up in his head and the slack-jawed gaze… those were the real clues.

So… that was another one.

"Something's coming out of the main access passage from within the ship!" someone screamed as guns blared on full auto and mags got swapped. Ulysses was moving from position to position, firing and trying to get an angle on what we might do next.

Even though, to me, hit again and already a bloody mess somewhere across my chest… there was nothing we *could* do.

I heard some… low screaming like an engine going psychotic redline. But it wasn't right, and it wasn't natural, and I was sure it was that thing… coming from farther down the passage.

"Where's the Old Man," I grunted in pain, and the Little Girl who worked my wounds and tried to assess what she could, and accept what she couldn't, didn't answer. She didn't look at me as she'd always done back when she was actually… the Little Girl. A potato-sack black shift dress. Oversized combat boots. Sometimes a faded military trench coat someone had given her. Sometimes a patchwork sweater. Dark hair and dark eyes. Pale skin.

She didn't look at me with those dark eyes. Convicting and condemning and… knowing.

"He's dead," she said flatly as she worked.

I nodded but my head went down and just slumped on my chest as I heard the gun battle all around go to what we call in the infantry… *final protective fires*.

Last-stand stuff.

It was that bad.

Ulysses was directing what little indirect we had. Someone in his team fired one of the anti-armor launchers. Brass and linkage clattered and danced their little dances on the mirror-black surface of the landing deck.

This is how it ends, I thought.

The first sergeant was in the rear portside cargo deck. He was going in with Voodoo and his task had been to get them in place accompanied by a small security team so they could do their thing.

Nether could displace and vanish stuff.

Cook would look for someone to break into their comms and download some kind of weird high-speed scramble audio code that supposedly hacked transhuman brain systems.

"We ran that scramble back at Dagon Five on a cult of transhumanists that broke off from the Monarchs. They'd been… priests… call 'em what you want… but they were the supposed keepers of the protocols and technology upgrades the Monarchs allowed for their inner circle of re-educated citizens, and the ones they kept back for themselves. If anyone was caught with tech like that… forbidden tech… they declared it heresy, Orion. Like they were some kind of freaky high-power ancient religion. They were kind of… inquisitors with detection gear, Orion. They moved among the worlds scanning and listening, trying to detect who was using that which was reserved for the elite themselves. Then they had capture teams from the Ultra Marines Seventh… the Black Widows as they were known because they were good at embedding in society and launching traps… and they'd bring them in for a full neural inquisition and then a public execution just to show the rubes they were nothing but cattle to the masters who could do anything, and I mean *anything*, Orion, that they wanted to. Grim stuff. I helped develop the code that could hack into transhuman brains and scramble them. Program was called *Operation Dazed and Confused*."

Then he went on about how he managed to create an audio worm that scrambled the brain for a half a second, accessed the most blissful moments of a person possessing transhuman heresy tech… and then the audio worm or virus or whatever it was hijacked the mRNA machines inside the body that came with the transhuman tech and turned on all the endorphin centers to overload. Like to full, and then some. Basically the person turned into an instant drug addict on the trippiest trip they'd ever tripped and made them easier to one, identify, and two, capture.

Nightmare stuff.

"Remember they were dangerous because they had that Monarch tech, Orion," intoned Chief Cook. "Seriously dangerous. Basically they were rogue Monarchs, and so while you might not approve of my time with Monarch Psyops or my involvement in some of the shadier operations… you should hear my story sometime… it'll scare the living hell out of you… Orion."

I did not want to and told him so. And had repeatedly told him.

He wanted to tell me.

I refused to listen. He was the only person in the company of whom I did not want to know their story.

"Well, Orion… these Dark Monarchs as they called themselves back then… were much, much worse. They had a whole real end-of-the-universe snake-cult vibe to them and their outfit. Bad stuff. Virgins wearing white dresses and sacrificing themselves so the 'true order' would rise and all. It was a good thing the Monarchs wanted them outta their way, and so I held on to that old code even though my friends back at Central Intel had me mind-wiped. I managed to keister the important bits anyway."

"Keister?" I asked.

"Oh, my sweet summer world child, Sergeant Orion. The things you don't know about the darker side of the universe. So anyway… I've reconstructed the code as best I can and once we can get into their system, post-boarding op insert… I can scramble their minds something real scary. Good times. Not. I added a whole visual trip to this one, this time. It's going to really be something… really, really special."

He laughed that evil knowing way he laughed where his widely spaced tombstone teeth never parted even as he grinned behind his mirrored sunglasses and his bald head remained perfectly still.

No one… laughs like that. No one. Ever.

It's disturbing.

"Bats?" I asked and didn't need to.

"You know it, Sergeant Orion. Some serious… bats."

"What's with you and the bats? It's always bats with you."

He gave me a look and then walked away telling me not to make eye contact if I saw them.

"That way lies madness, Sergeant. Madness like the end of the galaxy deeper and darker and more lost than that hokey old story Stink's always selling about his… 'Heart of Darkness.' Trust me, Orion. Never look the bats in the eye. Never. Ever."

And somehow… I believed him. I believed at least that part, of all his lies, was true.

Chief Cook was in rear portside with the first sergeant. As was Nether and Stinkeye, in the last dream before the Battle at Typhon.

Cutter was set up in his combat OR at the central lift on the cargo decks we called our troop assault bays.

There would be no wounded evacuated to the rear on this one. The ship was down and burning and still being shot to pieces despite Ulysses's efforts to fight on despite catastrophic losses.

In those final moments in that nightmare I knew, as I watched him moving among our pathetic defense… that had we survived this… he would have been our next captain. Someday.

A new… Old Man.

But… I wouldn't live to see that. None of us would.

And that was when the dream of us all dying badly on the *X*… got worse.

Much worse.

MUCH, MUCH, WORSE

In those last seconds I look up from the chaos of the last stand of the Strange Company... a fifty-meter rush into nothing but hot lead and death coming from every direction... Hauser stumbled through the gunfight. Several of Second were dead, and others dying.

The Little Girl had pushed away from me as it was clear to her I wouldn't make it. She had others to save. She was working on Bad Bet, who'd been hit bad, when she took a sniper round and fell over onto her back, rolling to her side...

I whispered, "No."

I could hear my own last breaths coming in quick gasps.

Ever die in a dream...? It's not fun.

She was dead. Her dark eyes going blank... finally staring at me now.

Saying... "You've always protected me. Sergeant."

Except I hadn't.

Ulysses was gone. I think... going forward attacking because he knew nothing but when it was dying time.

He'd never surrender.

Ultras didn't. So... he wouldn't. Even if it meant total annihilation.

The Pig Hauser carried was dry. Belt gone. It was smoking and the barrel was hot to the point of almost starting to glow.

Forbidden popsicle.

My friend the combat cyborg shucked out of the sling and threw the light machine gun aside like it was nothing at all.

His ammo was gone.

Hauser bent down over me. He was ruined. Massive wounds showing internal circuitry and damaged hydraulics.

"Sergeant Orion..." he said, in that calm and emotionless voice that was strong and quiet to me.

"Just... Orion..." I wanted to say, but my voice was nothing but a hoarse papery whisper and my gasps were coming faster and faster as I... died.

It took everything to reach out and grab his gloved hand he was checking my pulse with.

"Your vitals are not within parameters to maintain life, Sergeant Orion. Something is coming..."

A red autumn leaf fell between us.

But that may have just been a hallucination.

Others were starting to fall among our corpses. Dancing down through the bright tracers of incoming while other invisible rounds smacked into and destroyed everything in every direction.

This was the end of the company. And somehow...

"The assault has failed, Sergeant Orion. I have no contact with command."

It was all my fault.

I held the machine that was my friend's hand. My best friend. It was slick with the bio-synth hydraulic fluid that was his "blood."

"Damage to my systems has reached cascade level, and the clock inside me will activate shortly, Sergeant Orion."

Please, Hauser. One last time.

It's just Orion.

"Your… frien…d," I heard myself gasp.

"I am about to self-terminate, Sergeant Orion. There is nothing I can do to stop this. I am… sorry."

Whatever that huge, howling, dark thing that was coming into the bay to finish us off was… it was like the end of all things. Love. Good. Light. Us even though at times it felt like we were the opposite of all that. Whatever it was it was dark and ominous, like some unclean presence that comes into the room where you sleep in the night and scares the hell outta you.

It was nightmare.

Literally.

I couldn't see it, but I could… feel… it.

We had failed.

One of the attacking starships blew up out there beyond the entrance to the hangar bay as enemy missiles smacked into it from all directions. Other ships were detonating. Coming apart.

The loss of life was just… catastrophic.

We had failed. And someday… humanity would end because the Monarchs would come back as John Strange had said.

"I am sorry, Sergeant Orion. I will kill us all now."

Most of his face, or at least the synthetic flesh, had been shot and blown away by gunfire and fragmentary devices they'd used against Third.

He too, was the last survivor of his element. Like me.

"The clock has started for the last time. I cannot contain…"

I squeezed his hand, whispering… "It's… oka…y. Just… Oh-ri…on. Hause. Your… fr…"

Then he detonated and blew the whole thing and all of us to hell.

I felt it. And saw it. All of it.

I woke up screaming in my cage.

Panting and crying as I checked the time, my shaking hands fumbled a smoke loose and I was sobbing.

I got it lit and inhaled, just trying to feel nothing and telling myself that dreams and nightmares are lies.

That's all.

Three hours to jump-envelope insert at Typhon.

I sobbed one last time and lit another smoke, swearing like some old man who felt useless and used up at the same time.

Which is what I am.

I felt nothing like a small unit leader. Or a soldier even.

Or a friend. And somehow… that was the worst part.

Silence.

We have to be honest about these things.

CHAPTER TWENTY-SEVEN

I was back in the navigator's seat on the flight deck of the *Spider* when the fleet came out of the group jump envelope, homing in on the emergency broadcast beacon of the Andromeda-class super-freighter heading toward Typhon we'd received intel on.

By that time, including the *Winds of Change* that brought us all in its jump envelope to Typhon and not to *forever lost in the void*, so we had that going for us, we were thirty-some starships of different varieties, forms, utilities, and capabilities in the fleet of the Star Khans. This one wasn't such a hot mess, and we came out of jump as a fleet and spotted the *Dark Star* almost immediately.

"Look at the size of that thing," hissed Freako, who was running the defensive battery panels from the third row of crash chairs on the flight deck. He was in Gunny's platoon and he had some skill from past work on big ships.

"Stay on your screens. Things are about to get hairy," muttered XO from the flight officer's chair at the front of the bridge. Which was his way of saying, *Acknowledged… that thing is huge.*

Then he added, "This is looking like ship-to-ship combat if I've ever seen it, and I don't like the odds."

The odds.

I'll start with what we had as opposed to what we were looking at with total awe.

Thunderer was a refitted assault Antares Hegemony carrier acting as our fleet command-and-control ship.

Winds of Autumn as the lead scout vessel running target acquisition and battlespace development.

Michael G. Murdock, a Hellicon-class late-era battle cruiser, was our power hitter.

Sumotai, a Horseman-class light missile cruiser built during the long years of the Mangol Wars out along the starward arm of exploration thirty-five years back. She was carrying at least twenty-three one-hundred-megaton ship-killer SIMs. Space Intercept Missiles. Plus five scatter-pack launchers and forty drone batteries with over five hundred racks ready to rearm and launch as fast as she could. She had weak shielding and no close-quarters exchange weapons, but she was an absolute standoff killer, or so we'd been briefed thusly during the prior jump as we were expecting combat at some point in the Typhon system we were sure we'd run the *Dark Star* down in.

The prevailing tactical thinking had been that we'd reach the system first and have days if not weeks to lay down defensives… minefields, cloaked vessels, ambush forces… and even arm some of the asteroids in the system with light-burst pulse batteries and explosives, effectively turning them into giant rocks we'd just hurl at the last Monarch ship when we came close enough to exchange fire.

But that didn't happen. Getting there first.

Dark Star was already there and sucking everything she could out of an Andromeda-class super-freighter that had issued a distress call despite knowing that no one would ever hear out here far beyond human-controlled space. Even though we did.

The *Murdoch*, *Thunderer*, and *Sumotai* were our main capital ships. Around them lesser destroyers and corvettes and a few frigates formed up to make up most of the rest of the fleet.

The hospital ship was important. The jump-envelope ship was vital. Without it the journey back would take…

We're talking a decade at least of real time as opposed to clocked flight time.

The ad hoc destroyer fleet surrounded the *Thunderer*.

This was comprised of *Hammer*, a destroyer escort that had once been a part of the Monarch expeditionary forces, then was sold off to local pirates as a freighter. She was rearmed and turned out to be a big problem fifty or so years ago. She was recaptured by the Saturnian Batts, then sold off for scrap. The Technate of the Star Khans who'd been quietly building up their navies bought what was left of her and had her refitted with a B-class beam weapon and a huge power plant to provide energy to the weapon's energizers.

Asumasaryti was a straight-up destroyer with actual kinetic railguns, and a whole lot of them in fact. A private war vessel, she'd fought during most of the twenty years' war against the Monarchs in battles alongside the chimps' war hulks and the Star Khans' various fleets.

Most of which had been chewed to pieces in the battles against the last of the Ultra Battle Spires.

Where so many destroyed ships littered ravaged worlds or lay spread out in expanding debris fields over what had once been known as humanity's Bright Worlds, the *Asumasaryti* had survived.

Her crew was generational in that the whole ship was practically about fifteen families forming around some kind of crew-caste system.

Their world had been annihilated by the Monarchs' Battle Spire *Gorgon*, and the *Asumasaryti* had sworn what they called "Black Abyss" against the Monarchs. A vow that they would chase them into hell itself in order to settle the debt of their burnt world.

Two smaller destroyer escorts, light, nimble, and each carrying mauler-beams, battery-array-powered C-beams in the three-megawatt range, formed the vanguard for *Thunderer*. *Aston* and *Carnage* were once pirate interdictor vessels that operated far forward of the Monarch Expeditionary Fleet when they were surveying unincorporated worlds to add to the clutches of the once-powerful sovereigns of human-controlled space. *Aston* and *Carnage* were atmo-capable Bird of Prey–class vessels that could stack up their charge batteries off stars or local gas giants. Then they'd fly in on raids and take out pirate vessels with bad idents of marque that were most likely protecting the unincorporated star system the Monarchs had plans for.

That was how they'd operated.

Both had been dry-docked on Ceres IX when the revolt happened and the chimps captured them. They traded the complex raiding vessels to the Star Khans for freighters full of explosives and junky old AK weapons systems. And ammunition. Lots and lots of ammunition.

The chimps had their way of fighting the war, and it didn't include complex elite raiding vessels that could fire beams in the three-gigawatt range.

Aston and *Carnage* had cloaking devices that rendered them all but invisible to sensors, though they could be visually tracked.

Lynx was a DDM missile corvette, and she carried loads of racks of Savage-class missiles and four torpedo bays to get it done with.

Scorpion was an AGM destroyer with sensors and targeting data to coordinate all missile strikes within the fleet. She had very few defensive batteries and was mostly armed with chaff pods and sandcasters to defend herself. She did have one main kinetic gun battery that used wave-motion intercept tech to fire school-bus-sized dumb projectiles at two every thirty seconds if she needed to target an enemy vessel for destruction.

But her real power lay in the ECM and ECCM suites much of her decking was devoted to. The entire lower hull was one massive supercomputer running a once-illegal AHI, Artificial Hyper Intelligence. Under the Monarchs—only they could run actual real AIs—it was known as a BERTRAM Nine. A BERTRAM Nine could defeat most known ECM and could maintain target cohesion for fleets running at least fifteen thousand independent weapons systems. In other words, if *Scorpion* had the fleet resources available, it could order a targeting strike that could not be defended against by anything other than armor and shields. And even then, within picoseconds, a BERTRAM Nine could identify weakness from ongoing strikes and near instantly re-task inbound weapons systems to exploit hull, armor, and shield vulnerabilities that had appeared in the ongoing strike.

The chimps had linked nine of their war hulks to the *Scorpion* at the battle of Parcells in the Ursa Major conflict where the Battle Spire *Green Dragon* had gone down and simply overwhelmed the Monarch defensive system with info war attacks and coordinated strikes from all the monkey weapons the chimps had managed to weld to their rattleclap ships.

The chimps boarded and fought for six weeks against the Ultra Marines, who finally detted the *Green Dragon* and blew most of the hulks and all of the Ultra Marines to oblivion come.

The *Scorp* had already pulled back to a safe detonation distance once it became clear the Ultra Marines would not surrender.

Those, along with the freighters tuned up to either fight at broadsides or act as boarding vessels, tugs, or hospital ships closer to the action where we didn't want the *Nova* or the *Winds of Change*, were only some of the ships that surrounded *Thunderer* as we jumped in and saw the giant *Dark Star* finishing the pillaging of the super-freighter they'd raid before they left known space.

And that was a big problem because apparently the super-freighter had been on a long transit out through the uncolonized and un-surveyed worlds picking up returning deep-jump navigation probes, along with hauling whatever cargo they came across.

Those beacons had been sent out long ago, well beyond the reach of any ship, using combo fold/jump tech. Each probe contained the locations of many unsurveyed worlds hundreds of light years beyond the reach of any ship we, or anyone, possessed.

If the Monarchs cracked the probes, not a big problem. They'd have the coordinates to disappear far beyond our reach, without a trace, for lifetimes to come.

Except the words of John Strange about them coming back to finish the business with their former subjects came back to haunt me as I saw the detonation charges begin to crack the super-freighter into multiple sections.

The Monarchs had the probes.

The explosions were terrific and that was saying something. The super-freighter was the size of a large city.

But the Monarchs didn't need the ship, or her crew.

The *Spider* was in the attack cluster with Murdock group and now, as the *Dark Star* loomed in our forward observation window, a narrow slit at the front of the flight deck, we went to engines full as soon as the *Dark Star* fired her first beam weapon, clearly C-type, and just obliterated the *Asumasaryti* and her generational crew sworn to vengeance in the first ten seconds of the Battle at Typhon.

CHAPTER TWENTY-EIGHT

Battle Group Murdock was just coming around the massive command carrier *Thunderer* when the destroyer *Asumasaryti* went up like a candle and detonated terrifically in every direction all at once.

At the moment... sitting in the navigator's chair second row back on the flight deck of the *Spider*... I very much doubted any of our ships were going to board that massive Monarch ship, much less get close to it in the first place.

But... I guess we were gonna try.

Instruments chimed, feeds crawled, proximity alerts droned about navigation hazards from the expanding stellar debris field.

XO was committed.

"Nav... plot intercept and overlay on my controls. Engines... we're going redline to get in there fast. Activate the secondary pumps."

Our missiles were already streaking away from all three groups of the fleet, sidewinder in some cases, fracturing into multiple intercept vehicles in others, or just launching out of tubes like massive volleys of arrows in some forgotten long-ago battle when men wore armor and hacked away at each other with steel and flint knives if they could get close enough.

Things never change... even though they do.

All three attack groups were like swarms of tiny locusts, closing on a massive disc, a saucer, bigger than anything I'd ever seen before.

This was the *Dark Star*.

Just abeam our destroyer, the Andromeda-class super-freighter, a giant of a freighter, continued to explode.

The Monarchs had taken what they wanted.

They'd make sure we wouldn't have any of it.

And I seriously doubted we'd put boots on the deck of that monstrosity.

Seriously.

CHAPTER TWENTY-NINE

Okay... the *Dark Star*.

What can I say but that it was the largest ship I, or, bold statement here... *anyone*... had ever seen. Like every ship in space, it was small as we hurtled toward it breaking out of the jump envelope as provided by the *Winds of Change*. But within seconds as we faded from ultra-luminal speeds, the target we'd come for had suddenly become simply immense.

It was a disc. That was its shape.

Or a saucer.

Call it what you will.

It was so huge as we faded into space-time reality and came to a... weird word choice here but this is space and this is how space battles are... but we came to a hurtling halt. The braking effect of fading back into space-time from the jump envelope was so jarring it was like we were suddenly standing still.

I checked the overhead systems monitors above the NAC station running atop the ceiling of the flight deck across every row of crash seats and noted we still had power to the mains and were in fact... moving forward.

Suddenly the fleet chatter comm was alive with proximity reports, incoming fire, and exclamations of how "big that thing is!"

It was big. No understatement.

So the best way I can relate its impossible size is just to say this...

It was easily twenty miles across at its diameter. It was a saucer, but with a slightly oblong appearance.

It was thick by ordinary starship size. At least two kilometers high from central to dorsal points. Top to bottom that is.

As we closed and reality began to assert itself with all the speed and distance and thrust vectors of the maneuvering starships in the attack force of the fleet, Rogue Fleet, *yeeehawww, boys!!!*... it was clear that the disc's edge, the edge of the saucer, was "rough," and this was where the docking facilities and other external features ringed the craft. Bays. Hangars. Weapons systems.

The top and bottom of the giant disc were mostly featureless, smooth with a gentle curve, but side-scan topography of the *Spider* was reading features and feeding them to the CIC aboard the *Thunderer*, as was every other ship.

A tactical picture of the ship we'd soon be boarding, and dying on if my PTSD dreams were correct, began to develop.

The main beam weapons off the *Dark Star*, bigger than any energy strike I'd ever seen, fired and destroyed the *Asumasaryti* in an instant.

The battle was now on.

To an infantryman, riding a flight deck chair into battle made me feel helpless. Especially knowing this strange ship could straight up "dome" an entire starship with one shot.

The beam's pulse discharged from the leading edge of the saucer just after two powerful energy surges, glowing a violent red, swept around both sides of the massive disc, running along a channel at the top of the ring. As they met they formed the powerful beam that destroyed *Asumasaryti* in one remorseless instant.

I've seen death, close up and hard on the battlefield. Sudden death, in fact. A round out of the blue on a day you thought was gonna be a real nothing... then *zip* and someone's head gets vaped into bloody mist.

Back o' the skull turns to spray and without a word or even a look, the guy you just lost a game of Cheks to last night is dead without even a goodbye or a final summation of what life is all about.

Ain't no death speeches like in the spectacuthrillers.

Just... *gone*.

The weird thing is you keep expecting them to show up for days or even weeks later.

That you'll both laugh about what happened. But... that never happens.

Asumasaryti had a crew of seventeen hundred and change, including their families, when they went up in an instant.

But... it wasn't like the spectacuthrillers either when the big bad space laser gets fired and ends some ship or planet, everyone going silent in an instant...

Nope.

Because I was riding the nav crash seat on the flight deck running the plot intercepts and making sure we had all the proximity alerts tagged in the master attack section plot XO was flying...

Oh... tangent... Don't mind if I do. And c'mon... you've gotten used to this by now.

Here's how I do that. My table is a digital display graphed in orange and black. It shows near-space and an orange vector display overlay of the ol' *Spider*. Friendly ships are graphed in blue vector as our radar and side-scan reads them. Bogies are red. My job is to tag each ship every few seconds to make sure M.O.M. updates the plots and intercepts.

I do this with a stylus.

I know... this ship is old.

This data is then fed to the XO on the controls and allows him to fly the *Spider* without ramming any other ships.

In theory.

You'd think M.O.M. would be able to keep all the data straight, but she is a very old AI and the last battle at Marsantyium didn't do her any favors. Her core memory vaults were gutted and if the company can ever score big-time, we have double-underlined in the company command room "get a new ship's AI" and then we circled it in red.

Someone wrote "Get one that sounds HAWT!" and I can neither confirm nor deny that I know who wrote that. But no one in the command team erased it.

So, we have to be honest about these things.

Back to the death of the *Asumasaryti*...

Because I'm doing my job with plots and intercepts and playing what amounts to space bingo so our heavy and ponderous but fast-moving and deadly old destroyer doesn't hit any friendlies on the way to contact with a vessel the size and likes of which no one has ever seen... I'm also monitoring fleet comm, and the strange and powerful "death beam" that has just forked the *Asumasaryti* into several sections... is the hot topic of conversation.

And of course the Monarchs detted the Andromeda-class super-hauler just to add chaos and confusion to the mix.

Bets are now she's gonna spool up whatever she has for a drive and disappear. So...

We have to hit her hard and hope to disable her somehow.

I like infantry stuff. Throw frags at it. Hose it with the guns. Then assault and double-tap-stab.

Easy.

This looks like it could go real wrong all kinds of ways.

Spoiler, in about sixty seconds that's gonna be a real problem. The detonation of the super-freighter in near-local-space to the attack fleet.

But... again... back to the death of the *Asumasaryti*.

CIC was prioritizing rescue of the survivors off the stricken missile cruiser in seconds. About fifteen to be exact.

I shall now sum up space battles: decades of long boring flight through what seems like never-ending darkness... then sheer terror in under a minute.

All that cyber-drilling and sim-time running a digital *Spider* in the eighteen-month haul out here, never mind the time dilation effects, and it had become crystal clear that the *Spider* attack odds expected no space battle to last more than just over a minute.

And by "battle" I mean starships at beam-weapons and dumb-weapons range shooting into each other. Missile engagements are usually preemptive and get handled by a lot of ECM and maneuvering way off.

That is unless you surprise the largest ship ever and there's not time for missiles and suddenly it's beam weapons and ships' guns all at once. And missile spreads are getting fired off like Punch blowing chunks on a turbulent insert.

Which was what was happening. I'm sure of it. Reaper and the platoons were all stacked in the racks down on the assault decks.

Back to the space battle...

The *Spider* was in the attack section of the fleet. I listened as the *Asumasaryti* died across its various sections, engineers and junior grade officers trying to seal bulkheads or get families into the lifeboats and escape pods. The *Lynx*, our attack missile corvette, spammed the comm as she fired her full suite of medium-range missiles all at once.

This caused confusion. Much.

Lynx was just leading the *Spider* and suddenly all her weapons hatches blew open, venting internal oxygen and debris which meant they didn't even go through a pre-launch sequence. Instead they just freaked out and targeted the *Dark Star* and fired everything they had.

As a ruck hobo I understand this maneuver, as I too have found myself on an *X* with nothing but grit and full auto to get you off and under cover.

When in doubt, mag-dump the unknown.

It's not a great plan… but it is a plan.

Funny thing is if you go full rattle, and flip the selector to hard cackle, it's funny how that burns up all your ammo as you return fire and try to suck dirt or run for whatever looks like cover you spotted in the instant before the bad guys started murdering you.

Or big mistake… you do the right thing the wrong way. What do I mean? Attend and know wisdom, little hobos of the future who I'm probably never gonna meet…

The right thing, when you find yourself on an *X*, an ambush, like you're out on patrol or something, is to go ahead, identify where the enemy is, then… violently assault through their defense.

Supposedly the odds of survival are better with this tactic. But that may have just been written by some officer that just wants you to kill more and doesn't care if you survive.

But…

Listen, you're on the *X*. You're probably gonna die. Why not go try and kill a few and get in and among them and maybe, just maybe… it jams up their chi. Why not? Amirite?

Your mileage may vary.

So, right thing done the wrong way if you find yourself in that horrible situation and you're desirous of living through it… is to run into the enemy guns and kill everyone if you can. Solid plan. Good luck. As in good luck even having the balls to do that. But hey, can the infantry school of infantrying at the pro mongo level be wrong?

Uncomfortable answer: Yes.

The book is written by officers who, on a good day if you get a good one… are looking to die gloriously accomplishing the objective. Trust me. For the good ones, and a few of the awful… that's how they want to go.

Not like me.

I wanna go smothered by eel-girl flesh in a nice tropical lagoon listening to acid jazz. But hey, different strokes for different hobos.

Don't judge.

And don't @ me.

I'm probably dead already anyway.

So, the *Lynx* fires her weapons off like some new private on full auto thinking gunfire and thunder is gonna get them off the *X*.

Maybe.

But the pro move is to charge the emplaced guns and fixed fighting positions on single fire. Why? 'Cause you gonna need ammo once you're in and among them, and they gonna freak out so hard, they gonna start shooting, and chopping, and stabbing at you the second that happens. So: have some ammo ready instead of having to swap in a new mag if you ever find yourself in that particularly nasty situation.

That's how I got the scar on my thigh where they had to rebuild my quad. Ask me sometime and buy me a coffee and I might tell you all about how lucky I got and it was a good thing I had half a mag left.

But that's another story.

So there I was... in the nav crash chair on the flight deck and the assault fleet is suddenly going to full thrusters to close the distance with the *Dark Star* just like infantry suddenly getting ambushed... and then our lead missile corvette lets go with everything she's got and I know from having simmed fleet action on the way to Typhon that *Lynx* has a two-minute reload time on her missile racks to fire another salvo.

Again, battle and tac plan sims have assured us that space battles last no more than barely over a minute. The majority last less than fifteen seconds.

The vapor and exhaust trails from the sidewinders off the *Lynx* suddenly obscured everything in front of the attack fleet, and XO is yelling at me to update the plot so he can steer through the navigational hazard.

"Nav... loss on visual ID to target... Nav, update those plots or we're gonna slam into someone and this is gonna be one short attack!"

Oh, and now we've got missile alerts and locks ululating from the defensive station.

The *Dark Star* has targeted us as we streak in to attack and board.

And we know what happens then, don't we.

CHAPTER THIRTY

Lynx pulled out of the attack and nearly collided with the *Liberty*, a six-C-beam-gun frigate that had been part of the Monarch navy for a long, long, long time, and was due for the museums after having fought in a number of conflicts. Then her crew of junior-grade officers rebelled, spaced the captain and the political officers, and joined the Star Khans a few years back.

The crew was quick, took evasive action, and started to fire her portside C-beam guns into the *Dark Star* as she peeled off from the fleet attack vector.

I updated the plot.

C-beams are one gigawatt each, and the hot white burning red beams, ringed with quantum spiral-focused energy surges to keep the beam on target, immediately tore into the Monarch ship's shields and cut huge swathes of damage into the upper portions of the massive disc.

"We have damage!" someone over the fleet comm. "Registering internal strike on *Dark Star!*"

Comm operators cheered.

And yeah... impending doom got backed off a little. I felt it. We all did. Have to be honest about these things.

The frigate's beams lasted no more than three seconds on contact but carved at least mile-wide black slashes in the enemy ship as *Liberty* continued to take evasive action to avoid the reloading *Lynx* who'd broken off from the main attack to reload for the next missile strike.

Now the assault element of the fleet had something to work with. *Liberty* had punched shields, and for a moment as the array tried to recompensate, re-form, and get power from the enemy's main engines, or however the Monarchs had wired the *Dark Star* to work, the commander of the *Murdock* practically screamed over the already wild chatter-filled net, and don't forget the dying of the *Asumasaryti*... "Rogue Fleet... fire all weapons now!"

In an instant every forward-facing weapon system spat forth a variety of munitions from across all the ages of combat star flight at the looming *Dark Star*.

Some missed.

Some got deflected by shields.

Some breached and caressed armor and hull.

A few internal systems exploded across the enemy hull.

On the flight deck of the *Spider*, XO's voice was tense as he ordered M.O.M. to re-route all power from reactors one and two to the *Spider*'s two main guns.

Beast One and Two.

Oh, man… it was on now.

Ion disruption cannons that had been all the rage back in the Alpha Centauri Wars hundreds of years ago, which was when our ship had first seen action. The *Spider* had been a commissioned Monarch fleet destroyer back when that really meant something. A destroyer *then* was heavily armored, hit hard, and was relatively fast. Space combat was brutal and intense due to the fact that the long-range missile engagement systems were easily defeated by countermeasures and electronic warfare.

SI-AI—Super-Intelligent Artificial Intelligence missile systems—changed the whole game just like drone warfare had done a long time ago for a hot minute until we crafty humans learned how to shut that noise down.

Spoiler.

Shottys made a comeback.

Anyways, SI-AI. Imagine a high-functioning obsessive autist, then make it a weapon system and give it one purpose: to kill. They got rounds on target with missiles.

Missile combat got nigh undefeatable and very long-range. So… humans started up with space shotguns like chaff and PDCs. Point Defense Cannons.

Same as it ever was.

Think up a new crossbow and we'll make it obsolete fairly fast. That's humanity. That's us.

But before that, ion disruption cannons were the thing to have.

And we had two.

Beast One and Two, to be specific.

These are heavy-hitter railguns with energy disruption munitions.

Think a bunker buster for a starship and you're just about right.

We start firing, and the ship shudders as Beasts One and Two alternate fire.

They destroy *Dark Star*'s shielding in the first shots and then begin to devastate hull plating and armor as internal systems go off like a fireworks show.

But *Dark Star* is so huge… the damage is almost… underwhelming.

Still we continue to fire as we close.

The assault element of the attack fleet fires all her weapons at what space combat considers medium to short range as we are now on an assault intercept known as the *Close Shave*. We ain't boarding on this run… we're going to make a gun run just like some close air support aircraft in planet-side battle and dump everything we got. If things look good, according to the Star Khans' plans and *Thunderer*'s CIC, then we move to assault-boarding profile… which means fast attack, hard brake, hard contact, board and kill everyone for a beachhead.

The rest of the fleet… Support and Ranged… picks up the fire and begins to target the *Dark Star*'s external weapons systems as we go in for the Close Shave, drawing turret fire from the *Dark Star*'s ring.

Our shields are holding.

If all goes well and one of the assault elements manages a breach… then the rest of the fleet provides targeted fire and Ranged Fire takes out the main engines and any maneuver control the ship has.

Hopefully we can disable her before she jumps away to forever as far as we're concerned.

If all *that* goes according to plan… that's when the real fight starts. Bulkhead-to-bulkhead fighting until we take the ship and dust all the Monarchs on board.

There are problems with this plan, and the company command team is aware of those problems, and I shall, given the chance, illuminate further. Later.

In brief… we have questions about our allies in the fleet and we doubt all of us are of the same purpose, which is to kill the Monarchs and destroy the vessel.

Again… more about that later.

Right now, we dump all forward weapons into the *Dark Star* like Hauser going full ride-the-lightning on some bunker while the rest of Reaper maneuvers to the flanks for the ol' frag toss and double-tap-stab.

Listen… space warfare ain't wide of standard infantry fighting. I didn't know that even though I'd read a dozen books on the subject and had this weird unspoken dream about wanting to get a ship and go do some scouting. It wasn't until XO started running us through the combat sims that I saw how basic, easy, and stupid-lethal ship-to-ship fighting was.

Dark Star returned fire even as our outgoing weapons streaked away.

Both powerful kinetic shots from the *Spider*'s main offensive weapons thundered across all decks as the ship fired her guns, rhythmically, into the crazy maelstrom of outgoing fire.

Displays on the flight deck suddenly blinked.

We groaned.

Lights on several decks went out. Emergency lighting came on.

According to Punch, who'd unracked from the combat racks on the main cargo deck and gone to the deck's local mess to grab a couple of high-powered shakes to put something in his stomach as once again he'd heaved all over the deck during high-speed maneuvers to contact, threatening everyone that if they didn't look away he'd beat them within an inch of their lives when this was all over. If they survived.

No one looked away.

But no one called him "ghey," which is the standard hassle infantry use when any one of them does anything from using the restroom to getting dressed in the field.

No one says that because Punch has his tag for a reason.

Anyway, when the *Spider*'s main guns were firing and Punch was punching the buttons at the dispensary for his shakes… he actually got banana flavor and chocolate too which is crazy as the ship hasn't ever worked those flavors, or any, in my entire time with the company. It was a small miracle and when he told everyone in the racks, the rest of Reaper, it was received like some good omen that the battle would go well for the company.

We are simple mongos that way.

And…

Wolfy shouted, "Hotsoup is with us!" in his role of high priest of the Cult of Hotsoup, and everyone shouted…

Sigh.

"Hotsoup!"

I told you… I am the keeper of this log and I put everything in it. Even the things I hate.

At the same time the *Spider* fires her main guns, the *Murdock* erupts with four MKED torpedoes out of her forward tubes.

MKED. Mass Kinetic Energy Disruptor torpedoes.

Those torpedoes are already generating disruption energy when they streak and sidewinder past our hull. We lose power, backup kicks in, and that's what happened.

Then they continue on toward their targets.

The MKEDs... it's like watching four tiny suns burst into sudden life and tumble almost in slow motion given the currently incredible speed we're approaching the *Dark Star* at.

I will say this... a space battle is a beautiful thing. Like watching a quad fifty loaded with tracer fire.

But... way bigger and more.

Again... we mongos are amused by destructive forces. It's a ruck-hobo thang.

The MKED torps are moving slightly faster, and they manage to hit with three, each slamming into the superstructure of the enemy vessel like a dropped dumb bomb from the ages of long ago. Exploding volcanoes of sudden cascading damage. The hull is breached along the upper saucer of the giant disc now as components and probably crew and personnel are suddenly either immolated via being exposed to the intense star-like heat of the MKEDs, or vented into outer space. But internals are definitely scored as hits by the battle computers at the back of the flight deck of the *Spider*, crunching their numbers, or most likely on the giant "Looking Glass" that is the tactical sand table readout aboard the *Thunderer,* which I've seen on a couple of occasions.

To once more dive in and explain just how massive the *Dark Star* is, compared to the fleet of the thirty-some-odd ships converging on it... minus the *Asumasaryti*... those MKED torpedoes off the *Murdock* in battle simulations past against lesser vessels we were making simulated attack runs against... punched shields, superstructure, and game-overed the other side all on richly game-worthy-level graphics.

It was exciting to see, and it made us feel better about our chances.

In combat sim.

Now, seeing it in real time, up close and screaming in hot with more weapons to dump... it was again almost underwhelming despite the debris volcanoing up and away from the besieged *Dark Star* which was starting to get underway with motive power from her massive mains at the rear of the disc-ship.

Also, breaches in the upper hull were not optimal for our boarding needs, and already Tac Plan from the CIC aboard the *Thunderer* was telling us to disregard these points as possible boarding attempt sites and to stand by to make strikes against the ringed sides of the immense ship.

After *Murdock* fired her torpedoes, *Sinjon* and *Black Cat* fired their guns. Actually railguns that dumb-fired without smart projectiles like missiles are.

Sinjon was a twenty-six-railgun frigate with amazing computers that had been installed just before the collapse, and mutiny, of her crew who then joined the galactic insurrection. Her fire-control systems were the latest, and the ARCADE system, as it was known, could run firing plots and strikes for up to five ships using the AJAX auto-loader. Each of these railgun systems fired ten-meter rounds of core titanium tipped with a copper plate. When the round struck, the titanium savaged the actual hull armor upon penetrating, then, as integrity of the round collapsed in microseconds, expended a massive charge behind the giant copper disc that then surged forward into the breach area, ripping everything in front of it to utter shreds.

Applied explosive strength and kinetic impact could penetrate at least ten decks deep into an enemy warship.

Sinjon had twenty-six of these that fired twenty "rounds" per minute out of each gun for a total of five hundred and twenty per minute from one ship alone.

The display of firepower was utterly brutal.

Again, remember space combat lives and dies in under a minute… so this volume of fire was considered critical in the design and usage of the railgun platform vessels like *Sinjon* and *Black Cat*.

Black Cat had eighteen railguns and was considered, within the fleet, a light cruiser even though she was merely a heavily armored freighter that had been rigged by the technocrats early on as a Q-ship to fight pirates the Monarchs had refused to handle and were most likely financing as they tried to put pressure on some world they had designs on.

Black Cat was a bit of a pirate herself and had preyed on Monarch shipping through the war, taking in forty-eight prizes in the Vega Campaigns that had gone down during the company's long sleep to Marsantyium.

The Vega Campaigns had ended with the destruction of the *Dark Pegasus*, an Ultra Battle Spire, and the loss of the 54th Ultra Marine Legion.

Brutal losses to the Monarchs, and from history I've been able to put together, that was a turning point in the Star Khans/chimps war against the tyrants of human-controlled space.

Anyway, as I sat there in the crash seat, marking my intercept plots as all hell broke loose and *Black Cat* lobbed her fire, three hundred and sixty ten-meter copper-plated dumb rounds, plus the five hundred twenty off *Sinjon*, they looked like tiny silvery needles in space streaking straight in at the immense *Dark Star*, I was feeling better about this even though all that PTSD in advance told me we were still gonna lose.

Still, this… was gonna hurt… them. And maybe that would make a difference on those bloody decks I'd been plagued with…

Maybe?

Then we hit the blast wave of the Andromeda-class super-freighter the Monarchs had taken and just detonated.

Remember I said that was gonna be a problem?

Suddenly we lost all electronics and instruments as our hull flew through the streaking debris of one of the largest freight haulers the galaxy had ever managed to build. Something the size of a flying city with a gas refinery on board crewed by as little as eight people.

Some of the railgun rounds got through the blast wave as Beast One and Two kept spitting death.

The rest got ate up as the assault element of the fleet flew right into the sudden debris storm of the former super-freighter.

It was a clever play on the Monarchs' part, and as we lost power to the bridge and XO screamed at Fritz to pop the bus on the emergency batteries adding, "Slam your fist into it if it doesn't do it the first try"…

... I thought we were dead there for a second as we sat there in utter darkness, only the light show of destruction coming through the slit of the forward ob.

I closed my eyes, no power to the board, or station, I closed my eyes and embraced... whatever was coming next as a wave of tumbling debris slammed into the hull.

It sounded like all the giant hailstones that will rain down on the end of existence itself.

Breach alarms were already going off.

The ship listed hard to port... and everything felt...

Out of control.

Less than thirty seconds had elapsed since we'd attacked.

We were clearly out of action. A sitting duck. Destruction imminent. M.O.M. patiently instructing us to abandon ship now.

I was like...

"Really... that fast?"

CHAPTER THIRTY-ONE

Power to the flight deck came back online moments later. Maybe a few seconds. Or not even that. But in a battle between starships gunning away at each other with a weapons system that could just delete capital ships in one shot… it felt like forever.

There was also good news, and of course bad news.

Good news.

We had power, shields, guns, no serious breaches.

Bad news.

The *Lynx* didn't make it out of the debris cloud from the super-freighter's explosion. She was now tumbling away with the blast wave in multiple sections with distress beacons spreading out all over near-space.

That was bad.

And right now, observing the tac-plot… there wasn't much that could be done for people whose lifespan was being measured in under five minutes to a few seconds.

More screaming chatter that had nothing to do with life pods, escape boats, or rescue markers and just men and women screaming as their entire ship came apart about them.

"M.O.M.!" shouted XO from the pilot's seat, his voice a ragged heaving bark. "Filter out the non-essential comm. Tac and Movement only!"

XO is all business.

Alarms were going off.

Weapons fire alerts pulsing.

Breach indicators shrieking.

Shield warnings warning.

Reactor updates from our three working power plants. They were over-strained and close to redline.

And M.O.M.

M.O.M. was M.O.M.

"I am trying… dear. But currently there are five hundred eighty-three distress calls and assorted beacons. I can only do so much, dear."

Her voice matronly and calm. The passive aggression was there. But still, amidst all the chaos of combat in space, as seen through a simple ruck hobo's eyes, it was as though somewhere, wherever she was, it was afternoon, and there was tea almost ready, and perhaps freshly baked chocolate chip cookies you could sit with her over, and talk about things that didn't matter in the long run, but which maybe you needed some advice about now.

Losing yourself in something valuable you once had and can't remember how you lost it along the way.

Instead of… horrific death in the toe-to-toe combat that is space battle. Violent, and sudden.

"Punch… status?" I needed to check on my platoon down in the racks.

"We good, Sarge. No breaches. No injuries. Gunny tellin' us about the time one of his sister platoons in the Marines got murked all at once on an insert just like this one. So… you know… we got that goin' for us, Sarge."

Tortuga Cluster, a DL, light destroyer, configured with short-range direct-fire missile pods, swept in fast ahead of *Spider* on the forward ob and began to unload everything she had. Streams of hot lightning slammed into the immense hull of the enemy ship, ripping more plating and superstructure to shreds.

Impressive on the monitoring feeds as I watched impacts and continued to plot calcs and nearby intercepts as we closed… the *Spider*'s powerful main guns firing again and again in slow intervals compared to all that frenetic action going on all around us from the dozens of other starships in the fleet now swarming the *Dark Star*… but through the forward windows, scratched and pockmarked by time… so much time… the damage to the target vessel seemed minimal.

The truth was the *Dark Star* was simply a massive interstellar vehicle and even calling it a ship seemed… *inaccurate*. It was like a floating city. Or a small country on some upstart world we'd ruined long ago.

Victory and *Chaos*, two destroyers running overcharged B-beam batteries that could fire faster than the bigger C's, began to emit huge salvos from amidships as they closed in fast, ripping more hull plating away from the under-fire *Dark Star*.

In response, *Dark Star* opened fire from her waist with beam guns of her own, scoring hits on several ships that began to ululate damage reports over fleet comm.

We had one torpedo bay operational on the *Spider*, and it was now at this moment in the assault approach that XO ordered the weapons deployed.

That was my other job.

As the main weapons officer station was being run by Freako, torpedo launch management was done by M.O.M., except for the actual launching.

Which was my slot as the secondary weapons officer.

All M.O.M. did was run the weapon once it was live in space and tracking target.

I stood, worked my way out of my seat in EVC suit sans helmet, crossed the aisle between flight stations, and tapped in the release codes on an actual hard-key numerical keypad.

Old school. The numbers were even backlit.

Some allied vessel exploded and the ship rocked hard, but the weapons console received the command authorization and unlocked a small torpedo release panel. I flipped it open, hit three master arming switches, and pulled down the launch handle as I'd trained to do.

My work was done.

What did you do in the last great space battle against the Monarchs, Daddy?
I pulled a launch handle, son.

Not all heroes wear chest rigs.

Spider fired one more salvo as M.O.M. launched the torpedo weapon system and the *Spider* heeled hard to port, peeling off from the assault approach, automated waist batteries beginning to fire to little effect against *Dark Star*'s constantly regenerating shield systems.

Suddenly the ship's PDCs went to work. We had enemy vessel target locks almost instantly. All were screaming alerts as we were being tracked and engaged via missile fire off the *Dark Star*.

It was our turn now to take some serious attention from the enemy. I had this sick feeling in my stomach as I made my way back to the nav station like some over-bundled child on a wintery world.

"Torpedo away…" announced M.O.M. quietly through the entire ship, her voice echoing down empty passages as everyone was in their combat stations or the assault racks.

Then… "Fifteen seconds to impact." Her voice calm, reassuring. "Please move the ship to a safe distance."

XO ignored that. There was no place safe to run.

Us and two other ships were now going for broke and trying to shut down the *Dark Star*'s ability to jump… or space-fold, or whatever it was she did, we really didn't know, and she'd gotten here faster than we did, so there's that… to escape the battle.

This was all part of the carefully developed plan.

How were we gonna do that, you ask?

Hit her with sixty-megaton warheads.

The *Spider*, *Surriabas Maru*, and *War Cry* were each carrying three old-school multi-megaton torpedoes. Weapon systems once used long ago in other long-ago wars and battles not this one. Of course the Monarchs had kept them back for themselves, but they were almost nonexistent for private contractor or independent planetary government use.

Somehow, during those twenty years of war between and among the Star Khans, the chimps, and the Monarchs, the insurrection had hit some weapons cache where they'd found more than a few…

Several got used taking down the Battle Spires at various battles.

Three were held back for this final battle, and we had the honor of firing one as we were one of the few vessels that had launchers that could still fire these museum pieces.

In an instant the entire attack fleet was breaking off what had been the feint all along. Or what we would have called back in the infantry… the *probe*.

That was all this initial attack was meant to do.

The *Dark Star*, for all the damage we were doing to her right now, wasn't putting up a huge fight and we were wondering if she even had enough weapons to fight back.

Or was her plan just to get her Dark Lab engines up and disappear forever to some place we'd never find in our lifetimes?

This was our only shot to kill her.

So far she had that one starship-destroying beam weapon shot, but that seemed to be limited use and perhaps it was recharging before it could fire again.

And most assuredly, a lot of people were going to die once that happened.

So best to get it done in one, son, as Gunny liked to say.

That and *Fix yo'self at a high rate of speed afore I have to write yo' mama and tell 'er you died due to lack of motivation.*

So the plan had been to go ahead and make a quick attack with what seemed our main thrust, the assault section of the fleet. Support and Ranged were in position and ready. In about sixty seconds, if the battle lasted that long, Ranged was going to target *Dark Star*'s cyclopean engines with a full-spectrum missile engagement that, to this simple ruck hobo… had looked excessively apocalyptic.

I was all for that.

I'd seen planets that had been hit with that level of ranged missile fire strikes. They were little more than pockmarked hellholes burnt to a crust where the wind never stopped blowing that used to be megatropolises and Class A starports.

Really impressive stuff.

Now all a smoking pile of ruin.

No one called them this, but I did… I called them *Hollow Worlds*. As though beyond the utter savagery of a D-beam strike in the six-gigawatt range, old-school missile strikes like the one we were about to pull, could just flat gut a world on levels few had ever seen.

The first sergeant had seen them.

I was sure the Old Man, if what I believed about him was true, and of course Ulysses Two Alpha Six being an Ultra Marine, he had seen them too.

That was an Ultra specialty.

But the first sergeant had for sure.

"Engetti… saw one of those," he said one time. "Crisped the whole world like some buckshot road sign out in the middle o' nowhere. Everything targeted… roads, infrastructure, cities, canals, fields, assets… all of it just gone in under five hell-like-you-ain't-never-seen minutes. Expensive too, I'll bet. Not as utterly powerful and cheap as an Ultra D-beam, but a kinda hell I don't like to think about much these days now that I got older, young sergeant. These days… find myself pretty much just wanting to forget. Just remember what pretty girls looked like when I was young and the galaxy was a place where anything could happen and you wanted to be a part of it… not the way it'd become. Feel me on that, Sergeant Orion?"

"Yeah…" I told the first sergeant. He was getting more and more like this, going on about the past, and not liking the present and how it had turned out. I wondered how much we were all becoming like that.

Yeah, First Sergeant. I feel ya.

In an instant, *Dark Star* was now breaking away from our attack and lifting the side of the disc we were facing as she picked up a new course trajectory and fired her point defenses as though the combat intelligence that ran her systems knew there were three "fish in the water."

Fish in the water was starship slang in rough use across navy types regarding the use of nuclear-armed torpedoes.

"She's reading the threat!" shouted someone from across the comm.

At the same time, commanders were broadcasting the "EMP Harden" command as all systems were Faradayed or went offline to deal with the sudden aftereffects of one hundred and eighty tons of offensive nuclear yield being deployed in near-space.

XO was calling out seconds left to impact.

Half a second to det, one of the weapons ate the bright gloss of incoming from the *Dark Star*'s point defense systems, frenetic short-range lasers rather than actual dumb rounds like most of our PDC cannons in the Star Khans' fleet.

"Two left!" shouted a comm operator off the *Thunderer*. You could feel the desperation.

We'd already lowered the blast shields on our flight helmets and then there was a bright flash and XO shouted, "Impact!"

I closed my eyes.

Seconds later the *Spider* was hit by a colossal blast wave, as was the rest of the fleet. It was so powerful that we lost forward motive power even though the engines were operating at max maneuver thrust and we'd managed to get the sluggish bow into the blast wave.

Shields were at "Max full!" Batteries feeding the shields, the entirety of deck seventeen of the *Spider*… a place where Nether will often hang out because the raw power on that deck of the *Spider* will actually render him a dim shadow and he feels that's easier for people to deal with when they want to talk.

Very few people want to talk with Nether even though everyone says they "like" him. There's something about being "not there" that bothers them on some primal human level we haven't yet been able to figure.

I go.

We play Cheks and talk.

He takes a drag and burns my smokes in one go.

I can only take so much time on deck seventeen, and it's hard to get a good night's sleep after having that much loose power coursing through your system. You feel both high and wired for days to come and if you don't know how to handle it… it's… *unsettling*.

So anyway, the blast from the two "fish" that managed to strike the *Dark Star* drained our shields down to the last block of rows on the defensive screen readout. As the ship rolled on through the blast wave and tremored so hard it felt like the central spine would crack in half, I watched the critical warning indicators pulse red as the last block of shielding reached *CRITICAL* on the glowing readout on a nearby monitor, then reached for the reserve shield power slaved from deck seventeen in an instant.

But the shields held.

The bridge descended into darkness, and we could see nothing out of the forward ob for a long moment. Then the *Victory* went supernova off our starboard bow as her reactors overloaded and she just popped like a sudden Tiberian candle.

Other ships were dead or wounded badly and limping off the tactical plot.

Most survived though…

"Damage report," muttered XO as he tried to restore power to maneuver and weapons systems, hammering the master buses with his fist and swearing at the old destroyer as he did so.

"Number one reactor offline," reported a guy from one of the new platoons who was running the engineering panels and doing a horrible job of rerouting power here and shutting down power there to certain other decks we didn't need for this fight.

XO was yelling at him.

"Decks below nine are down. Integrity to cargo solid."

Cargo was what the "assault decks" were officially called on the ship's schematics.

We're elite like that.

Nothing but the best for us.

But that was good. Reaper and the other platoons were solid even though Punch was pinging me to ask what the hell had just happened.

I could see through the forward ob now.

Yeah, the *Victory* was now a bright star in the night sky. A stunning sight on any easy day.

But this was no easy day.

This was a battle unlike any of us had ever seen, and we really, as a fighting unit of private military contractors with a debt to the monkey Kong to fulfill, had yet to be in it.

The verdict was still out as to whether we'd put boots on the deck of the enemy vessel.

So, on a day like today, the sudden explosion of a Decider-class destroyer was nothing. Not even the six hundred lives that had gone dark in an instant.

We were too busy betting our lives on the next maneuver and phase of the plan.

Everything, in that first moment of looking out the forward ob at the front of the *Spider*'s flight deck, a high dark window below our instrument panels and flight stations, a flat, dark, uninspiring murder slit for a destroyer to see what it was intent on killing, as had been its design, everything out that slit seemed frozen in time for half a second as I watched it and flipped back the blast shield on the crash helmet that came with the flight station.

That helmet.

A bit of color. A note regarding the flight helmet that goes with this station on the *Spider* in this... account... of the Strange Company. It means nothing. It's not relevant to this tragedy I was given to write down as we approach... the event horizon of this portion of the company's tale of woe I am responsible for. But, there are old markings on it.

During sim time, when we were getting ready to run some combat scenario or some damage control procedure, and XO was giving his flight instruction class, I would study it and wonder at all the lost crew who wore it.

It's loose on me.

We don't have another one and one cannot be made for me.

M.O.M. won't marry any other interactive system to the nav station nor any of the other stations.

"These are original use design intended for this starship, dear," she'd say every time we tried. "I am sorry. But these belong here. With me."

The name of the original... *astronaut*... crew member... to use this has long been scratched off. But sometimes, in certain lights, I can make out a few letters. The name of an old corporation is there. The symbol of a red spider lies faded and scratched on one side.

Some old words I don't know and the databases can't translate because the Monarchs destroyed everything they didn't want to explain.

I think it's Latin.

Volare-Fuge-Win

Some old warrior motto for the unit that ran this ship when she first went out into the great big dark we call deep space.

Long ago.

No one knows how old the *Spider* really is. Like I said… we got her cheap because she was way past her operational prime and that was long before I signed on the dotted line to join the company.

It's weird to think things have been going on long before you showed up. Strange when you're young and you think you're somehow the main character in a big story. Odd when you figure out you're not.

Maybe not everyone needed that reckoning. But I sure did and it's part of how I ended up here.

Hopefully I'll have time to tell that story before things go… where I think they're going. But I'm not looking forward to it. Still hurts and you'll think less of me.

There are other stickers. Other markings. On the nav flight station helmet.

Some I have figured out. Old corporations. Old units. Slang and bravado. But there is one that eludes me and I have no idea what it means… though I am sure… it was once… *important*.

NASA.

Probably an acronym.

But I have no idea what it means.

So, that's just for color. A little bit of what the battle looked like and the hobos that fought in it, and some of the gear we wore.

For future generations. By that time… see *Not my circus, not my monkey*s.

Log Keeper of the next deeds of the Strange… I leave the riddle of the flight helmet and NASA for you if it's even interesting. I have a feeling it won't be. And I don't know how much longer the *Spider* can carry us to our wars where we fight for pay. After this battle we must've put a few hundred more years on her when we launched the HM185-TONW at the *Dark Star*.

HM185. Stenciled on the old torp when we loaded her in the launch tube below the bridge stack of the ship.

Heavy Munitions Class One-Eight-Five.

TONW.

Tactical Offensive Nuclear Weapon.

And below that…

Imperial Monarch Navy.

Factus sum mors.

Now… back to what I saw out the forward ob after the nuclear strike against the *Dark Star*…

I stared in utter horror at what we had done to that… *enigmatic*… and terrible ship that may have been our last link to *who*, or *what, we* once were. Every ship still operational in the fleet began to move in slow motion. Or that's how it seemed to me.

Slowly, as though time had stopped and we were all moving through syrup, struggling to be free. Struggling for time to resume…

Perhaps we'd broken time somehow? Perhaps the strange mad science on board the *Dark Star* and our sudden nuclear strike…

I don't know.

We were dealing with unknowns here.

That's all I can say.

But the fleet, blown and scattered everywhere, or at least the assault section was… was powering up, struggling back in for the kill on the big ship we'd hunted and run down.

It was clearly wounded.

In the distance I could already see the missile trails streaking toward it from the ranged section of the fleet. Firing their doomsday missile strike against the Monarchs' massive main engine systems at the aft of the vessel.

In the foreground… our ships, slowing getting back underway. Weapons systems that could fire opening up once again even as what appeared to be catastrophic damage to the enemy vessel was assessed.

And in the middle of it all.

The *Dark Star*.

A prize to some.

A kill to the company.

Simply put… the two nukes had blown a massive section out of the saucer on the nearest side. We could see hundreds of levels of open decking and venting oxygen even as fires roared from internal sections into the vacuum extinguishing them almost immediately. And still the onboard fires raged, for such was the volume of available oxygen within the behemoth of a starship.

Debris already trailed away like gossamer starlight disintegrated by nuclear fire.

In that half second… I thought…

We'd won. Maybe. It's done. Hopefully.

We won't have to live through what I'd dreamed we would in those PTSD nightmares.

We wouldn't have to board and fight compartment-to-compartment. Hatch-to-hatch. Stranger-against-stranger the deeper we went in.

The ship would just break up now, and we'd be spared the horror.

Or perhaps… whatever fantastic power system that made her what she was would go nova now… and do her in.

Game over, man.

In hindsight I could say we and everyone in the system, probably the colony and the gas giants too, would have been vaporized in an instant if that had happened.

That ship's power plant was… *interdimensional*. We would have all… gone… poof.

That's the simplest way I can explain.

But none of that happened.

And the ship was not totally destroyed.

Only a chunk was cut out of her by nuclear fire. A big chunk. A *massive* chunk. But still…

More than eighty percent of the ship was still intact and my guess is now… that had the doomsday strike from the ranged section of the fleet not totally disabled her huge main engines… engines three times bigger than any ship we were fielding… twice as big as a Battle Spire end-to-end if stood upright top to bottom to span the exhaust of the mains… then my guess is that ship would have been able to execute her space-fold, or whatever, and depart… even as severely wounded as she was.

That would've been my guess.

Now the doomsday missile strike slammed in across the huge main engines and destroyed them completely. Huge pox-like blisters erupted all across the aft hull of the disc, the missiles bunker-busting deep down into the titanic engineering sections of the massive interstellar vessel and exploding internally.

And again… let that sink in. The ship was so huge that bunker-buster ship-to-ship missiles exploded with high-yield munitions… and only left blisters on the outer hull.

Later we'd cross into those sections and see the incredible damage wrought by that apocalyptic strike.

But in that first moment, viewing it out the forward ob and on the feeds of all angles coming in from Ranged and other sections of the assault fleet… our weapons seemed ineffectual and weak. And when the ship did not come apart or explode and kill us all… my hopes of not having to compartment-to-compartment breach-and-clear, double-tap-stab… died.

I knew we'd be going in next.

And that many of us would die.

I'd seen it all before.

I unbuckled from the nav station, placed the flight helmet back on its peg above the workstation.

I felt weak.

I was on uncertain ground now. But I knew what I had to do next if we were gonna have any kind of shot at surviving the boarding action.

What did Gunny say as he ran us through the shoot deck again and again, making us aware of our deficiencies?

Fix yo'self at a high rate of speed.

CHAPTER THIRTY-TWO

In that moment… the fleet of the Star Khans dissolved in ways I don't think anyone beyond the captain and myself knew. The enemy ship was clearly wounded.

But we weren't a fleet now.

We weren't a new stellar "nation" like everyone in Rogue Fleet, *yeeehawww, boys!!!* had been going on about.

In the Strange Company we were mercenaries. All of us. We had no flag. No motto. No cause.

Everyone else in the fleet who'd been fighting to greater or lesser degrees the tyrants of human-controlled space for twenty years… suddenly seemed to realize they had the chance to take what had been denied them as the massive disc, one side of it badly damaged, failed to jump away as her aft sections got repeatedly pounded by targeted missile strikes.

All that patriotism and rah-rah freedom…

Died when the commanders of all those ships saw the potential to have what the Monarchs had stolen.

And their hearts were filled with darkness.

I have no idea where that comes from. It sounds like something that should be in a book, but it's not in any book I've ever read.

But dark hearts…

The company had them and was well familiar with the concept in others.

We'd come here to kill people and break stuff on a contract of sorts.

It was like the rest of the fleet suddenly figured out that angle as the boarding assault began and cohesive fleet chatter over the comm went silent.

Everything was OPSEC now.

More prizes for the survivors that way.

"Commence boarding operations…" went out over the comm. And then… it was everyone for themselves. Like some stellar frontier exotic mineral rush on some newly discovered world.

The only reason the command team of the Strange Company knew what would happen next was because we were mercenaries who gather about battlefields like carrion birds looking for an easy meal.

We have to be honest about these things.

We understood.

In an instant the grand plan to assault cohesively seemed… halfhearted, at best. The beast was clearly more wounded than anyone could imagine.

In an instant it was every ship for themselves.

But here was the truth and maybe this helps whoever reads this next to understand…

There was Monarch tech on board that ship. And whoever could get it… could be more than just… *filthy rich*. Or incredibly powerful.

They could become… *the Monarchs themselves*. But better this time, right? Few were able to resist the siren call of possibilities as boarding operations got underway. Small alliances and groups of ships swarmed in to where they thought "the meat" of the great beast was sweet and tastiest regarding Dark Labs tech.

Within hours no one was following commands from the CIC on the *Thunderer*.

Ships and their complements were going in… alone and in small groups. The slightest bit of strange super Dark Science tech off that ship could make someone… someones… rich beyond the dreams of avarice.

Far more than discovering a new world.

Far. Far. More.

I doubt most realized the paradigm shift of what this meant. Most thought they could get in, get out with something… then coast through the rest of their, and the rest of their grandchildren's… lives.

Some… shining… bit of… strange tech would do the trick. Forever.

The Monarchs had kept all the best for themselves. For the last run off into the dark.

Rumors spread like wildfire. And if we're honest about these things… they'd been spreading for the whole hunt.

It had been in our hearts all along.

Our *Hearts of Darkness*.

Stinkeye tries to scare everyone with something he calls "da Heart o' Darkness, Little King."

I got news for you… all our hearts are dark. That's what I've learned in this long trek across the stars. This tragedy.

We took whoever we were, thought we were going out there to be better, and ended up the same bunch of goblins in the dark doing dirty deeds.

Most of the fleet didn't even realize… *we were all enemies now*.

The company did. Knew it would happen in hushed discussions on the flight deck as we prepared for this mess. We'd planned for it too.

We're *people* people that way.

We knew what we had to do now.

We knew what our debt to the monkey Kong was.

Board. Then kill the Monarchs and their minions still waiting in that burning ship. Make sure nothing escapes… if we could.

The Monarchs would end here. And now.

Not even their strange magic would survive.

Nothing… could survive. Otherwise the galaxy would do it all again and if John Strange was right… it would end everything next time. Some perfect tyranny. Some unstoppable post-human civilization that knew neither love nor art nor anything we have that vaguely qualifies as a "redeeming quality."

Or… some perfect doomsday weapon next time. The one that just erases existence, and the universe while it's at it.

Theoretically it's possible.

Give the goblins time, and we'll figure out a way to destroy everything.

Ask a space merc how he knows.

So it was all... or nothing around the carcass of the *Dark Star* as boarding ops commenced.

I believe few understood what was really going on in that moment as all surviving ships swarmed the cadaver to board and kill their way to a fortune in forbidden tech or die trying.

And they would. She wasn't... dead. Just wounded.

We understood.

We'd been warned.

CHAPTER THIRTY-THREE

All the PTSD horrors of what would happen now came pushing into my mind as I unbuckled from my crash seat on the flight deck and made ready to reach the *Spider*'s troop decks and lead the assault I'd dreamed would be the end of the company.

We were going to die.

I'd seen that. Dozens of times.

Lived it.

It was... *real*.

My legs didn't want to move.

But I made them.

Only XO was left on the flight deck as everyone went to their platoons. He was flying the approach to the target even though we were taking heavy fire from *Dark Star*'s point defense batteries.

The *Spider*'s own PDCs were singing on low deep bass notes of chain-gun fire as they ate up incoming anti-ship missiles.

Long *braaaaaaaaaaaapppps...*

I wanted to say goodbye. And tell him...

Run. Live. Survive. Don't fly the approach, XO.

But... I knew this whole section of the ship was about to get hit by a railgun shell when we made the insert. And that XO would die here, doing his job.

Near-space around the ship was a hot mess of outgoing and incoming fire. Ships were jockeying for attack positions on the corpse of the great fish we'd run down.

Like some long-lost literary tale I'd never read but knew about of men and the sea.

And it was too late...

I knew what would happen next.

I turned and tapped my comm control on the left sleeve of the EVC.

"M.O.M...."

"Yes, dear. Hull integrity is holding at eighty-seven-point-four percent, but there is currently a problem with reactor two. Advise shutdown and immediate return to a Class One starship repair facility. Main guns are operating beyond parameters and Cyberdyne Armaments cannot be held liable for any internal discharges at this time... dear."

I had no idea who Cyberdyne Armaments was. Just another old corp that had contributed to the *Spider* long before any of us had ever been born.

In Olden Earth Days Long Ago, as the song goes.

Days... that were all but barely remembered myths now.

"M.O.M.... stand by to receive a priority access authorization..."

"Standing by, dear. Forward shields collapsing. Lateral controls failing..."

"M.O.M., initiate Nostromo protocol."

There was a short pause... and then her matronly voice came back.

"Confirmed, dear. Nostromo initiated. Please give the verbal password to initiate the sequence now..."

I cleared my throat and moved to the rear of the ancient flight deck, passing the last flight stations that hadn't been occupied in decades. XO couldn't hear me. But he was busy now, his ears filled with constant instruments and scratchy flight traffic.

"Nuclear Bolt... One," I said.

"Accepted," replied M.O.M. "Please enter the ID sequence..."

I'd already brought up the keypad on the EVC's sleeve. The ancient Numerica symbols.

I entered the code, desperately hoping I was getting it right. Forty-two, eight times.

Pause.

Had I gotten it wrong? My whole plan hinged on this. Otherwise... we were all gonna die on that hangar deck I'd seen too many times.

"Access granted, dear. What do you wish to do?"

I took a deep breath.

Then...

"Initiate self-destruct, M.O.M."

What I had just done was... *unthinkable*.

"Yes, dear. This operation will require the proper code string and authentication from flight command crew..."

I interrupted her.

"Flight command crew killed or missing in action..."

"Checking..."

I held my breath. I'd entered her Memory Prime, deep within the ship, to pull this hack. And to be clear... I am not trained in hacking multi-sequential alpha-level intelligences. So, there is that.

We have to be honest about these—

"Confirmed. Sergeant James P. Orion. Current senior-most surviving flight crew. Status... in command of vessel. Clearance to initiate self-destruct of vessel granted. But remember, dear, you must have all three codes from senior flight crew to initiate this operation."

"I have the codes, M.O.M. Stand by to receive."

Patiently and slowly... I gave the proper codes to destroy the ship.

"Destruct sequence 1, code 1-1 A."

"Destruct sequence 2, code 1-1 A-2B."

"Destruct sequence 3, code 1 B-2B-3."

Pause.

For a hot second I thought I'd botched it all somehow. It was a lot to remember, what with everything else going on. Space battle. Destroyed capital starships, last Monarch fortress waiting for us to assault... all that death, ours, I'd seen.

But she was back.

"Confirmed, dear. Destruct sequence engaged. Awaiting final code for countdown."

Aw yeahhhh, I thought and realized I was playing a very dangerous game here.

But it was the only ogre card I had. If you play Cheks then you know what that means.

"Code is zero... zero... zero... destruct..."

I held my breath.

"Zero."

My dark nightmares were somehow engraved in stone... the fabric of the universe... that is my mind.

What was I doing?

I'd decided to throw a little chaos into the mix and see if I had a play to make.

"Countdown begun..." replied M.O.M.

I tapped another string of numbers that would prevent her from announcing the countdown ship-wide and blowing my plan. Everyone else didn't need that right now.

Especially XO.

The ship was getting pounded by defensive fire.

If all went well... this would work.

And then... they'd have a lot more on their plates to deal with shortly.

"This vessel will detonate in five minutes and fifty-eight seconds." The countdown had begun in my ear only. "Please reach a minimum safe distance, dear. And have a nice day."

CHAPTER THIRTY-FOUR

The *Spider* was rattling and shaking as it entered the local gravitational well of the super-giant starship that was the immense *Dark Star*. Engines were throttling up to attack speed. Down below in the troop decks, last checks would be made. Motivation would attempt to be spread. Last words, and sometimes last texts, were sent… to whomever was still out there, somewhere in the great big galactic dark, who cared. Or once did.

Was waiting for some small words from across the galaxy on which to hang on by.

Even PMCs want that last connection to stay open. No matter how hard, how grim, how dark they've gotten. Or the circumstances of their leaving. Perhaps "someone" is still out there, down the line and long ago, waiting for a final word.

Or just… a word.

In that moment I couldn't think of anyone. But maybe that was the fear that had ahold of me bad for what I was about to do next.

"Dear… there are five minutes and thirty-three seconds to detonation of this vessel. Please move to a safe distance."

I left the flight deck and found Chief Cook standing there grinning at me in the passage to the lifts. His EVC was perfect. Bucket in one hand. Dark, mirrored sunglasses on even though the ship was under emergency red battle lighting.

They were as a part of him as Stinkeye's totem flask was of our drunken war wizard.

Incoming fire hammered the hull somewhere. Damage alarms in distant sections wailed. Bulkheads were being sealed.

M.O.M. rattled off damage reports and recommended safety precautions, advising us, as she always did, that some long-forgotten corporation was not responsible for loss of life, injury, and limb.

"You still want to do this?" asked the Voodoo psyops chief, grinning that tombstone grin of his. As though he was actually excited about what was about to happen next.

I tried to say something but my mouth was dry. Too dry to speak. I croaked something but the damage sirens masked it. That didn't stop the chief.

"All warfare is deception, Orion. Hell… do it right and you can even make them kill themselves for you."

I didn't agree with that, totally. I'd seen a lot of fights that were nothing more than just sheer violence and the willingness to hurt the other guys until they stopped and you got to go home that night. I get the deception angle… but honestly… you can overplay that and turn into nothing more than cheap liars fighting with cheap lies. Like children's birthday party magicians and starport carnies with "freak aliens" that are really just pathetically surgically enhanced humans who had nothing left to lose.

Lie too much and along comes the hard fist of reality breaking all your teeth and stabbing you in the guts while it curb-stomps your head. There's something to be said for reality... and violence. Because sometimes, as Punch likes to say... violence is the answer.

Or so has been my experience. Most lies die in the brutal light of extreme violence. Attend and know wisdom, young ruck hobos.

I nodded and said nothing again because my mouth was dry. My throat was a desert canyon. Already the smell of burnt leaves and the heat of dry winds was all about me even though they were not... *real*.

Then...

But I couldn't let the fear win.

"Let's get it..." I swallowed just to get some moisture into my parched throat. Just to fight back the invisible monster that was telling me this was the dumbest plan ever. Which was saying something for me. "... on."

Chief Cook laughed and slapped me too hard on the shoulder. His laughter wasn't a pretty sound. And there was—and this bothered me—genuine mirth.

Usually his laugh doesn't match his body.

Like he's just faking it.

Now... he was really laughing. And it wasn't good.

"There's a winner!" he shouted enthusiastically. "*All right all right all right*, Orion... let's go make some trouble for the commies. Like that old space bastard says... only good one... *is a dead one*."

Then we hustled through the bloody dark as collision alert klaxons wailed and incoming fire alerts ululated for attention.

We reached the lift and I slammed my hand on the button that would take us to the drop tubes.

"M.O.M.... this is the authorized commander of *Spider*. The bridge has been disabled and is under threat of capture/compromise. Lock out flight controls and assume flight command for the ship for the time being."

XO was about to freak out and I hated to do this to him but it had to be this way if we were gonna have a chance.

"Dear... sensors are malfunctioning on the flight deck...."

I know. I disabled them and didn't tell M.O.M.

"All flight systems nominal and functioning give current ship operational lifespan. Four minutes and nineteen seconds until this ship self-destructs, dear."

I cleared my throat. "M.O.M., run an integrity check on your Memory Prime."

"Running... complete. Data architecture suboptimal and below Cyberdyne operational minimums. But... dear..."

She sounded weak. Uncertain. Unsure.

I thought of my own mother and wondered what had ever become of her. I'd been gone from home a long time.

I hated myself for what I was doing to her. Yes. M.O.M. She's just an ASI. Artificial Super Intelligence. She's old and she's always taken care of us and if you were to ask any of the brothers in Strange they'd tell you she was just as much a real person, and a member of the company, as they were.

She was our... M.O.M.

And more than a few of the company had never had one. The galaxy is filled with orphans.

Though no one had ever formally articulated this point... it was generally accepted as grounds upon which knives came out and enemy *villes* got *laid waste* that M.O.M. was one of us. Even if we got a new AI we were gonna compartmentalize her and let her run the mess.

We're having meatloaf, mashed potatoes, and green beans, dear. And there's cherry cobbler if you finish.

That would be... nice. And the opposite of right now.

But right now... I needed to trick her in order to do what I was gonna do next.

"M.O.M.," I interrupted. "Your sensors and compilation algorithms are damaged. Trust me as senior flight officer of *Spider*... the bridge is under threat. Assume flight controls. Lock out the bridge and execute Attack Pattern Delta as I have programmed you to."

Long pause.

Like some old lady trying to remember if she'd put two sugars in the tea, or already offered you a cookie when you'd arrived by surprise that unexpected afternoon. I wanted to... cry.

I know I seem like a monster... but I'm not. You gotta believe me. It's just that I can't prove it.

I know, add Hauser in, and I got problems when it comes to artificial intelligences. It's like... they're small children to me. Naive and needing to be protected not just from the universe and all its darkness... but from us, and all our bad.

And even me. A wily NCO who's trying to get his platoon and everyone else off the *X* and will do anything he can so everyone can get another slice of birthday cake.

AIs and children... we don't deserve them.

"Okay... dear," she said, still uncertain. A quaver in her voice algos that... I don't know. Had someone written that in long ago? Long before any of us were ever born and this ship was launched when everything was different and no one could foresee all these things happening to us?

Or is the universe... just strange that way. Inserting itself in a small way to remind you you don't know everything.

"Flight deck locked down, dear. Flight systems under my command now," she said happily.

As though... we'd both seen that forgetful moment of her collapsing algos and impending computational senility, the second time the plate of cookies was offered again... and then we'd gone on with the playlet as though it'd never really happened. And that... everything would be okay, and time and memory wouldn't degrade, or eat us up.

That tomorrow wouldn't come.

She was happy to be doing what she'd always done.

Flying the ship.

Protecting the crew.

Taking care of us.

"Attack Pattern Delta confirmed. Engaging engines and weapons now, dear. There are three minutes and fifty-two seconds until self-destruction, dear. Please evacuate the ship."

CHAPTER THIRTY-FIVE

The *Spider*'s drop tubes weren't something the company had used in much of my career. They were not original OG installation on the Warhammer-class NewMax destroyer that was our ship as she'd originally been intended to be.

The company, long before my time, and well after the time of John Strange, had had them installed after ripping out the mine racks the destroyer originally came with.

Mine racks were awesome, especially for running gun battles and battles where the destroyer was outnumbered and wanted to canalize enemy ships into an attack vector that made them come right at the forward-facing direct-fire main guns which could cripple a cruiser with direct hits.

But… mines were expensive and getting harder and harder to find for private military contractors in the years after John Strange. They were impossible and idiotic to recover if they weren't used, and frankly they were a hazard to stellar nav if they weren't detonated.

Which came with all kinds of other problems too.

So the company on some world with a Class B starport and major refit facilities, flush with mem from a solid contract, had opted for the drop tubes.

The company had inserted via jump protocols into planetside combat zones before, or critical battlespaces, by simply conducting airborne operations off the cargo decks, making sure everyone went through the jump-sims and spent a week training in the swing-lander tower setup we could deploy inside the main hangar en route to our contract.

I had made three such combat jumps and only one was hot. The other two were merely made into areas within the combat operations area where the enemy wasn't.

The one that was…

The company doesn't like to talk about that one, and of the twenty of us that survived, all of us have scars and replacement hardware inside us from that day. And… we straight-up ruined a local cav screening force looking to flank our employer's armored columns thinking we wouldn't be where we were.

Surprise. We jumped with tons of AT, anti-tank weapons, and some portable air defense artillery. We came out of a dark forest at twilight as the enemy cav tried to work around the main force's flanks and ended up getting them committed to a twenty-four-hour fight that saw over a thousand of their casualties and two battalions of scout and helo light armor ate up in the process.

And then we got screwed on the bonus and barely made it off-world for some of the other stuff they asked us to do and didn't want to face the war crimes tribunals over. So… they burned us to the Monarchs and we had to pay a huge fine to avoid being hunted down by the inquisitors and their dogs, the Ultra death squads.

Not important… but company background.

So the "drops," or drop tubes, are located on the starboard side of the ship, about three decks up from the "cargo" or "assault decks." The drops are for a different yet similar style of putting troops where they're not wanted.

By the enemy, that is.

The drop tubes are small… to make this explanation easier… torpedo tubes you can climb into. Once inside you grab on to a racked sled that has just popped into place. Then you get launched via railgun-style magnets out into deep space, hopefully near a starship that needs to be boarded.

So… a couple of things to consider about why and when we use this method of insertion.

The target starship has to be disabled with her primary thrusters and engines offline. The tubes are basically direct fire, and the *Spider* needs to roll onto her starboard side to fire the tubes "down" onto an enemy vessel in near-space. And the distance can't be that far, so it requires a very close pass.

Which is difficult when high-speed engagement and flight maneuvering are going on in normal combat in space between starships.

So… we disable the enemy vessel's engines. The ship may still be under drift for her speed and the *Spider* can get close and match that heading and speed.

The target ship might have maneuver thrusters that can change her basic attitude, or position in space—still a problem—and many ships have many of these ranging from dozens to hundreds and even thousands in some of the capital ship classes…

We'd never attempt this on anything that had some kind of maneuver capability like the giant *Dark Star* currently possessed.

But hey… here I am about to pull something we'd never do. Which basically sums up all military tactics. So… honest about these things and all. We must be. You know how it goes…

Okay, so in theory… the *Spider* closes, rolls onto her side, and the first batch of Strange are in the tubes and they grab the next racked sled to pop up in their individual tube. They are in their EVCs because that's the only way this is going to work because of space and all, and the tube-guns fire the sled out at the target vessel that's hopefully not too far away.

Trooper rides the sled right into the enemy hull, fires the one-shot braking thrusters on the sled, and that should, if he times it right, either angle him right into the enemy hull, or smash directly into it. The trick with drop-tube operations is to bail off the sled ten to twenty meters from target, and go starfish, angling onto the enemy hull to perform a proper HLF.

Hull Landing Fall.

The sims assure you that if you "starfish" properly you can even survive contact with the enemy hull at the sled's max thrust velocity, which it shouldn't be at if you're doing this right.

The sims assure you of this tested fact. So you got that goin' for you.

I have never seen it work. I have seen guys go in hot and shatter their spines only to drift off into space, paralyzed and supported by the EVC until the batteries run out. If we can recover them before that, then…

... then there's that whole thing. Long explanation having nothing to do with what I'm about to do.

Usually the company is engaged in contact with the enemy and the guy with the shattered spine doesn't get recovered until the sled's batteries are all depleted.

Why?

As in why did the company long ago try to add this tool to their repertoire?

Boarding and interdiction were all the rage… a long time ago… and PMCs got paid every way possible to run starship boardings and get it on toe-to-toe inside some enemy hull.

The Monarchs were the ones really paying for this kind of action when I first came into the company, and we made some pretty good mem doing it. The Ultras at the time were strangely missing from the galactic scene, and word was they were handling some dark force of "Star Giants" who'd attempted to penetrate human space on the outer frontier.

Meaning… rimward.

Those are the rumors. Frankly… sounds hokey to me. C'mon… Star Giants? LOL!

So, the Monarchs wanted a taste of all the commerce between the worlds while they were… *absent*… and many PMCs in lieu of ground combat were picking up drop tubes to get in on the action. Infantry were the best suited, and so the company made hay while we could. If you were some mercenary armor or dropship unit then this probably wasn't your *thang* and you went broke as the Monarchs weren't funding wars while the Ultras were missing, and just trying to take their cut of galactic trade by any means possible by wars they were igniting and funding on both sides for their own profit.

It apparently made sense to them.

In time the Ultras took up the work and the PMC contracts dried up and the Strange went back to the mud, the blood, and the glory that isn't light infantry warfare on some planet hellhole.

We're glamorous that way.

I have hull dropped… *once*.

It's important you read everything that happens after this with that in mind. If the log ends… well… you know.

And *one time*… that's another one I don't want to talk about because that one was a dumpster fire too. I missed the main hull and had to fire the sled's emergency reserve grappling dart or go spinning off into the black forever.

Note… if the possibility of suddenly tumbling off into the black cold void of deep space is even remotely possible in some op… the moment it starts to happen, you are supremely aware of how badly things are about to go for you. Like you never, ever were… before. Spinning wildly, watching the target hull sweep by as you "fall" away from the enemy ship that's your only way out of this…

… and believe me that's a weird concept to ingest and it's best not to spend so much time on that…

Your mind instantly calculates how rotten everything has gone for you as your body breaks out into a cold sweat inside your EVC suit… imagine being suddenly immersed inside freezing mountain ice lakes inside a sub-tropical swamp… and your breathing begins to instantly hyperventilate as your heart jackhammers into cardiac arrest country.

It's like that.

But wait... there's more...

Suddenly the sim-brainwashing on how to perform this op kicks in and you run through your reserve dart deploy as you fire the braking thrusters on the sled, slap the dart reverse lever, check the alignment, thumb the trim tabs for adjustment and fire the grappling dart while you hold on to the spinning sled for dear life.

"Please wait for hard connect confirm," you can practically hear the hot sim girl telling you as you start praying.

Boom and thud.

Ask me how I know... well this is exactly what happened to me.

I got the *connect* message after performing emergency reserve dart deploy. Just like I'd been taught.

The dart stuck right into the aft engine drive of the target vessel with just twenty meters of hull before the deep dark black nothingness of forever swallowed young PMC Orion who'd only recently gotten his tag.

There's a story about that, but now ain't the time.

Twenty meters. That's all.

So... I confirm *hard connect*. Reach out and straighten the line, and now, this is the real hard part because you're dangling off a runaway starship by nothing but cable and a one-shot rocket sled you've been hanging on to like some drunk soldier hanging on to a whore at last call hoping she's not what she probably is and that everything is a little more magical than it really is at this very sorry state of affairs we find ourselves in... and now... you gotta let go of the ugly whore and face the reality of crawling up that line to get onto the hull and then find a breach and kill your way to a linkup with friendly forces already fighting to the death inside the enemy hull.

Hopefully the reserve dart doesn't come loose.

Oh yeah... did I mention that some ship captains, rather than be taken alive... are prone to det the ship and take their chances in the escape pods rather than face whatever mercy you and your team are inclined to dole out that day after you tried your best to kill them?

So... heavy things to have on your mind as you let go of that sled one glove at a time and begin to crawl up that steel cable, untethered, to the dart that punched in the hull.

Your only hope in this life at that moment.

Unless you believe in something.

And hey... pro tip from an old ruck hobo here... your mileage may vary... but don't look at that anchor the dart's got on the hull because it never inspires much confidence. It's pretty... thin.

So... that happened to me one time.

My only time performing a hull insert via the tubes.

So guess what I'm gonna do today to try to save my guys...

We reach the drop tubes and the deck is total darkness.

We haven't used this place in years.

helmet if only to get the imaginary smell of burning leaves
f my nostrils. I literally wave my hand at an imaginary leaf
f my faceplate.
with paranoid suspicion.
th him.

CHAPTER THIRTY-SIX

"I better shoot you up now... Orion," says the chief as I begin to tap in the secure access codes for the launch tube I've selected. At the same time, I'm watching the telemetry feed from the *Spider*'s flight deck. I've mirrored a small image inside the EVC bucket of the forward ob to see the ship's view of the *Dark Star* because timing is a thing here for me not to go spinning off into the void.

Did I mention I'm super bad at this type of math? But hey... M.O.M did the math for me despite her shotgunned algos.

This is such a bad plan, I think to myself. But then I remember the PTSD down payments on the company's impending lack of future and this is what I gotta do to get it done.

I have no idea if this'll work.

But, as my first platoon sergeant used to say... "You gotta shoot your shot."

So, there's that.

"M.O.M...." I croak into the comm, hearing the dry crack and trembling fear I'm trying to hide in my voice. "Roll ventral and prepare to execute drop-tube launch on target ship at pre-authorized and identified location on the enemy hull."

"Yes, dear. There are three minutes and four seconds left until detonation."

Chief Cook has his "special" booster pouch out and he has a very ghoulish smile on his face as he turns it in what dim light there is down there examining its dark, emerald-green depths. This booster shot looks like exceptionally vile venom off the worst pit viper ever to be milked of its toxins.

"Oh yeah..." he mumbles, almost trance-like. "We gonna party now, Orion. We... gonna... party."

"We..." I croak. Indicating I'm supposed to be the *only one* taking the booster to accomplish what happens next.

Chief Cook's mirrored sunglasses dart toward me like some fevered junkie's. I can only guess those hidden coal-dark eyes are dreaming dreams of higher oblivions.

A guilty second passes that we don't have time for.

"Two minutes and fifty-one seconds to self-destruct, dear. Minimum failsafe distance is now ten thousand meters."

"Yeah... about that, Orion. Mighta boosted myself a little in the lift when you weren't looking. Oh... *yeah*... this stuff's comin' on real *haaaard*. It's a..."

His jaw goes unnaturally slack for a long moment and I see his dark mirrored aviator shades tilt and scan the roof of the drop-tube compartment as though he's seeing something there. His head drifting like he's following the arc of a moon across the night sky.

I bet it's bats.

He slaps himself.

And then he's back.

"Had to make sure it wasn't gonna kill you, Sergeant. Outright. Tested it on myself. Just *aaaa*… taste. We dev'd this as a *poison* for diplomatic terminations but found it had some secondary benefits we repurposed for the Psyops program and this will… uh… *activate*'s the right word… latent Bishop powers in even the most low-level savant. So… here we go…"

He karate-chopped the air between us, suddenly muttering, "Damn bats are already here…"

"What?" I asked. He'd told me specifically this was not gonna take me to what he calls "bat country." He'd also promised me it wasn't poison.

And… I believed him.

I am… a sucker.

And right now all I was getting was the smell of fall. Burning leaves. The occasional fluttering leaf. I needed all of it. I needed all of what had come every time she'd summoned her friend…

The door opened and Stinkeye and the Little Girl walked in.

And for a moment… she wasn't the full-grown young woman that had become one of our medics. She was that lost little girl in the company of killers.

She stared at me with those dark eyes just as she had long ago, and I was reminded… of how much… all of us have been through in this long crossing since we met the Seeker.

It has been… a very long ride.

Everything I'd ever known… feels gone. Now.

And I wished it wasn't.

What had that quiet whisper asked me when I got hit back on Gateway… *How much can one man lose, Sergeant Orion?*

I was tired of losing. I'd lost too much. Too many of them.

Honcho, Crusher, and So-So.

Firsty, Farts, and Boom Boom.

Jax who never made it out of the hospital ship after the fight at Gateway.

And so many more… so many others…

"What're you doin' here, you ol' charlatan?" barked Chief Cook savagely at Stinkeye, then karate-chopped more "bats" in a sudden fury of knife-handed blows as though the unseen predators were all about him, flapping and taunting. "We can handle… this. Damn bats are everywhere!"

"You can't handle nothin', ya's cheap faker," hissed Stinkeye and took a deep gulp from his flask. "It's a two-fold power. Rare and rare like all the real good-uns are. He needs her close now to make the change. Become what she made him into when she come callin' for a Green Knight. Ah brought her… and now I'm gonna take her back to the fear and the Heart o' Darkness…"

Stinkeye turned toward the girl and was suddenly not himself. Not his… grim war wizard act anymore. Not the dark eyes who'd seen the darkness of the universe and its black heart itself.

"Ah'm sorry, girl. If ah could do it any way but dis…"

She held up her hand even as she moved to me like the medic she was now. She placed her small fingers on my vitals pad and punched through the displays, doing her job.

"I know…" she murmured, and her voice like we hadn't heard for years was back. She was a woman now. A warrior too.

Now… she spoke as the little girl who'd escaped the Dark Labs, living in fear, hiding, finding protectors among the darkest, hardest men she could.

Being as brave as she could be when she was scared to death.

Stinkeye nodded and then straightened. He took one last hot blast from his dented totem flask, an ancient canteen from the time when soldiers carried them long ago.

"All right…" he whispered. "Here we go den, Little Girl… da Heart. Ya's seen it… and ah seen it too."

He moved close to her. Slowly. Like a python in a trance.

Chief Cook inserted the booster into my EVC pic. He pushed it hard, his own eyes fluttering like this was just as good as boosting himself.

"Will there be bats, Chief?" I hissed.

"Probably, nah… well… there's always bats, Orion. So… just don't make eye contact, kid."

The psychoactive poison began to hit me almost instantly. Hard, too. It was like being slapped by an ancient stone column that just disintegrated to dust all around you. It destroyed you and was destroyed in the doing.

Time, history, you. All at once. That's how it felt. And that's as good of a description as I can give you as it took hold and coursed through my body and fever-brain.

"Copy…" I mumbled from where I was going.

I felt the Little Girl squeeze my arm. I looked up at her. I'd squeezed my eyes shut in the seconds after the boost as it came on hard and sizzling-electric all at once. Melting me. Exploring me. Whispering and hissing sweet lies. *That… music… can you hear it*, I didn't say.

"Roger that, Sar'nt Orion," said Chief Cook as he popped a couple of "combat multiplier pills" we used for extended operations where we needed to stay awake and fight for at least a couple of days. "You're a good man. Remind me of Ramerez. He was a good man too. Lost him at Vega to the commies, and the bats, Orion. Damn commies. Damn bats."

"They comin' for ya now," hissed Stinkeye in her ear nearby to us. She suddenly inhaled and whimpered like a small child as Chief Cook helped me into the drop tube…

I wanted to kill.

I was calm.

My body was far away and the EVC felt like one giant warm blanket on the coldest day of winter.

The world was changing all around me.

Blood. And death. Darker. Red.

The drop's lights in the tube ran through their pre-launch cycle.

I tried to open my eyes but the colors were too much.

I could still hear Stinkeye hissing in her ear, even though they were out in the room, reminding her she would be found no matter where she hid from "da Heart, girl." They would take her back. Back to the "Heart o' Darkness." She would never... *escape them.*

"Ya's never escape, girl. They know where ya's are. And they takin' ya now... back to da Heart. Heart o' Darkness at the center of the..."

She sobbed once. Fighting back the fear as her body began to tremble.

I wanted to kill Stinkeye. Hurt him bad. Real bad. Rage began to well within me.

The eel girl swam in like some representation of the person I'd always tried to be to the universe. Reminding me I wasn't a monster. Lying to me.

"We've always liked you, Orion," she purred in her long-lost French accent.

"You wouldn't like me," I grunted. "When I'm angry."

Slaughter. Death. Fields of dead. It was... everything now.

The launch tube opened and I could see the *Dark Star*. Burning, swarmed, and fighting back with everything she had. A maelstrom of chaos. Incoming and outgoing hot and streaking death.

The rail magnets in the tube fired and I was hurled out into deep space.

I was red hot, but calm and breathing like a bellows forging hot steel. I would murder everything, and everyone...

All of them. I would. Murder.

For her.

I heard her, her voice far away and small... calling me now. Calling who I really was...

"Wild Thing... I..."

And then... it happened like it had never happened before... this time I was ripped to shreds, and deconstructed.

"It's beautiful!" I screamed as I saw the Heart open and consume me whole. I felt the death weapon forming in my hands. My... gauntlets... grasping its raw power.

The Heart...

Black and nothingness and wanting to consume everything.

It was destruction personified.

"Operation... Warfare," said some voice that was familiar in my ear.

I was hurtling through the void and headed toward the *Dark Star* as missiles streaked across the darkness and hot searing beams tore into starships.

I'd never heard it before though. The familiar voice.

"Doom Eighty-Eight... you are cleared to engage. Weapons hot."

"Wild Thing..." she screamed. "I need you!"

CHAPTER THIRTY-SEVEN

How did we get here…

Spinning through space, shot out of the drop tubes and attempting to force the appearance of the Wild Thing… whatever that really was…

And save the company the fate I'd foreseen for all these months leading up to the Battle at Typhon.

Three things needed to happen for me to take a shot at avoiding the fate I'd seen.

It took a long time to come up with the plan and I didn't do it myself. Chief Cook and Stinkeye were involved. But it was strange how it happened. Of course it was.

But in short it went like this…

I needed to hack M.O.M.

I needed to become the Wild Thing.

I needed to board the enemy ship… ahead of the company… and then see how much of the waiting ambush that had killed us time and time again… I could disable and spring on myself, in order to give the company, and the ship, a shot of at least getting a foothold on the Monarch vessel. And surviving.

Hacking M.O.M. was the easy part.

I crawled into deep memory caches, a part of the ship no one I know has *ever* been to, and spent three days working my way through a hack that allowed me to install the command overrides that locked out flight control and gave me command authority to initiate the ship's self-destruct. Then I had to write the attack pattern that would wave the ship off its initial combat insert vector and instead make a run across the enemy vessel's hull, throwing everything, all power and reserves, into the ventral shields to absorb what I, as a mere infantry ruck hobo, would've called "ground fire" coming off the *Dark Star*.

There were huge amounts of incoming fire hitting the shields, bleeding out the battery reserves, and starting to score internals already as I launched out of the tubes. The ship was on fire with damage control alerts and automated hazard warnings of hull breaches and systems being knocked offline.

But she held through the attack run.

At that point in my plan, XO would be freaking out as I entered the launch tubes. The command team would be seeing that something had gone horribly wrong and they were not making the planned combat insert onto a hot LZ inside what the company and the *Thunderer*'s CIC had identified as our breaching point for the attack.

Hey… we got the long straw.

Other combat teams and private military companies were having to hit the external hull topside, or other unknown areas exposed and damaged by our initial assault, and breach by cutting into who knows what.

We at least knew we were going after an open hangar as an insertion point.

That has its benefits, and its negatives.

You know what you're hitting. You can prepare.

But also *they* know this is a likely insert point so they can prepare to defend with all they got.

The other inserts were more opportunistic. You got no idea what you're getting into. But… you got surprise. Which is always nice.

Some might have said we drew the short straw.

The company, one of the few PMCs possessing her own starship, was tasked with taking an identified landing bay and trying to anchor there so further combat operations could be conducted internally against the *Dark Star* and the Monarchs, and other friendly forces could be pushed through if they were denied access at their insertion target points.

But I liked what we drew. Even as I had visions of our destruction.

I can't explain why so don't @ me.

Of course the Monarchs were defending the bay. Heavily. It was one of four large ones that had been identified along the massive side ring of the saucer. One at each cardinal direction point. Fleet Intel was certain they'd defend it heavily once we attempted to board there.

Fine.

I'd seen our deaths and felt powerless to do something about it.

The question was… *why* was I seeing it?

Don't know.

But… it sounded like a warning to me. A warning from…

Didn't know that either.

Still. It was intel. Of a sort.

And also… there was what John Strange told me.

She picked you.

So I started planning. Or at least, trying to.

I executed my hack after I'd crawled into the vast glowing red memory core that crossed six decks of the *Spider*, vertically, like some giant and deep reactor. This area was so buried within the ship, and the security systems surrounding it were so tight, it took days to quietly bypass the code locks, scans, and finally manually unlock and crank open the bank vault hatch to M.O.M.'s inner sanctum.

It was an old deck.

Beautiful. Crystalline. Red. It glowed like a dull furnace in there and the air was alive with… computing power, information, data… And it was clean. Spotless. Every crystal-mainframe drive, and there were thousands of them stacked, was luminous and see-through, at the same time reflecting images of the myriad other crystal-crimson drives there.

It was… awe-striking.

Opposite of the grungy, ancient, solid, dark and dank and much-repaired NewMax Warhammer-class destroyer we'd lived and fought in.

It felt like a cathedral in there as I floated through the vast chambers and luminous wells of her "mind." I was reminded that much of the company's history, and perhaps humanity's, was lost somewhere in here. It was here… but it was unrecoverable because we never knew what to ask for, and she didn't know what to tell us.

But you could tell many answers and mysteries were there all the same. Waiting in the storage crystals.

We had a policy in the company of never messing with this area of the ship, or M.O.M. herself, unless absolutely necessary, as there was no way to repair her and the cost of a new ASI was beyond the company's means even if all the contracts ran solid for ten years straight. So… we left well enough alone and put up with her idiosyncrasies. We didn't want to cause the ship to be damaged and inoperable by messing with stuff we had no idea about.

But now the lives of everyone in the company were at stake and… I committed the cardinal sin of going into her prime memory. And messing around.

And if there was a sin among us sinners in the company… this was it. This was the big one the first sergeant would kill you himself for.

With that in mind I installed the hack and made myself the ship's secret senior flight officer by doing a little coding once I had root access.

As Chief Cook, and now Stinkeye and the Little Girl, prepared to launch me at the ship, M.O.M would now, after executing Attack Pattern Delta… roll from her ventral to starboard side as she approached the insert target, and other things that needed to happen and that I'd spent time badly coding in, would happen. The self-destruct sequence would be turned off and reset.

The ship would not blow itself to kingdom come.

But I'd needed the self-destruct sequence armed in order to complete the final hack and allow only the senior-most flight officer command authority to lock out the flight deck.

It was an emergency protocol within her code I found and took advantage of in order to allow me to assume command of the ship and order M.O.M. to execute my directives. But to trip it I had to activate the self-destruct sequence. It was the only way, and I spent an entire day, I mean twenty-four hours, in her memory, trying to find another way.

There wasn't one.

So imagine if I had been killed by enemy ship fire on the way down to the tubes. The ship would have continued its self-destruct and XO was locked out.

I would have killed everyone trying to save them.

But I had to do it. It was the only way under the circumstances.

Everything was accomplished now, and I was ready to launch. As soon as I departed the ship, M.O.M. would disable the nuclear space mine that would have destroyed the ship had the counter reached zero. Once I launched, she would, according to my programming and the hack I'd coded, then return flight control to XO after Attack Pattern Delta was executed.

Attack Pattern Delta would position the ship to fire the tubes into the hangar deck as the ship made her attack run over the enemy hull.

Then XO would be back in control.

XO, who would no doubt be freaking out as none of the flight systems had been responding, in the middle of a battle insert, as the ship seemingly went off on its own and took fire from the enemy vessel.

I can only imagine the stress.

The command team was gonna take turns killing me. I was sure of that. But... I'd had no choice.

My bet was once direct flight control was resumed by XO, the company would still go for the insert on the DZ.

I'd have maybe three minutes before they could attempt another landing on the enemy hangar deck to do what I could do to destroy the defenses there and give them a shot at not being cut to shreds.

The second thing that needed to happen was the hard part.

I had no idea how the third thing would go, so I chalked that up as "easier" than the second part as some kind of treat for myself because I'm a liar like that.

I know... I'm wired weird.

The second thing I had to do was become the Wild Thing now... in the moment before I inserted onto the enemy vessel at the hangar deck we were going to be murdered on.

That part took a bit... but in the end... I took the dive and we figured out a way to make it happen.

But first... I had to hear her story.

And I can tell you I always knew it was one I never wanted to hear.

But that's how it is. Sometimes you have to go where you don't want to go.

CHAPTER THIRTY-EIGHT

"Dere's tings ya's don' unnerstan' 'bout da nature of da galaxy, Little King," crooned Stinkeye tiredly in his ragged voice when we first began discussing "the plan." He seemed older now. Older than I'd ever seen him. Older than weeklong binges and much older than those times we'd asked him, without ever saying a word, to get our bacon out of some bad firefight we'd gotten ourselves into, and were already way in over our heads.

Those times cost him. There was no doubt about that. And perhaps that's why he got credit on Cheks debts and we sobered him up when he went too far gone.

Perhaps…

I don't know that everyone knew. But I knew. He always seemed older to me. Disappeared on his binges. Bet heavy on Cheks with money he didn't have like the action was something that could be felt, and tasted, and touched, as though in the end it might replace some of the power he'd lost spending it all on our behalf to cause chaos and destruction to the enemy and give us some small advantage in the knife-and-gun show that is private military contracting.

Perhaps.

"Every-ting costs something. Ya's got that, Little King, because it's a rule. Here in the starports and worlds you fight on, and fight for, never gaining, never growing, I 'spect sometimes ya's think 'sall for nothin' but da action, dem whores, and maybe some debt ya all think ya's settlin' up wit da big dark. Ya got that, Little King?"

I nodded that I did.

I'd found him in aft stores aboard the *Spider* on the long haul out to Typhon. He hadn't been himself lately. He'd actually been training with the company for the insert. Doin' the hull crawls in EVC. Clearing simulated compartments with a rifle on the shoot deck like he was one of the guys on the line instead of a warrant officer who didn't have to be anywhere or do anything except the magic they've always done for a fighting force on the move and looking to stack.

He'd even held his bitter cursings and promised bad luck hissings when Gunny barked at the old chief to get some bulkhead-to-bulkhead killing task done just right like we were expected to perform once we boarded the actual *Dark Star*.

If we boarded the *Dark Star*, I'd reminded myself in those moments after the cold shudder that came with all my visions of future PTSDs I'd been having.

No.

He was not the same Stinkeye on the six-month haul within the *Winds of Change*'s jump envelope out to that dark and mysterious system known as Typhon.

Out there, far beyond the edge of the known.

We have to be honest about these things.

Here be dragons, the star charts might as well have been marked.

And I guessed, as we trained and did our thing, that the chief warrant officer of Voodoo was as scared as we were, as I was, getting ready to face whatever we were gonna get into by getting himself ready to EVC in boarding combat.

Along with us. Because that's where the action would be. And that's where we'd need him.

My guess is he was having visions too, or whatever strange knowing that came with his powers.

I was reminded what Nether had said about him. Stinkeye was one of the most powerful Bishops he'd ever encountered.

Stinkeye got quiet too. No fighting with Chief Cook or much of anyone for that matter. None of his usual histrionics or theatrics.

Like he knew death was close on this one.

Weirdly, he even played Cheks better than he usually did, and there were a few in the company who actually owed him some money come payout, even though all his cards were ragged and horrible and barely worked.

Those debtors were practically lurking for the next epic Stinkeye binge, then they'd swap their debt for a marker to be paid.

Stinkeye sobriety among Cheks players began to be updated daily like some planetside weather report.

Unfortunately it was rain every day for them.

He didn't binge but a few times and only missed training on the training deck and hull crawls for a day at a time.

The Cheks players had their best cards out and waiting for him. But on those days he disappeared into the ship and wasn't seen until he was sober.

I tried to find him during those times but even when I placed a tracker on the tattered old OD-green patchwork messenger bag he always kept slung around his thin body, marked with old military units from Earth's past and other strange arcane symbols, I couldn't find him no matter how long I looked.

And wherever I looked.

He was just gone. Missing.

I knew the *Spider* better than most and was amazed after hours of looking through every passage, stores compartment, and engine room where few ever went, that I could not find him.

It was as though… he'd just vanished.

And I'd never known him to have that power. But I had known him long enough to not discount that he might have some such trick he could play when he needed it most.

He wasn't this old and this mysterious without a few tricks we didn't know about.

Even his worst enemy Chief Cook didn't discount him that way.

On those missing days Chief Cook got nervous and made bad jokes, trying to be near groups of us as he watched the shadows and dark corners for unseen wraiths.

He was unusually sober.

"Sometimes he goes down to the old rear gun deck, under the main drive, Orion," offered Chief Cook. "That's where he goes to hide when he thinks you guys will find out what a fraud he really is. That his powers are only Class Three on the official Monarch Psy-Can Scale. He's little better than a street con artist playing card tricks, Orion. Except he ain't got no rabbit to pull out of a hat and he's terrible at cards."

That's a new one. I'd never heard the Bishops were rated via a scale.

"Oh yeah, Orion. For sure they are. When I was with Task Force Two Nine Three, we ran the Psy-Can Testing and Combat Assessment Brigade for integration with the line units in the Ultras. Dark stuff, Sergeant. Dark stuff indeed. I was… let's just say… *assassinated*… for voicing dissent that the prospective Bishops were too unreliable to deploy into forward combat operations and just as likely to get our boys killed as do anything useful. Then Colonel Blood and Sergeant Major Hannerhan found out about one of my little 'side projects' to develop a weaponized version of Bantherium flu and… *overreacted*. Pure theater. I'd been splicing the fever with a little top-notch adrenalizers… read *speed*, Orion… that we could deploy via artillery shell during an arty prep, or orbital bombardment of an objective. They said I was, quote, 'sick in the head and mad to the point of high-functioning narcissist psychopathy for wanting to invite war-crimes charges under the extreme suffering amendment to article three-six-four, paragraph alpha, sub-note Charlie, which clearly states, *An attacking force shall not develop weapons of mass destruction that cause a target to question their personally held belief systems.*' Unquote."

He laughed dismissively.

"*Sooooo* I was drummed out of the Psy-Can Testing and Combat Assessment Brigade and for about a week I may have gone AWOL and been the subject of a search by specialized teams of Ultras and a few Inquisitors in order to face some trumped-up bogus charges."

Yeah, I thought as he told me this. *That makes total sense.*

"Joke's on them, Orion. I wasn't even on Aegyptus Nine. I was seven parsecs away hiding out in a safehouse I'd been prepping for just such an occasion. Royale Pleasure Dome Casino and Horse Track. Best week of my life. I combed the casinos as a life insurance rep for a bogus front company me and a few other like-minded guerillas had set up. Told all the rubes I was attending a seminar on risk management and sat all day in various casino bars playing Holo-Cheks and Zankou Chicken Poker. I was up twenty-five thousand mem by the end of the week before my contact at 'the company' came through and they pulled the 'Do Not Capture/ Terminate on Sight' order. Twenty-five thousand, Orion! I got assigned to the Five-Oh-Fourth Tac-Plan and Special Operations Command. Secret stuff there. I'd have to kill you if I told you anything about that. You understand, Orion?"

I did.

"So you think he's down in the old rear gunnery deck?" I asked Chief Cook flatly.

"Yeah. Probably gone fetal. Sucking on that canteen like some sociopath whose bad plans have all gone awry. If you find him down there, tell him I've got something waiting for him and if he knows what's good for him he'll stay away from his combat locker for about the next thirty-six years until that Altari mummy python I hid in there dies a natural death."

"Did you really do that?" I asked, trying to conceal my horror. Mummy pythons were nothing to mess with. One could kill the whole ship.

The chief smiled innocently.

"Oh c'mon, Orion. Where would I get a jade-green Altari mummy python in this sector? And *if*... big *if*... I did have one... I sure wouldn't waste it on him. The venom alone, when milked properly and treated with a carefully prepared mixture of sodium pentothal and *juuuussssst* the right amount of cyanide, will induce a high that will have you seeing the spirit world of the Atalatzi ruins in the *living-est* of colors for at least three weeks, Sergeant Orion. I wouldn't waste that stuff on him... but... he's drunk and stupid and afraid... so he's crazy enough to think I'm crazy enough to do it. You follow me?"

I turned to go to the rear gunnery deck and find our missing war wizard. My planning was nearing the phase where I needed to know some weird stuff only Stinkeye probably knew.

Then I stopped. I turned back to Chief Cook.

"Why do you guys hate each other so much?"

The chief laughed suddenly like a barking machine gun, or a sick dog. It was not... *a pleasant sound.*

"Ha, Orion... you're not cleared to hear that story. But if you knew... you'd understand. Yes... yes you would," he said confidently.

Then I was gone, leaving him to whatever mess and chaos he was working on next. When I'd come into his office to see if he knew where Stinkeye was, he'd thrown a black velvet cloth over his desk so I couldn't see what was there. I was sure it was bad and most likely *real* bad for us, and I wondered, not for the first time, if I shouldn't have just cut him deep there with my karambit just like I'd done to Sergeant Hannibal and a few other enemy combatants in my time in the company.

But I figured we might need the chief and his particular brand of weirdness in there, aboard the *Dark Star*, and the visions I was having of what we were facing outweighed my caution about killing him right there and now.

That's where we're at.

That's who we've become lately.

Or...

To be honest about these things...

That's who I am. Lately.

Honesty. These things. You know the drill.

I did find Stinkeye in the darkness of the old aft gunnery compartment. He was in the lotus position. It was dark and blue, and the gunnery windows, the guns long gone and sold off, cast strange hexagonal shadows across the dusty, dirty old place that was like some ruined holy place we never visited.

That's when Stinkeye said, "Dere's tings ya's don' unnerstan' 'bout the nature of da galaxy, Little King..." when I'd just entered and said nothing, standing there staring at him and trying to figure out how to proceed with all the PTSD and bare planning I had so far.

I hadn't said a word.

He'd just answered what was on my mind.

And then...

"Now... Little King... it's time to tell you how you been all's caught up in all'it for longer den you's knowed."

CHAPTER THIRTY-NINE

"Ya gots to imagine what it's like for dem... us, Little King. Every-ting costs something... but for us... to do our... gifts... and dat's what dey are... we gotta pay."

"So how am I..."

"Ha... not yet. I tell ya now... you won't understand and all ya do is be angry. Let me tell you what her life is like, was like... first."

I nodded.

"She ain't never told me nothin'. But I was dere in dem camps and da facilities too. Before you know me now and not all of it good, Little King. I was a bad man. I was a soldier. A killer. And even though I didn't know what I was there... lookin' back... I could see how I bent the outcomes ta the way I wanted things ta be."

The old war wizard paused for a long moment and that's when, by glow of the diffused warp envelope anomaly in space all around the hurtling ships, and the shadows created by the latticed gunnery windows where once the ship's aft defense guns had jutted out to protect the main engines from some ancient strike fighter or PT killer getting in on her six and lighting up the engines and the aft reactors jutting out, I could see that Stinkeye really was... *old*.

The warp envelope we were using to transit made a haunted weirdness of outer space, or the strange time-bending reality we were traveling through in order to beat the *Dark Star* to the ambush we had planned for her. The transit anomaly effect made ghosts out there in the dark-light. And rumors abounded that there were some on the ships in the fleet who saw something in that glowing white-noise light storm of dark light we traveled through. Some who said they saw inhuman shapes and figures, or alien faces, moaning and tormented within the white-noise storm that surrounded the speeding fleet.

Ghosts?

But here in the abandoned gunnery space, I sat facing Stinkeye whose coal-dark eyes burned like small fires between us.

I'd come to see what could be done about our impending demise. I needed answers from someone who had experience in the strange and the unknown.

Stinkeye was my only hope.

His ragged voice was deep, and lower than I'd ever heard it, but urgent now like some street preacher preaching that I must absolutely believe him if any kind of salvation is to be obtained.

Or a better life to be gained.

Or even... a shot in the dark against the inevitable.

"Dey snagged her outta whatever life she was in, Little King. Someone dimed her out on da powers an' she was taken to da camps. Den... to da facilities. Prisons really. Bad places like you ain't never seen."

Stinkeye cleared his throat and leaned closer.

"In da camps, Little King... dey see who ken survive da horrors no matter what dey power is. Ya know what a camp is... Little King. For what will become the Bishops?"

I didn't.

"It be hell. Ain't no vision of it. It just is. Da first camps, da ones I was in when dey pulled me outta da line units and figured out what Stinkeye really was... dey was hell like I ain't never seen and I'd seen Mars durin' da genocides. Bad stuff that... and dis was worse. Believe me... I'd already lived through hell on da last battles 'tween Earth and da Martian Insurrection. An' Alpha Centauri weren't no picnic neither."

If his stories were true... he was as old as John Strange.

But... now was not the time. The only thing that mattered was the future and mainly that LZ on the *Dark Star* we were gonna get murdered on.

"A camp is found on some world that's already inhospitable, Little King. It's real estate no one wants and hopefully... if men like dat bastard Cook have done dey intel right... it's got sumpin' real wrong wit' it... know what I mean?"

I didn't.

"Ghosts, Little King. Sins o' da past. Dat's where it works best. Where it comes out. Say... like a massacre or sumpin'... dey say tha's best fo' da dark magic to come to da surface. Some..." He hissed and spit. "Some... darkness or sorrow dat's all soaked into da ground by da spilled blood and tears. Dey say... dat brings out da gifts from inside us. Dem monsters don't know what dey talkin' 'bout though... but I do... 'cause ah seen da Heart itself, Little King. Ah seen it, Little King, and dat's what it's all about for us wit' da gifts."

I had no idea what he was talking about.

But I nodded and said nothing and this seemed to calm his bitter hissing-rattle voice he had descended into... like ghouls whispering, as he recalled these places called... *dey camps*.

"Da one I went into... Ah remember da day. It was rainin' iron 'cause dat's what it did on dat world... micro-particles dat rained like black water. Cut da skin like razors. Da day ah came dere was dark as night and da armored bus dey took t'ree of us out dere in was getting pounded so hard it felt like we were takin' incoming from God's machine gun Hisself. Dey had armor and MOPP too ta keep 'em safe. Dey pulled up to da gates and it was like some prison you ain't never wanna see no nevah. High towers. Guns. Artillery was facin' inward. Dat shoulda told me sumpin' dere. Told me dey was real scared to death about what was on da inside. Mean dogs dat ain't never played fetch or ball, howlin'. Like big *woofs* really. I 'member dey eyes all glowed red in dat dark afternoon as da steel rain stopped and I was hustled, chained I was, inside dat prison 'cause all ah did was take a stupit test one day. Worst mistake o' ma life dat was."

He stopped for a long moment. His eyes far away and distant like he was back there once more.

"Ah didn't understand it den, Little King… but I felt it real. Felt dat place's anchored to da Heart itself already 'cause dat's how it works even though dey didn't know it at da time. Felt da unquiet dead howling in madness up at us from da slit trenches dey'd been buried in… alive, Little King. Buried… alive. See… da Monarchs had known about da powers for… ah guess… a long, long, *looonnnggg* time before we ever started ta… manifest 'em. Maybe dey had 'em through all dey ages of *Old Urff*. Maybe always did. Usin' 'em all quiet-like to control us all along troo da history books and DVDs. It was dey way all along. But dat's over now, ain't it, Little King? We huntin' *them* now, and you seein' sumpin' you don't like for us. Ain't dat right?"

I said nothing.

He waved his weathered old chocolate hand as though driving that part of the conversation away for now.

"Dat's what dey say. Right? Dey all dead. We huntin' da last of 'em. Dat's what dey say?"

I nodded.

"They'll be dead soon, Stink," I murmured and didn't believe my own words. I'd seen the bloody hangar deck of the *Dark Star*. I knew what was coming.

Stinkeye laughed bitterly. Low and only to himself for a moment.

"Ha… ya tink so, den…"

Then he began to mumble something I couldn't understand for a few seconds.

"Dem camps… da Monarchs made 'em demselves. Dat site… dat was a colony ship dat gone missing fifty years back or so before I got dere. Ha… didn't go missing at all. Ultra Marines hijacked it and landed it. Den buried 'em all alive for no reason dey knew of. Just ordered to. Jes' followin' orders as the tools always like to say. Da Monarchs… ah, Little King, dey knew all along though what was what. Dey knew da injustice *done*… would… make da gifts surface."

He paused and closed his eyes.

"With jes' da right amount of suffering, and terror."

He smiled, but something wasn't right about the smile.

"So inside it's nothing but craters where dey had to fire an artillery shell into da camp to kill some candidate whose powers got all outta control all of a sudden with some new power dey never knew dey had… or fight dey way out during a psy-can extraction… I got a whole story about me in dere, Little King, but now ain't da time for ma story. And maybe dere ain't gonna be any more time on dis one ta tell it to no one. You gettin' da visions, Little King. I can feel 'em when you down there in your cage havin' 'em. Fun, huh?"

It wasn't.

"So… in dem camps it's nothing but survival. Everyone cuttin' and killin' for the food, da scraps and slop dat gets thrown over da wire ever' mornin'. Den after dat you wander 'round dat old crashed colony ship dat's been gutted of any ting useful you might use to escape, defend ya'self, an' try an' stay alive one day longer. Scared to death. Seein' tings no one should see. All da while… your powers startin'. Dey… *startin'*."

Stinkeye looked up at me out of his lowered eyes, the whites showing like some demonic goblin in the dark shadows.

"Startin' to *bubble bubble bubble toil and trouble*… Little King."

He laughed dryly. It was little more than a croak repeated.

"Ya's comin' online but you ain't one of us. You what's called… an anchor, Little King. Whatever that thing you can do… you startin' to feel it because the psy-cans near ya can do it. 'Cause ya need to feel it. See it. And den da killing starts 'cause you ahead of us. Seein' it. Like me in da camps after the first days… you stay safe doin' your trick, Little King… get da slop in da mornin' and hopefully it ain't rainin' steel, otherwise ya gotta find some collected water in da old rusty ship's hull to wash it off. Ya's start killin' in dose camps, Little King. However ya's ken. Some… dey make da fire wit' dere minds… others… telekinesis… others… strange and stranger powers that's got no names, Little King."

Stinkeye laughed again. But there was no mirth in it.

"Now… 'bout den dey usually pull ya out. But sometimes… if they wanna see what you can really do… dey let ya… *cook*… dey called it den. *Cook*… like you a dish dey gonna eat."

Stinkeye lowered his eyes again, sitting there in the dark like some mad monk who'd finally attained the opposite of peace, or whatever.

Cold madness.

Quiet revenge.

The hope of murder.

"*Let him cook*, dey'd say. See… dey wanna knows how far ya's gift goes once dey know what it can do. And da whole time, Little King… all dat terror and torment be jes' about finding out… findin' out so dey can use ya's against dey enemies. Dat's all. And to dem, dey Monarchs… everyone an' enemy, Little King. Even demselves. So dey jes' burn up yo' life ta find out. Dat's all."

He laughed a little, saying *Dat's all* over and over again, whispering until I couldn't hear it anymore.

The pause that followed was so long after that bit, I assumed he was done. But I sat there anyway because I still hadn't got to what I needed from him, and how to do it.

"I know why ya here, Little King," he croaked. His ancient muddy eyes closed. "Ya's here to use da gift she got you all tied up in."

He smiled slowly, his crooked teeth white in the shadows and ghost-light beyond the ship.

"Now… Little King… ain't nothin' wrong with dat. But now I gots to tell you how she became who she is, and ta tell you, dat is… how she escaped dem. And den… I gots ta tell you… *what* she really is. And dat part… it's too much for a man like you ta know… but you gonna know it anyways, Little King. You gonna know it anyways…"

CHAPTER FORTY

And then I was ripped to shreds and deconstructed…

"It's beautiful!" I felt myself screaming as the strange warrior's skin formed all around me and I hurtled aboard the drop-tube sled toward the *Dark Star*. But it wasn't skin… it was *his*… combat armor. I saw the Heart itself for a blink of a second open, and then consume me.

Stinkeye had warned me of this. Guessed it would happen. But then added a disclaimer. "But ah don't know… Little King… her power is strange and deep… deeper and wilder den mine's. My guess… it's more den any of us… and maybe even she… knows."

I felt the Wild Thing's death weapon forming in my hands. My… gauntlets. Felt the rubberized grip give just a little on the primary. It glowed in my new alien-like HUD. All bloody red.

An M99 Vulcan battle rifle. Ten-millimeter chain gun. Select fire mode operational… FULL AUTO.

These words flashed in bloody red script inside my new HUD.

The Wild Thing's HUD.

Doom88.

"Operation… Warfare," said some dry, smoke-stained voice that was… somehow *familiar*… in my ear. And I'd never heard it before all the same… but it was someone I knew?

"Doom Eighty-Eight… cleared to engage. Weapons hot."

An older man. A commander type who'd had his time on the line.

And then…

"Good luck, Black Ravens."

Reality beyond the Dark Heart of the Universe opened wide and we… there were others just like me… we were being pushed out… surging out… of a teleportation funnel.

I had no idea what a "teleportation funnel" was.

We don't have them where I come from.

Okay, so… ruck-hobo broken old PMC has never heard of a teleportation funnel. Got it.

But *me now*… the Wild Thing… *Doom Eighty-Eight… Strike Force Raven*… I knew what one was from the mission brief even though I had not attended the mission brief.

"Ya's probably come from another reality, Little King... when ya become him. He ain't from no future of ours. She snatched him from somewhere. But she needed an anchor..." Stinkeye had explained as we plotted out what would happen with my plan.

Still... I knew what the situation was. Doom88 and Task Force Raven's mission. How *we* were gonna do... the odds and they weren't good...

How *they* were gonna...

But they had to do it anyway. Their reality... depended on it.

"Teleportation insert good to go... Ravens... proceed to target." A dark and husky female comm operator.

EDF SOCOM.

Earth Defense Forces. Special Operations Command.

Never heard of it... and... I knew what it was.

Stinkeye had explained that this effect... *knowing* and *never having known*... might be part of "da swap."

We were running across hot brown sand even though the night sky and the cold stars were visible... and it was nothing but the interstellar map of all the stars that ever were and many we never knew.

I knew that.

Chatter from Raven Leader came through the armor's comm as he called out targets and movement points to engage.

The first of the Elder Titans were coming out.

What's a Titan?

I didn't know. Not immediately. But... when I saw one... I knew what it was and I knew what a Titan did.

The teleportation funnel had dropped us, Earth's last best hope...

This Earth... not the Earth of my... reality... timeline... call it what you will...

At the Oblivion Gate.

Above, among those unfamiliar stars, wheeled dozens of "other" Earths. All of them gazing down on the battlefield that was the Gate.

All of them were different. Some poisoned. Some burned. Some war-torn. Some... alien and overrun. Some... like ours... missing...

I knew, and... I didn't know.

It was a strange feeling as my mind... *synced*... with his. The Wild Thing. Me.

As the combat teams, in wedges, Task Force Raven, moved to target, we crossed through monolithic and crumbling ruins sinking in the sands of this strange moon...

I knew it was a moon. But it wasn't either.

It was a gate. A gate some ancient race... the Elder Titans... had built on a moon long ago.

The Oblivion Gate.

Tactical displays and maps began to come online in the bloody red HUD of the Wild Thing's armored bucket.

We already had KIAs. The Black Ravens. That was his company. My... company.

Earth Defense Force. SOCOM.

Task Force Raven.

13th Group.

Black Ravens.

Shock troops that served the ODA teams.

That... was where he'd come from. Who he *was*. Who I am... *now*.

"Titan eleven o'clock!" the team leader called out over the squad. Bravo Team Leader. "Gunner... transverse left and engage!"

Behind me a huge wheeled armored vehicle that had come through the teleportation funnel behind us opened fire from the gunner's turret.

The Elder Titan bounded over us infantry as hot brown sand plumes exploded in every direction. It grabbed the gun truck with one of its necrotic purple tentacles and crushed it instantly.

Just like that.

It roared like some ancient leviathan from the Saurian worlds.

I felt the loss of life instantly. He felt it.

"Keep moving forward, Ravens!" shouted the strike commander. "Almost there!"

The Elder Titan.

This vision I was having... lasted thirty seconds, maybe, as I transited toward the deck of the *Dark Star*, hurtling in on that drop-tube sled, praying I'd transform into the Wild Thing by the time I hit the landing zone.

We had no idea if it would work.

She was the Bishop. The Little Girl.

I was her anchor.

He... was her protector. The Wild Thing.

If I didn't become him... it was gonna be one short fight and then the company would land and everyone would die and Strange would be no more.

All I was experiencing right before I began to transform, and I could see the looming bulk of the *Dark Star*... was his memories.

Stinkeye had "theorized"... and this must be bracketed by the fact that as we worked this problem in the days after my meeting with him in the abandoned gunnery station aboard the *Spider*, Stinkeye had been bingeing non-stop from his canteen...

But... he was clear too. Clear like he was solving a problem so hard he'd broken out in a hot fever and even Cutter had mentioned he'd seen Stinkeye in the mess and thought he might be sick.

Stinkeye never went to see Cutter. Ever.

And Cutter... *didn't care*.

So... it was a push. As they say in Cheks.

But as we worked the problem, Stinkeye "theorized" that to fully input my consciousness into the Wild Thing and take control away from her... I'd need to be... vectored in... on the initial capture point in which she'd ensnared him.

We had no idea where that was.

Where, or when, she'd selected this... Wild Thing... to become her personal champion, and protect her in whatever dangerous situation she found herself in.

Even her memories had been suppressed and buried by the Monarch we called the Seeker. But we'd find that out later.

"I got nosy fer a long time once I saw her pull dat ting from wherever it come from, Little King... Dat it ain't from any-ting we knows, or has ever knowed to knows of."

He was referencing the Wild Thing.

"So where's it from?" I asked.

"Dunno. But… it probably be only two choices dis one, Little King…"

I waited as Stinkeye rubbed his old chin and the grey whiskers there. He was looking older day by day as we got deeper and deeper into this, and I worried about him. Or maybe that was because I was spending more time than I really ever had… with him. Note my long-standing policy not to be around Stinkeye at all… but hey… the company needed him.

"One may be… it's from da future. Which make her a time snatcher as we used to say back in da camps."

"A time snatcher?" I asked.

"Yeah… dey was high value. It was clear to da Monarchs and dem bastids dey called demselves scientists… dey wanted a time snatcher either dead… or on da ice. Ya's know… cryo-prison or maybe in coffin-sleep. Again… ah don't know what her story is, Little King… how she gots ha'self free… what power dey t'ought she had… but dey were happy to keep her in da camps and ready for da labs after. Dey must not of kenned she might be a time snatcher… 'cause if dey kenned to dat… den dey would've iced her one or da other way."

"For the record, Stinkeye…" I asked. "What is a time snatcher in… Bishop culture?"

Stinkeye laughed. "Ain't no Bishop culture, Little King. We slaves, boy. It was only survive best ya's could. But… dey time snatchers is Bishops who can bounce into another time, future or past, and bring somethin', or someones, back. Now, alone… ya's can see why dat kinda power scared da hell outta tyrants like dem Monarchs. Dey had ever-ting to lose. Snatch da wrong person and dey could not be da ones who ended up on tops. So dat's why dey either kilt 'em, or iced 'em and put 'em in da steep freeze-cryo on some asteroid base no maps tells of, Little King. Maybe someday dey needs a quick trip to da past, or future, to pull a mission. Dey bring one outta da steep-freeze and use 'em. But dat prolly fo' specials only."

The chief warrant officer of Voodoo thought about this for a long time after he said it.

Then…

"So… she was able to keep that power secret from dem… and ups to her for doin' dat. Like I said, da terror and torment of dey camps, den da experiments in da facilities… and finally… ah, boy, you don't want to know and can't imagine… da labs… for what dey called… *refinement* and *enhancement*… dat's where dey break ya… and turn ya's into nuttin' but a zombie workin' for 'em… all dat is designed ta get her, us, ta reveal our real powers and da true extent of what we can *really* do… through pain, torture, starvation, beatings, electrocutions, day afta' day… and… worse… boy… much, much worse like you ain't never seen. So, whenever she went gone walkabout on 'em… dey hadn't figured it out yet. Her power. My guess… she made it as far as da facilities and den she used her gift… if she is a *kind* of time snatcher… to escape."

"A *kind* of time snatcher?" I asked Stinkeye.

"Yas… dere's two kinds. One can snatch from a *when*. Dey others… and dey so rare I t'ought dey only existed in theory… but dose can snatch not just from *when*… but *other-wheres*."

Okay... every answer led to another question. *Other-wheres.* Other... *realities... dimensions... timelines?*

But I thought I knew where this was going...

Stinkeye hit his totem flask and laughed gustily. "Pure imagination, Little King. But... like I said... dat thing she can summon, he either from da future... our future but... Stinkeye don't think so... where he come from, dat day looks pretty dark by da look of his weapons and fancy getup if you ask Ol' Stinkeye... it's from somewhere else."

"Other-when," I murmured to myself. "Other-where."

He looked at me, suddenly serious, that low-grade fever making his dark muddy skin glisten as we sat discussing how we were gonna pull what we were gonna pull.

"Yas... Little King... that's what ah be thinkin' all this time."

Stinkeye set his dented ancient totem flask down. He pushed it toward me across the table. I'd been drinking coffee. It was afternoon, ship time.

I suddenly felt a cold chill like... like I knew where this was going all along and hadn't been able to be totally honest with myself about it. I didn't accept what he told me next.

But now... later, I realize if just by my intuition and reaction... that cold chill like I'd just suddenly stepped into the iciest of alpine streams and froze right to my spine and heart... I realize that probably this conclusion was the true one.

"Dere are..." began Stinkeye slowly, "Little King... other places. My guess... this lost one comes from one of those places. A dark place."

I think I knew what he was getting at. But, like many of us... sometimes when the truth just wallops you right across the face, whether you like it or not... you dismiss it and want to go back to the comfortable known that you *want* to be true.

If just because it's easier that way.

Easier to go on. Easier to go on thinking everything is neat and tidy and that even with war and chaos and death and entropy and, someday, the heat death of the universe... that it's all as you see it.

No... loose ends or seams in reality that don't quite fit.

Time-space navigation in the sims had clued me in to some of the messier and unexplainable parts of the mechanics of the universe, as far as we goblins with jump drives were concerned.

And to be honest... I'd let those go because... it was easier not to think too much about other dimensions and... other places. That's what the nav-comps were for.

Holes and tunnels and openings into... *other realities.*

"Dere is... da other twelve dimensions, Little King. And den... dere are... *other...* places. And... *other versions of...* places."

Stinkeye looked around at the mess hall. It was dark and empty save for the two of us.

I took a drink from the flask and it didn't hit me in the least even though it was pure jet fuel that day.

Who knew where he got it from.

No one.

I felt, at that moment, I was getting into something... far, far bigger and deeper and way darker than just the *insubordination*, by suicide attack, one-way mission stuff… I was cooking up to try and get the company off the *X* I saw coming in my nightmares.

Where I was heading… there might be real consequences worse than death.

"And den," crooned Stinkeye as though he were reading my thoughts, "… dere's da Heart, Little King. Da Heart o' Darkness itself."

CHAPTER FORTY-ONE

"So what are you saying, Stinkeye?" I asked stone-cold sober, almost… shivering.

I rubbed my hands together to generate some heat. I shouted at the ship to turn on the lights in the mess. The dark was too dark!

M.O.M. said nothing and the lights came on and for some reason that was deeply *weird* to me. No "*Yes, dear.*" Just… on. Stinkeye was staring at me like the voodoo witch doctor he really actually was.

No war-wizard act here.

"She snatched him from somewhere else because… she can do that, Little King."

He straightened up and took the totem flask into his gnarled old hands.

"Because she can. She just took him from whatever hell he was born in… and made him protect her. Because… she can."

And then he drank.

CHAPTER FORTY-TWO

The Titan bounded over us infantry. Grabbed the gun truck with one of its tentacles and crushed it instantly.
  I felt the loss of life.
  "Keep moving, Ravens!" shouted the strike commander. "We're almost there!"
  The Titan.
  There were a hundred in Doom Company in the Task Force Raven Strike Force. We were supported by an armor platoon. Thirty-Fourth Mechanized Armored Cavalry Regiment. The Basilisk Hunters. A scout platoon under Thirteenth Group Recon. The Shadow Stalkers. And three strange dropships from the Ninth Tac Air Wing. The Black Dragons.
  This was a one-way mission.
  I didn't need the HUD mission goals to tell me that. I felt it. Knew it.
  My brothers in… his brothers in… the Ravens had resolved to get this done or die trying.
  This was for all the marbles.
  I could feel that, and other things, screaming across his mind which was like a shadow in the sunlight of mine here on this strange moon of broken ruins.
  "Second Elder Titan entering the battlespace, Ravens. Stand by for fire mission, my grid. Nightmare, this is Raven Actual, drop danger-close my position! No time to adjust… send it!"
  This was the group commander.
  "Nightmare Three… firing for effect."
  The firefight was everywhere across the strange cinnamon sands ahead that were dotted with marble-white ruins like the bones of strange monolithic creatures half-buried in the regolith.
  I felt… knew… the mission was to seal the Gate that led to our… Earth… their Earth… but they called it something different… that's all I knew. That's what came along with the armor… vague memories and impressions. And oh yeah… the messages… that I'd just hijacked with the help of Stinkeye's knowledge of such things, Chief Cook's pharmaceuticals… and the Little Girl's buried memories.
  This is where she hijacked him.
  This had taken place a long time ago… but it was real right now and I wasn't just riding along… I was fighting. Pushing through the sand and dodging the incoming off enemy gun teams on the high chocolate dunes ahead.
  There were messages to him here too…

But I'll get to those later.

So, it took me time to figure this out... but this is what I think was going on now that I've had time to parse it...

This was that... other Earth's last attempt... to not end up like us. And she'd gone in there, after using her upgraded plus-one power of time snatching no one in the Dark Labs had figured out she had, and snatched herself a champion.

Doom88.

On this other Earth not called Earth...

The Titans were the mortal enemies of that other Earth. They had come through the Oblivion Gate that had opened on their moon.

I know that long ago, before Earth was destroyed by whatever the Monarchs did... or was done to them... that the Earth humanity came from... had a moon.

Monarch official history said there was never a moon. But sometimes it said there had always been a moon.

They controlled history.

That was how they controlled us.

Until they didn't.

I have no idea if our lost moon looked like this. Chocolate dunes, white ancient ruins, cinnamon sands. Some atmo... but it was thin. As in you could walk around without some type of environment suit... but you'd be breathing heavy and need Ox-Max boosters.

No big deal.

That towering Elder Titan that had just snatched up the armored fighting vehicle that had attempted to traverse left and engage, crushing it with one of its cyclopean purplish-black tentacles... was enormous. It was all black like... a widow spider.

Shiny like oil.

But huge. Huge like some of the larger Saurians on that world Boom Boom had come from. It was like a giant spider that stood on its two legs, its back legs, while the others... seeming delicate and almost artistic at this distance, but in reality each leg was the size of a wide column for a three-story building before it articulated at a joint and continued almost double that length... were just as huge.

These Elder Titans were leviathans.

And that should be the worst part, but it wasn't...

I remember thinking as I transitioned through this memory of her snatching... snatching from some *other-where*... that I definitely did not like this reality she'd jumped into to escape the Dark Labs facility where they'd been torturing her... escaped here to snatch her champion... her protector... me but not yet... *me*.

So that's an important part... *me*. And this is how Stinkeye theorized she did it. She used host life forms to draw from in the present, in order to anchor and summon her... hijacked champion. They needed certain criteria. Apparently, according to Stinkeye's drunken theories... I was a perfect candidate, and the Little Girl had identified me as such early on when we thought, for no reason we could ever remember, to take in and protect this orphan we'd found on a battlefield.

"Why did we do that?" I asked Stinkeye.

"Ah... she a mule, Little King. Dat's a power a lot a psy-cans have because dat's how dey protect demselves even when dey don't know dey have it. It don't make her none-special when she was in the labs. A mule can take a turn on da dial inside people and make 'em have da emotions she wanna have 'em have. She made da company want ta protect her. Dat power was what da labs thought she had. She was foolin' 'em because she had other powers she was either hidin'… or didn't know about. Smart girl. If dey found out about da time snatchin' dey woulda either iced her… or…"

Stinkeye drew his scarred old finger across his ragged bony throat.

Chief Cook confirmed this when we brought him in later because of his experience with the psy-can program.

"Oh yeah… Orion… she smelled simp all over you and anchored in like a Stygian brain worm. Feeding off your place in temporal reality to exchange and just gate her champion in from wherever he comes from and is. And… this is just my two cents, Orion… it ain't a pretty place, that's for sure."

I'd always felt weak and drained during those times when she'd… *summoned*… him to get our collective bacon, and really hers… out of some kinetic jam gone seriously pear-shaped.

I'd just chalked up the drain to that post-combat drop as the body and mind crash from the adrenal overload.

But… I did have that vague sense of… I don't know. Fall. Leaves. The smell of burning wood and stinking sulfur at times. And that low-grade burn of strange and hypnotic power-acid-jazz or whatever it was, like an earworm in my brain.

Like some song you can't quite get ahold of.

Now I knew. Now I knew why I had those feelings… that drained… essence. She was using me as an anchor to get the Wild Thing to come and save her.

We had KIAs already. On the cinnamon moon where Doom88 and Task Force Raven fought the Elder Titans and their forces. Dark Forces.

And re: those forces…

The Titan's… *implings*… if that's the right word… were now entering the battlespace as we pushed through cinnamon sand thick as dust and tried to stay away from the energy-bursting glare of the gun teams on the range.

These were LMGs. Light machine guns. They were firing rapid-pulse energy shots in the red spectrum and the impacts slammed into the other Ravens or fountained in the sands in sudden plumes of spent kinetic energy.

An attack drop came in low over the battlefield, and her anti-personnel guns began to spin up and engage the ridge, suppressing fire from there as we pushed forward into a cluster of the bone-white ruins ahead.

"Eighty-Eight… Nineteen… check that avenue and set up a base of fire if they come from that flank. Ravens keep pushing forward… We're almost there. They're depending on us!"

The implings, small, gibbering, wild and full of guns, surged out from the dust-swallowed cinnamon sands and ancient ruins that guarded the avenue to the Gate.

The Oblivion Gate.

I don't believe in such things, but…

They were… demonic. That's the only way I can put it.

So… hey, I'm not crazy. This is what happened.

They came on and made the leading edge of our gunfire, and we bled their surge in a massive wave of outgoing leaded death.

The carnage was overwhelming as the first assault of gibbering imps died even while the second Elder Titan took missile strikes from two more attack dropships while being saturated by arty.

The ground was shaking hard.

But then it got worse.

One of the Ravens near me got zipped right in the bucket and there was nothing that could be done for him.

"Leave the dead," grunted the platoon leader, a hulking version of the Wild Thing. "If we survive, we will bring them home on their shields!"

Above it all, the already shaking ground beginning to heave, a new Elder Titan advanced across the sinking sand ruins, its six other legs like arms dragging into the battle as the ruins got weirder, denser, and taller. More Raven commandos were getting drilled by hot beams of intense laser fire from the sands and dunes.

"Watch for snipers!" shouted the platoon sergeant and got drilled center mass.

From the Elder Titan's six tentacles, huge, chained whips that must've been bio-organic machinery... snaked out into our assault as all Raven elements closed in to attack the ruins near the Gate. Now the whip-tentacles were picking up Raven Troopers and hurling them off into the cinnamon sands or crushing them instantly.

M99's roared in response, cutting into the Elder Titan's shining carapace.

Someone fired an anti-armor spread that shot forth like hellish suddenly dying comets shrieking out on star-screams. The AT rounds rammed into the Titan's hideous body, or rather the armored carapace at its center, and exploded causing ineffectual damage, but the massive, bloated eye at the center of the obscene being I now knew as an Elder Titan... seemed to grow more bloodshot, more malevolent... more glaringly angry at our existence as though broadcasting its need to wipe us out here and now.

"Alpha Team moving in to take the shot..."

"Raven, get ready to hold the push... Strike leader out!"

"Negative contact on Team Six... they're just gone!"

The implings' mass wave-horde attacked again, and this was something I could do something about as me and Nineteen were pulled forward to join the main gun line, the hasty defensive positions being graphed out in bloody red by the platoon leader as he organized the defense of the blocking action we would perform with some element called Alpha going for the shot.

I had no idea what "the shot" was but I had a vague notion that Alpha Team was some sort of special operator unit that wore berets.

A picture of a green beret flashed in my mind as some kind of word-association triggered the memory. But where the image came from I didn't know... I'd never seen any unit that claimed a green beret.

The implings came on in a diarrhea-level torrent of three waves like pitchforks coming straight for our blocking maneuver.

The Ravens fought hard to hold the line, and it was warfare like nothing I've ever experienced in real life.

Maybe more like some over-the-top game I'd never had much of an interest in.

It was like a power-gamer's fantasy of incredible odds and savage violence.

"Raven legion... stand by to repel!" shouted the commander like some latter-day hero of some lost golden age we'd been cheated of.

Task Force Raven was using cover or down on one knee as the three massive elements of implings pushed over the chocolate dunes and into the cinnamon sands we'd been tasked to hold or die trying.

The demons came hopping and gibbering over the sands… their bodies all odd-shaped and no two the same, red like hot coals, their bulging eyes burning like dying embers. They surged over the fallen ancient bone-white-marble stones the size of mag-rail cars, stones that were covered in ancient swirling markings that glowed faintly and made my mind hurt if I stared at them too long.

They came like a flood and the first assault was literally hundreds, if not thousands.

Now I knew why the Wild Thing's M99 Vulcan battle rifle was what it was… a personal weapon of mass destruction.

The Gatling gun we'd theorized the Wild Thing had in all the times she'd summoned it, and we'd caught glimpses of the destruction it could produce on demand, was not mine to use as the implings surged into our line. The first gunners opened up from the flanks, simply vaporizing the jumping opponents in a single burst of utterly savage outgoing as though their primary was some close-support aircraft's *braaaapping* out its twenty-millimeter chain-gun fire. Demons exploded in every direction leaving smoking inkblots all over the pristine burnt-cinnamon sands.

Target engagement sequences and math began to develop all over my HUD and at first, as my mind struggled to comprehend the overwhelming nature, it suddenly dialed in and I knew… I just… understood who to kill first and how much I could kill as fast as I could kill it.

And it was… good.

Quiet rage that might have been madness surged within me… but I was in control of it. Like Stinkeye's berserking… but mine to use as I wished.

The Vulcan M99 wasn't brutal enough. I wanted to use the knife, and my hands, and my boots, and my… teeth.

I steadied the rifle, selected who would die, and prepared to engage at best range…

Lines and targeting reticles appeared like some symphony of ancient beings and mighty myths in my head.

I would bring damnation on them all…

I was… *damnation!*

I pulled the trigger… smooth… and was rewarded with the instant electrical thrill of death in mass quantities.

Target One took forty rounds in half a sec and came apart in slow motion within my berserk-fevered mind. I watched its cursed body parts flying away as blood spray caressed the permanent night of the moon and turned to spattered ink on the cinnamon sands. One of the rounds blew off the top of its knobby horned scalp and that was perfectly satisfying.

Target Two another half-sec later took thirty-five rounds by the frenetic combat math inside the bucket that was totally understandable as not just my seeing eyes but my thinking mind embraced it all and accepted it so that I might use it better. The spray of body parts was beautiful as the bloody red mist of its fluids painted the sand.

The next target took a full second as I drag-fired and spent two hundred rounds cutting that one in half.

The surging demons disintegrated under shimmering waves of our outgoing lead, coming apart in pieces—warty arms... bloated chests... horned heads... fanged teeth... clawed feet... ravening inferno eyes suddenly exploding and going dark. They didn't even know they were dead as I continued to kill the next, dragging the steady blaring chain gun across them all and landing the last furious dose on what must have been some kind of demonic NCO.

Bigger.

Larger eyes.

A chainsaw that was bright steel and dried blood.

I blew him to shreds.

Five point eight seconds. And they were dead.

And the rest came on and the killing continued...

I was a killing machine. A beautiful killing machine and this is what I was made to do...

Him. The Wild Thing.

Me... whoever I was.

The hot sand all around the swarming imp force fountained in kinetic impacts as our squad engaged on this flank and we destroyed them.

More came on, bubbling over their already dead and dying now under our death swarms of lead. Some of the Raven Troopers switched to pulsar grenades while others shucked automag longslide sidearms from thigh holsters and engaged at close range. The push despite the masses of dead was that close here in the cinnamon sands. Automatic thundering booms from the sidearm hand cannons left visible shock waves between muzzle and target.

And at target there was little left.

These rounds hammered through the demons' armor and exploded into the sands beyond the demonic force as they came down at us from a high dune they crested like some foul disease spilling out over everything. Tall, weird, mind-bending ruins jutted out over the tops of these dunes.

More Raven Troopers began to fail. To fall. The line was thin... too thin.

"Hold the line, Ravens... for them!"

An image came fast... I didn't know what it was... but later I did. But I didn't want it here... with these horrors. They were too... pure for that and so I swept it aside as Nineteen was dragged down to my left and stabbed dozens of times, the gibbering implings laughing maniacally, their voices echoing into oblivion.

But too many were coming straight at me for me to do anything other than weave that cone of leaded death coming out of the M99 at everything I could.

The demons mobbed the fallen troopers like a rat-pile piling, stabbing with blades that shined in the starlight of this strange moon I found myself on. Laughing wildly, madly, as they did so.

Hold the line... I grunted through gritted teeth.

More were coming through even now. And to me... even as the Wild Thing among Wild Things... it did not seem like we would be enough...

Enough... to stop the gibbering mad tide of these hellish creatures.

Or the Elder Titan whose every approaching claw-fall was like an artillery strike not far off and coming close.

"Hold the line, Ravens! Remember them! Do not fail the Hidden King!"

That was when I got the *OVERHEAT warning on Main Primary M99 Vulcan* in my HUD.

CHAPTER FORTY-THREE

I have no idea how the M99 reloaded, but I knew its ammo was not infinite and somehow it involved what was called a singularity-feed system that sucked in matter from all around me at a nano-particle level, and then created rounds on demand.

It was unlimited.

Fun, huh?

But the battle rifle could overheat. Forbidden popsicle just like one of our LMGs back in the company.

It was already smoking now as I waded into the impling press, vaporizing and ruining the streaming gibbering things that were overwhelming the Raven Troopers all around me.

The barrel was hot, but I needed to kill them all and I didn't care who sorted them out.

OVERHEAT WARNING was now flashing frenetically in my blood-red HUD.

The gun needed time to draw matter, and I had fifteen seconds' worth of total cone of outgoing lead destruction left as I took a knee and vaporized a cohort of demonic implings carrying what looked to be some pretty janky old-school AK platforms.

Dirty. Banana magged. Grip tape and bloody bandages wrapping the stocks and barrel. Everything gungy with dried blood and gore.

They had no fire control and just sprayed everything they were heading toward.

There had been incoming the whole time.

But… regarding the Wild Thing armor… we'd seen this effect it had on incoming in the company dozens of times when she'd made him appear for her.

The Raven Trooper armor that was the Wild Thing's… that swirling mass of autumn leaves or bats that was there, and not there, shimmering and impossible within reality… was a sort of personal point defense system for the Doomsday Armor, as it was called inside the bloody red HUD.

M13 Doomsday Armor System.

Including the M78 "Black Bat" butterfly defense network. The swirling autumn "leaves" that ate up some of the incoming. And what didn't get "caught" managed to ram into the armor with a solid impact the equivalent of an illegal ultraball block. The kind they banned for "player safety" after some of the old pros got their careers cut short.

Nothing to knock you down, not in the Doomsday Armor. But nothing to sneeze at either. Unless you were a Raven Trooper, which I had the impression were some kind of elite special forces shock troops like the Rangers of the Saturnian Batts the first sergeant had been part of back in his younger days.

Singularity feed mag empty. Reloading, flashed in my bloody-script HUD. *One minute thirty-seven seconds until quarter mag reload.*

The three spinning barrels of the chain-gun M99 battle rifle gyrated down to a subtle spin as ashy smoke drifted from the barrel.

I moved it to my off hand, shucked the primary sidearm, and began to blaze away, clearing off the last of the impling push.

There were two other troopers left with me.

The demonic dead littered the field.

"Eighty-Eight, move to the right flank!" called the newly promoted squad leader. Doom34. The HUD updated the chain of command instantly as the KIAs were recorded.

The smoke-stained familiar voice was there in our comm... "Raven element... eyeballs inbound. Set up a killbox on that avenue of approach while main body pushes on toward the Gate. Maintain the left flank at all costs. Alpha is going for the ball."

Highlighted positions and course tracks appeared in my armor's shadowy faceplate, and I could see the other two surviving troopers of our element moving to positions that would allow us intersecting fields of fire in the "killbox" we'd establish to eat up these... *eyeballs.*

But what in the hell was an eyeball?

CHAPTER FORTY-FOUR

Chatter from 13th Group Command came in that the main element was pushing on the Gate now. Two metallic dropships, each with wicked long guns hanging from underneath and racks of deadly missiles deploying from the extending pods along its stubby wings, swooped in low over the cinnamon sands as we made ready to continue the blocking action at the location we'd been assigned.

I was still marveling at the advanced state of the Doomsday Armor and its blood-red HUD, and I wondered if this was what the Earth we came from could've been like had things gone different. Had the Monarchs not stolen power and made slaves of the rest of humanity. I wondered this as high above, like some titanic Saurian beast from an elder age, the next incoming Titan to enter the battlespace emitted an otherworldly howl. Its titanic shriek sent a shiver through my armor and right down into my boots, and bones.

His...

Mine.

It towered high above as it strode over the sand-swallowed ruins of this strange moon. A huge necrotic purple beam radiated out from a gigantic bulbous eye in the center of its widow's-black armored carapace. The powerful beam lanced out and smacked into the trailing attack dropship. The troop transport exploded suddenly in all directions. Fragments and systems rained down in the shell-casing-laden sands, rattling off the ancient marble and falling into sands pristine and untouched by our bloody battle. In other places those same cinnamon sands were marred by the splattered guts and ruined body-part spray of the demonoid implings carrying the wonky AKs.

One of the fuselage sections of the drop landed in a nearby crater the arty had churned up in prep that must have rained down on the battlespace before I showed up.

The gigantic elder beast roared out in what must have been victory as more flaming wreckage fell across the enigmatic sands of this strange moon where dozens of Earths gazed down on this desperate battle I had no idea of.

And was I even sure if that was real... the other Earths...? How was that possible?

Like I said, Stinkeye had theorized I'd take over and get a glimpse of her initial connection moment with the champion she'd decided to snatch, and this was it. Somehow his unit, his "Earth," had been involved in a desperate battle that somehow involved the Oblivion Gate...

A bolt of realization shot through me… and I had no idea where it came from or why I knew it: the Gate opened into all the Earths. This moon was where their Gate was.

And then I asked myself, as contact came hard and fast… and very weird…

Where was *our* Gate? Our Oblivion Gate?

The eyeballs streaking in, hovering over the dark sands, were a sight to behold. I've read fantasy and science fiction novels, sure, even played games, that didn't do these horrid things justice… they were bizarre and inexplicable in ways… I can barely describe. But I'll do my best.

And I wondered how much longer this hijack of the connection between the Wild Thing and Little Girl would last, and if I would survive it.

I mean, I wasn't just watching a movie. I was running and gunning. She was not just a time snatcher… but she could take someone from *other-whens*… so had my hijack taken us back to a point where my actions could change the course of events…

… like, say, I get murked as the Wild Thing…

She doesn't get her champion.

She doesn't escape the Dark Labs.

They use her powers… to stop the insurrection.

The Monarchs… live.

At that moment I was suddenly and terribly aware that I had the potential, by trying to save the company… the potential to make things much… much… worse.

And my brain hurt just getting the flash of all the football-bat I could do with the slightest mistake.

Like getting murked by floating eyeball drones right here and right now.

According to Stinkeye, he would be influencing the hijack, and… if his theory was true… there was a reality shift and time travel involved and so technically… if I was in the past, it was in the past of another reality, yet one that, again according to Stinkeye, affected our… reality.

Oof.

Never tear down a wall without first knowing why someone put it up, my old platoon sergeant used to say. Points deducted against me for not listening just in case I ever ended up with the ability to influence the time-stream continuum for the worse.

Stupid ruck hobo… there are more important things than foot care and traversing fire.

But I had no time to think about these *terribles*. This was all way above my ruck-hobo pay grade.

The enemy came glaring at us.

Which… believe me… is exactly how it happened despite my feeble attempts to describe it. Go read ruck-hobo Hemingway if you want better.

With me… *ya get what ya get.*

So I started blasting. I engaged the eyeballs with the secondary while I let the battle-rifle death machine reload as it drew matter and nano-particles in order to reload its singularity mag.

M99 sixty-eight percent full appeared in my HUD.

But here came the monsters. The floating eyeballs were hovering armored orbs about the size of large exercise balls. The orbs were some kind of hovering drones, but the massive, bewildered eye in the center of each machine… was definitely biologic.

And the clawed tentacles that erupted from all around the orb's surface looked biological too.

Also, they muttered. The muttering was electrical in nature, but you had the feeling it was a language of some sort. They spoke in an almost insane and manically repetitive manner.

I shot the first one with an automatic burst from the long-slide sidearm that shared some kind of inspiration in this other reality with the legendary 1911 platform of ours. Sonic booms raced out from my weapon as the Doomsday Armor maintained sight picture and grip on the thundering "hand cannon" of a secondary weapon.

There were eight of these cobalt armored "eyes" coming through a sand-filled alley created by the half-sunken ancient alien ruins that was the wall of the Gate and the complex surrounding it.

I had a small map in the top left corner of my HUD, but it was confusing. The symbols made no sense and there was scrolling data I couldn't interpret. And I had eight hideous giant eyeball beings floating toward me, turning suddenly to glowering menace as we opened fire on them and they chittered one to another about the threat we presented.

I hammered the lead with fire from the secondary at a range of about twenty-five meters. The blood-red HUD cross-hatched targeting information and reticle track for each shot, showing me where I was aiming, and ghostly echoes showed where I'd hit as the weapon continued to thunder across the sands, creating near-visible shock waves between it and my targets.

That first eye imploded when my third shot rammed home, blowing its ocular matter, and what I assumed was a massive red brain, all over the caramel sands behind it.

Its bio-mech tentacles went all haywire as it plowed into the sand and began to roll, its eye glaring madly at me with each revolution, becoming more sand-caked with each turn.

Then its armored chassis erupted as though some kind of secondary damage had just cooked off an internal power plant… and the thing shot skyward like a popped balloon and exploded, sending metal and organs in every direction.

Yeah… it was pretty gross.

Other eyeballs were dying as we engaged hard on our killbox. Doom34 had been hit bad, but even so the last of these were firing back from their tentacled claws even as the blur of our primaries just disintegrated the rest. Still, they fired at us as they died and I had to suck sand to avoid getting hit. Their blasts were gray shimmering rays of… *white noise*… or at least that's what they looked like to me. Like when a monitor goes all static. These spat forth from some of their tentacled claws and managed to bring down Doom34 and slice him in half right there in the sands.

It occurred to me at that moment that I was not as covered as I might need to be.

From other tentacles, sprays of dancing lights shimmered forth and I could see these were disrupting our tactical feeds and targeting capabilities.

I was back on the primary now and dumping short deadly bursts of hundreds of rounds at the floating eyes as they shifted position and tried to disrupt our tracking with their dancing lights.

More eyeballs, a second squad, had entered the killbox, pushing down through the sandy alley at us, gibbering their electric madness.

Ice and fire shot forth from their tentacles, and in an instant the killbox was alive with fire and ice and even more white-noise rays lancing everywhere and cutting into the sands.

"Fall back!" screamed Doom105, who was the other trooper in the trio tasked with holding this flank.

Then he was gone as he got hammered by ice rays that slowed him, then was cut to pieces with white-hot lasers of fire.

I got off the primary, its three spinning barrels already smoking, popped a pulsar grenade, and flung it into the eyeball surge as more of them came down the alley, emitting those strange hums and electrical *snap*s and *pop*s like some clock that couldn't keep time even twice a day.

Everything about this reality was madness and I had a good idea there was much more, and much worse, than just here what I was fighting…

I shifted back for better cover down the sinking alley, getting on the Vulcan death weapon and ruining three more that tried to assault through the remains of the pulsar grenade I'd just blown a bunch of them to pieces all over the alley with. I barely got cover behind a spiraling white marble column whose twin was mostly buried in the cinnamon sands that were deep and shifting here. White-noise beams exploded all around me and my HUD struggled to deal with the suppression effect of these beams. It was as though each was a bolt of EMP… if that makes sense… which it doesn't to me.

This lone twisting column was all the cover I was gonna get as more white-noise bolts seared in at me. If I moved from it, those eyeballs and their slice-rays were gonna gut me to shreds.

I shucked another grenade and tossed it at them.

C'mon, Stinkeye… back in, I thought, tucking behind cover just as the pulsar grenade exploded like a small star going supernova in an instant. A bright bloody sun suddenly appearing and turning the attacking orbs into little more than burning ash and flaming paper as it flat-out annihilated them.

For a long moment the fire at the heart of the pulsar grenade hung there like a tiny stellar object suddenly come to life. More eyeballs rushed into the sands where we'd been defending and caught fire as they got too close to it in their mindless gibbering electric madness to slice and kill me.

Then the small star blinked out and still more eyeballs pushed in, an endless stream, glaring murder right at me.

I had nothing left to do but fight now…

So… I fought.

I fought for everything I was worth because perhaps there was a lot more at stake here than just my life.

I opened fire with the death machine gun I'd seen the Wild Thing ruin enemy bad guys with on many an occasion. Literally turning them to nothing but dust and flying fragments in a burst.

That's what I did to these things and I felt myself growling and then roaring the murder they intended for me right back into their hideous and malevolent eyes.

The gun thundered hard as it spat out thousands of rounds in seconds. And it was at that moment I felt like a swarm of bees blew right through me like a cool breeze as I held on to the trigger and rode all that death right into them.

It was glorious.

It was rock and roll... dialed to eleven. I traversed, and several eyes simply came apart under the swarm of killer lead bees I spat at them while others ruptured and exploded into the sands or rocketed off into one another.

More and more came, and I ignored the *OVERHEAT* warning and held on, spraying everything I could with the gun in the alley I'd inadvertently canalized them into. A long minute of hellish gunfire and the numbers seemed less than what had been pushed at our force through this gap in the flank.

They were hesitating... gibbering madness, questioning one another, and somehow I knew this... their mission, their existence, their supremacy against a mere mortal like myself.

Seconds left on the singularity mag and I saw my moment and pushed forward into it and them, spraying the hovering eyeballs that remained in the sand-filled alley between the cyclopean alien stones. I shot them as they came until the gun ran dry.

Fire spread across the sands from their beams. Ice lay on the walls in frosty clusters. White-noise beams had disrupted the sands and some stones, slicing them clean in half as though they'd just removed what they'd been aimed at.

Three floating death orbs were left, the eyeballs, and I was moving fast to kill them now as I let the apocalypse gun dangle on its sling and reached for the hand cannon.

I was faster than them. Faster than I even thought possible...

Was this an effect of the Doomsday Armor, I wondered, even as I went for them screaming bloody murder and rage, sidearm coming out and landing on the first.

It wasn't enough to just shoot them.

I needed to push the barrel into them... into the eye... before I squeezed the trigger.

I needed that level of violence.

That level of... retribution.

He did.

Me.

It all happened in slow motion now, and I remembered that about the Wild Thing. Sometimes it moved so fast it was like it was on fast forward, or at least twice as fast as any... human... I'd ever seen move.

But to *it*... him... me...

... in these suddenly boosted moments... everything would seem... *slower*.

Rage overwhelmed me.

Images from the messages stored in the HUD floated through my mind...

Messages for him.

Me.

My guess was the armor could either overpower my own human system and boost me as fast as my mind wanted it to, using the exoskeleton for short bursts of speed and attack, or the flickering doomsday armor could somehow perform pico-leaps through time, many in the slimmest measures of time, in order to think, move, and fight faster than anything it faced.

Some time-dilation trick inherent in its construction.

I didn't know. I didn't care.

I just wanted violence and all of it I could handle. That... was enough for me.

Him.

I surged forward at the three angry floating eyeballs, their clawed tentacles undulating like strands of slow-moving seaweed seeking something to strangle or annihilate with their beams.

I drilled the first one with a thunderstrike of outgoing fire from the hand cannon.

BOOM BOOM BOOM BOOOM BOOOOOM…

Death concussions of fractured reality expanded between us…

Yeah… that.

I know… weird, huh?

I watched as tentacles and eyeballs swung toward me in slow motion, intent on firing everything they had as they gained a targeting solution in their wild alien architecture of mind and biomechanical machine.

"Die!" I grunted from deep inside as I engaged the second one with more rounds from the hand cannon.

And I wasn't sure that was me. That ragged grave growl of a voice that had welled up within me.

A blade was in my other hand, drawn from off the armor seamlessly and without thought.

Like it was the most natural thing in the universe.

Thunder rounds tore the second one to shreds as I pushed the thundering barrel right into its eye and continued to hang on to the trigger as guts, brain, and carapace exploded away from the bulbous horror of that dark and *other* place.

The knife cut like hot lava through cold ice as I swung it wide in a killing arc at the third eyeball. I turned away from the ones I'd shot, twisted, and only caught the last orb in the lower half of its eye as I thrust the blade in, then dragged it to the left with a savage heave.

I roared as the blade pulled itself free of the armored carapace of the bulbous eye-being and I knew it was dead.

And more importantly… it did too.

It glared at me in horrific rage as it tried to float away from me in fear of what was coming.

One of its beams fired off…

I threw myself to the right, in an instant slashing with the death-blade like it was bayonet training back in the day with my old NCOs.

"What makes the grass grow!" they'd roared at us new recruits to the company.

I cut the eye in half and it exploded in my face throwing bloody guts and ruined eye in every direction.

"*Blood!*" the Wild Thing screamed and reveled as the last eye shrieked in its electric insanity indignation and murder because that's what this was.

Murder.

There was no fighting a Wild Thing.

When it came for you… it was murder.

It shrieked electrically again as though I was supposed to have mercy on it even as it covered my armor in flame from one of its tentacles.

I stabbed it and stabbed it and kept on stabbing it, driving it into the cinnamon sand beneath my bloody boots, the remains of the thing drooling out onto the red moon as I felt the death-blade push it deeper.

And… that's when I heard her.

"Help me!" she whimpered.

"All elements move on Objective Gate now…" echoed smaller and smaller in my comm.

The battle was being lost.

Orders, desperate ones… were coming from the strike leader.

I turned and saw the Little Girl as she was. Then, little. Oversized boots. Black potato-sack dress. Badly cut short hair. And those eyes… except now they were filled with fear.

"Remember them!" the Raven commander had shouted as we'd entered the battle.

And now, on autopilot, I heard the Wild Thing move toward her… shouting in his growl, "I got you, little girl. Hold on!"

I knew what was going to happen next.

I heard Stinkeye from across all the dark strands of the universe.

"Link is severed, Little King… Hang on now…"

Doom88…

The Wild Thing… reached out with his bloody gauntlet as she raised her tiny hand from out of the shadowy space she crawled into between the sinking sands and the huge alien stones scrawled with the writings of madness.

Above us one of the Earths exploded and cracked in half.

I felt the loss of life. It was… *catastrophic*.

"Noooo…" I heard myself whisper.

The blood-red HUD flashed with images as it scrambled and the messages of the strike commander became still more desperate, more urgent…

They were being slaughtered.

Strike Force Raven.

13th Group.

Earth Defense SOCOM.

And then… the HUD scrambled and died and I saw the Wild Thing's wife… and kid.

Doom88.

Whoever he was.

Her last message to him…

She was blond. Thin. Pretty. The child was… a toddler. A girl.

"This is your daughter, Marcus! Say hi to Daddy, baby girl!" her recorded voice said.

The Wild Thing took the hand of the little girl hiding in the sand.

He had one. A little girl.

And still… he'd gone on this one-way mission to save their Earth. Just as all of Task Force Raven had…

And now they were being slaughtered…

He'd rescue this one. This… little girl stranded on an impossible moon the strike force had been sent in to… *save*… that reality's version of humanity.

"Say hi, baby girl…" the pretty wife coaxed the toddler in the message recording. "Say hi… to Daddy."

"She ain't just a time snatcher… Little King," crooned the ghost of Stinkeye. *"She can go to other wheres. Find da perfect soldier… to save her from dem Monarchs. Keep her safe. From dem, Little King. From dem."*

The baby in the recorded message looked at the camera and tried to speak her first word…

"Da…"

"I got you," grunted Doom88 as he reached down.

Then the Little Girl took his hand… and he screamed as he was sucked away to where she needed him.

He roared because he knew where he was going. Because he knew they had lost now. And… because he had lost… *them*. Forever.

Da Heart, Little King. Dat's how she does it. She can anchor there. That's where she keep him… until…

Now I was in the armor. Hurtling through darkness…

Space…

The LZ at *Dark Star*…

That's how she does it, Little King. She take 'em from somewhere… and keep 'em for when she needs…

I was coming in hot on the LZ as the sled braked hard, rolled over like a glider, and slowed to landing fall speed.

LFS.

I was the Wild Thing now…

The blood-red HUD began to tag and highlight all the defenses on that enemy deck that killed all of us in all my dreams. And nightmares.

A cold cemetery wind blew across what I might have called my soul.

I would kill them all now.

"*Blood!*" I screamed as I hit the deck and slid in like some crashed starship, coming to one knee and opening fire with the death machine gun.

"*Death… to all of you!*" I growled.

CHAPTER FORTY-FIVE

I hit the deck of the *Dark Star* like a comet and left a trail of fire and blackened deck.

I'd come in hot. Literally.

The Wild Thing's HUD was dark and I realized my eyes were closed. For a moment there was nothing.

Sweet... sweet... nothing.

Silence.

A kind of peace that comes when you commit to a course of action and there's no turning back no matter how bad the plan is.

No *Sar'nt Orion, step on this problem somebody else made* or *Put out that fire the other guy started*. No *Lemme tell you my story, Sar'nt*. No Stinkeye and the chief trying to kill each other. No crazy war wizard and deranged conspiracy nut to deal with and avoid for continued slices of birthday cake. No unspoken command to do better with my charges from the silent weathered gaze of the old man, burning that heater and always watching... watching for an angle on how we could improve our roll.

Justified.

Urging me to be a better small unit leader than what he'd been dealt.

Seeming impossible most days.

I felt those things. Always. Always had since I'd been made an NCO.

I opened my eyes.

The blood-red HUD was offline.

I could see the massive flight deck of the *Dark Star*, the place of my endless nightmares in all that flight time out here, the infamous hangar we'd chosen for insertion that I'd seen long before it had even been chosen.

Our DZ. The place where I'd dreamed the company would die a thousand deaths, a thousand times.

It looked exactly as I had foreseen.

I felt my breath catch in my chest.

Perhaps... dumb as my plan was... it wasn't that wrong.

I'd burned in hot. Nothing felt broken but I wondered if I'd managed to do the one thing the Wild Thing had never done... broken the strange and enigmatic armor of the apocalyptic warrior we'd come to know as the Little Girl's pet.

Her... champion now that I knew the whole story.

Her... prisoner.

I could feel his rage...

But he'd been the company's ace of spades in a tight spot many times.

We... had profited because of his servitude.

Everything hurt.

I could see some of the enemy defenders... they weren't doing much. But there was activity...

I groaned, sure despite the Doomsday Armor's legendary status in our hearts and minds in the company, that something inside me was broken forever.

"Come on, Sar'nt..." I gasped to myself. We were dealing with intense speeds between starships even at near-space broadside combat. The *Spider* had been moving fast over the target ship. I'd been fired out of what was essentially a light torpedo tube. Aimed into a deck and slowed only to fractions of terminal velocity by a "space glider" equipped with one-shot retro rockets.

A space glider programmed and spec'd for EVC suits. The Doomsday Armor... who knew what its mass was? Everything about it was weird and... *other*.

Something has to be broken, that dark part of my mind we all possess shrieked at me as I tried to ignore it. As though M.O.M. were actually my mother telling me that's why we never play ball in the house after something valuable, some vase or precious thing... had been broken beyond the miracles of glue and the same thing available online somewhere.

A memory perhaps.

Strange...

I saw the dim shapes of the enemy running across the gleaming flight deck of the strange cathedral-like space that was the hangar deck. Ground troops. The *Dark Star*'s "Marines." We had no idea what these would be. The Ultras were all dead. Their divisions spent defending the destroyed Battle Spires. Who knew who, or *what*, guarded the last of the humans who'd made themselves our gods in their own eyes.

The clock was burning...

I had to straight-up wreck as much as possible, even if that meant getting wiped out as the Wild Thing before they attempted a second boarding insertion on the DZ now that they'd got back control of the ship I'd locked them out of.

The Drop Zone.

The *Spider* would be making her turn across the vast disc of the ship now, where already strange "cities" were deploying up into space as the massive starcraft entered defense mode. In seconds, as XO alerted the Old Man to the ship's status, what I'd done... they'd turn and attempt to board again. I had maybe three minutes before the *Spider* came within range of the *Dark Star*'s deck guns guarding the edges of the bay.

"Need to get those..." I gasped, heaving myself to one knee, dragging the Wild Thing's heavy assault gun up, using it as a brace to get to my boots. The armor felt heavy. I could hear the enemy boots thumping metallically across the hangar deck as they raced to see what strange creature had been torpedo-shot into their midst.

Still no HUD.

My head was hanging, looking at nothing but the once-gleaming charred deck I'd landed on. Came to rest along.

I was... tired.

I wasn't enough and I was pretty sure I was about to die. These weren't even odds...

It was me against the whole ship at this moment.

I'd need to do this now though, do whatever I could… even if the HUD didn't come up and the weapons didn't work. I'd brought one little surprise I haven't talked about… But I could deny the deck as an LZ and perhaps the *Spider* would select a new insertion site and have a better chance than the one I'd seen in the visions so many awful times before.

I'd brought a micro-bomb. I'd set it up in a det-ruck on the sled's equipment compartment. Usually reserved for more ammo or AT launchers we'd be jumping with.

I bent down and retrieved it, slinging it over one shoulder.

They were coming… they should've opened fire by now. But… I was just one guy. They could handle one guy.

They were about to learn how wrong they were.

Cumulative, fission feed, limited cascade. The micro-bomb. It was little more than a large grenade but when detonated would expand via molecular chain reaction into what amounted to something larger. Five hundred pounds larger.

It was an ancient piece of ordnance… but it did the trick when you needed to make sure that even if you lost… so did the other guy.

The *Spider* has a deep-stores weapon locker with weapons systems the company has acquired and accumulated over the years. Some of them are downright banned *weapons of mass destruction*. We're real quiet about those. Some are actually too deadly to even use. We keep those so no one else can get them is what we tell ourselves. Replitoxin gas canisters. Smart hypersonic missiles with nuclear warheads run by ancient AIs that are pure malevolence and that, when you run software checks on them, a company duty for a few, mainly the command team, the old weapons chatter on and on about old conflicts they're waiting to resolve… someday. They're like listening to barking dogs that just want to bite and tear and draw blood when you jack in to perform maintenance checks on them. There are other, darker things down there that I shouldn't even be talking about in the logs… so I don't. Again, the company just carries them so no one else can get their hands on them.

That's the lie we tell ourselves. Right?

But it begs the question… why haven't we destroyed them? And believe me… there's one we really should. Trust me on that one. It's too dangerous to even mention mentioning in the logs.

It's… inconceivable. And yes… I know the meaning of that word.

But we don't toss them into a sun. We haven't. And I suspect… we never will.

We keep them because… well, ya never know when it might be nice to use one on someone that's beating the crud out of you.

We are small and petty and vindictive that way.

It's best to be honest about these things.

Which was how the first sergeant put it one time when we were down there together. Only the first sergeant, XO, myself, and the Old Man have access to the deep stores weapons locker on Deck Nineteen.

Nineteen.

There's that number again. Strange…

We've disabled all access to that section of the ship and put in a lot of security. Gun turrets and laser sensors in the one passage that enters the secure weapons vault.

We only go there once per flight to make sure everything is as it's supposed to be according to SOP laid down by John Strange himself.

John Strange. Himself.

Then we close it up and try not to think of what's down there. Or at least I do. I don't know what the others do. We never talk about Deck Nineteen. Ever until it's time to go down there and do inventory as we call it.

So… I went in and got the micro-bomb after I'd hacked M.O.M. and had secret command authorization over the whole ship.

Man… if I live, the first sergeant's gonna kill me.

My plan is if the enemy closes on me… if I fail, I det the micro and take out the *Spider*'s DZ. Give the company a shot at life somewhere else, not here.

That's the best I can do, kids. Try to think well of me when I'm gone.

Spoiler… they won't.

The pounding metallic boots are almost on me when I look up and see the enemy we've come to put the hit on through the shaded bucket of the Wild Thing's forward visor. Nothing more than a black, lifeless slit in the armor when viewed externally. I have no butterfly defense field. No HUD. And the armor feels heavy beyond an unpowered EVC by orders of magnitude.

Maybe it's… outta juice…

Three minutes is what I gave myself to get it done… if not… then I det the micro-bomb.

It's that simple.

The bomb is an ancient OD-green thing with faded small yellow writing. "Military-speak" means nothing to me. From times I've never known and wondered much about.

M595 Major ASSET Denial Munition.

U.S. Army.

Aim Toward Enemy.

I like that.

It kinda sums up my whole… life.

Aim Toward Enemy.

But isn't that the life of every soldier?

Okay… I think… Let's get it on… c'mon, armor… do Wild Thang…

And then… that strange acid power chord thrums to life like some dark beast beginning to howl in the forest beyond the lights.

I feel hot. Irritated. Ready…

The HUD flickers to life, a blood-red imprint. Then it's gone, and then… it comes back.

I'm… pissed.

A personal message the Wild Thing has placed in the boot-up appears.

Do it for them.

I know who *them* is. I knew who he was doing it for when he went with the others, his brothers of Strike Team Raven in that *other us* we could have been. His wife. His baby girl.

"Say hi to Daddy."

My teeth are practically grinding as the rage… surges through me like a drug. Like… a swarm of bees…

"This is your daughter, Marcus."

Whoever he is.

Power... dark... holy... violent... surges through me as the armor comes online at last and I stand straighter, heaving the rifle of mass destruction to the ready as they come at me all at once... ready to lay the hate.

"Get it on," I growl like an animal to no one but myself in the Doomsday Armor.

Like some beast beyond the lights of civilization in the forest dark. Autumn leaves fall like rain across my HUD as the butterfly defense network begins to swirl and swarm about me like a tornado of nearly visible black-shadow bats.

Doomsday Armor Systems Online... appears in bloody HUD-script.

I jerk toward my first target and engage, pulling the trigger on the battle rifle as all three barrels begin to spin frenetically, vomiting out ten-millimeter rounds at three thousand feet per second, ripping the commandos to pieces.

Humanoid.

Their body armor is chimeric. Standard human body armor. Good stuff. Flexible armor carrier with mag pouches and gear. Armored shoulders and biceps. Armored greaves. Spiked assault gloves.

Humans inside somewhere...

The HUD graphs and targets everyone, prioritizing the murder that's about to happen.

The slaughter that's impending.

Their helmets are shaped like animals. Like black dogs with tall pointy ears. Like that ancient Earth breed Dobermans. Their "eyes," optical sensors, glow red indicating they have advanced visual and targeting systems.

"Good for them," I practically hiss.

A squad approaches me just as the spinning tri-barrel battle rifle of the Wild Thing comes up and begins to blare death itself.

Their armor is gold and black.

Their animal helmets purest polished black like obsidian stone.

Ornate and formal as though they are more ceremonial guards for some stellar... Monarch... than hard-bitten warriors tasked with denying a boarding operation by grunt space marines come to stack in mass quantities.

Sucks to be you...

The gun fires about three thousand rounds per minute.

The squad approaching me *was*, active word *was*, carrying small carbines. One guy carrying a shotty... all of them are just torn to shreds at ten meters as I point and destroy them with the battle rifle, turning them to red mist and flying parts and shredded armor in seconds as the gun whines and roars.

Oh mama!

What a rush!

I shift and engage the security element that was coming in to secure the perimeter from another section as I was taken into custody... or so they'd intended.

Instantly another squad is just shredded into little more than body parts and disintegrating flesh flying away at unexpected and sudden speeds faster than they thought possible.

No one on any of the gun teams on overwatch, other ground combat elements stacked nearby, defensive guns at the ready, drone operators to the rear... all the forces I have seen in all my waking PTSD-in-advance nightmares… none of them moves or responds, this has happened so fast.

"Good," I hear myself rumble bitterly.

Even as they came apart, my hyper-focused hyper-fast Wild Thing mind sensed they realized they were coming apart as they died and were aware of the hundreds of rounds savaging their bodies.

"Get it on," I hiss and begin to engage the rest. It's like being fed into a woodchipper fast, for them, but slow enough to realize it's happening… for them.

They're done and they know it as I seek and destroy with the M99 Vulcan gun.

I'm already moving fast, just like we've seen the Wild Thing do the times our bacon was in the fryer and she summoned him from wherever. But we know now… I push the implications of that away. No need to dive in too deep… I have targets to destroy.

People to kill.

I am the very word *predator* in ways I have never been.

A hunter in the jungle.

A killer in the dark.

The acid chords jam and blare as I roar red murder, muttering *revenge* and *death* as I begin to get my murder on… cream-style as Wolfy likes to say sometimes.

"Get it on!"

CHAPTER FORTY-SIX

My primary target is to take out the defense guns that shoot up the *Spider* as we try to insert onto the LZ in all my PTSD dreams.

Take those out and maybe we've got a chance… maybe they've got a chance.

Right now my odds look slim even with the Doomsday Armor.

After that I'll try to knock out the machine gun positions and other clusters of bizarre enemy infantry that absolutely ruin us when we try to get a foothold on this strange and fantastic ship.

It's nothing like we've ever boarded.

But I've seen it all before.

Most ships are tight. Narrow passages. Small compartments. Brutal security systems and automatic gun turrets. It's hell, and statistically, if you stack up the company's boarding operations versus our ground combat actions, one for one, we've lost way more men in these kinds of fights.

These are the worst. By. Far.

We generally don't do it and are little more than a light infantry company with a few shady tricks to pull. That's our *schtick*, as they say. Our *monkey trick*.

Now, as the Wild Thing, I go in hard on the two anti-ship gun positions at the edge of the hangar where it meets open space. Incoming is already trying to tag me. The butterfly defense system handles it and I eat up the defenders, more of those strange obsidian dobie-headed warriors rocking commando rigs as I close on the first position gunning everyone down indiscriminately.

The first gun position is a swivel-mounted twin pom-pom-style cannon probably firing railed eighty-eight arty rounds.

In those PTSD dreams these weapons systems wreck the *Spider* so much that the insert onto the DZ is little more than XO trying to maintain hover in a multi-hundred-ton starship, destroyer class, while we jump off the cargo decks we've turned into assault decks.

Oh yeah, in some of the more brutal "dreams" the eighty-eight positions adjust fire after they've put several smoking hulls into our starship home and turn their guns loose on the assault decks.

Many of us die and it's a bad death.

Torn to shreds by what is basically range-detonated anti-starship fire. Much of my platoon is torn to pieces right before me as my EVC boots hit the deck and we hurl ourselves into the interlocking fields of fire coming from the perimeter defense guns farther back in the massive hangar bay.

"It's real sporty," as Punch likes to say when the barroom brawl turns out to be a bit of a challenge for him. And he doesn't even drink. He just goes for the fights.

I remind myself as I go in hard with the M99 Vulcan rifle of mass destruction that it never happened. I am here to change things. It was all a dream, I tell myself as I engage a platoon manning their positions around the first deck gun I'm going after.

The *Spider*'s gotta be getting her act together and setting up a course profile to re-engage the DZ by now, so I am aware that the thin time left on the clock is already burning. I have no time to spare, and I open fire with the blaring anti-personnel gun that is the Wild Thing's battle rifle, cutting down any exposed defenders I can, then laying the hate on the defensive barriers they've erected.

These come apart like they are being erased from reality.

Cylinder barrels spin and I turn the first dobie-head to nothing but red mist from the waist up.

I'm taking fire but the butterfly personal defense system continues to eat up the incoming and I've killed another two more bad guys, shredding their bodies with high-dosage outgoing in just seconds.

What must be their squad designated marksman gets tasked with taking me out from a small nest of heavy-duty containers they've set up to defend him.

The rifle he's using is definitely heavy caliber and if I have to guess, it's some kind of short-barreled fifty cal with a very high-tech sleek matte-black design.

The box mag seated below the stock is the correct size to load that kinda thunder in the barrel, and for a half a second as I spin left toward him, dead dobie-heads still disintegrating from the cone of swarming lead I'm dosing them with... all in a kind of slow motion because in "Wild Thing world" you get to move, and think, and fight, faster than everyone else... I see the dobie-trooper SDM tap the mag, pull back the bolt, and prepare to engage me with some serious firepower.

Ruck-hobo me would suck dirt...

But I'm the Wild Thing now...

And I'm only vaguely wondering what a fifty-cal round will do to the Wild Thing's personal defense system and I have this suspicion it'll punch and hit and that... might be a bad thing.

But I'm too fast for the marksman.

Sorry, that's the breaks, dude, I think as I land the spinning tri-barrel on him and tear him to shreds before he can even complete the two-stage trigger squeeze.

In an instant he is hit by furious destruction and there is so little left of him it's as though he never was.

I am in awe of this weapon system.

And loving it.

Another commando comes up, and rounds slap into him, knocking him to the rear of the stacked heavy containers as bits of plate and chest rig explode out and away while bone matter and blood spray all over the back wall of containers.

Slow motion makes it all seem... cinematic.

Several rounds hit this one's slick SDM rifle and ruin it as one round in particular slams into his head and explodes the dobie-mask-armor bucket.

The body's just slumping as I turn and ruin two more popping up to put fire on me from the entrance to the deck gun pit.

The deck gun pit is defended physically by black synthetic sandbags probably filled with micro-thick anti-munition repellent. Or whatever the Monarchs' Dark Labs cooked up for them that's even better than the best I know of.

Generally this stuff, or versions of it, will straight-up stop most rounds and even some anti-armor. It's great stuff. Expensive though. And any contract we were on, it specifically got used wherever the generals had decided to establish their "forward" command post.

Which was often nowhere near where the tech would have been highly useful, say someplace like where the actual fighting was being done.

But this is a Monarch ship, the last one ever if this gets done the way it's supposed to, and my guess is… the best tech they have, the best ever known to man, is gonna be a big part of this operation… if the company can survive this very bad day.

"Why I'm here," I hiss in the ghostly armor as I luxuriate in the visual of the Wild Thing's Personal Weapon of Mass Destruction shredding the ablative dust bags, ravaging both the NCO running the gun team, and the gunner… in about three real-time seconds.

Feels more like sixteen seconds but the mission clock in the blood-red HUD says only three have passed.

This is…

… amazing.

It's like getting to sit in Monarch Class on some starliner. You can never go back to first, business, or coach ever again after that kind of experience. It all will seem so… less.

Sorry, Bastard, I think about my primary. But…

We have to be honest about these things.

The M99… is my new favorite jam.

Still… I gotta make sure everyone's dead because I don't need some "hero" coming in to "get the gun up" and defend the DZ as the *Spider* begins to make her final approach shortly in the next few minutes.

Which is something I could totally see myself doing if I was that guy on the other side of things. Something stupid that'll get you… bravely… killed.

Or Klutz.

The "brave" part is what you tell yourself right before you die. It's supposed to be a comfort.

And right there… I think of Hotsoup.

Soup on a bad LZ. Frightened to death and me yelling at him. And then he was dead.

Hotsoup indeed. And I can't believe as I march forward, letting my Personal Weapon of Mass Destruction cool with my off hand holding it by its barrel-mounted carry as I draw the auto-fire hand cannon and start shooting the other troopers inside the gun pit like I'm running a price-label marker-gun at some Dart Mart back on the world I came from… I can't believe thoughts of Hotsoup are hitting me as I'm living my best life… Infantry Space Grunt Marine with super armor and a Personal Weapon of Mass Destruction.

Literally… *unstoppable*.

I mean… I'm not ghoulish… but it simply doesn't get better than this in this line of work. And yeah… it's better than… eel girls in warm sauna grottos…

It's like feeling a swarm of honeybees blow right through you like a breeze… on a spring day. It's electric and you feel like you have the power of life and death in your gloves like you've never ever felt it before.

It's more than intoxicating.

It's… boosting.

One of the dobie-heads raises his assault-gloved hands and he's shrieking on audio… audio I'm picking up inside the Wild Thing's very wild bucket… he shrieks…

"No… No, no… you don't have to do this!"

Both gloves held out.

He's been shot, by me of course, several times. And yet…

I send a burst into his skull and then the gloved hands go limp on the bloody deck surrounding the anti-ship gun that had killed me and my friends over a thousand nights of PTSD on the long trek out to Typhon.

"Yeah, bro…" I mutter.

The Wild Thing's bucket makes my voice sound like the hiss of a snake. Or a long-dead mummy from some horror movie I never liked very much.

"I do."

CHAPTER FORTY-SEVEN

I gunned the second position hard. Didn't need to close and clean because the high volume of fire from the Wild Thing's Personal Weapon of Mass Destruction cooked off one of the HE rounds in the gun pit and the whole position, with still-living defenders fighting back, suddenly went flying in every direction as the gun's ordnance did what it did.

I was taking fire from… well, everywhere by that time.

I checked the massive port entrance into the flight deck from outer space and saw the *Spider* turning base to approach-landing flight profile, firing her massive reversers to slow some for an assault approach.

Now she'd get her chance to make the DZ without getting shot to pieces.

That was one half of the solution. Now, if I could shut down the defenders on the deck then the company could get off the ship, establish defensive position, and we could conduct operations with further push deeper into the target ship.

I moved toward the perimeter defensive guns, using as cover some of the loading cranes and ad hoc defensive positions the defenders had prepped the deck with to either defend or canalize us into an attack that sent us right into the meat-grinder of their interlocking fields of fire.

How, I'd asked myself dozens of times in the run-up to this moment, had they known to defend this landing bay so heavily against our targeted landing? The *Dark Star* was the size of a city. Bigger. It must've had hundreds, if not thousands, of landing bays all along the two-kilometer-high "sides" that ringed the circumference of the saucer.

But I'd never arrived at an answer, other than maybe… they just had that many defenders. Which… if that was the case… would be incredible odds and we would lose. The fleet didn't have the numbers to overcome those numbers.

Numbers are often the hard reality of battle despite the propaganda of spectacuthrillers.

But… once Stinkeye came into my planning, he explained their foreknowledge easily.

"Aw… dat one be no mystery, Little King. Dey got da Bishops of dey owns. And dem Bishops got all kinds o' magic powers from dreams to da insights to be able to smell out where we gonna attack. 'Member the battle at Tanang on Nessun, Little King…"

I did very well. Still got the gunshot wound on the meat of my thigh. First time anyone ever had to put a cat-tourniquet on me.

"I knowed them tribes were gonna come out the western gap and so ah told the Old Man it was so. Dey gots da same."

Stinkeye smiled smugly. Then Chief Cook launched his attack.

"Nice, Stink. We had drone recon all up in those hills and we saw that enemy force a mile off. I ran a standard capture-interrogation using my little friend sodium pentothal and that Bushi scout was singing like a little morning bird. It was me, you ol' fraud, that told the Old Man about the surprise. You came in, drunk and braying about dreams of fire and darkness in the hills you old con artist, just like you do every third day in any given combat zone during operations. Hoping to get lucky through guessing an impending attack all the time. Nice try. But that was all solid intel development and some pharmaceuticals which is how it's done in the bigs. But you wouldn't know about any of that."

Then the Psyops chief turned to me.

"Precogs, Orion. They for sure have 'em in spades and that's gonna be something we're going to need to deal with in there. I ran a precog test against a team of operators from the batts using nothing but cooks and mechanics as OPFOR. Sim of course. But with the Bishops specializing in precog we managed to wipe out the operators in three days of intense fighting in a forsaken swamp I still get the shudders from."

He stopped, shook out some small yellow pill from a secret canister, put it between his teeth and cracked it as he raised his head awkwardly and to the right. Then he growled like a dog and muttered, "That's the stuff."

For a second he was completely somewhere else and Stinkeye pointed at him and muttered, "See, Little King... he a drug fiend... tha's all. Can't trust 'im no never when."

Then Chief Cook was back, clear as day.

Behind mirrored sunglasses that is.

"Where was I... oh yeah... Orion... the battle at Shumago Moors... Yeah... precogs had a big hand in that one. And also... I mixed up a little batch of bathtub adrenamol and turned those cooks and mechanics into real bloodthirsty killers. The kind they make certain kinds of serial killer documentaries about."

Then the Psyops warrant looked around as though someone was suddenly listening in.

"Hey..." he muttered, coming in close. "*You ain't cheatin'... you ain't tryin'*, Orion. That's how it is in war. Precogs ain't cheatin'. If we actually had a Bishop besides Nether," he said ignoring Stinkeye, "then I'd use 'em even if I had to hook 'em up to a steady drip of oblivimox and tramazene... ooooh boy, talk about a good time. But we'd know and I'd do what they're doing to you in your dreams. 'Cept I'd do it better and we'd all be dead."

He seemed to miss the irony of that statement.

So, precog Bishops were the most likely reason why they had this docking bay so heavily defended in advance of our arrival. And if that was the reason... then I had very little hope the company was going to survive the further incursions we were facing as we went deeper and deeper into the X-ship known as the *Dark Star*.

But that was a tomorrow problem.

Today... wreck the DZ enough to get the *Spider* down and clear and everyone developing a defensive perimeter we could conduct operations from.

That's all.

Now I was stalking forward, shooting down clusters of the surging dobie-headed infantry tasked with defending this deck.

They were trying to assault and block my advance in different groups, putting up bases of fire from one direction while counterattacking from another. I was leaving them dead and scattered... and still... they continued to fight despite the withering amount of gunfire I was dosing them with.

Someone used an anti-armor rocket round on me but at the last second the round sidewindered away and missed, skirling off at the last second. The round detonated as the munition slammed into a shuttle on the deck and sent debris everywhere. The blast pushed me to one side and took my finger off the death machine's kill switch for half a second... and then I was back, cutting them down en masse and feeling the hot rage turn to cold, patient murder as the death-gun spun and whined and the long *BRAAAAP* resounded again and again across the cavernous deck as I wrecked as much of the considerable defense as I could.

The *Spider* was on final now. I could see her out there turning onto the base leg for final approach to the DZ.

I needed to destroy the perimeter defense guns now.

I moved fast, surging through the disintegrating destruction, feeling my black heart thunder like a pneumatic hammer in some heavy industrial weapons forge as I hosed positions and disintegrated bad guys in every direction. I roared as I turned and lit up another response on my attack against the interlocking machine gun pits that had begun to range me with their powerful AP fire.

The Black Bat butterflies were exploding like fireflies on a summer night as the armor-piercing rounds were taken out just micro-seconds from smacking into the Doomsday Armor.

The fluttering "autumn leaves" were swirling frantically about me like a tornado now.

More of these strange commandos died as I pointed and destroyed, the M99 gun radiating black invisible thunder-swarms of deadly "hornets" moving at speeds approaching three thousand feet per second. To their credit, these enemy commandos didn't halt, didn't hesitate, and instead... pushed straight on into the cone of destruction I was directing forward into the line of heavy machine gun pits that had ruined my company, and my brothers, in so many sweaty and shrieking night terrors leading up to this day.

I'd lived with enough deaths I couldn't change the outcome of no matter how hard I wanted to.

This... this was like getting that chance and I felt angry, and it was good too at the same time. And... I felt the acidic thunder music roar on devilish guitars and tribal drums, big and hollow that didn't just beat, they were pure thunder beaten by a maniac drummer who only lived to keep the rhythm and bang the drums harder than anyone ever.

The gun needed to re-arm, so I drew the auto-hand cannon and took rounds that got ate up by the swirling-mad butterfly defense as I sent short targeted bursts from the armor's secondary into the commander directing the next gun pit I'd made it to.

I left a trail of ruined body parts and bloody spray across the deck. Rounds from the sidearm walked across the commander's body in slo-mo as both intersecting bloody lines within the Wild Thing's target-computing HUD met center mass of his plated torso and revealed continuous engagement solutions.

I pulled the trigger repeatedly and tore him to pieces one part at a time.

Seemingly forever in Wild Thing time...

Seconds in real.

In that classic "commander" way he was knife-handing where he wanted his gun teams to fire, no doubt shouting within his red-eyed dog helmet that gave him all kinds of data and fire trajectory...

I scored hits like it was some kind of power-gamer fantasy.

Instead of the horrible reality it was.

And part of me... preferred the fantasy. Knowing full well it was all too real.

But it was nice to be on this side of the equation at least once in your life.

Monarch class.

Cream-style.

The sidearm spat rounds and punched him several times as I held the barrel, amazed at how little recoil there was as the Wild Thing's armor held the bucking and thundering weapon. I pivoted and ate up a rifleman once the commander was falling away from what was left of his body.

The enemy grunt's head exploded, fragments of his obsidian dog-head bucket coming apart as the back of his skull ejected a sudden spray of red mist and the body that had just been surging to defend... went flopping down across the deck as all life was gone from it.

The gunner and AG were trying to shift their fire onto me when I shredded them both and one died leaning over the medium machine gun, his guts and blood drooling out over the lethal-looking piece of deadly hardware, one hand smoking as it lay clutching the too-hot barrel. The other was shot so many times he came apart in pieces, flailing backward as outgoing rounds rocked him and he disappeared down into the ammo crates and spent brass along the bottom of the pit.

The gun pit was down when I got a combat cyborg team responding just in time as if they could stop me from pushing on the next and basically shutting down the whole defense with just a few anti-armor gun teams to clean up before the *Spider* dropped the company on the target DZ.

I knew the slang we used in the company for them... *terminators*... even as I saw them coming through the admin spaces at the back of the deck. Hulking and perfect "humans" as the Monarchs and their crazed scientists had designed them to be in the deepest and darkest of the Dark Labs.

Make us something that looks like them... but its sole purpose is to kill them, the Monarchs must've said. *Isn't that fun, huh?*

Like some villainous vampire with a penchant not just for cruelty, but theater, in this week's spectacuthrillers.

Hunter-killer combat cyborgs were no joke... see me almost getting killed on Gateway Station.

My heart was already jackhammering into what my mind was telling me was certainly going to be a heart attack...

But not because of them...

It was the rage inside of me. I wasn't afraid of them... I wanted to kill them harder. I wanted to kill... *everything*.

My breathing wasn't just the normal respiration of in and out... I was sucking ox like a bellows heaving, and then roaring out hatred and murder and violence and dark vengeance... I was... *growling*. Like some dangerous animal in the dark. Promising destruction. Hissing curses as I turned and saw the three "Hausers" coming at me, all of them carrying state-of-the-art energy and pulse weapons.

Advanced tech.

Stuff you never see in any of the sideshow circus weapons bazaars the company must avail themselves of.

Highly lethal tech usually reserved for the elites' personal protection details, or the Ultra Marines' special operations units. Heavy pulse guns. Plasma rifles. Stuff that just wasn't available... anywhere.

The ambient lighting was blue back there in the admin offices as the HK QRF team came through, the Doomsday HUD warning me about them...

Warning... Lethal cybernetic organisms approaching...

They were shadows. Jacked, perfect killing machines. Onboard targeting systems, reinforced combat chassis, skinned like dudes who spent all their time in the gym just to look like you and me if they were running an infiltration and mass casualty attack on some world the Monarchs had wanted to terrorize and prep for takeover.

They were hard to detect.

But the Wild Thing's armor had picked them right up. Neat trick.

I felt... not the Wild Thing's heart... but my own... catch for half a second. Cold fear, ancient and primal, deep and embedded by the Monarchs through centuries of terror and tyranny and teaching us to feel and fear their best killing machines, machines that looked just like us and could be anyone, I felt it course through my veins like ice water and for a hot second I thought about turning and just running.

No fear. No cowardice. Just... survival.

Beating these things as an ordinary grunt... impossible. Fact. No ifs, ands, or buts. I'd been lucky to take down one even when supported by a heavily armed squad that had already damaged it heavily by Hoser's gun fire from the Pig. I'd never met anyone who'd killed one alone, other than Hauser. And that didn't count. And I'd never met anyone who killed *just* one. Hauser killed three, all by himself.

I knew they were terminators because of their optical sensors. Their "eyes." in all that misty blue, the smoke of all the destruction I'd wrought, the diffusing of the thin available light making everything seem... distant and dreamy, their eyes glowed red in the dark. Like demons. Demon machines. Even as the dead defenders groaned and somewhere, someone, or *someones*, was still putting fire on me even as the butterfly net ate up incoming fire, catching bullets and destroying them with small electric *snap*s that were beyond my comprehension to understand... for a moment they could have been just three jacked operators in coveralls carrying near-mythical weapons...

That's all.

Light medium auto pulse gun. Charged particles the size of thirty-caliber rounds accelerated via mag rail to the five-thousand-feet-per-second speed with an impact matching that of a twelve-gauge slug fired from a shotgun. At point-blank range.

Absolutely lethal savage weapon system.

Usually crew-served when even encountered being used by Ultra Marines Special operations detachments.

The lead HK was carrying it like it was a Pig and as he paused in the blue misty shadows to the rear of the cyclopean and gleaming hangar deck, his red-eyed targeting optics pierced the darkness like some hate-filled demon.

He lay down a spread of pulse fire all around me.

I was already moving. Evading.

I could feel the butterflies in the personal defense net scattering to catch incoming rounds that wouldn't hit me. They were being drawn away by the volume of fire as though the terminator-thing knew that was how I could be taken out.

How?

No time...

Primary weapon system reloaded blinked repeatedly in my HUD and I felt all the fear and cowardice that had tried to consume me for a brief instant just flee, and be replaced by not just red roaring anger, but an almost gleeful feeling surging into my thundering black heart.

I wanted this fight.

Which was the opposite of what I wanted...

I skinned the sidearm, raising the personal death machine rifle in what must have seemed an instant, directing it at the state-of-the-art killing machines the Monarch supreme commander in charge of this battle must have thought could do something against...

Me.

The Wild Thing.

I dumped hot fire as everything went slo-mo. As though gallons of adrenaline were just being pumped into my body by whatever the Wild Thing's armor was...

A living thing, almost...

The opposite of them.

And somehow... the same as...

Things were getting... weird.

Certainly not just... gear. Armor. But something that seemed alive with hatred and destruction for hatred and destruction's sake...

I don't know.

Doomsday Armor.

The butterfly net grabbed incoming pulse rounds and hammered them into destruction in slow motion as I fired back and shifted position at the same time, the sound of all three barrels spinning slowly as though the soundscape had changed with the adrenal surge and everything was elongated and weird.

And... *other*.

Dark forces were at work.

I could actually see the incoming pulse rounds, bolts of pure lightning, disappear as the... bats... they weren't butterflies, but shadowy flickering... bats like autumn leaves... grabbed the rounds in their bat wings and enveloped each incoming pulse round... and destroyed it.

It was happening all around me in slow motion as I moved out of harm's way, chased by pulse fire, and returned accurately targeted fire at the same time.

I... was the killing machine now.

Look at me!

The arterial bleeding red bat-leaves were swirling faster and faster as more rounds from the HK's long-barreled pulse gun spat unlimited death at me. Tens and tens at first, bats grabbing, enveloping, and then encasing the deadly explosions about them, moving the kinetic energies into some other dimension. Within seconds it was hundreds of incoming rounds being defeated as the shadowy hulking terminator stalked forward, dumping long bursts of fire at me as though my destruction was… assured if more volume could be applied to the problem of me.

Imminent.

It was not… Wild Thing that was me smiled. Not even close, buddy.

Pro tip…

Pick a fight with a dude and he's smiling, back off.

That's exactly how I felt as all three terminators ran their game on me.

Base of fire off the pulse gun HK.

The other two were firing as they moved on me from opposite flanks.

Like pack hunters.

The M99 spat forth in shock waves from the spinning cylinders within my death gun. In seconds… it was a storm front of lead, and I watched in wonderfully horribly detailed slow motion as my rounds tore right through the terminator holding the long pulse gun. His synthetic skin erupted in a series of small volcanos as rounds from the Wild Thing's primary ripped straight through him. It was as if his armored combat chassis was made of butter, warm butter or even just water, as the rounds tore through and expanded the damage through sheer kinetic volume, shredding internal systems and vital components to pieces. The fast-moving rounds didn't stop. They just went straight out through his back, also heavily armored if you know your HKs, and spat off into the misty darkness beyond, shattering glass and doorways to the admin stations at the back of the hangar.

One of them lobbed an anti-armor round at me but it was wide and the butterfly net let it go. It exploded, tearing off the face of the terminator on the right who'd closed too fast, synthetic skin melting even as he began to unload with the chopped plasma rifle in the forty-watt range.

Fast-moving plasma-charged particles spat out in short bursts slicing through dozens of my "bats" in an instant.

But an instant was all he had left.

I roared promised murder, shifting the gun instantly onto this one even as the pulse gunner fell "dead" to the floor like some mere amusement automaton, no longer combat-effective because the Wild Thing's primary had just destroyed every system the thing ran.

Some of the last rounds had torn its "head" to pieces, destroying its combat processors instantly.

I was dimly aware of the micro-nuke self-destruct protocols but the armor was registering no surge or atomic energy signature.

And that was not a "right now" problem even as important as it was.

Right now I was vengefully disintegrating the guy on the right, watching as he disappeared in a cone of deadly shadow-lead-hornet fire.

The plasma rifle exploded after being rocked by multiple hits, blowing off the HK's arms even as he held it.

One got through my butterfly-bat-web.

I felt it. It was like getting struck by lightning. But the adrenaline-fueled hate that had taken me didn't care and as the final HK closed to within five meters, two sub guns blaring, rounds fleeing away from both ejector ports, I swung the death gun, held down the trigger and disintegrated this one with sheer outgoing fire as I watched hundreds of rounds just rip it to shreds until the demon-red light went out of its optics.

In the silence that followed, the Wild Thing's armor detected the retreat orders being issued to the enemy as it intercepted signals and interpreted them. The few commando riflemen, snipers, and anti-armor personnel that had survived my wave of mutilation, fled out of the hangar.

It was clear... there was nothing they could do against this asset their Bishops had failed to foresee.

The Wild Thing.

I turned... still the Wild Thing but feeling it fade now, wind down... ethereal mist beginning to soften everything as the strength ran straight out of me. I watched as the bat-shadows spun and twirled slower and slower, leaving their firefly tracers of blood and light, then seeming to fade into nothingness like dying comets falling planetward.

The armor was unwrapping around me like bloody bandages being pulled away... or an ancient mummy being unwrapped... even as the music faded.

I knew...

The *Spider* was deploying her massive landing gears now as she approached the deck behind me, engines howling, reversers cutting in.

I knew now...

The dead littered the deck in every direction. Shuttles and barriers burned.

In some places there were bodies. In others... only pieces.

I heard the gun drop but it didn't hit the deck with a clatter. It was just gone.

I knew now... what would happen next... just as...

Then, as I fell over... crashing hard... I heard that grim voice that had been me... roaring softly if that's a thing... like a distant ocean's surf, hissing, growling murder...

Whispering, tiredly...

Me...

"She's safe now."

The HUD... vanished like a bloody night-ghost fading at dawnlight as my eyes closed... and I saw the final image of the message he'd kept in his HUD.

The Wild Thing.

Marcus...

Some one-way-mission soldier laying it all on the line for something bigger than himself...

Just like all soldiers.

The pretty wife.

The babbling infant.

It all floated away like a dream... that never was.

"Come back to us," she whispered and I felt hot tears that weren't mine streaming down my cheeks and over my gritted teeth.

Come back to us.

CHAPTER FORTY-EIGHT

So there I was…

I had my head between my knees and had just stopped dry-heaving when the first sergeant began to yell at me.

That bean-and-cheese bar from the rations I'd thought would be a good decision to power in the oh-dark-prep-before-insert lay in greasy chunks all over the shining deck of the *Dark Star*'s hangar along with some coffee and a couple of rage-a-hols I'd powered as we got into our EVCs.

Oh yeah, and all the dead and shredded bodies…

"What in the ever-living hell did you think you were doin', young sar'nt?" roared the company's senior-most NCO as Little Girl in her medic role got the second IV bag dripping into me.

I watched as all elements of Strange pushed forward into the defensive positions around the *Spider*, threading the ruined corpses and the slaughtered dozens I'd made in my one-man assault as the Wild Thing.

No one got killed.

Except the enemy. They all got killed.

"Dayum…" exhaled Punch as he took a knee and came close to give me a report on First's position now that we had the LZ in hand. "You straight-up murked… like, everyone, Sar'nt. That guy over there is just… he's cut in half."

Then he started laughing as he muttered, "Guess he won't ever do that again."

Infantry humor.

The first sergeant continued on with his tirade informing me that after this was over he was gonna bust me down to his driver for a few years and other forms of punitive "training" I'd receive at his personal boots.

"YOU EVER DO THAT AGAIN AND I WILL… I REPEAT I WILL… PT YOUR DEAD BODY UNTIL YOUR DEAD FOREFATHERS' BALLS EXPLODE!"

Little Girl was murmuring my vitals, snapping open a pill container and stuffing several into my mouth as her dark eyes watched me.

She knew what had happened.

"Drink this," she whispered beneath the first shirt's promises of doom and suffering never-ending.

Then…

"Thank you, Sergeant," she whispered.

We both knew what she meant.

The captain was nearby.

"That's enough, Top," he said softly as he flicked one of his perpetual darts to the shining floor of the enemy hangar and crushed it out with his EVC boot.

There was oxygen here, so we didn't have to be in our buckets.

"Sergeant Orion got us a foothold. We'll deal with the lack of communication later. Right now we've gotta push in on the hull and shut down any attacks coming at us until we can get the perimeter defense systems set up. That's your bag, First Sergeant. Make it happen."

The first sergeant switched from raging demon of infernal judgment, his ancient face still florid with righteous indignation, to high-speed low-drag operations NCO in the blink of an eye.

"Solid copy, sir. We'll hold here..." He patted the flamethrower he had strapped for the insert. Just in case. "... come hell or high water. Those systems should be in place within twenty. Sir."

He turned back to me, eyeing me evilly, and hissed.

"We ain't done yet, Orion. No we are not."

Ooooo... I was in big trouble. Not an understatement. He didn't use my rank, and the first sergeant was generally the kind of guy that used your rank in formal, and informal, conversation because he felt it meant something and that was how he respected you. What he was telling me now was... I probably wasn't gonna be a sergeant much longer if he had anything to say about it.

I'd seen him do it to other people. And even then, I thought it was cold as ice.

But never me.

And now... yeah... ice-cold. Maybe I'd get killed before he could do it...

The first sergeant moved off, barking and yelling at the platoons responsible for setting up the perimeter defense equipment. Trip lasers. Anti-personnel guns. Gas mines. Heavy quad Mason Deuce fifty-caliber cannons we'd picked up on Marsantyium at the weapons bazaars that had formed as the chimps and other survivors of the battle looted the dead Ultra Marines and their weapons depots.

"Deep scan up!" shouted one of the guys from Gunny's platoon, the Devils, in charge of setting up an internal hull-scanning lidar system we'd use to make our maps.

Remember we had no idea what the internal layout of the *Dark Star* was. Now... with the lidar scanner up we could figure out the terrain and where they'd come at us from in order to dislodge us off the DZ we'd carved into their ship.

There was a sudden rumble. Some distant explosion far deeper inside the hull.

And at that moment... there was that to consider.

What, you ask?

The possibility of instantaneous death despite our best efforts. The possibility that the Monarchs, surrounded and besieged, might just go ahead and det their whole ship with all on board and trying to get deeper into the hull in order to kill them.

Which was our mission.

It wasn't the fleet's mission. And that had become more and more apparent as the pursuit across the stars and into the unknown had progressed. But more about that later...

"A ship-wide det will never happen," Chief Cook had brayed during our many briefs as we discussed how the company would crack the *Dark Star* once we finally boarded her. "They are… narcissistic sociopaths," he guffawed. "They'd never commit suicide willingly. Trust me, I know. I am one! To them that would be an admission that they had been beaten by someone lesser. And that's just not in their programming. It's why I never give up."

But now the deck of the leviathan ship was rumbling and for a hot second… *yeah,* it felt like they might just do themselves and take us with them. Out of spite.

The chase was over.

The battle was here and now, and already, as the captain shook out a dart for me and lit it, I could see the battle beyond the open hangar doors out there in near-space… it was winding down. I was on my knees and still kinda heaving but nothing was coming up. Defensive fire off the *Dark Star* was definitely less now. Smaller support and boarding ships were sweeping in with patrol fighter cover, streaking in toward their marked "beachheads" aboard the *Dark Star* that the fleet's commanders had selected.

Remember this ship was the size of a city. Bigger. It wasn't gonna fall in just a few hours of breaching compartments and taking main engineering and the bridge, wherever that was.

We had no idea.

This was gonna be a long fight and we always knew that. And… if I was really honest with myself… I had no idea how long it would last. Maybe three days. Maybe weeks. And yeah… if they did decide to det… then they either needed a massive nuclear space mine, an actual munition every Battle Spire carried, an MNSM as it was known, strapped and ready to go somewhere near the main reactors… or they'd need to cascade all those same reactors across the entire ship into an overload explosion that would just tear the ship apart and send it flying instantly in every direction.

Which was what they'd need to do to kill us.

In the case of an ordinary reactor overload, which could take up to a day to effect, six hours minimum… "We'd detect that surge," XO had noted during the run-up briefs. "M.O.M. would detect that kind of power surge and I would advise the company to pull back to the ship and we'd depart the battlespace until det."

But, in the case of an MNSM detonation… we had…

We didn't know what we had. Only that it wasn't enough.

"What do we do then, XO?" asked the Old Man in the brief, smoldering dart-drifting-grey-smoke phantoms from his scarred fingers across the flight deck plot table, beneath the glare of the overhead light and the constantly updating and talking systems from the flight stations.

The XO laughed briefly which was uncharacteristic for him.

It was a bitter laugh. There was a lot of that going around lately.

"Run, sir. Run as fast as you can. I need five minutes to get the ship gears up and reach a safe distance on emergency burn to escape the blast radius. So… you get the call to *pull back*… run. Just… run, sir."

So… we had that going for us.

The Old Man let me take a drag off the smoke as the platoons secured their sections of the perimeter around the destroyer.

Then he told me what was what.

"We were going to die, weren't we, Sergeant?"

I took a long drag as I thought about telling him all my PTSD dreams right then and there. Crazy, crazy stuff. Real crazy. There was every chance he'd realize, or think, that I was crazy. And maybe I was. Maybe… none of that would have ever happened.

Maybe…

I looked around at the maimed and ruined defenders, reminding myself they were us.

"Yeah, sir."

Then someone shouted, "Got a live one!"

It was time to see if we could get some intel. I followed the commander to where a wounded commando lay sprawled against some defensive crates that had been arranged near one of the forward positions the enemy had established in order to answer our impending attack.

"Got vitals and he's… talking," said Klutz enthusiastically. He was my medic. And I was sure he'd want to save this guy because that was the kind of dude Klutz was. He was always looking to be a hero because that was the right thing to do. He just wasn't… very coordinated.

That's not a crime. But sometimes you can still pay the price like it is one especially in the military.

In his defense he'd been blown up several times during his prior service with a local military on some planet. Technically he had two TBIs.

Traumatic Brain Injuries.

But the first sergeant swore that if he could sign the contract straight then they'd let him merc with us. And well… here he was.

The commando still had his dog-headed bucket on. Obsidian-black and unmarked by my attack. He'd been shot several times though across the rest of his body.

I burned the smoke as they worked on him, thinking distantly, *Hey, I did that*.

Chief Cook appeared like some unwanted ghost, already popping open his interrogation kit.

There were a lot of needles.

I hated this part.

CHAPTER FORTY-NINE

"Kill me... kill me... please..."

All we could hear was his voice, coming through the black dog-headed mask that was clearly some kind of ballistic armor helmet with enhanced environmental protection features. No doubt a HUD on the other side.

"Probably like our EVC buckets..." grunted Punch. Most of Second and First Squads had taken up position here. Third was on our right. Fourth on the left. To the left of the platoon was Gunny's platoon... the Red Devils, or just Devils, or sometimes Devil Dogs... and that pretty much covered the hangar deck.

The *Spider*'s massive engines were still spinning down as steam and gases came off the ship. The massive cargo doors for the assault decks were open and all the defensive gear was being lugged out in preparation for being set up to defend the LZ on a long-term basis.

The first sergeant was barking furiously, stalking around with his flamethrower like some perpetually unhappy mythical dragon that might just roast you alive if you weren't fast enough with those ammo belts and crates for the Mason Deuces.

"He's delusional," muttered Chief Cook as he worked on the wounded commando. "This oughta bring him around."

The warrant officer reached into one of his EVC pockets and took out a small yellow ampule with a microinjector.

"This is from my personal stash... real *Happy Time* stuff... but hey... we need answers and this guy has obviously been through some fifth-cycle mind-control programming. Real deep. He can't kill himself... then he'll beg the enemy to do it according to the protocols he's been indoctrinated with in order not to give up any vital intel to us. Well... we'll just see about that my little red friend. We did the same thing back in the Subartu Kush in '89 but you didn't hear that from me and I won't admit to it in open court. Top-secret stuff."

He jammed the *Happy Time* injector into the guy and a moment later the suffering slob started to giggle.

Klutz had an IV bag attached and tourniquets applied to what remained of both arms.

Apparently, I had blown both hands and some of the forearm off to varying degrees.

Good shooting, me.

"Bro..." said Punch to Klutz as Klutz got ready to remove the guy's ballistic dog-headed mask and start some oxygen. "Why ya doin' all this...? We're just gonna ice this guy once we got what we need."

Klutz turned around. Horrified.

"Bro..." said Punch confidentially, leaning in. "That's what we came here to do. Kill them. Break their stuff. We ain't rescue personnel."

Klutz shook his head like he couldn't process this right now and turned to take off the wounded man's mask.

"I wouldn't take that off..." mumbled Chief Cook, the creepy gravitas of the infamous warrant officer making Klutz jerk his hands away suddenly.

"Could be booby-trapped. *Aaannd...* most likely it's keeping him alive to some degree or the other. Again... fifth-cycle reprogramming. You... uh... ain't gonna like what you find underneath either. But that's just my two cents."

Now the guy was laughing and it was a sickening sound. Like a dog hacking up something it couldn't digest. Then he started to cough suddenly, his whole bullet-riddled body heaving.

"The... uh... mask... it's based on some ancient earth deity. Remember the psych profile I did for you guys on the average Monarch," opined Chief Cook. "They believe they are in fact gods. So their servants are often denoted via some supporting mythic structure as either heroic, mystic, or deity-like. Like our boy Achilles over there... the Ultras always reclassify their soldiers using some mythic-heroic identifier. Ajax, Achilles, Bauer, Conan... then the numeric identifier... and that's standard Ultra stuff. But the farther you go up the chain, or the closer you get to the... uh... 'gods' themselves that is... as they would have you believe... then you get their old god names and liveries. Ancient stuff no one remembers anymore. And then there's that..."

The guy was heaving now, aspirating it seemed, as he laughed harder and harder. Like...

"Mighta given him a *liiittttle toooo* much of the *Happy Time...*" said Chief Cook, starting to work again. "Okay, I can get him straight. Let's hit him with a little bleakapan and bottom him out. That should do the trick and put him right in the headspace to start answering some real tough questions..."

"He's choking!" shrieked Klutz suddenly, and before anyone could stop him he reached up and pulled the ballistic faceplate away from the rest of the mask. It came away with a small pneumatic hiss.

Then Klutz heaved his pre-mission rations all over the place once he got a good look.

It was omelet and veggies.

I woulda too once I saw what was underneath the mask... but I'd already lost all mine coming back down off being the Wild Thing.

So I just dry-heaved and gagged.

I'm a veteran NCO that way.

CHAPTER FIFTY

Underneath the captured dog-head's faceplate, what was probably his combat helmet… I thought at first were worms. Living, crawling, twisting, slithering, bioluminescent worms. Crawling and entwining about each other in a kind of undulating horror.

His eyes were gone. But you could clearly see where contact points surgically emplaced within the empty sockets would interface with the optics unit in the mask Klutz had just removed.

Klutz who recoiled in horror and now just stood there with his jaw hanging open and his surgical gloves bloody.

He dropped the mask.

"Neural scanner assembly…" commented Hauser as he studied the poor soul with his standard grim killing machine efficiency, Hauser's own optical units and processors always scanning and assessing all he was seeing.

"This is technology well beyond my design parameters and like nothing we've encountered before. We are dealing with higher-order cyborgs here. The combat cyborgs Sergeant Orion terminated were different also. More human-like bio-technological systems and no micro-nuke to cause self-detonation. They operated a battery system in the two-hundred-year lifetime range… this is several cycles ahead of anything I have ever encountered. And good for us as they would have destroyed the drop zone upon termination."

Chief Cook as usual was more than willing to add his doom-and-gloom two cents to make sure he had the street cred to compete and hold his own with a terminator like Hauser.

"It's a control device more likely, Hauser. See only what they want you to see. We experimented with this back in Monarch Special Unit Psyops R&D. It was rude and crude, but it got the job done when you wanted the perfect killing machine to stay focused on target and didn't have your kind available to do the dirty work. We called them Shake-and-Bake." He laughed nervously. "I posited a plan in which we'd test these on an entire division of Ultras and command them to wipe out a Monarch-loyal planet using only ground combat forces. We'd feed their neural-optical interface with images of enemy troops in order to see if we could use that should we ever need to quell a loyal population base… for… y'know… *reasons*. Of course command shot it down and said I was dangerously psychotic and bleated about *what kind of monster would come up with a plan like that* and all. Secretly though… I knew they liked it. I'm sure this went into design and what we're seeing here is where it went. Of course no credit for the guy who thought it up… damn Monarchs were always cheap that way."

The man on the ground's bioluminescent worms that were really cyborg parasites writhed around the empty spaces where his eyes had been removed.

Not something you want to take credit for, I thought. But that was Chief Cook. Sociopath.

But… he was our sociopath, as they say.

Klutz dry-heaved a little more, omelet and veggies already on the deck, and adjusted the drip on the guy as we all stood around waiting to get some answers about what we were gonna face going in further on the *Dark Star*.

Intel. Disposition of forces. Locations. Command and control.

It really, really helps to know what you're facing. Trust me on that. We needed anything and preferably something useful.

"Were there bats in your plan, Chief?" someone muttered as an aside.

Chief Cook continued to work, getting the right interrogation protocols injected into the wounded man as he watched Klutz's vitals reader and muttered to himself about something.

I heard, "Of course there were bats. There's always bats, idiot."

But that didn't seem to have anything to do with what we were facing.

And what we were facing, as our warrant from Voodoo Platoon got down to the not-so-pretty business of quick intel development via chemical interrogation on the battlefield, was not… *pretty*… by any stretch of the imagination.

The guy whimpered like a child in a nightmare as the drugs took hold.

"What in the Hells of Suth are those worms crawling all over his damn face?" muttered the first sergeant.

Chief Cook grunted and laughed, getting the final dosage before he started questioning… just right. He kept dropping the doses and injecting again and again, murmuring like he was whispering sweet nothings to some starport hoochie he'd seduced in one of the many hoochie houses we'd tried to forget our work in.

"Those are cybernetic organisms, First Sergeant," said Hauser flatly. "This man is parasitically controlled and these devices…" said Hauser, pointing a thick finger into the man's exposed face, following one glowing green bioluminescent worm as it crawled through ashy grey skin and open sores that seem to have been made long ago, and remained open, "… control his actions and thoughts through direct interface with the brain, via pain-reward centers throughout the human body to reinforce control. It is very effective on your kind."

"Awww hell… I don't think I like that at all," rasped the first sergeant. "Tell you what… I seen a lotta horrible stuff and I'm glad I'm gettin' near the end of things because I don't think they're gonna get much better ever again. And that's a damn shame when you consider how good it used to be."

No one had a response for this.

"All right, here we go…" muttered the chief quietly, almost to himself.

Then…

"Hey buddy… hey buddy…" cooed the chief, nice and sweet. "You in there? Can you hear me, buddy?"

The guy opened his dry and cracked lips which were crusted with white… *debri*s… and blood.

I'll be honest… he was one of the more horrible things I've ever had to look at. So I looked away and saw a deckload of ruined corpses just like him. Dead that I as the Wild Thing had created. I had the distinct impression that all of them, all the ones I was seeing right now covered by their fancy black dog-head combat buckets, savaged and ruined by high-volume gunfire from the Personal Death Machine, were like this same dude underneath that mask.

Crawling with biosynthetic parasitical mind-control worms.

Slaves beyond any kind of slavery man could think up. This was… demonic.

That was the only word that occurred to me and it's not a word or concept I use much. But I'd seen those… things… implings… and the Elder Titans… strange beings… in that other version of us where the Wild Thing came from.

Doom88.

Marcus.

"Come back to us."

Now we'd be facing slaves fighting to the mindless death for the last of the Monarchs who even now were being hammered all across the hull by a flotilla of angry warships looking to score some next-level tech.

Their lives… this guy's life, I thought as I stared down at him and burned the last of the smoke the captain had handed me… *must have been a living hell.*

"Yeah…" groaned the man crawling with worms.

"Who are you?" asked Chief Cook intently.

Then back to us, "Gotta establish a friendship first. Works better than just upping the pain center reactions with a little sensadrox and hitting 'em with the ol' Edison medicine. But if this don't work… then…"

There was a long pause and for a moment the man made what looked like a silent word, a name perhaps, with his tired and cracked lips.

But no sound came out.

Then his whole body arched in pain and his vitals spiked.

"Don't… remember… anymore. Not… allowed…"

Long pause.

"To…"

Then…

"Kill me. Please."

CHAPTER FIFTY-ONE

"*Awww*... can't do that, buddy," lied Chief Cook like he was the nicest guy in the world. "Not just yet... maybe we get some answers about what's going on here... then we talk about killing you."

I... I have no words. You think you'll never be a part of the areas where things get gray... but here you are listening to a wounded man get chemically interrogated and the reward is we ice him if he tells us what we want to know.

Life comes at ya fast.

The chief's victim groaned as though in bone-deep pain.

Then...

"It'ssss... hell," mumbled the man.

Chief Cook smiled.

"Yeah... I bet. I can do something about that, but... here's the deal... I can only do it once, buddy. So... you're going to need to give me something I can use to justify the expense of getting you into a more... let's call it... pain-free state. How's that sound?"

The Voodoo warrant turned and leered at us, then winked like it was all a big joke we were in on.

It was a good thing the guy couldn't see without his faceplate and optical assemblies.

"Like... what-t-t?" mumbled the man.

"Oh, you know... troop dispositions. Numbers. Weapons. What we're facing here in this section of the ship. Who's in charge. How 'bout that one? Seems easy enough. Who is in charge of forces? Who's your CO? Who's the big guy or gal?"

The man screamed loudly, and suddenly.

Then he was silent as his body stopped twitching and heaving.

"Can...t..." he panted breathlessly. "Can't. No...t... her. Never... her..."

Chief Cook made a face as he studied the vitals. Then he flipped open his field needle pack and thumbed through a few layers of vials, his long fingers hovering over various toxins as though considering the potential of each.

"You do that again..." whispered Klutz at the warrant officer, "and he's gonna peg out."

The chief turned back toward the suffering man.

"Okay... cool down, buddy... all right let's stay away from that one. What unit are you with? How about that? That's easy and there's a big gooey award if you tell me right now."

The man groaned again and started breathing rapidly as though he were fighting something.

"Gotta... kill me. Serious."

"Can't. Not 'til you tell me something we can use. Buddy."

Rapid breathing increased. The worms crawled.

"You want... something... you can use?" the man said rapidly, sweat breaking out through the bits of grey, almost mortified flesh we could still see where the bioluminescent cyber-organisms weren't crawling. "After... after... you kill... me. Do yourself. Trust me... easier... that way."

Chief Cook smiled patiently.

"Okay. I get that. Again... what unit... are you... with?"

The man took several deep breaths and Chief Cook hit him with something that was a deep tranquil blue. A quick shot into his temporal lobe.

The man smiled suddenly, then mumbled. "Oh... that's nice." Then... "I missed you... baby. Thought they... got you," he whimpered for a moment.

Chief Cook held up a hand.

"Okay... you see her now, buddy?"

A tear ran from the man's eye socket. He nodded in the affirmative.

He was seeing *her*. Whoever she was.

"Listen, buddy, I can let you talk to her some more. All the way to the end. And... I'm sorry. But I gotta have some answers first. Then... I promise... I'll bring her back. Back to where you are. And she can stay until it's time... okay?"

The man shook his head but none of us thought that was anything. It was more like he was trying to shake off whatever bad dream, nightmare, his life had become under the chief's chemicals.

"Where are you at when she's there?" whispered Chief Cook with none of his... *him*... in it. Like he was actually concerned. Like... he cared.

The man whimpered again. More tears ran from his eyeless sockets.

"Beach... beach at Nampoor."

His chest heaved a great sob that was like watching some giant beast shake the weight of the stars off its back.

"Best... best... day... ever," he sobbed softly.

"I know," the chief lied soullessly, his voice a sweet sick poison I'd never heard before and never wanted to hear again. Like some pimp convincing a used-up girl to go out one last time for him because *didn't she love him like he loved her?*

I've felt dirty before. Sometimes because of things I've done or sometimes because of things I've seen. This was... worse in certain ways.

"Okay... beach at Nampoor," crooned the chief. "I got ya. Just... give me something and I can bring her back. Back to the beach. Back to the beach at Nampoor, buddy. Just you and her... best day... ever."

He was practically whispering in the man's ear. Getting more intimate. More close. And... that made it... worse. For me.

The man heaved again, another huge sob that sounded like some... wounded leviathan of the seas calling out to its own kind that had long ago been hunted to extinction. It was a horrible sound. And one I never wanted to hear again for as long as I lived.

The sound of being totally... alone. Now.

"Twenty... fourth commando..." grunted the man through gritted teeth that were long uncared for. "Under... No... no... no... can't say... her... name."

"Good, okay dam's breaking, kids," he said to us. "I'm getting through the mind control programming and he's ahead of his own internal protocols. We can get some info now."

Chief Cook administered three more syringes, each more toxic-looking than the previous.

Klutz looked shocked as each one went in and I was sure he still thought we were gonna try to save this guy instead of just soak him for intel and then off him.

Oh, my sweet summer medic. The mercenary life ain't for you.

And I wondered if it was for me and why I'd done it for so long now. There was a place I used to call home and I wondered if I could find my way back there.

I wasn't sure anymore.

Wasn't sure it was even there anymore.

"You know what you're doing, Chief?" asked Klutz naively.

Chief Cook grunted and sneered. "Kid, I was doin' this when your daddy was tryin' to learn to tie his shoes. Shut up or I'll dose you to the eyeballs next time I get a chance and yeah... I promise you'll see some bats like you ain't never seen, kid. Just keep an eye on that heart rate, medic. Hang on..." he said manically as he bent back to his victim. "And... Here. We. Go."

The guy on the ground visibly relaxed when the last syringe went in, and the cyber-organisms actually ceased writhing, undulating slower and slower until they too were tranqed. Chief Cook barked at Stinkeye suddenly, fierce like some starship scrapyard dog.

"Gimme your damn flask, you old sideshow clown! Now we're gonna see some real psychological warfare instead of that hokey black magic you're always tryin' to shop around. Stand back!"

Stinkeye had the totem flask to his old lips as usual. Frozen, his eyes went wide at suddenly being addressed. He considered the situation, then without ceremony, handed the iconic flask to his archenemy who promptly splashed the toxic contents all over the man's face. The worms crawled away from where they'd been splashed and some even began to burrow back into the grey and ruined features.

We could see more of him now. Our prisoner. What kind of man he'd once been before the Monarchs had gotten their hands on him and turned him into a killer slave to defend them one last time for all the marbles.

Chief Cook upended Stink's flask and took a huge gusty gulp. Then he howled like a wolf and took out another injector we thought he was gonna stick the guy with. Instead, he spiked himself with it as he pushed it in and moaned.

His grin was psychotic as he got down in the man's face and then... touched his bald forehead to the man's gray sore-ridden skin.

"All right..." he said to us as if from very far away, "... get ready to take this down... They got... maybe a brigade to defend this section of the ship. Anubian commandos they call 'em... like him. Cybernetically enhanced meat shields for the HK teams operating in this sector. Five teams. Oh... that's real bad. They've got Bishops but that access is classified and above his clearance level. Sector commander is definitely a Monarch. They call her... Lady of Death. No visual on her... his optical sensors aren't allowed to record her apparently. Okay, digging down deeper past his frontal and headed into the cerebellum where the good stuff gets cached… Sergeant Orion… reach into my injector kit and hit me with the first vial, row three… uh… page five… should be purple like a Smack-a-Pop… Do it now…"

Then… he was back to the prisoner.

"Hey buddy… let's go on down to the beach… Yeah… I'll show you how to get back to her. She's there… I think… waiting for you. Okay…"

The man whimpered and sobbed. His wounded left foot, the one I'd shot, began to shake and twitch like the kind of autonomic nerve response I'd seen in guys when they got switched off.

"Hurry, Orion…" muttered the chief, almost *sotto voce*… I'm going down deep into his cerebellum where they wrote in the orders… and I need him to relax now."

I fumbled with the injector and got it in. Pushing hard like I was pissed at him. Which I was.

"Done," I said flatly and stood back.

The man was sobbing again, whimpering as Chief Cook fed on his mind, throwing open mental doors long locked in darkness by the Monarchs' mind control machines as the Psyops warrant looked for what he needed.

"Vitals are spiking… his heart rate is approaching one-eighty," said Klutz indignantly. "You're gonna kill him first, Chief!"

"I know… almost there… hey buddy… we're at the beach now. She's over there… see her…"

The man started to convulse as he grunted savagely, "Muh-muh-my wife, my-y wife, mmm-y wife…" over and over again as he sobbed.

Chief Cook hissed.

"Got it… they need to prevent us from reaching the inner hull. High priority targets are to protect the displacement drive there and a few other targets. They're putting everything into protecting the inner hull and we can't reach there. If we do… it's over for them. I got everything I need… coming out!"

He said this as the man continued to chant about his wife.

Then Chief Cook… the man I probably hate the most in all the universe… did something… *unexplainable*. Something I never thought he'd do. Or was even capable of. And for a moment, maybe forever, my opinion didn't quite change, I won't go that far… but I realized how much… I really don't know.

About anyone.

The chief held the man, wrapping his arms around him, whispering, "She's here now, okay. You are together. Everything is going to be great… from now on."

The man blubbered hard and uncontrollably as joy and sorrow spread across his ruined face at the same time.

It was hard to tell if he was laughing, or sobbing. Like when the worst almost happened, but it didn't… and everything turned out okay. Normal. And not… let's just say as bad as it could have and how, in the moment of terror… it seemed it would.

A close call on some highway.

A bad dream in which someone was gone forever.

A serious pain that comes… and then goes away like it was never there.

"I m-m-m-issed you… s-so s-so… much," he heaved. "I thought I'd lost you… f-f-forever."

Chief Cook pulled back slowly, kneeling above the man who kept speaking to a woman who'd been... *who knew?*... killed, abducted... years ago when the Monarchs did whatever the Monarchs had done to a world with some beach called Nampoor where two lovers had begun to love one another forever...

Those two lovers, and all the rest.

Chief Cook reached into his upper sleeve pocket. I'd been with him long enough to know that was the pocket where he kept the good stuff. The stuff for personal use. His stash.

He pulled out a clear vial with an injector already attached as he whispered words to the man, some of which we could not hear. He was still chemically linked with the man's mind.

"You're here now. With her. Both of you. She's beautiful. It's all good now."

"She is," mumbled the man through snot and tears from eyeless sockets. "The most... beautiful... ever... I love... you," he moaned to the ghost of her.

Chief Cook inserted the injector, then gently... depressed the injector. Like an artist making the final brushstroke. A surgeon the final cut. Some actor the final gesture.

Forever.

"It was all just a bad dream," whispered the chief softly. "Tell her... it's all better now."

The man was smiling.

The bad dreams were over.

The man was mumbling to that long-gone woman, his breathing slowing until it was barely visible, and then he was dead.

On the beach at Nampoor.

CHAPTER FIFTY-TWO

Gunny's platoon, the Devil Dogs, was already heading further into the ship and reporting some deeply weird stuff as Chief Cook came down off… whatever he'd been on and downloaded a quick intel update regarding what we were facing in this sector of the X-ship.

Strange's command team had already formed around what was quickly becoming the tactical operations center for our activities in and around the DZ. Which was basically some arranged munitions and ordnance hard shells and a bunch of tactical boards and field CPUs set up to run comm, intel, and operations.

It was where the Old Man led from as the action aboard the *Dark Star* began to spool up.

But it was really "the First Sergeant's Hut" as it was often referred to.

Or just simply *The Hut*.

"This is what we're facing, sir," intoned Chief Cook like some pagan high priest calling the faithful to attend and know wisdom. This was his church. His sermon. And he was in full role as he told us what was what.

And it wasn't good.

We were facing at least four thousand of what the interrogated man had called the *Anubian Corps*. Brigade-sized elements tasked with stopping our way through the outer hull, which roughly comprised the entire ring of the saucer for at least three miles in toward what was called… the inner hull.

All across the outer hull were enemy brigades assigned to sectors and tasked with preventing any attacking unit gaining access to the inner hull.

Those sectors were other boarding combat teams' responsibility. Ours was this sector.

The interrogated man's mind had no memory or knowledge of what lay within the inner hull, but it was clear that was where we'd find the Monarchs in their nest if we could breach that deep into the massive vessel. It was there we needed to go and do some *breaking and entering* and *smashing of stuff* along with a lotta wholesale life-taking in large doses.

"Problem is, sir…" intoned the chief with as much Mil-Intel Dark-Side gravitas as he could muster, "is that the Monarchs are often field commanders in these types of situations… just like our friend the Seeker was one at some of those big battles in the Sindo. And in this case, they deployed the one called Lady of Death to run operations in this sector of the ship. Now… I don't know for sure, but it seems like all the heaviest defenses are around the outer hull and lookin' to scrap real hard to prevent access to the... uh... lair of the beast if you will. If that inner hull is as important as his pre-programmed orders indicate that it is vital we do not breach... then I might have a little something I can make things easier with if we can breach. But... I'll have to get a little cook going on in my field lab to make the stuff I'm thinking might do the trick, sir."

The captain gave Chief Cook a look.

"Honest, sir... no fun stuff. We gotta go biological strike here. This is pure lethal what I'm thinking, fast-acting, and it's just as likely to kill us as them... might even be a last resort... but... it could make things easier, or just get it done if we can't, sir. No drugs, sir. I mean... well..."

Then he started mumbling.

XO had come off the ship to join the intel brief. He gave me a look that a serious payback was coming my way as he wiped soot, dirt, grime, and grease from his carved face. The ship was still smoking from anti-ship fire she'd taken coming in. Black smoke poured out from one of the main engine housings near the rear of our destroyer.

But she'd held.

The *Spider* had taken PDC fire and made the approach getting us onto the DZ. There wasn't much she could do now for a PMC light infantry crew ready to attempt to bust open a hull with heavy compartment-to-compartment fighting and all the bonus weird the Monarchs had managed to loot on their way out of human space. But she could still act as a hospital. Cutter already had wounded, a supply point, and... if we got the call to dust off... an extraction LZ.

Now XO, after giving me some serious murder eyes, interrupted the chief's brief with critical intel.

"To that point, sir, re: our combat sector. I've notified fleet we're down on the DZ and starting operations. *Javelin* and her troop freighters have secured a secondary smaller shuttle port three decks down on our left flank in this section. They've got their lane of attack plotted and all we need to do is send the scouts out to mark off our lines, so we don't end up in a crossfire hurricane."

The Old Man studied the tactical displays and burned a dart, his tired old grey eyes crunching the numbers and doing the fatal math we were walking into.

There was a lot of unknown. We had no map of the vessel beyond less than a hundred meters past this compartment.

"What were *Javelin*'s losses going in?"

"They didn't report, sir," the company XO stated flatly. Which spoke volumes about what was soon about to develop during the siege of the *Dark Star*.

Purposeful lack of communication.

The Old Man made eye contact with XO for a moment and then returned to studying the maps our barely hull-penetrating field lidar was giving us so far.

"I have tactical comm established with their operators and I'll route all traffic to Top through the ship. They have our call signs. I suggested they feed those to the small unit leaders on our flank. They acknowledged the traffic. Nothing else, sir."

"What about the right?" asked the captain, eyes on the hull maps that were developing even more and more now by the second.

"That explosion, sir, about thirty minutes ago... that was the *Sins of Solari*. Her beachhead went so badly, the hostiles started a boarding action after our friendlies lost all their troops on the DZ. The DZ there was a landing platform that served some sort of either beam weapon launcher, or a tube for what I might guess is patrol fighters that could be launched from carrier bays deeper within the target hull. Anyone's guess. Radar and lidar could not penetrate the hull more than a few thousand meters down the tube. Some sort of signal jamming. *Solari* detonated and destroyed herself to prevent capture. Escape pods are now drifting all over the battlespace, but there was most likely catastrophic loss of troops as she was carrying the Five-Oh-First heavy marines out of the Horse Worlds. Three battalions total. What they didn't lose on the beachhead inside the *Dark Star*'s beam tube, they lost on the det as they in no way, shape, or form had enough escape pods for all the troops she was carrying. Most likely the crew used those for themselves. Sir."

The Old Man sighed.

Different day. Same mess.

"I'll keep scanning for comm, sir, but I've studied the maps. That tube on our right flank is sixteen decks high and just as wide. It's solid like it's a gun barrel of some sort, and the position of the tube blocks off most passages into our right flank. I can use the engineers we've developed from the new platoons to go over there and booby-trap the passages I've marked. Set up detection sensors and sentry turrets. That should allow us some security on the right as we move into the hull in our sector. But… it is what it is, sir."

And the unspoken was… it wasn't good. Nothing on our right flank meant we had to keep that in mind as we pushed forward.

The Old Man nodded. Then he turned to Chief Cook.

"Continue."

The chief inhaled deeply as though he needed to re-gather his lost gravitas and launched in where he'd left off.

"But that's not the worst of it, sir. Those five HK teams, four now still in operation, are what we might consider SF. Combat cyborgs. Priority is to locate and deal with them as we go in. And if that's not bad enough, sir… there are several Bishops, and no, I do not have any idea what kind they are. So… that's a real big, bad unknown. The control systems the man was wearing prevented him from seeing them. But he knew they were there, and he was deeply disturbed by them. And that wasn't just mind control protocols in effect. He had a real deep fear of what they could do. Sorry for all the good news, sir."

The Old Man flicked his latest dart to the deck and crushed it out with his EVC boot.

"That all?"

"Negative, sir."

The chief took another deep breath.

"There's another element in this bunch, and my intel… frankly, sir, I—my profession… who I am—is all about *knowing* what's out there. What's coming at us. I pride myself on that. I've always seen that as my role in the company, sir. Contrary…"

He cast his mirrored gaze around at all of us.

"… to popular belief… I've done my best for the company. But there are sometimes intel fails, and I take that… *personally*. Sir. This is one of those situations. We have Inquisitors in the mix. I do not think these are the same as the Inquisitors that followed the Ultras around when the Monarchs were King Daddy. Same name, but these are something new... the interogatee's only impression was they're true believers of some sort and they are as deadly as they come. The man I—and just so everyone knows, that was a chemical interrogation and that's how it works... there was nothing... *unseemly* about how I... conducted it."

"Bro... you hugged a dude," said Punch, and suddenly for an instant, Chief Cook snarled like a mad dog on a leash.

Punch didn't move, which was, in my experience, the Punch you got right before you got the most dangerous Punch there was.

Stinkeye laughed gustily, spraying his caustic flesh-burning irritant of liquor everywhere and all over some.

"Yasss... ya silly spook. Thought ya'd found ya'self a new boyfriend," cackled Stinkeye maniacally.

Chief Cook reached for his gleaming highly polished sidearm but he didn't draw.

The Old Man stopped him with a clearing of his throat.

Both warrants gave each other the murder-eye promising that this time... some bridge that could never be crossed, had finally been... crossed.

But then again they always did that.

Punch remained still, quietly waiting for his chance to choke-slam the chief.

The first sergeant, who'd been monitoring comm traffic, barked for everyone to *shut the hell up.*

"Sir... we got us a situation. Devil Dogs is in trouble already up-hull."

Up-hull. Deeper in.

Down-hull. Closer to the outer hull.

"What kind of trouble?"

"They're in an area we've identified as the sector cooling tanks, and they're tangled in a firefight with something. They're surrounded. Requesting support to effect a break contact."

The Old Man swiped both hands over the local tactical display. Our field lidar resketched the expanded area in blue vector. He expanded Gunny's platoon's position. I saw all the markers for our guys.

Yup. They had wounded.

"Sergeant Orion..." said the Old Man as he studied the routes in and out from our position on the hangar deck. "We'll move through this passage and come in on their four o'clock. Get your squads ready to move out in two. I'm going with you."

Showtime, I thought and left without comment, already alerting my squad leaders it was time to earn some pay.

Two minutes and ten seconds later we were stacked at an emergency access door that had been cyber-locked and sealed by the enemy. It was another passage through the hull that came at the developing firefight from an asymmetrical angle.

Rockstar and Solo, who'd picked up the art of demo from Jax, set the breaching charges. Ten seconds later Rockstar called, "Execute execute... Here come the BOOM!" and we blew the hatch inward.

"Get it on, Strange," I muttered over the comm, watching everyone do their jobs just the way we'd run it all those months on the shoot deck.

If things could just go this way the whole time, I thought naively and watched as Fartsack pushed past me with extra belts for the squad Pig and a new patch on the back of his EVC bucket with a cartoon bomb that said *Hang in there… it gets worse*.

Yeah, I thought. *That's what I needed. I was almost happy. Don't wanna be that, now do we.*

"Thanks, Farts," I said, following him into the smoke and dark.

He didn't ask *For what*, or for me to explain. It was like he knew and just answered, "Ya welcome, Sar'nt. My pleasure."

Punch, on point as usual, led the way for us into the smoky blast area, our targeting lasers sweeping all sectors.

Scanning for targets.

Get it on, Strange.

CHAPTER FIFTY-THREE

The first fight we got into was hot and hasty. Punch rocking the breaching shotgun ran into Nether who'd gone ahead, coming back down at us along what looked like a shadowy hexagonal passage with subdued blue floor lighting.

Very high-tech.

We had small barracks rooms, or what we assumed were barracks, off to our right and left at two-meter intervals. They were beneath the deck passage, as in the hexagonal door hissed open and you stepped down into the barracks room.

"Boss... I got Nether," said Punch over the comm. He was twenty meters ahead of his squad in the lead of our element. "Says we got bad guys stacked in the next compartment beyond the bulkhead."

He was whispering and we were moving swiftly, not fast, to relieve Gunny's platoon.

Nether couldn't rock any kind of commo so he had to run back and forth when he was doing his scouting thing, walking through passages and sealed bulkheads, incorporeal and near invisible, in order to scout and report.

I was at the back of First when Punch signaled the short halt and gave me traffic he had an update from our Voodoo scout. Once we'd started our way up the passage, Nether had gone ahead of us almost instantly, merely whispering in that smoky hush of his that he was headed "in" to see what we could find.

Without him... we woulda been murdered on this one. And from the sounds of it, Gunny's platoon had walked into a real knife-and-gun show.

I was monitoring the fight, and it was going from bad to worse by the second. I had a small feed from off Gunny's EVC camera and much of it was nothing but gunfire, flying brass, and his guys screaming as they got it on.

They were falling back, carrying their wounded, but under fire and that was making breaking contact difficult.

"Shorts is down, man! They just took his freaking head off!" someone shouted hysterically over the squad comm.

Automatic gunfire.

This was getting bad.

"Fall back to the stairs... fight from there," thundered one of the corporals. "Where's the damn medic? Where's Drips?"

"Drips is gone, man!" someone shouted back.

Repeated shotgun fire thundered as one of the corporals, a solid dude I'd seen Gunny elevate, his tag was Whisper because he was a low-talker, moved in on some dark hulking shape I couldn't see and started dumping slugs, rocking the titanic thing inside the chaotic gunfight through sheer kinetic excessive outgoing force.

In the feed Whisper turned toward someone in the dark and there was a sudden burst of bright fire from nearby. Their gunner shouted, "Dammit! Hold the line right here while I get Drips outta there!"

Drips looked dead to me, but the EVC feeds were pretty grainy and we were getting a lot of hull interference.

Gunny was issuing orders, barking mechanically and laying down bursts of savage gunfire from the S16 shorty he preferred as he tried to keep the enemy push back.

I heard him shout a second later, "Heads down, Devils... frag out!" Then I saw his feed visually inspect the frag he'd just popped the spoon on.

"Eat this, chungos!" he growled and hurled it into the dark where more hulking shadows were coming down the dark passage.

Seconds later there was a deafening explosion and more gunfire.

All that was going on as I pushed us up after our short halt along the passage. I made my way through First Squad, arriving at Punch and the barely visible Nether.

"What you got, Neth?"

"Two gun teams set up in a blocking position to prevent anyone coming through and trying to relieve Gunny's platoon."

His voice was the usual ghostly rasp. But there was an urgency in it.

"These those same commandos?" I asked.

"Affirmative, Orion. Looks like light machine guns. Six of them. Two gunners each. Two security teams. Their NCO dropped back up the passage, so he might be bringing in more to stop us."

"What's the compartment shape?"

"Circular, Orion," rasped Nether. "Elevated platform runs all the way around. The gun teams are staged at the far end with interlocking fields of fire behind what looks like a local atmo control station for this section of the ship. They shut down all power, so it's dark in there, and my guess is they locked the controls. Make of that what you will."

I made of it what it was. They were locking us out of atmo control and intending to vent atmo in order to deny access or at least make it difficult. We were in EVC posture four. We could handle hard space. And if they shut down the gravity generators, or they failed, we could deal with that too.

It would just be more difficult.

But hey... when wasn't it?

Stinkeye was right behind me and of course his bucket was off and he was drinking from the flask.

"Stink... you need to—"

I was gonna tell him to get his bucket on.

"Ain't got time for dat noise," he hissed foully. "Listen... I can already hear 'em in dere and dere's sumpin' I can do on dis one fo' ya's, Little King..."

Anything he could do would be good because walking into two gun teams with interlocking fields of fire in what looked like a standard medium-sized ship systems control compartment... was gonna be murder.

No two ways about that.

Shoot deck sims always put us at fifty percent minimum casualties on something like this.

But there was no other way in sim... Gunny wouldn't let the warrants do their voodoo.

"All dat hokey make ya weak," he'd bark when Stinkeye tried something for us in sim. "Ain't got no circus freaks in the Corps. You breach and clear like a man. Watch your corners. Violence of action. Smoke everything that moves. Then do it again until they all dead. That's how we gonna do it... just like in the Corps. That's how it gets done every time. Casualties... that's what corpsmen are for. Gotta give 'em something to do."

Right now... I'd take Stinkeye's magic. I didn't like throwing my guys into the face of automatic gunfire. Even if I did have medics.

Gunny couldn't stop calling 'em *corpsmen* and even Klutz, out of sheer terror, had started calling himself one whenever Gunny was around.

"All right... what you got?" I said, knowing I was gonna probably regret what came next.

Stinkeye laughed gustily, smiling like the evil gutter cat he was.

He hoisted up a recoilless rocket launcher he'd lugged along with him. Then patted the MeGoosa.

"Dis some heavy-caliber magic, Little King. Best kind sometimes. Rocket go boom shaka laka boom!"

CHAPTER FIFTY-FOUR

"Bruh..." I said to the chief warrant officer whose proper rank I would never use because I'd seen him face-down in his own vomit and filth so many times I could not begin to count the number. "This is compartment-to-compartment fighting. Overpressure's a thing in here, Stink. This close to the surface of the ship and we could breach and depressurize the whole section. Get sucked out if someone's not clipped in with the frog-tango... *which*... would be a real hassle right about now to put it not mildly enough. Did you get hit in the head? And... hey, last time I checked... aren't you... a space wizard... amirite, Stinkeye? Not an anti-armor gunner which we generally do when say... facing armor or bunkers planetside. Hell... I'd rather call for the first sergeant and his ridiculous flamethrower than deploy a recoilless rocket round inside an enclosed hull. You'll kill us all."

"I knows, Little King, I knows all da tings 'bout breachin' and clearin' starships. Was doin' dat 'fore humans reached Alpha Centauri itself. Was a gunner too at Cestus, but dat's another story. And don't worry... dey gonna be magic. Right, Nether...? He gonna see to that overpressure and backblast, ain't ya, Nothingboy?"

Nothingboy was Stinkeye's personal name for Nether who... Stinkeye, like everyone else, was kinda creeped out by. But with Stinkeye... it was more like fear than anything else. And I'd never really figured out why. Rarely did our Space War Wizard want anything to do with our barely visible Voodoo operator who could pass through things and make...

Oh, I thought at that moment. *I get it.*

Yeah, Nether could make mass and energy disappear inside certain volumes. I didn't totally understand his power, but...

"Can you do something about the overpressure in here, Nether?" I asked.

"Yeah," Nether rasped. "That's not a problem. It's a solid plan, Orion. You guys will get chewed to pieces by those guns. I like this one better. But if he vents the deck to open space... ain't much I can do about that."

A point about Nether. If you've read enough to get here, then you know his story. Next to Hauser... he's the best asset this company has. Both would do themselves to save any one of us.

Fact.

So with Nether... I've seen him absorb volume, energy, mass, make it disappear... or whatever it is he does with all that freaky-weird voodoo quantum... and I've seen him do it to the point of frying the negative battery he actually is.

If it's for us... he'll do it.

"You sure?" I asked him. Back on the LZ at Marsantyium he'd almost fried himself into oblivion... or... what he told us was the Oblivion Gate.

And yeah... I'd been thinking about that and what John Strange had said and where I hijacked the Wild Thing.

Each one near something called the Oblivion Gate.

Strange had even warned me I was entangled and there was a possibility that the closer I got to it... I could be sucked in and lost.

And right now... I had a feeling if all the things were adding up... we were very close to it.

So I was worried about Nether because his powers were innately tangled with it. According to him.

The shadow of the man that once was one, nodded and rasped, "Yes, Orion. I got this. I'll be fine."

I didn't have time, or room, to call him a liar. And what would that do... the lives of two platoons were on the line.

Nether was one man.

I hate the math of leadership.

"Then do it," I said, and Nether was gone.

Thirty seconds later Stinkeye whooped, not a pleasant sound, and screamed, "Fire in da hole, losahs!" when he should have called "Backblast area clear," and depressed the trigger on the launcher, firing the rocket into the gun-team-laden compartment forward of our position.

We'd just blasted the door inward five seconds earlier.

Rockstar and Solo were heads down at each side, and Solo was screaming over the comm... "Ain't no party like a high-ex party!" as the round streaked past them and into the compartment, Stinkeye raggedly laughing with glee.

You could feel those gunners inside waiting patiently to murder us in high staccato violence. Intersecting and plunging fields of fire all ready to go... just hoping we thought we were clever with the breaching and that we were pushing into some dark and unsecure hull section instead of the major X they had waiting for us.

But we had Nether.

And a recoilless rocket launcher with an eighty-four-millimeter high-explosive, fin-stabilized, dual-purpose anti-armor round fired by a drunken war wizard.

Your move, Universe.

The rocket streaked down the passage on our side, its motor lighting up both stacked squads, First and Second.

We had to let Stinkeye fire it as he wouldn't let go of the launcher and whined pathetically, while at the same time cursing us drunkenly, that it had been his idea and he got to "fire the Carl!"

We had no idea what a Carl was. Old-man stuff from wars no one ever heard of.

Some of the younger guys laughed.

Half a second later the blast detonated, killing both gun teams and their security elements.

Nether was already in position as blossoming flames and waves of massive overpressure, with nowhere to go, raced back down at us through the open hatch...

For a moment I saw Nether in front of that wall of flame where the rocket had detonated. Between us and the compartment where the gunners were being roasted alive, or at least what was left of them...

His arms and legs outstretched making an *X* of my invisible friend. He was just a shadow. But a shadow you could see now because of the detonation.

It was like he was trying to will himself to be bigger than he was, shadow hands and fingers splayed as though he was trying to catch, or grab, all the displaced violent energy he could absorb.

And protect us from. As though that was his sole purpose for existence.

The blast... *bent*... into him.

Curled.

Was sucked into.

Flames and destruction... as though it was being inhaled into a void within him... going somewhere else... somewhere *other*.

The Oblivion Gate.

For a moment I felt a ghost walk over my grave.

Come back to us.

It was just a moment.

The voice on the message inside the Wild Thing's HUD.

And then Nether collapsed, disappearing, and I wasn't sure if he was dead and gone, or finally fritzed out into the negative void forever.

I was his friend. Sure...

But I didn't have time for that right now.

We were breaching. I am the breaching unit's leader. I must think of all my men and not just the one...

"*Go! Go! Go!*" I shouted.

Punch pushed in and immediately I heard his breaching shotty thunder-humping one of the unfortunate survivors who'd managed to live through hell for a few seconds.

The whole compartment was cooked. Gun teams down. Wounded got cleaned up.

Ten seconds.

Then we had a new firefight, running up from the next passage beyond the ambush they'd set.

They had enough assets to push in just in case we got through.

Now it was all flying brass and barking guns.

Organized murder.

Nothing but chaos.

"Catboi engaging."

I was indeed... here for the violence.

CHAPTER FIFTY-FIVE

The push up the passage and into enemy-held compartments was on. Punch and First had finished pulse-checking the survivors of Stinkeye's recoilless rifle shot as more of the enemy pushed down from an opening just beyond the next intersection.

Pulse check.

You shoot a dead guy again to make sure he's really dead.

War is not pretty, don't let anyone tell you anything different.

We have to be honest about these things.

Later, we'd find that these compartments deeper into the ship and farther up this passage were some kind of huge medical diagnostic center filled with advanced medical suites like reclining surgical couches surrounded by auto-docs and workstations. From the ceiling hung spidery auto-docs like you'd find in some of the more high-end surgery centers back in the Bright Worlds that no longer existed due to chimp invasion, and lay trillions of miles behind us.

In the first few minutes of fighting it was clear the Anubian commandos had been staging here just for the counterattack we were conducting, assuming we'd eventually overcome the two ruined gun teams Stinkeye had destroyed with the Megoosa and Nether.

They were probably hoping for higher casualties on our side before they'd need to repel. Instead we were pushing through on them in full and the firefight here started in earnest and almost immediately as both First and Second pushed through the space and engaged in a gunfight with the lead elements of the reserve force.

First took the right and Punch set up a base of fire as I listened to my two squad leaders interact.

"Down and suppressing, Reaper Alpha Two!" shouted Punch.

Alpha Two was Ulysses's callsign.

"Two moving!" called out Ulysses as his squad pushed into the space and advanced, forming a gun line on their half of the large compartment and moving forward dumping mags on full auto, using what cover the medical workstations, surgery couches, and spindly auto-docs provided for cover as they advanced.

It's hard to be agile in the bulky EVCs, as in "sucking dirt" or even just basic crouching, but in this kind of combat, compartment-to-compartment aboard starships, you tend to use larger cover and spray heavily with your gun as agility and quickness are compromised.

Goods started to lay the hate with First's Pig, opening with short rattling bursts as he tore a cluster of Anubian commandos just forward of their position to shreds. Itchy ran the belt and fed the death machine as Goods got on it, reshouldering the gun after the first burst and shouting, "Hotsoup, losers! Come get some!"

Then he opened afresh and raked the entire front with a long burst as Second continued to maneuver forward.

The rest of First engaged individual bad guys out on the flanks and deeper back with select fire which Gunny had taught us to use to effect during this type of operation. Covering fire was targeted. Movement fire was full auto and burst and almost more of a suppressive action.

Jingo, who I'd never much really liked—he'd been one of Hannibal's scouts—caught a round right in the faceplate and died right there with little fanfare. Of course Klutz was on him, grabbing the drag handle at the back of the shoulder collar between suit and EVC helmet connector ring, dragging the dead man out from under fire even as the rounds of the Anubian commandos started chasing him.

He pulled Jingo's body back toward the center where I'd pushed in with Fourth to make sure it was clear and was now directing Hauser's squad to come in and set up a new base of fire to cover First's move forward into the fight to take the compartment.

My intention was for First and Second to bound forward through the half-an-ultraball-field-sized space in order to close and destroy the staged defenders. Third under Hauser would set up our base of fire as that squad had two light machine guns. Hauser carried a spec ops Pig, and Slash had the main LMG for the squad.

That made them the heavy hitters.

That was when I saw Jingo's skull and brains blown all over the inside of his EVC bucket.

And I realized I'd liked him more than I hated him. And that really... I'd just been annoyed by his personality more than anything.

But he was dead now.

"Klutz... my man..." I said as I swapped in a new mag doing my best EVC gorilla crouch. "He's dead. Forget him and get ready to push behind your squad leader."

Gorilla crouch. In EVC it's your best shot to avoid being a target by finding cover and getting down behind it by doing a basic squat.

Getting on the ground is harder to shoot from, and harder to recover from. But sometimes... *needs must*, as they say.

Klutz gave me this look for half a second as hot incoming smashed through the air around us, destroying medical stations and exploding monitors and equipment.

The look was... *I guess you're right, Sar'nt.*

Like he'd thought just before my words that it wasn't as bad as it looked and if he could've just dragged Jingo to some place and gotten started on him then death could have been staved off.

But that is not the case when your brains are all over the back of your bucket. This is not my first rodeo.

Still, my medic hesitated.

Because death was... abhorrent to him. Klutz hated death like some men hate politicians.

"It's all good," I told him. "I got Jingo now. I'll take care of him now."

My medic nodded, seemed to accept he needed to hear that, then adjusted his bulky aid bag and crawled back toward First on the right to see what he could do there, where the incoming was heaviest.

And honestly, I wouldn't have my medics any other way. Haters of death. Lawyers bargaining with everything they've got for a lighter sentence than the one you've been dealt. Crawling right into all the bad because maybe they can help when all of us are trying to hurt.

We do not deserve them, I sometimes think.

I get it… sometimes I complain about everyone. But in these horrible moments where all the opposite of what I'm experiencing is staring up at me through the remains of a bloody mess of an EVC bucket… I think…

Man, I have been blessed beyond any belief I don't possess to have had medics like Klutz. Yeah, I'm probably gonna buy it on this one, or the next one… but to have a medic who straight-up middle-fingers death even as it laughs at what it's taken already…

That makes me happy.

And then Klutz is gone and for a moment it's me and our first casualty, as Hauser's squad pushes in, some of the guys asking, "Who's that?"

"Jingo got it."

"Man… that's bad. He was into me for two large on Cheks!"

And.

"Serves him right!"

And…

"He wasn't so bad."

And…

"Yeah, bro… he was. Ever tell you about that time in the bar in Fall's End?"

And…

Yahtzee in the SDM role falling in last, taking up a position behind a surgical couch and stabilizing his slick rifle as he readied to engage.

He leaned down, patted Jingo's arm, and said something I didn't catch.

But I bet it was something to the effect of… See ya soon, buddy.

They'd both been scout-snipers trained in Ghost back before we got into this mess.

Then he engaged his scope's feed in his bucket, bent toward the eyepiece anyway, took a breath, let it go, mumbled, "Die, chungo," and blew the head off an Anubian commando out there.

Get it on.

Strangers to the universe.

Brothers to the end.

CHAPTER FIFTY-SIX

I watched as Ulysses Two Alpha Six moved swiftly forward, leading his squad in a combat wedge as they shot down commandos and overran positions forward of our base of fire.

Then they were down and covering, switching to suppression and calling out for First to push forward now.

Like a well-made watch, my platoon ran their game as Third came online and began to suppress the fire we were taking from the far end of the compartment.

First with Punch in the lead wove through the surgical stations, Punch working the shotty he preferred for internal ship combat like it was some pneumatic killing machine. I watched as he swiftly came around the side of a medical station that seemed more advanced and tightly packed with diagnostic equipment than the others nearby. Anubian commandos were firing from here, three of them. Punch pushed in, slam-firing the shotty and ruining all three in a thunder-spray of blasting fire, all lead and concussive thunder.

They were shredded to scraps and he took the bloody position and pushed his troops into fighting positions there.

That position was considered *overrun* and I heard Ulysses order his squad to deploy their frags forward of it to soften up the next line of defense.

We had half the compartment now, and with Fourth, my squad, on rear security, we shifted Third forward, Hauser just standing up and leading the wedge into the next phase of the battle as he burned an entire belt from his chopped Pig just to keep the enemies' heads down as his squad repositioned.

Also… combat cyborgs fire incredibly accurately even when *pray and spray* is in effect.

The Anubians had no idea who was hitting them and from what direction at any given moment. For half a hot second I had a feeling we were gonna do better than all my dark visions had promised me we would.

Then they threw their first Bishop at us.

I was still getting chatter from Gunny's platoon as they retreated out of the sector cooling towers under fire, pushing for an intercept passage where we could come in and relieve them.

They were pulling a fighting retrograde and bleeding the enemy bad… but again… the enemy had the numbers. If Chief Cook's drug-induced intel was solid… we were facing a brigade here.

One company versus what was in effect at least three battalions... weren't great odds.

But as every fighting unit ever has said to itself at some point... *We know it's gonna suck. But we're gonna go and do it anyway.*

Their Bishop came at us, supported by fresh Anubian commandos with sub guns.

All we saw of this psy-can operator was a shrouded figure, lithe to the point of gaunt, tall like a specter, appearing at the far end of this hospital compartment for this section of the vast city-sized starship, bigger, we'd come to board.

Punch was pushing forward with First when the telekinetic Bishop began to tear apart... everything... with unseen forces, hurling it all into a developing micro-tornado within the room, right here on a starship.

Computers, data drives, sharp surgical scalpels, injectors, needles, personal medical scanners, all of it was instantly collected into the sudden windstorm that hurled and swirled itself into an evil black maelstrom within seconds. Almost becoming like some living heaving-and-breathing sand devil out of ancient lost tales of genies and devils as everything was sucked up and began to spin dangerously around.

There was some electricity in the air... some bad vibe that made you feel like imminent doom was approaching and it seemed to reach down into your guts and grab you right where the bean-and-cheese rations didn't sit well.

Stinkeye was with Fourth, and he recognized the Bishop's powers and entrance into the battle within the compartment almost instantly as he sprayed hot liquor and swore.

"Dat's one of 'em!" he shouted gustily to my squad. Which... apart from Hustle and Hoser... is composed of some new guys, guys I'm not sure about, and the let's just say... the skittish.

Catboi watched the dust-devil of sharp knives and heavy things spin up and said nothing. I wasn't sure if that was good or bad...

I had NCO stuff to do.

The tornado turned into some kind of living demonic thing bellowing and heaving like a mad bull, and then it drove itself suddenly right into First on the right.

At the same time a massive internal blast door on our left flank irised open and Anubian commandos, armored in black and gold with their dog-headed buckets and glowing red eyes, surged into the room firing small compact battle rifles.

Punch was grabbed by the demon tornado even as he blasted it with the shotty like that was gonna do anything...

It didn't. But A for effort.

The summoned wind demon, which was all I could think it was, tore through First Squad, picking up my men and flinging them in every direction.

I swore. Because that was all I could do seeing as shooting it wasn't gonna work... which, honest about these things we must be... I was considering doing.

Second was getting hit by fire, and flashbangs were being tossed into their midst from the enemy forward of their position. Both my flanks were being rolled up almost instantly—and just seconds ago things were going my way.

"Hauser!" I shouted over the comm, hearing my voice ragged and gasping in the bucket against the suit's ox feed. "Support Second. Fourth is gonna push in on that Bishop and we'll see what we can do."

Then I turned toward Stinkeye as I got a terse and emotionless "Copy, Sergeant Orion," from Hauser. "Engaging forward."

"What the hell can you do to that thing?" I shouted raggedly at Stinkeye who still didn't have his EVC bucket on even though I'd told him to repeatedly regardless of his outranking me.

He shrugged helplessly.

Some war wizard.

"Fourth!" I bellowed over the platoon comm. "Follow me. Target that tall dude and waste him!" I shouted at Hoser with the squad Pig. "Use the whole nine yards!"

Sometimes when an LMG starts to just cook off rounds, at that point you got two options... break off the belt... or ride the lightning.

I chose violence.

Hoser bellowed back as he got on the gun and got ready to unload long and steady on the Bishop and his security force, "Got three belts linked, Sar'nt. But heads-up... I can no longer make responsible decisions!"

Then Hustle and Hoser started to unload. The volume of fire was cacophonic and loud... and long. The area where the Bishop was turned into... *destruction in progress*. A disaster area. A slaughter.

Explosions, flying equipment, rag-dolling bodies... more explosions and much, much more destruction erupted across the focus of the gun team's hate.

Indeed... bad decisions were in effect.

But... this was my dumpster fire to run.

The Bishop's commando security team died en masse but the Bishop moved like a ghost that couldn't be hit. Fast and effortlessly as though he were just floating off the deck of the compartment. Even though he was tall he wove between medical diagnostic stations and an elevated walkway at the end where huge data servers were arranged like sentient giants, still glowing their indicator lights as data traffic monitors surged and pulsed in weird arcane patterns that were meaningless to this simple ruck hobo.

I put targeted fire on him as we advanced, thinking I'd do something and watched as rounds passed harmlessly through his fluttering grey shrouds.

Were we, in fact, fighting a ghost?

Was that a psy-can power like Nether's?

Above my pay grade was the answer I'd have to live with as I swapped in a new mag on the Bastard and raised it to engage again, muttering, "Die already..."

Nope.

Another squad of Anubian commandos in turn returned fire and I had to actually go full suck dirt to avoid taking accurate fire.

My squad, moving in twos, bounded forward and engaged any commandos who got near the shrouded Bishop, killing some, missing others.

I struggled to my feet like a fat man who'd fallen into a wet gutter on two-for-one large pizza day...

The wet gutter feeling was the swamp my suit had turned into as sweat broke out all across my body, what with all the incoming trying to put the murder on me.

On my feet and in my push to murder this dude, I got too close as I kept dumping rounds on him, hoping my eyes were deceiving me, or that something else was at play and in some way I was actually doing real damage to him....

Nope.

A commando came at me from out of the maelstrom gloom created by the howling demon windstorm-being the Bishop had summoned that was currently tossing First Squad in all directions.

I was getting hit by debris and struggling to stay on my boots and hold sight picture on the thunderstick I call the Bastard. My bolt had just locked to the rear indicating my mag was bone-dry.

Catboi had followed me in… with none of his usual narration… and now he said, a little more urgently than usual… "Catboi picking up the slack…"

And dumped a load of well-timed but rapid bursts of fire on multiples coming at us.

"Tango down, Sar'nt. Catboi… half cat, half boi," which was a thing he muttered, and which we could not break him of, every time he murked someone.

He'd done it in sim.

Now… he was doing it for real and the question I had often asked myself, in sim, of how this would play out under fire, if I could live with this or was it gonna be the next "Hotsoup Forever" that would send me over the NCO's edge…

Was answered.

Hells yeah. He just smoked a dude, accurately, under fire that probably would have put several holes in me.

I wiped the sweat from my face that had suddenly broken out, remember I was wearing an EVC bucket, and fumbled inserting a new mag on the Bastard as I got flat-out surprised by another bad guy.

This one fired his sub gun at near point-blank range… but at someone else. He had just appeared out of the dark to my right. Probably low-crawling forward, he came up and around my cover to attack, engaged some target farther back, saw me, and turned his attention thusly to the new threat I posed.

It was that close and hot, and now a ranged firefight had suddenly turned into an up-close and personal brawl. "A real knife-and-gun show" we sometimes call them. According to Gunny this was fairly standard in compartment-to-compartment fighting—given the short ranges and spaces, fights tended to get real close, real fast. They were also short, and very violent. He'd taught us to work with our secondaries and knives in these kinds of situations and said that was sometimes better than being on full cackle with a primary.

This was not a religion that appealed to me, but I saw and understood the tenets of its faith.

I even carried a second combat knife on my chest rig that I could get to easier in tight quarters like the situation I was in now.

Without thinking I threw my torso to the left and savagely kicked out with my right leg, landing the blow right in the dude's thigh. The sub gun jerked up and discharged a round. The bullet creased my EVC bucket, leaving a huge integrity-compromising gouge.

I slammed my rifle in his gut. Hard.

Motion causes motion and he went down, doubled over on himself. I brought the butt of the Bastard down heavily on the back of his bucket, uncertain if that would crack his skull.

It didn't, but it drove him down on the deck, and faster than I gave myself credit for, I got the mag in, let the bolt slide forward, and blew his brains out all over.

It was brutal fast.

This was… for all the marbles and birthday cake in the future.

The lights in the data servers were pulsing frenetically, wild, and really… manically. I'd been on enough starships to know what equipment looked like under normal operation, and these servers were acting anything but normal.

Like they were being affected by some local magnetic, or signal, interference… or even undergoing a hack…

We'd had our briefings on the Bishops. Their powers verged on not just the paranormal, but the supernatural.

Apparently there are differences, but to me… it's all the same.

One of the identifiers of their power usage is that often digital equipment might start to act… *strangely*.

"Sometimes, little children…" Stinkeye had said, dead serious during the "Bishops brief" as we trained up for this insert. "Dey takes dere needs from power systems, and sources. Certain types… *manifestahs*… dey get way more powerful 'round certain types o' machines."

The ghost Bishop… was weaving in and out of combat, but he was staying near the immense sentinel data mainframes at the back of the compartment as their lights and readouts went insane while the heaving demon windstorm had its way with my squad and turned everything around First into a winter squall.

Then… all of a sudden, the wind demon bellowed like it was a living thing… emitting a long mournful bone-chilling howl… and hurled itself into Third. I turned and saw Hauser, a dark shadowy hulk in the gloom holding the barking Pig, cutting down the attack force on the left flank pushing into Ulysses's squad.

Hauser's eyes, seemingly normal under average lighting conditions, glow red in the dark. A feature the Monarchs wanted to inspire terror. But at the moment my friend's optical sensors, his "eyes," were shifting colors through red and white spectrums.

The thing was "hacking" our combat cyborg.

And… that's bad. Real bad.

The command team has discussed options in this event… and none of them are good.

For a moment I thought it was just a trick of the light. But I knew it wasn't as I heard his Pig stop its rattle of fire.

Stinkeye was down on the ground, crawling like a snake to reach Hauser. He'd never dare poke his head up in a firefight. And the times he'd done so he'd screamed like a child, cried, and claimed he was as brave as they come afterward.

"He's figurin' him out, Little King… takin' all o' his power to use against us!"

I turned toward the frantic data servers and saw them wildly visually ululating their lights and manic readouts. That's where the Bishop was drawing his power from.

Now he was looking for new power sources…

I took a knee, popped a frag, and hooked it into the servers calling out, "Fire in the hole!" with zero warning 'cause I'm pro like that.

Stinkeye screamed as incoming destroyed just about everything all around us.

Less than five seconds later the frag exploded among a rank of towering servers and instantly live and wild power was in the air, snapping and cooking off with electrical cracks and hissing sizzles.

For a moment I wondered if I'd made a mistake as huge electrical snaps cracked through the air and electricity arced out and fried nearby machines with just a lightning bolt's touch.

Then I saw the ghost of the Bishop flicker.

It wasn't a shroud. Nor was it tall, or gaunt. Those were just images it had placed in our minds with its unreal powers. Playing with our perceptions, displacing its image.

Tricks of light, shadow, and mind.

The Bishop, in reality, was a slight, stoop-shouldered young man with huge dark-circled eyes. Haunted almost. His skin was corpse-white to almost blue by the explosion-light of the data servers. He blinked and shuddered as each machine erupted violently all around him.

Hoser roared madly and worked the Pig, cutting down the remaining commandos as Hustle egged him on.

The shadow of the Bishop-thing looked about wildly, uncertain and... afraid.

I knew enough about fear to know the look. Fear I'd seen in others. Fear I'd experienced.

His fear wasn't just that he was about to die... that his power had fled... but that he had failed... *someone*. And that the fear of the failure... was greater than the fear of vengeful infantry all about him.

"Nooooooo!" he wailed pathetically.

I raised the Bastard in the fireworks display of destruction and the gloom of his dying wind demon. He was just a ragged slave, and what I think made him even more pathetic to me, was that he was wearing... what doctors call... scrubs. As though... he was just some medical experiment. Some patient.

A sick person.

It was just the flicker of a moment of realization in my mind.

I felt my finger caress the trigger of the Bastard knowing I could, and could not, kill him.

I saw tattooed bar codes running across his cheeks. Haunted, pale, concentration-camp features.

He wasn't the enemy. He was just... a tool. Of the enemy.

I lowered the Bastard even as he flailed his scrawny arms wildly, his long fingers seeking any strange power left within the compartment he could bend to his will to serve his dark masters once again, the Monarchs, a little bit more at the end of himself. Now.

I couldn't kill him.

And... trust me... I have no problem killing.

I lowered the Bastard, uncertain of what I'd do next. Probably just walk forward and bash him with the butt of my weapon. Take him prisoner. Interrogate him. Maybe... give him some kind of life like the one he'd never had.

All those stories of Stinkeye's about the camps, about the labs...

The experiments.

A living hell like none of us had ever experienced.

Nether had gotten close to it, in his work, and destroyed the lab he worked at, rather than become one. Or one of them. Monarchs.

And it had cost him, if you've read these logs... *everything*.

Stinkeye was yelling at me to "shoot him, Little King! Shoot dat devil before it kills us all!"

But I couldn't.

I wouldn't.

And I knew my days as a paid killer, a contract mercenary, were coming to an end. Sooner than later.

Stinkeye had rolled over onto his back, slithering up against a Frankensteinian surgery table with an auto-doc crouching over it like some hideous nightmare.

With little finesse and much fumbling Stinkeye shucked his personal firearm.

I have rarely ever seen him fire it.

Usually he only fires it at range time which he reluctantly shows up to, and only when ordered by the Old Man. He shows up drunk too. And in the occasional firefight he's gotten close enough to, where suddenly we're trying to save our lives with final protective fires, he's usually just blazing away at nothing in the general direction of the enemy with his eyes mostly squeezed shut.

That's his best.

Stinkeye, at heart... is a coward.

And as he'd tell you, "Ain't nothing wrong with dat, boy."

He is not ashamed of his cowardice and need for constant self-preservation.

Stinkeye fumbled the ancient sidearm out as the mainframes exploded, aiming it at the pale skeleton of a medical experiment that was the kid.

"It," he called the Bishop. Shrieking for me to kill it in fear.

And Stinkeye shot him repeatedly until he was dead, screaming raggedly incomprehensible gibberish as he did so.

The kid kept saying, "No, no no no!" as Stinkeye shot him dead.

But I think not because he was being hit.

But because he had failed... *someone*.

Finally.

Utterly.

As though there are fates worse than mere death.

That was when I knew the *Dark Star* was a ship of horrors like none I'd ever boarded, or seen, or even heard of.

That was when I knew how much trouble we all were in.

CHAPTER FIFTY-SEVEN

We had wounded. But everyone could still walk and fight after what could be treated was treated. And yeah, there were some gunshot wounds, but Gunny's crew had fallen back from the main cooling towers into the processor stacks and were now fighting for their very lives as they got pushed from all sides.

So we had to move now otherwise they were gonna get rolled.

First was pretty beaten up, but Second was ready to go. I usually only moved Hauser and Third to the front if I knew we were gonna push hard like an assault right into the face of a prepared and dug-in enemy, a situation I avoided at all costs, and then hit the flanks with my other squads.

I liked Hause in reserve because he was my ace in the hole. How many other platoon sergeants had a terminator as their best friend and primo squad leader?

None that I knew of.

So I left First in the rear as we mounted up and pushed past them, moving Fourth into the follow-on behind Ulysses and Second.

We pushed into the halls and passages beyond the brutal battle we'd just fought in the surgery center, or whatever it was. Probably something far worse, knowing what we knew about the Monarchs. It felt more like a Dark Lab they'd decided to take with them to wherever they were off to.

And that sent shudders through my soul.

"Place feels like a torture chamber," muttered Hoser as he stalked past me, the Pig low-ready and looking to lay some hate.

You could feel it. We were itching now to hit them hard. This... has been a long time coming.

"Yeah," said Hustle. "Gives me the creeps. We should burn it."

They were right about that. The whole place didn't feel so much like the starship we'd anticipated storming, as much as some city we'd never wanted to sack in the first place.

And one we knew needed to be burned to the ground, then salted, and left to die forever.

What was gonna happen here... felt ancient and primordial to me. I don't think the others realized it... but I'd read enough illegal history to know that that was what was coded into the human hard drive regardless of mRNA injections and societal engineering.

And this was odd...

Damage done in the firefight to the surgery center had hit something that caused the whole place to come to life for a moment. Automatons that weren't ruined came back online, as did the machines and readouts that hadn't been shot to pieces.

As though someone somewhere had wanted to send us a message from some command center deep in the ship that they were still in charge.

And then... as soon as they had started up they fell silent, frozen into immobility in their last bizarre configurations.

I gave the order for us to get our hump on and conduct the movement to contact in the passages ahead.

Then I turned and gave the gruesome place... it was gruesome to me now that I had some suspicions about what it was really used for... one last look.

A deathly quiet had fallen over the place after the last of the Anubian commandos had been pulse-checked and we'd declared the area clear.

It was lifeless.

"They know we're coming," muttered Punch, who'd been shot in the chest plate of the EVC. It cracked, ablated, and redistributed the damage. But he was coughing up a little blood here and there and when Klutz tried to come near and help him, the First Squad leader glared and waved the naive medic away with the fingers that remained on his maimed hand.

Punch comes from an infantry background that is almost spartan. Weakness of any kind is seen as an admission of defeat. Even first aid.

Me, I like a little bandage and a couple of painkillers. Life is rough. Try to make it bearable.

That was when the weird music suddenly started up as one of the processors began to spark and snap, its shot-riddled front system diagnostic lights showing operational run-ups.

The music was dark and haunting. Like you were listening to something at the bottom of the deepest ocean on the loneliest world ever found. So deep, so dark, so lightless down there in the blue shadows of a cold world... that where this music played, the light of a star had never shined.

It was that dark.

Holographic messages, huge block-white letters, swam through the air all around us as some of the auto-docs began to articulate once again, their needle-like spindly limbs slicing and dicing whatever had been placed on the surgery couches beneath them. One commando had died halfway over the surgery couch, and the auto-doc picked him up, laid him on the couch fully, even gingerly... then began dissecting his brain faster than I'd thought possible.

"What in the..." muttered Ulysses.

Which was rare. My Second Squad leader never said much beyond orders and back-briefs.

I didn't know what I was amazed at more. The darkly horrifying surgery on a dead man I was watching. Or the fact that my squad leader had actually remarked on something not job-related.

Ulysses, as I have mentioned before, was the company wonder boy. Formerly an Ultra. Now a merc. He was just like the captain in many subtle ways. And to hear any stray word from him that wasn't about the mission, or task, or purpose... of what we were about as a PMC company... was rare.

"It's an MK update center," hissed Stinkeye and dragged from his flask, his chocolatey-mud eyes dull and far away. "MK stand for… mind kontrol, Little King. Update center is how dey make sure everyone runnin' da proper protocols and da software and hardware ta match. Back in the Labs dey were called… garages. Here's where dey make sure everyone tink da right tings dey want 'em to tink, Little King. Dat's where all civilization ends… when it gets here. Endgame. Heart o' Darkness take dem all, damn dem."

Gentle words… a woman's voice… gentle but utterly cold, and loveless… echoed out all around us.

"This can be that. That can be this."

Her voice was clear. So clear for a moment it seemed like it was right in our EVC buckets as we cast about, our suit lights shining on all the surgical horrors, trying to see where she was coming from.

"Weakness is strength."

"Obey your gods."

"You will never be free."

"Lose yourself in us. That… is your destiny."

Other strange and bizarre words and phrases swam about us, in our ears and minds, that had no meaning to men like us.

Killers… I thought at first.

But then I told myself *no, that wasn't it.* Free. Words like these meant nothing to us. And never would. If they did… then we wouldn't be us.

Free.

Then Punch walked over to the processor that had lit up and shot it three times with his shotty. Pumping and blasting until it was "dead."

Zero emotion on his hard, tired face that was always up for a mission, a fight, or just violence on demand.

He turned toward us in the silence and muttered, "That's enough of that."

CHAPTER FIFTY-EIGHT

We pushed into the next passage and worked the corners and dark spaces, passing through tight hatches that suddenly opened out onto vast canyons that showed the cyclopean and enigmatic internal systems of this vast starship.

The route we were following in toward the intercept point would suddenly dip down into a sub deck and pass through rows upon rows of tight cells, each blocked by what looked to be a small bank vault door. There were small shadowy windows in each door... and when I chanced a look inside one I saw gold bars stacked to the ceiling.

Soon enough everyone was reporting in whispered hisses some insane level of wealth or strongness within these guarded chambers. But it would take time to hack or blow these doors and we needed to keep moving if we were gonna relieve Gunny's boys.

There seemed to be no locking or unlocking mechanisms or panels in these solid hexagonal doors either. And it was clear they were bank-vault-rated. You could tell just by touch how heavy and thick these sturdy panels were.

And they were filled.

Gold.

Diamonds.

Weapons in some cases.

Hard currencies bundled in shrink wrap and packed tight, stacked in pallets.

Mem bearer-bond certificate plates. Planetary levels of trade exchange. Gold-stamped. Worth billions if not trillions of mem on the worlds that could still cash them.

"This passage alone is worth a planetary fortune," whispered Bad Bet incredulously. "Imagine how much is on this whole ship," he whispered over the comm as we worked the solutions that allowed us to pass through this area.

"Looks like a bank heist," replied Rockstar. "That went off without a hitch."

No one else said anything when I told them to shut it and concentrate on what we were doing as we made our approach to contact.

But Rockstar was right. It did look like the haul from a crime. Because it was. The biggest one ever.

We passed out of the area in a patrol column, Catboi constantly muttering his non-stop autistic narrations with each movement of the patrol.

"Catboi on your six."

"Catboi covering the LDA."

"Catboi pie-ing this corner. No tangos. Room clear."

And so on, and so forth.

I muted his comm, constantly, but often I needed to communicate with everyone and for some reason the EVC kept unchecking the block feature I'd set for him.

At least he kept it to a low whisper.

I had him pulling security for Wolfy who didn't seem to mind the constant thread of narration much.

I asked Wolfy why Catboi didn't get on his nerves as I'd taken to pairing the "half cat, half boi" with the SDM.

"I build attachments, Sar'nt... like Hotsoup may his name live forever... so I can detach when I shoot people."

Uh...

"Why?" I asked.

"Because you get good at this kind of work and you can lose yourself, Sar'nt. See everyone as a target. That way lies madness. Know what I mean?"

I did now.

So... that explained the Hotsoup thing, a little, but not how it had come to almost replace *Get it On* as the company motto for getting into a fight.

And...

I was so tired from the waking PTSD I was having when he told me this—I'd asked him during Gunny's shoot-deck runs on the cargo decks, that it kinda went in one ear and out the other—that I think, at the time, I just tiredly mumbled, "Okay... that makes sense," and then moved on to the next NCO task in a never-ending list of them...

Such is my life.

But later, in my weapons cage deep down in the dark of the ship where everyone knows I hide and pretends not to know where it is unless they really need something from me... it's a game we all play... I thought about what my SDM had said as I smoked and drank my special stash of coffee. I may have been adding something to that but that's not germane to these confessions.

I build attachments so I can detach when I shoot.

Wolfy and his three-wolves t-shirts. Wolfy the head of the Hotsoup cult. Wolfy my SDM who was so good at it that Ghost had tried to come and poach him back on a number of occasions and I'd held them off because at the end of the day, having a solid squad designated marksman who could get it done in a tight spot... saved you a lot of work if you had to storm a position.

So I held on to Wolfy. But what he said... that bothered me. Later.

And that's when I started putting him with Catboi. I mean... not right when. I went back at him the next day as we arrived on the training deck for another one of Gunny's... *Y'all done died of stupid. Now let's run it again and this time don't be stupid. Hell, Marines, guys who eat crayons for snacks, can figure this out...*

"Hey, Wolf..." I said. "That thing you said the other day... what did you mean by that?"

"By what?"

I sighed as I tried to recall the exact phrase even though it had bothered me so much I could have spat it out like a computer feed right back in his smiling zenned-out face.

But that would have said more about me than I wanted anyone to know. Or so I told myself.

Wolfy's got bushy, curly hair. He looks like a hippy. No one would mistake him for a soldier. Maybe a musician.

And yet... he can kill you dead with that rifle and not bat an eye.

"Uh... it was something like, uh... *I build attachments so I can detach when I shoot.*"

I said that too slick.

I should've messed it up. A little. To show him he hadn't gotten under my skin in any way, shape, or form.

Because to do that to me...

I don't know. Maybe that says a lot about me too. Man, this is getting uncomfortable and I'm ready to delete my Warts And All policy for running the company log and start lying.

No.

What I got next was... not what I'd expected or prepared for.

"Hey, I don't have a story, Sar'nt."

I was taken aback.

Ha. *Taken aback.* Never thought I'd write those words in the company logs. Logs which are merely supposed to be a record of where we've been and who we've killed.

And yeah, I get that I've turned it into some kind of... *account.*

But *taken aback* is a little literary and even I have to admit that. See... I'm capable of introspection. I'm not totally flawed.

So there I was... *taken aback.*

"I'm not saying you do, Wolf."

"Well I don't," he said flatly.

"Okay," I floundered as we all got ready to run today's game of compartments and passages of fatal funneling. In hindsight, events aboard the *Dark Star* made me wish I would've taken it more seriously instead of being... *taken aback.*

But hey... I'm me. *Taken aback.* Anyways...

We have to be honest about these things. Okay? Believe me, I write that a lot more for me than whoever bothers to read this mess.

Can I get a Hotsoup?

"Uhh... well, what does that mean," I dialed in, refusing to let him go on this. "*I build attachments so I can detach when I shoot?*"

Listen... soldiers are some of the deepest people you'll ever meet. No joke. People who kill for a living have been exposed to wisdom and physics and levels few ever get the chance to experience.

Both, wisdom and physics, are great teachers... if you can survive the first lesson. Trust me on this.

And soldiers have a lot of time to think. It's not all gunfights and fast-roping off slick dropships to save the mission.

It's a lot of radio-watch. CQ. Waiting in general. We talk about booze and hoochies and spending our life insurance policies never really doing the math that for us to get paid out on them we have to be dead... but sometimes that's just to give our minds a break about the things we've had to learn the hard way.

And keep rucking.

Never make the mistake a politician makes of thinking soldiers are just dumb grunts.

They really aren't.

Socrates, some ancient philosopher the Monarchs tried to erase... I found an old half-burned book about him in a weapons bazaar, he'd been some great thinker fundamental to Earth civ long before we hit the stars and tried our act on the stellar road... he was a soldier.

Some of the hardest most truthful things I've ever learned have come from guys who ordered others guys to kill, having done a bit of it themselves, or the guys who did the killing.

Uncomfortable truth for those who think they're smart or educated.

Your mileage may vary. Mine doesn't.

"It doesn't mean anything, Sar'nt," said Wolfy with just a hint of exasperation. "It's not some clue to my jacked-up past that led me to being a mercenary."

I was looking at the shoot deck, but really I was parsing all this and trying not to show what I knew was probably a *dumbfounded* look.

Pro tip... NCOs should never look "dumbfounded" in any situation, save one. That one situation is when one of your guys has managed to do something so impossibly dumb, most likely adding or subtracting to the local civilian population, or something definitely illegal and warranting stiff penalties, that a general and most likely the local authorities have become involved.

In such cases, look as dumbfounded as you possibly can, even though you knew this guy was gonna do something exactly like what you've just been called in on the carpet for.

It's your only defense.

Ask me how I know.

"But that's not what this is about," continued Wolfy. "See... everyone knows, Sar'nt Orion. They get that somehow you do this other job besides being Plat Daddy, by trying to find the nobility in all of us and getting our stories down. Everyone knows you can do that for us and especially after we're gone."

Spoiler... I don't always find it. The nobility. Some guys are just *seriously wrong*.

"But just because a guy is messed up don't mean he ain't a shooter, Sar'nt Orion," the first sergeant would say. Usually when he'd just contracted some problem child he knew was gonna be a problem child and dumped him on me so he could be *my* problem child.

Being an NCO is really glamorous. One star. Would not recommend even to my worst enemies.

"Like somehow how the things we do... killing for money..." continued my SDM, "some bit of our past when you mark it down in the record... will justify our crimes and horrors. It won't, Sar'nt. Has nothing to do with it. It's just a job. We kill lifeforms for money and that's as old as... as old as it gets. Listen, I just shoot things. I'm really good at it, and I don't mind the pressure. In fact... ain't really a thing for me. So much so, my parents wondered if there was something wrong with me."

Then he held up a hand like...

"Ah! You almost got me, Sar'nt. Got me to tell you my dark secrets."

"So there are secrets. Dark ones?" I said too eagerly as internally I congratulated myself on being right that everyone has dark secrets.

I am a small and petty man.

Honest. Things. We have to be.

He shook his head and smiled that patient, tired smile of his.

Universe-weary.

"Nah, Sar'nt. There ain't. Average kid. Took up performance shooting in school. Good enough to win medals. Good enough to get the attention of certain Ultra recruiters even though I was considered too old for indoc. They had a program that would have... taken care of that."

Pick my mouth up off the floor.

He looked... away.

"See... I'm downtown one day, after practice... shooting team practice. There's gunfire and a robbery goes real bad. Cops pin the guy on the street and because it's a peaceful world they ain't got the arty to respond and the guy's got a juggernaut EOD suit with a mobile cyber-skeleton on. That way he can move relatively fast. Plus, he's strapping some heavy artillery himself. I see two cops go down and my truck is getting hit by that time. Girl... she's screaming."

Here's the dark secret, I hear myself telling me. The girl was the love of his life. She gets hit and he gets galvanized to make a difference out here in the dark. Every shot he takes is one that might bring her back.

Swing and miss, bitter NCO.

"I don't love her," he continues. "I like her. Sure. We'd just gone to the big Colonization Day dance. She's the prettiest girl in school, and when she starts screaming, I realize at that moment I don't really love her, and I know I never will, and the way she's screaming and crawling onto the floor pathetically like it's the end of the world... is well... was really... *ridiculous*."

He looks at me.

"It's like this, Sar'nt Orion... in that moment I didn't feel anything. For her. For anyone. I wasn't afraid. I had no fear even though this guy's laying down some serious heat on the street to make his escape."

Swing and miss, Orion the storyteller, I tell myself.

"But I see this cop get hit and he was one of us on the team right when I started shooting for medals. He graduated, big man on campus, got a job with local law enforcement. He was too new to be on a tac team but he's out here responding to that day's level of crazy and the shooter just tags him hard."

Wolfy looks back at me and without missing a beat continues his story. This is the Wolfy I know in a hard spot. Clear. Rational. Emotionless. Sniper firing so we can get off the *X* or maneuver.

He too is another ace in my hand as a wily ruck hobo trying to get everyone through the day and to their next slice of birthday cake.

"So, I get my competition rifle outta the truck and without even stabilizing the shot, I chamber a round and do the guy in the eyes because he was wearing a full armor helmet with jaw protection and everything. Eyes were the only place I could punch him. So he's dead and that's when the trouble starts."

Okay... here we go... I think. *This* is where it gets dark.

Yes. I am sick.

I just let him talk. Like I do.

"The Ultra recruiting team comes to the school, from off-world, once what happens hits the networks and they find out and all. I get the day off from school and they take me out to the range and give me some time to shoot. They observe and say nothing. Then an Inquisitor shows up and puts me through a psych eval and he's smiling... and it's not a pretty sight when that kinda guy smiles. Chief Cook, know what I mean, Sar'nt?"

I do.

"So they show me the results and say I have what it takes to enter the Drop-Start Program for the Ultras. The big things they say that're in my favor are... one, I can shoot well. And two, I don't get emotional about it. Which is important to them as that usually needs to be suppressed in the standard indoc trainee through meds and shots, which starts much younger around fourteen and sometimes as young as eight to make a perfect Ultra Marine sniper. Or so they think."

I say nothing.

"See... shooting is just math to me. I really don't... hate anyone, Sar'nt. Not even the bad dudes that have tried to kill us. It's just a game, and sometimes you win, and sometimes you lose. Except... I've never lost, Sar'nt. So... my parents were aware of... the way I think early on, and they were worried when I shot a local blue-eyed raptaar, which is a beautiful flying bird, gorgeous colors and huge eyes... it's very... as they say on our world... *cute as all hell*. It's kind of a rite of passage when your dad takes you hunting... you kill it and there's an... emotional response because it's so beautiful and when it dies it makes this real mournful mating call..."

He stopped for a moment... hearing it. Hearing that dying love song long ago on that world he was from. Something mourning that it has lost the ability to have the most important thing of all... not life. But love.

A tear starts in the side of my eye because... this hits too close to my story and no you are not going to hear it here and hopefully... never.

So I open my eyes wide and rub the tear out quickly like there was some grit or something in it.

Damn. I haven't thought about that for... years. And then suddenly... *whammo*. Emotional IED. Surprise, loser.

"They say, Sar'nt, it's like hearing everything that's wrong with the universe. Like... it's a cry for help against something that can't be helped ever again. Seriously. Guys talk all tough about how it's not gonna get 'em, and then go out and shoot it and they come back bawling their eyes out. And I've thought about that a lot since I left home, and I don't think that's a bad thing. Killing something... you should think about that. It's a life. And you ended it. You go out and kill one of those, it stays with you and haunts you. And I think whoever is in charge of the universe... got that right."

But...

"But it didn't haunt me, Sar'nt."

Wolfy shook his head.

"Not at all. And that's when my parents worried about me and took me to see a shaman. We have shamans on that world as medical practitioners. Shaman says there's nothing wrong with me... I just don't see killing the way others do. I see the shot, the math, the game. And... I'm cool with it. Even the results. And that that too is part of the universe."

I close my mouth because... this is one I've never heard, and I have heard every merc story there is to hear.

Including the one where the guy had to join up with us because he ran over a guy who owed him money and that guy was his twin brother.

Long story. That guy bought it on Blue.

"So... fast forward to the Ultra recruiting team. My parents will be tax-free if I sign the contract. They get to vote in the senate, not that it counts for much back in those days. If I join. If I become a killing machine for the Ultras... the Monarchs. For... them."

Silence.

I have learned... when it reaches this moment... say nothing. Don't try to explain it for them. They'll shut down and back out of the story.

Let it happen.

Let it bleed.

"We're different on that world, Sar'nt Orion. We're peaceful. But that offer was... *life-changing*. And my parents knew it. Having a kid who's an Ultra... that's... as they say... *something*."

"So what happened?"

Wolfy looked down and made a face. For a moment his eyes started to water and then... he was back. Peaceful. Himself.

And yes, when his eyes started to water, I almost shouted, *Aha, got you!*

But I didn't.

I am... unclean. Look away in horror.

"My dad took me to the starport... bought a forged ID and put me on a freighter outbound for one of the new worlds."

Wolfy sighed.

"It was early morning, still dark, when the freighter issued last call to board. Rain coming down light like it did in all the mornings I'd ever lived on that world. He gives me all their money and says, "I didn't raise you to be a killing machine. I get that... I get that you're good at what you do. That you have potential they can max, son. And I get that you like the shooting. But not with them. That's not you. And it won't be you anymore by the time they put you through that program... So... go. Go and live and be whoever it is you wanna be. But don't come back here. Not here. Not ever."

Pause.

What... do you say?

Answer: nothing. Sometimes... there just aren't words.

"I stood there, Orion. I wasn't crying. But I've thought about it since... and... I wish I had."

Yeah. I know that moment too, kid.

"So I start to go, and he says before I do... don't be afraid to make friends, don't be afraid to love people, son... and care about them... okay?"

Wolfy stops and adjusts some strap on his gear. Studies his rifle for a long second.

"I said I wouldn't. But he's looking at me real serious now, Sar'nt. Then he says, 'No... I mean... do those things, son. Ruin the killing machine they want you to be by caring. That way... if they ever find you. You'll be no good to them. Okay?'"

I said I would.

"So why become a shooter? A PMC?" I asked after a long moment to digest this revelation.

He shrugged. "I like the work, Sar'nt. The shooting. I think... I'm helping, Orion. Helping the people that don't want to... be them. The slaves of the Monarchs. The ones we're going onto that ship to kill. But..."

He hesitated.

"There's more to it than that."

I waited.

"I read books... on how to... form attachments. At first... I was faking it. But eventually... I figured it out. And it helps to form those attachments, here in the company... so I never doubt that I can be me. Detach... and just make the shot like I did that day I..."

He trailed off. I'd seen that look many times before.

He was there again on the day when everything changed. All of us, for the rest of our lives, go back to that day. Sometimes, as the years go on, less and less, and then as I get older... maybe more and more.

It's like visiting a place you miss now and understand better.

But maybe that's just me, even though I don't think it is. I think... it's all of us.

"The day you saved some lives in shooting?"

"No," he whispered. Then he looked at me... and this... this was the confession. The dark secret. "The day... I destroyed my family."

Then he just turned and went off to another side of the deck, falling in easily with a group of Hotsoupers, letting go of the *who*, or *what*, he'd been with me in that moment of complete... revelation.

Honest.

No lies.

No evasions.

Just... the math of what we do, the shots we take, and the trajectory of fatality.

The arc... of *descent*.

"Yeah, Wolfy..." I said to no one in his absence. "You got a story. Everyone does."

Even me.

CHAPTER FIFTY-NINE

We hit the next section of the ship and knew we were getting close to the running gun battle Gunny's platoon was involved in.

We ran into our first survivors, Devil Dogs helping the walking wounded to get out of the firefight while the rest of the platoon kept falling back in teams, burning ammo and bleeding the enemy push.

Ulysses and I had gone forward, putting the platoon into a halt while we connected with one of Gunny's NCOs, a squad leader everyone tagged Jake Canada.

I didn't know much about him other than he was prior some service, worked hard, and never slept. Or it seemed like he never slept. He was known to work at weapons maintenance and combatives at odd hours of the night. It had become known among anyone on duty or watch that you could usually find Jake Canada doing his thang with a hot brewpot of coffee you could hit to keep going and finish out whatever you had to get done before racking out.

Generally, if it was work of some kind he'd jump in and help you. Solid guy.

Why he was tagged Jake Canada I had no idea, that was a Gunny's platoon internal thing. Someday I'd get the story and I'd mark it down in the logs.

Jake Canada was helping a guy tagged Scribbles down a passage, away from the firefight and toward the rear. It was clear Scribbles had been badly wounded but was doing his best to help out with his own evac.

"What's the situation?" I asked Canada.

"We lost five on initial contact. Ended up in a gunfight with those commando dudes. Thought we got outta there and then all the sudden... those things started showin' up. Tore us to pieces."

"Where's Gunny?" I asked.

We could hear gunfire and shouts deeper back in the darker sections of the warren of compartments we'd found them making their way through.

Canada had a broken chem-stick glowing to lead their way through the dark.

Their imaging systems in the EVC buckets must have malfunctioned. When I mentioned this Scribbles grunted, then groaned and hissed, "They had a damn Bishop with them... some chick who can basically generate a localized EMP wave like... like a flamethrower... 'cept all you see is blue waves that are barely there. She hits you with it and you lose all electronics... comm, targeting, even the optics on your weapons. We had to fight our way outta there on iron sights. Bad day *gettin' worse.*"

First time? I felt like asking but didn't have the time.

Ulysses had his weapon out as he stood sentry taking in the info and scanning the dark they'd come through. But I had a feeling he was about something else.

And I liked that.

We have to be honest… as I like to say… about things. I liked Ulysses because he was pro. Pro in ways I'd never be. Yeah, he was younger, faster, newer, and brighter than me… but he had that old soldier feeling that comes with having been trained by one or several. There were times I found myself unconsciously deferring to him.

Truth was…

He wasn't just a great soldier.

He was… a great warrior.

There's a difference. Don't @ me.

"Take Scribs back down that way, and start shouting…"

I shuddered as I paused before I gave them the password.

I hated this part.

But the platoon had insisted.

This was our response when needing a code phrase to use for security situations.

Sometimes it becomes painfully apparent that I'm not really in charge at all.

"… Hotsoup."

Scribs and Jake Canada looked at me, gunshot and bloody, orange chem-light burning hellishly to illuminate the dark internal space.

"That's awesome! Soup was da man!" Jake Canada roared.

Of course he is. Of course the cult had spread to Gunny's section. One day we'll no longer be Strange Company.

We will be Hotsoup PMC Ltd.

They were off and just as Ulysses started laying out the plan he'd already formed, to me, I could hear Jake Canada calling out, "Hotsoup, boys! Hotsoup, boys! We comin' in. It's Canada and Scribs from Devils."

But Ulysses was already downloading his plan in that concise, perfect, low thunder was his voice was.

"Listen, Sergeant. This is how we can do this…"

I don't have an ego. I really don't. I just want everyone to survive. And it'd be nice if I did too. Ulysses has proven to be what we all think of him as… a wonder boy. A super-soldier. A tactical genius. And hell… I'd make him the next captain of the company when it comes time to vote.

"Go forward and interface with the platoon sergeant, Sar'nt. Tell him to conduct a retrograde through this section…"

He drew a line through the dark compartments and the three passages that threaded this unused section of the ship. It looked unfinished and abandoned to me. There was something about this whole place that felt… forlorn, and… unclean. I didn't like it here.

Ulysses continued anyway.

"I'll go back to the platoon and get them set up in ambushes here and here…" He pointed to two locations. "With reinforcement staged down that passage. Once our guys make it through, we'll conduct an ambush and give Gunny's element the time to pull back behind our lines near the DZ. Then we'll break contact, fade down that secondary passage back toward the DZ. Copy, Sar'nt?"

Again… I outranked him. And here he was running my platoon, and I had no problem with that. His plan was solid, and I'd always tried to get everyone, top to bottom in my platoon, training for the job above them. Some days during training, I'd flip positions and put the new guys in leadership positions and get them to get a feel for the role and the responsibilities.

First Sergeant taught me that. Said it was a thing in the Saturnian Batts when they went through their qualification schools and got the tab. So I adopted it and here it was… actually executing because of course, Ulysses was involved.

"Solid copy."

What else was I gonna say. It was a solid plan and I didn't have a better one and our guys were in it and needed to get out of it.

"Let's roll."

We covered a few signals and made it happen.

Twenty minutes later, when all was ready, Duster detonated micro-claymores via remote and savaged the first teams of Anubian commandos trying to penetrate this section. I'd already hustled Gunny's platoon through and the hulking ex-Marine and I hunkered in a dark passage, smashing out a few of the sensor readouts and indicators that had flickered in there just moments before the attack began.

I listened as Wolfy picked up the Bishop girl. She was cloaked, slim, and hooded by some kind of anti-thermal soft armor, but he spotted her anyway through the scope of his SDM rifle. He was looking for her once we'd apprised the shooters to be on the scope for her because we wanted to shut down her action as a combat multiplier for the bad guys we were facing.

We needed better odds.

He domed her with one shot as Hoser and Hustle opened fire from their position while Mad Max opened up with the Pig from Second and interlocking fields of fire were suddenly ripping the commandos to shreds.

Now came the targeted fire on anyone even looking like a Bishop, or a commander, or small unit leader of any type, as the rest got savaged by the gun teams.

For half a hot second I thought we had it done and Gunny's unit effectively disengaged without us getting caught…

"What hung you guys up in there?" I hissed at Gunny not meaning to as we hugged wall inside the shadowy passage watching Ulysses's ambush do its killing work. I'd pulled off my EVC bucket because it was creased and the integrity was bad. And because I was hot. And sweaty. And tired of breathing my own stink.

Gunny, sweating heavy and black-skinned, held the shotgun he'd worked savagely trying to kill his way out of the X.

He was thumbing rounds in and it was still smoking.

His EVC was splashed with someone else's blood.

And… some*thing* else's blood.

"Those damn things…" he muttered.

And then I saw them. Spider-like bio-mechanical scorpions the size of large dogs, scuttling along the ceilings of the passages above the ambush.

They were black like an oil slick and seemed to be armor-plated with some kind of tough insect shell that was probably more carbon than insect. They chittered and clicked to one another, but electronically like old-school eight-bit gambling machines.

I watched them race over the heads of the *X* we'd arranged for the commandos to die on, and sweep, fast, toward my emplaced platoon.

Punch spotted them first even as I alerted them on comm.

"Watch the ceiling for tangos!" I shouted.

Punch's shotgun started exploding them almost instantly as their claws opened wide and sprayed slimy saliva all over the flank security team, encasing them in a fast-developing crystalline web.

"Got somethin' for 'em this time," hissed Gunny and started popping ThermaPhos grenades down into the machine-gun-ruined dead on the *X*.

ThermaPhos is a phosphorescent grenade that burns like thermite after emitting a short-radius explosion that merely spreads the phos all around instead of any kind of meaningful concussion and frag.

Marines tasked with hull breaching favor them because while being highly destructive to lifeforms, they don't rupture compartments. Which is especially helpful when you're boarding an enemy vessel and don't want to suddenly hull breach and get vented into open space.

They're also great at denying avenues of attack to the enemy because anyone who knows what this stuff is stays clear of it.

It gets on you… it doesn't stop burning and you need a medic who knows what he's doing to shut it down.

But venting right now was not a serious problem according to our deep scans of this section. We were now deep into the immense vessel. Board a corvette or a fast gun frigate and deep dark cold interstellar space was sometimes just meters away.

Marines, especially Ultra Marines, used low-caliber ammo and even energy weapons along with ThermaPhos grenades which ate up any kind of environmental suit or armor in a heartbeat, to get their work done.

Gunny started popping the hellish munition as he ordered me to cover him.

I flipped the Bastard to bark and started dumping bursts into the dark ceiling where the creepy crawly bastards were coming for my platoon.

I didn't have my EVC bucket on, so I'd lost imaging. I thumbed on the Bastard's scope, which was pre-selected for thermal, and got a blown-out image that was no good because of the intense heat sig coming off the deployed phos.

Close to fifteen hundred degrees Fahrenheit.

I swore and went to night vision because it was so dark in there.

ThermaPhos started to explode all over the compartment and passage. The gun teams were far enough away and so were most of the security.

The SDMs were further back, in the darkness, just shadows stabilizing their weapon systems on piping, smashed terminals, or whatever they could find to put rounds into the targets they'd been ordered to engage.

Rockstar, Bender, and Solo were the security team that got enveloped in mucus-web. They were struggling out of it as Yahtzee engaged from behind them at near point-blank range on the first of the scorpion spiders to come for the enveloped team.

Not a solid role for an SDM, but Yahtzee was a shooter hence the tag. Even point blank he engaged solid and steady, destroying the crawling things on the ceiling as they came for our security team.

Three scorpions anchored themselves to the spray of hardened web, then began to draw the entangled security team toward them as though ready to haul them back into the darkness they'd come from.

Solo, Rockstar, and Bender were being dragged into the darkness by the hideous things.

Bender began to scream.

Hauser, running the reaction force just meters off to their left, let his gun dangle on the sling and simply strode into the web, reaching down and grabbing a handful of burning ThermaPhos, then dropping it into the webbing.

The synthetic flesh on his hand instantly melted away in great dripping chunks, revealing the near-indestructible gleaming combat chassis beneath.

Instantly the whole mass of web was alight as the flames crawled around the now all three screaming soldiers. Hauser pulled them loose before the flames could reach them, yanking them out of harm's way.

Solo was the last to get free, our combat cyborg literally heaving the soldier like a flying bundle down the dark passage to the rear of the position and away from the battle.

Some who have been through the first day of military basic training will understand the action, having been thrown off cattle-transports by their drill sergeants.

Then Hauser strode from the burning web almost effortlessly, batting out the flaming strands still on him as though they were nothing.

He popped a frag and tossed it just meters behind him where more of the fiendish scorpion spiders were clustering to vomit more webbing. Then Hauser turned his back, absorbing the blast seconds later in order to protect the men he'd just rescued.

All this while the gunfight continued to escalate despite the ambush.

With the ThermaPhos burning like hell itself, the passage quickly became enveloped in white smoke. I ordered the machine gun teams to pull back and the platoon to break contact.

"Reaper, we are leaving!" I shouted and made sure I had a head count as Ulysses and I held the rear.

He was out of mags when I was satisfied we'd left no one behind.

I lent him two of my last three and we boogied.

In other words... we ran for our lives.

That... was Day One of the boarding of the *Dark Star*.

We barely made it back to the firebase forming around the *Spider*.

It didn't get any easier after that.

CHAPTER SIXTY

Over six weeks of brutal compartment-to-compartment fighting later… on Day Forty-Seven… we finally broke through.

The last of the Anubian commando defenses, around a nexus of the *Dark Star*'s internal flight systems and engineering that served one of the main maneuver drives of the strange and cyclopean starship, collapsed.

The battle at that sector control node had been brutal. Three hours into the fight both sides were out of ammo even though it was being pushed forward as fast as possible.

Their sappers were shooting up our resupply along Route Vega, and Ghost was creeping in and doing the same to them. Three hours in and it devolved into hand-to-hand combat. Though there were more knives than there were hands.

Even EVC buckets got used.

But we finally broke through their fortifications along what we'd taken to calling Route Vega.

Vega had been a huge and desperate battle in the early history of the Strange, long before any of us were part of the company. John Strange days. Early stellar exploration by the vast human diaspora exploring more by trial and error than anything else.

Occasionally, on other contracts, as we developed our theater of operations for the mission we'd been given, when we wanted to focus on areas the local maps had not defined or named, we dove back into the company logs for reference points and used those in our tactical planning.

Route Vega was the avenue of attack we'd pursued for six hard weeks of compartment and passage fighting to reach what the company had determined was its first objective in carrying out the overall operation, which was to destroy the Monarchs once and for all.

As we penetrated deeper and deeper into the hull, breaching and clearing hardened compartments one at a time, close-quarters fighting with the commandos resulted in instances of extreme and sudden gunfire, or defusing complicated IEDs left to blow a whole element to pieces in one fell swoop, which was how we lost one of the new squads on Day Nineteen, as we developed Route Vega.

The hard way.

We had dead. Yes.

Everyone was wounded to some greater or lesser degree. Our EVC armor was shot to hell by then. Patched twenty times over to the point of being a useless exercise, we did it and wore it anyway. Many of the personal weapon systems the company allowed us to use were no longer useful in that the ammo for them, especially if they were specialized, had gone dry in the company stores.

Battered but well-maintained S16s were handed out in replacement, and Chungo the company supply sergeant laughed heartily as he chomped down on his ever-smoldering stubby cigar.

"They always come back to Daddy," he rumbled like some great sweaty ogre. "Best weapon system in the world. Stoner. Cleared all the First Worlds back in the day. Great then. Still great now. Take your pick, kids, got lots of 'em."

Then he laughed like the devil you'd just signed your soul over to as he handed you a battered, scrubbed, and no-frills combat rifle.

And yes. He was right. I chose the S16 because it always went "bang" when I needed it to. And I'd learned that was probably the most important feature to have when you and the other guy were trying to kill each other.

Fancy guns were like fancy girls… you had to get 'em in the mood to have a good time.

The Bastard was a slut and she'd do it anytime I wanted, anywhere I wanted.

And it felt that was crucial to extended slices of birthday cake.

We have to be honest about these things.

I didn't like the supply sergeant, but he was right. The Bastard was a tricked-out S16. And Chungo had gotten us thousands of them. No matter how many times we'd tried to can them because of some material malfunction, loss, or destruction in combat… there was always another down there in the weapons racks.

Rumors abounded in the company that Chungo had a secret weapons locker somewhere on the ship where he kept the rest. And… that the locker was the size of a dropship hangar.

Rumors.

The company would face its last fight someday, desperate, surrounded, outnumbered and outgunned… and Chungo would happily be handing out S16s like you won the lottery.

Some religions have their end-of-days scenarios… that was ours. Or at least, mine.

He was proud of the S16. He could do this really cool trick with it. And yeah, I had to give him props for this because to look at the fat bastard you'd think he possessed no soldier skills whatsoever. But the first sergeant told me Chungo had been with Second Armored Cav at Gerault as a tank commander and apparently he'd gotten some big-deal award for holding a ridgeline against thirty-two other tanks when the line was real thin.

I hated Chungo too much to ever ask him if this was true for fear that it was, and then my hatred would just be petty and small. I was sus of the hero tale if only because I disliked Chungo and his commitment to profiteering at the company's expense.

I guess there's a lot of that going around now that it feels like we're coming to the end of… something.

Me?

The company?

This… chapter of our story?

Okay, so that trick Chungo could do with the S16. So, invariably some New Guy would get an S16 he said couldn't be zeroed.

That basically means… shoot straight.

New Guy would return it and Chungo would take it.

Guy would complain and show the target-sims and how the S16 in question would always, no matter how much adjustment in the iron sights applied, shoot this way or that way, wrong, and invariably off.

Then Chungo would clamp his ever-smoldering cigar between his fat wet lips, take the battle rifle from the kid with his fat stubby fingers, without one word, and then head toward the range he always kept nearby.

Then he'd shoot a perfect zero and shove the rifle back at the kid, saying, "Works for me."

Every. Time.

I thought that was cool.

So Route Vega… forty-seven days to clear all the way to the last stand of the Anubian commando brigade that had been tasked with guarding this section of the ship.

Along the way we faced a rough hump and a couple, one in particular… very bad days.

We'd iced most of the Bishops our early intel had developed in the sector. But there was still one known active one left and the captain had a bounty out on her. And there were who knew how many unknown.

We were pulling a lot of currency and precious metals, along with some other strange assets, out of the sector of the ship we'd cleared. If we survived and made it to another world… this would be one of the most profitable contracts we'd ever done.

It figures I had a pretty good idea I wasn't making it off this one.

And as XO reminded everyone… "We have no idea if they haven't pushed more Bishops into the sector."

So… Fartsack's sticker on the back of his EVC was still valid.

It gets worse.

But we hadn't seen any evidence that they had pushed in more Bishops, and so we prepared for the final assault against Terminal 95 at the edge between the outer hull of the *Dark Star*… and what we'd come to understand was called… the inner hull.

A forbidden zone to most of the *Dark Star*'s slave crew according to the captured commandos we'd interrogated. Or from intel we'd seized by data capture or hard acquisition of sensitive sites and materials.

The first Bishop we met after the one Wolfy domed was a dude that could start fires with his mind. He almost roasted Reaper, but we backed out of the PDC munitions stores compartment we'd been breaching, dead Anubian commandos shot to pieces and blown apart in every direction from the frags we used to pry them out of their ad hoc bunkers. That's when the flames started to ignite on almost every surface in the room and the temperature started to climb.

With PDC munitions stacked three stories high.

It was an automated stores, and there was a robot system that could draw and elevate the munitions up the PDC gun system it fed on the outer hull.

An explosion here would have destroyed most of the sector, and it was almost as if the Monarchs wouldn't have minded the loss.

Route Vega was growing.

The *Dark Star* was huge.

Losing this section but taking us out was... let's just say the command team could see the benefit of such a denial-of-route attack.

But we had to make it work. Keep it open. It was our only way into the inner hull and mission accomplished.

Inside munitions stores that day as the firestarter Bishop started to raise the temp and flames were everywhere...

Hatches we'd cracked suddenly re-hacked and shut closed, sealing us inside the passage and compartments that served the ship as a munitions stores area for this sector.

We'd just cleared a warehouse stack that had food, supplies, a huge cavern of stocked goods the company had identified as a resupply point should the fighting drag on into months...

Some of us wondered if it would go on for years. Or at least that's what it felt like as each day we arose and got tasked with either clearing Route Vega forward or keeping it open. Day or night, operations of breaching with the only reward that you dragged yourself back to the secured LZ on the hangar deck for four hours sleep, re-arm, hot chow, and back out to clean another passage filled with sentry guns enemy sappers had set up at key junctions, poison-gas mines, snipers positioned at each bulkhead, or even laser trip-wired IEDs camouflaged like decking or terminals or interface panels along areas of the route we'd already cleared.

IED was how we lost Tags on Day Five.

I never knew his story. And now... *I never will.* He will merely be listed in the company records by his contract date and his KIA date.

And yet...

Strangers to the Universe, Brothers to the End shall be noted at the end of his file. As is our way.

I'm finding little comfort in that lately.

But there's some. Still.

And even other things as I become convinced like some faith in a religion... that we will die in this hull...

"He went Total Hotsoup there at the end when he pushed on us, Sar'nt. Got on the gun and didn't forget the Soup. That's how I wanna go, Sar'nt," they will say to me as we stand on the cargo deck with their boots and rifle and say goodbye. Spacing them off the hangar.

There's a lot of wreckage out there now.

Very few of the Rogue Fleet, *yeeehawww, boys!!!*, talks to each other anymore. But that is another story.

And I wonder how much of it is left.

We still hear distant booms across the superstructure. Get occasional traffic. Trade supplies.

The siege of the *Dark Star*... is a lonely one.

I never expected that.

But... here we are.

That's what I think when we say goodbye to our dead.

And then *Hotsoup* and *Brothers to the End*.

Don't underestimate the power of the little things. They keep ya goin' when the suck is in full effect.

So back in the PDC munitions stores on Day Fifteen, Fire Guy lights the chamber on fire and starts surrounding us with flames that are just coming from seemingly nowhere.

I'll be honest… we freaked out. Everyone lost their collective cool.

See enough guys burn to death in vehicles after roadside IEDs and you'll be a true believer in the power of fire.

Hauser. Hauser saved our bacon that day.

Again.

Route Vega was slowly growing, day by day, twisting through this section of compartments that led toward Terminal 95 which is the main, and final, fortification of the last of the Anubian Command.

The Monarch acting as their sector commander. Guarding the inner hull from Route Vega.

Chief Cook assures us daily he has something special for us if we can make it.

He looks worn, tired, desperate. And… coked up on starport speed.

When Hot Stuff tried to roast us alive on Day Fifteen in the oven he'd created in the munitions stores, Hauser, running "detailed schematics" we'd been developing of the *Dark Star* as we stormed different sections and were able to access mapping and routing directories of at least the local area, Hauser was able to see that Route Vega was right up against the main gun tube that had been our sector barrier in this section of the massive disc ship.

That gun tube, or whatever it really is, is open to deep space. The supernatural flames inside munitions stores started crawling and licking at us almost instantly as we backed away. Some of the guys' EVC suits had suddenly even started to catch fire for no reason I can explain. Hauser overrides the comm across all squads and tells us to go to posture four immediately and brace for "explosive decompression."

A note here.

Explosive Decompression. This is the most feared aspect of hull breaching. A sudden breach can suck you right out into deep space, and if you're not tethered, or there isn't some kind of rescue and recovery crew, and ship, on station, there is a pretty good chance you're going to be lost in the void forever.

Even with an EVC suit and a working beacon.

No more cake for you.

Further note… ACE reports are currently reporting fifty percent of my platoon's EVC suits do not possess operational beacons.

So… we got that goin' for us.

But there's nothing that can be done about that. So that's not even a "tomorrow problem."

Our EVCs have been shot to hell but that's better than your body being shot to hell. They're punctured, repaired, smell bad, are covered in blast soot, cordite, and possess a veritable raft of "tattoos" that are, in reality, repair work done with sprayplas just to maintain suit integrity in case we end up in a hostile environment courtesy of something, say, like… an explosive decompression.

"Get to posture four, Reaper. Now. Stand by for explosive decompression," orders Hauser in that voice of his.

"Hause, what you got—"

"No time, Sergeant Orion. It's the only way to extinguish the flames and prevent a catastrophic explosion. If the stored munitions here detonate, the entire sector, including the *Spider*, will be destroyed."

Did I mention I'm breathing like a jackhammer to get enough ox as I seal my EVC and look for something secure to clip into.

And making sure everyone else is doing it too because apparently that's my job as an NCO.

I saw what Hauser was intending to accomplish. Venting to space would immediately extinguish the flames the Bishop was trying to roast us alive with. And my guess is the Monarchs were willing for their slave to det the sector in order to prevent us from reaching Terminal 95, and then the inner hull.

Mind Kontrol of their slaves.

Explosive decompression would prevent us from burning to death inside our EVCs. And blowing a giant hole in this ship and ending John Strange's company right here and now.

No more logs.

No more cake.

And I still was not, as they say... *heartened*.

Let me explain. Explosive decompression inside a hull in deep space. Go outside during the next tornado and try to hold on to anything. If you fail, then you get sucked into the black void with no hope of recovery.

With seconds to decide... we didn't have much of a choice, and the combat cyborg, correctly and immediately, thanks to his onboard tactical processors, diagnosed the cure to what was about to ail us.

I scrambled to get my frog tango clipped into a heavy brace with brackets that was attached to a bulkhead in the passage.

Then I began to assess my squad's efforts.

We were sealing and getting our EVC buckets locked in place as Hauser slung his belt-fed Pig, reached into Duster's EOD ruck, and pulled out the big door charges we'd created for some of the more bank-vault-sized hatches we'd needed to breach in the clearing of the very dangerous, and very deadly, Route Vega.

Duster had specifically created "these babies" as he called them to tear apart those huge doors and force the blast outward toward the compartment beyond, instead of back all over us with a bonus of brain damage from overpressure.

"These'll breach hull any day that ends in Y," Duster had proclaimed proudly.

Well... now we were gonna see if that was so.

Flames crawled all around us as Hauser placed the charges and armed them. The Bishop was obscured by smoke and flames as oxygen began to burn.

We had fifteen seconds before we burned alive to seal up, go to EVC posture four, and grab on to something or get out the EVC airframe clip and flexy-cable onto something...

Again, more notes... I'd seen the airframe clip straight-up tear out of the suit, and I'd seen the flexy-cable both break, and not break and instead sever a limb it had entangled with.

That's what I mean when I said I was not *heartened* by Hauser's plan.

So all this fun circus of terrible outcomes was running around in the ol' plat daddy's head in that fifteen seconds as Hauser slammed both sizable breaching charges against the compartment wall he calculated gave access to internal systems that were most likely depressurized and exposed to deep space between there and the massive gun tube, or whatever it was that was on our right flank through Route Vega.

"Hang on... the compartment is about to depressurize," stated Hauser emotionlessly as everyone swore and complained about *not signing up for this* to varying degrees of vulgarity.

We tried to cover and hang on as best we could. Everything not nailed down went straight out through the breach including me, as my clip and leash both broke. Hauser grabbed me, holding on with one hydraulic arm to the starship bulkhead, just meters before I entered the vacuum and got carried off into the black void.

Emergency hatches and damage control bulkheads sealed a minute later and we made our way back into the pressurized hull sections of the *Dark Star*... barely.

Hot Stuff didn't get it that day. But two days later, Day Seventeen, we set up an IED with pyro gel and cooked him good when he tried to get in behind us and start another fire that wouldn't allow us to breach or pull back to sections we held.

Apparently, he wasn't immune to fire.

Weird.

CHAPTER SIXTY-ONE

We fought hard for Route Vega through a section of the ship we'd learned was identified as Delta Sector. Advanced Navigation Interface Engineering for the *Dark Star*.

Again… it must be said this ship was massive. All across the wide disc of its hull the battle raged as the rest of the fleet tried their best individual efforts to plunder the ship. The fighting thundered and there were some nights and days it sounded positively apocalyptic as the heaviest munitions the fleet had brought along were used to breach whatever lay in the way of our former allies' routes to the inner hull.

And wealth and power beyond imagining.

And on that note… the fleet.

Rogue Fleet, *yeeehawww, boys!!!*

I still have the t-shirt. It's pretty raggedy.

By the third week the fleet didn't exist anymore and whatever joint operations being conducted of the rapidly diminishing forces and ships were uneasy alliances at best as the Star Khans of the Technate realized what was to be had inside the treasure ship that was the *Dark Star*…

Fantastic technology only even barely conceived of by the most brilliant minds.

And endless wealth beyond the dreams of avarice, some overheated and long-dead wordsmith chungo might have put it… Certainly not your humble ruck hobo, Keeper of the Company Log.

We had become like pirates here for the plundering as we crawled in, on, and through the cursed ghost ship that was the *Dark Star*.

And there *were* ghosts… just like those killing fields on that contract. Guys on watch saw things. We fought horrors and that… became the norm.

But…

Our purpose was still our compass. Stack the Monarchs. There was nothing else but this debt for us.

And…

The rest of the fleet had lost its way.

But… the company did not.

In the first few weeks, the bulk of the fleet that had been rebuffed in their efforts to insert along the outer ring of the massive *Dark Star* had instead gone in hard along the upper hull where strange brutalist fortresses and slender almost alien-like towers rose. The heavy hitters in the fleet had gone in there using dropships to take the towers and fight brutal battles down along the length of these structures, floor by floor, spec ops teams rappelling down the lengths of the elevator shafts never to be heard from again. Heavier units were pushed down through meat grinders floor by floor... and few ever reached the hull itself. It was as though the towers along the upper hull weren't towers at all... but merely seductive structures designed to be nothing more than attractive canalizations for opposing forces thinking these were key objectives to take and plunder.

When in reality they were perfect death traps.

No wonder my PTSD dreams had indicated they'd defend the large hangar bays like the one we'd been assigned so heavily.

Those *weren't* traps. They were weak points in the Monarch defense of their ghost ship.

And furthermore...

It wasn't long before the fractured alliance started fighting each other when they realized the fantastic and powerful tech to be had. Exponential advances in science, interstellar travel, weapons... even energy-based weapons like nothing we'd ever seen.

And medicine. Even the hospital ship *Nova* couldn't resist the lure of that life-saving, life-extending... *life-altering*... Dark Labs technology. The details of the *Nova*'s fate weren't conveyed over the sporadic comms. Only that... she met it.

And that the fleet no longer had a hospital ship.

We'd seen the R&D labs indicating the designs... we'd fought major battles to open Route Vega through these. We'd stormed fabrication forges and seen some of the parts.

Whoever owned this ship... they could have it all.

Yeah... it would take not just years, but decades to understand... but they would *become* the Monarchs.

And, I thought to myself, telling themselves the whole time that this time... *things would be different.*

But as John Strange had told me... it wouldn't be. And this battle, the battle to take the *Dark Star*... this would be the last chance to stop this kind of madness.

What kind of madness, I'd asked myself, and Preacher, the company holy man, one time, but now just to myself as I lay in my rack after three days of ops forward trying to clear Route Vega of IEDs where it went through the water tanks and filtration section of this giant nightmare ship...

Brutal work. The most stress I can ever remember being under.

"The madness that we can become gods," I heard Preacher answer in my mind.

I had talked to him about this, all of it, the dreams and John Strange. On other days and not this night I couldn't sleep, as it all began to come together in my mind whether I liked it or not.

Spoiler... I didn't.

"It's a madness we've always had, Orion. I doubt we'll be free of it until we actually meet God. Then we'll know... we... we aren't Him. That... will be abundantly clear."

"But then why your devil?" I asked Preacher. "If he knew God, had met Him... then why did he think we'd worship him as a god instead of God?"

I thought I was being clever. Finding the lie in his whole religion.

Preacher just smiled and said, "Madness, Orion. Men and angels have both been possessed by it. And if you're trying to figure it out... you won't. That's the point... it doesn't make any sense. And that's why you struggle, Orion."

"Who says I'm struggling, Preacher?"

He said nothing. Just put his hand on my shoulder and gave it a gentle squeeze. Then...

"Keep fighting, Orion. Keep knocking, keep asking. That... is the opposite of them. They... they thought they knew. They were wrong and went mad."

That was after the ceremony on the back deck of the *Spider*. Five pairs of boots that day.

I told myself I was done asking questions.

I lay in my rack... asking questions.

I hate Preacher.

In those first weeks of the fleet assault on the *Dark Star*, every three days or so there was a conference between the individual captains and the fleet. I attended with the rest of the command team in *listen and observe* mode only.

But from the get-go, as we AAR'd the group comm... it was clear to the Strange Company command team the fleet was fracturing.

The three guys who ran the fleet and the big ships that had taken the center of the upper hull were asserting dominance and trying stunts like issuing directives that stated "all tech needs to be safeguarded in the super-carrier *Thunderer*."

It was pretty naked what they were up to, and of course it didn't fly with anyone.

A week later there was only one guy and the other two were reported dead. A coup apparently. A week after that, on the final official call of Rogue Fleet, *yeeehawww, boys!!!*, everyone was accusing everyone of holding back tech finds and poaching on lanes of assault into the inner hull where they'd made some headway.

The final conference ended badly and an hour later *Warbird* fired on *Covenant* and crippled her. Her surviving crew evacuated to the *Thunderer* and it was clear after that... that everyone else was out for themselves from here on out.

And probably... *winner take all* more than a few were thinking.

So we were on our own now.

Communications broke down.

We were all very tired. No one trusted anyone anymore.

Mark that line down because I have some suspicions that somehow I've heard it before in one of the older logs or somewhere... the company long ago ended up on an edge world fighting against a shapeshifting alien and I think the Log Keeper used it before everything went seriously sideways and the company was said to have escaped that ice world with only two surviving members.

I need to review those logs again...

But... that was long before my time and maybe it's just some old sim I've run in the long sleeps between this war and that conflict we were getting paid to go stack in.

I don't know anymore... and I'm too tired to go digging in the logs between missions to open up and secure Route Vega to the inner hull.

Maybe I'll do it during the Big Sleep after this gig.

But right now people are giving better odds to Stinkeye with his pathetic Cheks cards than to our survival.

Everyone in fact is betting heavy on Cheks because there's a serious chance no one's gonna collect.

The sharks are cleaning up, which is why I don't play. Plus… my cards are terrible.

Nothing but a Red Queen and a stack of rando gobs.

But that's another story…

Here's my typical day regardless if it's shipboard day, or shipboard late night.

Note… I need a world. I need soft sand and real grass. I need to hear the roar and retreat of an ocean. I need to just sit and stare at all its power and unknowness. And I don't know if I ever will again.

My day starts with four hours of bad sleep. I get shaken awake out of my rack by a patrol leader coming in to get me up and ready to go back out.

Half-asleep he briefs me on what they did while, if he's cool he hands me a coffee while I light my dart, they were out there on Route Vega. Then he tells me I'll get the day's op order from the first sergeant because the Old Man is probably forward with Ghost making mischief or leading a hit on a fortified position we don't want an enemy reaction force coming out of to stall our push, our drive, on the objective that is the inner hull.

If we can get there, then I think it's over.

Chief Cook assures me that will be the plan. But… and this is saying something… he looks more deranged than usual. Like he's living a fever-dream.

He has disappeared for days at a time and there's even been one command team meeting to find and locate him.

Perhaps the cult finally got him and spaced him, I thought.

But they're too tired and we found him in one of the bio-medical labs wearing a full hazmat suit dosed to the gills on starport meth.

He said he was working on his "secret weapon" and that everyone better stay clear. "This is real, real, dangerous stuff… Orion. Kill ya dead and make ya wish it'd been faster."

I had to ask.

"Will there be bats?"

"Oh boy you betcha, Orion… like you ain't never seen. This is gonna be beautiful. This time things'll be different. Much different."

His eyes were wide and mad.

I reported his status and whereabouts and got what rest I could before going out again.

So after I get the coffee and dart and listen to the patrol leader, I let everyone sleep for another hour while I check the wounded, grab chow, and listen to as much gossip as I can get from everyone else who's been down-hull for whatever it's worth.

Generally they're tired if it's been IED work and wired if it's been a gunfight.

Meaningful intel is like pulling teeth, but I take all I can get because you never know what's going to keep you and your guys alive.

Here my hopes die every time someone says, "Didja hear what happened last night, Sar'nt?"

What are my hopes, you ask?

My hopes are that the last remaining Bishop in the sector got smoked by the Ghost Hunters last night. Who are the Ghost Hunters? The captain's personal goon squad out hunting them down the hard way…

The hard way, you ask?

Crawling through the overheads of crew compartment spaces, sometimes in hard vacuum… to find bad guys and take a shot before fading like they were never there.

Usually it's just sapper teams that get hit. Bishops would make my day. Next would be the combat cyborg HK teams that are still out there… there were six in the sector when boarding ops got underway. We thought there were five… but there were six. More on that later.

The Wild Thing… Doom88… *me*… took out the first team on Day One, leaving only fifteen highly effective combat cyborgs roaming our sector of the ship.

Fifteen HKs with cold red glowing murderous intent.

So we got that goin' for us.

Rare is the day I am rewarded with such good news as a Bishop or an HK getting dialed. But I smoke my dart, drink my third coffee, aiming to get as much in my system before I have to jock up in my shot-to-hell EVC and lead another patrol down hull along Route Vega.

My EVC is covered in yellow sealing plas.

Within three hours of waking, we get the brief of what the Old Man wants us to hit via the first shirt and then we do weapons and armor checks, final gear prep and inspection… and then we pass through the automated defenses surrounding the ship at the LZ and down into the hull heading through the marked-out Route Vega.

At any time, sappers could have come and placed an IED… they are really clever at this, making it look like a terminal or system, or a sniper could be set up down some intersecting corridor off the clear route.

The route…

We have made some of these markings that show the path along Vega. Other squads and platoons have made their markings to "the Snake."

Which is what we call Route Vega. Informally. The Snake.

It twists and turns and it's very dangerous even cleared.

We mark Route Vega with orange rattle-cans. There are about thirty boxes of it down in stores aboard the *Spider* for reasons none can explain. But Reaper uses it and marks the route with our standard marking, a rude spray-painted scythe and then the code we use for notes about directions, things to avoid, and precautions to take.

Gunny and the Devil Dogs mark with spray-painted devil horns.

The other platoons have theirs, but they don't go down-hull much on their own as they have a tendency to get chewed up and their numbers, consequently, are dwindling and there's talk of disbanding one of the platoons and reinforcing the others.

Sometimes they follow on as a hatchet force to exploit breakthrough or just support by fire. If there's maneuver room for those kinds of games.

During inspection I overlook the usual games… vampire teeth, ceremonial daggers, new things they've written on their gear… I even remark on some of the wittier ones…

Caps to Pop, Bodies to Drop
Belt-fed Baddie

World's Okay-est Sniper

Hug Me on their 'nades. Or some such…

And of course Punch has written *Negativity Cleanser* in white marker on his frags. The penmanship is precise.

Hustle and Hoser do their standard pattycake routine shouting, "Load the Pig, load the Pig, mow 'em all down, we got graves to dig!" a little more enthusiastically given the umpteenth hump into an enemy hull full of IEDs, snipers, enemy voodoo warfare specialists, killer cyborgs, and whatever other horrors the ones who called themselves our "gods" can think up…

During prep I'll turn to Klutz and ask him if he's good to go on suit patch and pressure dressings because of course I have to and he nods enthusiastically… why? I don't know… and says his standard, "Livin' the dream, Sar'nt."

At which point I remind him that, "Nightmares also are dreams, Klutz."

Then we head down into the hull.

Yes, we've cleared the route. Yes of course Anubian commandos have sniper teams, and they too are crawling through the sub hull, the outer hull, and the non-crew compartment spaces to set up a shot on one of us, bonus if they can potentially ice command and control which is how I got hit on Day Thirteen. Plate caught the round and I had three broken ribs to show for it.

The carry back to the rear CCP was a real picnic.

Plate got replaced… yes, we are running out of those and no days off because Route Vega must remain open. Ulysses of course stepped in and ran the platoon while I was down, much to Punch's smoldering. I followed along like a football-bat as best I could.

Oh yeah and the holes in my EVC got sprayed with more sealing plas and I was thankful the round hit me in the chest carrier and not in the balls because the plate there deflects badly and manages to spare your junk but the spray-plas makes you look like you just pissed yourself and spray-plas only comes in bright urine yellow because why else wouldn't it.

And you realize this is the way you'll fight the rest of this battle in this forsaken hull where you'll probably die listening to everyone stop using your tag and call you Pee-Pants.

I'm a positive thinker that way. A real little Jennie Sunshine on some days.

If it's not the sniper teams… and generally if Nether's not busy with the captain, then the forward-clearing unit gets him, screw Nether and his need for rest. Nether will never tell you he's tired because he's, thankfully, helpful that way, terminally so, I suspect sometimes… but if you have Nether's services, you get a jump on the snipers and you can run a game on them.

Which takes a bit of planning.

Now, the IEDs are another thing…

Nether can't trip those and he's not actually great at spotting them because, though he is a private military contractor and technically a soldier… he ain't one. He's a scientist and he's not the most… let's just say *combat aware* dude.

So, the big leadership mistake you can make in the game of small unit warfare is to assume that just because you have a non-corporeal guy who can go forward, invisibly, and find enemy troops set up and waiting to kill you, you cannot, in fact, assume he's spotted the IEDs on the way in, because due to his incorporeal nature, he cannot set them off, and so he didn't set them off.

I am so... tired of it all. Tired of the vampire fangs and bad jokes. Tired of the petty fights that break out between dudes who just a few hours later will be blazing away at bad guys while the guy they've got a hangup with heaves on the drag handle on the back of their armor to get them out from under fire and off a very bad *X*. I am tired of this unending route through hell and nightmare... tired of the constant "Hotsoup" this and "Hotsoup" that... in general... and in fact... I am tired of it all and just waiting for some fast-moving twenty-four-hundred-feet-per-second death to just smash through my faceplate and end this waking nightmare of having to clear this route and board this ship of the damned...

But...

You cannot be tired. Nope. You are in charge of this dumpster fire.

You must remind yourself of all the little details of a platoon full of killers, and a brigade full of bad guys on home ground... no one's infantry math ever... you must remind yourself that Nether cannot trip IEDs.

The enemy sappers are disguising the IEDs in the ox-flow valves at every intersection.

The enemy snipers are working in teams of three, so don't just go after the first guy because there's probably two other snipers watching his position and looking for a shot on the assaulters.

The HKs like to throw choke-smoke before they hit and run so don't commit to an assault through the ambush... pull back. Set up security. Send a MeGoosa round down there. It's the only way to be sure.

Punch wants to kill this guy today.

Catboi is getting on Hoser's nerves.

Klutz ran out of spray-plas and nasal tubes in case we get a traumatic breathing injury like we did three days back...

And so on, and so on, and so on...

A million other things you're too tired to remember.

But you must remember. Whether you like it or not.

We have to be honest about these things.

On Day Thirty-One we caught another Bishop. But not before he killed Fartsack and New Guy One who we'd started to call Bull.

Someone had started to call him Hangdog. He didn't like it. He had a naturally sad, long face and everyone constantly would ask him, "What's wrong?" even though they knew nothing was wrong. They just did it to bug him once they figured out it bugged him. Infantry... they are like that. One day... he made the mistake of letting them get to him and said he wasn't "Hangdog" about anything. Really blew up. We'd had a bad day before when a major IED detonated and almost killed us all. We managed to get behind a bulkhead just after we found it and the sapper running the ambush just blew it since we'd discovered it. Our ears rang for days. So Bull blew up about "Hangdog" because he couldn't hear.

Bull then said, in fact... that he was very happy to fight any of them. To the death even. If they ever said it again.

So... of course, them being infantry and dudes in general... they said it a lot and all the time to him in the days that remained of his life.

Punch I had to order not to say it before he even could because Punch was just looking for a fight to practice in and work off some of the tension of route clearing.

Understandable, but still, I had to tell him not to.

His response… "You get me, Sar'nt."

Then I had to take New Guy One slash Bull slash soon to be Hangdog aside and tell him that "Hangdog" was most likely going to be his tag and he told me he sure hoped not because everyone had called him that back where he came from and he'd practically run away from the world he'd come from and joined a local security force just to get away from the slur.

I felt his plight and told him he had one week to come up with some way to get them to call him something different. But I didn't think that was gonna happen and truth was… he'd brought this on himself.

"What should I do?"

"I don't know."

I wanted sleep. I didn't want to deal with this level of small and petty because I needed to seethe about some other minor grievances I was upset about and of course… the big picture of us getting killed here, the Wild Thing, and… the Monarchs pulling the fade and ending human civ as we knew it… someday… which is a lot for a lowly ruck hobo who asked for none of this. This was after a patrol into the hull in which we'd spent the day clearing a passage, painstakingly slow work, of plasma mines with thermal detectors for triggers.

Fun stuff. Not.

"Maybe pick the same rations every day," I suggest. "And get them to call you that."

Bull Hangdog New Guy One thought about this for a long moment in which I kept wondering if the conversation could be over now.

Then…

"I like the tacos one. Maybe I could be Taco or Nacho…"

"No," I shouted, a little too irritated. "They all like tacos. They would never let you, or anyone, have anything cool like that. Pick the one they hate and be really excited about it every day. Make a big show of it when we do chow. Like… Ham and Eggs. *Oh man… this is my fav!*"

Ham and Eggs… literally the nastiest ration pack we have. Not ham and not even remotely eggs. No one knows why Chungo got so many of them. And, to top it off… they're like forty years old and marked as Star Rations.

Seriously… your guts explode every time after one of those. Great way to lose weight and contemplate poor life choices like joining the company and picking Ham and Eggs for your rats that day.

"I hate that one," New Guy One Bull Hangdog whimpered.

I sighed. Seriously…

"I know. That's the point," I lectured pedantically. "That's what makes them tick. Maybe… just maybe… they'll call you the *Ham and Egger*. That's pretty cool. Make you a gunner in time and you could make a whole rep out of it. *Here come the Ham and Egger…*" I whisper-screamed like he was some kind of ultraball star. "*Yeahhhhhhhhh!*"

He was crestfallen.

I hated myself and my job.

"I know," I tried. "But it is better than the other thing and at least you're not Fartsack."

Funny thing, I thought at the time. Fartsack loves being call Fartsack.

Further funny thing that's not so funny I'll think later when I gotta stand there on the aft cargo deck while Preacher does his thing and we space them off the hangar.

Strangers to the Universe, Brothers to the End.

They both die on the same day.

So I got that goin' for me. Shame and grief together. Wheeeeee!

So that was the last week of his life. A living hell for his bowels as he totally committed to his platoon sergeant's plan to launder his impending bad tag and become known as the... *ta da*... the Ham and Egger.

He lost eight pounds he told me the morning before he got killed.

It probably wasn't gonna work and he'd get called Hangdog for the rest of his time with the company.

Then he died and they called him Hangdog and voted to award him the tag he hated. Posthumously.

They actually did this out of respect, and not their typical malevolent humor because he really owned up in the last seconds of his life and went after the Bishop we'd run into on Day Thirty-One knives out, as they say.

"Cream-style," Wolfy likes to say now for no reason anyone can figure out and I don't have the heart, or will, to ask.

I told them all, on the day we spaced them off the back deck, that I'd mark Hangdog down as such in the logs. Instead, I marked him down as the Ham and Egger.

And then added, hearing my scarred fingers tiredly tapping the keys in the silence after everyone had racked out...

Brothers to the End. Strangers to the Universe.

I was tired.

And it wasn't until later I realized I'd reversed it in my fatigue.

And that was his story and there wasn't much of it. But here he is. That's it.

And then I put down how he and Fartsack got killed.

CHAPTER SIXTY-TWO

That morning, we humped into the Navigation Engineering section of the *Dark Star*. This was an area of advanced tech like nothing any of us had ever seen before. There were giant gleaming obsidian-black computer balls at least two decks high. When the ship was underway and navigating... we ruck hobos theorize... the balls act as quantum data calculators and engage in some kind of weird dance in which they roll around this vast computational space and make direct contact with other giant balls.

Stellar maps holographically appear across the floors and ceilings and change with each interaction.

It was a pretty amazing show if you could get past the fact that these things could crush you...

... and we had to pass through this space to continue to develop the route.

Somehow... these interactions calculate the incalculable on a quantum interaction level and this allows the giant ship to move through stellar distances supposedly faster than any ship known.

Pretty incredible stuff.

No wonder we didn't beat them here. Time dilation and all.

They were stone-still like megalithic statues when we got tasked to clear a route through. But we weren't about to assume they'd stay that way.

Hauser hacked into one of them and downloaded everything from its internal core processors. It took him four hours to effect a total data capture... which, believe me, is incredible because his onboard CPUs can calc incredibly fast... but he was able to figure out how these giant dark balls did this level of math, and what that math actually did.

Navigate unknown distances by drawing a calc between known points never attained by human starships.

Hause explained it this way...

"Cyborg models like mine have known problems calculating quantum mathematics because of the unknown and illogical nature of this type of equation. It was felt, by the designers that created me, that it was best we did not have access to those methods as they might have difficulties for our killing algorithms which are based on Von Neumann math. Simple. Efficient. Lethal. Sergeant Orion."

It's just Orion, Hauser. We are friends.

So, we were in what we'd called "The Ball Room" when that Bishop came at us on Day Thirty-One and killed Fartsack and New Guy Bull the Ham and Egger.

This Bishop was like Stinkeye. Powerful and dangerous. And not like Stinkeye... drunk all the time. The killer enemy Bishop made its attack in the Ball Room where the strange orb-like computers rolled and touched surfaces to compute the mind-numbingly vast spaces the ship's jump engines and computers needed to reach the distant darknesses where the Monarchs would hide, if they got their way, and bide their time for their next shot at enslaving us all.

And Command, once I'd told them about the encounters with John Strange... knew they couldn't let that happen. The company was caught up on things... just in case I bought it.

For whatever that was worth.

"You're like the high priest of this here outfit now... no offense, Preacher," said the first sergeant after I'd tried to tell them as much as I could about the dream-like encounters with the company founder, and... becoming the Wild Thing thereafter to destabilize the enemy assets on the target DZ.

"No offense taken, Top," said Preacher gently with his usual stoic smile as he continued to eye me. "I'm here for their souls. The rest... that's just noise that'll come and go in the big picture. Reality... is stranger than we imagine, First Sergeant, and if something... let's just say *other*... has decided to communicate with our company Log Keeper... that's above my pay grade. I just bury 'em proper, Top."

After that, the Old Man had the final say on the matter.

"I don't know much about the supernatural, Sergeant Orion. But I know these bastards can't ever come back from the grave. That's what we're here to see to. Their final burial. Nothing... and I mean *nothing*... of the Monarchs survives this run... because it's all poison. And it's time for it to be purged."

That was... an uncharacteristic amount of words from our company commander. *Aaaaannnnd*... something else I couldn't quite put my finger on.

But he'd meant every word of it. It might as well have been carved in stone on some mountain somewhere as far as we were concerned, and he meant it to be.

We had our orders. No matter what.

But that was when an uncomfortable topic came up. All the tech looting and salvaging from the other ships in the Rogue Fleet, *yeeehawww* and all, even though we were no longer a fleet... all that was Monarch tech. If nothing survived, or was supposed to... then what were we supposed to do about them, our former allies?

"So," began the first sergeant slowly as he seemed to catch the captain's drift. "You sayin' sir... none of it... heads back to human space? Or anywhere else for that matter? I read that order right, sir?"

The captain was silent, the smoke of his perpetual dart drifting between us all. I was smoking too. The first sergeant was working a cigar he'd gotten from Chungo that he didn't like much. "But a stogie's a stogie, as they say, young sar'nt," he'd said to me regarding Chungo's stinky heaters.

The captain spoke and what he said might as well have been the epitaph of all the Monarchs, and any of our enemies, that ever were.

"I said what I said. We burn 'em all, First Sergeant. Only way to be sure. No tech survives. Wherever it is and whoever's hands it's in. It's poison. We're the cure."

So I had that in my heart as I contemplated these strange rolling giant black ball computers that were unlike anything, any flight system, on any vessel, I'd ever seen, or even heard of.

We were operating in the unknown now. Far beyond the perimeter of anything we'd ever known or considered home.

A cold wind ran over my soul.

The deeper we progressed into this ghost ship of the damned, the stranger, and almost alien, tech of the Monarchs got. Near the established LZ we held, the *Dark Star* was much like any ship—if you discounted the sheer gigantic nature of the vessel, and the highly polished and state-of-the-art features and interfaces. It was clean, pristine, almost robotic in the passages, decks, and compartments.

Most starships, even when they're large, are industrial, utilitarian affairs with small compartments because space is premium. And all starships smell like circuitry, old fabric, and dust. They are usually dark, and the lighting is generally subdued due to the nature of interstellar travel. The instruments *thrum* and *tick* constantly as readouts on every possible datapoint on a myriad of panels and displays constantly update flight information.

That's standard on every ship I've ever been on.

But the *Dark Star* was like some strange utopian vision of what starlight should be. Clean, magnificent, but in a sinister way. Almost perfect. Threateningly malevolent. Terminals at stations were the best I've ever seen and often far advanced beyond anything I'd worked with. There were cyclopean wall panels of clean grey and highly polished black, several decks high in the hangars and gleaming white within the inner passages. Yet often the compartments, smaller as we threaded the initial section of the outer hull on the way through the developing Route Vega, were much like the starships we knew, except when they weren't.

Then they were…

Sealed tombs of forbidden advanced tech.

Vast storehouses of supplies.

Vaults of wealth plundered from all of human history.

Strange labs and enigmatic ship's systems that defied logic and our small understanding. We breached and blew our way into heavily shielded compartments where we found ancient pieces of art, ornate artifacts, carved and beautiful of ivory, silver, and gold. Statues. Idols. Old, actual dusty books.

In these moments we just stood there, shining our EVC targeting lights into the quiet, untouched darkness, staring in wonder at what the Monarchs had looted from our collective history for the final fade.

I wasn't alone in that these finds made us… *uneasy*. It was like we were staring at all the things that had once been… *us*. Who we'd been before the Monarchs declared our home system holy unto them only. A sacred place the rest of humanity was forever banished from.

Cast out.

Fallen from.

Rejected.

Staring at these lost wonders and ancient treasures, the books especially, I had no idea what any of it meant, and that made me shockingly angry because I wanted *to know*… and I knew now, truly, that I would never know who we once were.

I was surprised at my simmering rage.

But now… I understand it and I bet you do too whoever you are that finds this tragedy of the Strange Company.

It is the tragedy of us all.

All these... lost things. All these missing memories. All these tears in the rain.

My fists were clenched in rage as we stared at all of it each time we breached some new forbidden vault.

That we'd blow the ship... and everything in it... to prevent the poison of the Monarchs from ever festering again... I knew that.

I wanted that.

Didn't I?

I felt the cold tendrils of temptation to do... what was wrong. To... just have it. Save it. Surely... I could be trusted, I lied to me.

It was a sweet hiss in my soul and I felt... unfinished.

The command team of the company had heard the Old Man's orders.

And so it would be.

I pushed all that away. But not the rage. Not the simmering rage that they had forced us to do this to them.

I killed a guy once in a battle back on a contract. I was a scout with Ghost and had gone forward to see if some houses hit by arty were empty. So had the enemy scout. We started shooting at each other through the shot-out remains of the house, missing. Shooting harder. Trying to get closer through all the disaster and shattered plaster and someone else's lives. Burning rounds, swapping mags, and angling for an advantage on each other.

It wasn't even two minutes but I got him. I'd been cursing at him in my mind the whole time we shot at each other.

Two minutes is a long fight. Trust me.

But when I finally got him, swearing at him the whole time, I tapped him once and he was down on his back, dropped his weapon, and was both scrabbling to get away to cover and get his sidearm out. I advanced through the rubble, shooting him again and again...

It was dawn.

And I was screaming at the top of my lungs, "You made me do this!"

He was dead by the time my mag was empty. His eyes vacant and far away.

And I just stood over him, swapping in another mag and breathing raggedly, contemplating shooting him even more, mumbling, "You made me do this," over and over again until my breathing calmed down.

That's how I felt, looking at all the things the Monarchs had taken from us, and that we would destroy.

You made me do this.

It wasn't an answer. It was just... unfrozen rage.

So... the giant cybernetic balls in the Ball Room were insane.

The Bishop activated them when we were midway through the immense compartment. So now they could crush us and they kept us busy not being crushed. Great time to spring an attack. The vast internal chamber was easily three decks high and when we'd entered, the black mirror-surfaced balls, at least two decks high, had been motionless and stable.

No projected routes or stellar constellations.

Route Vega had already navigated this passage through the compartment, but we needed to keep it open and we were still another hour's march from our objective where we'd continue to thread slowly the route forward. Hacking terminals and breaching compartments, clearing IEDs and watching out for snipers or enemy counterattacks, as we closed on the last of the outer hull.

The inner hull just ahead. Always… just ahead.

And then… the end.

For someone.

The scouts, led by Sleeper, had come through three days ago and cleared the chamber. Operations continued forward on the subsequent days and in all reports the giant dark balls had not moved or done anything but stay totally motionless.

Hauser had gone forward the day before with his squad and breached the Astrogator's Watch, as it was known in the terminal directory. This was a small upside-down cupola located high in the ceiling behind cantilevered windows.

It contained standard, though highly advanced navigational computation stations and holographic interfaces with another ship system known as… *the Displacement Drive*.

Sounds ominous.

But Hauser explained what it, theoretically, would do.

"This type of interstellar drive system will allow the starship to execute her final jump that will put her well beyond our reach. For at least several of your human lifetimes, Sergeant Orion."

It's just Orion, Hause. We're friends.

But I didn't say that.

"Then what kind of drive system have they been using to get here faster than we could if we hadn't had the quantum jump-envelope ship?"

Hauser, of course, didn't miss a beat as he explained it all to me.

"This starship is X-tech-capable, Sergeant Orion. Both of the main engines located aft, destroyed by the missile strike from the support fleet, are Duality TransJump Comet8000s. An experimental concept developed four hundred years ago and classified as… deniable technology."

I understood.

"They kept it for themselves, Hause."

"Affirmative, Sergeant Orion. This gave the Monarchs a significant research advantage beyond just the ability to jump-skip at faster than normal warp speeds. It also allowed them a research tree not accessible to the rest of humanity or any of the other star-faring races as they had no idea this branch of the tech tree even existed. They have done this many times before with different areas of research, which is what allowed them to maintain their grasp on the reins of civilization."

I swore.

Punch punched an ammo crate because that's what he does. Hence… Punch.

"So now that the Comets are disabled from the support fleet strike, Hauser… they're stuck here at Typhon?"

"It would have seemed so, Sergeant… but given our discovery of the Displacement Drive, that would appear not to be the case. Now that I was able to hack into the Astrogator's systems and see that they've run several computation simulations for their *displacement jump*… it is clear they are not, in fact, 'stuck,' Sergeant Orion."

That cold chill… it was here now.

"Then what are they doing? Why not just... *displace* now and leave the fleet far behind? Why not make their escape, Hause?"

My friend the combat cyborg studied me for a long minute. Like he does when he finds some fascinating new lifeform or tries to understand why a man loves a woman, or any of the other myriad of intangible things that seemed to fascinate the machine that he is.

He is... human in ways we should strive to be. But don't. My friend.

"I do not know, Sergeant Orion. But if I access my primary directives as..."

He paused.

Since Hauser had hacked himself, he didn't like referring to himself as what he'd once been when he'd served them on kill teams.

A killing machine.

A combat cyborg.

A hunter-killer that looked like one of us. The apex predator of apex predators.

Soulless.

Remorseless.

Without pity, or mercy...

It is hard to know those things and reconcile them when you look at and observe Hauser's actions on behalf of the company. He was... once... one of them. One of those things.

But he is my friend. And so... you do the work of taking them at face value... instead of what your programming says.

It's what... makes us human.

Hauser looked off but his head didn't move, and neither did his eyes. It was just a moment he had where he ran another file inside his processors that he'd coded... it allowed him to bypass and deny what he was.

It allowed him to be free when buried problematic code from his killer past tried to assert itself in his decision tree.

I called it *looking off*. And waited patiently.

In these moments I always reached out and put my hand up on his massive shoulder. And squeezed it.

All good, buddy?

Then Hauser came back and looked at me, as though the interlude had not happened. Even though we both knew it had.

"Warfare doctrine protocols allow me to tactically surmise what the enemy might do in a particular situation, Sergeant Orion."

"And what would they do, Hause... what do your protocols indicate?"

"There is a thirty-seven-point-three-percent chance they will not displace because they are currently overrun by enemy forces and do not want to reach a new destination and give enemy forces an opportunity, though a communication system may not be currently technologically active, for their new hiding place to be reported back even if it is on the other side of the galaxy which is currently well beyond the reach of any of our starships for several generations of stellar flight time."

I heard all that and it made sense until my mind replayed the percentage.

Thirty-seven point three was awfully low.

Hauser waited for me to figure it out.

"But that's not what you think they're doing, right, Hause?"

He shook his head slowly.

"Negative, Sergeant Orion… I do not think. I only calculate. I would assign a much higher percentage to another strategy we used in certain situations in which the enemy felt victory was within reach and we wanted to deny that outcome by luring them to a pre-planned killbox and engaging the enemy in an ambush with explosives and heavy machine gun fire. This is called *Scorched World*. And it is designed only to deny victory to the enemy even if there is a catastrophic loss of assets to implement. For HK combat cyborg teams we would be authorized to deploy… chemical, biological, and even nuclear weapons to effect mission success. This strategy was used by HK Team Q-5-6 at New Strasbourg and resulted in a planetary loss of life in order to defeat the insurrectionist revolt that had overrun three Monarch systems ready for advanced strip-mining development."

I'd never heard of New Strasbourg.

But of course… the Monarchs had won. And the winners always rewrite the history.

I thought of those treasure and tech vaults… and all the lost history, our lost histories, for better or worse, good or bad, that could be known or at least guessed at now.

In one… we'd found ancient paintings, secured behind thick plates of hyperplastic sheets. They were racked and stored and as our weapon lights played over them it was clear I was looking at lost works of art, probably once highly prized beyond any value a simple ruck hobo could imagine. I read some of the computer-tagged titles that had been etched into the shipping plastic.

Holographic and blue… I could barely read the ancient language. But my EVC bucket recorded them and I mark a few down here.

For posterity.

Corner of the Quarry by someone named Cezanne. Apparently.

David with the Head of Goliath by Caravaggio.

Edouard Manet: *Berthe Morisot with a Bouquet of Violets*.

I looked at these, trying to find some moment of connection with them… feeling some rage that I couldn't… and yet… should.

We pulled back, leaving that tomb of lost art.

And then, just before we resealed the door, Hoser popped a plasma grenade, muttered, "Fire in the hole," and threw it in, slamming his ham-sized fist on the closed door panel, sealing it shut.

The explosion was muffled within, and I looked through the shadowy safety glass of the slitted viewing port and watched as all those ancient beautiful works were suddenly consumed in a conflagration that filled the sealed chamber within seconds.

All I could see was smoke and bits of drifting ash. I turned away and we were moving deeper into the hull again.

Rinse and repeat.

I'd seen us do this before.

Burn and destroy. It's what we did best.

We'd do it again and again until there was nothing left… of us.

Ever have to demo your life…? It's a hell of a thing. Trust me.

We have to be honest about these things… and yes these things haunt me more than just some small words regarding how I deal with my reality.

We were angry. And the company wanted to lash out. So I let it happen because those things had to be destroyed, and… they no longer meant anything to us. To the company, and to what humanity had become out among the stars.

We burned what we found. Even as we yearned for it.

It was just the stuff of the Monarchs now. And we were here to break it and kill them.

I was thinking about those things when the cybernetic orbital computers began to shift and roll about the Ball Room as we called it.

Shifting and adjusting quantum unknowns to develop a jump… or displacement… calc.

Strange stellar maps, larger and more beautiful than anything I'd ever seen before, startling in their sudden revelations and display, threw themselves across the gigantic chamber, adding to the developing chaos and confusion as the crushing balls began to roll at us from every direction, colliding and revealing new mad solutions to the probability of vast stellar distances and worlds and stars we'd never known before.

But really, it was a Bishop getting ready to lay the smoke on us. An attack was coming, and we were sitting ducks.

CHAPTER SIXTY-THREE

On Day Thirty-One… when Fartsack and Bull New Guy Hangdog got killed… the Bishop had remotely started up the sleek black glass computer balls, using his strange psy-can powers. Instantly they began to roll slowly about, caressing each other, and this was a weird thing and maybe only I felt it…

… but you could feel the sudden… *connections* and for a moment you could feel that the universe wasn't all that big, and that perhaps… it was connected simply by… math.

With each connection there was the sound of pool balls striking one another and then giant sprays of stellar maps were suddenly broadcast throughout the area as the sacred math was crunched and some impossible travel solution reached.

But that part about the universe being connected by… math…

It was like an explosion going off in some never-used-before part of my brain.

This utterly stunned me for half a second and I could feel the whole platoon moving as I just stood there, dumbfounded by what I'd realized.

I'd spread everyone out into three combat wedges covering all sectors forward and the flanks as though we were conducting a movement to contact across some terrestrial battlefield instead of an interstellar map room the size of some industrial-grade shipping warehouse.

I had Hauser and Third in the rear on security, and again we were just transiting this area to get to our day's work farther ahead.

Clearing Route Vega forward.

So, a good NCO and not me of course, should have been prepared for an attack. Wide-open spaces, cover for the enemy, a place where you thought you could let down your guard and just hump your gear and weapons across the vast empty space save for the strange computer balls.

But I'd been distracted…

The balls began to roll, gently, and it was easy to get out of their way… which effectively broke up my wedges instantly.

Aaaannd that's when the incoming… started incoming.

Light machine gun fire forward from the end of the chamber where previously undetected ports like hardened gun bunkers opened up.

First things first.

We did not assault through ambush and storm the bunkered enemy positions.

It was immediately clear that wasn't gonna happen, and the first burst of fire from the enemy MG teams was ranged. Rounds smacked a few of the computer balls and tagged a few guys on the right flank as bright fire seemed to erupt all across our front.

Only one serious penetration wound.

Duffy in First.

He caught it right through the shoulder as it deflected off his chest plate and tore a nice groove through some flesh and muscle and a little bit of bone, which caused him to freak out immediately in pain and scream that he was dying as he struggled to scramble away from one of the giant rolling black computer balls that had suddenly adjusted course and then come directly for him like it was some bizarre alien predator.

Like it was just gonna roll over and crush him.

Punch reacted, grabbing Duff by the drag handle and yanking him to the rear as he screamed, let his slung weapon dangle, and then began to turn his shrieking into gunfire with his sidearm, firing offhand as he was dragged away from getting crushed.

At that point we noticed the Anubian commando teams fast-roping down through portals in the ceiling one by one.

They had sub guns.

But… there was really no one there.

More about that in a sec.

All the mean little firefights we'd been fighting in the days before had devastated the commandos in this section after Ghost had crawled deep into the overhead wiring bundle tunnels and conduits and inched their way through two kilometers of pure darkness to achieve a position to dome the sector commander with one shot from Sleeper's rifle.

Then they faded even as the Anubian commando brigade sent in tunnel rats after them. These were small killer sentry drones. Duster, our EOD guy who'd once been in Hannibal's company, went with Ghost on that stalk and made sure the follow on the fade was littered with mines for the tunnel rats.

That hit on the sector subcommander, we'd later find out in an interrogation from a separate ambush, had ruined enemy operations in the sector for the moment.

So that was why we were pushing Route Vega harder than we should have and felt we had a little room to breathe.

And why I let us get sucked into this ambush and get two of my guys ending up KIA.

Developed intel after the fact indicated that was when Lady Death pushed forward one of her better Bishops like some chess piece on a board, supporting him with two platoons of commandos and a gun team each.

This Bishop created illusions in your head. His specialty was making you think there was more of the enemy than there really was. His opening move was to create an illusion of fast-roping Anubian pipe hitters coming down on us just as things got weird. Most of my platoon reacted to contact thinking, basically, "This might as well happen," and started engaging like we'd just hit the ammo store on half-price Tuesday.

But if you've ruck-hoboed long enough, you know no one fast-ropes into a firefight unless some junior-grade officer just ordered them to and managed to bypass every level of common sense and tactics that allowed him to either be in a position to do this, i.e. dropship support, or that his platoon sergeant had suddenly turned into a spineless low-IQ jellywhale and hadn't pointed out this was a dumb move even for an LT.

Beautiful creatures on Ataru. Jellywhales. But stupid as all get.

No, you fast-rope into a critical situation, or drop in via airborne operations, where the enemy *isn't*, in order to be able to attack from where the enemy doesn't want you to be.

You generally don't fast-rope down into a gunfight because everyone will shoot at you while you're trying to get down the rope and not break your back.

Which, *shooting at you*, was what my guys were doing in adult-sized doses.

But there was no one there because it was just a psionic illusion created by one of the Monarchs' Bishops.

In our defense we were tired and this was Day Thirty-One of the boarding op.

Most boarding ops take about two hours to take a ship or get killed trying to take said ship.

Day Thirty-One was a record somewhere where people kept records of such records.

So you don't drop right into the heavily armed teeth of a reconnaissance force currently being performed by a platoon of veteran stackers who've been fighting you recently at three-to-one odds, minimum, and winning.

My mind called *horse-pucky* on the fast-rope right in on us when I could clearly see Anubian pipe hitters, slick gold-and-black armor, obsidian dog-heads, red eyes and red targeting lasers dancing from their sub guns as they came down fast.

It was too dumb to be true.

Hustle hefted the Pig and just sprayed the "sky."

Punch knew it was bogus and so did Hauser once he figured out we were seeing something his sensors did not detect.

But Third was to the rear on security and support and so Hauser didn't key in on our collective deception at first.

Punch did because he'd been… "briefed" for want of a better word by our space war wizard who was drunk as a skunk and shaking with either a bad case of the DTs or the willies, when he told us he was "picking up" one of the Bishops in our sector.

"Whaddya mean… picking up?" asked Punch with zero tolerance, or patience. Of which he has none for Stinkeye. And never has.

"Da ones like me… we seen da Heart and we can… ya's knows… smell each other out dere and workin' da magic likes we do."

"Likes ya do," said Punch flatly.

Then my First Squad leader rolled his eyes and gave me a look that basically indicated… *Do I have to be here for this?*

I ignored this and indicated yes, he did.

In Stinkeye's defense he'd been in a bad firefight with Gunny's platoon when they made it across the bridge of the onboard water reservoirs for this sector of the ship.

That had been a defining moment for the clearing of Route Vega. Gunny's Devil Dogs had pushed through heavy gunfire to reach the far side of the bridge and wipe out hastily erected enemy bunkers there in what quickly became little better than close-quarters trench fighting through a concrete-and-steel maze.

Stinkeye had been forced to go in with them to provide… what it is he did.

The gunfire was brutal and from all directions forward of their line of attack, and half of Gunny's men had been hit or wounded to some degree, and instead of calling for medics they just picked their wounded up and dragged them forward toward the bunkers because that cover, if they could take it, was closer than the cover to the rear. The wounded engaged as best they could as they were dragged or hauled into the battle.

Stinkeye's magic that day...

Fireballs.

Yeah. Fireballs like an actual game, or movie, wizard. I'd never seen him, or heard of him, doing anything like that. Throwing giant palms of flaming napalm like some battleship torpedo system at any of our enemies. Ever.

And yet, on that very bad day with Gunny's platoon he'd gone forward... *casting*... is that the right word? ... like he really is some wizard... fireballs right into the enemy bunkers, or against them.

To hear Full-Up, one of the NCOs in Gunny's platoon, tell it was hilarious. And... kinda awesome.

"Hear this, Sar'nt Orion," crowed Full-Up. He got tagged Full-Up because he was always "full up" on everything stupid or badly executed, during compartment and hull breaching training. He was prior service and he and Gunny spoke the same language. "That damn drunk warrant gots to be dragged into the fight and Gun Team One is shifting forward under direct and intense fire while Two suddenly needs a barrel change. It's bad and I'm already full-up on everyone's nonsense. Sar'nt Gunny turns around... slaps the tar outta Stinkeye who's shakin' and cryin' and practically pissing his fatigues and orders him to do his *thang* right there and right now 'cause we all gonna be diced and shredded by enemy gunfire in about the next five seconds. I mean... full-up, Sar'nt Orion. Drunk Stinkeye, he be sobbin' his heart out and screamin' we're all gonna die out there and ain't nothin' can be done. And I'm thinkin'... that boy ain't wrong, Sar'nt. Lookin' real bad at that moment. So anyways the chief warrant officer shouts all ragged-like some swear word I ain't never heard... calls us all a bunch o' damn *ladyboys*, sucks at dat flask o' his and throws back his arm like he's gonna heave a pitch at an ultraball double header... then he spits the liquid and throws this invisible pitch all at the same time and this big ol' ball of fire just streaks out like a damn Thunderfire anti-tank round. Hits one o' the enemy positions. 'Cept 'steada explodin' an' all... the flames just wrap themselves all around the position and cook every one of them damn commandos all at once right down to their skeletons, armor and all, inside the bunker. Hell... I saw guys still walking around like flaming skeletons before they finally just fell over. Ya ever seen a man do that, Sar'nt Orion... throw a fireball? I ain't. Hell no I ain't never."

I close my hanging-open mouth as this is told to me by Sergeant Full-Up.

"Anyhow," continues the NCO, "Stinkeye thinks he's done his trick and he can... shall we say... pull back to the rear... uh-uh... neg-a-tive, Sar'nt Orion. Sar'nt Gunny, he full-*up* now! He grabs Stinkeye and shoves him forward barking, 'Clear that position or I'mma cave in your damn skull, you freak!' And Sar'nt Gunny got his trench gun back like he's gonna do it, Sar'nt Orion. Hell... Full-Up believed he was about to see some good ol'-fashioned war crimes. So Stinkeye curses Gunny, something about never being able to make love to a woman ever again, and Sar'nt

Gunny shouts, 'Don't care, war wizard. Got two ex-wives and no money anyway! Do your *thang* or you won't make it off this assault!'"

Sergeant Full-Up pauses and leans in, dark eyes serious. "I do not have to reiterate to you, Sar'nt Orion, that all this is goin' down while we takin' some serious full-up incoming dialed up to all levels o' cream-style as that dumb kid in your platoon says."

I swear and curse Wolfy's name. But the narrative continues.

"*Allll right…* you son of a worst whore on Busseco…" says Sergeant Full-Up in his best *sotto voce* of Stinkeye's ragged curse scream, which, of course, I know all too well.

And also…

If you know Busseco that's really sayin' something.

"Ya's all gonna see the Heart o' Darkness now and wish ya'd nevers!"

Oh no… not the Heart of Darkness schtick.

Sergeant Full-Up nods.

Everything is "da Heart o' Darkness" with Stinkeye. Bad chow. Losing badly at Cheks. Showers onboard the *Spider* are out of hot water. It's always "da Heart a Darkness."

Trust me… it gets old.

"So now he's advancing forward ahead of the gun teams…" continues Sergeant Full-Up, "standin' straight up like he ain't afraid of nothing, swilling twice from his canteen and hurling them damn napalm strikes all over the bunkers at the end of the bridge."

"Twice?" I ask.

"Yeah… I think he was drinkin' the first and usin' the other for his Heart of Darkness magic. Anyway we make it up on the bunkers and head in. Some of the guys get hit by some of Stinkeye's magic nape coming off the strikes and they're all butt-hurt 'bout it and ol' Stink, he just turns and howls, 'Suck it up, whores, 's called splash damage!'"

We both laugh at that.

"Sergeant Gunny runs that pump like it's a bodily function and we're blasting through the entrenched commandos and those improvised bunkers sideways, Sar'nt Orion. Cleanup takes thirty minutes and when we come back Stinkeye's drunk and crying, fetal really, and we got to get the medics to come forward and carry him to the rear because he's downright helpless by that time. Pretty pathetic. Honestly… don't blame him though. He wasn't hit or nothin'… but I had to run a check on him to see if he'd been hit and three places on his gear had taken rounds that needed just a smidge more to tear into him. So… he brave and all… but he drunk brave, if you know the type, and that don't ever last, know what I mean?"

I knew the type. I knew what it meant.

I'd seen Stinkeye do shades of such sudden bravery in the past. But the fireballs was a new one.

And I was kinda pissed he'd held out on us. We could have used that one a time or two…

So, back to the briefing our Voodoo chief downloaded on me and Punch right before that day when we were going out to clear forward on Route Vega and ended up fighting for our lives in the Ball Room.

Which will explain why a few of us disbelieved the Anubian fast-rope into the battle. And which will explain how Fartsack and Bull Hangdog New Guy One got killed.

I know… I recount what happened in a weird way.

Don't @ me. I'm doin' my best.

But… there's a lotta moving parts here and this is the best way to complete the log. Even if it does sound like a story told by a drunk with super-freighter levels of ADHD. Trust me… it's all part of the firefight that erupted in less than six seconds.

Stinkeye's response to all of my bitterness that he'd never used his fireballs before… "Just "cause I know how's ta fight don't mean I have ta like it. 'Sides… I went and showed 'em da Heart o' Darkness, Little King… what more do you want me ta do about it? Ya's have no idea what dat kinda power costs…"

Then he looked at me.

"But you be findin' out, Little King. You'll see it before dis over, Wild Thing. Then you come at me all high and mighty soldier-man and *rah-rah* and all's… you'll know da cost den."

Then he hit his totem flask.

"Until den… pound sand, Little King. And Punch… I seen da end o' ya's… and it t'ain't no good. You go screamin' and beggin'."

This was a common tactic of Stinkeye to make people think he had precognition… the ability to see the future, see people's deaths… but as far as I knew… he did not. And to watch him play Cheks was to watch a man who had absolute zero knowledge of how the cards would play out for him.

Punch, unfazed and cold as murder-ice, merely grunted and said, "Long as my paws are around your throat and takin' you with me… it'll be a good day to die."

Then they both spit at the ground around each other's boots and parted ways.

This was standard for their interactions.

So Stinkeye, before things had gone sideways in the Ball Room, had told us about "smellin' one of 'em out dere on da night winds dat's blown troo da devil ship."

I told him there were no winds blowing through the ship and Punch reminded him it was always night in deep space and that time was just a conspiracy of clockmakers agreed upon by the rest of us so we could do business and remain relatively sane.

"Dat's how little ya's really know. Dat night winds not like any wind ya's ever tasted or smelt an' felt against yer skin comin' off da seas of some angry and cold and cruel world ya mother never thought ya'd end up on. Ya's got to have da gift ta smell it, and if it's tuned right… we can smell each other and sometimes… da powers we might possess. Dis one… da one comin' at ya on da next patrol… he had da time… maybe he might have been as powerful as me… or…" He rubbed his scraggly old chin and cast his theatrical evil eye all about. "Maybe… even more so, Little King."

Then our war wizard warrant officer shook his staff and all the dog tags and bone-and-teeth necklaces, and ancient unit insignia he'd looped about it, dangled and rattled like ancient dried wind chimes for a moment…

"Bah… but he ain't seen da Heart. Dey didn't show dis one like dey did me and so he's only got da cheap trick o' da mind-trickery. Which… 't'ain't nothin' once ya's seen da Heart. Bah… what are tings comin' ta?"

So we were to be on the watch-out for mind-trickery.

"What the hell is mind-trickery, Sar'nt?" asked the ever-practical Punch as we walked away from Stinkeye because we could smell chow being set up on the cargo deck of the *Spider*.

And we were hungry.

Which was something as there were a lot of dead bodies rotting out there all over Route Vega. The stink of them was beginning to get pretty ripe.

But where were we gonna put 'em?

We'd made 'em.

To haul them back to the hangar deck and space 'em was a not-insignificant effort that would have drawn resources for the route clearing, or the defense of the LZ around the *Spider*. And the more we cleared Route Vega, the more they stacked up out there where we'd made them.

Your EVC, if it hadn't been creased like mine had, or outright destroyed like a few had been, could keep out the death-funk. But eventually you had to take off your bucket to eat, clean up, and try to sleep and not think of the horrors of the day... or the fear of the next.

Klutz had taken to sleeping in his bucket claiming the smell of the death kept him up.

So there was that.

"What the hell is mind-trickery, Sar'nt?" Punch asked me again as we reached the chow line. Chungo had some heating trays out and a few of the guys from the new platoon had been tasked out to run the kitchen on the *Spider* and keep us in hot chow.

It's the little things like hot chow that keep you in the game. Awards, glory, all pale compared to heated-up rations and maybe some bread and butter and hot sauce. A cup of coffee and a minute to listen to the talk and think...

There are other worlds than these.

Which, I suspect, is the unspoken mantra of all mercenaries.

Normally chow was suck duty.

But lately, after the horrors of clearing Route Vega, not a few of the Strange were starting to ask when they were gonna get their rotation at KP duty.

KP.

Kitchen Patrol.

"I don't know, Punch, what mind-trickery might be as demonstrable in a combat situation..." I told him as steaming corned beef and hash were heaped onto our trays. There were even instant scrambled eggs that looked yellow and rich like real eggs.

Not like the ration-pack "eggs" at all.

I kinda wanted to cry but I thought that might not reflect well on me as a small unit leader. So I just held that tray of eggs and hash like some orphan who'd never been given anything might hold a richly wrapped present some tech tycoon might give to the orphanage, all wrapped and beautiful.

The present was enough. I didn't even need to tear it open.

I asked the cook how he got those that way. The eggs. Fluffy and rich.

"Lotsa butter. Just the right amount of heat and stirring it but not too much, and not too little."

I thanked him for his service with a profound sincerity I haven't even used on guys who've actually saved my bacon in a gunfight. He generally seemed pleased that

I was looking forward to covering his eggs and hash in hot sauce. Extra salt. And a slice of sourdough toast.

And for a moment, I couldn't even smell the death we'd made out there permeating this sector of the ship. Our route of battle into the inner hull.

And the horrors that lay ahead.

"Ya know…" I said to Punch halfway through my third bite, half the plate already gone. Of course, Punch had already eaten his whole tray in one bite, maybe two, I don't know, it's his superpower, and now he was sitting there staring baseline murder into the nothing as we waited until it became time to go out and stack more along the route. "… ya know how Stinkeye can get inside people's minds, Punch. Like that time he convinced the mercs working for the Monarchs on the Verishaw Moons that it was us coming through the gap in the crater and they dropped mortars all over the swamp along the river bottoms thinking it was us conducting a probe when really it was their own guys going out?"

Punch laughed grimly and muttered, "That was awesome."

"Yeah, you couldn't convince them their own guys weren't us and they couldn't even see Stinkeye walking around whispering inside their minds to ignore the radios to adjust fire off their own. If what this Bishop we're about to run into is like… that… then reality won't match what we're seeing. If so, we need to detect the faults in reality, and call it out. Otherwise… we're the dead guys this time."

Punch gave me a look that was basically the equivalent of asking me if I was serious. How were we gonna do that?

I nodded and worked on my corned beef hash and eggs. The eggs were… great.

I wanted to have chickens someday.

Once I was done with… *this*.

I'd eat eggs every day.

There are other worlds than these.

"Yeah… if this guy can mess with reality, we could end up shooting ourselves in the foot… literally."

So we discussed strategies on how to detect this kind of attack, once enemy contact was achieved. How this Bishop might be affecting the outcome. And the consensus we came to was basically, *If it don't smell right, then it probably ain't.*

Hence the dialed-up operators fast-roping into a firefight when in reality they wouldn't do that unless they trying to take a fixed position. We were on the hump through the hull along Route Vega.

An insertion like that would have taken place to our rear and we wouldn't have noticed it until they started shooting us in the back.

So back in the Ball Room…

"Mind-trickery, Punch!" I screamed over the comm and I ignored the illusory incoming off the sub guns coming from the dark shadows of death rappelling down all over us while the dark cybernetic mainframe balls rolled and tumbled like strange giants.

"Oh yeah, baby! Gotcha, Sarge!" whooped Punch back as he dragged Duffy to the rear and handed him off to Klutz.

CHAPTER SIXTY-FOUR

Hauser moved his team forward to set up a base of fire distant enough from the gun teams in the walls trying to hit us with plunging fire despite the giant black glassy rolling balls which we were now using for moving cover to stay out from under the glare of the enemy gun teams.

Hauser, using his advanced targeting, wiped out one gun team with a full belt, turning the inside of their slit-windowed bunker halfway up the compartment wall into a torn-apart body-littered horror show we'd find later once we closed for breaching and clearing.

The first sergeant even came by that time with his flamethrower and we cooked a few of the secondary fallback positions their reaction force had fortified in the four hours it took us to stage the counterattack once we got off the *X* this Lady Death had planned for us.

The second gun position got nailed by an anti-armor round from Solo in Second who'd taken to carrying two light anti-armor Penetrators instead of the MeGoosa.

Small disposable munitions tubes that did anything but destroy armor. They were badly designed, and so of course Chungo had picked them up in bulk for cheap. And while they couldn't kill a tank or a mech… they had a great interface system for very effective targeting and wireless control that married with our EVC buckets after a few homemade patches. They were good for bunkers and compartments we'd breached and needed to pull back from. So I'd had each squad carry two and assigned them to a gunner.

Solo had yet to miss with a round, he was so adept at optically controlling the outgoing round with his eye as it tracked across the faceplate of his EVC bucket.

All the expanding circles, telemetry, and targeting crosshairs appearing like ghostly hieroglyphics in my bucket hurt my head and so I didn't like using them.

But Solo was a pro.

"Score! Direct impact!" he crowed and dropped the expended tube as I told him to hit it again just to be sure.

Money was exchanged between squads or at least the reminder of the debt that Solo could, or could not, hit it again.

Those not running from the rolling black cybernetic balls as we pulled back, or covering behind them to avoid fire, either whooped or swore.

The betting pool had been raging since Solo's hot streak had started with LAAPs.

Another *whoosh* and I had my squads out from under fire as once again Solo crowed, "Direct impact, direct impact for effect… pay up, boys!"

He'd begun betting on himself, *high on his own supply* as they say.

Now we had two minutes until both Fartsack and New Guy One, or Hangdog, or the Ham and Egger if he could have just choked down one more ration packet of the foul stuff, or so I liked to think to myself now and then, he *might*... have been known by... would be killed in action.

But those are the dreams of NCOs in which they fantasize about getting right all that they have gotten so wrong.

CHAPTER SIXTY-FIVE

So what we didn't know is... the Bishop had fallen in behind us, and at times, just as though he had the same equivalent powers as Stinkeye, he'd gotten close enough to us to start convincing our minds he was one of us, beginning to worm his way into our minds so he could convince us that when the Anubian brigade sprang their attack on us, our greater threat was the mind-trickery platoons suddenly coming down on us out of the top of the compartment, and not the gun teams trying to range and engage us.

But Punch and I grabbed on to the trick and ordered an immediate pullback. Fartsack and New Guy soon to be Hangdog unless he could find some more Ham and Eggs rations to convince everyone they were his favorite, got ordered by me to pull back past Hauser's squad and secure the last compartment we'd breached just before hitting the Ball Room.

And... they ran smack dab into the Bishop. The guy was dressed like an Anubian commando and he had a det ruck with him. He was busy setting up a line of tied-in claymore-style mines for us to run right into.

Fartsack's last transmission alerted the comm that we had bad guys in the rear and he was engaging.

I got a, "Catboi moving to support, Sergeant."

As near as we can tell, the Bishop smoked Farstack with a sidearm and New Guy One got a jam on his S16.

Normally... a very reliable weapon.

But we'd been using them a lot and New Guy probably hadn't been cleaning his as much as he needed to get on it, and instead... thanks to me... he'd been eating Ham and Eggs until his guts exploded and he puked up what was left. And no, I will not feel bad about this because the standard Sar'nt Orion refrain is, "You got time to do... whatever useless thing I catch you doing... you got time to clean your weapons."

I'm good.

Anyway... starships for some reason really gunk up kinetic hole-punchers which is why most respectable operators prefer energy rifles of some sort.

But that's rich people money.

And don't ask me why the Monarchs' Anubian commandos didn't have 'em. My guess is we'd run into them later.

If we made it that far. Maybe the inner hull.

So New Guy, Hangdog, the Ham and Egger, gets a jam on his primary and just jumps the Bishop, shucks the official "operator" knife Chungo lays on everyone as part of their basic issue, and starts stabbing like a sewing machine gone haywire.

It's a real fight, there's blood everywhere, and to be honest, it's a real hassle to fight hand-to-hand in EVC posture four.

But he did. He straight-up went after it.

The fact that in EVC posture four you can really hear your own breathing hyperventilate, and your heart jackhammering like it does in a real fight, doesn't help matters.

The Bishop, who was not so encumbered and has been trained not just to do... *mind-trickery*... but EOD ambush stuff and hand-to-hand apparently... he really is some kind of commando... gets the advantage over New Guy who was built like a bull as has been discussed, as we're pulling back under fire out there in the Ball Room and not expecting to retreat right into a bunch of daisy-chained mines ready to really brighten up our day with mass casualties.

The Bishop stabs New Guy...

Ham and Egger...

Hangdog...

Bull...

Call him what you want, and here's us coming into the det area.

Both guys are cut up and bloody and Fartsack was probably dying from gunshot wounds...

The Bishop reaches for the detonator and it's pretty clear our guy, New Guy, knows what's gonna happen next.

Mass casualties.

Our guy kicks the detonator even though he's experiencing massive blood loss, pulls the pin on a frag, and hugs the Bishop so the bad guy can't get it.

Klutz who's just dragging in Duffy sees this happen, and New Guy...

Hell... he's the Ham and Egger because he went out baller... shouts... "I'm gonna blow, get back!"

Klutz yanks Duffy's gunshot body savagely back into the Ball Room, throws himself over the wounded man because of course he would, as he's always trying hard to be a hero for the sake of us, and us alone...

And the Ham and Egger dets and kills himself, and the Bishop. And thankfully the daisy-chained claymores don't go off.

Duster goes in to secure the whole mess and disarm, and even though we're taking fire, we have cover and we're able to pull back and get the rest of the company forward to storm the Ball Room in earnest four hours later.

With our bloody dead watching us.

So of course we go full Strange Company on them.

Medieval.

Bronze Age.

Salt-the-earth style.

What the Ultras had called *First Pass*.

No quarter is given and we shred them with brutal and excessive gunfire, and if that isn't enough, we enter with shotgun shells because we want this to hurt as we storm the final defensive positions in the further compartments on the far side, screaming, "Hotsoup and Hangdog Forever!"

The first sergeant goes with us and gladly sends hot jets of flaming fuel into some of the tougher compartments held by the commandos, shouting, "Eat it, you dirty bastards! This is for Fartsack! See you in hell!"

When one of us, or a few of us on this occasion, get it like Fartsack and the Ham and Egger did, the company has a tendency to get... *excessive*. Like this is how we laugh right back at death, then spit in its eye. Glad it is not us being bagged by the medics and carried to the rear.

Call it a coping mechanism. Our slaughter.

Alive, for now, even if it is on a horrorshow death ship full of the smell of death at the deep end of the universe where there is nothing but fear, and death and the unknown, we live to fight another day.

We win.

The excessive gunfire reminds us of the thin line between death, and life.

Fartsack.

The Ham and Egger.

Strangers to the Universe, Brothers to the End.

That was Day Thirty-One.

On Day Forty-Seven we breached the inner hull. There weren't any good days between now and then, and the worst was yet to come.

CHAPTER SIXTY-SIX

Before we finally cleared the route to Terminal 95, the last stand of the Anubian commandos and their Monarch Lady Death… the final access to the inner hull of the *Dark Star*… we had to deal with the last HK team, and the battle they drew us into along Route Vega.

Spoiler… they weren't actually the last. But we didn't know that then.

We'd already smoked four. HK teams. Combat cyborgs. Hausers. One in the early days of the op. Heavy losses and I should get that fight down in the log too but when a boarding op goes on for forty-seven days of pro-level suck it can be… challenging to log everything. Choices have to be made. Most days it's all a ruck hobo can do to live through it and come out the other side with time to rack down and do it all over again.

I did jot down a note though.

Day 7. Smoked HK team.

Looking back, those three words are some of the best three words I've ever put down so let's just leave that one at that.

Another team because we knew they were operating in the energy lines that fed power from the sector reactor, just waiting for us to come in there and either try to use the reactor as a weapon against the *Dark Star*, directly… or, power it down and deny power to the sector to even up the odds.

Chief Cook-led interrogations yielded solid intel that the HKs were in there, waiting for us. And side note… the Voodoo psyops warrant had run out of interrogation drugs… or so he claimed… and was beginning to resort to more crude methods of information-gathering from the captured.

War crimes stuff.

But only if you're caught. And we were too far beyond the limits of human space and anything remotely recognizable as law and order… so anything goes.

Which works both ways some told everyone else that didn't listen.

We were fighting for our lives here. That had become apparent. So we voted for our survival and listened in as he got anything out of the captured between tormented screams and pathetic crying that might get our bacon through this one.

Then there was the inevitable gunshot to the temple they'd begged for. Not just because we'd captured them and were interrogating them… the Monarchs' technological slavery had done that part to them.

They only wanted death.

The hard part was keeping them from it until we could get some intel out of them. So… the medics had to do that part and they were not happy about it.

The Old Man stood right there and did it with them, running IVs and boosters to keep them talking.

Leadership… even when it's… awful.

Listen… we have to be honest about these things.

So, once we developed enough intel that a combat cyborg team was near the sector reactor and allocated to deny us that asset, we crawled in through the upper passage wiring bundles, met the scouts who'd been in there watching and waiting from nightmarishly claustrophobic crawlspaces, and then set up a basic L-shaped ambush to engage the combat cyborgs on a patrol they ran twice a day around the reactor subsystems and maintenance levels. They came down a midnight corridor, their optical sensor eyes glowing red like demons in the dark. Pie-ing corners and stalking forward like the best three-man recon team of mechanical killers that ever was. Then our dirty-trick ambush ate them up the moment after we detonated our emplaced mines and tore their synthetic flesh right off their chromed and bloody combat skeletons.

Wolfy had written a note for them right where we wanted the *X* to ignite.

It was a salvaged databoard that was supposed to look like it was dropped by one of the scouts making a probe into this sector.

The repeating loading screen had a numerica-encrypted puzzle that would have taken a normal human brain one hundred years to decrypt. The terminator had it unlocked in fifteen seconds and was rewarded with something other than the intel of our comm and data links it thought it was gonna hack into.

DUCK appeared on the screen, and we actually saw the terminator on point, a hulking synthetic curly-haired titan carrying a chopped light machine gun with a huge cylinder of drummed high-caliber ammo, turn to the others as though he was silently asking them what the hell this meant.

Then Duster whispered, "Execute, execute, execute," over the platoon comm as he triggered all our mines at once.

I squeezed my eyes shut.

The deafening blast ripped throughout that section horrifically.

Understatement.

And they still put up a fight, but they were already badly savaged by the detonation and the heavy gunfire we applied liberally seconds later. Then we moved in and did them with slugs from our shottys as they tried to crawl away from the battle with what few of their remaining gleaming articulating mechanical appendages were left.

That was one team down. Two left to go.

The second-to-last one… they paid us back good when they hit the *Spider*.

But they didn't survive.

And it cost us bad. Real bad.

The last HK team left in our sector aboard the *Dark Star*, what we thought was the last, the one that was operational forward of the final defense at Terminal 95, came running their A game. Now that was a real knockdown drag-out fight.

After that we were ready for the final push on Terminal 95 and an attempt to crack the inner hull. Chief Cook was going on and on, rather madly about his "secret weapon, Orion… she's a real beaut."

I had high hopes, honestly, for this "weapon."

If the inner hull was anything like the crawl through Route Vega… we weren't gonna make it.

But the second-to-last HK team that infiltrated the LZ…

Yeah, they almost killed us all.

And in a way… they really did.

CHAPTER SIXTY-SEVEN

Five days before the knockdown drag-out that killed the last enemy HK team forward of Terminal 95, one of the new platoons that was barely hanging on came in through the wire at the LZ around the *Spider*.

The LZ was the center of the initial docking bay hangar we'd taken during the opening assault on the wounded Monarch starship.

Traffic with the rest of the fleet was now mostly nonexistent. Rare was the day we even heard gunfights or explosions from distant places across the hull.

This state… let's call it that… was understood but not discussed. What could we do? We'd always known we were alone on this. We'd only used them to get close enough to board. Like Heraclitus's killers…

We have to be honest about these things.

The platoon coming through the wire around the LZ had been forward clearing Route Vega that day and had little contact.

The platoon was challenged by the other new platoon pulling LZ security, running the laser trip wires and automated sentry guns we'd put out. Every passage and compartment that led into the LZ had been covered with remote-det mines and fully loaded sentry guns with security parameters dialed into their interfaces that were set as high and as intolerant of enemy presence as could be set.

Oftentimes at night they'd go off and nail a rat or even sometimes got triggered when the ship experienced the now-rare detonation of some catastrophic munition in some other battle being waged by other elements of the former fleet of the Star Khans.

It was every ship for itself now. Tech and plunder were too rich to share.

Huge ordnance had been used, but less and less often lately and I had to wonder about those other battles we'd know nothing about. Their stories, their logs… their losses.

But I'm a positive thinker like that.

A lifetime, and many lifetimes in fact, of unlimited riches back in human-controlled space, was on the line out here if some of the stories of fantastic tech being hacked out of the ship's networks or taken as plunder in the onboard Dark Lab R&D sites we were hearing of was to be believed even just a little.

I heard things that I cannot verify that sounded like straight-up magic and myth.

So the new platoon came through the wire giving the appropriate countersign to the signs and they were dog-tired because walking through IED country on Route Vega, head on a swivel and constantly waiting for everything to just go suddenly south in one hot second of kinetic incoming with a round in it all with your name on it, kinda takes it outta ya.

We have to be honest about these things.

Reaper was on downtime, and I was on the flight deck talking with the command team, dog-tired myself and getting ready to go out on another push in three hours to keep the crawl of Route Vega through mines, ambushes, technological horrors, supernatural terrors, and whatever else this ghost ship could throw at us… crawling.

Gunny and the Dogs were far downrange and about to get hit in a coordinated effort to entrap them where they were at and deny the LZ a quick reaction force that could come in and peel the enemy forces off of the main push.

So, back at the wire, someone in the new platoons didn't run a bioscan for some reason once the platoon threaded the perimeter, and the new guys running security didn't notice the three hulking gunners who'd just come in with the platoon, actually giving the password and countersign…

The HKs had been watching and listening.

And that scared the hell outta me after the fact because… it just felt… sinister.

I'll tell you… combat cyborgs are as creepy as it gets. Real live killing machines with no souls, unlike warriors, soldiers, mercenaries, and even alien life forms we've tangled with in what some call war and combat.

It's always little more than a brawl with all the marbles on the table. No need to dress it up with fancy words that are supposed to mean something noble and have something to do with glory.

But combat cyborgs are killers and nothing else.

I've only felt the same kind of level of threat from apex predators on some of the worlds I've been to.

Just killing machines that will kill you dead and not think twice about it. Can't be reasoned. Can't be bargained. Hard to kill.

Hauser, my friend… is rare. He rejected the programming. And it only cost him all his runtime. Every minute of his life is lived with the knowledge that he only has fifty-eight point three seconds left.

After these encounters with the killing machines trying to kill us, I'd be lying if I didn't look at Hauser sometimes and wonder how easy it might be for him to just flip back into what he'd been designed and built to do.

Kill. Kill humans.

I think sometimes he catches me studying him, wondering those terrible thoughts, and in his own, ironically innocent way he'd ask me *what the matter was*.

What thoughts caused that look to appear on my face? Even though I said nothing. It was there.

One time he seemed to… *read my mind* isn't something he's capable of even though he'll tell you he has detailed psychological profiling algorithms installed into his mainframe in order for him to engage in predictive behavior programming assessment.

"Why?" I asked. As in… *Why did they give you those files about our behavior patterns?*

"To kill your kind more efficiently, Sergeant Orion."

Yeah, I thought when he told me that. *That makes sense.*

Another look must have crossed my face. Horror. Horror that some human had… conceived that idea. Brilliant. And terrible. Give the killing machines files that help them to understand humans better so they can kill more humans.

A human designer thought that up.

That was the look that crossed my face and Hauser seemed to *sense* it.

His math, his algorithms, his *detailed files*… doing the work. The same math and algorithms and *detailed files* he was designed to use, and to kill, with.

Then…

"I will never allow you, Sergeant Orion, or any of the company, to be harmed."

That was his way of saying… *I will never kill you, Sergeant Orion. You are my friend.*

"It's just Orion, Hause," I said. Because he is my friend. A killing machine.

So… that very bad day for the company, Day Thirty-Six of the boarding of the *Dark Star*, the three combat cyborgs made it through the wire because they'd garroted two guys on rear security and fallen into the patrol column as it came through the ever-scanning sentry guns and deactivated laser trip wires for the anti-personnel mines.

The bioscan didn't get run, as was protocol, and who knew why they got cut that break. But they did. And they made hay with it. They were probably going to go ahead and go kinetic right there if the alarm got tripped. At least take out that security site.

Instead… jackpot for them. They got inside the wire.

The *Spider* loomed above them and they immediately went to their ambush positions to ensure maximum casualties, and a gut shot to the company, even though they'd had no idea they'd effect that that day on Day Thirty-Six.

The perimeter inside the wire was busy with its tasks of downtime and prep.

In about ten minutes we were gonna find out they had three companies of Anubian commandos in the passages behind them, ready to hit the perimeter and draw us to the defense outward, while they were inside and busy.

It was brilliant.

Savagely, terribly brilliant.

Ending that security checkpoint, hacking the anti-personnel mine control and taking out the turrets, would have given their force a chance against the LZ and the ship with her PDCs which were effectively our final protective fires on the LZ.

Instead, they caught a break because some slacker didn't do his job with the bioscanner and they made it through. Because they were combat cyborgs, they immediately communicated with one another via their own private network and updated their plan to do even more damage, using those *detailed files* they too had, making the thing way worse for us instantly.

And really forever after that.

They would leave a wound in the company for a long time to come.

One terminator "lingered," actually setting down the light machine gun he carried in, just beyond the bunker that overlooked that security passage on the LZ. Another immediately started for the *Spider* with most likely the intention of disabling our ship and/or blowing it to kingdom come, killing all of us at the LZ instantly, or stranding us on board a hostile enemy starship with no hope of resupply or rescue.

Not optimal.

One star... would not recommend.

Later, some of the survivors reported noting that they should have clocked something was going seriously sideways by the way the guy, in reality a combat cyborg, was walking fast and determined, making straight for the cargo deck of the *Spider* like no one ever just coming off a tense pump beyond the wire.

Add by the fact no one had ever seen him before. He was dressed in a shot-to-hell EVC suit the HK team had mocked up pretty decently, however they did that.

"Subterfuge and insertion camouflage are part of our infiltration protocols, Sergeant Orion," explained Hauser patiently. "They would go to great lengths to make sure they could... casually... pass as one of you."

Also... EVC suits hide a lot of details.

The last terminator to cross into the security perimeter this side of the wire at the LZ went kinetic two minutes later, shooting up the security position they'd just inserted through and killing nine as it just raked the position, hip-firing because its optical sensors interface with the gun and targeting software. It used the advanced light machine gun it had humped in. Onboard targeting software allowed effective kill shots and damage as it just sprayed everyone in the observation bunker we'd set up to watch the gate. It cut everyone to pieces in mere seconds.

That was the opening of their attack, and it was savage, brutal, and sudden.

We were already behind the power curve as things got going and we tried to react to what we were hearing all across the LZ.

An attack. Inside the wire.

It took return fire, but this was too little to be effective to a combat unit of this type. Return fire only drew its attention and that... is not a good thing.

Those guys died next as more gunfire began to ring out across the LZ inside the hangar.

Ulysses, Hauser, and Punch, my squad leaders, had just received my WARNO for what the captain wanted us to do out there that day, and were aft under the main engines dealing with loadouts, assignments, and positions for their squads.

We were going to hit a supply route the commandos were using to fortify the left flank of Terminal 95 in what was identified as ship's stores for this sector of the *Dark Star*.

This would be a major blow and might open up the route into our main objective.

Large apartment-block-like warehouses surrounded by a network of "streets" where transport and delivery vehicles could pull supplies from stores and distribute them across the sector. It was ripe for ambush, but taking it out had been deemed a priority by command.

So Reaper got to be the hitters.

We were worried about the "streets" because Ghost's scouts had reported actual light tanks moving along the main artery through the stores section and that meant we were gonna need to hump in some serious anti-armor to deal with one of those.

Add in there was no air support because we were inside a ship, not planetside like we were meant to be, and this had us nervous.

Light infantry problems. Light infantry fears.

A tank bearing down on you with nowhere to hide.

So we were dealing with that when the combat cyborg goes kinetic on the observation bunker far side of the perimeter, shooting the emplaced team down in hot sprays of bright fire that rang out almost rhythmically inside the vast ship, which is looking, and smelling, more and more like a planetside war-torn city on any given day than some bright X-tech of the future.

Gone is the pristine starship we'd stormed weeks ago.

Lotsa damage, black scoring, holes, and stuff that doesn't work. The enemy has pushed in on the LZ in surprise attacks three times and gotten wrecked for their efforts.

Those PDCs on board the *Spider* are hard to argue with.

So my three squad leaders react and go after that cyborg attacking the checkpoint, as do various other elements from across the perimeter.

Which was exactly the HK team's plan.

Draw our attention away from where they were bringing in their main force, stationed in the shadowy corridors and unguarded compartments out there in the dark of the ruined ship.

We'd figure out later they'd been stacking for about six hours in order to support the HK attack. We were about to get hit hard. Real hard.

And... we had bad guys, the worst bad guys, inside the wire.

That cyborg at the perimeter checkpoint will survive another five minutes before Hauser, using the Pig, manages to get into a position to put a full belt of AP, armor-piercing, on target, savaging its combat chassis.

Ulysses, staged with Punch, will toss three frags at the thing as it skulks away from the fight, shooting down some of the platoon members who have no business attempting to flank it, dragging a useless leg assembly torn to pieces by Hauser's AP fire. The 'nades det and Punch goes in with the shotty loaded with dumb slugs, slam-firing up close and personal at the thing glaring right back at him with one lone soullessly evil mechanical red-eyed optical sensor.

Internal systems spray out the back of the killing machine, but it's not "dead" until Ulysses mag-dumps at close range, watching it recoil mechanically as Wonder Boy shoots it in "the belly," the power plant really, while Punch moves in thumbing in more slugs, then blasts it in the remaining "hand" and once again in the armored cranium where its... *detailed files* for killing humans... are kept.

Gunfire erupts further inside the perimeter as the "lingering" terminator still outside the ship gets detected when someone actually asks it, "Never seen you around... what platoon you with?"

It had positioned itself near our small QRF force comprised of New Guys we kept in reserve just in case the enemy tried the wire and managed to breach.

So... the HKs had been watching us and they knew what this force was.

For a few nights after this incident I was bothered by that. The fact that they'd sat out there in the dark and ruined parts of the starship, watching us from the shadows and empty spaces, figuring out how to get in and kill for maximum effect.

And I wondered if there was another team out there... doing the same thing...

So the guy next to it, next to the combat cyborg that had positioned itself with the New Guy reaction force, a kid tagged Drinker, swears and just screams, "Terminator!" and immediately goes full rattle with a light battle rifle. Points for focus and reaction. But five-five-six won't do anything and the terminator just punches Drinker so hard in a split second that its fist sinks straight through Drinker's chest cavity... and right out the back.

No more Drinker.

Then, wordlessly, it picks up the chopped Pig it had set down and begins to *'scunion* for the high score on the reaction force and everything else in sight.

Sergeant Hot Round, the New Guy platoon's NCO, gets everyone going right at the terminator even as dudes are getting shot to pieces, swearing murder. Sar'nt Round gets cut in half by a burst of fire from the cyborg's chopped LMG.

But his platoon, New Guys and not responsible for dropping the ball in allowing the combat cyborgs through, picks up that ball and engages the terminator full-tilt. Someone also has the presence of mind to re-arm the mines and sentries.

And that really saves our bacon because the supporting force of Anubian commandos who'd been stacking out there in the dark of the ship had immediately begun to make for the wire and the checkpoint as soon as the attack started.

Perimeter mines go off and the sentry guns start to bark automated murder at the Anubian commando force quietly creeping close to the checkpoint.

So if this all seems organized and understandable... it wasn't at the time. Trust me.

It was total chaos. Instantly.

Meanwhile that last combat cyborg of the murderous triumvirate not under fire is already inside the *Spider* and heading toward deck fourteen.

Main engineering.

The only place you can overload all four of the ship's reactors and set them into cascade mode for immediate self-destruct.

So... that was gonna be a problem pretty quick.

CHAPTER SIXTY-EIGHT

"He's heading for main engineering," said XO, casting desperate eyes at the rest of the command team who'd assembled at the flight deck to discuss the current situation in and around the *Dark Star*.

It was heading toward main engineering.

The current situation in and around the Dark Star...

More about that later.

But it wasn't good.

Mission-critical problems abounded.

Now things were going from bad to worse.

"We don't need this," said the first sergeant, shrugging into the harness of the flamethrower he'd been running for the whole op. "Sometimes the only way to put out a fire... is with a fire. Flame on, boys."

I ain't lyin'... that thing made me nervous. The man-portable nape-thrower. But... here we are. A real nightmare combat cyborg running amok... inside the *Spider*.

Our only hope of getting off this ghost ship.

Our last fallback position.

Trust me... in infantry terms... it doesn't get much worse than this.

"Hell," I swore as I grabbed the Bastard. "I thought today was gonna be normal and I was just gonna get shot at or blown up."

"I can lock him down on deck twelve for a few minutes," shouted XO, "but if he hacks into M.O.M. he'll be able to reroute through her subsystems and gain access to Main."

Main engineering.

The absolute heart of our starship. Our *Do not pass go, do not collect mem* spot on the board.

From there, it could det and blow us all to hell.

Fun times.

Which, as Hauser had often reminded me, is a combat cyborg HK team's secondary mission.

Denial of assets.

Their primary mission was to kill humans.

So... that'd be a double dip for this one, I thought grimly and didn't voice what I found mildly funny at the worst possible moment.

They weren't human, as Hauser had reminded me every time the enemy HK special ops teams came up in intel.

"Remember, Sergeant Orion..."

"Just Orion, Hause. We're friends. You can override protocols. For once just—"

"It can't be bargained with, Sergeant Orion. It can't be reasoned with. It does not feel pity, or remorse, or even fear. It will not stop... ever, until you are dead, Sergeant Orion. I know this. Those were our prime directives hard-coded into our neural net processors. It was our primary function. Know this, and live..."

He struggled to override formality and protocols... for a moment.

But then...

"Sergeant Orion. I repeat this because you are this unit's friend. I want you to live. Forgive me."

There are fifty-eight seconds and change left on his runtime clock. My friend. And he is worried about me?

Yes. Of course I forgive you for reminding me to live. Always.

The life of a ruck hobo is hard and thankless, and even more so if you've been unlucky enough to live long enough and make NCO.

But then sometimes... I have been given more than I ever deserved in a friend like the killing machine I have ended up with. And this company who calls me a brother... even if I want to punch some of them in the face on any day that ends in 'y'.

So there is that.

We must... we absolutely must be honest about all these things.

"Sir," says the first sergeant, straightening up and getting the load of the fuel tank higher on his back. "We'll deal with the tin man down there. They need you on the defense out there. Sounds like it's goin' from bad to worse by the second."

It was. The gunfire was apocalyptic. I had no idea who was winning but then the PDCs engaged and I felt like that was for the best... unless it wasn't.

In the dim lighting on the bridge, a bare overhead bright white light shines down on the plot table and the notes we've printed out as ghostly blue graphs and maps of local space and the *Dark Star* herself update quietly with each pulse of the ship's sensor sweep...

The captain looks like a statue of himself that was never carved long ago by some race of mythic heroes better than we'd ever be. Or maybe that's where I hold him in my mental architecture. He looks hard and ancient. Old and determined to see it done come hell or high water.

He looks how I want to feel on all the days I know I'm not enough for what's coming to kill me. And my platoon.

If he is the measure of a small unit leader by which I have tried to hold myself accountable... then I have failed mightily.

Here at the last... I was not enough, I thought as I desperately wanted him to come up with some plan that stopped this doomsday-cascade-in-progress our morning had suddenly, out of the blue, become.

"Copy, First Sergeant," says the captain in that grave-gravel voice of his as he reaches for his primary on the table and slings it over his EVC, the dart still burning in his mouth, his washed-out tired blue eyes never leaving the first sergeant.

Then... he scans the rest of us for a quick second we cannot spare.

"Let's put this fire out so we can make room for the next one. XO… if that thing down there starts the reactor cascade, pop the eject on the emergency override and flush the jump core."

Damn.

That's cold. Hardest decision we could make and he just made it.

Without the core we'll be on dumb-thrust back to the nearest inhabited planet.

And we are so far out here, that'll take hundreds of years.

The cryo-coffins have an increasing rate of failure as flight time extends.

Not good.

But there was no other option than the one he chose.

Me… I couldn't have made that decision.

I'd have gambled. Kept the core.

And we'd all be dead.

CHAPTER SIXTY-NINE

The first sergeant was on the hump fast into the lower decks. But now... now that I look back on it all, on him... he always was fast about things. Or maybe he was just smooth. Always racing about in whatever ground vehicle he'd commandeered, all-wheel mule, five-ton crawler, hover tank strapped and loaded with belt-fed defense guns, beans, and blankets and sometimes even a one-twenty main gun for, as he would put it... *"to get it done in one, son."*

We moved aft of the bridge and took the main lift down to deck twelve just forward of the aft weapons computer stacks. Once XO got a hold on the lockdown, that would put us in position to go after the state-of-the-art killing machine with just the two of us.

Outside, the firefight for the LZ went psychotic as the Anubian commandos pushed for all they were worth, attempting to exploit as much gain as the HK team had purchased for them from inside the wire. I could hear calls for medics and NCOs overriding the chatter to focus forces and react to contact.

It was chaos.

But the Old Man was going out into it, and my squad leaders, especially Ulysses Two Alpha Six, were leaders born for that kind of hot dumpster fire that is command under fire.

So we had that going for us as the worst was about to happen.

"Lemme take point, Top," I said as I slapped in one of my AP mags on the Bastard. I still wasn't in my EVC suit for the pump forward and was just wearing my chest rig and no plates.

But honestly, I was sick of the EVC suit. It was so shot-to-hell and plas-sealed it was on the verge of utter uselessness that it wasn't funny.

In fact... there had been a general murmuring about that among the company and the consensus was we needed to shuck it and use our mobility to get the last push done.

Ditching it would let us move faster and with more agility under fire. Ditching it would also mean having almost zero chance to survive a hull breach or explosive decompression.

There were life-support stations all over the ship where we could survive these incidents if we were extremely close, and extremely lucky. And we were heading deeper and deeper into the hull where the chance of collateral damage that resulted in being exposed to open space was less and less likely.

But it was never zero.

We have to be honest about that. We are on a spaceship, surrounded by the stuff. Space.

It's absolutely unforgiving.

Plus there was the chance the Monarchs could go biologic or even chemical on us inside the hull.

EVC would help. In theory. If theory didn't account for the shoddy condition of my EVC and most of the rest of them besides.

"Lemme take point, Top."

The first sergeant looked at me. He was working dip and his eyes were far away and focused like he was planning how to come at the combat cyborg just right and get our kill on without us getting killed… *maybe*.

He looked pretty homicidal. Like the hunter-killer team attack on the *Spider* and the DZ had been personal to him… and he was definitely taking it that way.

Guys from the batts are like that.

Just straight-up murder cult.

Note… Top was a great first sergeant. He was also a vengeful son of a gun. So I could read him. And he wanted to make that thing pay good for this attack.

He looked at me like I'd just slapped him. Then shook his head angrily and tightened his grip on the flamethrower's gun.

"Nah… bastard's gonna pay, young sar'nt. Ever tell you 'bout the combat cyborgs we had to fight alongside at Hamado? Bastards kept turnin' on us. Batt commanders wouldn't take 'em after they killed a bunch of us in a firefight. I get that you got one as a friend and all, Sar'nt Orion… but I'll be honest…"

We were approaching deck twelve. XO had triggered the battle stations alarm aboard the ship and M.O.M. was advising all personnel to be ready to engage in combat. And… to have a nice day. "Dear."

"I'll be honest, Sar'nt Orion. Never liked your boy because at the end of the day he's just a machine. And them machines… there's something… not just wrong, but evil… about 'em. Maybe that's just me and the things that happened to us at Hamado in the Saturnian Batts… but I lost a good brother there. So I got that axe to grind against them and that's on me."

I disagreed with him. And I didn't.

Hauser was different.

And yes… there was something wrong about combat cyborgs. They were a cruel mockery of us. Perfect versions of us… but coded for cold murder… on us.

So I said nothing and went with *why* I wanted to take point once we went in after him.

'Cause… I had this feeling.

Gotta be honest about these things.

And the PTSD dreams hadn't stopped. I'd seen other things, yeah, but that wasn't the worst of it and some of those things didn't come true and so I haven't put them down here.

The worst parts though… for some reason… were the Wild Thing's real life.

I saw… clips of it.

He was a real man.

Wife and kid.

Come back to us, Marcus.

Those were the ones when I woke up and my face was stained with tears. They were the worst.

But I had this feeling hitting deck twelve like I'd seen this one too... and it wasn't good.

"Solid, Top. Listen... I got the gun. I put rounds on it and suppress if we get up on it. You get around and flank it... then barbecue its metal butt. It'll prioritize gunfire and engage on me and I'll cover. My primary ain't gonna do jack against him. But that flamethrower... that's another thing. Then you hit him with the nape."

The first sergeant nodded at me once.

"Yeah, young sar'nt. Works for me. Good plan, Orion."

Then the door slid open on deck twelve and it was nothing but whirling damage control lights and shadowy darkness.

It looked like a storm in there and I, to be honest, bad vibes included, did not want to go in there.

Incoming message from ship's executive officer, prompted M.O.M. I tapped my mic and opened the traffic.

"He's hacked in," said XO. I could hear key-strikes slamming the terminal he was working at as he talked. "He's taking the maintenance tube up to deck fourteen now."

Damn.

"Tried to lock him out. If we're going to eject the jump core I need to start that procedure now..."

"He's probably locked down the bulkhead security doors and the lift," I said. "How can we get into reactor control?"

"Take the portside passage to tool stores. The door will be locked but enter 95-85 and it'll force open. Back of the benches is a hatch. It's dogged. Crank it open and you'll get a ladder up to deck fourteen. You'll come out behind reactor control in main engineering near the drive stacks. If he's gonna do an overload he'll go in reactor control and do it from there. If he seals himself in, there's not much you can do. I'll have to eject the jump core. It's not the worst-case scenario... but... it's pretty damn close."

Yeah. I've told you the crawl back to human space at sub-light will take hundreds of years. I actually did the calc during flight sim. Specifically, it's four hundred. Years.

Coffin-sleep has an incidence of fatality at above eighty percent over that stretch of time.

Not... even suboptimal.

Very few of us would make it home.

Yeah... but the worst-case scenario... the terminator dets the ship and blows those of us still inside to smithereens, stranding anyone outside the blast area on a hostile starship with probably no chance of rescue or even survival.

But at least you got a shot to run up the score.

And sometimes that's all you play for.

CHAPTER SEVENTY

We went into main engineering, me following the business end of the Bastard, the first sergeant's flamethrower's blue light hissing on a low deadly note reminding me, along with the smell of gas, there was every chance I was gonna get burnt to death getting this done.

Not my favorite way to go.

I'd seen it enough times. One star. Would not recommend.

I did not have any frags.

We threaded through the dark monolith-like calc-drives which managed the engines and power plant. M.O.M. alerted the ship that "the captain has activated the jump core eject protocols" and all crew were to stand by to evacuate the aft engineering deck where the jump core was located.

We just paid for that thing, a small part of me thought as we exited the calc stacks and entered the industrial warrens of main engineering.

Piping and steam created a misty nightmare mixed with the warning yellow hazard lights strobing incessantly.

M.O.M. was warning that radiation levels were escalating and immediate cooldown procedures were recommended as continued operation at this level would result in a loss of life.

The combat cyborg was starting to overload the reactors. It would take time. The killing machine had to break through a lot of encryption and run the start-up sequence just right to get the reactors to cascade independently of one another. Twenty minutes... and things would be well beyond our control.

I held up my fist, indicating a halt, and pointed at the engineering boards and terminals for Reactor Four.

We could see him in there.

The hulking giant's hands wove across the holo-terminal faster than human-possible as he raised engine power levels and turbines faster and faster.

There was a deep and ominous cyclone of intense humming starting to build.

This did little for my nerves.

Visions of how catastrophically bad this could go danced through my head like some children have visions of sugar plum fairies.

Mine all came with nuclear blast waves.

Again, M.O.M. warned... "Critical systems are now operating past standard parameters, and maintenance violations should be reported to the chief engineer on duty. Continued operation at these levels will result in the destruction of this vessel, and a catastrophic loss of life. Thank you, dear."

I nodded at the first sergeant to go to the right through the interstellar motivator interface machinery that connected the power plant management, where the terminator was working, and into the systems to the jump drive.

I'd learned a lot about this ship recently. More than I ever thought I'd know.

And part of that knowledge was it was about to go *booom* really hard and take us all with it.

The clock was on fire, as they say.

Going right would put the first sergeant in a position to cut off the combat cyborg if he bolted for reactor control overwatch. From there, if he could no longer overload the reactors individually, he could just break them down by overspinning them and make them tear themselves apart via the superconducers.

It wouldn't cause a catastrophic cascade, but the resulting explosion would rip through several decks, perhaps killing some of us inside, wounding or even maiming... but the ship would survive.

It's just, again... the jump drive would no longer work. Which was a certain death sentence in the long run for at least most of the company.

The main engines would also be unpowered. Motive power would be down to thrusters, and those were slaved to the ship's batteries. Other than being able to possibly maneuver our attitude in space, I doubted we could do much.

We could get a tow from a heavier vessel in the fleet up toward lighthugger speed... but still... four hundred years and certain death in the cryo-coffins loomed.

The *Winds of Change*, the experimental jump-envelope vessel that could create a displacement field for a fleet to move even faster, had perished with all hands when the *Dark Star* targeted it with a Scorpion anti-ship missile strike and it got rocked straight-up like it was in a hurricane.

Now... there was no "fast" way back to the space lanes we'd once known.

In reality... without vessel assistance we'd be stranded. Forever, if the fleet, or what was once the fleet, didn't destroy the ship with us still docked inside.

Chances of survival... still not good.

We had to kill it here. Before it got to crime scene number two. Reactor overwatch.

The first sergeant on the move to flank, I counted to ten and moved in to engage.

The killing machine turned and engaged me with the chopped light machine gun it was carrying and almost riddled me with very accurate fire.

Because I am a wily hobo, I sucked "dirt," hitting the deck and rolling behind an astrogation interface display still running calcs for an optimistic jump back to human space.

Someday.

The critical device absorbed a heavy dose of hard gunfire as it came apart in sprays of smart-glass shards while I did a fast high-crawl-scramble for better cover.

The age-old problem for infantry, even in the age of starships... better cover from which to return fire.

I rolled upright, popped a flashbang, and tossed it in what I thought was his general direction.

It could have shifted.

Now... bangs are excellent weapons against combat cyborgs. Fries their optics and messes with their systems for a hot sec. Yeah, they reboot faster than a human and there's no disorientation effect to their equilibrium because they don't have ears...

... but it *do* stun them for a good three to five. And I'll take what I can get.

I used this to reposition, hunch-running for a new position to push it into the first sergeant and the nape thrower. I slapped in a new mag hearing the old one hit the rubberized decking of the ship.

I told myself I'd come back and get it later. If I survived.

Then I flipped to single-fire and put hot accurate fire into it as it came back online.

It cut loose with a long burst and faded back deeper into main engineering, trying to suppress. Now it was headed right at the first sergeant who was ready to hit the damned thing with four thousand degrees of flaming napalm.

Yeah... there'd be damage to the ship's systems. But there were backup control stations all across the ship, and at the end of the day M.O.M. could either set up a new holo-station in sim... rerouting to flight deck control stations... or just run it herself.

We'd take the chance.

And that was when the killing machine pulled a fast one on us and went right inside the reactor control station. This was a heavily shielded area I highly doubted we could penetrate with rounds, or even the standard high-ex we carried on the hump.

Which I currently did not have.

The first sergeant had almost hit him with a jet of flame but the combat cyborg reacted quickly and diverted away from that display-laden passage, now covered in burning gel, and made for main reactor control.

Now it was in there and there was every chance it had good cover, and that it could seal itself in tight if it chose to. It also had enough of a handle to override all the security systems and lockouts, thus preventing us from getting in and getting after it.

From there it could start the cascade overload on at least two reactors, maybe three but not all four, or just destroy the reactors by overspinning them.

Dealer's choice...

The first sergeant came down the passage he'd set on fire with a jet burst of nape. The close flames didn't seem to bother him even though the heat was intense and M.O.M. was already sounding off about a fire in this section as fire alarms, blaring and insistent, started up, unrelenting in their own special way.

Add in the battle stations warning she was sounding.

Damage alerts.

It was all getting rather busy.

"He's in main control!" I practically shouted at the first sergeant, hearing the ragged desperation in my own voice choke.

The firefight on the LZ was in doubt out there at that very moment. Elements of the lesser platoons were pulling back and there were requests for fire from the ship's PDCs right on the gun line.

XO was stating, "Negative at this time," wisely refusing to spin up the powerful point defense cannons and spray six thousand rounds a second to intercept incoming missile fire. While effective as demonstrated at the LZ on Marsantyium, it was pure homicidal suicide in this situation that close. Command had decreed they only be used as final protective fires should the LZ be overrun and the need to depart be abundantly clear.

The PDCs had been armed and had been engaging elements further out in the hangar and supporting compartments. Not closer.

Even with this, there was a chance we could bring down the superstructure of the hangar and the surrounding starship on the *Spider*, permanently trapping us, or compromising the integrity of the hull and the hangar force barriers…

Note: destroying the force batteries would vent the deck to open space and many of us would be sucked out and probably die drifting in space as our EVC suits ran down.

It got worse and worse by the second.

"He's in main control!"

The first sergeant stalked forward at me through the flaming passage, avoiding contact with the fires and licking hot tendrils spreading even as local fire suppression systems kicked in.

"We'll have to go in, Top. There's only one way in and it's got it covered most likely," I was barking.

Breaching the chamber and going in, even if it hadn't locked us out, was going to result in the fatal-est of funnels to take it out.

We were going to die getting it done.

In other words we'd be walking into a hail of gunfire coming down a tight narrow alley through control systems with nowhere to cover or hide, just to even get rounds, or jet fuel, on him.

The first sergeant seemed to ignore my concern as he barked, "Check that hatch over there and see if it's open, Sar'nt Orion. Maybe we can just squirt some flame in there and cook him."

I saw the problem even as I moved to hatch control and had to shut my mouth.

Three green lights indicated the hatch was wide open and neither dogged nor locked out internally. It was closed though. All I had to do was slam my fist onto the metal button that would cause it to pneumatically open.

Either the killing machine hadn't had the time to lock us out… or it didn't assess that it could… or XO had thrown down some system override that prevented the thing from locking itself down internally.

"Reactor breach in progress… startup sequence alpha delta nine," stated M.O.M. flatly over the hiss of the fire suppression systems and the blare of the damage klaxons.

Back to that problem I'd seen…

The fatal funnel into reactor control was a short alley, a dogleg attack avenue into the main chamber. Getting the nape in there was still going to require us to try that alley he was probably set up on to unload at us.

We wouldn't make it ten meters. There was no changing that.

And if he wasn't… he could still hit us from the exit through the control systems alley and then the dogleg turn into the main chamber where he could be waiting to hit us again.

That was when the first sergeant slammed his open-hand palm into the back of my skull at the base of my head, intending to knock me out.

I stumbled, kinda stunned, hadn't been expecting that… and went down on one knee now knowing the first sergeant was going to try to prevent me from going in there and getting killed with him.

I looked up in bewilderment as he kicked my support leg out from under me, grunting as he did so.

He was fast and he'd lost nothing over the years even though I'd heard him complain often about his pains and aches and not being what he once was.

As though he'd deceived us all those years just in case he'd need an edge someday when it mattered life-and-death-style.

Here was that day.

He played his card and whammied me.

"Knew I was gonna buy it on this one, Sar'nt Orion," he barked quickly as he stood over me. I was still dazed. "Company's yours now!"

Then he turned and sparked up a jet of napalm from the tip of the gun connected to the gel-tank, letting a little fire fly off into the dark passage into the reactor control chamber.

"Rangers lead the way!" he shouted one last time and threw himself into the fatal funnel that was the entrance to the chamber.

I wanted to throw up from the blow to my head, but I knew I had to go with him, whatever happened…

No matter what…

As I staggered to my boots I heard the long bark of gunfire, then the gusty eruption of the first jet of liquid burning napalm coming from the tanks, ignited into a living crawling flame monster.

I can still smell the tang of that gas.

I am haunted by that moment… forever.

I lurched to follow him in and the security door slammed shut. I heard the first sergeant laughing madly as he spat out more jets of flame from the tanks, then screaming as he roasted himself alive, and the terminator with him.

I watched it all happen through the reactor control windows.

Later…

M.O.M. took the station offline after the damage sensors indicated a shutdown that bypassed the cyborg's lockout hack. Reactor control was rerouted to a secondary station.

But the first sergeant was gone by then.

CHAPTER SEVENTY-ONE

Later I watched the footage from inside reactor control. The first sergeant went out like a boss. The hunter-killer combat cyborg hit him with a savage burst of direct gunfire, up close and personal, but by that time they were both cooked.

The flames were everywhere as the first sergeant covered everything in burning fuel.

The first sergeant went down, but the killing machine was already fully engulfed. Its threat dead, the combat cyborg turned back to its work at the panels and terminals to overload what reactors it could as though it were not completely covered in burning fuel, its synthetic skin and hair dripping off in great flaming chunks. It attempted to put all the power systems it could into a runaway cascade that would have destroyed the *Spider* one way or another.

The synthetic flesh dripped and melted away, burning, in great blobs along with the EVC its team had mocked up, but the nape wasn't satisfied... its gleaming metal frame and armor plating began to warp and twist as the nape-tank itself caught fire in the burning mass of the first sergeant's remains and exploded inside the small chamber.

In the end... the cyborg just fell over, its work unable to be finished.

The feed on the chamber filled with grainy black-and-white smoke and fire as the suppression systems finally kicked in.

A day later we held the funeral for the first sergeant and the others who'd died in the HK team's attack on the LZ.

We'd beaten them back and held the line. And the LZ.

We had wounded, and dead.

Our losses were represented by rifles and boots just below the ramp of the aft cargo deck.

Preacher said his words. We stood there in our patchwork EVCs. Shot to hell. Some wounded attended. Those that could.

We looked rough.

I'll be honest... the news was getting grimmer and grimmer by the second and this didn't add to the good vibes in the current events section of the Strange Company logs.

Preacher finished saying things he always said, things I couldn't listen to anymore.

I just kept asking myself... or some voice inside my head kept asking... *How much can one man lose?*

I felt empty and hollow and I wanted to feel… mad. But I couldn't. It was just… too much.

There're too many dead in Strange Company these days, and for a lot of days… and due to the nature of my job as company Log Keeper… I feel more keenly aware of that than most.

I suspect.

I felt selfish and small for thinking of it that way. Everyone was grieving for the first sergeant like a parent you never thought wouldn't be there to bail you out of your latest jam.

We were orphans now.

No matter how bad that suck was…

He embraced it and somehow convinced us, believed in us… that we could too.

And now he was gone.

I needed it to rain. But it doesn't rain on starships. And so it didn't.

We have to be honest…

The Old Man walked forward and climbed the ramp to the cargo deck we were using as a kind of speaker's platform for our… memorials.

Preacher stepped aside. Done with his words I couldn't hear anymore.

It was time to cut and run. That's what the Old Man was gonna say.

We hadn't even breached the inner hull. Our numbers were down. We still had to hit the terminal and deal with an actual Monarch.

Then… whatever the inner hull was… we had to make it to one of the vital ship-killer systems there and det this beast.

Or put our faith in Chief Cook… L. O. L.

I couldn't even and I have had to *even* through a lot of suck.

And right now, this morning, standing there with my head aching where the first shirt cracked my skull in order to save my life…

Everything seemed… impossible.

"Damn," I muttered like some old starport hobo still pissed at deeds done to him long ago. No one listening. No one caring. Just an old man burnt out by the haul and down on his luck, same as it ever was.

Punch was sobbing hard.

I felt bad for anyone who was gonna make fun of him later for this.

He'd probably kill them this time.

But… I didn't think anyone would.

We all wept in our own ways.

The captain studied us for a long moment. No coffin nail smoldering in the side of his mouth. No quiet gaze appraising us. No… perpetual look of indigestion that makes all such commanders. Real commanders.

He was looking at us. Looking inside us.

His eyes were almost as dead as we felt.

There was no speech coming. No praise for the first sergeant. No resolve to pay them back for what they did to our brothers.

Our… First Sergeant.

That wasn't the captain's way, and I'd never heard him make such disingenuous speeches.

It was always the truth with him, whether you liked it or not.

If the rumors were true, he was an Ultra Marine from long ago.

I didn't know his story. No one did. Only myths and rumors and the occasional hint abounded in the company scuttle.

Then...

He, the captain, Company Commander of the Strange, reached up and disconnected from his EVC armor, breaking the docking collar for the helmet he hadn't brought up there with him.

He zipped out of the suit... and just let the dirty, smelly, patched and ruined, shredded and bullet-creased armor... fall around his boots.

He had weathered fatigue pants and combat boots on.

His chest was a crisscross of ancient scars and old gunshot puckers.

It was a star chart of hard times.

Just like ours.

Scars like those made by a whip crossed his chest in wide slashing X's. When he turned around later, I saw it was even worse on his back.

Someone had once really laid into him. And I wondered if I'd ever know the story... his... story.

The captain stepped out of the old and ruined EVC armor and stood before us, ramrod straight. Grey close-cropped hair unmoving. Washed-out seen-it-all done-been-there-and-got-the-gunshot-wound blue eyes just watching us.

He nodded. And now we knew, without a word, that our time laboring in the EVC suits... was over.

Guys were already stripping out of theirs, sighing as the heavy load fell away, silently hissing at the stink of themselves, kicking their dirty armor as they shed themselves of it and returned to their natural state of light infantry.

Half-naked ugly savages with every bad starport-tattoo-shop ink, ancient gunshot pucker, badly sewn-up knife slash from vengeful pimps and rejected whores, and a variety of other old wounds, finally revealed.

In the end I stood there, with my brothers, free.

We'd be infantry now, unencumbered by armor. Naked and ready to kill, inside a hull that was a thin layer between us and death by deep dark black vacuum.

As though we were saying something...

We'd bet it all to take the advantage of agility and lack of encumbrance to get it on better.

Committing to something because of what had been done to us, the taking of the first sergeant...

The captain straightened up even straighter, fixed his iron glare at all of us, or so it seemed... and then...

"We finish this now, Strange Company. No one gets outta here alive."

It was personal for us now. No debt to the monkey Kong, no contract or prize money... it was *vendetta* now.

And only three times in the entire company history had we engaged in a vendetta.

All three were the stuff of legends and well before my time. All three were deadly serious.

In the company regs... the words... *to the last man* are used to show... we are serious.

Then the captain turned and entered the ship.

Ten days later we would hit Terminal 95 after we got sucked into a battle by the last HK team which revealed the route of attack we'd need to exploit to lay the hit on the final objective.

Now, even on a starship, we were light infantry once again. Silent, hard, murderous and on the move at dawn.

Maybe Chief Cook's secret weapon…

Maybe compartment to compartment all the way through the inner hull. We were gonna do it, even if it meant with knives. No matter what. Even if it cost us everything.

Punch wept for the man he'd considered his father. We all did. In our own ways.

To the last man now.

Our enemies were unaware death was coming for them now. We were, and didn't care to count the cost.

Vendetta.

For the first sergeant.

Strangers to the Universe, Brothers to the End.

CHAPTER SEVENTY-TWO

We, the command team… minus the first sergeant… reconvened. After the battle.

His new absence was… *profound*.

The holos, feedbacks, and data crawls of what we'd been meeting regarding before the attack on our perimeter still scrolled on loop. Our business unfinished despite the attack, counterattack, and loss of our own.

We awkwardly discussed ACE reports. Casualties. Ammo. Current defense posture.

The captain was the first to speak as we tried to get underway because the topic we'd been discussing prior to recent events had been… *pretty important*.

But first he opened with new, and unfortunate, company business. Because of course… despite current events, the company must go on.

Just as it always has.

Same as it ever was.

The silence of the first sergeant's constant wry wisdom and hard embrace of the suck with at least a smile's take on soldiering… was deafening now.

He was gone.

The silence was deafening.

Ask anyone who's ever lost someone they cared about.

It roars that silence.

"In light of current operations…" began the Old Man. "We will forgo appointing a new Company First Sergeant until we smoke these bastards and get off this nightmare vessel," said the captain bitterly as he shook out a dart and lit it with all his practiced motions so rote as though he were some high priest doing yet again the rituals of the faithful.

He stared down at some data crawling across the tabletop we were supposed to make sense of.

"Master Sergeant Chungo will handle supply," he began again abruptly. "XO will assume operations. I'll pick up… his… duties when I'm not forward. Right now I need every small unit leader right where they're at for what's coming next."

No one disagreed.

In lieu of numbers due to the rise of casualties, leadership was gonna have to get real creative.

Honestly, we were too shocked. It was as though right then and there he'd just walk onto the bridge and start telling us problems that needed to be solved and wayward troopers that needed some NCO time.

But he didn't. And we were less without him.

Sergeant Gunny cleared his throat, his voice a deep rich rumble as he spoke through clenched teeth. An unlit short cigar in the side of his mouth as he watched the updated map of Route Vega.

All business… but the respect for the moment was there.

"Sir… bi'ness at hand and all… I think ah got a insight to what's going on out there."

The captain indicated Gunny should go on.

Gunny pointed toward the feed of the *Thunderer* we'd been contemplating.

She was one of the few ships that hadn't docked with the *Dark Star* in some form or fashion. She was the last remaining major capital ship in the battle fleet that had gone hunting the last of the Monarchs what felt like so long ago.

Now, in the holo-feed, grainy and blue… she was dead in space.

Six hours ago the Monarchs had played a card and instead of fighting *Thunderer*'s extensive "ground" forces investing the upper hull of the target vessel, the Monarchs had instead launched a small strike fleet of shuttles and drones.

The drone wave had been huge. Massive. Warning alarms had started shrieking even on the *Spider*'s flight deck which was docked internally aboard the *Dark Star*. The drone wave came out of hidden launch bays all along the underside of the *Dark Star* and swarmed the *Thunderer* holding position just above her beachhead on the dorsal, or top, of the *Dark Star*'s hull.

The fleet scout vessel, *Raven of Winter*, had been destroyed in early fighting and many of the smaller ships had either been chewed up in the initial assault, or gone rogue and boarded the larger target vessel, their captains understanding the potential of any dark tech salvage off the last Monarch ship. Small cabals had formed around some of the medium-class vessels, but once the alliance had broken up, infighting began, or the cabals had gone radio silent, too busy to be bothered with mutual defense as they tunneled deeper and deeper into the fantastic of the *Dark Star*.

The starship debris field around the *Dark Star* in orbit around the massive purple storm-laden gas giant Typhon was now a legitimate navigational hazard.

There was even an orbital debris wake.

We had PDCs and they were mostly full up. Blue Sky always indicating them at ninety-eight percent. For now. That was enough to get clear of the debris field and figure out how to get back to human-controlled space now that we no longer had a jump core.

No one had said it… but… I'd already thought of a solution and I'd need to sell it to the captain. Note… I'd do this in about an hour, after the meeting, and XO would be there and he'd shoot the plan down. There was no way we had the technical expertise or equipment to get a salvaged warp core out of one of the wrecked vessels, get it installed and balanced for jump operations.

"We do that, Orion, and we could tear the ship apart in two different directions, each one moving away from the other at light speed. This ain't drop-in technology. A jump core is carefully timed and balanced by scientists with serious calibration equipment for each vessel. Like back on Blackrock, it's a six-month job by people who know what they're doing with the right tools, big tools… you're talking a starship hook… to get it done. We don't have any of that, Orion."

Meaning it was going to be a four-hundred-year crawl back.

Did I mention the fatality rate in the coffins?

Eighty percent.

I say... why not go for it. We got Hauser... he can become an expert on anything with the right databases.

So, back to the dead-in-space *Thunderer*... the drone wave slammed into the basically unsuspecting carrier because she had no sensor support or defensive ships that weren't docked and trying to haul out the tech shipside that had been salvaged off *Dark Star*.

Apparently the pickings were pretty good up there along the upper hull and that's why the fractured elements of the fleet had started fighting one another.

The drone wave knocked out critical systems on the *Thunderer*, then started hacking into the vessel's internal security and defensive systems.

The captain, of course, pulled a last-ditch trick known as a pulse defense.

And now I quote from the book of starship combat.

"In the event drone-based hack attacks are conducted in direct contact with the vessel, the captain may order the reactors to conduct an EMP pulse to deny the attack. Be warned... this will shut down most systems and require a critical hard-boot that can take anywhere from two minutes for minor systems, to upwards of four hours for the standard jump drive interface."

Note... sensors take about twenty minutes.

So the Monarchs anticipated the captain of the *Thunderer* would play the pulse defense card, and when she did... they struck with their actual attack fleet.

Combat-cyborg-led teams, reinforced with Bishops and leading a division of commandos, these had cat's-head helmets instead of dog's heads according to hijacked feeds scooped up by our ship, launched off the *Dark Star* on full burn and boarded the *Thunderer* within twenty minutes.

There's about four hours of distress transmissions as the crew fought compartment to compartment, finally falling back to main engineering in which they declared an intent to self-destruct.

Then nothing happened and Hauser who was part of our meeting bluntly stated...

"The cyborgs have taken the engineering section and disabled the self-destruct. They are in control of the vessel and the crew is dead."

XO objected.

"Only the senior-most officer has the final self-destruct-control code string, Hauser. If she wanted that ship blown to bits all she had to do was off herself or refuse... no matter what... to divulge the code that would stop the procedure already initiated," stated the XO in certain disbelief of Hauser's blunt assessment of what had happened instead of a catastrophic explosion and a bright momentary star on our battlefield.

Hauser's only response was, "They have methods of retrieving secure data despite these kinds of obstacles."

We have to be honest about these things.

So, we were watching the death of *Thunderer* and seeing no longer the massive armada we'd come in with. In fact, other than the debris field, there was very little left to see.

No one was talking to anyone. Comm and chatter were dead. There were ghost signals. But... those could be automated.

Alive, dead, still engaged in combat or active salvage... there was no intel about what was really going on out there.

In reality we could be the last ones left and frankly it wasn't looking too good for the company right now.

That is, if anyone kept up with current events.

"Sir..." said Gunny. "Beginnin' ta think this ain't so much a siege as... sumpin' else. Sumpin' bad. Real bad."

Gunny sighed. It was more of a growl as he worked his cigar to the other side of his stone-faced mouth.

"This is a damn trap, sir."

"How so?" asked the captain after a moment of silence. I hadn't considered what Gunny had just indicated. A trap we'd thought was a siege. But in seconds... I think we all started to see it for what it really was.

"Back in the Corps, sir... we had scenarios like this we had to train for. Run a ship down... especially if it was one o' them Q-ships we took for a blockade runner... we'd board thinking the Navy boys had shot 'em good and hard with the ship's guns. Yeah, we'd have some fighting. But the ship was ours, little by little. 'Cept this one time and I wasn't part of that op. But it happened in the Troja system during the insurrection there when the Monarchs were sending us in to take over the trade routes there."

He moved the stubby cigar around and his eyes were far away for a long moment.

"Ship called the *Bucephalus*, assault corvette running three platoons of legit heartbreakers outta One-Nine Marines... goes inta the Q-ship and once they penetrate they walked into a real crap show o' defenses. Assault corvette was chasing two other freighters and the commander wanted to gun their engines and get them dead in space. Then we'd get around to them. So One-Nine Heartbreakers go in there and get in way over their head real fast. Can't get no call for support out because part of the ship's trap was to jam signal besides all the heavy internal defenses. So... in the end they got killed and *Bucephalus* swings back around and gets no comm. Security elements board, and suddenly Q-ship fires off a hidden main gun at C-beam strength cutting straight through the *Bucephalus*'s engines, disabling them. It was a one-shot, which is why she didn't fire them in the running battle. Batteries were forward and tied to the rear engines. Gun tube had been cored into the ship's spine and fired only aft. *Bucephalus* had come in and taken up a standard rear guardian position and took that shot direct right into the engines. Now she's dead in space, no Marines, and she can't run. Boarders off the Q-ship stormed the corvette and butchered everyone."

Silence.

"It was a trap all along, sir. Never was a boarding. They lured our guys to board because that was the plan all along. Took about two years to figure out what really happened and get it installed inta Marine Corps doctrine as what was eventually called *the Macross Gambit* for no reasons I can tell other than the strategy brain who came up with it based it on some old sci-fi show about a super defense fortress that gets left behind as a 'gift' for the enemy. In this case they left the Q-ship which *Bucephalus* took as an ordinary freighter loaded with goods. In the end, the two gunships that ran got away and came back as the corvette tried to get underway using emergency power from the impulse engines. Spoiler... they didn't, sir. Like I said, they butchered 'em all. But... no worries... Three-Nine went in and paid them back old school. We went Ultra Marine on 'em for what they'd done to our boys."

The captain lit another dart.

"So..." his eyes were far away as he worked the "math" of what Gunny was saying, and what we all knew now. "The Monarchs knew the game was over back in human space. The chimps were too much for them. They also knew we'd chase them wherever. So they led us all the way out here, way past where any of the chimp hulks could make it, then set the trap by letting us think she was disabled and then boarding her."

Silence as we all just... took this in. It all made sense now. Why they hadn't activated that jump system that was controlled by the Ball Room.

"And the trap is this ship. They weren't disabled. They could probably still jump," said XO in a hushed voice as he stared incredulously at the massive ship rendered in holo in the near-space navigational display on the plot in front of us. "They *wanted* us to board. They wanted us to turn on each other..."

Stinkeye, lurking in the shadows, croaked, "Aye, Exec-u-tive Officer. Dey got da right Bishop, piped into a... call it a power source... and dey could have been low-grade running dat troo certain brains as we made da attack. Pretty clever for da Dark Hearts."

Dark Hearts.

Hearts of Darkness.

Theirs or ours.

Vendetta.

Come back to us, Marcus.

I pushed all that away and tried to get my mind wrapped around all this.

I'd never heard him use that term before.

Dark Hearts.

"So they are destroying us, battle group by battle group... and then once they're done... they salvage the destroyed ships, or have some technology, to get back underway and off to where they're going to hide until it's time to reappear," said the Old Man.

"If all elements are destroyed here in this system," said Hauser flatly, "then it would be impossible for any other elements wishing to engage and destroy them to know their final destination point. They will have effectively won if the... phenomena Sergeant Orion is experiencing are correct."

Silence. We considered the feeds, the data, and the maps in this new light.

Our fate.

The fate of the universe.

Stinkeye spoke once more.

"It was our greed dey used to trap us here. Countin' on us ta not leave until we had all we could plunder, like pigs at da trough suckin' it up and gettin' all fat for da slaughter... knowin' dey'd destroy every one o' us before dat happened. Damn, damn der Dark Hearts."

It was all crystal clear now.

Yeah.

The captain leaned forward into the blue light of the map displays. Hovering over the feeds like some relentless warlord the galaxy had never figured into any of its plans.

"Doesn't matter," he said finally. "They were dumb enough to let us get our hands around their throat, then we're gonna take 'em with us."

He pointed toward Terminal 95 on our maps.

The end… of Route Vega.

"We find a way in here and strike. Then we gain access to the inner hull. We're inside them now. They jump to the farthest quadrant, we'll be right there with them. Inside their wire."

He paused and straightened up, a shadowy form now looming above all the bad news in ghostly blue holo.

A variable of chaos in the most-certain plans of others.

"Then we kill them where they think they're safest."

And…

"They will never escape the Strange, gentlemen."

Like it was a law.

A promise.

A prophecy.

CHAPTER SEVENTY-THREE

We developed the intel to hit Terminal 95 just days after we'd finally cleared the route far enough to see the cyclopean terminal down the huge corridor through the massive bulkhead at the end of Route Vega that led to what hacked terminals revealed to be… the Ring.

The Ring was a central transportation tube that circumnavigated the entire inner hull of the fantastic disc-ship that was the *Dark Star*.

The Ring, though internal, was several decks high… at least thirty, cylindrical and heavily armored to protect the inner section of the ship. It was almost like some moat surrounding an ancient fortress. As though the Monarchs had wanted this primeval touchstone somewhere within their escape ship of the future. Even though none of the fleet's beam weapons, or even some of the high-yield major explosive devices, had managed to penetrate remotely close to this far down into the ship's outer armored defensive shell.

It was as though the entire ship surrounding the inner hull was designed to protect that final, most sacred to them, place.

And it was there we had to go and kill them all.

Decks above and below the Ring were so heavily impacted with flight control systems and flight operations equipment for the vessel, they formed more walls within the ship that guarded the inner hull from above and below as well.

These areas were impassable.

And where this mass of critical systems and machinery wasn't, there was pure armor and heavily shielded bulkheads that couldn't be cut into with conventional breaching tools.

This wasn't new news to us.

We'd figured this out after hacking terminals and downloading schematics of the ship as we progressed along Route Vega, capturing control nodes. These hacks weren't always all-telling of what we were fighting our way into… but they gave us clues and pieces to the map we were navigating by fragments… that helped develop a picture of the mysterious ship we'd come to destroy.

And how to destroy it.

Information within the Monarch system was heavily compartmentalized and classified. We're an infantry company. Not hackers. But… due to various past *shenanigans*, we'd developed… how might one say… *a certain set of skills* that came in handy for these types of sensitive site collections.

It was surprising to see which guys had developed the most affinity for Monarch system hacking. Punch was their leader. A brawler and a guy who talked more with his fists than his mouth... and it was always odd to watch him bust out a portable deck and collapsible field keyboard as he started rooting through attachments in his shoulder cargo pocket that would interface with the input devices into the system he was hacking.

Then he'd start muttering hacker-speak to himself...

I'm in.

Breaking crypto.

Running the hack.

Pay dirt... root access here, ha-cha!

And invariably...

Here come the anti-virus bots... ten more seconds before they burn the terminal. Copying to download...

Each squad had at least one, and sometimes two, who were at least adept at this work and it got done even in the middle of a firefight as we built our digital sand table of Route Vega, and the *Dark Star*, back at the *Spider*'s flight deck.

So far, this was what Route Vega looked like.

A series of hangars and external flight controls mixed with defensive batteries along the outer hull.

We'd secured that on Day One.

Then we got into the large compartments with munitions stores, shuttle repair facilities, vehicle storage hangars, gantries, elevators, living quarters and support systems for crew.

We took those areas in the early hard-fought battles against the Anubian commandos. Bloody, no-holds-barred, compartment-to-compartment fighting with sub guns, full-auto mag dumps on the primaries *spray-and-pray* style, and of course shottys at close quarters to clear their last-stand fighting positions.

Anubian armor was weak and punchable by fast-moving lead. Our EVC armor, heavier, bulkier, made us move slower, but it deflected a lot of shots and absorbed a lot of damage.

And then there was urine-colored spray-plas to keep it going.

In those compartment areas was where the EVCs had gotten really chewed up with the fighting being brutal and day after day.

After that we pushed Route Vega into the admin district and labs in this sector of the ship.

We'd learned there were ten sectors within the ship in the outer hull. Each was commanded by a commander and a brigade of commandos. We had no idea what was in the inner hull.

Only suspicions...

These admin districts, and the labs, were lonely places, devoid of any sign of life... this is where the Anubians switched over to IED warfare, and ambush.

But... this was our jam. As light infantry with long experience on hostile worlds with local guerillas resorting to this type of warfare, we knew how to get down and dirty with these types of operations.

So we moved slower, cleared safely, called for anti-armor teams to just devastate anything that looked like an ambush, and pushed farther and farther into the *Dark*

Star and along Route Vega day by day, rooting out nests of commandos, storming them as my guys called out "Hotsoup," and went in throwing frags and machine-gunning everyone they could.

Nether was especially useful.

Stinkeye was all but broke and drunk most of the time, muttering to himself and disappearing for days.

Chief Cook... he disappeared. We couldn't find him.

But, in the process of looking for him we figured out Stinkeye wasn't broke. Wasn't useless. He'd been going forward at night and messing with the nests of commandos before we hit them the next day.

Doing his magic.

Whispering his lies.

It was costing him and everyone knew it. So command started to just say he was drunk and useless and couldn't be found like all warrants can never be found when you need one.

The truth... that he was exhausting himself out there making mischief... it was weird... it was like after the first sergeant... we didn't want to think that perhaps Stinkeye, the oldest member, and then some if you believe very old logs, was at the end of things.

We couldn't lose him. That would be... *too much.*

How much can one man lose, Sergeant Orion?

And...

Come back to us.

"I'll go with you, Stink," I told him one day when I found him behind a large supply crate, back in the shadows just sitting there sipping from his flask.

I'd run my platoon, get an hour's sleep, and go back out with him. Just to keep him safe.

Yeah... I needed the old war wizard too.

Any... is too much. Loss that is.

He waved me away and said, "Nah, Little King. Dis is what I do. An' soon... you gots ta do what ya's got ta do. Don't ask me for help on dat one... ain't no comin' back from where ya's headed, Little King. I knew it from when I first met ya's. Now... I see it. And... I'm sorry, Little King. I am sorry 'bout dat."

It was like having a shadow pass over your grave when he said those things. And... I'm not holding back, but I understood what he was saying. It's just... the log isn't ready for that yet and I'm too tired to put it down what with clearing Route Vega.

And maybe, the ruck hobo lied to himself... maybe it won't happen.

Come back to us.

So in the admins and labs it was boring work punctuated by moments of terror, chaos, and gunfire as we started our ambushes and left our own surprises for the commandos.

It became a game of attrition.

They had more to lose, but we had to bleed them. We cannibalized our first platoon and distributed them out among the rest.

I never put their name in. It was a cool name. It should be used again and the record should reflect that the platoon didn't fail, or was cursed by bad luck... the name should be used again.

Outlaws.

That's a cool name for a platoon.

But we disbanded them and distributed the survivors.

Morning pumps forward along the route cleared the day before would find the ruined remains of Anubian sappers sprayed and shredded all over compartments, bulkheads, cargo elevators between decks, and sometimes small tubes used for maintenance and deep system penetration.

Our IEDs were merciless.

Duster was a master of the high-ex surprise.

Many was the time we didn't even go look down some tight tube that led to a series of remote mines we'd left down there knowing they'd tried to infiltrate Route Vega that way.

We just knew by the smell.

No need to crawl on your belly for half a kilometer in claustrophobic darkness to find ruined body parts and ship's rats having a good ol' time at the remains.

I have learned... sometimes it's best you don't look.

Catboi proved to be a great point man.

His attention to detail was phenomenal. He had a few rough edges... but he could spot IEDs and traps like no tomorrow.

"Catboi forward, Sergeant. Catboi has eyes on trigger device and explosive, Sergeant. Catboi marking with chems. Catboi moving on."

We'd mark and Duster would disarm.

And the squad... really took Catboi under their wing. He'd saved them a lot of hassle.

And again... only I was annoyed by the narration. Everyone else loved it.

They even started doing it one day.

Then I PT'd them after a pump forward. We weren't doing PT then. We were too tired from the mission. So they stopped.

I am a small and petty man.

I... have to be honest about these things.

After the admin and labs district we reached the big supply warehouse and the stand-up fixed battles began again as we cleared the blocks of warehouse the Monarchs had stuffed with all the supplies they could loot from their fallen empire that had turned on them. Supplies they'd use out there in the vast unknown to start a new worst nightmare, somewhere we could never find them for a very long time.

And then, according to John Strange, if we didn't do our work here... they'd be back.

The company slogged forward. Intent on the kill.

There were days it seemed... so far off. Never-ending. That we would be on this ship forever.

"That's not true, Orion," Nether told me as he inhaled one of my darts. I'd confessed my fears that this... would never end.

We'd lost the gun team for First that day. Goods and Suckitup. Commandos threw a frag into the compartment they were firing from and killed them both. Goods died on the way to the casualty collection point.

We had to carry our wounded back down Route Vega. No dustoffs here.

He didn't say anything. He was just gone.

Rough day.

I told Nether I thought there would never be an end to this…

He was silent for a long moment.

Then, just before he would say, "Time to go, Orion," which he did as a courtesy because you couldn't see him, he put his hand on my shoulder.

It's not a pleasant feeling. But… he is my friend. And even shadows need… contact.

Then he said, "This too shall pass, Orion. All things… come to an end."

"You sound like Preacher," I said.

He laughed a little.

Then, "Time to go, Orion." And he was gone.

It's okay to have rough days. That's what he was saying. We all do.

And yes, there will be good days. And sometimes you just have to navigate by those dreams of a better tomorrow.

These warehouse districts were huge decks, high storage areas the fighting rarely penetrated into. The fighting took place in the "streets" between these gargantuan blocks of spoils houses.

The streets were throughfares and avenues supply and transport vehicles coming off the *Ring Internal Transportation System*, as the Monarchs' ship designers had tagged the Ring, used to either deliver or transport supplies, or take crew and personnel between sections of the ship.

The streets were three vehicles wide and often as tall as the six-deck-high warehouses along them. Ground vehicles and hover vehicles like cargo versions of dropships we'd used for combat ops could come down these streets and rendezvous with the cargo and storage facilities.

We saw some of the stranger drops still docked on their landing and loading platforms.

Again… this ship is big beyond definition.

Understatement.

There probably has never been a ship as big as the *Dark Star* nor can I ever conceive that one will be built. Each day as we patrolled forward doing the clearing or fighting work, I ruminated that soon, if the company did what it said it was gonna do… *all this*, I thought looking around me, would be nothing but an expanding debris and vapor trail in the universe.

But only if we succeeded.

If we failed…

I pushed that away and thought of a better expanding debris trail called *tomorrow*.

"Look on all my mighty works and despair…" Nether said to me one time when he was working forward with us, advancing non-corporeal and invisible along the route to spot ambushes. He'd come back and caught me considering a massive warehouse that was six stories high, seeing the small landing pads and docking stations along its brutalist edges where those dropships could come and dock and load cargo.

It was impressive. I stared upward, slack-jawed, wondering what it looked like under normal operations.

Seriously... I was keenly aware few humans had ever seen what we were seeing. For all our faults and weaknesses... we could get up to some serious shenanigans when we set our minds to it.

We should be fighting in some third-world hellhole for nothing but land against some equally desperate mercenary company.

But here we were, the hounds of hell pursuing our former tyrants.

The low bringing down the once-mighty in their own undeniably fantastic realm.

I was eloquent. Forgive me. These are supposed to be just logs.

But...

Maybe they're supposed to be something more. Something I leave behind to say that... *I was here.*

And then there will be a new company Log Keeper.

"What's that from?" I asked Nether and shook out a dart for him.

I lit and he inhaled, rasping and killing the smoke in one go because that's how he affected the material plane.

"An old poem about the hubris of those who would ever think themselves... *great*, Orion. Gods or something that they should be remembered after they are gone when the rest of us are so often not. Most of history is littered with the forgotten, Orion. And what we remember, or hold on to, is really not that much of the whole that was. Think about it sometimes."

I repeated what Nether had said.

"*Look on all my mighty works... and despair.*"

Then...

"I get it, Nether. I understand."

He was silent in his own way, and I could hear him softly rasping. That's how he breathes in and out.

Then...

"You would, Orion. If anyone would... it would be you. I think... maybe that's why you're here. To mark it down. Their fall. Their... arrogance. Their... defeat."

I laughed and heard myself. I was dry, hollow, spent. Just moving forward now to get to the other side of this. If there was one... that is...

"Nah... I'm just here for the violence. Like Wolfy says."

But we both knew that wasn't true, and soon enough we were back at it, focusing on possible ambushes and IEDs to the point our skulls ached, and our eyes popped, or felt like they were going to, as we scanned every dark passage, every shadowy corner, and anywhere they could try and kill us from.

This was for... *all the marbles.*

Not just our lives, unremarked... or even theirs... vainglorious like some sunken head in the sands of time... but for that better tomorrow in which they would never participate, and we would never know.

That... is what history is really about. Your mileage may vary. But thus sayeth the ruck hobo.

The route pushed forward until we made it in sight of the terminal that would give us access to the Ring.

What was next… was in sight.

For better, or for worse.

Come hell, or high water.

Beyond the Ring we could penetrate the inner hull. We didn't know what was there… but we knew the last of the Monarchs were hiding there.

And once they were dead…

We were done.

That's it. That's all. Perhaps the company would be no more just like the rest of humanity that had pushed things forward without getting a big broken head in the sand to be unremembered by.

Perhaps…

All things come to an end. Even the company.

This too shall pass.

The warehouse district gave way to a monolithic bulkhead twenty decks high. Ghost pushed in on the stalk and saw there was only one passage through the bulkhead from the main service route that served the warehouse district.

Terminal 95, our objective, lay beyond this massive sector bulkhead.

And it was impassable.

Impassable except for that one passage through. A long access highway, a tunnel really, going right into the Ring, covered by emplaced guns that led to Terminal 95. Pure murder funnel. Featuring special guest star *us* as the murderees.

We called it the "Highway of Death." We are good at naming things.

So yes, impassable.

We did not have the numbers to push.

CHAPTER SEVENTY-FOUR

Scouting the cyclopean bulkhead that blocked us was like discovering some giant alien ruin to keep out monsters of the long ago. Some spectacuthriller about a jungle planet a ship full of impossibly beautiful people never should have crashed on. Alien and fantastic, almost... too mind-blowing to grasp. But we were just grunts looking to get the job done. So we crawled, searched, and probed for some other way through this section that would allow us to get at our objective from an unguarded angle.

We didn't have the numbers to make a direct hit. We had to get wily.

It was during this search we got hit by the last HK team, leading a company of commandos.

Long story short, they'd come through a secret route into the warehouse district. They went after Gunny's platoon as they scouted the warehouse and supply corridors along the alley nearest the giant wall of the bulkhead on our right flank.

Reaper was three clicks off Gunny's flank doing the same work in what had become a dark and gloomy haunted house of soulless blocky structures and lonely roads where nothing moved and everything was wet.

The whole place was creepy and... it even "rained" here. We theorized the ship had taken damage during the initial fleet assault and either a fire suppression system hadn't been repaired... or actual water piping to supply the crew and personnel in this sector had been damaged and was now slowly drizzling down into this forgotten and abandoned area.

Whatever it was... there was constant misty rain here and now that we'd shed our EVC armor we were wet, cold, and it was dark and scary.

I know. *Dark* and *Scary*. But yes... even infantry get the creeps. Try being out in the woods at night with no lights or people for miles around.

You can hear some very strange things that will flat-out freak you out.

Troof!

Not all the lighting worked here either, and occasionally some supply alleys had flickering lighting, or just one lone light... and the whole scout here was unsettling.

Chief Cook appeared long enough to have a theory. Though he'd lost weight, not that he had much to lose, he was sweating heavily. He looked... *distracted*.

"They're messing with us, Orion. They broke some pipes. Playing with the lighting. Little games, Orion. I don't really have time for this, got some... uh... big stuff cooking in this latest batch and we are *sooo* close... so very close, my sweet little infantryman... but I went in there... recorded ambient sound and came back to the ship and put it through the computers... laugh out loud..."

Which he didn't.

He waved at something that wasn't there. Cursing it.

"They've got a very low ambient frequency running in there we used to use for interrogations to get prisoners in the, shall we say… the *right frame of mind*… ah yes. Sweet, sweet paranoia, my old friend, with a little dash of the ol' impending doom. All that real fun stuff, Orion. Not always a great way to go… hell, better interrogations through chemicals as I always say… but if the interrogated doesn't freak out and off himself on you… and you can convince 'em to talk a little… tell you the secret plans… hell, then they won't shut up if you put them in the right… *frame of mind*… Orion."

He laughed weirdly. Don't ask me to describe it. It was just weird.

It was just… weird.

Then he was gone. Couldn't find him after that.

The command team stared at our deranged warrant officer as he wandered off… nothing new there. But still… every new trick in this battle made you literally want nothing to do with this.

They were trying to freak us out in there.

Why?

The captain was staring off into space, murder eyes in full effect.

"They don't want us in there," he said after inhaling his dart and letting the grey smoke spill out from his nostrils.

"My thinking exactly, sir," added Gunny. "They don't want us in there, sir."

So… we went in there even harder. Poking around more.

That's when we got into the fight and figured out how they were getting into the district without using the MSR that we were steering clear of, what would have been the last leg of Route Vega all the way to Terminal 95 if we'd had the numbers to withstand all the murdering we'd take.

MSR.

Main Service Route.

I liked "Highway of Death" better.

The fight would lead to a way in, but the time to use it was definitely limited.

CHAPTER SEVENTY-FIVE

"*Awww hell no...*" said Sergeant Full-Up over the company comm I was monitoring as we probed this section of the warehouse district looking for a way through to hit Terminal 95 and cross into the inner hull without having to go down the impassable Highway of Death through the sector-behemoth of a bulkhead that blocked our way in toward our final objective.

The inner hull.

"*Awww hell no...* they comin' down like spiders..."

Sar'nt Full-Up had his mic open and I was catching local traffic from his platoon comm as I ran my platoon in the hunt for a way through the bulkhead.

"Contact... HK team down on the ground here and securing their insertion point," rumbled Gunny over the comm. "They don't see us."

"Say again, Devil Six..." I said as I stared up into the rainy gloom inside the massive ship that sometimes seemed to me more like a floating world... than an interstellar vessel. "... say again, *coming down like spiders.*"

Yeah... I was gonna need clarification on what we were about to get into, seeing as automatic weapons and high-ex were gonna need to be used.

Now that we had that HK team.

I was acutely aware of the squad's lack of a recoilless MeGoosa.

I swore.

I'd had that *expect contact* feeling in the pit of my stomach all day. Everything felt edgy and weird. Not bad like it usually did... but more like... *hey, maybe we're getting a break in the clouds, or the opposite of that.* Maybe an opportunity to avoid the certain death my dreams and nightmares and every pump inside this vessel had been confirming to me.

Or... that certain death life had been promising me lately.

You know... *edgy* and *weird.*

Like... call me crazy... but something good was gonna happen even if I was hearing that something was coming down like spiders... that couldn't be good... and that an HK team... which meant combat cyborgs... had established an insertion point.

Or... nothing good was gonna happen.

See... both edgy... and weird.

We'd wiped out most of the Anubian sapper teams and ambush elements in this sector and if our KIA numbers were solid there weren't many of the enemy left in what we were told by interrogations was a brigade-sized unit.

We'd stacked.

But the enemy had other sectors to draw from, and they were now all guarding one final position that *seemed*... impossible to attack.

Seemed being the active word.

In my infantry experience... very few places are truly impossible to attack. Everything's got a weakness.

You just gotta find it and then exploit the hell out of it.

We are playing for all the marbles after all.

"Ain't that right, Big Sarge," said Punch. My chief exploiter of exploiting the hell out of the enemy.

Ghost Platoon, scouts and snipers, had eyes on Terminal 95 right now, from a distance, straight down death-tunnel Murder Highway, and we had rough numbers there. One company of hardened defenders. And that Bishop and a Monarch. A. Real. Live. Actual. Monarch.

Crazy...

But that's another story.

"Reaper Actual... Devil Six..." It was Gunny on the comm. "Listen here, Reaper... we got us a company-sized element of commandos coming down along the bulkhead seam and sector wall..."

Uh... that was twenty decks high here in the corner of the sector.

And... that was an impressively asymmetrical move by the enemy. Color this wily ruck hobo impressed.

They'd gone up and over the bulkhead, probably cutting through it or some access route up there purposefully hidden by the ship's designers. Unconsciously, I stared up into the rainy mist and gloom hanging over the whole warehouse sector. Lighting was currently *little* to *none*. We were running night optics and thermal but the rain and ambient temperature was interfering with vision beyond medium engagement distances.

So... I couldn't see the enemy force coming down the bulkhead. I would guess they had to be using ropes...

My eyes tracked the darkness off to the left finding where I thought the main bulkhead, a cyclopean wall, was... and where the sector seam of the ship met.

I could see nothing but blackest darkness and inky gloom.

Reaper was on the short halt, watching their sectors. Staring into clean, abandoned alleys that ran through the monstrous warehouses and security doors from which we might get contact if that was to happen. Earlier in the clearing op we'd taken sniper fire from a team of commandos. But their shooting was awful and Wolfy got the angle on the element shooter and his spotter and did them both. They were up on top of a warehouse that was five stories high so we had to breach the warehouse and take the internal stairs up to confirm the kills.

Both had been domed.

Again... Wolfy was here for the violence.

Soaking wet, his three-wolf moon t-shirt clinging to his lean torso, he came close as Punch took a squad up to confirm the kills. Wolfy whispered to me as we waited...

"That was for Soup, Sar'nt."

He then whisper-roared and fist-bumped me.

So that ruined the day.

Later, when I got that contact alert from Gunny that an HK team was on the ground and about to engage, with a company-sized element of commandos coming down the side of the bulkhead wall, descending on ropes twenty decks' length… I don't know… maybe it was the lack of EVC armor… but that felt like a break.

I decided to let go of the weird and whatever I was feeling and just… think positively like all those books say I should.

Hell… why not.

I was taking deep breaths. It was like I could breathe for the first time in years, and if they were here now, I was ready to get our kill on.

And then exploit that.

They'd gotten here somehow.

We had them boxed in at Terminal 95. We couldn't hit. They couldn't leave.

Highway of Death works both ways.

But now… here they were.

So… I was counting this as a break in the clouds.

Don't @ me.

This too shall pass, right?

Eventually this ghost ship was either gonna eat us, or we were gonna turn it into an expanding vapor cloud.

I voted for the expanding vapor cloud.

I motioned for Hauser to come over and began to apprise him of the situation.

"I am aware of the traffic, Sergeant Orion," he told me. "I monitor all company channels and all open EM bands. This is a standard asymmetrical insertion operation by the HK team. They are going to try and set up an ambush on Route Vega. They will use the commandos as a diversion for their real attack."

Hauser knelt down, stared at the wet deck beneath our worn boots, and broadcast a holographic map from his eye creating a simulated sand table with all our hacked information and mapping. This was a trick he could do for us.

He pointed toward Gunny's element.

"Sergeant Gunny and his platoon are here. HKs are here. They will separate from the commandos and use them to attack from this direction if the hunter-killer team leader follows standard combat cyborg attack protocols for this type of operation. They will maneuver here, form a gun line, and attack the platoon from this direction where we do not expect them to be. With this information we can flank them here, Sergeant Orion, and eliminate the team."

I studied the glowing blue map on the wet deck. Everything my friend the killing machine said… was solid.

"All right…"

I tapped the platoon contact and opened a channel.

"Reaper, we got contact ahead. Punch, need you to take your guys and Second forward three blocks up. Stack in these sub-maintenance alleys and stay down until the firefight starts. Hauser and my guys are going in straight at them up the street as they move on Devil. I'll alert Gunny and tell him rear security needs to set up a crossfire. Once that's established, the terminators will fade right into you and you hit them from both sides. Copy…"

Both squad leaders copied and got on the hump.

Then I was on the comm again to Gunny.

"Sar'nt… Hauser says it's going down like this. They're going to push that company-sized element right into you. Go ahead and set up a defense. But… I need your rear security to be ready to set up a crossfire with my guys because you got HKs coming in at your six once contact goes kinetic. Don't worry… we got you, fam. We're gonna roll them from the flank and push into an ambush. You down to clown, Devil Six?"

Long pause. Gunny was pretty SOP in all things. He wasn't Strange-loose yet.

That good feeling I was having between doom and victory… *hovered*, telling me it could go either way.

"We down, Reaper. We definitely down to clown on these tin cans. Devil Six out."

Right then, inside my tiny black heart that's gotten so jaded and so… shriveled… the sun broke out and I felt the same way I did the first time some girl back home said she'd go out with me one night.

I was young then. I felt like I'd conquer the galaxy if such a thing could happen like that.

And it wasn't some girl.

Her name was Cheri Karmen. I never forgot her. It didn't work out. We actually never went out. Stuff happened…

But at that moment… I felt like everything could happen.

I felt like that kid again as the light infantry around me, my guys, Reaper, hustled into the misty rain and gloomy dark, ready to get their mischief on.

Maybe good things can happen… sometimes…

Maybe.

Maybe we could win.

The first rule of war is… you gotta show up.

After that…

Anything can happen.

Even something good.

CHAPTER SEVENTY-SIX

We straight-up chewed them up and spat them out.

Gunfire from Gunny's element went hot in the darkness a few blocks to our right by the time we were in rough positions.

My squad leaders in the ambush positions gave me two clicks as Punch whispered into the comm, "We ready to get our murder on, Sar'nt."

Enemy commandos came at Gunny hurling frags and moving forward in elements. Gunny's gunners patiently dosed them with Pig fire, ruining them as they pushed.

But… they had the numbers.

Four-to-one against one platoon.

The commandos sent in anti-armor force and punched warehouses in tremendous explosions that rocked the sector. Gunny's SDMs opened fire and shot down the anti-armor gunners as the second wave pushed into battle.

That's when we saw the three-"man" team of cyborg killers stalking forward in a wedge. Each had an LMG and a secondary weapon on its back.

Like hulking dark predators, sentinels of war, moving forward, red eyes glowing in the gloom and mist, they pushed in on Gunny's men as we made ready to engage.

They had no idea we were here.

A small jammer Hauser had rigged up was playing hell with the local radar, as was the inherent electromagnetic signature of the ship.

That's when I told my gunners to hit 'em with the three-piece.

Three-piece. Just some slang we use.

"Engage," I whispered with a channel open to Gunny's rear security who I'd just told to be ready with a "Here they come, Devil Six."

Two clicks and a "We ready, Reaper."

"Rage *hawt!*" shouted Slash, the gunner from Third. He would open fire, then my gunners, Hustle and Hoser, would respond as we got the guns to "talk." Then Hauser would engage opportunity targets and pick up their belt changes to keep the volume of fire steady.

Bright tracer fire came suddenly screaming down the dark misty alley from Gunny's rear security team as Slash's fire found the lead terminator and sprayed him with outgoing lead.

"Hits on target," Slash's AG alerted over comm as the *dakka dakka* of the guns spooled up.

Seconds later Hustle laid it on nice and thick all over one of them, his range almost good instantly. He knocked that one down immediately even as the lead 'borg was being rag-dolled by Slash's fire.

Number three opened fire with one hand, moving to the downed number two cyborg and dragging him back for the cover of the building they'd just crossed into the intersection from.

Hauser engaged and used the whole belt on the lead one.

This was a murder and I liked it.

One round must have actually hit the thing in the neck because the head came off and the cyborg just sat down in the middle of the street.

Didn't think that was even possible. I'd never... seen anything like it. And it made me wonder if these HKs, this last team appearing that shouldn't even have been here according to our intel, had been hastily called in from some dusty back storage room where the Monarch engineers kept their damaged wares and maybe not exactly their finest work.

Condition as-is. Buyer beware. Absolutely no returns.

And if that was so... we'd bled them more than I thought, the defenses in this section of the *Dark Star*. They held Terminal 95, which remained... untouchable. But that *she-said-yes* ray of light burned just a little brighter.

Hauser ordered more fire on the 'borg saying it could still pop frags.

By that time Three was dragging Two down the alley and off our *X*.

I clicked the radio over to my two squad leaders.

"Here they come."

Both squads moved up from their positions in the alleys and straight-up wasted both killing machines. Two never regained its boots. Three got shot up so bad it ended up sitting with its back to a warehouse being shot from every direction as it tried to load another belt, its synthetic skin and clothing tearing away and ravaged by our gunfire.

In the end its red glowing eyes just powered down and it sat there with its gleaming skull on its chest... like it was deep asleep and dreaming its soulless dreams of a universe with no biologic life ever again.

Or whatever it is killing machines dream of.

Good things had happened and from that moment, I knew we'd just gotten a window to turn things around and maybe end this.

But still... there were all those dreams and nightmares.

And what Stinkeye had said to me.

"*Don't ask me for help on dat one... ain't no comin' back from where ya's headed. Little King.*"

CHAPTER SEVENTY-SEVEN

In the aftermath of the battle in the supply warehouses and distribution alleys that fed the ship in this sector, it was clear we'd been dealt a solid card finally.

It was Hauser using his tactical analysis combat simulations inside his onboard CPU that spelled out what my tired mind was already catching up with as we consolidated forces, pushed the wounded to the rear in the hands of the medics, and made ready to declare the bulkhead no longer impassable in this sector.

"Negative, Sergeant Orion," stated Hauser as we gathered around the shot-to-hell terminator with its back to the wall. "The failure of this HK and commando team has opened a small window in which to use their route into our primary objective as a means to hit their base. But that window will close if their commander follows standard warfare and planning doctrine."

"Yeah, I see what the tin can is sayin'..." muttered Gunny around his clamped cigar. "We go up and over and follow their route back into their base 'fore they figure out these all dead."

I tapped the comm for the commander.

While I waited, Hauser continued as my squad leaders looked on. Gunny's platoon was still blocking from their position up the street. They'd overrun the badly positioned Anubian commandos and were making sure no more were coming down the ropes we could now see as we peered up through the mist and gloom inside the cyclopean starship, a view that barely hinted at the monstrous size of this vessel even though the mind did not want to accept the fact of its size.

"I estimate we have under four hours before the enemy commander will declare the team dead and seal off the alternate route taken into the sector," stated Hauser. "Most likely the team went dark and even turned off their own comm and transponders to avoid our tracking and sensor systems in order to conduct this operation."

I stared up into the dark, wiping away the falling "rain" coming off the broken water system in this section of the *Dark Star*.

"Hause... that's a combat climb and we're not sure if they disabled the ropes higher up in order to circumnavigate some hatch or cut made into the bulkhead up there..."

"Affirmative, Sergeant Orion. Combat climb protocols will need to be followed to surmount the obstacle... but this unit calculates a sixty-seven-point-six percent possibility that the hunter-killer team command unit left the ropes in place in order to effect a quick disengagement route off their mission profile."

I stared at Hauser in what he probably took for disbelief, or so his human interface software probably reported that this was most likely my response.

I was just tired. Post-violence come-down hitting me harder than usual as I shook out a dart and contemplated conducting a platoon-sized combat climb assault up into what was unknown and unsecured territory… with a difficulty level of… *fall and you're dead.*

Pancake time.

"This route was their only way out, Sergeant Orion. They would have left the egress viable to be used swiftly."

This was the very epitome of things not to do. Tired. Unsupplied. Small force.

But…

"Tin Can's got that right, Sar'nt Orion," grunted Gunny. "My boys can go up and we can follow the route in and hit them from above at the terminal if this leads that way… or wherever it drops out. Or maybe it leads somewhere along the Ring and we got access to the inner hull. Trick is the timing, Sar'nt Orion. Max effect would be if we can get the commander to gin up a direct assault so their forces at the terminal are drawed off and occupied while we come in from above. Then our hit's far more effective and hey… every Devil Dog got his day… we get lucky… maybe we take the terminal."

I smoked and added it all up.

Then…

And I didn't like the numbers at all.

But…

This was our one shot to do it with some surprise instead of what it was shaping up to be… right down the Highway of Death.

Excessive casualties. No two ways about it.

How much, Sergeant Orion… can one man lose.

Even a little, one guy… is too much. I've written enough Strangers to the Universe, Brothers to the End… to hate that phrase.

I… don't want to lose… anyone… ever again.

"Negative, Gunny. Reaper'll do it. Some of my guys have combat climb training from our time on Blue. You guys are hullbusters. We'll need you to go ahead and throw yourselves into those guns at the front and then clear the forward bunkers. Once we get over and in and put fire on them, you'll have a puncher's chance to push down the highway. Copy?"

Gunny hissed and spit some tobacco off into the rainy dark.

"Thanks, young sar'nt. You a real peach that way."

What can I say… I'm a giver.

And before you think worse of me… that climb was almost certain death. Looking up at it scared the hell outta this ol' ruck hobo already, and truth be told… I'd rather push up on those guns waiting at that murder funnel we hoped to crack open from the other side than do the impossible Reaper was about to attempt.

Climb into the dark and unknown… in the rain.

"Hotsoup," I hissed like it was a curse word.

Because it was.

CHAPTER SEVENTY-EIGHT

Warlord, the captain, said we were going for the plan and that he was personally spinning up an assault force to rendezvous with Gunny's platoon near the end of Route Vega.

They'd make the push together if we could put pressure on the terminal.

That is...

If we made the climb up into the top of this sector, found the route through the bulkhead, and then came out in a position to hit the terminal with an advantage... then we'd stack for the attack while the main element under the Old Man, coordinating with Gunny's platoon and supported by all the heartbreakers in Ghost... would start the final attack on the terminal.

Enough *ifs* in there to make this... questionable.

But it was all we had.

And there was that Monarch defending that station against the invaders.

Which was us... the company.

Strange Company.

When the day's pump had begun I'd thought we were at least a week away from the final assault. And I was dreading that day. Now events had changed. We had a small window to go for it.

The anticipated dread was quick to return to the pit of my stomach despite all the "Hotsoups" being handed out as we got our climbing gear ready.

And by *ours*... the gear we'd taken off the dead commandos.

We hadn't brought any as this was not anticipated on today's training schedule.

But life comes at ya fast.

And you're either the xeno on the forward view of the speeding assault trac... or you're the forward view.

The odds our tac plan computers back on the *Spider* had been spitting out at us had never been good for a frontal assault down the Highway of Death. They had been... worse than bad. We didn't have time to input the new intel and data and crunch some numbers and then run some sim variants...

On what we are about to do. But looking up into the gloom at those wet ropes, with most of my guys not combat-climb rated...

Not good.

Still... this felt like an opportunity and just like every commander back to the age of spear and shield... you had to smell it, and feel it, and in the end... let the dice fly and throw your men into the meat grinder to see if you would echo in eternity or something or other.

Or the crows would eat your eyeballs.

If you were a good commander… then you led the spear and shield into the meat grinder… from the front, telling them lies about glory being all that mattered.

When in reality it's just this…

It's gonna suck. But we're gonna do it anyway.

The Old Man didn't say anything over the comm, things were happening too fast, but he didn't say anything about glory. Just that he was going in first against enemy guns set to flat-out murder in high doses.

He'd broken his back for the company and laid it on the line for all of us, and me personally a time or two, well beyond the count of mere numbers.

So I got my guys organized and swore to find some advantage, and take the hell out of it. Hit the enemy harder than they'd ever been hit before.

As Punch likes to say, "Wipe the teeth off their smile."

If just to save a few lives, and the Old Man's, as they threw themselves into that thankless meat grinder to get it done in one, son.

Hotsoup.

The first sergeant.

Whatever.

There is no glory.

I haven't found any yet in this PMC biz.

But I got brothers. And… that means more than I ever thought it would when at first I began.

So whoever gets to be the next keeper of the company logs… here's all my chips. That's all this broke ruck hobo's got left.

Push 'em all in on this one.

Please. Whoever you are.

I have lost too much.

And…

Sometimes you pray, even when you don't believe.

We started up the ropes in the dark and the wet…

CHAPTER SEVENTY-NINE

Just before we started the climb up into the superstructure to reach some kind of position from which we might hit the enemy objective and lay some hate...

Or as we used to say around here until the Hotsoup cult... *Get it on.*

... XO fed the command team a distress signal from another ship.

The last ship in the fleet still broadcasting.

The rest were gone, destroyed, or docked and unable to leave the death-trap ghost ship that was the *Dark Star.*

Oh, Rogue Fleet, *yeeehawww, boys!!!*, I hardly knew ye.

"... chief engineer of the *Dogstar,*" I heard as Reaper made final gear prep to start up the ropes. "We are being overrun... bad guys flexing on our last positions. Bridge crew is... all dead, or... captured by those... monsters. Say again... this is Al... chief engineer of the *Dogstar*. We are preparing to..."

There was a pause, and the signal went all broken and distorted as "Al" came back, his voice warped by the local space-time effects, sounding hollow and distant like he was down at the bottom of some dark elevator shaft he was never gonna get out of.

"... say again... all vessels this vicinity... I'm gonna pop the bottles on the mains and blow *Dogstar* to kingdom come. They're comin' outta the walls! Say again... all ships... brace for impact or move to a minimum safe distance at this time... we are preparing to..."

So there must have been other vessels out there they had sensor pictures of...

Or at least... as of the moment of this last broadcast off the *Dogstar.*

Signal interference asserted itself over the channel in a sudden snowstorm of white noise and I felt something inside me want to reach out and up the gain just to hold on to this guy and let him know he wasn't alone. That we... were with him.

If he was gonna do this...

Then Al was back.

"*You want some, you sons o' bitches... come get some!* This is my last transmission... Go humanity... Don't let these bastards get away with this! Make 'em pay, boys. Navy is with you! *Anchors aweigh, you bastards!*"

Then nothing.

Nothing.

Nothing...

The seconds felt like hours...

Thirty seconds later the *Dogstar*'s blast wave shook the superstructure of the *Dark Star* like some final last angry vengeful blow from a dark titan.

All of us fell silent for a long moment, staring at one another as our minds imagined the worst.

I felt somehow less now, even though I'd never know who Al was.
Fair seas, Al. Whoever you were. You went down legit to the last.
Go Navy.

CHAPTER EIGHTY

The death of the *Dogstar* and her engineer… probably taking an entire Monarch boarding force with him in those last moments… calmed me.

Like any NCO handed a change of mission, hell… like any NCO on any given day… I had that *nothing-will-go-right-and-everything-will-go-horribly-wrong* feeling.

Fine.

Adding in a combat climb into enemy-held territory didn't necessarily… *hearten* me.

Fine. I deal with this too.

There were a myriad of possibilities how everything could go wrong on this. Horribly wrong.

A fall could kill someone. And… could take multiple someones with them. Contact right now, somewhere in the upper reaches… was not, to say the least… *optimal*.

We have to be honest about these things.

Strung out all up and down a vertical surface, we'd be sitting ducks as we went up.

Yeah… the fear had gotten good and deep in me and I ain't ashamed of that. Been there, done that, got the gunshot wounds to show for it.

But Al, whoever he was, surrounded and low on ammo to the point of harsh but accurate insults, hadn't flinched to kill them all given the chance.

Even if it cost him his ship, and his life.

Engineers think of the hierarchy of needs in those terms. Or so it has been in my humble experience.

Ship. Then lives.

So if Al could get it right in the face of certain death… then yeah, this ol' ruck hobo could get it done as best he could until… that same moment of certain death… came to collect on the debt.

My rated climbers were of course Hauser, Punch, Hustle and Hoser, Yahtzee, and surprise surprise… Ulysses Two Alpha Six.

As an Ultra Marine operator of an undisclosed level—he'd said nothing about his experience, but it was clear he was well trained beyond even the average Ultra—he knew his way around the ropes and techniques of combat climb.

I put Punch in charge of providing an incredibly short course on combat climbing for the rest of the platoon who were not skilled at climbing… about ten minutes, congrats, you're now as combat-climb rated as you've got time to be… while the rest of us checked the ropes, made our plans, handed out the D-clips Punch carried by the dozens, distributed some ascenders, and made sure everyone's assault gloves were able to handle the action.

We had to swap out a few on some of the newer guys but again Punch and Ulysses came to the rescue with spare climbing gloves.

Or as Punch put it... "You got one, you got none. You got two... you got one. Simple."

He and a very few others packed spare assault gloves. We got these where they needed to be, and then I organized the climb.

The climb.

Here's how it looked to me from what I could see of it... and Hauser was contributing via his onboard radar and superior optics system...

We were going vertical at first.

Straight up.

So, that's not necessarily the hard part. Near-vertical, or just steep, would have been best. But the ropes dangled through sheer darkness and rain up above five decks high.

This was along a support beam for this section of the hull... a main structural rib, actually. From there we had no clue where the ropes would go. But we were pretty sure they'd need to work over onto the bulkhead wall that separated this vast compartment of the gargantuan ship from the Ring. Then somehow it would need to go along until there was some kind of breach, or maintenance doorway up there where we could not see, that accessed the Ring and gave some way to get a look at Terminal 95 that wasn't ringed by gun positions with interlocking fields of fire and wide-open kill zones.

A gunner's paradise.

We had no idea other than that the OpFor had come this way to ambush us. Now we were gonna use it against them, and backtrack, to surprise attack them.

And if they were smart, they left ambush teams up there, or snipers on overwatch who were already sit-repping command, or mines, or IEDs, or portable auto-turrets... or whatever horrors the Monarch Dark Labs had cooked up to guard against us doing just what we were about to do.

I took my squad up first. We'd secure the first rest high up along this rib, then see what we had to work with up higher.

The clock was burning. We were already approaching three hours until the HK team would be declared overdue, according to Hauser, and then this route in would be considered compromised. At best.

At worst...

There would be an ambush waiting for us.

The captain and the main force from the *Spider* were already on the hump through Route Vega to rendezvous with Gunny's platoon in order to start the diversionary push into Terminal 95.

"Get it on, Strange," I said. But it was really a hoarse whisper.

I hate climbing.

It's... unforgiving.

It was a caterpillar crawl up five stories.

That meant entwining your boot around the rope and using that to push yourself up, then reverse boots and do it again. One after the other. Slow going.

Rest and you clip in, double knot the rope, and let the acids in your muscles disperse.

Then back in and crawl… upward. One foot at a time.

At first the new guys struggled, but in time, because they're younger than me, they got the hang of it and were riding my butt as I peered up into the darkness waiting to see some combat cyborg's red eyes lowering to a scope, ready to dust me from the shadows.

My body dangling as my brains drooled down along my guys…

Fun, huh?

We unhooked our chest rigs, clipped them to our rucks, and let our assault packs dangle ten feet below us as we hauled ourselves up, higher and higher.

Five decks of open-air dangle turned to a major rib of the ship's structure and we had a near-vertical surface to send along.

Klutz lost his grip, flailed and let go… but he was clipped in and only fell twenty feet to dangle into open air, barley missing taking Catboi with him.

Catboi deftly dodged the falling medic and then muttered in his usual autistic monotone… "Catboi… half cat, half boi."

Defeating death was considered worthy of his motto.

I… agreed with that.

I had a different motto and with less polite words.

We got Klutz straightened out. Hauser, who I had following us with his squad, was able to get him back on the ropes and settled. Hauser handled that as I climbed up another five decks along a rain-slick near-vertical rib to reach a "lip" or wide groove in the mammoth ship's curving support rib.

This would be our first rest.

No snipers or combat cyborgs here.

Breathe. But… too much stress. So… wipe sweat or rain away. Look at what's next.

I scanned for mines, IEDs, and other traps before pulling myself up onto the rain-slick lip.

My muscles were screaming from sheer fatigue.

But, by the time we made this section we'd already burnt an hour on the ascent.

Sitreps from Main Force indicated they were halfway up Route Vega now.

Hit times and LDAs were starting to be coordinated on the fly.

Never good. But… all we had.

That clock… she burnin'.

XO was reporting all quiet among what was left of the great fleet we'd pursued the Monarchs all the way out here with.

This felt like… a last shot now.

No one else was gonna get it done.

No one was gonna come save us.

So, I dangled there at the lip of the rib, scanning the dark of the groove above and seeing how I'd get up in there. Looking for those traps perhaps the attacking hatchet force had left behind…

I saw nothing and muttered, "Well… here goes nothing… Reaper Six going in."

No one said anything and I could hear them holding their breath over the comm.

Waiting for the deafening det that signaled the end of the platoon sergeant.

I coulda used a smoke.

Once in the groove of the rib I scanned the rib and watched it climb toward the roof of the compartment. Less steep, but still steep. I saw the knotted rope lying in the gutter of the groove the attacking force had left behind when they'd come this way.

The Bastard was on my ruck. I shucked my sidearm and bent down, muscles trembling, hands shaking like I had the DTs.

I tested the knotted rope, giving it a good tug.

It was secure.

Now we had a very steep ascent, with the aid of a knotted rope. This would prove to be tricky what with all the slipping and the IEDs we had to clear.

But an hour later we pushed through the opening they'd cut in the bulkhead.

Another ten stories higher.

"Don't look down, Sarge," Punch said to me as he came up. "Ain't good for yer mental state."

I tried to say something but my voice was too dry to make sounds.

I just nodded.

And he was absolutely right.

It was... quite a view considering you could just fall to your death instantly on one wrong rain-slick step.

The structure up here was so thick. They must have used industrial-grade plasma torches rated to cut starship hulls in order to sneak into the areas we'd taken from them.

On the other side of the cut was a landing used for hull inspection.

And below...

Terminal 95.

All defenses were in view.

The massive tube of the Ring, like some cyclopean subway system of space giants, stared off into vast misty differences here inside the ship.

Our target, Terminal 95, was about halfway up the near side of the tube. There were multiple rail lines running the length of the tunnel, roadways too, and a large open space in the center where it was clear dropships and small cargo freighters could fly.

A bridge launched out from the terminal on this side and through the various rail lines and across the vast open space to a wide platform preceding a massive armored blast door that led into the inner hull.

That was where we'd need to go.

And that massive circular vault door was currently... wide open.

As though Lady Death had no need for additional defenses beyond the impassable Highway of Death and Terminal 95.

Monarch arrogance. Why change now?

Through that open doorway... lay our objective. The inner hull.

All of our intel-gathering had given us no... intel... no insight... into what we would find inside the inner hull, this secure ship within a ship. And the sight of it... of what was so preciously protected at the very heart of the massive experimental disc *Dark Star*... was... mesmerizing.

And...

... extraordinary.

CHAPTER EIGHTY-ONE

When the Little Girl got killed everything went pear-shaped.

But that would come later, after we assaulted the right flank of the objective, Terminal 95, as Main Force started to push up the Highway of Death that was the last of Route Vega.

"Main Force" was the call sign we'd established for the combined elements of the captain's reserve forces pulled from the LZ around the *Spider*...

... PDCs were now spun up to full and only a few personnel led by XO held the line back there. Even Cutter had moved forward to do what he could do for the soon-to-be badly wounded...

... and Gunny's platoon, who'd moved into position near the Highway of Death's entrance through the massive sector bulkhead and into the final objective before we hit the inner hull.

Terminal 95 was the objective.

The inner hull just beyond across a bridge through the Ring.

What we'd do after that...

Well, we'd cross that bridge when we got there.

If, that dark part of my mind, the fears and dreams and PTSD on down payment, tried to tell me.

I told it to shut up.

It was Lifetaker time. Heartbreakers only.

"You look like ya gonna kill someone, Big Sarge," said Punch as we worked our end of the captain's plan just before we moved to our assault positions.

"Looks like it," I grunted and moved on. Time... I had none. Funny how you think you have lots at points in your life, and then sometimes... you are acutely aware of how little you ever had.

When my Oma died... funny what you think about right before it's time to shoot people to decide who gets more slices of birthday cake... when my Oma died, right before she died I held her hand one afternoon. We all knew we were saying goodbye now.

She said, like in a dream, she'd been sleeping a lot, she said to me, "I was born. I was a little girl, and then... now I'm here... dying. It all moves so fast."

Then she was gone.

Funny what you think about in the moments before zero hour.

Plans were made, hit times were agreed upon, and then my element, Reaper, four understrength squads, went up and over and through the sector bulkhead one last time. Then we made our way down along a crude maintenance stairway the HK-led ambushing force had used to infiltrate our held areas of the ship.

We went dark after breaching the bulkhead. No comm. No transponders. We were doing it old-school now. Hit times, LOAs, and marks for contact.

We had to avoid detection for the Old Man's plan to work.

The plan... Main Force would start what was supposed to be a "dedicated attack" up the Highway. In truth it was really just "sound and fury" and a cautious advance using whatever cover could be found, or improvised, to make it look like a badly stalled assault the enemy might want to come out and take advantage of.

Listen, most of all warfare is stupid tricks that work. Especially if you are infantry.

As this happened, Reaper element would come down the stairs that wound along an internal rib of the superstructure of the ship, fan out into three combat wedges, and storm the right flank of the enemy positions, taking up position inside the terminal from which to shoot at as much of the enemy as we could.

The commander's intent was this would cause enough forces to be pulled away from the forward defense for Stinkeye to pull some... *magic*... try that in your next op order... then Main Force would storm the front defenses with extreme violence of action while bad guys were occupied by us.

Speed.

Surprise.

Extreme overwhelming violence.

In other words once the enemy thought they had bad guys in the wire... hey, that's us, Reaper... they'd freak out and want to stomp us out with all they could spare in order to maintain integrity of their forward line.

They'd shift assets at us and... here's the fun part... we'd have to hold out for a hot minute. No picnic. Trust me.

Now comes the speed.

Main Force had to get up that highway *fast*. Stinkeye could play tricks, yes, and he even had those fireballs he'd held out on us about...

I am still pissed about that.

But the fighting still needed to be done by our guys.

So they'd move up fast, probably still under solid fire, and use indirect fire to saturate the defenses, "walking" whatever they had to throw indirect-wise as they moved danger-close to the exploding ordnance.

Chungo was even coming out with his mortar drones and if he could get them in through the murder funnel, that would make this part much more effective.

Just had to get past the emplaced gun teams and everyone on the *X* pointing their various bang sticks at that opening through the sector bulkhead.

Chungo's problem... not mine.

Now came the surprise part.

Surprise, we're climbing over your defenses and shooting you and stabbing you. A lot. Which was what Main Force led by the captain was gonna do coming through the front door at the same time we hit from the sides and above.

This is also the violence-of-action part. Meet violence with overwhelming violence. And then some.

If it worked, we'd split a hardened defense into two parts, then roll them up at the center.

See *plans are great until the enemy is met* for smarter people than this hobo's thoughts.

If it didn't work, the plan, then we'd probably both get whacked individually in our elements, and especially hard for the element that held out the longest as the enemy defense forces would now angrily reconsolidate on our survivors and... pretty much show no mercy.

Not that we asked for any.

But it was pretty clear this was our last shot. Failure here and we'd have to pull back to the *Spider* and evac. We did not have the numbers to continue this operation.

That was clear.

And I doubted many would survive even a successful op like this, much less a failure.

There was talk of uncoupling the NSM, nuclear space mine, from the *Spider*, and carrying it from its place in aft stores, into the *Dark Star*, and detonating it as close as we could get to the inner hull.

Again, this ship had already been hit by three nuclear weapons and minimal damage had been done to one sector. Confidence was *not* high that the NSM could do any better.

The NSM is a last card we keep just in case we want an immediate self-destruct, and it is a highly guarded company secret. So secret that in the logs I've never referred to such a weapon other than those of the same type, the MNSM, massive nuclear space mines—theirs are necessarily larger—on Monarch Battle Spires. But now that we are at a point of no return... yeah. We got one too. We never talk about it and only to refer to it in the command team as... *that thing*. It can only be manually detonated, which is why the combat cyborg infiltrator couldn't find it in the system when he hacked into M.O.M.

It isn't in the system. It's just in the ship.

Back to the plan...

If it, the plan, failed... then we probably failed. If the log doesn't continue... whoever finds this... then I probably got it on the X.

Nice knowin' ya.

So we moved down the maintenance stairs along the darkness of the rib twenty decks down and into the gargantuan Ring tube itself.

Literally one of the most amazing things I've ever seen.

It's hard to believe humans could build such a thing.

With twenty minutes to go before the hit, we set up a patrol base and I went forward to do a quick leader's recon of what we were hitting.

I'd had a pretty good look from high above. Most of the enemy defenses were pointed right down toward the Highway where our guys would soon be pushing.

The terminal was on the near side of the tube. In the center, mag-rail tracks, several of them, entered from left and right continued on the loop around the entire ship, I assume, to deliver cargo. There were even landing platforms for light cargo drops and small ships and I assumed all this was conducted during normal operation, and not a ship under siege-boarding status.

We saw no traffic, rail or drop.

All quiet on the X.

Hauser and I went forward and did the scout, identifying the entries and sentries we'd need to pop to infiltrate the station and get in position. I targeted the gun pits we could put fire on from where we were gonna set up, then we went back and briefed the platoon about what was gonna happen next.

Everyone backbriefed me on their parts.

And... they did it Catboi-style. Even Punch.

And... quietly, in our own way... we laughed a little at ourselves. It broke the tension because we knew we were about to do some heavy lifting, exposed and surrounded.

It had been a tough crawl down those stairs mostly on our bellies just to avoid detection on the insertion to the hit.

Five minutes to said hit.

I'd lead and take Catboi with me on point. We needed to do two sentries on the far edge of the terminal. Then the platoon could infiltrate and we could kick things off.

Catboi might be a high-functioning autist... but he was a hitter. I handed him a suppressed sidearm but he already had a can for his Catboi secondary that had buxom catgirls laser-etched all over the barrel.

What remained of my platoon waited there, stacked and ready, hunched down underneath their overloaded assault rucks, carrying all the gear we could don for what was about to come.

One of Punch's guys asked him something and I heard him say, "Livin' the dream," in the dark and cool of the giant tube that rose up all around us.

Then I heard Mad Max the gunner from Third say, "You know, a nightmare's also a dream, Punch."

I studied my watch. Old-school. Everything was turned off. I always... carry a watch.

"Yeah," rumbled Punch. "Heard that somewhere."

The hands got closer to the time hack.

There in the massive tube that was easily thirty decks high... all was quiet, shadows, and blue dark. The moment before battle.

I wanted wind in my hair. A horse under me. I wanted to howl a war cry.

The mammoth ship hummed on some long low note I'd never really listened to. And now did.

I tried to give my mind a rest for a half a sec... but it was useless. There was too much to think about.

I looked at everyone in Reaper. One last time.

One minute to go now.

I studied every one of them, checking their gear, but really... stamping their faces, living and alive, scared, ready, bored and whatever... but alive this one last time when it was just us.

After this... we would be different forever.

How much, Sergeant Orion...

Some would...

Come back to us.

Thirty seconds.

Everyone has someone like Marcus's wife and kid out there. Someone who just wants you to make it back.

Everyone...

Or at least I like to think that's so.

The mark passed and on cue I heard the first sounds of our guns down the distant Highway of Death.

Then the gun teams of the enemy, closer to us, opened up in response.

Now it was on.

"Get it on, Strange," I hissed in the dark. And we stood and moved in, as quietly as possible, with murder in our hearts.

CHAPTER EIGHTY-TWO

She got hit early in the fight. The first time she got hit.

I… should have pulled her back.

But…

I didn't have time to get to her. Hustle and Hoser were taking rounds and Hustle got hit pretty bad as we began to engage from the flank.

We were about a minute or two into the fight but it already felt like forever. I was on him, trying to plug a hole and keep pressure on it. She and Hobo Mike were dragging Rockstar out from under fire when she took the first round.

Rockstar looked bad, but he'd make it. He was out of the fight though with a shattered leg.

If Cutter hadn't been close by, he would have died. Cutter was just behind Main Force pushing up the Highway now.

But in those first moments it felt like forever away and I saw how they might never make it and we would be surrounded and cut off forever.

I'd watch everyone die just like I had in my dreams.

I saw her take one right in the chest plate from the enemy infantry now being redirected in at us to seal the line and retake the right flank of their defense.

Hustle and Hoser had opened fire on the rightmost gun pit and killed the commandos there, in the first moments of our surprise attack. Then they'd started engaging the defenders forward there.

The insertion had been perfect.

Catboi and I had crept up and smoked the two sentries to the rear of the right flank, then directed the rest of the platoon to their fighting positions.

Then we opened fire.

It's never this easy, I was thinking when it all began to go sideways.

Ain't that how it always is?

I put Mad Max and his AG, Bad Bet, covering the inside of the terminal which led to the center of their defense and then their left flank. Their gun was ringing out loudly in the vast empty space of marble and chrome as they engaged the first responders to our incursion. Belt-fed baddies, they cut down commandos in bulk. And still more got pushed in. Shattered glass exploded in every direction as the enemy returned fire at us.

Now there were two fights going on for the enemy.

One forward.

And one against us.

It was here, as she and Hobo Mike dragged the badly wounded Rockstar out from under fire, that she got hit.

Little Girl.

She fell, tried to get up but couldn't breathe due to the impact being so traumatic against her plates.

Klutz dashed through incoming fire doing that hero thing and dragged her back for cover.

"She's hit!" I was screaming as Hustle bled beneath me.

"I'm good, Sar'nt. Go... go... help her!" grunted the AG. But he wasn't *good,* and I couldn't take my hands off the pressure dressing I had down.

Nearby, Hoser, now running the gun on his own, hefted it, swung it over to a new angle, and engaged a cluster of enemy troopers coming up the steps on the front side of the terminal to kill us.

His raking fire brutally cut them down with little fanfare.

"Hang in there, Huss... need ya on the belts, buddy!"

"Doin' my best, Hose... but I got some holes, man..."

I looked around. Catboi was nearby, covering behind a large carved stone trash receptacle that looked more modern art than utilitarian.

"Catboi, get a belt in that gun!" I shouted.

"Catboi moving..."

He ran, grabbed the belts and with some help from Hustle got it done. Hoser began to fire, training Catboi right there in the fight how to AG at the pro level.

"Keep the belt straight!" he barked.

"Catboi straightening the belt..."

"Keep the brass away from the barrel! Make little piles, Catboi!" grunted Hoser, teeth gritted and hard face full of *get it on* murder as he reshouldered the Pig and engaged with a long burst on a new group. Brass and linkage frenetically flew away.

"Catboi making piles..."

Klutz came up on me fast, tapping my shoulder and trying to get as much cover as he could in the improvised gun position we'd created.

More of them were coming in at all angles. The incoming was thick.

"I got this, Sar'nt," said Klutz, taking over Hustle's pressure dressing. "Get back in the fight!"

I looked up and scanned for Little Girl. She was back and working on Rockstar to get a tourniquet around his wounded leg, across the concourse from our position.

"She took it in the plate," explained Klutz. "She's okay, Sar'nt. Maybe a cracked rib."

But I saw blood...

Her fatigues were dark and wet near her ribs...

My gun teams were under fire.

I had wounded.

We had to hold the line here or else the whole plan, and perhaps the company... were done. The outgoing fire toward Main Force had gone from absolutely apocalyptic to... half that. It was happening. We were drawing them off and the main assault was pushing forward.

Then the enemy started tossing frags in at us. The terminal was suddenly alive with deafening explosions. The gunners stayed on the guns anyway, blasting away at the positions outside, taking fragments, getting cut up and in one case... took out a gun team.

Most of the enemy was now repositioning to get away from the kinetic glare of our gun teams where there shouldn't be gun teams, hoping to still be able to engage forward against Main Force.

Surprise was now in full effect. Next came violence. And lots of it if we were gonna pull this off.

The jury was still out...

The verdict was in doubt...

Armed conflict can change in half a second and I knew that more than anyone...

Hell... I'd used it to stay alive a few seconds longer more than a few times.

I got cut by frag in two places, but it was just blood, and it ran down from my forehead into my eyes.

One frag killed my last New Guy as I tried to get a bandage around my head and hope my brains weren't leaking out.

Another grenade knocked out Slash and Runs. Both gunner and AG were badly wounded and the gun was canked. They'd been placed in the middle of my defense and Hauser was there with his Pig to engage forward and pick up the slack.

Grenades were going off like fireworks as Hauser stood there and held the line, getting ripped to shreds by blasts, Pig blaring away like a death machine at anything he could.

The frags suddenly stopped.

Our ears were ringing despite ear pro.

That was when the Little Girl left her spot with Rockstar, who was stabilized, and moved forward to help the gun team.

Runs was screaming bloody murder and Slash was out. From here... they were lower than my current position... it looked bad.

She got to them and then got drilled by someone.

That was when she began to die even though she kept working on Run who was bleeding out everywhere.

His arm was gone below the elbow.

I had my SDMs, squad designated marksmen, looking out for two HVTs. High-value targets. We knew there was a Monarch in play. We also knew there was one Bishop.

Yahtzee.

Eights.

And Wolfy, of course.

The frags had stopped now and that meant we were about to get pushed really hard. Grenades are usually deployed preparatory to an impending assault to take, or retake, a position.

"Cover me!" I barked at Hustle and raced forward to get to her, hearing that little girl she once was telling me in my head, *You always look out for me, Sergeant. You always have.*

I had to get to her before the next push came.

Bloody red autumn leaves began to fall across my vision... or maybe it was the blood drooling down into my eyes.

My ears were ringing, or maybe it was that hell music that came when the Wild Thing decided to show up...

Not now, I thought, thinking I needed to manage the battle and lead my men, instead of going the full apocalypse beast mode of Doom 88...

Come back to us, Marcus...

Deep red, arterial-bleeding blood drooled away from her as she tried to do something about the screaming and thrashing Runs who was fighting her as she tried to save his life.

Slash looked dead.

But he wasn't.

And that Monarch.

In about two minutes Chungo was going to make it rain steel on their front line. Main Force had pushed through the sector bulkhead and were ready to make a final rush toward the last defenses themselves.

Chungo's drone-mortars had made it through and were deploying, throwing out their mag-plates and getting ready to auto-load munitions to lob at the enemy. Meanwhile Chungo had a recon drone up and was tagging enemy positions for his indirect spread.

In two minutes he was going to score a direct hit on Lady Death who was directing the attack from a fortified bunker near the action.

Killed dead instantly.

One of Chungo's drones was gonna drop an eighty-eight in there and kill everyone there in the pit.

Including her.

No *Big Boss Fight*. No epic spectacuthriller moment. Just death from above courtesy of the mortars.

And if you ask any infantry... well, they'd tell you that's how it's done, son.

Enemy SDMs were trying to drill Chungo and anyone else moving, but Chungo is surprisingly agile when he needs to be.

It didn't stop them from shooting at him, though. And he was sucking dirt when he needed to, his terrible cigar clenched and mashed as he muttered, undoubtedly, "Got somethin' for ya..."

Their gun teams were at half strength and seemed to have trouble both "talking" their guns and keeping the belt changes staggered.

Talking... interspersing the six- to eight-round bursts so a continuous rate of fire can be kept up across separate elements with a combat team.

It's a skill and when it's done right... thing of beauty. Ask any NCO.

One gun team was blaring away frantically and it actually sounded like they were just riding the lightning.

Their gun had gone runaway on the belts, now just firing without the ability to be stopped.

Sounds fun, and it is... not good tactically, though.

So, I thought as I rushed forward, we were gonna get a break here...

Thought the ruck-hobo NCO optimistically.

Silly ruck hobo...

If it can go wrong... it will.

Then the Bishop appeared, coming in through one of the tall, shattered glass apertures of the terminal from the left flank.

Preceding the assault like some frag grenade... which she was... of a kind.

I saw her... she lowered her head, pulled back a ragged cloak, revealed a shaved perfectly sculpted head, otherworldly eyes, and touched her temples with long porcelain fingers...

... then my brain exploded in a sudden bright white light.

I was... somewhere else for a long moment...

I woke up on my back, with the worst headache I've ever... ever... had.

Fun, huh?

Especially in the middle of a fight.

By now the Main Force was pushing in, double-tap-stabbing the last of the commandos. I rolled over, my skull on fire like it was filled with broken flaming glass.

I must have been out for at least a minute, maybe two... which is forever in a battle.

Yahtzee had domed the Bishop.

Her body was sitting down with her back against a chrome column, half her skull missing. Red-mist spray about halfway up the column.

... I'd been somewhere else for a moment in the mental blast. Forgotten all about the battle...

... My mind was swimming through cotton and cloud...

Now I remembered the Little Girl. Our medic who'd become a woman and joined the company.

She'd been hit.

I jerked my head to where she'd been last.

She was there, lying over Run who was still screaming. Her body was utterly limp, looking like all the life had gone out of it.

But she'd gotten the tourniquet around what was left of Run's arm.

Saving him.

Cutter could work with that.

"No!" I shouted and ran for her, feeling like I was gonna throw up. Knowing I didn't have time for that right now...

You've always watched out for me, Sergeant.

CHAPTER EIGHTY-THREE

Not to the bar did I go...

When the Bishop blasted me with what Stinkeye would later tell me was "da psionic blast, Little King. Powerful, dat one."

But to the Wild Thing's moon orbiting the well of destruction at whose center is the Heart of Darkness.

His memories...

His timeline...

All I can say is the blast, that mental blast of the Bishop was like... a *download*. It unlocked the Wild Thing, all his memories... all his grief, for me.

The constant observer.

Marcus...

He was aware they were waiting for him... but... the Little Girl had ensnared him so hard... that he could not leave her, could not forsake her.

Come back to us, his wife had written in the text he kept in his HUD when he'd gone into battle as Doom88.

Part of his powers were just... the Little Girl's, were just stepping into all those strong emotional ties he had for his wife, and the baby, his... *little girl*... and making them about her.

A... defense mechanism for a powerful orphan with no one to protect her.

Which was odd.

"*She kinda a mule*," Stinkeye had told me. But I had no idea what that meant.

As a woman, a medic in the company, she was not like that. She was... pretty selfless.

See how she'd just died...

I didn't know about that yet. Hadn't yet seen her death on the *Dark Star*. But here... with Task Force Raven... Earth Defense Force... beside the Oblivion Gate...

Here I already knew. Here I... felt.

My mind tried to process that.

But it couldn't in this place of his memories and bloody autumn leaves raining down across my eyes, and soul.

I have one.

He needed to go home now.

She'd wrapped what looked like tendrils, or ragged grave shrouds... about him in that moment he'd "rescued" her...

The lost little orphan somehow on this strange cinnamon moon.

But something close by... on this ship... was unraveling those shrouds.

The *Dark Star*.

A neutron star at its heart. Its power. Its... there was more but I couldn't understand that now...

I heard Stinkeye's ragged voice.

"Da heart, Little King..."

Whatever we were near... it could disentangle him. Free him.

The Heart of Darkness.

He could... go home...

Come back to us, Marcus...

When he was not... *summoned*... to defend her... when he was not summoned he wandered that other strange moon, among the dead and demons, waiting for her call. Her call to summon him back once more.

To slay for her as Doom88.

Her champion.

It was like... he was trapped in amber here in this time on this moon swirling about this mad maelstrom of other worlds that were us.

"All Ravens... the evac to the LZ is on final... Pull back... Pull back..."

Chatter and comm in his bloody HUD.

But he would not.

He has not.

He... protects her.

He waits.

Even as the inky shrouds come loose.

Even now.

I watched all this from his mind, near him, following his boots through the cinnamon sands of that strange, other, moon.

Like a ghost here.

I can see the drops in the distance...

Soon they will leave.

If he disentangles, he can return...

If he doesn't...

Stinkeye was there with me now, but stone-cold serious, and sober.

Like a Stinkeye never seen before.

"He close enough, Little King... It can suck him in... and you... in both forever now. No dustoff at the LZ. No more protecting her... Look..."

He pointed his bony scarred old muddy finger at the Heart of Darkness that all these other Earths were swirling around like some maelstrom, or whirlpool at the center.

Even now Earths we'd never known were being sucked in and destroyed.

Crushed into nothingness.

All those other... *us*.

The shrouds, black and ethereal that were wrapped around the Wild Thing, and the Little Girl as she was walking in front of him, her leading, he the eternal sentinel following... were coming undone...

He could leave soon.

But if he didn't...

The Heart of Darkness would take him.

"And whoever else he anchored to," said Stinkeye. "Da Heart will take dem both."

I knew that was me.

That was what happened after I got blasted.

There are other worlds than these.

CHAPTER EIGHTY-FOUR

Stinkeye was there, on the *X* now, watching what was happening like some junkie gambler who'd bet it all on some janky horse race beyond the limits of the shadiest starport... fists clenched, eyes intent like he could will his bet to pull ahead of the pack and claim his final ticket that would make all the wrongs... right.

One last time.

I was throwing up and crawling toward the medics working the Little Girl...

And the red leaves were gone now.

Now... I looked on in horror as they swirled about Ulysses Two Alpha Six...

Who was standing there in stoic... rage.

Gripping his weapon tightly.

And then I knew...

He... loves her.

The black shrouds no one else could see were flying up from her dead body.

I was supposed to...

No one else was seeing this.

Protect her.

And...

I had failed.

No one could see the tendrils that were like black veils, or strands of deepest space...

Certainly not Klutz who was working on her, muttering, "Come on, girl... you got this..." as he continued chest compressions and Bender got ready to hit her with a booster of some sort.

She was on her back, staring lifelessly up at eternity.

She was gray and turning blue...

She was gone now.

I've seen it enough to know.

You've always protected me, Sergeant.

I don't think anyone saw Ulysses becoming the Wild Thing... transforming...

I did.

Or the black shrouds...

His rage as he dropped his weapon.

Or the swirling bloody autumn leaves...

He was... screaming silence...

Makes no sense. But I could hear it.

Maybe just me and Stinkeye. Maybe.

"Stay with me, girl," said Klutz. Working hard. Sweating. Doing that hero thing. "Gimme another two hundred, Bender…"

"Ain't gonna do it, Klutz… she gone, man…"

Klutz swore. He never swears. Bender got the dose ready.

"New force coming down the bridge," said Gunny striding in, weapon at the ready, like some duke in a play after the slaughter of all the main players. Justice arrived. Normalcy restored. His men like wolves came in.

I watched her on the ground and wanted… to wail.

To tell the universe it was made of stone!

Down near the enemy gun pits and defenses the other wedges of Main Force were still sweeping and shooting.

"Cap'n says we gotta hold," grunted Gunny, eyeing the bridge the next counterattack was coming down.

We did not have the numbers.

Stinkeye came near.

"Ya didn't know, Little King…" he said wickedly. Mischievously. Malevolently.

This was a lot to process.

Understatement.

Ulysses turned like some dead zombie and began to walk toward the bridge, the same bat-like butterflies wrapping around him now.

A dark sudden storm no one else but the war wizard and I could see.

The apocalypse armor forming. Wild Thing. Doom88.

His soul… just *screaming* for her.

An Ultra is almost a monk. There is no love for Ultras. There are girls though. Prizes. Slaves. Rewards.

But never… love.

I could hear that scream of his and it's a thing I never want to hear again. I don't think, what with all the chaos of the battle and going right into another one… I don't think anyone else could.

"I cast ma powers all over him, Little King. Made he love her," crooned Stinkeye wickedly. "Now he gonna hijack dat Wil' Thing o' hers and take it right into da Heart o' Darkness. Big explosion comin'… Little King. Dis one… dis for all da marbles, Little King…"

He laughed like a maniac.

Maniacally.

Then Stinkeye turned toward the bridge like some high priest of chaos and whooped as the Wild Thing's primary of mass destruction came online and began to eat up the enemies I could not see down there.

The last counterattack had no idea what it was getting into.

Mass slaughter.

Death.

Revenge.

"We got Inquisitors!" someone shouted from the defense the captain was trying to get up and going before this counterattack came down on us hard. We hadn't seen them before. Inquisitors. But Cook's interrogations… and there were… more of them than I'd like to say… Cook's interrogations had given us a description. And these psionic warriors… the counterattack coming now forward across the bridge to meet us here at the last-stand defense of the inner hull across the Ring from Terminal 95… these met that description.

We had two choices now.

Fight.

Or run.

Only a fight would get us what we'd come for.

"Ah…" roared Stinkeye. "Dey gonna get a fight now, Little King. We gonna blow this ship to kingdom come now!"

Then he turned and spat at the bridge, and the inner hull on the other side of it, and the micro-neutron star swirling inside it they used for a power core… and more…

Fantastic to imagine.

Utterly.

Mind-blowing.

"Now ya's gonna get what ya's long deserved, ya miserable bags o' bones!" he called out at the Monarchs still hiding behind the last big door to the inner hull.

He hooted, hollered. He raged.

"You…" I started to say, head pounding, world swirling… spinning… all of it into the maelstrom that was the heart.

"YES I DID, LITTLE KING!" raged Stinkeye, his voice ragged and hoarse as he did an impish little devil jig right there on the *X*.

"Iss my back pay for what dey done ta me and all'a us, Little King. Is my back pay!"

Then he came close.

"I couldn't lose ya, Little King… so I swapped him out for da Ultra. He'll go in dere and kill 'em all. Entangled… he'll destabilize da Heart's gate and blow dis ship right into da maelstrom…"

"The Heart's gate?"

"Yasssss… Little King… dat star in dere is a gate to where da real Heart is chewin' up dem worlds. If he goes in… pure death localized. Death for all dem damned Monarchs dat's left in dere doin' what it is dey do. Evil. Destruction and terror. Dis my back pay, you sons o' da devil!"

The last force of the Monarchs, the Inquisitors, their final hole card we'd been warned about through field interrogations, came up the bridge.

And there was no craft or guile, or tactics… in this last attack.

It would be a brawl.

Them against the Wild Thing.

I threw up again.

Klutz told the dead girl to, "Stay with me!"

There was… real ache in his voice.

What is a hero… someone who keeps going when no one else does. Maybe. I don't know.

The Inquisitors were the Monarchs' last best defenders.

Psionic warfighters, they were all but unstoppable. Supposedly. Shooters with battle rifles they'd pursued the art of with feverish religious devotion. They also had limited ability to mess with your mind to attack.

Vision disruption.

Distraction.

Fear of your darkest secrets.

We'd had strong concerns about messing with these when it came time to breach the inner hull where they were supposedly stationed.

Now they were being pushed out.

The Monarchs had some idea how bad things were.

We'd deal with that when the time came, we'd told ourselves in the briefings.

Talk of using the NSM abounded.

When in doubt... go nuclear.

Attend and know wisdom.

There weren't any war crimes anymore.

There was just war.

Which... is really what it's always been.

Inquisitors wore ragged rust-colored cloaks that covered spartan frames and chest rigs full of mags.

They chanted code.

They had grenades and wicked knives and they were basically holy warriors for the Monarch cause.

The final devotees.

Long feared, myths of rumors really.

Finally revealed.

Not a lot...

"Gimme another two hundred cc's!"

"Klutz, man... give it..."

But enough to ruin our assault and get us to pull back to the LZ.

Mission over.

Fail.

Except now Ulysses as the Wild Thing was going in after them.

Because... unbeknownst to me... he and the Little Girl, or our medic as a full-grown young woman, had been having... a thing.

No Stinkeye magic needed.

It just... happens.

Who knew...

Apparently a few did, I found out later.

And now she was dead and Stinkeye had somehow planned all this with the intent of aiming the Wild Thing at the Heart of Darkness, or the gateway to it, that was at the center of this strange, fantastic, cursed ghost ship of the universe's tyrants.

Okay... lot to process.

Apparently... love was the secret weapon we never knew we had.

I...

Then Chief Cook showed up on the *X*, right in the middle of our chaos and mess... with *his* secret weapon...

And then... things got *really weird*.

CHAPTER EIGHTY-FIVE

"What's in the canister, Chief?"

There was a fifty-gallon canister marked for dangerous hazmat chemicals destruction. Various wires and timers had been added.

And Chief Cook had written on the side in permanent marker, *The Only Good Commie, is a Dead Commie*. I recognized his bizarre penmanship as I'd seen it before in a series of cryptic notes he'd supposedly not written making death threats against his own life.

Long story, no time right now.

Chief Cook inhaled deeply inside his mask and as he did, faint wisps of stinky smoke drifted up from it. There were hints of sandalwood. He was wearing a full bright yellow engineering room reactor suit straight from the *Spider*'s engineering section.

No one wore those.

But they were there in case we ever had an engineering section again.

Around his waist was of course his spartan pistol belt and two skinned forty-fives. Holsters highly polished.

Inside his mask… he wore mirrored aviator shades. Now he was smiling that soulless tombstone smile of his like he hadn't a concern in the world.

Like he was holding a pair of Red Dragons in a high-stakes game of Cheks.

His voice was muffled, and we had no idea what he was saying because of the thick rubbery mask he wore. Our ears were still ringing from all the explosions inside the terminal and… a whole lotta gunfire that had gone along with it.

Out there, on the bridge… the Inquisitors were being cut down by Ulysses the Wild Thing.

Suddenly Klutz shrieked, "Got a pulse! I got a pulse!"

He started ox on her, working the rubber diaphragm slowly.

"Well…" I muttered, seeing some color start to flood back into her cheeks. I thought she was dead.

Thought… I'd… failed her.

Her eyes fluttered, focused, and then seemed to lock in on me for a moment as the two medics worked on her and the company readied itself for another fight even though the Wild Thing was out there cutting everything that opposed us down.

The chief ripped off his gas mask.

"Pure nightmare fuel, Sergeant Orion. That's what's in this little beauty!"

He sounded… very confident.

He patted the hazmat drum like it was some neat new toy. But he talked about it like it was our salvation come at last.

I was… spent. My head ached. It was looking like some kind of fight was headed our way… and this wasn't over.

I had little left to give at the moment… but hell, why not, I thought.

This was most likely his… *secret weapon*. The one he'd been working on for most of the boarding op. Disappearing for weeks. Surfacing looking mad and wild-eyed.

It was probably gonna get us killed.

"*Aaand*… what are we supposed to do with it, Chief?"

"Clock's burning, Sergeant Orion. That giant bank vault of a door is gonna close the minute they realize their Inquisitors ain't no match for the Wild Thing. And that ol' drunk's doomsday weapon ain't gonna do the trick if my math is right. We gotta find a transport now, load Dr. Good Vibes' special gas canister, then roll it right into the inner hull. If we're lucky… this will do the trick and there won't be any airlock between the deployment-infection point, and… the rest of the Monarch lair… whatever the hell that crazy scene is in there."

I'd seen the scene in there too. On the other side of the open massive door into the inner hull. It was… crazy.

"So tell me what it is, Chief."

"No time, Orion. We need to get the hustle on."

Then he seemed to dance a little and hum to himself. The Dr. Good Vibes sign was bad. It was an alter ego he only used when he was at his most… insane.

Read… dangerous.

It had surfaced here, now, at… what we were in the middle of. Not good.

I thought to myself, *This might as well happen.*

The medics were getting the Little Girl ready to transport. Cutter was coming up. A collapsible stretcher was being rolled out. The rest of the wounded were being organized.

Out there on the bridge, the battle between the Wild Thing and the Inquisitors… sounded like the end of existence itself.

If he didn't kill them all, they'd come for us… and we… did not have the numbers. Fact. No two ways about it.

"I'll secure a cargo loader from the rear of the station," said Hauser. "We can secure the weapon and take it downrange to the vault door that guards the entrance to the inner hull. We can deploy it there if we can penetrate the enemy line of advance."

"See, Orion…" crooned the chief, suddenly back from whatever thug-life concert he'd just been grooving to. "Hauser's a real team player. Less talk… more *chop chop*, Orion."

Thirty seconds later… we were driving a very small electric cargo loader down the bridge.

A bridge littered with torn-apart pieces of Inquisitors who had died very badly opposing the Wild Thing's advance in the name of love and revenge. He'd hijacked my weapon… or rather… love had. Even now, ahead in the distance, we could see the shadowy dark undefeatable warrior engaging furiously forward, intent on reaching the mammoth circular blast door…

Where the last of the Monarchs wait for us…

Time is indeed… short.

A shoulder-fired missile streaks in at him and the Wild Thing Ulysses pivots the personal weapon of mass destruction and just vaporizes its inbound flight with a swarm of outgoing lead. It explodes like a sudden firecracker, illuminating the scene on the bridge. He is surrounded by the shadowy-cloaked Inquisitors dumping all they can with their primaries to get through his butterfly defense.

He turns and directs the glare of the horrible weapon at a team moving in on him… they are just vaporized by the fury of outgoing lead, coming apart in a spray of what they once were.

I don't know how long he can last…

The Wild Thing never sticks around for long…

But I doubt he can clear the forces at the door…

Or even go beyond it into the Lands of the Monarchs, the inner hull, and waste them for us.

I am dead tired, but an NCO can dream. And in my dream as the little electric cargo loader whines its way down the bridge to the fight at the end… I dream that this is over.

And…

I can save him, I think to myself from the TC position in the vehicle as Hauser drives and the chief, splay-legged like he's on the deck of some ancient wave-rolling sailing ship, stands on the transport deck of the electric vehicle we are riding into battle.

He is singing what I think might be some kind of sea shanty.

Like we have come to hunt some deep-water leviathan too big for this little boat that we are.

Doc Good Vibes in full effect.

And… we are in big trouble.

Stinkeye has come too.

"You told me you wouldn't follow me in…" I'd said to him as our space war wizard climbed onto the rear deck of the cargo loader, letting his worn ancient jump boots hang off the sides, clutching his war wizard staff of dangling dog tags and other grim war trophies, hitting his totem flask as we began the "hunt" as Chief Cook was now calling it.

"Ah told ya's that… but… as dey say… here we are, Little King. Da universe is strange indeed. Plus… now I wants ta see 'em die up close. Dem Monarch bastards. Dis crazy chief tinks it's gonna be his drug-gas… I tink it's gonna be my missile-man… we see now, Little King. We see what we see, says ol' Stinkeye."

Yeah.

"So what's in the gas, Chief?" I ask as we weave around a particularly gruesome pile of slaughter. We are halfway across the bridge now.

The corpses the Wild Thing has made are starting to pile up. It's like they really tried to stand up to him here.

Sucks to be them.

Across the great ship, titanic klaxons, like the collision alert sirens on battleships, are resounding throughout the superstructure.

The Monarchs… are worried.

I can feel that now.

The *X* they laid for us has turned into a trap they can't get out of now.

Maybe… we win.

Still in doubt though…

Ahead I can see the Wild thing blasting everything in sight. His gun, going *BRRRRRAAAAP* on long notes… destroys clusters of surging operators. He has almost reached the other side of the Ring, the massive blast door leading to the inner hull. More Inquisitors throw themselves into the fray.

And now, finally, the Monarchs recognize the threat. The… impossibility. Unconsidered due to its absurdity. That their elite fighting force, the Inquisitors, might be defeated. That the inner hull, their inner sanctum… might be violated.

They see it now.

And the gigantic, decks-high circular door begins to move. Slowly rolling, grinding into position over the gaping aperture that is a sudden vulnerability within this invulnerable vessel…

The slaughter approaching this mess is beyond comprehension.

Bodies hang in the gossamer wiring of the sculpted bridge. Or lie spread out all over the roadway. Pieces, parts, wholes.

It's… horror show.

"Back in the Kilgali, Orion… I've told you about that… sixty-eight it was… best years of the Sindo… we were upcountry in a basin, running a little… shall we say… psychological warfare operation."

Stinkeye snorted in derision.

"Trickies and games, Little Man… ya's know nothin' of the power of da Heart."

Cook ignored him. Maybe Doctor Good Vibes was cruising on a victory that didn't involve the petty ongoing war between Cook and Stinkeye.

I don't know. But he didn't take the bait and Stinkeye came off as petty and small.

Ask me how I know sometime.

Hauser was intent on the road ahead as we approached the rear of the battle. I was intent on the grinding blast door and the shrinking view of the impossible beyond.

It was slow, or the massive door and our narrow window of opportunity would already be shut. As it was, we had a minute, maybe two, before it closed fully.

The captain was busy pulling the entire company back to the *Spider* now. XO was prepping for dustoff. Reactors were spinning up.

We… were leaving this ghost ship.

Either our warrants' insane plans were going to work…

Or… we had failed.

Either way… the company had done its best, and there was nothing more that could be done.

We'd pioneered Route Vega, paid for in it blood in fact, and that had gotten us close enough to take this asymmetrical and weird shot.

Weird stuff.

Voodoo Company stuff.

I'm just a light infantry ruck hobo. Way above my pay grade.

Later I'd find out the captain had been briefed by both of his warrants about their insane plans and that he'd then counseled with Nether, the most rational and sane of the three Voodoo Platoon warrants.

"It's a plan, sir," rasped Nether as he no doubt burned one of the captain's darts. "It's all we've got. If not, what else can we do but fly the *Spider* into the superstructure closest to the inner hull... somewhere near the top I'm guessing, ramming speed..."

Which is a thing in starship combat except it's real, real slow and no one would ever perform this maneuver. Or at least... no one in their right mind.

"Then det the NSM," hissed Nether. "But I doubt that would work, sir."

The captain had no idea Stinkeye was going to use Ulysses as the missile. He was told only that Stinkeye would attempt to hijack the Little Girl's Wild Thing.

When I asked Stinkeye why he chose Ulysses Two Alpha Six to be the missile he said, pathetically...

"Ah already got you broke in, Little King. Him... I don't know so much. He new. So... why not, says I."

But... I think he was lying about that.

And it's not important now. But I'm putting that in the logs so... I can be right about it later?

Yeah. Why not.

"So... back in the Kilgali, Orion... we discovered... way up in this basin... these *frogs*. Now... they weren't ordinary frogs... they were flat-out psycho frogs, Orion. Real mean bastards... for frogs, which if you know frogs... is sayin' something. So... long story short... someone in Dirty Tricks, which was the OP team up there, was a real psycho... total craven drug addict... he licked one of them to see what would happen... frogs on many worlds have these... uh... shall we say... properties... Orion. And no... it wasn't me. Anyway... guy killed twelve people on an A-Team out there doing their... uh... operation. We went in, did the reconstruction and found out this toxin, when... *applied*... will absolutely turn on the berserker-impulse buried deep inside most human beings. It also elevates the homicidal sociopathy right off the Freen Index by a factor of twelve."

Pause.

We were getting close.

"Yours truly, Orion," continued the chief, "put forth that this *substance* should be weaponized. There were some... shall we say... problems along the way though. Shame about that."

"Like what, Chief?"

"Well, they're not really *problems* as far as I was concerned, Orion. One... ya never come down off the stuff. Net benefit as far as I'm concerned. Two... contact. Contact spreads it. Basically it has to wipe itself out through mass slaughter to go dormant again. Program was considered too entirely dangerous for weaponization and I was sent to a reeducation ring for six months to forget it even existed."

"How come you didn't forget it, Chief?"

"Re-education rings... ha, child's play for someone like me, Orion. That's like a vacation. I enjoyed it and it was a much-needed break. Drug cocktail juice boxes, twenty-four-hour state-of-the-art mind control propaganda everywhere you looked, isolation boxes, sleep deprivation... it was thrilling! I came away a new man, Orion. That's where I met Doctor Good Vibes. Anyway, I'd mentally keistered the chemical recipe from the psycho-frog toxin. That's what I've been working on this whole time, Orion. That... and I've made a few... shall we say... fun... modifications."

"Like what, Chief?"

"Replicar Number Five. Long-lasting. Now it will never go away even though I've aerosolized it. It's shelf-stable and will survive even on non-biological surfaces. It's here to stay once we deploy this baby!"

He laughed maniacally for three seconds, then abruptly stopped.

Hauser was slowing. We were getting very close to the battle. Time to dismount.

"Anything else, Chief?"

"Ah... well, I may have thrown in a little cocktail I call Nightmare Fuel. A psilocybin mix with some definite bad trip possibilities. In fact... it's the worst bad trip I've ever had. Found it in the shooting dens near the Black Pit of Waatayahari. Terrible, terrible stuff. Death, endlessness, hopeless black despair... the heat death of the universe... then a nothingness like you can't imagine. It's like being stuck in a sim that's only a grey room for ten thousand years. I only use it occasionally. To come down off... stuff. You know, Orion."

We dismounted.

"And you mixed all this up, Chief... and what now?"

He began to undo the straps we'd secured the drum with. Hauser was out of the vehicle and had his Pig ready, scanning for any of the Inquisitors who might try and go for us.

The gunfire of the Wild Thing was spinning down.

There were only wounded and a few shooters left. He had the primary hand cannon out and was going around shooting them where they lay, or stepping on their necks and heads with his heavy boots.

"Well... now we go in, Orion," said the chief. "Roll this stuff through that aperture and start to leave. Once we do... I'll trigger the bottles inside to mix, then it will disperse and spread."

How... underwhelming considering everything we've been through.

I turned to see the Wild Thing Ulysses.

He was just standing there, heaving, guns smoking. There were dead everywhere.

The giant decks-high blast door was almost closed.

"Better get a hustle on... we ain't got much longer..." said Chief Cook as he and Hauser got the drum off the loader transport.

"Why does this work, Chief?"

He stopped the work and looked at me, throwing his hands and arms wide.

"Because they'll kill *each other* now. It'll turn them against one another. Like they been doin' to us. Except... now they'll just have each other to tear apart. It doesn't go bad. It spreads... and it's a real bad trip."

Stinkeye stood up and whooped.

Then he reached up and handed his flask to Chief Cook.

"Hot damn!" Stinkeye hissed like a salamander. "Now dat's a plan. Dat... is... a... plan. That's perfect for dem bastards in there. I gots ta give it ta ya's, you ol' fraud... dat is a good one indeed!"

Chief Cook was stunned.

Stinkeye held out the flask like he meant it.

Then... Chief Cook nodded and they both laughed as he took the flask... and drank.

Then the three of them, yes even Stinkeye, were working at the hazmat drum.

Hauser would carry it there.

They would all watch it roll into whatever was in there.

I didn't care.

I thought I would.

I thought I'd wanted to see their last, in the inner hull, their most sacred space… the inner sanctum… those who thought they were our "gods"… the ruiners of so much of our history…

The almost-destroyers of the human race. And so much more.

… Like I thought I would understand why they'd turned on us if I did… as though it would make sense of all the chaos and madness… and… all of it.

I didn't care.

Now they would tear themselves apart inside this hull they could not escape and as they did so, over time, the orbit of the *Dark Star* would kiss the gravity well of the giant Typhon out there in near-space… and then suck them down into a dark swirling madness this wreck could never be retrieved from.

Like some kind of hell there was no rescue from… ever. No end to. Just a howling, mad, lonely storm that never ended.

That was perfect.

I turned and walked toward the Wild Thing…

Ulysses.

FINAL LOG SLICE

The Tragedy of the Strange Company

We are thirty-seven days out of Typhon.

The gas worked.

Within days, after pushback and gears up... the *Spider* limped away from the *Dark Star*... and the last Monarch ship's orbit began to degrade into the super gas giant Typhon.

A sure death sentence for any ship.

Yesterday, far faster than expected... she broke up and burned in, pieces of her sinking down into the crushing depths of the gas giant's gravity well.

I can think of few places more unforgiving than the deepest depths of a super gas giant.

Back at the bridge within the *Dark Star*'s Ring...

I went to the Wild Thing...

Ulysses Two Alpha Six.

I could see the strands, black like beautiful scarves flowing from the quantum entanglement of the Heart of Darkness... and the Little Girl.

Because we were near the Oblivion Gate...

... they feathered and fluttered about the two of them.

Ulysses and the Wild Thing.

I don't think anyone else could see it.

Just, my recent experiences had allowed me fading impressions of what was happening at the time on the quantum level of things.

I could see both men.

Pure quantum. There... and not there at all.

Ulysses.

Marcus.

Soldiers.

I said to Ulysses...

"She lives. It's time to go back now, Two Alpha Six."

Nothing.

"She's safe now, Marine. Time to go back to her and take your place next to her, watching over her now..."

Nothing...

Then he stepped away from the armor... and just fell, collapsing on the ground.

Passed out cold.

Same as I had when my ride as the Wild Thing was over.

The Wild Thing stood there in all his horrific beauty... a weaponized apocalypse...

Cautiously I took a step forward. It's a fearful thing to behold. The armor.

"Marcus..."

He nodded slowly.

I think I was speaking inside my mind. Our minds.
I thought of...
His wife.
She was beautiful.
His baby daughter. An infant.
"Say hi to your baby girl, Marcus... say hi to Daddy."
"You're done here, Marcus. She has a new champion."
The Wild Thing didn't move.
The butterfly-bat web spun about him, growing and hissing... like the terrible thing it was.
But I wasn't afraid... even though I knew I should be.
"They want you to come back."
Come back to us, Marcus.
His chest armor heaved.
Like he'd just taken some great breath... sighed some great weight... shaken some epic task... off his shoulders.
Off of him.
Doom88.
I pointed toward the blast door. Now lowering slowly down over the last of the opening.
"The drops are still at the evac LZ on that moon. Go now," I ordered.
He was close enough now to the Heart... the star... the Oblivion Gate... to sever the strands of entanglement...
And like all strands, and entanglements... we must cut them ourselves.
No one... can do this for us.
"Go home, soldier... your time here is done now."
And then, the thing all soldiers want to hear.
"We... won."
The Wild Thing took one last look back across the bridge. In the direction the medics were no doubt carrying the Little Girl to the rear.
To Cutter who would save her.
I took a step closer to the Wild Thing, reached out my assault-gloved hand, it was bloody, held it hovering over his shoulder which was higher than mine...
And then...
I whispered... "It's okay now."
Which is something I always say to the boots and rifles when Preacher does his ceremonies.
It's the last thing I say to the company dead.
It's okay now.
That shadow-smoke visor turned and studied me for a long moment.
And then he began to walk toward the closing blast door. Leaving. Going. Severing.
I didn't follow.
They'd already rolled the canister in, and Hauser, Stinkeye, and Chief Cook were headed back to the vehicle.
I bent down and got Ulysses over my shoulder. I carried him back to the vehicle and laid him on the cargo deck. Then I got on and we made ready to leave.

As the vehicle turned around and headed back, just before the giant blast door closed... I stole one last glimpse of the inner hull.

And this is what I saw...

The inner hull of the Dark Star was one giant space. Miles across. An entire world...

The Wild Thing began to fade.

The shroud-wraps of quantum entanglement were cut loose and flapping like mad pennants in some strong breeze.

Then he was gone.

Beyond that I saw the Heart of Darkness itself. Though really I was just looking at a gate that was a splinter of the actual thing. A micro-neutron star.

Nether explained it to me later.

It was a giant black sun that was more a hole of nothingness in reality inside the chamber, spinning slowly, glaring rage and anger and contempt at all who gazed at it.

And beneath its glare, a sprawling city of strange dark pyramids and obscene monuments carved in black obsidian rose up that the Monarchs had built for themselves, of themselves, to themselves. Erected to wait out the long ages until their next bid... to do it all again.

To rule.

To ruin.

To enslave.

The lands within weren't vast gardens or awe-inspiring pleasure domes... just hard cruel red rock and sands spreading away beneath it all... beneath the petty monuments to themselves.

Beneath the Black Hole Sun.

The canister was already emitting a toxic yellow gas. Spewing the weaponized hatred and berserking everywhere. It would grow and replicate and it was a death sentence if there ever was one.

Now they would fight amongst themselves as they'd made us do so they could maintain control over all of us.

It was a fitting end.

We drove away and the giant door to the inner hull closed, sealing them inside with the deadly gas that would make them kill one another.

Mission end.

We are thirty-seven days out from Typhon and headed to a series of worlds well beyond the frontier.

It's a gamble.

But when hasn't it been for the company?

XO has picked up transmissions from some united systems called the Reef Worlds.

We have no idea what's there.

There have always been rumors of other smaller civilizations well beyond the farthest known frontier. Secret civilizations trying to escape the ever-reaching tyrannical grasp of the Monarchs who went farther out and started micro-empires out there.

The Monarchs would have gotten around to them eventually... until the company finished them off.

Now... they have a chance.

We will go there now because it's closer than the long haul back to Chimp Space. We will see if there is anyone to fight for pay.

If not... then maybe we'll beach the ship on some tropical island in southern seas and learn to fish.

Because the jump core was ejected during the HK attack on the LZ, we are back to dumb-thrust and light-hugging.

The long, slow crawl into the dark.

Literally primitive Space Age flight.

It will take thirty-seven years to reach the Reef Worlds, and we have no idea what we'll find there. We only have a few transmissions to go on.

Trade.

Commerce.

Discovery.

Thin soup to make a meal out of private military contracting on.

But... humans are humans and eventually they fight each other for resources.

That's where the Strange Company comes in.

Preacher buried our dead, spacing them off the deck as we prepared for full burn to our destination.

Gear was seen to.

The ship's maintenance was done.

The logs updated.

We cryo-coffined our wounded.

Said goodbye to our dead.

I am finished with this last log-slice for this section that began with the Seeker *getting involved*, and that ended with the destruction of the *Dark Star*.

I had a feeling it was important.

I'm surprised we lived and that the company continues.

That's the whole story.

The long-distance sleep narcotics are flooding the coffin chamber as I finish the log and slice it for emergency storage... I'm fading. I've asked M.O.M. for a starship-sim. A romp. Adventure. Hot alien babes. Treasure. Light speed. I want to live in a universe of starships and exploration and space combat.

I need a break from ruck-hoboing for a while.

I hope she doesn't...

... Faded there.

Almost... asleep for the long haul now...

Funny... in the end... it was love that was our strongest weapon. Ulysses... the Little Girl.

It's like... destiny or something... dunno...

Orion... out. Log-slice here. Cut and add to Tragedy file. Final entry...

M.O.M., begin sim.

A FINAL DREAM

In the dark before morning light, a company of soldiers are on the move through the darkness. The moon is long gone. We are just shadows in the night. Infantry on the move. I can smell the dirt and the thick scent of sage in the air. The air is cool.

We are silent as we move across the dark lands.

Silent as we halt beneath the pass ahead and above.

Dawn will soon be here.

The first sergeant comes up along the column and stops next to me. A dark shadow among shadows. He is old and his eyes just search me, looking for something within. I am humping a heavy ruck, my feet are tired, and we've been moving all night. We've been moving all our lives. The first sergeant watches me.

We are soldiers moving in the dark as all soldiers have. There is nothing but the quiet world around us, and the experiences that are ours and ours alone.

Boots.

Ruck.

Weapons.

Mission.

Brothers.

We have been moving through the shadowy hills in the early morning dark. All night long. Above the halt lies a pass between two hills. Dawn… will soon be here.

It will rise through that notch.

The first sergeant tells me he will go on ahead now, into the first light of dawn, even though it is still dark.

And that soon, I will too.

Strangers to the Universe…

Brothers to the End.

The End

STRANGE COMPANY
WILL RETURN
IN
THE STAR GIANTS

www.ingramcontent.com/pod-product-compliance
Lightning Source LLC
Jackson TN
JSHW060252160425
82676JS00003B/3